'Til We Meet Again

'Til We Meet Again

'Til We Meet Again
by Pamela Griffin

Eliza
by Mildred Colvin

Precious Jewels
by Nancy J. Farrier

Thanks to a Lonely Heart
by Elaine Bonner

HeavenSent
FROM
Crossings

All Scripture quotations, unless otherwise indicated, are taken from the King James Version of the Bible.

'Til We Meet Again
Copyright © 2000 by Barbour Publishing, Inc.

Eliza
Copyright © 2004 by Mildred Colvin

Precious Jewels
Copyright © 2003 by Nancy J. Farrier

Thanks to a Lonely Heart
Copyright © 1999 by Barbour Publishing, Inc.

This edition was especially created in 2006 for Crossings by arrangement with Barbour Publishing, Inc.

Published by Crossings Book Club, 401 Franklin Avenue, Garden City, New York 11530.

ISBN: 1-58288-208-8

Printed in the United States of America

'Til We Meet Again

'Til We Meet Again

by Pamela Griffin

Thank you to my entire family for their love, encouragement, and support. In particular I wish to thank my "editor mother" and "computer genius father," Arlene and John Trampel; and Lena Dooley, for her patience and mentoring.

And thank you, Brandon and Joshua, for being patient when Mommy was on the computer so often. I love you both!

I also wish to thank Philip Hind for his permission to use the wealth of information I gleaned from his web site.

But most of all, a special thank-you goes to the Master Storyteller, without whom this book would not have been written. It is to the Lord that I dedicate *'Til We Meet Again*.

1912

teasing breeze played with Annabelle's dark curls as she stood on the sun-splashed deck of the eleven-story ocean liner and watched the activity all around her.

She didn't look over the white balustrade toward the bustling English town below. Nor did she watch the pale-skinned, rosy-cheeked children as they gazed up in awe at the huge ship readying to depart from port. And she didn't pay attention to the few photographers and reporters on the wharf, snapping their black box cameras or writing furiously in their small notepads.

Annabelle Mooreland had had enough of the town of Southampton—all of England, for that matter—and she was anxious to leave. She had especially had enough of a certain Englishman who'd pulled the wool over her eyes.

Feeling terribly naïve and stupid, Annabelle grimaced. A hint of pink tinged her creamy skin when she thought of Roger Fieldhall. Best not to think about his kind or she might cry or scream or do something else embarrassing; she certainly didn't want that.

She tilted her head and, shielding her eyes from the brilliant sunshine with one hand, watched as a huge wooden crate was hoisted upward with ropes and pulleys; it swung past one of the towering smokestacks and was stowed in the hold of the ship. All around her, hundreds of well-dressed people stood and waved to those on land, many of them oblivious to the preparations taking place behind them.

Ladies wearing linen and silk day dresses and enormous wide-brimmed hats and men dressed just as extravagantly in silk and serge suits and wearing bowlers on their heads stood along the railing, strolled the decks, and investigated their home for the next week. Still others went below, seeking out their rooms.

One family had one of those new cameras that took moving pictures. It sat on a rickety-looking tripod, the man behind it winding the crank at the side and filming the day's events.

Annabelle noticed a distinguished-looking, silver-haired gentleman wearing leather gloves and carrying a gold-topped walking stick. Briefly she wondered how her father was faring. Totally unaffected by this milestone event in ocean travel in which he was playing a small part simply by being a passenger, he had retired to the men's smoking lounge to smoke his pipe and talk politics with anyone who would listen.

Annabelle sighed. She loved her father but hated the rank smell of his pipe—even though the tobacco was imported and some of the most expensive to be found, as her father had told her countless times. In deference to his daughter's "delicate smelling apparatus," as he teasingly called her nose, he had agreed to remove his "smelly old pipe" from her company. But his twinkling eyes had shown her he wasn't one bit angry.

Annabelle knew that in his blustering, awkward way, her father was simply giving her time to come to terms with her broken engagement. He'd never before demonstrated the slightest concern about smoking in her presence, but the reserved Englishman obviously recognized his daughter's need to spend time alone now.

Skirting knots of excited passengers, Annabelle escaped the noisy crowd and pulled her short, fitted jacket closer around her waist. She walked past the wooden lifeboats to the other, less-populated side of the ship that faced the sparkling ocean.

Actually, she would have appreciated a hug before her father left. But he'd never been the demonstrative type. As a child, Annabelle used to wonder why her American-born mother—a spirited, fiery woman—had married the staid Englishman. However, as she grew older, Annabelle learned to appreciate her father's hidden qualities. Although he hadn't mentioned the fight she'd had with Roger, her father had been sensitive enough to realize Annabelle was hurting.

Again Annabelle flushed with humiliation.

She should have known the dashing, young yet penniless Roger Fieldhall—famous polo player—had only been interested in her for her father's money. Though Annabelle assumed she was rather pretty from what her reflection in the mirror revealed, she knew her looks weren't anything spectacular. And while her personality was agreeable, she wasn't charming and flirtatious—not like the blond, delicate Mary Flossman, in whose arms Annabelle had found Roger upon her surprise visit to the stables a week ago.

She clenched her teeth, trying to maintain her composure, and again berated herself for her folly. Her friend Patricia had often told her she would be a fool to marry someone who didn't share her faith. At least Annabelle had discovered the truth of that statement before it was too late. She knew she'd been wrong to get closely involved with a non-Christian; but for the most part, hers had been a lonely life, and the possibility of spending her future as an old maid had no appeal. When Roger had proposed a year ago and offered Annabelle a part in his exciting life of fame, she quickly agreed— though she didn't love him. Only one man had ever held the key to her heart.

Annabelle impatiently flicked a tear away. No. She mustn't think about him, either. It had been four long years since she'd last seen him, and now he was promised to another.

Sighing, Annabelle tightly clasped her hands, forcing herself to concentrate on something else as she watched a gull soar and dive over the sparkling water.

When he'd seen how upset she was, her father had decided to leave for the States months sooner than originally planned and take Annabelle with him. He'd made the last-minute arrangements quickly and easily. Indeed, it seemed that when one had money, all manner of things were possible—even obtaining first-class cabins aboard a luxury ocean liner a day before departure and another in second class for Annabelle's maid, Sadie.

Annabelle knew she should be looking forward to this voyage, as Patricia had so enviously told her. But she wasn't.

Lord, is it my lot in life to be alone? Is there nothing else for me? She stepped back from the rail, intent on seeking out her stateroom.

A small blue-and-gold object suddenly came hurtling toward Annabelle, striking her and almost knocking her down.

"Oh, my!" Annabelle teetered backward, grabbed the rail, and regained her balance. She reached up and straightened her broad-brimmed, gaily beribboned hat, which had been knocked slightly askew. A small pink and white face, with two of the bluest eyes—like cornflowers—turned upward.

"I'm sorry," murmured the little girl, who looked to be no more than five, as she backed a step away. "I have to fin' my dolly."

Annabelle knelt down to the child's level. "What's your name, sweetheart? And where's your mommy?"

From under the soft round hat a cascade of blond curls swished over the navy-blue wool coat as the child shook her head back and forth. "Not s'posed to talk to strangers."

Annabelle bit the inside of her lower lip and looked around the deck, hoping to find an anxious face searching for a child. An olive-skinned, black-haired woman with fearful dark eyes caught sight of Annabelle and the little girl from about twenty yards away. Her face relaxed as she walked quickly toward them. Annabelle studied the woman curiously and then the fair child. The stranger certainly couldn't be the little girl's mother. They weren't a bit alike.

"Missy! You must never run off like that again," the woman said breathlessly with a Spanish accent. "If your mother knew what you did, she would be worried. *Si?*"

Chastened, Missy nodded. "But what about Helena?"

"She was probably packed with the luggage by mistake. I am certain when we reach our cabin, she will be there."

The woman seemed to notice Annabelle for the first time. Though her manner wasn't unfriendly, it became very reserved. "I wish to thank you for your help. If you had not stopped her when you did, Missy may have left the boat. *Gracias.*"

Annabelle smiled and glanced at the little girl. "Well, I can't take all the credit. Actually . . ." Missy's big blue eyes cut quickly to hers, silently begging her not to tell of the near mishap. "I was glad to help," Annabelle quickly ended.

The woman nodded, though her expression was curious.

After a grateful smile to Annabelle, Missy turned to her companion. "Maria, do you really think Helena's in my trunk?"

Instantly a gentle look touched the dark eyes. "*Si*, little *señorita*. Perhaps we should go look now—yes?"

Missy nodded, then looked at Annabelle. "What's your name?"

"Annabelle."

"Ooooh. I like that," Missy trilled. "I want to name my next dolly that." Her fine brows raised. "Are you a stranger?"

Annabelle quickly glanced at the reserved Maria, who looked on silently, then back to Missy. "Yes, Missy. I suppose I am."

The little girl looked puzzled. "But how can you be a stranger if we know each other's names?"

Annabelle was flustered. She didn't know how to deal with children. She'd never had any brothers or sisters—none that she remembered anyway. Her older sister had died in a sledding accident when Annabelle had been only four, and her baby brother—born much too early—had died a few hours after his birth.

Maria took over and reached for the child's hand. "Come, Missy. Perhaps, we will see Miss Annabelle again during the voyage, and you can talk to her then, hmmm? We must go now."

Annabelle watched them walk away. Missy looked over her shoulder and smiled. Annabelle smiled back. What a delightful little girl! Though Annabelle had little experience conversing with children, she looked forward to talking to Missy again. That is, if her nanny, or nursemaid, or whatever the exotic-looking Spanish woman was to the child, would let her.

Maria was a mystery. Her fine clothes spoke of wealth—definitely not something a domestic would wear—and her voice had been well modulated. As Annabelle looked back at the silver-tipped water, she wondered about her two new acquaintances. . . .

ॐ

On the pretext of studying the ocean, Lawrence casually leaned against the rail and looked instead at the pretty young woman standing several yards away. She was modestly outfitted in a long, pinstriped traveling dress and matching jacket. There was something familiar about her face—what he could see of it.

He searched his mind trying to place her but came up empty. Perhaps she'd been one of the many guests at his mother's soirees and balls in past years. He'd attended such functions only because it was required of a viscount, but he had always made excuses to leave at the first opportunity, wishing to evade the simpering young ladies who always sought him out. But this woman didn't look like one of their kind. There was a sweet innocence about her that enchanted him.

His eyes narrowed when he saw her flick away another tear. She'd been silently crying before the little girl had run into her, too, so he knew the collision hadn't caused the tears.

Was she married? Lawrence wished he could see her hand, but she was wringing both of them, her forearms lightly resting on the rail in front of her. He watched as she hastily lifted an arm and clutched the top of her straw hat when a sudden gust of April wind mussed her dark curls.

His heart lightened. No band of gold shimmered on her left hand, which he could now see clearly.

Lawrence wished he had the courage to approach her; but that kind of thing simply wasn't done, as far as he was concerned. Though in this day and age, he noted, many of his peers didn't have the gracious manners that had been instilled in Lawrence by two very proper English parents. Some men might not consider it too forward to talk to the pretty woman without benefit of an introduction—especially since she seemed so familiar. . . . But no, he couldn't do it.

Sometimes Lawrence felt as if he should have been born in an earlier time—a time when honor and chivalry abounded and the young maidens were pure and innocent and sweet. Not money-hungry flirts like Frances.

His dark brows pulled down in a scowl, and he shifted his gaze to the rippling water. Frances had been more than willing for a marriage to take place between them, but Lawrence had always disliked her wild, uninhibited ways. Good thing, too, when he discovered the real reason for her interest.

Surprisingly, his father had agreed with his decision, although

Lawrence hadn't told him everything concerning the fight he'd had with Frances the last time he'd seen her. Her father also was wealthy, and a marriage between her and Lawrence would join their lands in Fairhaven—a fact that Lord and Lady Caldwell had often pointed out to their son. But when Lawrence firmly told them he couldn't marry her, his father had offered little objection.

Even more astounding to Lawrence was the fact that his father hadn't been against his taking this voyage. He had told Lawrence that perhaps once he had seen some of the world he would be ready to settle down and live the life of a nobleman in the Caldwells' sprawling Tudor manor.

Though Lawrence loved his homeland and knew he must return one day, he doubted it would be anytime soon. The thirst for adventure was strong in his blood. He wondered if one of his ancestors might have been a daring adventurer, such as a captain on the high seas or perhaps a buccaneer or a swashbuckler accomplished with the sword and always at the ready to rescue fair maidens. Lawrence often likened himself to the fictitious Sir Lancelot because he shared the famous knight's name—Lancelot being Lawrence's middle name. But where was *his* Guinevere? Had she found and wed her Arthur?

With a deep sigh, he pushed away from the rail and whisked slender fingers through his dark hair. He was becoming entirely too fanciful. No . . . more like ridiculous. Ever since this past winter, when he turned twenty-five, he'd given more thought to the idea of marriage. But if he were honest with himself, he'd have to admit he probably never would have married Frances, despite his parents' wishes. She wasn't his type. And her unscrupulous behavior had given him the reason he needed to terminate the relationship.

He turned toward the woman and hesitated, watching as the salty wet wind played against her, molding her linen dress to her slender figure and whipping tendrils of black curls about her rosy face. *Why does she seem so familiar?*

The question bothered him to no end, and, almost as though his foot had taken on a life of its own, Lawrence took a step in her direction, then stopped, suddenly realizing what he was doing. Forcing himself to turn away, he shoved his hands deep into the pockets of his overcoat, dodged several fellow passengers, and walked to the first-class companionway in search of his room.

၆✍

Once the tall gentleman moved away from the rail, Annabelle relaxed, letting a soft sigh of relief escape her lips. She'd been more than a little aware of the frequent glances he'd cast in her direction and was glad to see him go. She hadn't taken a good look at him while he'd been watching her, for to turn and stare back would have been considered much too bold, not to mention highly embarrassing. But now it was her turn to watch.

Annabelle easily picked out his tall, slender form in the charcoal-gray overcoat as he wove his way among the people strolling along the boat deck. Suddenly he stopped and picked up a reticule a middle-aged woman had dropped, turning sideways and doffing his bowler hat courteously as he returned it to her.

Annabelle's eyes widened and her heart gave a little flip as the years rolled back and she was a young girl in her uncle's house once again. *No . . . it couldn't be!*

Clutching the rail for support, she studied him in disbelief, noting his handsome profile, his gracious smile to the woman—who was now all a-dither, her face beaming. Though his shoulders weren't broad, his carriage was commanding, erect. He looked strong, capable, and dependable, much like . . . but that was impossible! *He* was a Caldwell—heir to the family title and a vast fortune. What would he be doing embarking on this voyage?

It had to be someone who strongly resembled him. Yes, of course that was it. Her brief thoughts of him earlier must have caused her to see his face in that of a stranger.

Annabelle's frantic pulse rate slowed to normal, and she relaxed her tight grip on the rail. Idly studying the retreating figure a moment longer, she almost jumped when an earsplitting blast from he ship's whistle signaled it was time to depart.

Not wanting to join in the festivities, Annabelle hurried to the deck below, escaping the excited shouts and cheers of other passengers, who stood at the rail and watched as the *S.S. Titanic* slipped away from the dock, ready to embark on her maiden voyage.

$$\textbf{2}$$

*A*nnabelle pulled a long, gold-trimmed evening gown with short sleeves from her trunk. She slipped it on, fastening it in back with only a little difficulty. It took longer to dress without Sadie there, but Annabelle managed. She finished by pulling on a pair of long white gloves. Looking into the mirror mounted onto the carved dresser, she critically studied her reflection.

The soft material of the gown gently molded her upper body, then fell in a straight line to her matching satin pumps. The color was the exact hue of her eyes—what Annabelle felt to be her one outstanding feature. She wore her mother's emerald pendant and matching earrings, and she'd swept her hair up off her neck and pinned it to the back of her head in what she hoped passed for an elegant style.

Annabelle walked to the curtained porthole and looked out at the black ocean below, at the twinkling stars and hazy moon in the nighttime sky. Bright yellow splashes of light from hundreds of portholes and windows along the ship shimmered on the dark water beneath her. Perhaps after dinner she would take a walk along the promenade and enjoy the beautiful evening. However, it did seem a lonely thing to do without someone by her side. A pair of ice-blue eyes in a handsome face came to mind. She hadn't been able to stop thinking about *him* since she'd mistaken that stranger for him earlier today.

With a disgusted sigh, she hurriedly turned from the romantic view. Rifling through her jewelry box, she plucked out a green rhinestone comb and slid it over lustrous black curls now contained in a French twist. Or rather, what she hoped passed for a French twist. She didn't have a lot of experience when it came to fixing her hair. At least her curls were natural, the one thing she'd inherited from her English grandmother. And the salt air seemed to give the ringlets even more bounce, Annabelle noted as she pulled away tiny tendrils with her comb, allowing them to dance about her face and neck when she moved.

Her maid had been sick upon boarding, and Annabelle had told her to stay in her room until she recovered. Annabelle remembered being seasick on the voyage to England eight years ago. But that couldn't be Sadie's problem; the ocean was calm.

A light knock sounded on her stateroom door. Annabelle put down the silver-plated comb, took one last look in the mirror, then walked across the cream-colored carpet to join her father.

ع

When the door opened and Edward Mooreland saw his daughter standing there, he tensed. It was amazing how much she reminded him of Cynthia—Annabelle's mother—who had died years ago. Though Cynthia's hair had been straight and the color a deep russet, the emerald eyes looking up at him from beneath thick, dark lashes and the sweet smile on his daughter's rosy lips were the same as her mother's.

Lately, now that Annabelle was maturing into a young woman, Edward noticed that his daughter resembled Cynthia more and more with each passing day. It hurt him to look at Annabelle or be in her company, though he was ashamed to admit it. Even eight years after losing Cynthia, the pain was there, sharpened when he looked upon her likeness.

Annabelle took his arm, noting its stiffness, and glanced up at him. He gave her a shaky smile before looking away.

ع

As they silently walked down the carpeted corridor to the lifts that would take them to D-deck, where the first-class dining room was located, Annabelle again sent a prayer heavenward, asking God to heal the breach between her and her father.

Upon entering the luxurious dining area, Annabelle inhaled softly, her eyes opening wide in wonder. The accommodations were magnificent! Carved white pillars, towering from floor to ceiling, stood sentinel throughout the spacious room, and tables of various sizes were grouped all across the brightly patterned linoleum. Covered with pristine white cloths, matching napkins, patterned china, crystal glasses, and silver utensils, they appealed to the eye, beckoning the people to come and dine. From one side of the oak-paneled room a band softly played music for the dinner patrons, who were rapidly filling the area.

A black-coated waiter led Annabelle and her father to one of the tables near the middle of the room. Those they would eat with had not yet arrived, and so for now, Annabelle and her father had the table to themselves. The waiter pulled out one of eight cushioned, red leather chairs, arranged around the table in twos, and she sat down and thanked him. After taking their orders for the first course, he bowed graciously, then left.

Annabelle turned to face her father, who'd been seated next to her, and voiced something that had been on her mind since they'd left Southampton. "Father, doesn't it bother you that the *Titanic* has never sailed before this voyage? I mean, it's all quite elegant, but this is her first time out to sea—the ship is completely new! I even noticed several painters disembarking before we left the pier, obviously having just completed their job, judging from the fresh smell of paint in the corridor."

"Annabelle, you worry too much," he gruffly reassured her. "Several men I've recently met told me she is virtually unsinkable. In fact, of all the ocean liners we could have chosen, the *Titanic* is by far the safest." He gave her a smile, and she relaxed a bit.

"Earlier today I met a gentleman by the name of Thomas Andrews," he said. "Incidentally, he oversaw the construction of this ship, and I heard him reassure another gentleman—who had questions similar to yours—of the absolute seaworthiness of her. Why, are you aware the *Titanic* is four city blocks long and took three years to build?" he added, obviously awed by the information. She shook her head, and he continued. "Captain Smith has been with the White Star Line for twenty-five years and has an outstanding record with them.

I've heard this is his last voyage before retirement. So you've nothing at all to fear, my dear. You're in good hands."

Annabelle nodded, though she still wasn't thoroughly convinced. Yes, she'd seen a demonstration of the Captain's prowess when, upon leaving the waters of Southampton, a collision with a steamer called the *New York* had narrowly been avoided. In horror she'd stood at her porthole and watched as the small steamer had come closer and closer to the black hull of the *Titanic*. However, Captain Smith had somehow managed to avoid a collision. Still, to Annabelle's way of thinking, it hadn't been a great way to start an ocean voyage.

Forcing herself to stop her musings, Annabelle lifted her glass to her lips and stared out over the bustling dining room. Studying the elegant decor, she turned her head and watched as a well-dressed man approached their table. The small smile froze on her lips. Her mouth went dry as she stared in shock and realized the impossible was indeed possible.

The newcomer briefly looked at her fixed gaze a little oddly, but gave a polite nod. Then he saw her father. "Mr. Mooreland, I believe?" he asked in that rich, cultured voice she loved so well.

Edward broke into a smile. "Lord Caldwell, as I live and breathe! Sit down, sit down. You remember my daughter?"

Lawrence stiffened, his ice-blue eyes going wide as he turned his head to look her way again. "Annabelle?" he murmured in shock, as he slowly sank to the chair on her right, never taking his searching eyes from her face. "Is it really you?"

At her hesitant nod, he continued. "I sincerely doubt I would have recognized you had it not been for your father."

She gave a nervous laugh. "Considering I was in pigtails and pinafores at the time, I wouldn't wonder." She twisted the linen napkin in her lap, hardly daring to believe this was really happening. The love of her life was here, on board the *Titanic*, sitting next to her!

"How long has it been?" Lawrence asked, his voice soft.

"Four years."

"Four years . . . ," he repeated, his words trailing away. Annabelle swallowed, staring into his beautiful eyes. The contrast between them and his coal-black lashes and dark brows made them appear like ice—though the expression in them was very warm.

"It's lovely to see you again, Lord Caldwell," she managed.

"Please, Annabelle, cease the formalities. Considering the friendship we shared, to you I'll always be Lawrence."

His words warmed her, but further conversation was halted as a waiter appeared at their table, an elderly couple trailing behind. They took their seats across from Annabelle and her father and introduced themselves as Mr. and Mrs. Isidor Straus. Less than a minute later, the last couple waltzed in and took their places at the table.

Annabelle inwardly cringed when she saw the young woman. She had heavily rouged cheeks and lips and hair the color of fire. A cocoa-colored gown covered her hourglass figure, and a matching feathered plume waved from the top of her piled-up curls. Annabelle was shocked at the woman's low-scooped neckline, which clearly exposed a bit too much flesh, to her way of thinking. Judging from Mrs. Straus's horrified reaction, she, too, thought the woman was dressed inappropriately for the occasion.

The man—also flamboyantly attired—sat down beside her at the other end of the table, facing Lawrence. He introduced himself as Eric Fontaneau and the woman as his sister, Charlotte.

Annabelle took an instant dislike to her. She was too much of a flirt, as evidenced by the shameless way she leaned across the table and spoke to Lawrence during the meal. Much to his credit, he barely gave anything more than a polite reply to her questions and didn't stare at her as many of the other men in the dining room were doing. But then, he'd always been a perfect gentleman. It was one of the things Annabelle loved about him.

The memory of a shy eleven-year-old peering through the banister rails at a ballroom full of splendidly dressed dancers came to Annabelle's mind. She had sat huddled on the carpeted stairs, her bare toes peeked out from beneath her long cotton nightgown and wrapper, and tried to stay hidden, hoping her absence from the bedroom wouldn't be discovered. Feeling as if someone were watching her, she had looked sideways toward the bottom of the stairs and had spotted Lawrence leaning against the wall.

At first she'd been awed by the tall, handsome young viscount whom she'd admired from afar, as well as a little fearful he would angrily demand to know what she was doing there and send for her nanny. Being out of bed past midnight and spying on the guests would've gotten Annabelle into trouble with her strict uncle, whom she and her father were living with at the time.

But Lawrence had neither yelled nor gone for assistance. Instead, he walked up the stairs and sat next to her. "Hello," he said softly. "You must be Annabelle." At her slight nod, he offered a friendly handshake and smile. "I'm Lawrence."

To her amazement he had spent the next few minutes conversing with her, harmlessly joking about several guests dancing below them and making Annabelle laugh—something she hadn't done in a long time. It was then that her little girl heart began to see him as special. The fact that someone so handsome, so sought after by the pretty girls at the dance, would leave the party and spend time with her, a mere child, endeared Lawrence to Annabelle, making him a hero in her eyes.

Because her uncle and Lawrence's father were good friends, the families got together often, and each time she saw Lawrence, he made a point to spend time with her—talking with and reading to her, riding horses with her, and sometimes helping her with her studies. He treated her special—always seeming to care about what she had to say and how she felt—and a strong friendship developed between them, a closeness which, for Annabelle, had led to love. But Lawrence had never known of her strong feelings for him; it was a secret she'd closely guarded in her heart.

A waiter came with the third course of poached salmon in mousseline sauce, and Annabelle hastily took a helping, realizing with embarrassment that she'd been openly staring at Lawrence. He probably hadn't noticed, though, since he was discussing business with Mr. Straus, cofounder of Macy's in New York.

She took a few tiny bites, then turned her head and noted with dismay that Charlotte's interests were now focused on her father. And he didn't seem to be dissuading her, either.

"I miss the freckles," Lawrence said softly for Annabelle's ears alone.

She turned to him, startled, certain she'd heard wrong. Her stomach did a little flip when she met his eyes. "What?"

"Your freckles. I miss them."

Embarrassed, she blushed, her lashes briefly flicking downward. "I lost most of them when I turned seventeen two years ago. I'll soon be nineteen, you know," she said a little shyly.

"Nineteen . . . ," he said with a teasing grin. "Why, it seems like only yesterday you were romping over the grounds at Fairview Manor and begging to ride Thunder."

She frowned at him. "I never romped. Romping is for boys. I skipped."

He gave an easy laugh, his eyes crinkling at the corners. "Ah, Annabelle. You always were such a delightful child."

Something clutched at her heart. *A delightful child.*" And did he still see her as a child? Did he still equate her with the freckle-faced urchin with a cloud of unruly dark hair who had often come to the Caldwells' stables to ride the horses? *Oh, Lawrence, open your eyes— I'm a woman now!*

But it didn't really matter what he thought, she supposed, feeling a hint of despair. He loved another. Idly she wondered how Frances felt about Lawrence taking a voyage to America.

A lilting laugh sounded across the table. Annabelle looked at Charlotte, who was talking to her father. His cheeks went ruddy, and he gave the woman next to him a grin. What could that painted woman have said to make her staid father react like that?

Distressed by his unusual behavior and disappointed that Lawrence still thought her a child, Annabelle somehow managed to sit through the next five courses, eating little of what the waiters offered on their silver salvers.

Foregoing dessert, she pleaded a headache, and her father excused himself and turned to her, offering assistance. To Annabelle's dismay, the Fontaneaus also rose, claiming they, too, were ready to depart. It helped that Lawrence accompanied them, but when Annabelle discovered that the Fontaneaus' rooms were on the same corridor as her and her father's rooms, she softly groaned.

Upon reaching her door, Annabelle said good night, stressing the word when she said it to her father. He didn't appear to notice, but nodded and gave a cheery "Good night, Annabelle." But Lawrence seemed to notice.

"I hope you soon feel better," he said softly. He gave her arm a squeeze before dropping it, showing he understood, and she offered a weak smile in return, thankful for his consideration and support. At least she still had his friendship.

Before Annabelle closed the door on the retreating figures, she saw Charlotte take her father's arm and smile, fluttering her long, dark lashes. In disbelief Annabelle watched as the woman sidled up to him, steering him away from his room and toward the grand staircase. Annabelle just managed not to slam her door.

Turning, she looked at the cheery pink and blue furnishings, the delicate Queen Anne furniture, the white marble fireplace—and she wanted to scream. Sinking onto the plush blue sofa, she plucked up one of the round pink cushions, clutching it to her breast.

"Lord, how can Father not see what type of woman she is? If that French accent is real, I'll, I'll . . ." Annabelle looked around the room. "I'll trade in this luxurious stateroom for one of the third-class rooms in steerage!" She threw the pillow down. "And that can't be the natural color of her hair; no woman has hair that color! Why, Mama was ten times prettier than Charlotte Fontaneau, and that's the truth!"

The words stabbed like a knife blade to the heart, and her eyes closed. Was Annabelle jealous of the interest her father was showing Charlotte because Annabelle thought he was wronging her mother's memory in some way . . . or was she jealous of the attention he gave the woman because he rarely showed any interest in his own daughter? Her eyes opened wide at this new thought, and she silently admitted the latter.

With only the care of a stern uncle, a distant father, and an aunt who had "more important matters to take care of than spending time with a runny-nosed child," it was small wonder Annabelle had clung to the sweet friendship she'd shared with Lawrence while growing up.

And she must learn to be satisfied with *only* friendship, she reminded herself yet again. Frances was the woman he loved.

Sighing, she rose from the couch and changed into a white, ruffled nightgown. Then, grabbing her Bible, she climbed onto the soft mattress. But she was too upset to concentrate on nightly devotions. Laying the Bible on a nearby chair, Annabelle stared at the electric fireplace that took the chill out of the room.

Unfortunately, it did nothing to take the chill out of her heart.

efore dawn the next morning, Lawrence rose from bed, groomed, and hurriedly dressed. He wanted to take advantage of the ship's gymnasium. A believer in the value of physical fitness, Lawrence almost took it to the extreme. Horseback riding, fencing, canoeing, lifting weights—he'd enjoyed all of these at Fairview, his ancestral home, and he was anxious to see what the *Titanic* provided for the athlete.

He walked up the stairs to the boat deck, easily finding the large gymnasium. Making his way toward a rowing machine, Lawrence again thought of Annabelle. He still found it hard to believe she was the woman he'd been staring at before they'd left Southampton. He remembered last night, how she'd shyly told him she was approaching her nineteenth birthday. Annabelle Mooreland . . . a young woman. Unbelievable.

He thought about when he'd first seen her at Mooreland Hall—a little waif cowering on the stairs during the Harvest Ball, afraid of being discovered. His mother had told him Annabelle had recently sailed to England with her father, having lost her mother several months prior to the voyage. He had seen the pain and uncertainty in her wide emerald eyes and pinched white face and had made an effort to befriend the lonely little girl. His kindness had been prompted by sympathy, but as Lawrence got to know her, he'd thoroughly enjoyed the independent little miss—her feistiness, her sweetness, her innocence—and had treated her like the younger sister he'd never had.

However, the feelings that had raced through him upon seeing her again were *not* those one would feel for a younger sibling. Ridiculous! He was six years older than she was; at her age, she probably thought him an old man. Still, he would like to renew their friendship, if she were agreeable. . . .

The muscles of his chest strained against the thin material of his shirt, and his strong arms glistened with sweat as he pulled on the oars of the rowing machine with steady strokes. After about ten minutes of rigorous exercise, Lawrence mounted one of the mechanical bicycles and gave his legs a good workout. He lifted a few weights, then rolled down his sleeves, shrugged into his coat, and headed for the freshwater bathing pool, Annabelle on his mind the whole time.

ॐ

"Good morning."

Annabelle looked up from her book, shocked to see Lawrence standing there. He smiled and motioned to the empty chair next to her. "May I?"

Eyes wide, she nodded.

"I missed you at breakfast," Lawrence said softly as he sat down and faced her. "Your father said you still weren't feeling well. I hope you're much improved now?"

Her heart fluttered. Had he sought her out at breakfast? That's what his words implied. "Yes, I'm feeling much better. I had a small headache, but it's gone now. This wonderful salt air and sunshine are invigorating."

Lawrence nodded and took off his hat, pushing his fingers through his thick dark hair. "It's fortunate the ocean is so calm. Otherwise you might have to deal with being seasick—a most unpleasant sensation, from what I've heard."

"Yes, I know." Annabelle grimaced. "I remember having that problem on the journey to England eight years ago. And I believe my maid must be dealing with the same thing, though with the lovely weather conditions it does seem a bit strange. She's been sick since we boarded at Southampton."

"I'm sorry to hear that," Lawrence said sympathetically. "Is Mrs. Reardon still your maid?"

"Mrs. Reardon was my *nanny*," Annabelle said, stressing the word. "I have a *ladies' maid* now. Father secured her services not long after I turned sixteen."

"A ladies' maid." He chuckled. "Let's hope you don't put frogs in *her* blankets before she retires for the evening," he teased, reminding her of an incident she'd once confidentially shared with him concerning her nanny.

Annabelle bristled. "Lawrence, really! I was twelve years old then. I'm not a child any longer!"

He straightened, the smile leaving his face. "Of course you're not. I was merely jesting, Annabelle. Please don't take offense." He looked away, wondering why she'd gotten so angry. Whenever he'd made such remarks in the past, he'd elicited a giggle out of her, which often turned into shared laughter between them. But the green eyes flashing at him now held no laughter.

After an uncomfortable silence, he looked down at the book in the lap of her dove-gray dress. "Might I ask what you're reading?" he said lightly.

She gave a faint smile, embarrassed to have reacted so crossly to his teasing comment. She realized he hadn't meant any harm by it. It wasn't in his nature to hurt someone's feelings. But oh, how she wished he would really look at her and see how she'd changed! "I visited the ship's library and found a copy of *The Pilgrim's Progress* by John Bunyan. Have you read it?"

"Ah, the adventures of Christian," Lawrence said, nodding. "An excellent book."

"Then you *have* read it?"

"Oh, yes. I think every Christian should read *The Pilgrim's Progress* to help enhance their spiritual journey."

Annabelle's heart soared. Roger had never wanted to discuss spiritual subjects, claiming they were much too deep and philosophical, and there were more exciting things in life to talk about. And Annabelle's father, though he'd once given his life to the Lord, rarely engaged in such discussions. Only with Lawrence had she been able to talk of spiritual matters.

"I like to think that when Christian arrived at the Celestial City," she said excitedly, "he prayed for Christiana, and through his prayers, she developed the desire to follow him and be saved."

Lawrence glanced out over the ocean and watched a gull dive over the sparkling water. He paused, considering. "An interesting concept. I'm not certain if there's Scripture to back up your theory, but I do know without a doubt that Jesus Christ is our personal intercessor to the Father."

She smiled, thrilled to discuss spiritual things with him again. She had so many questions, so many things she didn't know. The church she'd attended in Fairhaven was confusing and strangely empty, though it had been packed with the well-to-do of the area. "Does that mean, then, that we—those of us who are on the earth—aren't to intercede if Jesus is doing it for us already?" she asked, her words coming out a bit hasty in her excitement.

He looked startled by her question. "My word, no! Didn't the good Lord tell us how important it is to constantly be in prayer and thanksgiving and admonish us to pray for one another daily? Saint Paul also spoke of it in his many letters. I feel that if it weren't so important for us to take an active part in intercession—especially for the unsaved—then it wouldn't be referred to as often as it is throughout the Scriptures."

The morning passed quickly while they talked. The sun was directly overhead when they pulled into Queenstown, off the coast of Ireland, their last stop before heading out to sea.

Annabelle's hand flew to her mouth. "Oh, my! It must be close to noon," she exclaimed. "We've been talking for hours!"

Lawrence smiled warmly. "I can't think of any way I would prefer to spend the morning. I've enjoyed our conversation, Annabelle. I've missed them," he added softly. "That's one thing I would have liked to have had at Oxford—someone I could really open up to like I could with you. Oh, I had friends. . . . But with you it was different somehow."

She lowered her head, her cheeks warming. "I've missed you, too, Lawrence."

He smiled and held out his hand. "Would you care to take a turn around the deck with me, Annabelle? For old time's sake?"

She swallowed hard and nodded, allowing him to assist her. He replaced his hat, and she clutched the book to her breast as they began to stroll together along the sunny deck, reliving old memories and watching as hundreds of seagulls soared and dived in the *Titanic's* wake.

&

Annabelle stuck the end of the pen between her teeth, wondering what to write next in her letter to Patricia. She looked around the room at the other ladies, the Georgian-style furniture, the carved paneling, the exquisite décor of the light and airy reading and writing room—obviously designed for feminine tastes—and contemplated her dilemma.

Looking down at the ivory sheet of paper only half filled with flowery writing, she sighed. Should she tell Patricia about seeing Lawrence again? No, perhaps not. Annabelle had met Patricia at a banquet Annabelle had attended with Roger this past year, so Patricia didn't know Lawrence. And to tell her about him at this point would steal something away from the special friendship he and Annabelle shared. Her brow wrinkled.

Despite knowing Lawrence didn't have a romantic interest in her, it bothered Annabelle that he still thought her a child. Otherwise, wouldn't he have asked if she would like to visit the Café Parisian for tea and scones instead of inviting her for hot cocoa and macaroons? True, they'd been her favorites when she was a child, but she was a woman now! When would he see that?

Almost furiously, Annabelle began to write. A huge blob of black ink splotched the paper, entirely covering several of her words. "Oh, drat!" she fumed under her breath.

"Somethin' the matter, honey?"

Annabelle looked up at the handsome woman who sat across the table from her with a book in her hand. Bright blue eyes set in an oval

27

face that spoke of strong character looked back at Annabelle. A cloud of dark reddish hair covered the woman's head—a gargantuan hat, loaded with flowers, covering it. Wearing a stiff navy blue dress with a white ruffled inset, the plump woman looked to be in her forties.

"I'm afraid I've ruined another sheet of stationery," Annabelle explained ruefully.

"Don't worry. I'm sure you can get another one. A ship like this one is bound to have plenty o' supplies."

Annabelle looked at the three crumpled pieces of paper at her elbow, the result of previous mistakes. "Yes, I know . . . it's not that. I simply don't seem to be able to focus on what I want to say right now." She sighed. "I suppose my mind is on other things."

"Your young man, for instance?"

Annabelle's head shot up at the woman's gentle query, and she looked across the table into laughing eyes.

"Forgive me if I'm a little too blunt, honey, but I couldn't help noticin' the two of you talkin' to each other this mornin' as I walked along the deck."

Annabelle blushed. "I notice you're an American," she said hastily to change the subject. "I, too, come from America—Manhattan, New York—though I've lived in England for the past eight years."

The woman nodded. "Newport's my home. Name's Mrs. Margaret Brown—but you can call me Maggie; everybody does." Her eyes twinkled. "You remind me of a young lady I met in Denver once—a sweet young thing. Met her not too long after James an' I met—that's my husband, you know, though now we're what people call 'estranged.' Strange word, isn't it? Strange—estranged. Get the connection?" She let out a loud laugh, eliciting disapproving stares from a few others in the room.

Annabelle was shocked at the boisterous behavior of the woman, though she thought she detected a look of sadness in the blue eyes and wondered if Mrs. Brown was really as indifferent concerning the situation with her husband as she appeared to be.

Maggie again took up the conversation but was stopped when the six o'clock bugle sounded the call that it was time to dress for dinner.

They parted, Maggie issuing an invitation to get together for tea soon. Annabelle nodded vaguely and smiled.

At the moment, all she could think about was that soon she would see Lawrence again.

4

*S*adie, you should go back to your cabin. I don't think you're well enough to be up yet."

"I'll be all right, miss," the young blond quickly assured, though her tired hazel eyes belied her words. "At least let me do up your hair. I feel absolutely awful that you had to do it last night. And however did you manage your stays this morning?"

"I received help from a stewardess," Annabelle explained, fluffing her dress as she critically eyed her reflection in the mirror. "After you finish my hair I want you to go back to bed, though—and this time, I want you to stay there until you're one hundred percent better." She smiled at her maid. "Okay?"

Sadie nodded, and Annabelle sat down in a cushioned chair in front of the vanity, allowing Sadie to comb, weave, and sweep her hair up into an elaborate style, elegantly displaying her shining curls. Sadie was a skillful hairdresser, and Annabelle was secretly relieved for Sadie's expertise tonight. A jeweled hairpiece, sprinkled with tiny diamonds, provided the final touch as Sadie slipped it over Annabelle's head.

After Sadie left, Annabelle studied her reflection in the mirror. She wore a taupe-colored satin gown that shimmered in the light. The neckline was Grecian—gently gathered in shimmering ripples below the collarbone to fall in numerous folds down her back. Her mother's antique diamond pendant circled her neck, matching earrings dangled from her small ears, and long white gloves and satin pumps matching the gown completed the ensemble. Annabelle smiled at her reflection, satisfied. She hardly looked like a little girl now!

As she walked into the dining room on her father's arm and greeted other passengers she'd previously met, Annabelle glowed with the shocked look of approval and admiration Lawrence gave her, and she was pleased she'd taken the extra effort with her preparations.

Even Charlotte's eyes opened wide. "Why, you look simply lovely, mademoiselle," she remarked, her green eyes taking full inventory of Annabelle. She turned to Edward, who sat beside her. "I can see where she gets her looks—*oui?*"

Edward's face turned ruddy, and Annabelle's mouth grew grim. Was it to be another night like last evening, with Charlotte fawning over her father the entire time?

Monsieur Fontaneau spoke up. "My sister speaks ze truth. You are truly a vision, mademoiselle. Perhaps you would care to accompany us to ze reception room after dinner? Your father has agreed to join us, so you will not go unchaperoned."

Annabelle looked to her father, but he ignored her. "I—I'm rather tired tonight, Monsieur Fontaneau, and directly after the meal I plan to retire to my stateroom to rest," she said quickly.

He nodded, but his ocean-deep blue eyes seemed to burn through her, demanding . . . what? Annabelle hastily looked away.

Lawrence watched the interchange between the two and a nerve ticked near his jaw. He didn't trust Eric Fontaneau one bit, whether he was the son of a French count—as Eric had told them last night—or not! And Lawrence certainly didn't want him around Annabelle. There was something about the man that seemed dangerous, phony—as if he were trying too hard to impress.

"Since your father has made other plans, I'd be more than happy to escort you to your stateroom after dinner, Annabelle," Lawrence said smoothly.

"A splendid idea, Lord Caldwell. So gracious of you to offer," Edward piped up immediately.

Lawrence's silver-blue eyes turned toward her. Eyes that reminded her of warm ice. Though the term was an odd one, it fit. His look seemed to melt her. "Annabelle?"

Annabelle nodded. "Thank you, Lawrence. I would like that very much."

The meal passed rather comfortably after that, except for one incident. Monsieur Fontaneau ordered a bottle of vintage wine, insisting everyone drink. Not willing to consume any form of alcohol, Annabelle declined and was pleased that Lawrence did likewise. But her father gladly accepted, much to Annabelle's dismay.

After the seventh course had been taken away and dessert served, Annabelle noted with disgust that Charlotte was now acting tipsy. True, wine, champagne, and liquor routinely flowed freely throughout the sumptuous meals—a waiter always at the ready to refill an empty glass—but tonight Mademoiselle Fontaneau seemed quite intoxicated. Had Annabelle imagined it or had Charlotte moved her chair closer to Annabelle's father's?

Annabelle angrily bit off the end of her chocolate éclair, wishing it was a certain woman's head. She forced herself to chew the cream-filled pastry, but when she was only halfway finished, she pushed her plate away and took a sip of water. Though *that* woman had ruined her dinner yet again, Annabelle refused to leave the table until everyone else did. She wouldn't go running off to her room like a silly child as she had done last night! She would show Lawrence she was a mature adult, capable of dealing with difficult situations.

Her heart sank when the waiter brought a bottle of champagne to the table at Charlotte's request.

Lawrence, seeming to sense her discomfort, said softly, "It's such a lovely evening. Shall we take a walk along the promenade before I escort you to your stateroom, Annabelle?"

A loud burst of laughter erupted from her father, and Annabelle turned her head, shocked. His whole being was focused upon Charlotte, who was speaking in husky, low tones, making it impossible for Annabelle to hear the words.

"I think I'll go now, Father. Lawrence has asked me to take a stroll with him before I retire for the night. Father! Did you hear what I said?"

"Hmmm?" Edward asked, turning to his daughter. His eyes were dull, his expression dazed. "A walk, you say? Oh, yes—fine night for a walk. You might take a wrap, though. A bit chilly."

"*Good night*, Father."

ॐ

Lawrence wondered if he had been the only one who noticed the frosty tone of Annabelle's voice. Together they left the dining room. His hand on her elbow, they climbed the stairway to the next three levels and the covered promenade, which stretched out along the length of A-deck. They walked in silence, passing several couples strolling in the other direction.

"You don't like Mademoiselle Fontaneau, do you?" Lawrence asked thoughtfully, noting how Annabelle stiffened at the mention of the woman's name.

"Why do you say that?" She stopped and looked at him.

"Because of the way you react whenever she's in the vicinity . . . and speaks to your father."

"Speaks to him!" Annabelle blurted, her green eyes flashing fire. "*Throws* herself at him would be more accurate. The woman is nothing more than a cheap floozy dressed in satin and jewels!"

Her cheeks flushed and she turned her head away. "Forgive me, Lawrence. Father has often warned me that my tongue is my own worst enemy. I shouldn't have spoken so. You must think me without any refinement whatsoever," she said dully.

Lawrence smiled. "Think nothing of it. Now and then everyone speaks things better left unsaid."

"Really? Even you, Lawrence?" She looked up at him, her emerald eyes brilliant. Her back was to the calm ocean as they stood in front of one of the well-lit windows lining the deck. The bright light played over her features, emphasizing the soft curves of her cheeks and forehead, her lustrous curls, her rosy mouth.

Mentally he took a step backward, away from her, though his feet didn't move. "Perhaps we should continue our stroll now," he said, a bit gruffly.

Annabelle nodded, confused. This time he didn't take her arm when they continued to walk, and a pang went through her as she wondered what had made him so distant all of a sudden.

❧

Lawrence sat on the sofa in his stateroom, blankly staring at the intricately carved paneling on the brown walls. When he'd purchased his ticket, he'd chosen Italian Renaissance for his room from the variety of décor available to first-class passengers. He wondered what Annabelle's stateroom looked like. Probably something soft and feminine like her. . . .

"Lawrence Caldwell, stop this nonsense right now!" he ordered. "Six years' difference is a lifetime to someone her age." He chuckled dryly and whisked his fingers over the back of his hair. Now he was talking to himself.

Perhaps he should go to the smoking lounge and see if anyone was about. He didn't smoke but would rather seek out company there than sit all alone in this confining room with its dark furnishings and his depressing thoughts.

Lawrence left his stateroom, ascended the grand staircase, and walked down the corridor to the dimly lit smoking room. Upon entering, he saw Edward Mooreland sitting slumped over at a green, felt-topped table and strode across the carpet in that direction. He waited for the other man to notice him and finally cleared his throat. "Excuse me, Mr. Mooreland. I see that you're alone; would you mind if I join you, sir?"

Edward, eyes bleary, looked up from the brandy he was nursing between clutched hands. "Oh. Hello, Lord Caldwell. Alone?" he repeated wryly. "Yes, frightfully so." He looked down into his amber-colored drink.

Lawrence felt that Edward's enigmatic words went a lot deeper than the moment. Without invitation, he sat down in the dark brown leather chair across from Edward. The older man fiddled with his crystal brandy goblet, a grim expression on his face, then picked it up and downed the rest of the contents in one gulp. His hand shaking, he set it back on the table.

"Don't pay me any mind, my boy. I'm afraid I've had a turn of bad luck with the cards. Perhaps tomorrow night will prove more profitable." His eyes flicked upward. "Do you play?"

Lawrence shook his head, and Edward sighed. "I quit shortly after I met Cynthia—my wife," he explained. "However, Monsieur Fontaneau can be rather persuasive when it comes to the game, and I must admit, I was rather easy to persuade."

Lawrence's mouth narrowed to a straight line. Here was yet another reason not to like Eric Fontaneau. "I trust you didn't lose much." The statement was posed more as a question.

"A mere pittance." Edward waved a hand in dismissal, but Lawrence could clearly hear the undertone of anxiety in his voice.

"Then I'm glad, for your sake as well as your daughter's."

Edward's eyes misted. "Ah, Annabelle. She's a good girl." A small grin cracked his mouth below his trim mustache. "Though she's a bit spirited, like her mother was. Unfortunately, Annabelle has a habit of speaking her mind without considering the consequences. But I'm certain, after spending time in her company these past years, you've already found that to be the case."

"Actually, I find your daughter quite refreshing."

Something in Lawrence's tone alerted Edward, and he studied the younger man intently. "Annabelle is still a bit of a child, and though she will turn nineteen in a matter of weeks, she thinks like a little girl much of the time. Perhaps it's my fault. Perhaps I should have married so that she would have had a mother to raise her and teach her all the things a woman should know." Edward paused and cleared his throat before continuing. "It will take a strong man to take my daughter in hand. I know what a handful she can be."

"I don't think you have any reason to fear for Annabelle's future. Your daughter is a genuine lady. She doesn't hide the truth behind fluttering eyelashes and flirtatious speech, as do some of the women I've met," Lawrence said bitterly, thinking of Frances. "With Annabelle, a man knows what he will get."

Upon hearing Lawrence's quiet words, Edward flushed as a picture of Charlotte came to mind. "Don't be too certain of that! Perhaps you don't know her as well as you think. There's a lot more to

Annabelle than meets the eye." He paused a moment, considering. "If I may be so bold, Lord Caldwell, do you have a personal reason for speaking thus?"

"I'm concerned for her welfare—nothing else," Lawrence said firmly. "She's always been dear to me, like my own sister."

Edward's eyes narrowed as he studied Lawrence, who seemed a bit too adamant, his eyes bright. Edward had a feeling the young man's interest went a lot further than he'd stated, whether he realized it or not, but Edward trusted him with Annabelle. He knew Lawrence's family well and had always been aware of the strong friendship between Lawrence and his daughter. In truth, he would have welcomed Lawrence as a son-in-law, but it was more important to Edward that his daughter find a man who truly loved her as he'd loved Cynthia. Especially after what that scoundrel Roger Fieldhall had done.

"Fair enough," Edward said, nodding.

Lawrence smoothed an imaginary crease from his black pant leg before speaking again. "Perhaps this is none of my business, Mr. Mooreland, but after our talk tonight, I feel I may be bold enough to discuss something else with you."

Edward inclined his head, his expression curious.

"Are you aware that Annabelle's behavior has been a bit, shall we say, strange lately?"

Instantly Edward's eyes flamed. "What do you mean by that remark, Lord Caldwell?" he demanded gruffly.

Lawrence paused, realizing he was going about this all wrong. "She's concerned for your welfare, sir."

"My welfare?" Edward exclaimed, incredulous.

"Yes." Lawrence looked him straight in the eye. "Your relationship with Mademoiselle Fontaneau has disturbed her greatly. Annabelle hasn't told me in so many words, but I detect that she's fearful your interest in the woman is deepening."

"Deepening?"

"As in marriage."

"Marriage!"

Upon hearing Edward's loud bellow, several of the other men in the room turned briefly to look toward their table. Edward straightened in his chair and lowered his voice. "I can't imagine why she would think such a thing! You must be mistaken."

"Perhaps. As I said, she didn't actually say it in so many words. I certainly don't expect you to confide in me, Mr. Mooreland, but since your wife died, have you paid as much attention to any other woman as you have to Mademoiselle Fontaneau?" *Including your own daughter,* he added silently, remembering how distant Edward had always been with Annabelle.

Edward's face turned ruddy, answering Lawrence's question.

"Perhaps you should talk with her," Lawrence suggested kindly. "It seems there's much that needs to be discussed between the two of you."

"Yes. Perhaps you're right," Edward tiredly conceded. "I'll talk to her tomorrow after breakfast."

5

*A*nnabelle woke early and quickly dressed. Not bothering to wait for Sadie, she again secured a stewardess's help to lace her corset. After donning a pale green dress bearing a white-ribbed front and high collar, Annabelle attached a cameo to her throat—her father's birthday gift to her when she turned fourteen.

Loosely pinning up her hair, she studied her reflection in the oval mirror. Satisfied, she picked up her hat, then changed her mind and laid it back down. Not today. She wanted to feel the hot sun on her head and shoulders and allow the breeze to sift through her hair. She wished she could take it out of its confining pins. But, of course, that wouldn't be proper.

Excited with the approach of a new day, Annabelle left her room and walked down the corridor to ascend the magnificent grand staircase. Starting at the boat deck, the ship's uppermost level, dark, lacy wooden banisters and rails, which matched the color of the paneled walls, wrapped around the upper balcony in a semicircle and angled downward. At each end of the semicircle a short set of white stairs edged in gold led down to a small landing, then turned and widened into one long stairway that swept down, fanlike. On the wall in the middle of the landing, an intricate carving bore a clock in its center. A bronze statue of a cherub holding an electric torch stood on a pedestal at the end of the rail, at the bottom of the stairs. High above, a domed skylight shed a soft white glow on the room below.

To reach the next lower deck, one only had to do an about-face after descending the last stair, walk a few feet, and turn, where another flight of stairs led downward. The layout was the same on each level.

Annabelle lifted the hem of her dress with one hand and held on to the rail with the other, as she made her ascent to the boat deck. The ship also offered three passenger lifts, located opposite the stairway. Annabelle and her father had used the elevators when going to dinner the previous two nights, but this morning she preferred to walk.

Upon reaching her destination, Annabelle noted a chill in the air and was thankful she'd brought her thick shawl. Turning toward the stern of the boat, she gasped in awe at sight of the red disc of the sun just beginning to touch the sky and flood it with graceful ribbons of shimmering color. Annabelle walked toward the stern until she could go no farther. Clutching the rail, she stared, losing herself in the beautiful artwork of the Master Painter.

"Fantastic, isn't it?"

Startled, Annabelle turned and looked up into eyes that had always reminded her of warm ice. Her pulse rate increased when she saw how close he stood.

"Forgive me," Lawrence apologized softly. "I didn't mean to frighten you, Annabelle. I was going down to F-deck for a workout when I noticed you walking in this direction." He smiled. "I'd forgotten how you enjoyed early morning. . . . I remember when you and your family stayed at Fairview for several days after the Christmas party because a snowstorm made the roads hazardous—I was on break from university at the time. Do you remember, Annabelle?"

She nodded. How could she forget? It had been one of the last times she'd seen him. She'd just turned fifteen, a most awkward age, and had dressed and tiptoed down the stairs one morning to view the sunrise through the huge picture window facing east in the front parlor. When she noticed a light coming from the open door of the study, she panicked and quickly turned in flight. Stumbling, she caught her foot on the edge of the second stair and fell, ending up on her derrière in a most disgraceful manner, her gangly legs sprawled out in front of her.

Annabelle had been mortified when, upon hearing her soft cry, Lawrence hurried from the study and had seen her in the embarrassing position. But he hadn't said a word about her clumsiness; instead, he anxiously inquired if she were hurt.

When she shyly assured him she was all right, he helped her up and followed her into the parlor. Together they had watched the sun rise over the crystalline white world and afterward had indulged in hot cocoa and macaroons—a forbidden luxury to Annabelle at such an hour. But he'd put his finger to his lips and teasingly whispered, "Our secret."

The memory of that shared morning with Lawrence warmed her now, and she smiled. "I always have liked to greet the new day. I feel that if God goes to all the trouble to start each morning with beauty such as this, I should be grateful enough to see and enjoy it."

He nodded, looking to the east where the sky was now a mixture of muted violets, soft pinks, and pale yellows surrounding a rose-colored sun, hazily reflected in the rippling wake of the *Titanic*. "Though I think it hardly any trouble for one so powerful as He," he said slowly and softly, almost as though he were speaking to himself and had forgotten her presence.

"What is it the Scriptures say?" he continued. " 'Bless the Lord, O my soul. O Lord my God, thou art very great; thou art clothed with honour and majesty. Who coverest thyself with light as with a garment: who stretchest out the heavens like a curtain: Who layeth the beams of his chambers in the waters: who maketh the clouds his chariot: who walketh upon the wings of the wind: Who maketh his angels spirits; his ministers a flaming fire: Who laid the foundations of the earth, that it should not be removed for ever. Thou coveredst it with the deep as with a garment: the waters stood above the mountains. At thy rebuke they fled; at the voice of thy thunder they hasted away.' "

Lawrence's deep, melodic voice sent tingles down Annabelle's spine. Her eyes widened in fascination. "I don't remember reading that," she murmured. "How wonderfully poetic! And you know it so well! I must find and read those verses. By any chance, do you know where they are found?"

"I learned that Scripture when I was a lad under my tutor's instruction. If I remember correctly, that Scripture is found in the Psalms." Lawrence shook his head ruefully. "I forgot to tell my manservant to pack my Bible, so I can't look it up. I'll have to secure another when we reach America."

"I brought my Bible with me!"

Lawrence marveled at how her face seemed to light up from within and her eyes sparkled as though with inner fire. He cleared his throat before speaking. "Why, that's wonderful, Annabelle. Perhaps later, after breakfast, you can bring your Bible and we can meet here?"

"Yes, that would be lovely," she said, suddenly shy.

"I must go now," Lawrence said. "I made an appointment to play squash with Mr. Frederick Wright, the racquet attendant. Otherwise, I would stay."

Annabelle felt her cheeks go hot and she knew she was blushing. His words and the way he was looking at her caused her to feel a little breathless, renewing dreams for a romance between them. "Until this afternoon, then."

"I look forward to it, Annabelle." He tipped his hat to her with a smile, then turned to go. She watched him stride away, his carriage erect and certain, until he disappeared through the companionway and she could see him no longer.

ॐ

Though she was nervous, Annabelle managed to eat a breakfast of shirred eggs, grilled mutton, scones with marmalade jam, and fresh fruit. Lawrence was quiet, and Annabelle hoped he didn't regret his hasty invitation to her earlier this morning.

She was relieved to see that Charlotte and her brother weren't in attendance. It didn't really surprise her, though. They hardly seemed the type to be early risers. Of course, the *Titanic* offered other dining options, and Annabelle supposed they *could* have visited the à la carte restaurant. But she didn't think that was the case. Given Charlotte's extreme interest in Annabelle's father, Annabelle doubted the flashy woman would dine anywhere but where he was.

Annabelle's eyes cut to Lawrence. With a sinking heart she saw that his face had a grim look as he sliced his tomato omelet. She had looked forward to their getting together for hours now, and she worried that he no longer felt the same way. He had seemed quite anxious to spend time with her earlier; perhaps he was thinking of Frances and now regretted his impulsive act. But no, he still thought Annabelle a child. She was no threat to Frances.

Her father blotted his mouth with his napkin, then turned to her. "Well, I'm for the Turkish baths I've been hearing so much about. What will you do this morning, Annabelle dear?"

"I, uh . . ." She hesitated, caught off guard by his sudden question after thirty minutes of silence.

"Perhaps we could talk for a bit then," Edward said with a smile. "That is, if you can spare me a moment."

"Of course, Father," she hastily assured him.

Lawrence rose from his chair. "If you both will excuse me, then?" He looked directly at her. "I look forward to our Bible study, Annabelle. I'll meet you on the boat deck at twelve o'clock, if that's agreeable with you?"

Annabelle flushed, feeling her father's curious gaze light on her. "Yes, that would be lovely," she said, relieved. It was obvious Lawrence was still in favor of the idea.

"Bible study?" her father asked incredulously, after Lawrence had left the table.

Annabelle picked up her cut-crystal glass and drank the last bit of orange juice, allowing time for her cheeks to cool.

"Yes, Father. Lawrence has always shared my love of the Scriptures," she said, setting her glass down on the table. "This morning he recited a remarkable Psalm about our mighty God making the clouds His chariot and walking on the wings of the wind, among other things. He has promised to show it to me."

"I wasn't aware the two of you met earlier today."

Annabelle felt her cheeks flame again. Why? It had all been perfectly innocent. "I was on the boat deck, watching the sunrise, and he came from the gymnasium. We met and talked." She idly ran a finger along the rim of her glass, staring at it.

"Ahem, well . . ." He cleared his throat. "Let us go into the reception room for a little more privacy, so that we may talk without interruption."

Nodding, Annabelle followed her father into the adjoining room. However, it was crowded, many people partaking in an after-breakfast coffee. Obviously frustrated, he led her up the staircase to the next level, where they found two empty chairs not far from the stairway yet far enough from a few other couples to allow them a private conversation.

"Whatever is the matter, Father?"

Edward slowly rubbed his thumb and fingers over his jaw and mustache. He studied the curved staircase, the oil painting on the wall, the muted lighting. His gaze lowered to the white tiles, interspersed with decorative dark brown tiles, beneath his feet.

Part of his mind appreciated the luxurious surroundings, while another part struggled with how to proceed with what he wanted to say. Finally, his gaze came to rest on his daughter, who looked completely baffled by this time, and he cleared his throat. "Annabelle, it has come to my attention that you don't approve of Mademoiselle Fontaneau. I wish to know why."

Now it was Annabelle's turn to squirm. She bit her lip and studied her hands. "She reminds me of a black widow spider."

Edward's eyes widened. *"What?"*

"They lure their mates to their webs, and when they're done with them, they kill them."

Edward shook his head in exasperation. "Annabelle, really! You're a young woman now and should act like one. Such fanciful imaginings are more suited to the mind of a child."

Annabelle's mouth narrowed, but she didn't respond.

"Mademoiselle Fontaneau is an interesting dinner partner, nothing more. Like me, she is lonely and seeks companionship. However, I've no desire to further the relationship."

Annabelle's ears perked up. "Really, Father?"

"Of course not." He reached out and awkwardly patted her hand. "It's been eight years since your mother died and left me, but on the slim chance I might be able to find someone as wonderful as Cynthia, don't you think I would seek your approval before taking the relationship to another level?"

Annabelle looked down at her lap, feeling suddenly foolish for having so little faith in her father or his judgment. "I'm sorry, Father. I know I've behaved abominably."

"I understand, my dear. If anything is bothering you in the future, I trust you will come to me with it."

She nodded. Edward hesitated, wondering if he should tell her about last night's losses in the card game with Monsieur Fontaneau. No; now was not the time. Besides, tonight he planned to win it all back, so there would be little reason to speak of his embarrassing folly.

ْ&

Once Annabelle reached her stateroom, she picked up her Bible and *The Pilgrim's Progress* from the table, left her cabin, and went up the stairs to the boat deck. She was much too excited to do nothing until twelve o'clock, so she headed for the sunny deck early to wait for Lawrence.

Annabelle had read only two pages from her book when a childish voice piped near her ear, "Hello."

Looking up, Annabelle saw Missy standing next to the deck chair and smiled. With a fluffy blue bow in her blond curls, the little girl looked absolutely adorable. She wore a white linen dress with a square sailor collar that was lined in dark blue rickrack. A blondheaded doll with a painted porcelain face was clutched tightly in her arms. Annabelle noted that the doll wore a dress similar to its owner's. She put down the book.

"Well, hello, Missy. How are you enjoying the excitement of being on a ship?"

The little girl shrugged. "It's okay, I s'pose. I've gone on one before when we went to Spain. This is Helena." She thrust the doll out for Annabelle's inspection.

"What a pretty doll. I see why you didn't want to lose her."

Maria walked up behind Missy. "Good morning, Miss Mooreland." Her tone was frosty and her dark gaze cool.

"Hello, Maria. Won't you call me Annabelle?"

Maria's eyes widened in an unguarded look of surprise, then narrowed perceptibly. "It is not—how do you say . . . proper—for me to do so. I am only a governess." Her tone was bitter.

"But that's not true! You're my cousin—daddy said so."

"Hush, little *niña*," the exotic woman hastily inserted, avoiding Missy's puzzled gaze. "You mustn't speak so. Your mother, she would not like it."

Annabelle was clearly interested, almost to the point of being rude and boldly asking what the child was talking about. But a sense of propriety saved her at the last moment. "Please, sit down," she said, motioning to the empty deck chair beside her. She'd been saving it for Lawrence. The sunny deck was crowded today, and Annabelle was grateful she'd found a spot early.

"We must be going, but thank you," Maria said quickly.

Blue eyes wide, Missy pouted and looked up at her governess. "I asked Mama about strangers; she said once you meet someone, then she isn't a stranger anymore."

Maria exhaled, exasperated. "It's not that, Missy. Your mother made it clear that you were to have a nap this afternoon."

"But I don't want a nap!" the little girl insisted. "They're for babies. I'm going to be five tomorrow." She straightened proudly, looking up at Maria. "Besides, Helen Lorraine doesn't have to take naps!"

"Tomorrow's your birthday?" Annabelle asked softly, noting the rebellious pout of the rosy lips and the blazing blue eyes and trying to divert Missy to a happier topic.

Missy nodded. "And Mama is having a party for me in the res'raunt." Instantly she brightened. "Can Miss Annabelle come to my party, Maria? Please? I'll be good and take a nap."

Maria looked totally flustered. "Missy, I—I am certain Miss Mooreland has other plans."

Missy quickly turned to Annabelle. "Do you?"

Always honest, Annabelle admitted, "Well, no, not at the moment."

"See!" the little girl demanded of her nanny.

Annabelle felt bad to put Maria in such a position and quickly spoke up. "Missy, your mother and father don't know me. Perhaps they would prefer to have only the family celebrate."

Missy shook her blond head furiously. "Daddy's not on the boat with us—he's in Spain. And Mama already said she wants to meet you. Oh, please say you'll come!"

Annabelle looked helplessly to Maria, who looked resigned. "The party will be at the Café Parisian at 12:30 tomorrow afternoon," she stated indifferently. "If you want to come, I am certain *Doña* Ortega won't mind." She took Missy's hand. "Come, Missy. We have taken too much of Miss Mooreland's time."

"Bye, Miss Annabelle." The little girl looked over her shoulder as her nanny pulled her away. "I'll see you tomorrow!"

Annabelle watched and wondered. There was certainly a mystery there. She looked forward to going to the party tomorrow and meeting the as yet unseen *Doña* Ortega. So . . . Missy's father was a Spanish don. Strange that none of his dark looks showed in his golden-haired, blue-eyed daughter. And why wasn't he here? Missy had said he was in Spain. . . .

"Hello."

Startled, Annabelle turned and looked up into Lawrence's amused blue eyes. "Oh! Is it twelve o'clock already?"

He sat down in the empty deck chair beside her. "No, only eleven-thirty. I came early."

His soft-spoken words seemed deep with meaning, or maybe she just wanted them to sound that way. Feeling her cheeks warm, she looked down at her lap.

"I see you've brought your Bible," he said quickly. "If you'll allow me, I'll show you the Scripture passage I referred to this morning."

"Oh, yes! Please do," she said with a smile.

Lawrence took the black leather book and flipped through the thin pages. Annabelle watched, noting his strong hands and slender fingers. A gold signet ring bearing his family crest gleamed from his right hand. Her gaze lifted higher, to his face, and she studied him as he perused the pages.

He had taken off his hat when he sat down, and the ocean breeze moved through his thick dark hair, teasing the locks as they played over his smooth forehead. His eyelids beneath straight brows were lowered, shielding his remarkable eyes. His nose was straight, his jaw strong, his lips well shaped, sensitive. Not for the first time Annabelle wondered how it would feel to be kissed by them.

"Ah! Here it is—Psalm 104." He raised his head, fixing her with his warm gaze. Quickly she lowered her eyes to the page, flustered.

Lawrence wondered why her face turned red and why her hands shook when she took the book, but he didn't comment. Instead he intently studied her as she bent her head to read the passage.

She really had changed in four years' time. She still had the same pert nose he'd always thought so cute, and her lips were pink—a little fuller perhaps. A few dark, curly strands had come loose from her up-swept bun, and for the first time he thought it a shame that fashion required women to wear their hair up. He remembered what a thick mane of it she had. Her face had lost all the baby fat and had thinned with maturity, bringing into relief her delicate cheekbones. The freckles were gone, but on closer inspection he was almost relieved to see a few light ones sprinkled over the bridge of her nose. A strange desire filled him to touch her cheek and see if it was really as soft as it looked—like satiny velvet. Her thickly lashed, emerald-colored eyes lifted to his face, and he swallowed—hard.

"Oh, but this is simply fascinating!" she exclaimed. "I never knew this was in here. The Psalms are quite beautiful."

"Annabelle," he said softly after a moment. "Please don't tell me you haven't been keeping up in reading the Word."

She lowered her eyes, a trifle sheepish. "Just the Old Testament. It's always been a bit difficult for me to understand—except when you explained the verses to me. You always had a wonderful way of making the Scriptures come alive, Lawrence. But when you didn't come home from university your last year, there was no one to talk to. And then we left Uncle William's house, and, well . . ." She shrugged and looked away.

But Lawrence understood and felt bad. During his last year at university, he'd gone with his roommate, Theodore, to his home during breaks. He supposed the least he could have done was write a cheery letter or two just to let Annabelle know someone cared. How lonely life must have been for her these past years!

He remembered the heavy atmosphere at Mooreland Hall, the constant animosity between the brothers—Annabelle's father and her uncle—and the huge, empty rooms devoid of children . . . except for one lonely little girl. Later his mother had told him that Annabelle and her father had moved to the empty caretaker's cottage on her uncle's property. And last year when he'd taken Frances to the annual spring soirée at Mooreland Hall, Annabelle hadn't been among the guests. He'd never forgotten her—their friendship had been too special for that. But once Lawrence had graduated, Frances had consumed most of his time.

He gave Annabelle's hand a gentle squeeze. "Well, I'm here now. So allow me to give you a brief lesson on the Psalms. They were mostly written by King David and deal with praising the Lord. However, there also are many Psalms that deal with crying out to the Lord in times of trouble. One thing the Psalms all have in common, though, is that they abound with poetry." He smiled. "If I remember correctly, you excelled in that area."

"Oh, yes! I loved it when we read from my book of sonnets together." Her eyes danced as she met his gaze. "But how I despised Latin! I'm quite sure I never would have understood it if you hadn't helped me, Lawrence."

"That's what friends are for," he said softly. "And I'll always be your friend."

Her face instantly clouded, and she looked down at her lap.

"Why the sad face all of a sudden, Annabelle?"

She shook her head.

"Annabelle? Don't you want to be my friend anymore?" he said in a mock-sad voice, trying to lighten the situation. He gently put his hand under her chin, forcing her to look up, and for one brief moment he was able to see what bloomed in her heart.

His eyes widened. "Annabelle . . . I . . ."

She rose before he could say more. "I have to go now," she murmured. But before she could hurry away, he grabbed her hand.

"Annabelle, listen to me—"

"Please, Lawrence—don't." She looked beyond him, refusing to meet his eyes, and noticed that several other passengers had curiously turned to look their way. "Let me go. We're drawing attention," she said quietly. Immediately he dropped her hand.

A group of rowdy boys raced by, laughing as they chased each other down the deck and abruptly stopping a few feet away when an officer blocked them and sternly reprimanded them. The incident was just what Annabelle needed to make her exit. Turning, she escaped to the nearby companionway and disappeared before Lawrence could rise and follow.

6

*A*nnabelle took a small bite of her watercress sandwich, her mind a million miles away. She picked up her teacup and put it to her lips.

"And how's that nice young man o' yours?"

"Excuse me?" Annabelle almost choked on her tea and set it down quickly on its saucer, avoiding Maggie Brown's shrewd eyes.

"The man I saw you with on deck yesterday mornin'. A gentleman if ever I saw one. When I was goin' to the lounge, he gave a little bow as I stepped off the elevator and moved aside for me to pass. Made me feel like royalty, he did!"

Embarrassed, Annabelle looked away. Two young children sat on the floor nearby, playing a game.

"He's not my young man," Annabelle said softly, watching as the tots rolled a ball back and forth. "He's just a dear friend."

"Hmmm, a pity. He looks like a right fine catch," Maggie said, her sharp eyes lowering to Annabelle's slim fingers tightly gripping the handle of her teacup. "Well, never mind."

Annabelle picked up the silver teapot and managed to pour more into her cup without spilling it, though her hands were shaking. "Do you have any children, Mrs. Brown?"

"Oh, please, call me Maggie," the older woman said. "'Mrs. Brown' sounds like you're talkin' to my husband's mother."

Annabelle allowed a small smile. "Maggie, then."

"Yes, a boy and a girl—Larry and Helen."

"And what does your husband do for a living . . ." Annabelle broke off and bit her lip, suddenly remembering what Maggie had told her the other day. "I'm sorry. I shouldn't have asked that."

Maggie chuckled and waved her hand, shooing away Annabelle's worries. "Now, honey, don't you fret. Ain't nothin' you can say to get me riled. You're much too sweet a child." Maggie reached for another sandwich. "James discovered gold quite a few years back—made a fortune off it. I'd say he probably uncovered enough gold to choke an elephant!"

"Really? How interesting," Annabelle said softly, now accustomed to Maggie's sledgehammer wit. She'd been in the woman's presence long enough to know Maggie Brown was in a class all her own, and Annabelle rather liked the older woman's colorful character. When she wasn't asking personal questions, that is.

They talked a bit longer, about family and friends, and Annabelle told Maggie what she remembered of Manhattan and her aunt who lived in New Jersey, making a mental note to check with her father and find out if he'd sent Aunt Christine a telegram informing her of their expected arrival time.

Unable to locate her father, Annabelle gave up and walked to her stateroom to study her Bible. She was looking forward to reading a few more of the Psalms. Upon entering, Annabelle found Sadie laying out her things for dinner.

"Sadie, you don't have to do that now," Annabelle said as she scanned the room for her leather-covered Bible, finally locating it on a chair by her bed. "Dinner is hours away."

Sadie blushed furiously, averting her gaze. "Well, actually, miss, I wanted to get everything ready now. I, um . . . ." She wrung her hands. "I have plans for this evening. That is, if you won't be needing me," she hastily added.

Annabelle studied her flustered maid. "Not at all, Sadie. Feel free to take time for yourself. I'm relieved to see you up and around and feeling better. You deserve some private time."

"Thank you, Miss Annabelle," Sadie said, lowering her eyes.

Annabelle studied her critically. "Why, I think you look better than you have in months. You're positively glowing! This ocean air must be good for you."

Sadie flushed an even deeper red but didn't respond except to say, "Yes, I feel fine now. I'll return at six to help you dress for dinner, Miss Annabelle. And thank you again."

Annabelle watched as Sadie hurried out, then turned to look at the silk dress hanging on the door. Cut simply, the gossamer ivory gown was trimmed with subtle threads of shiny silver, a silver satin underskirt shimmering beneath it. The filmy capelike sleeves were made of the same gauzy material as the dress and ended in a ruffle above the elbows. The gown, when it caught the glow of the electric torches, shimmered like trapped moonlight.

It was one of Annabelle's favorite dresses, making her feel like a princess whenever she wore it. She approved Sadie's choice and decided on the jewelry she would wear.

Afterward, she picked up her Bible and began reading. Poring over the poetic Psalms, she wondered about the men who wrote them, all the while being drawn closer to the One about whom they'd been written.

❧

During dinner, Annabelle noticed that Charlotte seemed rather highstrung, laughing a bit too strangely and doubling her efforts to attract the attention of Annabelle's father. As if that were a problem. However, Annabelle did notice a reserved air about her father tonight; he still smiled at Charlotte and paid a great deal of attention to her, but something in his manner toward her seemed to have changed.

Annabelle took a bite of her peaches in chartreuse jelly, chewing thoughtfully. Several meaningful looks passed between Monsieur Fontaneau and his sister, puzzling Annabelle. He seemed to be quietly demanding something, and Charlotte seemed . . . fearful? The woman suddenly let out a gay laugh, no sign of fear on her face, and Annabelle felt certain she must have been mistaken.

Lawrence's smooth, rich voice disrupted her musings. "You're rather quiet tonight."

Annabelle turned to face him, her eyes briefly fastening on his collar before looking beyond him. "Am I? I suppose I've nothing to say," she said, realizing she sounded a bit rude, but still embarrassed about their earlier encounter.

Lawrence wanted to bring up the afternoon's conversation, but with a feeling of frustration, he realized now was not the time. "Oh, you're wrong, Annabelle, you've always had plenty to say," he drawled, though not unkindly. She looked at him sharply, which was what he'd intended. At least now she wasn't avoiding him as she'd been doing all evening. "Tell me, have you read any more in the Psalms?" he asked, now that he had her full attention.

Annabelle bit her lip, then nodded, carefully setting her spoon on her plate. "Yes, I have. King David certainly was a poet, wasn't he? I know He was gifted with the harp and often sang beautiful songs to the Lord, like you once told me—and so many of the Psalms are filled with praise to the Creator." Her fine brows drew together in puzzlement. "Still, I was amazed to see how many Psalms deal with God delivering David from danger."

"You must remember, David often had to flee for his life from his enemy King Saul. David knew what real danger was, having come up against it countless times." She nodded, and he continued, "We could take a lesson from him in how to deal with danger, if the time ever comes for us to face it. Even in his most trying times, David never lost faith, always trusting the Lord would save him."

Annabelle idly picked up her spoon again, her expression thoughtful. "I find that amazing. I've never personally dealt with anything life-threatening. Not like my sister or my mother did." She looked up at him. "Have you ever experienced real danger, Lawrence?"

"I was thrown off a horse once when I was learning to ride," he admitted. "But besides cuts and scrapes and the few broken bones I acquired—as rambunctious boys often obtain while growing up—I've never faced any real danger."

"Were you really rambunctious?" Annabelle asked with a smile. "Somehow, I can't picture you that way. You've always been such a gentleman."

He leaned back, relieved that she was herself again. "Oh, yes, I was quite a little scamp. But I suppose most young boys go through that stage." He studied her, a mischievous light dancing in his eyes. "And I remember what a little hoyden you were, always tearing your new pinafores, climbing fences and trees, riding the horses with total abandon. I don't envy your maid her job. You always were such a spirited thing," he teased. But she wasn't one bit amused.

"Lawrence, must you always see me the way I was years ago? Take a good look. I've changed, in case you haven't noticed. I'm a young woman now—I enjoy teas and crumpets and balls. I prefer Paris fashions and Elizabeth Barrett Browning sonnets to pinafores and Mother Goose nursery rhymes. I was even engaged up until two weeks ago. . . ."

Shocked that she'd revealed such a thing and in such a way, Annabelle hurriedly looked down at her plate. She hadn't meant to tell Lawrence about Roger. But her words had come so fast and furiously—she was so frustrated with his constant little-girl comparisons—that it just slipped out.

There was a long pause before he spoke. "Annabelle, I apologize. Please understand that the image of you I had in my mind up until a few days ago was that of a little girl just on the verge of womanhood, and it may take some time for me to fully accept the changes. I can certainly see you're a young lady now, and I didn't mean any disrespect." She lifted her head and noticed how uncomfortable he looked. "I hadn't realized you were engaged," he added. "Do I know him?"

She shook her head. "I don't think so. His name is Roger—Roger Fieldhall. I met him at a party at my uncle's house."

"The polo player?" At her nod, he asked, "What happened?"

She grimaced. "I became aware he wouldn't be the type to keep his wedding vows once we married. It's no longer important," she said, not wanting to discuss Roger with him. "I'm just relieved I discovered the truth in time."

"Did he hurt you?"

Annabelle felt warmth flow through her at the almost angry, protective tone of Lawrence's voice—evidence he must still care about her a little. She looked back down at her dessert plate. "No, he didn't hurt me—not really. It was more a case of wounded pride and embarrassment. I never loved him and even told him so, but he seemed to think I'd fall for him in time. I'm ashamed to say his offer of a partnership in the glittering world of his stardom is what caused me to accept his proposal in the first place." *That and the fact I knew your love was for another, Lawrence*, she added silently.

Her eyes nervously flicked upward; she feared she'd see his expression filled with disdain for the fickle creature he probably now thought her to be. Her heart fluttered at the soft look he gave her. "I'm sorry you had to go through something like that, Annabelle. I know firsthand what a rotten experience it can be."

His words alerted her. "What do you mean?"

He looked around the dining room and watched as several guests departed for the adjoining room before answering her. "It appears dinner is over. Would you care to join me in the reception room? We can continue our conversation there."

She nodded and turned to tell her father, realizing with shock that at some point he'd torn his attention away from Charlotte and had been observing her and Lawrence. Annabelle's face grew hot. How long had he been listening?

"An excellent idea, Lord Caldwell. I'd like to visit the reception room myself and listen to the musicians play," he said, his eyes twinkling first at Lawrence and then at Annabelle. "Yesterday, when they played near the grand stairway, I was in rather a hurry to reach my stateroom and didn't pay much attention. And during dinner they play so softly, it's a bit difficult to hear them. I can scarcely hear them now."

Annabelle looked at him, shock written in her eyes. Except for the day they'd boarded, her father usually went to the smoking room for brandy and cigars after dinner. Why was he acting so out of character? Unless . . . unless he thought she needed a chaperone because Lawrence was romantically interested in her. *Oh Father, if only you knew.*

And yet, what had Lawrence meant by his cryptic remark earlier?

7

$\mathcal{A}$nnabelle moved with the others to the spacious reception room, barely aware of the group of talented musicians playing a gay tune. At the moment, all she was aware of was Lawrence by her side, his hand above her elbow where the long glove ended, as he guided her to a small table next to a tall plant with long, slender green fronds. Her father walked behind them, Charlotte clinging to his arm like a love-starved octopus, and Eric beside her.

Lawrence took the seat next to Annabelle. "They are rather accomplished, aren't they?" he asked after a few minutes had passed and the orchestra had moved into another song.

"Yes," Annabelle said a bit impatiently, wishing he would continue their earlier conversation.

After a few awkward minutes had passed, her father abruptly spoke up. "There's Colonel Gracie—quite an interesting fellow. Wrote a book on Chickamauga—one of the battles of the Civil War in America," he added for the women's benefit. "I need to discuss an important matter with him. If you'll excuse me for a moment?" He nodded to the others, then rose from his chair.

Annabelle looked across the room to the dignified gentleman with the bushy dark mustache. Colonel Gracie seemed to be deeply engaged in conversation with Mr. Straus. Did father really have business with the colonel, or was he merely trying to find a polite way to escape Charlotte's clutches?

Eric whispered something to Charlotte and they excused themselves, moving to the doorway. Annabelle turned to Lawrence. "Please tell me what you meant earlier when you said you knew firsthand how terrible an experience such as I went through with Roger could be," she asked, a little breathlessly.

Lawrence sighed. "Do you remember Frances Davenport? Her father's estate adjoins Fairview."

Remember? How could she ever forget? She nodded dismally. "I'd heard you two were engaged."

His eyes widened in shock. "Who told you that?"

Annabelle looked down, embarrassed. She didn't want to tell him she'd overheard one of the servants at Mooreland Hall gossiping with another a few months before Annabelle moved with her father to the cottage. The handsome viscount's activities had often been secretly discussed among the people of Fairhaven, though Annabelle never took part in such talk.

When she didn't answer, Lawrence said, "It's true my parents wanted us to marry, but Frances and I were never engaged."

Annabelle quickly lifted her head and saw the sincerity in his eyes. "You were never engaged?" Her heart stopped, then began to race, keeping time with the tune "Glowworm," which the musicians were now enthusiastically playing.

"No." He leaned back in his chair, his eyes going to the few dancing couples on the floor. "I never felt comfortable around Frances, though for my parents' sake, I did try to make a go of it with her. But she wasn't the lady everyone thought her to be." He looked toward Annabelle then. "A few months ago I discovered she was secretly having an affair with a married man. She only wanted a union between us because she was Davenport's stepdaughter and wasn't entitled to the large inheritance her stepbrothers were. She was attracted to the Caldwell fortune."

"Oh, Lawrence, I'm so sorry," Annabelle murmured, vividly remembering the haughty blond she'd seen dancing with Lawrence at the Christmas ball five years ago. His news about Frances didn't surprise her; but his news that he wasn't engaged did.

"Don't be, Annabelle. I'm not wearing my heart on my sleeve, I assure you. I never loved Frances and am grateful I found out her true character before it was too late."

Her mind a whirlwind of conflicting thoughts, Annabelle nodded as if in a daze. All these years she'd thought Lawrence loved Frances, that they were engaged and would one day marry. For so long she'd yearned for Lawrence to look at her with eyes of love but had thought it hopeless and had avoided his company, resigning herself to the idea of a loveless marriage with Roger. Up until a few months ago, she and Lawrence had been promised to others . . . but now they were both free.

"Annabelle, are you well?" he asked, his voice laced with concern. "You look a little strange."

She blinked and smiled at him. "Oh, yes. I'm wonderful."

He looked at her oddly, obviously puzzled by her sudden giddiness and the dreamy way she'd spoken, but he only gave her one of his boyish grins. "Something just occurred to me, Miss Mooreland," he said formally. "In all the years we've been acquainted, we've never danced with one another. Would you care to join me in a waltz?"

Her smile grew wider. "I shall be more than happy to, Lord Caldwell," she answered, just as formally. Her head was in the clouds as she took his arm and walked with him across the tiled floor.

Lawrence took her right hand in a warm clasp, at the same time lightly placing his other hand against her waist; then they began gracefully moving to the music of the stringed instruments. Annabelle followed his lead, though in her nervousness, her feet fumbled twice. She could feel the heat of his hand through the material of her dress and had to remind herself to breathe.

Dancing with him was as wonderful as Annabelle had always imagined it would be. The look in his eyes nearly melted her, and she felt her cheeks grow hot while her head slowly started to spin. They moved so well together; Annabelle was sorry when the Strauss waltz ended and the musicians went into a ragtime tune. But he didn't let her go. A few other couples twirled around them while they stood motionless in the middle of the floor and stared at one another.

"Oh, Lawrence, I love you," Annabelle breathed.

Her mouth dropped open in shock when she realized she'd spoken her thoughts aloud. Startled, he stared at her, his eyes growing as wide as hers now were, and she hurriedly broke away from him, almost tripping on her gown in her haste.

"I—I mean I love being with you . . . in your company," she blurted out, her face bright red. "I enjoy the friendship we share." She bit her lower lip. "I'm suddenly feeling quite weary. I think I'll turn in now. Good night."

He shook his head. "I can't let you walk unescorted this late at night, Annabelle," he said, his voice soft.

"Oh, no, please," she put in hastily, inching backward. "I know my way about, and there are many stewards and stewardesses throughout the ship—that is, if I should need assistance of any kind, which I'm certain I won't. But thank you for offering, Lawrence," she said quickly, her words falling over one another in her haste to depart. She almost tripped on the hem of her gown again as she took another quick step backward. "I'll see you at breakfast in the morning."

Turning, she escaped across the wide floor and up the grand staircase, like a startled doe in flight.

Stunned, Lawrence watched her rapid ascent. Had she really meant what she'd first said . . . that she loved him? He remembered the other day on the boat deck when she'd run away. For a moment he'd thought he'd seen something in her eyes when she briefly looked at him. Later, he was certain he'd been mistaken; yet her behavior afterward had been rather strange . . . as it was now.

He had practically convinced himself they could be nothing more than friends, certain Annabelle would be uncomfortable with the six-year difference in their ages. But what if he were wrong?

Lawrence made a hasty inspection of the room, searching for Edward to tell him Annabelle had left, so he wouldn't worry if he couldn't find her later. However, Edward was nowhere in sight.

Striding across the wide floor and up the grand staircase, Lawrence hurried after Annabelle, uncomfortable at the thought of her roaming the huge ship alone.

❧

Annabelle's heels clicked a sharp staccato across the smooth, polished floor as she hurried in the direction of her stateroom. She couldn't believe she'd actually blurted out to Lawrence that she loved him! She had thought it so often, and the shock of realizing he wasn't engaged to Frances coupled with the wonderful feeling of being in his arms must have loosened her tongue. Oh, how could she ever face him again?

He already thought her immature; now he probably thought she had a silly schoolgirl crush on him after the way she'd acted. But it was so much more than that! How could she avoid him these next few days? Unless, of course, she stayed in her room and starved. . . . She wondered if the ship offered room service. Surely a ship as luxurious as this would.

Her mouth turned grim. *You're acting just like the child he thinks you to be, Annabelle Mooreland. Stop being so dramatic! There is a little less than a week of this voyage left, and then you'll probably never see him again.*

Ignoring the pain this thought produced, she stopped walking, suddenly remembering she'd not spoken with her father about the matter of contacting her aunt. Should she discuss it with him in the morning? But what if it slipped her mind again? It wouldn't do for them to arrive unexpectedly. Yet she just couldn't go back down there and face Lawrence right now!

She bit her lip and peered down the carpeted corridor that led to her room, then she looked toward the elevators. To her surprise, Charlotte stepped off one of the lifts, alone, and hurried away, not noticing Annabelle. Which most likely meant that Annabelle's father had gone to the first-class smoke room.

But that presented yet another problem. Women weren't allowed inside the gentlemen's private sanctuary, where the men often retired after dinner to smoke cigars and drink brandy. Yet she had to talk to him. Annabelle took the elevator to A-deck, approached the door to the smoke room, and stopped, having second thoughts now that she was here. She supposed she could send a steward to fetch her father, but would he consider her errand frivolous and become irritated with her for interrupting him?

Well, it's too late to back down now, Annabelle thought determinedly as she looked at the door to the wealthy gentlemen's inner sanctum. Glancing around, she was dismayed to see none of the stewards who usually were in abundance wherever one looked. Frustrated, she walked around the upper balcony to the corridor, relieved to spot a white-coated steward coming from one of the rooms, an empty tray in his hand.

"Excuse me?" Annabelle queried, motioning to him.

Immediately he walked down the aisle. "Yes, miss?"

Annabelle paused, a bit embarrassed. "I was wondering if you could deliver a message to one of the gentlemen in the smoke room—a Mr. Mooreland—and tell him that his daughter desires to speak with him right away?"

"Of course, miss." He gave a slight bow and quickly walked into the smoke room. Soon Edward Mooreland's silver head came through the door, and Annabelle hurried up to him.

"Annabelle! What's this all about? Couldn't it have waited 'til morning?"

She blinked and bit the inside of her lip. She should have waited. Oh, why hadn't she waited?

Running his fingers over the lower part of his face, he gruffly cleared his throat. "I'm sorry if I was abrupt," he said, his voice now controlled. "Now tell me, what's the problem?" He took her elbow, steering her away from the door.

Annabelle relaxed, though her father still seemed a trifle uneasy. Perhaps he was just tired. "I wanted to know if you'd contacted Aunt Christine," she explained hurriedly, now feeling her mission wasn't as important as she had first thought and wanting to be done with it. "The rooms of the house will need airing, and the servants need to be notified of our arrival."

His face took on a strange expression. "The house . . . of course . . . the house," he said under his breath as though he were speaking to himself and had forgotten her existence. He blinked and shook his head. "I'd forgotten that little detail. Don't concern yourself, Annabelle. I'll send a wire tomorrow."

"Very well, Father," Annabelle said quickly, taking a few steps backward. "I'll see you at breakfast, then. Good night."

Edward gave a vague nod. His mind was so involved in the interrupted card game, he was unaware that Annabelle had hurried away unescorted. Abruptly he turned and entered the room, striding across the patterned carpet to his table. With barely concealed irritation, he noted Monsieur Fontaneau was no longer there.

Upon his return, a gentleman at another table turned and, after taking a puff off his cigar, nodded to the other empty seat. "Monsieur Fontaneau also had urgent business that warranted his leaving. He said to tell you that he would try to finish with it as quickly as possible."

Resigned, Edward nodded, sat down, and lit his pipe.

ॐ

Annabelle hurried down the stairs, relieved when she had reached B-deck. However, she'd taken the staircase closest to the stern, rather than the one she usually took near the bow of the ship where her room was located. So she still had a long walk ahead of her.

The corridors remained empty, and Annabelle felt completely isolated, her senses heightened by the eerie stillness of the long, carpeted hallway. Most of the other passengers were in the restaurants, reception areas, lounges, or on the promenades, and many had already retired for the night beyond these very doors. But that fact didn't make Annabelle feel much better.

"The Lord is my light and my salvation," she breathed, "whom shall I fear? the Lord is the strength of my life; of whom shall I be afraid?" It was all she could remember of the Twenty-seventh Psalm that she'd read earlier that morning, but it helped to ease the tension a little. However, when Annabelle reached the grand staircase, her uneasiness returned and multiplied. Monsieur Fontaneau walked down the stairs, heading in her direction.

"Good evening, Mademoiselle Mooreland," he said smoothly, his eyes roaming over her, making her shiver. "You shouldn't walk unescorted zis late at night. You never know what manner of man may be lurking on ze ship."

Annabelle's blood turned to ice in her veins. "If you'll excuse me, Monsieur Fontaneau, I must be going to my room now."

Unmoving, he stood in front of her, blocking her way to the corridor that led to her room. She swallowed and looked up into his dark blue eyes, her heart hammering at the bold look in them.

"You have left ze dance early. Such a lovely woman as you should not confine herself to her room so much of ze time."

Her throat went dry at his silky words. He lifted a hand to her cheek, brushing it with the back of his knuckles, making her shiver again. Then his hand dropped to the diamond pendant around her neck, lifting it with his fingertips. "Your beauty rivals even zese exquisite jewels you wear and zose shining from your hair."

Annabelle took a step backward, her hand nervously fluttering to her tiara. She said the first thing that came to mind. "They were my mother's. They've been in the family for generations."

"Ah . . . rare jewels for rare beauty. Zey are privileged to be in ze company of one such as zeir mistress."

Annabelle swallowed, her eyes darting around the empty room. "Excuse me, Monsieur Fontaneau, but I really must bid you good night."

She stepped around him, but his strong hands flew upward and firmly took hold of her upper arms. Her head snapped up, and she stared at him in shock. His face loomed closer; his eyes were electrifying, dangerous. . . .

"Annabelle?"

At the sound of Lawrence's brusque voice, her would-be attacker let his hands drop from her arms and took a step back, his head lifting to look behind her. Annabelle exhaled a shaky breath, and turning, she hurried to her rescuer, clutching his upper arm in panic. "Lawrence," she breathed in relief, forgetting her former humiliation with him.

His brow drew down into a frown as he looked at her, then at the Frenchman. Annabelle studied Lawrence's rigid, unsmiling features.

She glanced Eric's way, then turned back to Lawrence. The look of challenge passing between the two men was obvious; she knew conflict could ignite and flash out of control in a moment—unless she stopped it.

"Is there a problem, Annabelle?" Lawrence asked softly, dangerously, never breaking eye contact with Eric. "Was this *gentleman* bothering you?" He said the word sarcastically.

"No, no. I'm all right—really," she quickly assured him. "Monsieur Fontaneau was merely warning me of the hazards of walking unescorted this late at night. I suppose I became rather anxious, which explains my unusual behavior."

Lawrence broke his stare with Eric to study her face. "Are you certain?" His voice was steel wrapped in velvet.

"Oh, yes. It was of no matter, Lawrence, I assure you."

Eric spoke for the first time. "I will take your leave now, Mademoiselle Mooreland. Remember to be more careful in ze future." He nodded to both of them. *"Bonsoir."*

Lawrence watched Eric make his way up the staircase, and Annabelle clearly saw a nervous tic in Lawrence's jaw. Realizing she still tightly grasped his arm, she dropped her hands and took a step away. "I should go now. It's been a rather long day."

Without a word, he took her elbow and walked with her down the carpeted corridor to her room. She silently admitted she was grateful for his protection; her heart still pattered madly against her rib cage from the narrow escape. Or was it his close proximity that caused her heart to race?

At the door to her stateroom, they stopped. Annabelle felt her cheeks grow hot. Suddenly feeling a bit awkward, she looked down. "Thank you, Lawrence."

"It was my pleasure, Annabelle. I hope you have pleasant dreams." His low, soothing voice brought her head up. Flustered, she watched as he took her gloved hand in his and slowly raised it to his lips, his ice-blue eyes never leaving hers. "Good night."

"Good night," she said on a shaky breath. Turning quickly, she slipped into her stateroom, shut the door behind her, and leaned

against the smooth wood. Taking a few deep breaths, she told herself that his unexpected gesture had been nothing more than the customary act of a gentleman escorting a lady to her room and bidding her good night. Still, she hoped it was much more than that. . . .

8

"iss Annabelle? Ma'am?"

Annabelle groggily pulled the covers closer around her ears, trying to drown out the insistent voice. "Go 'way."

"But Miss Annabelle. It's ten o'clock in the morning. . . ."

Sadie's words were like a dousing of ice cold water. Annabelle's eyes flew open and she quickly sat up. "Ten o'clock, you say? Oh, how could I have slept so late," she moaned, throwing off the covers and hastening out of bed.

Sadie quickly gathered Annabelle's things together and helped her dress. "I'm sorry, miss. I suppose it's my fault—you missing breakfast and all. I—I didn't get to my room 'til late last night and didn't wake up 'til fifteen minutes ago."

Pulling on heavy stockings, Annabelle shook her head. "No, it's not your fault. I didn't retire until quite late myself."

She'd lain in bed last night, unable to sleep, her mind a hodge-podge of thoughts. She'd relived the frightening encounter with Monsieur Fontaneau but also the dance and the wonderful feeling of being in Lawrence's arms while they waltzed, and later, the look in his eyes when he'd kissed her hand. Had it been her imagination, or did he, too, desire more than friendship?

After Sadie helped her with her corset, Annabelle slipped a lilac dress with a white lace inset and long lace sleeves over her head, and Sadie fastened the pearl buttons running along the back. Suddenly Annabelle stiffened as she remembered something.

"Sadie, I'm in rather a dilemma. It seems I've been invited to a party—a child's birthday—and I've no gift to bring."

Sadie's brow furrowed. "A child's birthday, you say? Hmmm. I know of nothing . . ." Her voice trailed away, then her eyes suddenly brightened. "Wait a minute! I met the most delightful young woman on the second-class promenade. She crochets and knits all sorts of things. She told me she has a few items she's finished and hopes to find a place to sell them in America. Maybe she'd sell some of her work to you."

Annabelle's eyes gleamed as another thought came to her. "Oh, please find out, Sadie! The party is only a few hours away. See if she has a blanket—such as a baby would use."

"A baby?"

Annabelle laughed at her maid's stunned expression as she stopped in midflight. "Yes, a baby! Go on, I can fix my hair."

Humming to herself, Annabelle braided her dark tresses and wrapped the silky rope around her head, pinning it in place, then added a wide-brimmed hat loaded with lilac and cream blossoms.

Knowing she'd missed breakfast in the dining room, she ate in the expensive à la carte restaurant, which catered to special tastes. It was quite lovely with its deep pile rose carpeting, floral tapestry chairs, and light walnut furniture and paneling.

Annabelle wondered why her father hadn't come to her door to escort her to breakfast as he usually did. Remembering his abrupt behavior last night, she reasoned he might be ill this morning. Perhaps he had one of those nasty headaches that sometimes plagued him. She should check on him.

After a light gourmet meal, Annabelle hurried to her father's stateroom. She knocked on the door and waited, but he didn't answer. Mildly puzzled, she turned away, assuming he must have retired to what had become his favorite room—the men's smoking lounge. With a resigned sigh, she went to her room and retrieved her Bible, then climbed the stairs to the boat deck. She was sorry to have missed yet another sunrise and promised herself she wouldn't sleep late again while on this voyage.

A blast of cold air attacked her as she opened the door of the companionway. She pulled her jacket closer around her and easily found a chair. The boat deck wasn't crowded this morning, and few people strolled along the deck.

Annabelle shivered and opened her Bible to the Psalms. But the teasing wind snatched the page from her fingers and caused the rest of them to flutter madly. Sighing, she closed the leather cover, giving up. She looked out over the barely rippling ocean, half hoping Lawrence would come. But after ten minutes passed with no sign of him, Annabelle decided to seek warmth and went below.

❧

"Oh, Sadie! It's lovely," Annabelle murmured, holding up a snow-white blanket with tassels bordering its edges. Delicate pink flowers had also been embroidered along the edge. "And you even brought something to wrap it in—how clever of you!"

Sadie blushed as she handed Annabelle the brown paper and string. "A—a friend of mine is a steward on the ship, and he gave me this when I told him about the situation."

"How thoughtful of him. Please thank him for me."

Blushing, Sadie looked away and nodded. Idly wondering why her maid was acting so strangely, Annabelle shrugged it off, knowing she would need to leave soon for the party. She grabbed her reticule from the table and took out a couple of pound notes. "Give this to the woman and tell her for me that I think her workmanship is extraordinary. Get her name and where she will be staying; I may be in touch with her after we reach America."

Sadie took the generous amount of money and stuffed it in her bodice. "Her name is Myra Flannigan. I'll ask for her address." She bit her lip. "If you won't be needing me . . ."

Annabelle nodded. "Go and enjoy yourself. All too soon this voyage will be over, and you'll want as many memories as possible to share with your grandchildren someday."

As Sadie hurried away with a word of thanks, Annabelle wrapped the blanket, hoping Missy would like the small gift.

❧

Upon entering the Café Parisian, Annabelle felt as if she were seeing it for the first time. She'd eaten here the day they'd left Southampton, but she'd been upset then.

The lights were dim, the carpeting a dark brick red. Carved white walls and ceiling matched the wicker furniture. Ivy-covered trellises along the walls provided a splash of refreshing color. Several young couples sat at the tables, eating delicate sandwiches and sipping coffee and aperitifs while listening to the low strains of music coming from the band in the adjoining reception room.

Annabelle easily spotted Missy, who looked adorable in a dark-blue velvet dress and crocheted white-lace collar. An image of what Missy would look like in twenty years sat beside the little girl, talking to her. Maria stood on the other side of Missy, picking up bits of discarded paper. Several other children sat around the small table and at the table next to it.

One of the children, a girl no more than four years old, shyly walked up to Annabelle. A huge ruffled bow sat atop the girl's dark hair, and she studied Annabelle with curious eyes, a finger in her mouth. Annabelle smiled, receiving a shy smile in return.

"Lorraine, dear, come here," a dark-headed woman sitting nearby said softly. The child turned and ran to the woman, but instantly turned her head, looking back at Annabelle.

"Miss Annabelle!" Missy exclaimed happily, receiving an instant rebuke from her mother to hold her voice down.

Annabelle took the remaining steps to the table and handed her package to Missy. "I'm sorry I'm late, Missy." She turned to the blond, who curiously looked at her, obviously wondering at the appearance of a stranger at her daughter's birthday party. "I'm Annabelle Mooreland," she said with a smile.

Doña Ortega nodded regally. "Missy has talked a great deal about you. It was kind of you to come." The words were gracious, but the woman's Dresden-blue eyes were cool, as was the expression on her smooth, china-doll face.

Annabelle's gaze shifted to the exotic woman standing behind Missy. "Hello, Maria."

"Miss Mooreland," Maria said with a deferential nod.

An excited squeal erupted from Missy's mouth, earning another stern reprimand from her mother.

"Oh, Miss Annabelle," Missy gushed, blue eyes sparkling. "Now my Annabelle will have something to keep her warm!"

Annabelle raised her eyebrows, puzzled at the child's words, then smiled as Missy lifted a new, elegantly dressed doll with long, dark ringlets of hair for Annabelle's inspection.

"What a lovely doll," Annabelle said, relieved Missy had known for what purpose Annabelle had intended the gift.

As she watched Missy lovingly wrap the fuzzy material around her new doll, Annabelle felt grateful to the mystery woman who'd made such a fine present. She tried to recall the name Sadie had given her. Meg? No, not Meg . . . Myra. Yes that was it, Myra Flannigan. She fully intended to get in contact with the woman upon reaching America. Maybe Annabelle could help her set up her own business. Such craftsmanship shouldn't go unnoticed.

A smiling stewardess served red punch and thin slices of iced cake to the small party. Annabelle took a small bite of the rich cake, idly wondering at the strange relationship between Missy's mother and Maria. Not once since Annabelle arrived had Doña Ortega addressed Maria, except for a few curt orders. For the most part, both women ignored each other, and Annabelle could sense the dislike simmering between them.

Though Missy's mother was stunningly beautiful in her powder-blue, gauzy gown, there was a frosty look in her eyes and a downward tilt to her delicate mouth that warned of a cold nature. After several futile attempts at conversation with Doña Ortega, Annabelle wished Missy a happy birthday and left, grateful to escape the heavy atmosphere in the room.

ॐ

Annabelle tried to focus on the printed page, but her mind refused to concentrate. Where could her father be? She hadn't seen him all day—neither had anyone else she had asked.

She had hesitantly introduced herself to Colonel Gracie, upon seeing him leave the first-class lounge; he'd been sympathetic and had offered to go and look for her missing father. Annabelle hastily assured him that wasn't necessary, the memory of her father's angry behavior the night before coming to mind.

Not knowing what else to do, Annabelle then went to her room to retrieve *The Pilgrim's Progress*, deciding to visit the lounge and finish the last few chapters of the book. She'd easily found an empty chair and sat down, opening her book.

But as she sat there now—her eyes had skimmed over a paragraph three times and yet she still didn't know what she had read—she realized that trying to concentrate was futile. Sighing, she lifted her head to gaze out the curtained windows and studied the calm ocean.

"Hello, Annabelle."

Her heart jumped to her throat upon hearing the deep voice she loved so much. Willing her pulse rate to return to normal, she turned and looked up into Lawrence's serious gaze.

"May I join you?" he asked. Annabelle nodded, and Lawrence pulled a chair back from the table and sat down. "I was concerned when I didn't see you or your father at breakfast," he said as his eyes studied her, questioning.

A dread Annabelle couldn't name rose within her. "Father wasn't at breakfast?"

"Why, no. Didn't he eat with you? I'd assumed when I didn't see either of you that you'd both dined elsewhere."

She clenched her hands together in her lap and looked down. "Actually, I haven't seen him yet today."

Lawrence obviously sensed her distress, for his voice became soothing. "I'm certain there's no cause for alarm, Annabelle. Likely as not he's in the smoking lounge, or perhaps he went to visit the Turkish baths again. I wouldn't concern myself."

"Yes—yes, you're right. There's probably a simple explanation." But she knew she didn't sound very convincing.

"Would you like me to go look for him?"

Annabelle bit the inside of her lip, then raised her eyes to his. They were concerned and sympathetic, causing a warm glow to radiate inside her, chasing the gloom away. She smiled. "No. I'm probably overreacting. It's likely as you said, Lawrence—he simply made other plans without telling me first. His behavior was rather unusual last night."

He gave her an encouraging smile, for which she was grateful. There was a moment of companionable silence before he spoke. "I see you're continuing your studies on the pilgrimage of Christian." He nodded to the book on the table.

"Yes," she said with a small sigh. "Only today I can't seem to concentrate on the words. I'm afraid I can't get Christian through the Enchanted Garden. Every time I try, I lose concentration, and I fear he's doomed to stay there forever."

He grinned. "Perhaps what you need is a good dose of fresh air. Would you care to take a walk with me around the deck?"

"Oh, but it's so cold." She bit her lip, uncertain. "I suppose I could get my coat from my room, though. . . ." She really *did* want to walk with Lawrence.

He stood and held out his hand. "Shall we, then?"

"All right," Annabelle said a little shyly, still uncertain how things stood between them. Were they just friends or had their relationship entered another level? Oh, how she hoped it was the latter!

Before going to her room, Annabelle tried knocking on her father's door again. When she received no reply, she gave Lawrence a little shrug, acting as if she wasn't concerned. But she was. Somehow, she knew something was terribly wrong.

&

Edward heard the insistent knocking attacking his brain and came out of his alcohol-induced sleep, groaning. He sat up and swung his legs over the side of the bed, wishing the terrible throbbing pain would stop. He didn't remember drinking *that* much.

The events of the previous night played themselves over in his fuzzy brain like some form of sadistic torture, and he dropped his head into his hands in agony. "Oh, Cynthia! What have I done? *What have I done!*" Rasping sobs shook his body as heavy chains of guilt wrapped around him, squeezing ruthlessly.

In one wild, reckless moment, he had succeeded in destroying his young daughter's future.

9

*O*oh! It is rather cold, isn't it?" Annabelle gasped, pulling her fur coat closer around her.

"Would you prefer to go below?"

She looked sideways at Lawrence and saw a hint of disappointment in his eyes. "No, I'll be fine. I do enjoy the outdoors," she said with a smile.

"I know. It's something we've always had in common," Lawrence answered so softly, she almost didn't hear him.

They walked in companionable silence for a few moments, looking at the still ocean over the white balustrade.

"Isn't it unusual that the sea is so calm?" Annabelle asked, more to start a conversation than for any real desire to know. In the silence, terrible thoughts concerning the whereabouts of her father had clamored through her head, and she didn't want to give them free rein. "After my first voyage, and after hearing you read *Moby Dick* years ago, I was expecting at least one small storm."

Lawrence seemed thoughtful, then nodded. "Yes, I overheard several gentlemen—obviously well-seasoned travelers—talking yesterday. They, too, were commenting on the strange phenomenon. However, I think it rather a blessing, don't you?"

"Yes. It is a relief not to be tossed to and fro."

He smiled at her. "I agree. But I was referring to the fact that the captain has made remarkable time. We covered more miles yesterday than on Thursday, and, from what I understand, we will probably exceed yesterday's distance today. Because the waters are so calm, the ship is able to travel across the ocean much faster," he explained.

"Therefore, it's a strong possibility we'll reach the shores of America sooner than planned."

His words brought a stab of pain to Annabelle's heart. Soon they would arrive in New York Harbor. And what then? Would she have to part ways with Lawrence? Would he just tip his hat and say good-bye? *Please, God. Don't let me lose him again.*

"Why so melancholy all of a sudden, Annabelle?" He stopped walking and turned to her. She stopped also.

Swallowing the tears threatening to choke her, she managed a small smile. "Was I? I suppose I was wondering what your plans were once we reach America. I was quite surprised to discover you aboard the *Titanic*. I mean, I couldn't possibly think what business a Caldwell would have in the States."

"Not business . . . pleasure. I've always had the wanderlust in my heart—the desire for adventure. Father realized it and encouraged me to take this voyage and visit friends who live in Manhattan. He hopes this bit of excitement will satisfy the adventuring spirit in me so that I can soon return to England and resume my duties as heir apparent," he said, with a boyish grin.

Remembering the stories Lawrence read to her before he went to university—of courageous knights embarking on dangerous quests, often rescuing damsels in distress, and ruthless pirates fighting daring captains on the high seas—Annabelle doubted the earl's plan would work concerning his son. Even now she could remember the gleam in Lawrence's eyes while he read to her.

"My mother's home is in Manhattan, also," she said softly. "That's where Father and I are going."

"Really . . . ," Lawrence said, seeming to consider something. "Would you mind if I called on you at your home in America?"

She held her breath, hardly daring to believe she'd heard him correctly. "As a friend?" she murmured.

He nodded, taking the wind out of her sails. But his next words buoyed her spirits again. "We will always be friends, Annabelle. But I was hoping to call on you as a suitor. That is, if the age difference between us doesn't concern you," he added quickly.

"Age difference?"

"The fact that we're six years apart."

Her look turned incredulous. "You're hardly an old man, Lawrence! Why, Father was eleven years older than Mama," she added, obviously surprising him, judging from his shocked expression. She nodded as if to emphasize her point. "He was thirty-five and she was twenty-four when they married. And they loved each other dearly.

"Oh, I'm certain they fought at times, but I've no recollection of them doing so. I do remember Mama telling me about a conflict between them a few days after I was born, though. You see, Father wanted to name me for my grandmother—his mother—but Mama insisted on naming me after her mother and sister, and for a while, Mama and Papa weren't even on speaking terms. Can you imagine? Over something as silly as a name?"

Annabelle giggled, realizing she was babbling inanely, but she was giddy with the knowledge that Lawrence was romantically interested in her, and she couldn't seem to control her tongue.

"However, in the end they compromised, and Father had his way," she continued. "Why, I'm probably the only woman on this ship with four names."

Amused, Lawrence smiled, his eyebrows lifting. "Oh?"

"Yes. My birth certificate reads Annabelle Christine Guinevere Mooreland," she said with a dramatic flair.

He looked at her so strangely that Annabelle blinked in confusion. Had she said something wrong? He cleared his throat. "Did you say Guinevere?"

Eyes wide, she nodded.

He continued to stare at her, the look in his eyes causing her heart to race as fast as the ship sailing across the ocean.

"Guinevere . . . ," he murmured, his tone incredulous, wondering. "I never knew. All this time . . . I never knew."

Feeling her cheeks go hot at his probing stare, she lowered her gaze. After a moment, Lawrence spoke again. "You're shivering. Perhaps we should go inside and order something hot to drink."

"Yes, that sounds like a good idea," Annabelle agreed, only part of her aware of him taking her arm and steering her toward the companionway. The other part of her wondered. . . .

&

During dinner, a strained silence settled over the table, and Annabelle ate her meal in confusion. Her father had finally made an appearance less than an hour earlier; however, Annabelle couldn't help but be shocked at his slovenly attire, so unlike his usual impeccable grooming. His silver hair was unruly, his collar wasn't buttoned properly, his tie hung askew, and his jacket had a rumpled appearance, as if he'd slept in it.

Annabelle tried to make eye contact with him, but he avoided her numerous stares and only muttered a few abrupt words in response to her curious questions. And then there was Lawrence. . . .

Except when she asked him a question, Lawrence barely said a word. What was he thinking? Did he wish he'd never asked to call on her? Was he having second thoughts? He had mentioned something earlier about their age difference, something that had never been a concern to her. But maybe it bothered him. Maybe he had changed his mind about courting a nineteen-year-old, unable to get over the obstacle of seeing Annabelle as anything other than the child she'd been. And the way she'd foolishly chattered about her parents earlier probably hadn't helped him see her as a mature adult either.

Annabelle tried to concentrate on and enjoy her glazed roast duckling, but it was hopeless. She may as well have been eating sawdust. Feeling a bit dejected as well as rejected, she lifted her head and idly studied the diners across the spacious room. Waiters inconspicuously weaved among the tables with their large platters, offering passengers a tempting array of foods from which they could choose their next course.

Colonel Astor and his new bride, Madelaine, sat a few tables away. Sweet and dainty, she was the same age as Annabelle, though her husband looked to be in his fifties; yet *they* seemed to be happy, despite the difference in their ages. Annabelle sighed and took a sip of water. She had briefly met Madelaine earlier in the voyage, while trying to compose yet another letter in the ladies' reading and writing room, and had learned that Mrs. Astor was with child.

Annabelle's gaze wandered to the right. She noted the polite and helpful Colonel Gracie escorting three women past the doorman and out of the dining room . . . and there were Mr. and Mrs. Straus, who, after the first night of dining at the Mooreland's table, had not eaten with them again.

Annabelle's father had managed to strike up an acquaintance with Mr. Straus while visiting the smoking lounge, he'd told her, and had found that he, Mr. Straus, and Colonel Gracie all shared a fascination for talk of the American Civil War, which had taken place almost fifty years earlier.

Annabelle could hardly blame the Strauses for not wanting to eat with them, after remembering Charlotte's shocking behavior the first night. Again the Fontaneaus were not in attendance, causing Annabelle to wonder. As a matter of fact, she hadn't seen Charlotte all day, except for a glimpse of her earlier that afternoon. . . .

"Annabelle?"

She turned toward her father, wondering about the desperate tone of his voice. "Yes, Father?"

"As soon as you've finished, I'd like a word with you."

"Yes, Father. Of course."

She resumed eating, suddenly apprehensive, and at last gave up, laying down her fork and knife. Her father must have noted her action, for he pushed away from the table and helped Annabelle from her chair. She rose and noticed that her father's plate was still full, the roast sirloin and creamed carrots apparently untouched. Annabelle allowed herself a curious glance in Lawrence's direction.

He looked up from his plate and gave her a small smile, which boosted her spirits a bit. But she was still anxious concerning her father. What did he have to tell her? It obviously was something terrible, judging from his behavior. She wondered if it had to do with Aunt Christine. Had her father sent a wire today only to receive bad news in return?

Annabelle bit her lip and tried not to worry as she walked beside her father past the other diners and through the door.

When the Moorelands were almost at the exit, Lawrence set down his utensils and watched Annabelle's retreat, still a bit stunned. All day he had mulled over his talk with her. Was it merely a coincidence that he'd been searching for his Guinevere and Annabelle just happened to possess the name? *Lord, is this a sign from you? Is she the one for me? If so, then . . .*

Closing his eyes, Lawrence shook his head, disgusted with himself. He knew better than to put his trust in fleeces, as Gideon had done before he fought the army of Midianites in the book of Judges. In Old Testament days it had been acceptable to ask for miraculous signs for affirmation before proceeding with a given action. But that was before the Savior had come into the world. The Holy Spirit now lived inside Lawrence's heart and was his direct connection to the Father. Lawrence would pray about his relationship with Annabelle, as he should have done concerning Frances. If he had turned to God first instead of trying to please his parents, he could have avoided a lot of wasted years courting a woman he would never marry.

Lawrence had always thought Annabelle special. They had shared a friendship that some may have considered unusual; but he'd never connected with anyone as he had with her, despite the differences in their ages. Of course, he'd only thought of her in terms of friendship and had looked on her with eyes of brotherly love . . . that is, until a few days ago when he discovered her on board the *Titanic*. And strangely enough, except for a momentary shyness on Annabelle's part, they had bonded immediately, as if four years of separation hadn't existed between them.

Lawrence motioned a nearby waiter to the table and ordered a coffee. He had developed a taste for the drink while traveling on the *Titanic* and wondered if he would ever go back to the everyday ritual of drinking English tea.

Lawrence thanked the waiter, who set the steaming cup in front of him. He took a sip of the strong brew as he considered his life. One day he would have to return to Fairhaven; he had no choice in the matter. At some point he would become earl, and his duties lay at home. But for now he would stay in Manhattan, instead of touring the country as he'd planned to do before leaving England. And he would earnestly pray to God concerning Annabelle, starting tonight.

Lawrence drained his coffee and left the dining room, not interested in the remaining courses of his dinner. Ascending the stairs, he went to the boat deck, desiring a walk before retiring for the evening.

The frigid air took his breath away momentarily. He paused, looking down the length of the deserted deck, wondering if he should return to his stateroom for his warm, fur-lined overcoat. Before he could turn back to the door leading to the stairway, however, something at the stern caught his eye.

Annabelle? he wondered incredulously. He studied the lone woman wearing a fur coat. Staring out over the calm sea, she stood by the railing, her gloved hand holding one of many thick ropes that were attached to the waist-high ledge and traveled up to the tops of four tall smokestacks along the ship. Her back was to him, and he couldn't be certain it was her—there was little light. But it did look like Annabelle from this angle.

Hurriedly, Lawrence walked to where she stood, his steps loud on the silent deck, and he watched as she turned to face him. It was Annabelle! And it looked as if she'd been crying, though it was too dark to be sure.

"Lawrence," she breathed in a shaky whisper. "What are you doing here?"

"I might ask you the same thing," he said quietly, noting her gloved hand quickly swipe at her cheeks.

"I—I needed time to think," she stammered.

Lawrence watched her nervous movements as she began pulling at the fingers of her white gloves. "Do you need a shoulder to cry on, Little Belle?" he asked softly, applying the pet name he'd used for her when he'd offered comfort in the past.

She shook her head. "I'll be all right, Lawrence," she said in a wobbly voice that belied her words.

"Annabelle, this is Lawrence you're talking to, remember? We've known each other too long for you to expect me to believe that. Let's go somewhere warmer and discuss it. And might I be bold enough to suggest hot cocoa and macaroons if the ship has them?" he teased, hoping to get her to smile; he remembered how she'd lit into him the other day after he'd invited her to the Café Parisian for the childhood treats she'd so favored.

But she didn't smile. She only looked at him with huge, tear-filled emerald eyes, causing his heart to wrench in pain.

Gently taking her elbow, Lawrence steered her back to the companionway. Feeling her arm shake, he sincerely hoped there was something he could do to help her. He knew it wasn't only the frigid air that caused her body to tremble.

10

*U*pon reaching the Palm Room, Lawrence spotted an empty table and led her to it. Immediately a steward came, and Lawrence ordered coffee, waiting until the young man had left before turning to Annabelle. "Now, what seems to be the problem?" he asked softly.

Annabelle clasped her hands in her lap and looked down at the table for a moment. Lifting her head, she anxiously met his caring gaze. "My . . . my father—" Annabelle broke off as the steward came with their coffee, her eyes nervously flicking back down to the table.

Lawrence resisted the urge to snap at the unassuming steward and made himself smile and thank him instead, before turning his gaze back to Annabelle. He watched as she took a sip of the black brew and grimaced. Either she wasn't accustomed to coffee or she didn't usually drink it black. He waited, trying to remain patient. A few silent minutes passed before he gently insisted, "Annabelle, please tell me what's bothering you."

She shut her eyes.

"Annabelle?" he prompted.

She opened her eyes and looked at him. Taking a shaky breath, she shook her head. "I've no idea where to start."

"How about the beginning? That's always the best place."

She nodded and took a sip of the strong coffee. "My father, before he met my mother, had a problem with gambling. He became a Christian shortly after he married Mother—it was Mama who introduced him to Christianity—and he gave up playing cards." She paused, then went on. "When Mother died, Father withdrew from me and everyone around him. I think at the time he even withdrew from God. He was so unhappy, so angry.

"During these past eight years he mellowed, but was never quite the same—at least not how I remembered him to be when Mama was alive. Two years ago he took up playing cards again with his old friends at an exclusive gentlemen's club where he's a member, but I didn't really think he had a problem. Not then."

With a pang, Lawrence watched as tears again formed in her eyes, but he waited patiently for her to go on, knowing that if he interrupted now, she might not finish the story.

"This past year he became even more withdrawn from me. It was painful, but I understood the reason for his behavior. It hurt him to look at me. . . . I've been told I greatly resemble my mother," she added with a quaver in her voice. Annabelle took another quick sip of coffee, then her eyes flicked upward to intercept Lawrence's encouraging, sympathetic gaze.

"My mother came from a very wealthy family," she continued. "She was the eldest child, and when my grandparents died in a train accident, the house went to her." Annabelle bit her lip hard. "That's where we were going when we reached America."

Lawrence's dark brows raised in question. "Were?"

"My father gambled the house away in a card game the other night, along with a great deal of money," she blurted. "Almost everything we have—had—now belongs to Monsieur Fontaneau."

Lawrence inhaled sharply. Obviously embarrassed, she looked away toward the high-arched window, where a view of the dark ocean could be seen between the openings of the covered promenade.

"Father had the deed to the house. He brought all his important papers with him. You see, we didn't plan to return to England. We only went there eight years ago because everything in America reminded him of Mama, and he couldn't stand it," she explained dully. "But as you know, my uncle and Father didn't get along, even after we moved to the cottage, and months ago, Father decided it was time to move on—to return to the States.

"But now we have nowhere to go. Unless we stay with my aunt.

But she's a recluse and blames Father for Mama's death—though it wasn't his fault," she added, fresh tears pooling in her eyes. "So now I've no idea what will become of us."

Annabelle felt his hand cover hers and turned to face him. Her heart began to race at the warm, almost possessive look in his eyes. She also detected a glimmer of anger in their depths, but knew it wasn't directed at her. Who, then? Her father?

"I know what Father did was wrong, but I don't blame him," she said softly, noting Lawrence's surprised expression. "You see, I understand what he was trying to do, in a way. Gambling is a sickness, a disease that makes the gambler think he can win with the next hand of cards. Father told me he was certain of his turn of luck when he put the house up for stakes. He'd already lost a great deal of money and was trying to win it all back. He was so positive he would win . . . but he didn't."

Lawrence nodded, admiring Annabelle for taking up for her father, even though she was now homeless, thanks to Edward Mooreland's stupidity. Lawrence had never gambled and didn't understand what would send a man to a card table to lose his money and eventually, in many cases, his honor. Oh, he knew there were those who won, but those cases were rare.

Several on board the ship were professional gamblers, Lawrence had heard, luring the unsuspecting to bid ever higher so that the professionals could line their pockets with the other men's wealth. But Lawrence wondered how those greedy, crafty men could spend money they'd dishonestly won and still live with their consciences? Didn't it bother them to reduce a man to nothing, to prey upon his weaknesses? What of the wives and children of the victims?

Lawrence felt Edward had been set up and that Eric was, indeed, a card shark, and his sister probably was in cahoots with him. Though Lawrence didn't know much about the gambling world, he was fairly certain no true gentleman would agree to such high stakes. And the little he'd seen of the smooth-talking Frenchman convinced Lawrence that Eric fit the mold of a professional gambler.

"I should go to my room now," Annabelle said, looking down at his hand still covering hers. "Thank you for listening, Lawrence."

"Little Belle, do you trust me?"

She looked up, surprise evident on her face. "With my life."

He smiled. "Then please believe me when I say I will never let anything bad happen to you if I can help it. You'll never want for anything as long as I'm alive. Let's pray, Annabelle. God has the answer. Nothing is impossible where He's concerned."

She nodded and Lawrence offered a quiet prayer, asking God to show them light and lead them in the way they should go.

A few minutes later, Annabelle walked with him to her room. When they reached it, she turned to him. "Thank you again, Lawrence. Thank you for being there for me."

"Don't worry, Annabelle. We've prayed and now we need only trust the Lord to show us His direction," he said, his tone encouraging. "Will you attend worship services in the morning?"

Her brow furrowed. "I wasn't aware there were any."

"Yes, in the dining room after breakfast. May I escort you?"

"I'd like that," she said softly.

He bent over and kissed her forehead. "Good night, Annabelle."

Her heart racing, she leaned against the door after entering her room and replayed the last few moments. As if an icy gust of air had suddenly blown into the room, the warm feeling was doused as her mind stubbornly reminded her of her plight. She looked at her reflection in the oval mirror of the dresser.

Tired, fearful, anxious, excited—all these labels could be placed on the girl who looked back at her with wide green eyes.

ಕ

Sunday morning as Sadie helped her dress, Annabelle wondered if she should tell her maid that soon she would be out of a job. Seeing Sadie's beaming face, Annabelle decided to wait.

Remembering how cold it had been yesterday, she opted for a brown velvet skirt and long-sleeved white blouse, attaching her mother's cameo to the shirred high neck.

Strangely, in the quiet hours of the night, Annabelle had come to accept her fate with a calm that surprised her. Whether Aunt Christine allowed her homeless brother-in-law and niece to come live with her wasn't an issue to Annabelle any longer. If her aunt didn't offer her home to them, Annabelle had already decided what she would do.

Although she was grateful for Lawrence's offer of help, she couldn't accept monetary assistance from him. It wouldn't be proper, even though they were good friends.

Her father didn't tell her how much money he'd lost, but Annabelle assumed it was a great deal if he'd needed to put the house up for stakes. They might be practically destitute. She was thankful her state-room was paid for in advance. At least she wouldn't be kicked out of it. But upon reaching America they would need money soon, she was certain, and her father wasn't as young as he used to be. He may not like the idea of her working, but Annabelle felt certain there was some position she could acquire that he'd look on as acceptable. Perhaps Mrs. Brown—*Maggie*, Annabelle silently corrected herself—would know.

Annabelle pulled on white gloves and pinned a wide-brimmed hat loaded with russet flowers to the top of her head. Her gaze went to the velvet-lined jewelry box sitting on the dresser.

Every year on her birthday and at Christmas—starting when Annabelle turned fourteen—her father had given her a piece of her mother's jewelry. And Annabelle treasured each gift. Each time she wore the jewelry, Annabelle felt close to the woman whom she'd known such a short time. Though the gems would probably bring a small fortune, there was no way Annabelle felt she could part with them, selfish as that made her feel. At least not yet.

Resisting the urge to cry, she turned to her maid and held her arms out from her sides. "Well, Sadie, what do you think?"

"Oh, Miss Annabelle—you're truly a vision, you are. Why, I'm certain you'll be the envy of every woman who sees you."

Annabelle smiled. "Well, I'm not certain I want that, but thank you for the compliment, Sadie. You may go now."

Sadie bobbed a curtsey, though Annabelle wasn't royalty. But when her maid did that it made Annabelle feel special—just like when Lawrence stared at her with his icy-warm eyes. . . .

"He's no longer for you, so stop this nonsense right now!" Annabelle said sharply to the dreamy-eyed girl in the mirror. "You could hardly allow Lawrence to court a penniless, homeless waif! Especially after the experience he had with Frances."

Turning away from the plea she saw in the green eyes, Annabelle hurried to the other side of the room to snatch her shawl from the trunk.

ॐ

Annabelle curiously looked at her father over her glass, still surprised he had asked her to join him early in his stateroom for a light breakfast of fruit and scones. From the despairing way he'd acted when she'd last seen him, Annabelle had thought her father would spend the rest of the voyage isolated from everyone, including her. Today his appearance was much cleaner, neater, though there was still a look of hopelessness in his eyes. She set down her juice and covered his hand with her own. He looked at her, obviously surprised and a little anxious.

"Father, I want you to know I forgive you for losing the house. We'll get by."

The ghost of a smile he managed was hardly encouraging, but Annabelle refused to again fall into the pit of misery she'd wallowed in most of last night. Like Christian in the Slough of Despond in *The Pilgrim's Progress*. Or David, when he'd been a fugitive fleeing from Saul's wrath. It had taken hours of prayer and poring over the Psalms to regain hope; but like King David, she, too, had cried out to God, knowing that somehow, some way, He would help her.

"You're a good girl, Annabelle. No man could have a finer daughter," Edward said, his eyes lowering from her steady gaze.

"And I'm glad you're my father." He gave a snort of disbelief, and she nodded briskly. "I mean that; you're a good man. Mama must have thought you were very special, too. She loved you very much; I remember that."

At the mention of Cynthia, Edward's expression softened, then took on a guilty look. "I've failed your mother," he said before looking away.

"Nonsense," Annabelle was quick to reply. "You made a mistake— everyone makes mistakes. But you know how easy it is to be forgiven. . . ." She paused, until his eyes again flicked to hers. "Come to church services with me today. Please."

Edward hesitated. It had been a long time since he'd gone to church. Not since God took his Cynthia away. . . .

"Please, My Papa."

Upon hearing the endearing term she had used as a little girl, Edward felt a touch of nostalgia, and his eyes misted. "Your mother would be proud if she could see you now," he said softly.

The cameo Annabelle wore at her neck was the one Cynthia had worn when Edward first met her. Oh, she had been a beauty! Except for Annabelle's dark hair and a few other details, it was almost as if his wife were here with him now. He closed his eyes, willing himself to return to reality.

"Father?"

Seeing the pleading, expectant look on her face, he knew he couldn't refuse; he owed her this favor and so much more besides. "All right, Annabelle. I'll come to church with you."

She squeezed his hand, and they both smiled.

Her heart felt infinitely lighter, and she silently thanked God for this breakthrough.

11

*A*s Annabelle entered the dining room on her father's arm, she studied the people gathered for the worship service. She was looking for a certain face. He was already there, as she knew he would be. But there wasn't time to talk now; she and her father were late, arriving just as the service began. It had been worth it, though. They had talked—*really talked*—about so many things. Never could Annabelle remember a time when she and her father had been closer.

Annabelle turned to number 418 in her hymnal. A warm feeling filled her when she looked down at the words and sang, her husky alto blending with the other voices. She closed her eyes, letting the encouraging words of Isaac Watts minister to her spirit. She knew God would take care of her; God would find them a home. He would help her no matter what life might bring. Boldly she sang the last verses:

> Before the hills in order stood,
>> Or earth received her frame
> From everlasting Thou art God,
>> To endless years the same.
> A thousand ages in Thy sight,
>> Are like an evening gone
> Short as the watch that ends the night,
>> Before the rising sun.
> Time like an ever-rolling stream,
>> Bears all her song away
> They fly forgotten as the dream,
>> Dies at the opening day.

O God our help in ages past,
Our hope for years to come
Be Thou our guide while life shall last,
And our eternal home.

Afterward, Annabelle felt as if the warm breath of God had blown over her, comforting her, reassuring her. For her, the song alone made the service worthwhile. It was exactly what she needed to hear, confirming everything she'd read in the book of Psalms.

Feelings of doubt had crept in this past hour. Like the man Christian, trapped in Doubting Castle, Annabelle had begun to worry about what was in store for them. But the hymn acted like the promised key to open the door and free her from her dark prison of uncertainty. God was omnipotent; He had a place for them to live and a future for them to enjoy. She would trust Him to lead and protect her, just as the Psalms said He would.

Annabelle tried to concentrate on Captain Smith's message, but with her peripheral vision she could see Lawrence's puzzled gaze upon her. She hadn't been kind to him, she knew that. She had agreed to let him escort her to the service and then she hadn't been there when he came to pick her up. And he probably wondered where she'd been during breakfast as well. It hadn't been her idea to eat in her father's stateroom, but she was glad they had. If they hadn't sought privacy, they might not have talked about personal matters, and her father might not be sitting next to her now.

She stole a glance at her father and noted his erect posture and his intent expression as he listened, tears in his eyes.

It had been a mistake to look at her father, Annabelle realized, for suddenly her eyes cut to Lawrence and his gaze caught hers, trapping her. Tingles raced up and down her arms and her cheeks grew warm. He gave her an uncertain smile. She managed to smile back, then quickly faced the front, focusing on the commanding figure of Captain Smith. But no matter how hard she tried to concentrate on his words, thoughts of the man sitting a few chairs away kept invading her mind.

After the service was over, Annabelle felt guilty that she didn't even know the subject of the captain's message. She determined that she would read several extra chapters in her Bible to make up for her lack of concentration this morning.

As she had known he would, once the people were dismissed, Lawrence quickly came to her side. "Hello, Annabelle."

"Hello."

"I missed you this morning."

Annabelle looked to her father, who'd spotted Colonel Gracie and was now talking to him. "Father and I had breakfast in his stateroom," she explained. "We had much to discuss."

Lawrence nodded. "Would you care to take a walk with me?"

"No, I don't think so. It's much too cold." And it was. Annabelle had risen early to view the sunrise, but upon arriving on the boat deck, had decided against it. Maybe tomorrow.

"Annabelle—"

"Oh, there's Mrs. Brown!" Annabelle interrupted. "Won't you please excuse me, Lawrence? I'm sorry, but I really must ask her something. I'll talk to you later." She hated to be rude, but she really needed to talk with Maggie. As she hurried away—her mind imprinted with the surprised, hurt, and confused look on his face—Annabelle managed to paste on a smile and greet her friend. "Hello, Maggie!"

"Well, I do declare. Don't you look like a bright ray of warm sunshine on this cold mornin'," Maggie said with a smile when Annabelle stopped in front of her. Her dark eyes cut to the tall man in the background, wistfully looking in their direction. "Isn't that your nice young man?"

Annabelle couldn't help the flush that she felt warming her face. However, she chose to ignore Maggie's question. "I really need some advice about something. Could you help me, Maggie?"

The woman didn't hesitate, but nodded and steered Annabelle toward the lift. "I need warmin' up. Let's go fetch us a cup o' tea, and then we'll talk."

Once they were seated at one of the tables in the Café Parisian and had given their order to the young stewardess, Maggie turned to Annabelle. "Now how can I help, honey?"

Annabelle hesitated, wondering if she was doing the right thing by confiding in someone that she hardly knew. "I have a bit of a problem," she explained. "I may need to look for work when we reach America, but I don't know what sort of jobs are available—or acceptable—for a woman. I–I wouldn't bother you with this, but I don't know who else to ask." Annabelle's gaze lowered to her clasped hands on the table in front of her.

"Why do you need to look for work?" Maggie asked.

Annabelle's face grew warm. "It seems that . . . well, the fact is . . ." She broke off, embarrassed, unable to continue.

Maggie reached over and patted her clasped hands. "That's all right. You don't have to talk about it if you don't want to." There was a small pause. "Let's see . . . about your question. Hmmm. A governess position is respectable, or a teacher—but I think you have to have a certificate to do that. . . ."

Annabelle's heart grew heavy as Maggie ticked off different occupations on the fingers of one hand. It seemed, according to Maggie, that one either had to have special schooling, or credentials, or references, or a certificate, or *something* Annabelle didn't have.

Later, in her room, she sat staring out the porthole, her Bible open in her lap. She'd considered her plight. She wished she had some kind of talent, like the unknown woman who'd made the lovely blanket. But Annabelle had never excelled at embroidery, sewing, drawing, or painting. Not like Patricia had.

Patricia had been gifted with probably every artistic ability in existence. She was even an accomplished musician, playing the harp. Annabelle had tried learning to play the piano once, but her uncle soon put a stop to that, tiring of all the jarring, discordant notes she banged out.

A knock at the door interrupted her musings, and Annabelle turned her head sharply at the unexpected sound, bidding entrance. Sadie walked in. "Sorry to interrupt, miss, but I . . ." She lowered her head.

"Yes, Sadie?" Annabelle asked, puzzled by the strange way her maid was acting.

Sadie raised bright eyes and looked directly at her. "The fact is, Miss Annabelle, I have something important to discuss, and I wanted to speak with you first, before I talked to Mr. Mooreland." She fidgeted, shifting from one foot to the other. "You see, miss, I met a nice young man. . . . Well, the truth of the matter is, he, uh . . . he asked me to marry him."

Annabelle's eyes grew round, and she drew in her breath swiftly. "Sadie, I don't know what to say. . . . How long have you known him?" she asked, suddenly realizing the stupidity of such a question. It couldn't have been long; this was only their fifth day on the *Titanic*.

Sadie began to wring her hands. "I met Hans the day we boarded. He brought things to my door when I was sick—he's a steward on the ship—and we started talking. Later, after I got better, I spent more time with him when he was off duty."

Seeing Annabelle's skeptical gaze, Sadie hastened to say, "Oh, Hans is a good, kind Christian man, miss! We attended church services in second class this morning—he was off duty—and he proposed right afterward.

"You should see him, miss. He's tall and blond and has the most dreamy blue eyes—like the ocean, they are. . . ."

Annabelle sighed. "And you love him."

Sadie hesitated, then nodded.

"Sadie, I can't tell you what to do concerning your personal life, but five days isn't a great deal of time to acquaint yourself with anyone. Especially someone you think you may want to marry!"

Sadie bit her lip and nodded. "Yes, miss. I'll think on it more." She looked down, uncomfortable, then up again. "I want you to know, miss, I've enjoyed being in your employ. And if I do decide to marry Hans . . . I'll–I'll greatly miss you."

Annabelle felt the tears prick her eyelids. Sadie had been with her for almost four years—ever since her father had decided she was no longer a child and needed a personal maid.

"I'll miss you too, Sadie."

Sadie nodded and brushed away a stray tear. "If there's nothing you need me for, Miss Annabelle, then I'll leave. I'll be back at six o'-clock to help you dress for dinner."

Annabelle smiled and assured her that she would be fine. As she watched Sadie's slim form disappear through the door, a fleeting thought went through her head. *Well, that would take care of the problem of having to let Sadie go.*

Actually, Annabelle hoped it would all work out for Sadie, and that her young man was everything she thought him to be. Remembering the sparkle in her maid's eyes, Annabelle was glad Sadie had found love. Lawrence's handsome face materialized in Annabelle's mind and she closed her Bible a little more forcefully than she had intended.

Perhaps a walk on the covered promenade would help her to think of other things. She must resign herself to the fact that there could never be a future for them together now.

Annabelle reached the grand staircase and spotted her father at the same time he caught sight of her. After excusing himself from the bearded gentleman with whom he was conversing, he walked her way. "Annabelle! I thought you'd retired to your room."

"I tried, but I'm restless. I can't seem to concentrate on the Scriptures today," she said, happy to see a marked improvement in her father's carriage and expression. "I thought I'd take a walk on the promenade. Would you like to join me, Father?"

"No, dear. It's much too cold for my old bones."

"Oh, Father. You're hardly old and decrepit yet," she said with a smile. "But I do understand your abhorrence of the cold. The temperature has dropped sharply since we boarded." Something suddenly occurred to her. "Have you contacted Aunt Christine?"

"Blast it all—no, I haven't. I suppose I should wire her and tell her of my folly and ask if we might stay there for a time . . . ," he said, adding a defeated sigh. "I'll go right now and do so. Don't worry, Annabelle. There's still plenty of time before we reach America."

ॐ

Edward walked to the boat deck, wishing he'd worn his long overcoat before braving the elements. The sea was flat as a sheet of glass, which, according to one of his well-traveled scientific comrades, was unusual.

According to his friend, the winter had been characterized by storms that regularly whipped the seas into a frenzy; its placid appearance now was quite uncommon. He also had told Edward he'd heard that other ships had telegraphed reports of iceberg sightings in the area, which was strange because they usually didn't float this far south.

Edward mentally shrugged, not all that concerned, and his mind switched gears. What would they do upon reaching America? Could he find work when he wasn't qualified for anything, having been raised to a life of wealth and luxury as the youngest son of a shipping magnate? At least he knew Annabelle would be taken care of, come her twenty-first birthday, thanks to Cynthia's parents. But what about until then? He supposed they would have to move in with Christine. That is, if she would let them. He wished Cynthia were here to advise him of what to do. Of course, if she were here, none of this ever would have happened.

Stop it right now! Face up to your own guilt and stop trying to blame others, he harshly told himself.

Cynthia had so wanted another baby—though the doctor had warned her it would be dangerous— and she had died happy, not knowing her son would follow his mother a few hours later. Edward supposed he should be thankful for that, anyway; baby Henry hadn't died before his mother, causing Cynthia grief.

It had helped to go to church with Annabelle. In that brief hour, Edward had felt convicted concerning his behavior these past years, and he had felt God's love warming his heart, urging him to forgive, to let go.

But still he held back. All these years, he thought he'd blamed God; but now Edward realized it was really himself he blamed—he'd welcomed the chance to have a son, despite the doctor's dire warnings after Annabelle had been born. Perhaps Christine was right; perhaps he *had* killed Cynthia. . . .

An officer hurried over to him, his cheeks red from the cold. "Something I can help you with, sir?"

Edward forced his mind off the past. "Yes. I need some directions. I want to send a wireless."

"I'm sorry, sir, but the radio broke down about an hour ago. The chief operator has assured us it will be working again, soon, though. May I suggest you try again this evening?"

Frustrated, Edward gave a vague nod. He should have sent the wire yesterday, as he'd told Annabelle he would. But he'd been too busy wallowing in self-pity.

After thanking the young man, Edward hurried back down the companionway, intent on ordering a cup of hot beef broth. He would try again later.

$$\left(\begin{array}{c} 12 \end{array}\right)$$

*A*nnabelle pulled her fur coat closer as she walked along the covered promenade. Few people were about, having more sense than to be out in the freezing cold, but Annabelle didn't care. She needed privacy, needed to be away from all the noise and confusion. There were decisions to be made . . . a future to plan.

She toyed with the idea of offering her services to her aunt. She could be a companion to the old woman, give her medicine when she needed it—if she needed it. Aunt Christine was a bit of a hypochondriac, always believing she was suffering from the latest ailment present in Newark at a given time. Ninety-nine percent of the time she wasn't.

Annabelle sighed, pulled her fur collar closer around her ears, and looked at the calm ocean. The sun shone off a glimmer of white far away on the horizon. She stepped closer to the opening of the promenade, craning her neck to see. An iceberg?

Annabelle had never seen one, but would like to. Sadie had told her that she'd spotted an iceberg floating by her porthole window the previous night. However, what Annabelle was seeing, or trying to see, was too far away. Probably a mirage (did they have those at sea?) or a trick of sunlight on water. A shiver ran down her back, and she decided it was high time to return to her cabin. The temperature must have dropped several degrees just in the few minutes she'd been out here.

Annabelle had just reached the corridor to her stateroom when an annoying, familiar voice stopped her. "Miss Mooreland! Please wait one moment; I would like to have a word wiz you."

Annabelle halted, wishing she could flee down the hallway to her room and escape an unwanted conversation. However, against her better judgment, she waited for the redhead to approach. "Hello, Mademoiselle Fontaneau. I was just going to my room. I'm rather tired," Annabelle tried politely.

She thought she detected a look of alarm in the cat green eyes, but wasn't certain. It had passed so quickly. "Oh, please wait one moment. I would like to talk wiz you about somezing important." Charlotte twisted her slender fingers in agitation.

Annabelle hesitated. The woman did look distressed, almost . . . desperate? Terrified? But why? "Very well, mademoiselle. What did you wish to say?"

Charlotte cast a quick look down the corridor. "Oh, please, not here in ze hallway. Someone may hear."

Annabelle sighed, growing a little impatient. "What would you suggest, then?"

Charlotte pointed to a stateroom door a few yards away. "Zat is my stateroom. Let us go zere—eet is more private. I promise, I will only take a few minutes of your time."

Annabelle grudgingly nodded. She didn't want to spend any more time than she had to with a woman like Charlotte Fontaneau, but curiosity overrode common sense. Annabelle followed her into the room, idly taking note of the furniture and decorations. French Provincial—what else? Even the colors of the décor fit Charlotte. Olive greens, muted golds, and rich creams.

Charlotte motioned to a chair, and Annabelle obediently sat down, waiting. Charlotte began to slowly pace, smoothing her fiery hair, wringing her ivory hands. "Miss Mooreland, I . . ." She broke off and turned, looking straight at Annabelle. "I want to apologize for what Eric did to your papa. I had no idea he would do such a zing. You must believe me."

Annabelle shrugged, and Charlotte seemed to wilt.

"I know you do not care for me. And I can understand why." She turned and took a few steps toward the porthole, her gaze focusing on the sea beyond. "I wish we could have been friends," she said so softly that Annabelle almost didn't hear her.

Charlotte gave a despairing sigh, causing Annabelle to feel a bit of grudging sympathy. Looking at the woman, Annabelle saw traces of unhappiness clearly marked on her face. Had they always been there? Annabelle had never taken the time to notice before. Feeling as if she should say something, she cleared her throat. "I don't blame you for what happened to my father. He's a grown man who knew better than to do what he did. But sometimes he makes stupid mistakes. We *all* do."

Green eyes wide, Charlotte turned to her. "But how can you be so—so forgiving, so unconcerned? You have lost your home."

Annabelle nodded sadly, but her reply came firm. "Yes, that's true. However, I have the assurance that God will take care of me and will find me a new home. It's only because He's a part of my life that I'm able to survive this calamity. Without Him, I would be reduced to a quivering, frightened child—and at first I was, I'll admit. But now, I'm no longer afraid."

Sinking into the chair across from her, Charlotte looked intently at Annabelle. "You are good—a lady. But not all people are good." A flush of rose tinted her cheeks. "Some people are very bad and God wants nuzing to do wiz zem. If someone like zis has troubles, what can zey do? Tell me, what hope do zey have?"

Annabelle thoughtfully studied Charlotte, and suddenly words seemed to pour from her mouth that she knew weren't her own. "In the first place, you're wrong about God not wanting to have anything to do with those people," she said softly. "It is His desire that all come to know Him. He sent His Son Jesus to die for the sinners, not for the saints."

At Charlotte's look of surprise, Annabelle continued. "It's true. He knew it was impossible for man to keep all the laws of Moses. So He sent His Son to redeem us so that everyone who comes to know Him is under grace and no longer under the law, which leads to death."

"Does zat mean, zen, it is all right to have sin in one's life?" Charlotte asked, incredulous, yet hopeful.

"Of course not! It means His blood can wash us clean from the sins we commit. The Bible tells us 'all have sinned and come short of the glory of God.' Only by accepting Jesus and what He did for us on the cross can we be set free."

Charlotte's head lowered despondently. "But what if someone is born wiz ze sin and it can never go away, no matter how much zey want it to?" she whispered.

"What are you talking about?" Annabelle studied her, perplexed. "The blood of Jesus washes *all* sins away."

Charlotte opened her mouth to speak but was interrupted by a loud knock at the door. Her eyes widened, and Annabelle thought she detected fear in their depths. An immediate change came over the woman—her manner now panicked, yet commanding—as she suddenly leaned across the table toward Annabelle.

"Miss Mooreland," Charlotte said softly, quickly. "I must warn you. Stay away from Eric—he is an evil man."

Baffled, Annabelle watched as Charlotte then turned and walked to the door, opening it. Eric walked inside, his dark blue eyes instantly lighting on Annabelle. "Good afternoon, Miss Mooreland. What an unexpected pleasure to find you here," he said smoothly. "I've seen so little of you since we've boarded. Perhaps, later, you would care to take lunch wiz me?"

Annabelle gave him an incredulous look. Did he actually think after what he'd done to her father—to her—that she would desire to spend time in his company? And yet . . . perhaps she could sway him to forget the debt her father owed and allow them to keep the house. Were such things done? Judging from his elegant dress and grooming, as well as that of his sister's, he had plenty of wealth. Would he listen to Annabelle if she pleaded with him?

Annabelle looked into the frightened, warning eyes of Charlotte, who stood behind him, and then her eyes cut to his. Beyond their dark-blue color, Annabelle sensed hardness, ruthlessness, and yes . . . evil.

Annabelle shivered, instinctively realizing he might do as she asked, but he would expect a far greater price in return—something she wasn't willing to give. What intuition told her this, she wasn't certain; perhaps it was the Lord gently warning her. She knew she must heed the voice, leave this place, and seek the safety of her room as soon as possible. She rose from the chair. "I'm sorry, Monsieur Fontaneau, but I don't feel well. I think I'll return to my room now and lie down."

"Perhaps later—"

"No, I don't think so. I have plans for later in the evening. If you'll excuse me?" Annabelle said as she quickly walked past him and to the door. Without waiting for a reply, she made her escape and hurried down the corridor to her room, not relaxing until she was inside and had locked her door.

On shaky legs she walked over to the bed and sank down upon the satin coverlet. Grabbing up the pillow from underneath the bed-spread, she held it close and prayed to God for protection. She wouldn't feel safe until this voyage was over and Monsieur Fontaneau was out of her life for good.

Lawrence's face came to mind, and for a brief, wonderful moment, Annabelle dreamed of a future with him. "But no," she told her-self for probably the hundredth time since he'd left her at her door last night, "it's impossible. Totally impossible."

Annabelle tossed the pillow aside. Perhaps it would be better if she avoided him for the rest of the voyage rather than put herself through this misery. Up until a few days ago, she'd never thought a future be-tween them could be possible anyway. So maybe she could blot out the brief time they'd shared when he'd looked at her with eyes filled with something more than friendship. She would get over him . . . eventually. Besides, soon he would return to England to take over the family duties, and she would remain in America. And she'd always have her cherished memories of their years together, when Lawrence had been her dearest friend. No one could ever take that away.

Annabelle sighed and picked up the pillow again, burying her face in its softness and allowing her tears to wet it. "Oh, God, please help me get through this," she cried softly. "I'm alone again, always alone. And I've always been so afraid to be alone! That's one reason I wanted to marry Roger. But You already knew that, didn't You? I sup-pose I wasn't fair to him either. He wasn't the only one in the wrong. Forgive me, Lord.

"I turned my back on Your will and agreed to marry someone who didn't know You so I could attain popularity and the worldly pleas-ures of this life! But after losing almost everything, I realize earth's riches are fleeting. Please forgive my vanity, Lord . . . and help me to release Lawrence. I'll always love him, but I know he's no longer for me. Perhaps he never was. Maybe I'm destined to remain alone forever. Please give me the grace to accept my lot in life." She sighed and raised her head to look at the gilded walls.

My child, you are never alone. I am with you always—even until the end of time. . . . I will never leave you nor forsake you. Nothing can pluck you from my Father's hand, and nothing can ever separate you from My steadfast love. . . .

As the soothing voice spoke deep within her parched spirit, bringing forth its living waters, Annabelle felt ten times lighter—though she now had no home, no money, and no chance of a relationship with Lawrence. It defied human reasoning, but Annabelle felt a sweet peace.

ॐ

A few hours later the warm glow had faded somewhat, but the fear hadn't returned. However, Annabelle knew she must steer clear of Lawrence. It wouldn't be fair to him to do otherwise. She'd been selfish this past year in agreeing to marry Roger when she knew it was wrong to do so, and she wouldn't think of her own interests again—especially when it concerned someone she loved. Lawrence needed so much more than she could ever give him.

Annabelle walked to the ladies' reading and writing room, *The Pilgrim's Progress* in hand, and noted that there weren't any empty chairs. She sighed. Perhaps in the lounge.

But even the lounge was full. However, Annabelle spotted an empty chair near the window and made a beeline for it. She supposed the bitter cold outside had something to do with the crowded rooms. She sank onto the comfortable chair and opened her book. But the steady hum of voices floating around the room was distracting, and she finally closed the book, having read only two paragraphs in fifteen minutes.

Annabelle glanced around the room, observing those about her. Men and women sat talking, reading, drinking coffee and tea, and generally having a good time, judging from the smiles and soft laughter. Annabelle's heart seemed to stop as she saw Lawrence walk through the door.

Quickly she opened the book and lifted it to eye-level, shielding her face and hoping he wouldn't notice her. She wasn't ready to deal with him just yet.

"Annabelle?"

She swallowed hard and lowered the book, finding him standing directly in front of her. Her heart gave a little jump.

"Oh. Hello," she said, wishing her voice didn't sound so strange. At least there were no available chairs nearby.

Almost as though he'd heard her thought and wanted to provoke her, the elderly man in the next chair closed his book, checked his gold watch dangling from its fob, then slipped the timepiece back into the pocket of his silk vest and abruptly rose. Lawrence immediately sat down and turned to face her.

"How has your day been?" he asked.

"Fine, thanks."

"A bit cold, though."

"Yes, it has been." She fidgeted with her book.

"The temperature is dropping even as we speak."

"Really?"

"Yes. I'd advise you to dress warmly tonight."

"Thank you, I will." Annabelle bit the inside of her lip, uncomfortable with this inane conversation, even more uncomfortable to have him sitting so close. "If you'll excuse me, I think I'll go to my stateroom for a bit of a rest."

She rose and almost succeeded in walking away, but suddenly felt the searing heat of Lawrence's hand as he grasped her wrist, stopping her. She turned her head and looked at him, shocked.

"Annabelle, have I done something to offend you?"

Shame coursed through her when she heard the puzzled tone in his voice. "No, of course not," she assured him.

"Then why are you avoiding me?" he asked bluntly.

She bit the inside of her lip, knowing she had to tell him. He deserved the truth . . . but not right now. She needed time to think and pray, time to formulate her thoughts and plan what to say to him. She needed time to compose herself, to be in total control of her feelings; it simply wouldn't do for her to break down and cry—as she wanted to do at this moment.

"Lawrence, I know I've behaved rudely, and I'm sorry. Tonight, after dinner, we'll talk then. I really must go now," Annabelle said softly, so those nearby wouldn't hear.

He nodded, his eyes seeming to melt her, as he released her wrist. "All right, Annabelle. I intend to hold you to it."

Annabelle turned and hurried away, wondering how she would ever get through this night.

๚

Lawrence watched Annabelle hurry across the patterned carpet, her velvet dress swishing around her ankles. Why was she suddenly so distant toward him? Lawrence knew the events of yesterday weighed heavily on her mind. However, before, they'd always been able to talk to one another, to confide in each other, but for some reason she was now shutting him out.

He had prayed long into the evening last night, getting only two hours of sleep. But he'd prayed until he believed the Lord had clearly shown him an answer, and he planned to seek out Edward Mooreland tonight and discuss it with him.

The idea of a lifetime with Annabelle gave nothing but great pleasure to Lawrence, and he wondered just when it was he'd begun to deeply love her. Perhaps subconsciously he'd always had strong feelings for her and had known that one day she would be his. Maybe that's why the idea of an engagement to Frances, or any of the other young ladies he'd met, had never appealed.

Of course, he would spend the required amount of time courting Annabelle, and later he'd propose. They would marry and return to Fairview, where his mother could train Annabelle on what was expected of a viscountess. They would raise their children in the English countryside, where generations of Caldwells had been born, and they would remain best friends all the days of their lives and grow old together. . . . He smiled, staring at nothing in particular, imagining how Annabelle would look as a bride. . . .

Lawrence sighed. He was putting the apple cart ahead of the horse again, as his nanny used to tell him. Before he planned their entire future, he ought to tell Annabelle how he felt and make certain she returned his feelings. Then, too, remembering her independent streak, he didn't think she'd be too thrilled about Lawrence leaving her out of the plans he was busily making for them. But he hoped to remedy that situation very soon.

*A*nnabelle randomly selected a necklace with onyx and diamonds embedded in its elaborate setting and fastened it around her neck. Usually she rifled through the jewel box, trying on one piece of her mother's jewelry after another, holding them against her throat, studying, deliberating until she reached a decision. But tonight her mind was far away.

She looked into the mirror. True, the necklace she selected matched, but it was rather much to wear over the detailed velvet gown with the wide silver lace running along its square neckline.

Blowing out a breath of frustration, Annabelle snatched the necklace from around her neck and threw it back into the box. "Oh, I don't know what's wrong with me tonight, Sadie! I can't seem to think clearly."

"If I may suggest, miss . . ." Sadie pawed through the velvet interior of the ornate silver box. "I think this will complement the blue-gray of the gown quite well."

Annabelle took the simple silver necklace interspersed with tiny dark-blue sapphires and held it up to her throat. "Yes, Sadie, I think you're right," she said, relieved. "Please fasten it for me; the catch is too small."

Annabelle studied her reflection in the mirror while her maid fastened the necklace. Her face was too pale. Because she'd inherited the creamy white skin and rosy cheeks of her Irish grandmother, she usually never bothered with cosmetics, except for a dab of rice powder on her nose and lip rouge for her mouth. But tonight she definitely needed something!

Annabelle selected a pot of lip rouge, popped off the cap, and then to Sadie's obvious shock, judging from her expression in the mirror, dipped her finger and dabbed colored circles on her cheeks. She tried to blend the color into her skin, but the effect was hideous. She ended up with bold red blotches on either side of her white face. "Oh, Sadie! Go get me a washcloth! And hurry," she cried in horror.

Sadie left, and Annabelle clutched the top of the vanity. Vain— yes, that's what she'd been. Why did it matter how she looked? Soon she would tell Lawrence of her decision not to see him anymore and why. She knew he'd likely offer protests, but in the end he'd see it was for the best, and they would part with fond memories. She looked in the mirror sadly; their romance was over before it had even begun.

Annabelle's wistful expression turned into one of relief as Sadie walked in, bearing a wet washcloth. Annabelle took it gratefully and scrubbed it across her cheeks. The streaks were gone, but now she looked even more like a clown.

"Oh, Sadie, what am I going to do?"

Sadie studied her thoughtfully, then reached for the rice powder and opened the lid of the canister.

"Of course! Why didn't I think of that?" Annabelle took the puff, dipped it into the chalky powder, then swished it over her cheeks. The ending result was better, but still Annabelle wished she had let well enough alone in the first place.

A knock on the door interrupted her perusal. "Well, I'm ready, and just in time—there's Father. Please let him in, and then put the jewelry back in the safe after we've gone."

Annabelle scanned the room for her mother's silver lace fan with the little mirror in the middle. Finding it, she snatched it up and turned toward the door. "Lawrence!"

He stood on the threshold behind Sadie and smiled at Annabelle. He looked so handsome in his black silk evening clothes and white bow tie; the sight momentarily took her breath away. "I asked permission of your father to escort you to dinner tonight," he explained softly.

She held out her arm to him in a daze, and Lawrence took her hand and placed it in the crook of his arm. It was impossible not to notice how she trembled, and he turned his head and looked down at her, giving her an encouraging smile.

Annabelle felt as if she were in a dream as she walked down the carpeted corridor to the grand staircase with Lawrence as her escort. This wasn't supposed to be happening! How was she to maintain any kind of distance with him when her hand was wrapped around his arm and he walked so close? She was more than a little aware of his muscular strength and his vitality, and it made her want to melt against him. She put space between them and almost bumped into a couple just walking out of their stateroom.

"Careful," Lawrence warned as he gently tugged on her arm, bringing her back closer, to avert a collision.

They headed for the lift. Annabelle knew it would be sweet torture to be alone with him in such a confined space, but the lift was faster than the stairs, and so they would reach their destination that much sooner, she assured herself.

The lift was confined, but they weren't alone, as two other couples and a small child walked on at the last moment. Annabelle held her breath as Lawrence drew her closer to him to make room for the others.

"Are you not feeling well?" he asked in concern when the man working the lift pulled back the grilled gate upon reaching D-deck, and they walked out into the spacious room. Annabelle never thought she would be so glad to see wide-open spaces with plenty of room to walk.

"I–I'm fine," she said while briskly fanning her face. "I think I just need to sit down."

Lawrence took her arm and led her past the beveled glass door into the dining room. American beauty roses and white daisies in crystal vases were in abundance throughout the room, their sweet aroma filling the air. Her father already sat at one of the covered tables, next to two empty seats usually occupied by the Fontaneaus.

I hope Charlotte is well. The automatic thought surprised Annabelle, especially when she realized she meant it. Something had happened earlier in the day in Charlotte's stateroom, causing the animosity Annabelle felt toward the woman to flee. Perhaps it was the hopelessness, the yearning Annabelle had seen in Charlotte's eyes when Annabelle told her about God's love and mercy.

Annabelle had seen a side of Charlotte she hadn't even known existed. Gone had been the flirtatious, happy, sometimes tipsy woman, and in her place had sat a frightened little girl, anxious to be loved and accepted—yet sadly resigned to the idea she never could be. Especially by God. *What happened in Charlotte's life to make her feel that way?* Annabelle wondered as she sat next to her father.

She bowed her head to say grace quietly, as she always did, and was surprised when her father's large hand covered hers. Stunned, she looked at him and noted that he, too, had bowed his head. Annabelle felt as if a small ray of sunshine had brightened the gloom, and again she silently thanked God that her father had attended the worship service with her.

The three tried to do justice to the sumptuous eleven-course dinner, but they had too much on their minds to partake in most of the tempting dishes served or to engage in anything but trivial conversation. After dessert was served and sparingly eaten, Lawrence turned to Annabelle, his eyes hopeful, expectant. "I believe we have something to discuss."

Annabelle suddenly felt as if furry caterpillars were crawling in her stomach. She took a quick sip of tea, hoping it would help. It didn't. Nervously, she nodded to her father before walking away with Lawrence.

ॐ

Edward thoughtfully watched as Lord Caldwell escorted Annabelle away from the table and to the door. He would make a good husband for his daughter. Edward liked the young man and, in the eight years he had known Lawrence, believed him to be dependable, responsible, and a true gentleman. And most importantly—he was a man in love with his daughter.

That fact had been obvious when Lawrence had visited him in the smoking lounge earlier and had asked Edward's permission to court and eventually wed Annabelle, if she would have him. Edward wasn't blind and could see Lawrence was sincere in his love for Annabelle. Much as Edward had felt about Cynthia.

He sighed, picked up his spoon, and finished his Waldorf pudding. At least he would rest easier, knowing Annabelle would be well taken care of, come what may. He only hoped his daughter had enough sense to say "yes" to Lawrence's proposal.

ॐ

Dreading the next few minutes, Annabelle walked beside Lawrence along the covered promenade to the Palm Room, and distinctly felt the sharp chill in the air. She was relieved to arrive in the warm, brightly lit room and hear the ship's band playing next door. Now there would be less chance of her and Lawrence being overheard by others.

Lawrence ordered them coffee, and this time Annabelle made it a point to add sugar and cream to hers, remembering the bitter brew from the previous night. She idly listened to a few notes of the bouncy ragtime song the musicians played, while wondering how to begin with what she had to say.

"Annabelle? I have something I need to discuss with you. . . ."

"No, Lawrence, please let me speak first," she pleaded. "I–I want you to know I've enjoyed knowing you—the times we shared in England, the talks we had, the Bible studies, the stories you read to me, everything. And being with you again these past few days has been wonderful. I shall always hold the memories dear to my heart," she choked. Her gaze lowered to her cup. She stared at the brown liquid as if she'd never seen it before.

Lawrence stiffened. "This sounds a lot like a good-bye," he joked, intently studying her bent head.

"It is."

His brows drew down into a frown. "Annabelle, I—"

"Lawrence," she said, her troubled gaze lifting to his, "please hear me out."

Frustrated, he opened his mouth to speak, then closed it and nodded, his eyes never leaving her face.

"Perhaps if things had been different. If—if certain things hadn't happened . . . perhaps then . . . ."

Lawrence straightened in his chair as understanding dawned. "This is about what happened to your father, isn't it?"

Annabelle hesitated, then nodded slightly. "Yes," she said in a soft whisper, barely heard above the stringed instruments.

"Annabelle, I don't care about that!" At her look of hurt surprise, he hastily inserted, "I mean, I care that you were victimized and that you lost your house, of course, but all of that has no effect on the way I feel about you—"

"Lawrence," she interrupted, raising a hand. "Please don't say anything else. I've thought long and hard about this, and I've decided it's the best thing for both of us."

"Oh, really," Lawrence said a bit sarcastically. "You decided, did you?"

"Yes. Considering your former relationship with Frances . . ."

"What does Frances have to do with us?"

She looked down and bit the inside of her lip until she tasted blood.

"Annabelle?"

"Lawrence, don't you see? If our relationship was to deepen . . . and we were to marry one day . . ." She broke off momentarily, her cheeks growing uncomfortably hot. She knew she really was assuming a great deal since he'd never told her he loved her. But she had to make him see the truth. She forced herself to continue. "Then you would always wonder if I were only interested in you for your wealth, like—like Frances was."

"Annabelle, I—"

"It's true," she insisted. "Maybe you wouldn't feel that way at the beginning. But one day you would start to wonder, to question, to regret the day you talked to that little girl on the staircase many years ago at the ball."

"Annabelle, this is ridiculous. . . ."

"No, it's not—you simply don't see it yet. But later, when you think about what I've said, you'll realize I'm right, that it would be better if we didn't see one another anymore," she ended on a whisper, her heart twisting in pain.

Lawrence pushed a frustrated hand through his dark locks, disturbing his impeccably groomed hair. One errant strand lay against his forehead, reminding Annabelle of the young man she'd met eight years earlier. His eyes had a pleading, almost desperate look to them that tore at her heart.

"Please understand, Lawrence," she whispered, "I could never bear for you to look at me with suspicion or derision. And now that I no longer belong to the wealthy class, it's entirely possible one day you would think I had ulterior motives. I'm certain even your family—"

"This isn't about my family!" Lawrence interrupted angrily. "This is about *us*. We've known one another too long, Annabelle, and we've shared a closeness I've never experienced with anyone else. Do you honestly think I can let you just walk out of my life?"

"We've made it through the past four years without one another. It may be hard at first, but I'm sure we'll manage," she said, picking up her spoon and stirring her coffee, though it didn't need it.

"When we were friends, we were young and innocent, not bound by propriety's demands," she continued. "Now we're adults, and the world expects more from us—from you. You're wrong if you think this has nothing to do with your family. Eventually you'll receive the title of earl and one day, perhaps, duke. The Caldwell name is well respected—many look to your family as an example. What would people say if you were to marry a penniless woman? It was different before we lost everything. At least then I had my mother's inheritance, even if I didn't have a title. But now I have nothing to give—no dowry, nothing. And I don't want you or your parents to think of me as another Frances Davenport," she said, shaking her head sadly.

"Annabelle—"

"I'm sorry, Lawrence; you'll never know how sorry." She rose from her chair, tears clouding her eyes. "There's nothing more to say except good-bye. God keep you always."

"Annabelle . . ."

Before he could say more, she turned and walked hurriedly past the other tables and out the door.

ॐ

Lawrence fell back in his chair, stunned. Had tonight really happened? Had she just walked out of his life?

He had been a fool to tell Annabelle about Frances—he could see that now. Of course, he'd merely been sharing a confidence with her, trusting her as she'd trusted him with her painful revelation about her ex-fiancé. He'd had no idea at the time that his words would boomerang and hit him smack in the face.

Groaning, he ran a hand over the back of his hair, his eyes going to the window and the dark Atlantic Ocean. Vaguely he noted there was no moon tonight. How fitting. The light had just fled his life as well.

The steward came to see if he wanted anything, and Lawrence almost told him to bring him a scotch from the bar, but he declined at the last moment and ordered another cup of coffee instead. Though the temptation to get roaring drunk was great, Lawrence had never done so and didn't care to start now. Besides, he needed to maintain a clear head, to think through this unexpected turn of events and decide what to do next.

He drank the black coffee, feeling as bitter as the strong brew tasted. *And to think, I was going to propose my plan tonight and tell her I love her,* he thought wryly. Suddenly he straightened, eyes going wide. He never told her he loved her! Of course, she hadn't given him much of a chance to say anything. Would it have made a difference if she'd known the extent of his feelings? Probably not. She'd been determined, stubborn, insistent, impossible . . . and oh, so beautiful.

Very well, then. Lawrence would leave her to her solitude tonight and give himself time to think, time to invent a believable argument opposing her ridiculous claims—one that she couldn't possibly refute. He would make her see the truth, and then he would tell her of his love for her.

Tomorrow morning Lawrence would execute his plan at the first opportunity that presented itself. He would seek her out and have his say—even if he had to tie the beautiful, independent Miss Annabelle Mooreland to a chair until he finished speaking what was on his mind.

The likelihood of him executing such a stunt was slim; still, the thought brought a grin to his lips, and, hopeful again, Lawrence finished his coffee and left the Palm Room.

14

*T*earfully, Annabelle hurried down the hallway, half hoping Lawrence would come after her. He didn't. *Of course, it's better this way,* she told her traitorous heart. *Better to end it all neatly and not prolong the pain.*

Annabelle descended the grand staircase, hoping she wouldn't run into Eric again. Upon reaching B-deck, she practically flew down the carpeted corridor and hurried to her room. Once inside, Annabelle relaxed, and then the tears came in earnest. She threw herself on her bed and cried for all that might have been with Lawrence.

After a few minutes, when the torrent had subsided, she sat up and wiped her eyes. Strangely, she felt somewhat better, though her heart still lay like a heavy stone within her breast. Seeing her Bible lying on the table and remembering her vow after the church service to spend time in it, Annabelle sheepishly walked to the chair and sat down. After turning the pages to where she'd left off, she began to read the Ninety-first Psalm and felt a sudden strong desire to memorize its verses.

Lawrence sat in his cabin and stared at the four paneled walls. He prayed to the Lord for wisdom and mentally rehearsed what he would say to Annabelle in the morning. Sighing, he rose from his chair, slowly stretched his arms high above him, then rolled his head to remove the kinks in his neck.

For the past couple of hours he'd required solitude. But now, even though a glance at his pocket watch showed him it was fast approaching eleven-thirty, he desired company. Perhaps he would visit the smoke room and see if any of the other gentlemen with whom he'd acquainted himself were also playing the part of a night owl. He grabbed his jacket and shrugged into it, then looking into the mirror, he adjusted his tie and used the twin brushes on his hair. Satisfied, he grabbed his coat as an afterthought and left the room, hurrying along the corridor.

Upon entering the dimly lit smoke room, Lawrence was surprised to see quite a number of men there, most of them playing cards and smoking cigars at the green felt-covered tables. And there alone in one corner, smoking his pipe, sat Edward Mooreland. The older gentleman motioned for Lawrence to join him and greeted him fondly. Once he'd sat down, Edward came straight to the point. "Well, how did it go with my daughter?"

Lawrence started, not expecting such a blunt approach, but quickly recovered. "Not well, I'm afraid, but tomorrow I will try again." At Edward's puzzled look, Lawrence explained, "I was hardly able to get a word in edgewise. Tomorrow she'll have to listen to me, though!"

Edward's eyes twinkled and he gave a deep chuckle. "She's more like her mother every day." He grew a little wistful as he stared into space, then abruptly he shook his head. "Never mind. I warned you, my boy. Annabelle has a mind of her own. She's always been rather independent, as you know. But if you want the truth . . ."

A slight jarring sensation made the tea in Edward's cup slosh over onto the saucer; puzzled, he broke off in midsentence, looking down at it.

"Hey, boys, we've just grazed an iceberg!" a loud voice called into the room a few seconds later. Lawrence shared a look with Edward. Upon seeing a few men rush outside to the promenade deck, the two rose and followed them.

It was incredibly cold. However, no matter how hard they studied the still ocean, both toward the bow and stern, they couldn't see anything. Lawrence looked long and hard, but it was no use. He returned to the smoke room, a bit disappointed. He would like to have seen an iceberg, never having seen one before. Oh, well, perhaps tomorrow he'd get another chance. He'd heard there'd been recent sightings.

They returned to their table, and Edward ordered another tea, his having gone cold from sitting too long. Lawrence was relieved to note that Edward wasn't drinking an alcoholic beverage tonight. Not since the evening of the fateful card game had Lawrence seen a drink in Edward's hand.

Suddenly all was quiet as the ship came to a complete halt.

The men looked at one another, puzzled. There was silence in the room, a silence never before experienced on the ship, and several of the men again left the tables to investigate the strange occurrence.

Lawrence wasn't certain how much time elapsed, but soon the *Titanic* began to slowly move forward again, but very slowly. He leaned back in his chair, relieved the problem had been fixed. However, his relief was short-lived. Once again the mighty ocean liner stopped and sat still and silent on the calm sea.

"I don't like this one bit, Lord Caldwell."

"I'm certain there's no cause for alarm," Lawrence said, trying to reassure the older man. But he too felt a strange unease.

"I'm going below to check on Annabelle."

"If you don't mind, Mr. Mooreland, I'd like to come with you," Lawrence said. Edward nodded and the two men left.

ã

Annabelle sat up, wondering what had jolted her awake . . . an impact of some sort. Puzzled, she rushed to the porthole and turned her head from side to side to look. A dark, craggy form toward the stern drifted away as the boat passed it. However, the night was pitch black and Annabelle couldn't really tell what it was.

Curious but not alarmed, she closed her Bible, which she'd been reading before nodding off. She was still dressed in her evening clothes, though it was probably quite late—she felt as though she'd been asleep for a long time. When Sadie came to Annabelle's room earlier to help her get ready for bed, Annabelle had waved her off, too intent in the Psalm she was reading. It dealt with how God had rescued David in a time of great trouble.

Suddenly an eerie silence filled the room as the boat stopped moving. Now more than a little curious, Annabelle walked to the door, grateful she was still dressed, and looked out into the corridor. Several other passengers left their rooms, everyone asking one another what had happened. Most were still in nightdress with wrappers tightly wrapped around them. A small child began to cry. "Hush, Ida, it's all right," a mother softly crooned.

Annabelle walked down the corridor, intent on finding a steward. After a moment, she spotted one.

"Miss, you should go back to your room before you catch your death of cold. There's no need for alarm—a simple malfunction. It will be fixed in no time," he promised.

Annabelle turned away, feeling reassured but tired. She decided it was high time to retire for the evening. When the boat started moving slowly forward, Annabelle breathed a sigh of relief. She reached her stateroom, pulled the pins out of her hair, and thought about Lawrence. She hadn't really been fair to him—hadn't let him say a word. And would she ever forget the pain in his eyes when she'd left him? *I wonder what he'd wanted to tell me,* she pondered. But it didn't really matter. There was nothing he could say to change her circumstances. Still, she supposed she should have let him have his say. She brushed her thick hair with long, fierce strokes.

Again the boat stopped, and all was silent. Confused, Annabelle laid down the brush. Hearing several people rush by her door, she walked to it and opened it. She looked in each direction, then left her cabin. After walking down the corridor, she found the same cabin steward she'd spoken with minutes earlier.

Recognizing her, he said, "I'd advise you to return to your room and retrieve your life belt, miss. It seems we've struck an iceberg." Seeing her eyes widen, he hastily added, "Oh, there's no reason for alarm. The captain has asked that everyone go to the boat deck. Merely a precaution, you understand."

Annabelle nodded, though her heart skipped a beat. She reached her room and slipped into her fur coat, then grabbed the bulky life belt out of the closet and slung it over one arm, letting it dangle. *Merely a precaution,* she told herself. *He said it was merely a precaution.*

Annabelle hurried from her stateroom toward her father's room. After knocking at his door and receiving no answer, she paused, then tried again. She turned the knob and opened the door, peeking inside. The room was empty. Obviously he was already on the boat deck. They must have missed each other when she went in search of the steward. Oh, well, no matter. She would find him.

She descended the grand staircase, deciding she would first go to the lower deck and wake Sadie, if she wasn't already awake. However, as she passed Charlotte's door, Annabelle paused, uncertain, then lifted her hand and knocked loudly. When she received no answer, she tried once more. Thinking Charlotte had already left, she turned to leave. The door slowly swung open. Annabelle turned to the French woman to relate what the steward had said, but her words died on her lips.

Charlotte stood quietly, an emerald-green wrapper wrapped tightly around her body. A terrible bruise blackened one eye, coloring the skin a dark purple, and her lower lip was swollen to about twice its normal size.

Annabelle forgot about her mission, her eyes opening wide. "What happened to you, Charlotte? Who did this to you?"

She shook her head, as if to dismiss Annabelle's words. "It—it's nothing. I ran into a door. A foolish mistake."

Annabelle eyed her critically, doubting her words. But she knew it wasn't any of her business. "The captain has asked everyone to bring their life belt and go to the boat deck. The steward says it's nothing to be concerned about—merely a precaution. I—I just wanted you to know," Annabelle finished, suddenly uncomfortable.

"Thank you, Miss Mooreland. It was kind of you to tell me." She hesitated and opened her mouth as if she wanted to say something more, then quickly closed it. Saying another soft "thank you," she closed the door.

Annabelle paused a moment, wondering. She turned away and walked toward the grand staircase in search of Sadie. As she descended the stairs, it suddenly hit her.

Charlotte had lost her French accent.

❧

Edward and Lawrence walked hurriedly down the corridor as several people wearing their life belts rushed past them. When Edward knocked on Annabelle's door, no one answered. Seeing the door slightly ajar, he pushed it open and stepped into the room while Lawrence stayed discreetly in the hallway.

He returned quickly. "She's not here. Her life belt's missing from the closet; she's probably gone up to the boat deck along with everyone else. If we split up, we have more chance of finding her. However, I'd advise you to first go to your room and retrieve your own life belt, Lord Caldwell."

Lawrence nodded reluctantly, and the two men took off in opposite directions. Lawrence ascended the stairs, overhearing two men conversing in front of him. "The foredeck is littered with it. The steerage passengers are having a grand time tossing it at one another. Keep it as a souvenir," one of the men joked, handing the other man something.

Lawrence curiously looked over their heads to see what the man was holding. It was a piece of ice.

"What do you think about it all, Stewart?" Lawrence heard the other man ask.

"I don't know what to think really. A bit of a nuisance, certainly. I'm going to my stateroom and pack my bag. Doubtless we'll be transferred to another ship close by. I heard William say the squash racquet court on F-deck was flooding with sea water. Said it was over his shoes when he went down there a few minutes ago. And the mailroom is flooded as well. The postal clerks have been kept busy moving two hundred bags of mail from the sorting room on G-deck to a drier place. . . ."

A pang of alarm raced through Lawrence. What *did* this mean? The *Titanic* was supposed to be unsinkable! He stepped up his pace, searching for Annabelle.

❧

Annabelle walked down the corridor of C-deck to Sadie's room. After knocking on the door, she received no reply. Frustrated, she turned the knob to find the room empty. She shut the door. A woman came out of a stateroom a few doors down, dressed to go outside, a carpetbag in her hand.

"You lookin' for Sadie?"

"Yes."

"She left here about five minutes ago."

"Oh," Annabelle said, disappointed to have missed her. "Thank you."

"I'm headin' up to the top deck. I'd advise you to do the same. The sooner I get off this boat, the better."

"Oh, but—there isn't anything really wrong, you know," Annabelle was quick to say. "This is all merely a precaution. The steward told me."

"Then he lied or didn't know no better. I heard steam escapin' in my room and that's not normal. Mark my words, there's somethin' wrong. We struck an iceberg, you know," she threw over her shoulder as she hurried past Annabelle.

"Yes, I heard," Annabelle said softly under her breath. She moved down the corridor toward the stairs when she heard her name being screeched by a frantic voice.

"Miss Mooreland!"

Annabelle turned to see Maria running in her direction, a frightened look on her face.

"Have you seen Missy?"

"Missy?" Annabelle asked stupidly.

"*Si! Si!* We were almost to the boat deck, when she turned and ran away. I could not catch her! And now I cannot find her," Maria said hysterically. A stream of rapid Spanish flowed from her mouth as her hands waved wildly in the air.

"Maria, calm down! Please! This isn't the time to lose your head. . . . Now, think," she said when Maria calmed a bit. Annabelle thought hard as well. Something suddenly occurred to her. "Did she have her dolls with her?"

Maria's brow puckered, but she shook her head. "I think she only had one. Yes, I'm sure of it!"

Annabelle sighed in relief. "Then she's probably gone back to her room to get the other one. You know how important those dolls are to her."

However, when Annabelle and Maria arrived at Missy's room they found it empty. The snow-white baby blanket Annabelle had given her for her birthday lay on the floor near the entrance.

"She had that with her, I remember," Maria said firmly. "That means she's been here."

"Yes," Annabelle said, relieved as she picked up the blanket. "And she's probably gone to the boat deck to look for you. Come, Maria, I'll help you find her." She put a hand on the Spanish woman's arm.

Maria paused a moment. "Thank you, Miss Mooreland. You are different than what I thought," she admitted, shamefaced.

Annabelle gave her a small smile, and they turned to go. As they walked down the corridor, Annabelle detected a slight tilt in the carpeted floor and wondered what it could mean.

*L*awrence walked along the port side, searching the faces of those who stood on the boat deck. Most people were calm, assured, a little perturbed—thinking this only to be an annoying inconvenience—and they patiently waited, hoping soon to be told they could return to their rooms.

Lawrence looked over the railing at the black water below. Bright yellow spots of light from the many portholes and windows along the *Titanic* shimmered on the ocean's calm surface. Was it his imagination or did they seem a bit closer to the water than before?

Hurriedly he moved from the rail and began to weave through the crowd. He vaguely noted that multimillionaire John Jacob Astor was reassuring his wife, who sat on a deck chair while her maid stood next to her and helped her to finish dressing. Under normal circumstances Lawrence might have stopped to chat; he'd made the gentleman's acquaintance on the second day of the voyage. But these were not normal circumstances.

He walked past crowds of people huddled in small groups, talking and shivering in the chill night air and waiting for the order to return to their rooms. He hurried past them all, praying to see a certain face.

જ઼

Annabelle walked along the starboard side of the boat, following Maria. They still hadn't found Missy.

"Miss Annabelle!" Relieved to hear a familiar voice, Annabelle turned and looked into Sadie's sparkling eyes. "I looked for you in your room, miss, but I couldn't find you," Sadie said with a grin.

"We must have just missed each other, Sadie. I looked for you, too, but you'd already left."

The maid gave a nervous giggle and flicked her thick blond braid back over her shoulder. She wore a long black coat over her white nightgown. "This is quite a bit of excitement, isn't it, miss? I only hope I'm able to go back to sleep tonight."

Annabelle gave a small smile, thinking she could do without this particular kind of excitement. "Sadie, do you remember the little girl whose birthday party I attended? Have you seen her?"

"I don't rightly remember ever seeing her, miss." Sadie's eyes lowered to the white blanket on Annabelle's arm and her face grew solemn. "Is that the blanket?"

"Yes," Annabelle said, watching curiously as several members of the crew uncovered a few of the wooden lifeboats. Loud sounds of creaking and clanging filled the night air as one of the boats was readied and lowered over the rail with ropes and pulleys. After it had been lowered partway over the side, an officer turned to face the people. He spoke loudly to those around him, trying to be heard over the terrible noise of steam escaping from a vent on one of the huge smokestacks.

"Women and children to the boat, please. Men, stand back from the boats. Women and children first. No need for alarm, just a cautionary measure."

Many women demurred, preferring to stay with their husbands, and several men were allowed into the boat instead.

Sadie's eyes grew round as she watched an elderly gentleman move over the rail and step inside the boat suspended a great distance above the ocean. "Miss Annabelle . . . have you noticed how few lifeboats there are?"

Actually, Annabelle hadn't noticed. In her walks with Lawrence the past few days, she'd barely given them a second glance. They'd become a part of her world, there, in the background, but were hardly worth noticing. Her brow puckered as she mentally counted them, trying to remember how many she'd seen in her previous walks along the boat deck. "I'm sure there'll be enough for everyone." But her tone wasn't very convincing.

"But, Miss Annabelle . . ." Sadie's eyes were wide and scared. "There aren't *any* in third class. This is all there is."

The women stared at one another in silence. Annabelle swallowed. "I'm certain the captain knows what he's doing, Sadie. He has a very reliable record. If you'd rather go on, I'll understand. There's really nothing to worry about. I have to find Missy and my father, and then I'll be right behind you."

"I'd rather not, miss." Sadie bit her lip, her eyes cutting to the boats one last time before turning back to Annabelle. "I—I need to find Hans first; he's working in third class tonight."

Annabelle hesitated, her first instinct to deny Sadie permission. However, one look into Sadie's pleading eyes was enough to convince Annabelle she couldn't do that. "All right, Sadie. Go find Hans. But afterward, you must come back and get into one of the lifeboats until they fix the problem."

"Yes, miss, of course. Thank you." She paused a moment, then, in a burst of uncharacteristic emotion, gave Annabelle a quick hug. "I'll see you soon, miss."

While Annabelle silently watched Sadie's departing figure hurrying toward the third-class section, a man whom she recognized as Thomas Andrews walked up to her. "Excuse me, miss. But Officer Murdoch has asked for all women and children to enter the lifeboats. Purely a precaution until the damage to the boat is rectified," he assured her.

"Thank you, but I'm looking for someone. I'll go later."

He paused, then nodded. "At least put your life belt on. It might help keep you warmer. It's rather cold tonight."

"Yes, thank you. I will," Annabelle murmured as she obediently slipped the well-padded jacket over her fur coat.

She looked up into the velvet-black sky twinkling with thousands of stars and noticed the moon was nowhere to be seen. It had hidden its face from them; but her heavenly Father hadn't done the same, of that Annabelle was certain. "Dear Lord, I need Your help right now. Please show me where Missy is," she whispered. Instantly a thought came, and she rushed away to find Maria.

∂∾

Lawrence continued searching the port side of the boat. With a pang of alarm, he noticed a lifeboat being lowered over the side and overheard a man speaking to his young daughters.

"You must both get into the boat and row around until the damage to the *Titanic* is repaired." He took the girls by the hand and walked with them the few steps to the lifeboat, which was now being filled. As he handed them inside, he added, "It does seem more dangerous for you to get into that boat than to remain with me here, but we must obey orders."

Lawrence looked into the boat, hoping to spot Annabelle. But she wasn't there. However, he did see the woman who'd been with Annabelle after church services. "Mrs. Brown," he called, doubting she could hear him over all the noise. He felt momentary relief when she looked up. "Have you seen Miss Mooreland?"

She shook her head, lifting her hands in a shrug, and he sighed. Well, there was still the other side of the ship. He hurried down the deck to the starboard side.

∂∾

"Maria!"

The Spanish woman turned, her expression hopeful. But when she saw no golden-haired child running alongside Annabelle, her face fell. Annabelle hurried to the governess, her words coming out of her mouth before she'd even stopped to catch her breath.

"Maria, I need you to show me where Missy's room is. I can't remember the number."

Maria shook her head. "We tried there already."

"No, Maria, we didn't. We only looked in the door. *We didn't search the room*," Annabelle said, stressing each word.

A hopeful light burned in Maria's dark eyes. "*Si!* You are right! Come, I will show you."

The women hurried down the first-class companionway, only just missing Lawrence as he rushed from the port side to the starboard side of the boat.

ॐ

Lawrence scanned the deck, growing anxious. *Lord, please don't let anything happen to Annabelle. Please help me find her and get her safely off this boat.* For, as he had searched, Lawrence realized the horrible truth; there weren't enough lifeboats for everyone. And the ship, the mighty *Titanic*, was going down—despite what the crew was telling the passengers, to avoid a panic, more than likely. Certainly the crewmen and officers, who made sailing the sea their life's work, must know the truth.

"Lord Caldwell!"

Hearing Edward's voice, Lawrence turned, hoping to see Annabelle beside him. But Edward stood alone.

"No luck yet?" Edward questioned gruffly, though the answer was obvious.

"No. I haven't been able to locate her."

He gave a brusque nod. "You stay up top. I'm going down below. We'll find her," Edward said and hurried off, leaving Lawrence to scour the boat deck once again.

ॐ

Annabelle and Maria quickly walked down the corridor of C-deck. They passed a stewardess who loudly knocked on one of the doors. As it opened, Annabelle heard her say, "Please put on your life belts and go to the boat deck. Captain's orders."

Maria threw open the door and turned on the light in the stateroom; Annabelle rushed in behind her. Maria looked in one direction and Annabelle the other. There was no sign of the missing child. Biting the inside of her lip, Annabelle scanned the room carefully and noticed an inch of material sticking out from underneath the curtained bed.

She dropped to her hands and knees, lifted the pink spread, then gave a relieved sigh. "I found her, Maria." Carefully, Annabelle pulled the sleeping child from underneath the bed. Missy groaned, clutching both dolls closer to her chest.

"Missy, wake up!" Annabelle insisted softly.

Golden eyelashes flickered, then cornflower-blue eyes opened wide and looked at her. "Miss Annabelle!" the child cried, jumping up and throwing her arms around Annabelle's neck. The dolls dropped to the carpeted floor. "I was so scared! Everybody was talking so loud, and I had to find my dolly. And then when I tried to find Maria, I got lost and came back here. I want my mommy," she sobbed against Annabelle's shoulder.

Maria knelt down and pulled the little girl close to her. "Hush, little *niña*. We will go and find your mother, *si*? She must be worried. You must never run off like that again!"

The blond head nodded up and down against Maria's chest. Maria stood, pulling Missy up with her, then looked up. "Thank you so much . . . Annabelle," she said softly, her eyes saying more than her words.

Annabelle smiled and picked up the two dolls, relieved that all had ended well.

Lawrence completed his search of the starboard side with no success. People around him were beginning to look more anxious and puzzled, though there was still an outward show of calm.

The sound of stringed instruments suddenly carried over the cold night air as a band began to play a cheery, bouncy song. It provided a strange accompaniment to the noises of creaking and clanging, hissing and groaning of the dying ship, and of many lifeboats being hoisted and lowered over the side. Lawrence looked up to the top platform of the boat deck where bandmaster Wallace Hartley stood directing his seven musicians, giving a party atmosphere to the bizarre situation. Several of the passengers relaxed, and some joked with one another, smiling.

A man turned to his comrade. "If the orchestra has come up here to entertain us, certainly there could be nothing terribly wrong with the ship. It's a mere annoyance, nothing more." However, the look in his eyes belied his words.

Lawrence listened as a few men began to persuade their wives to leave them and get into the lifeboats, assuring and comforting their women, telling them, "As the officers said, it's only a precaution. I'll take another boat and meet you later."

Though several women agreed, others shook their heads, stating they would rather stay with their husbands on the steel decks of the huge liner than take a chance out on the freezing water in flimsy lifeboats. Lawrence clenched his jaw, praying he would soon find Annabelle and get her to a boat.

જી

Annabelle walked to the boat deck, Missy clutching her hand and Maria on the other side of the little girl. They brushed by a couple of gentlemen blocking the stairs, and Annabelle tried to move past them. "Excuse us, please."

The men turned and stepped aside while recommending that the women head for the lifeboats. "Merely a precaution," one of them added. Annabelle thanked the men and had taken only a few steps across the floor when she heard her name being called.

"Annabelle!"

"Father!" Annabelle dropped Missy's hand, turning at the sound of the familiar voice, and walked quickly to her father, who was rushing toward her. She received his uncharacteristic hug with pleased surprise, almost dropping the dolls she still held.

"We must get you into one of the lifeboats, dear."

Annabelle nodded, then turned back to Missy and handed her the dolls and blanket. "You be a good girl, now, and don't give Maria any more problems," she said firmly, though her eyes were gentle.

"Aren't you coming, too?" Missy whined.

"I'll come later. You go find your mother. She must be worried sick."

Missy reached up toward Annabelle, who bent down. The little girl wrapped chubby arms around Annabelle's neck and gave her a kiss on the cheek. "Thank you, Miss Annabelle."

Smiling, Annabelle briefly watched the golden head until it disappeared amid the groups of people standing in the room.

"We really need to hurry, dear."

She turned back to her father. "I'm sorry, Father. You're right, of course. We should get into one of the lifeboats until the damage is repaired. The thought doesn't give me much comfort—they're so flimsy—but it can't be helped, I suppose. Father . . . ?" She trailed off, curious at the solemn expression that had come over his face. His eyes avoided hers.

"They're only letting women and children into the lifeboats."

She shook her head. "Earlier, I saw several gentlemen get into a lifeboat with no problem whatsoever. I'm certain they'll let you come, too."

"No, Annabelle. I won't be going." His voice was firm.

Her brow wrinkled. "Why not?"

"Because it's time for me to go now to be with your mother. I've made my peace with God, and I'm ready."

Uncomprehending, Annabelle blinked a couple of times as she studied him, then her eyes widened in horror. "What are you saying, Father? Everyone has told me the lifeboats are a precaution. When the damage is fixed, everyone will return to the ship. You *must* be mistaken."

Edward remembered the deadly green sea water he'd seen rushing through one of the lower levels when he'd descended the stairs in his search for Annabelle and shook his head. "No, I'm not mistaken. In view of all that's happened these past few days, I can see you've matured into a strong young woman; I believe you can handle what I'm about to tell you.

"This ship is doomed," he said, lowering his voice so those standing nearby wouldn't hear. He didn't want to start a panic.

"But—"

"You must go now, Annabelle," he insisted gruffly. "You have your whole life ahead of you. My life hasn't been the same since your mother died; I want to go and be with her. Please, Annabelle, don't make this harder on me. Release me."

Tears clouded her eyes, causing his face to swim before her. What was he saying? Could it be true? Was the ship really going down? But it was unsinkable! And yet, looking into her father's eyes, Annabelle saw the truth written there.

How could she leave him to remain behind—how could he ask this of her? True, she'd known he hadn't been happy, but she didn't want him to die, especially now that the breach was so recently healed between them! But at the same time, she was proud of his courage in the face of death. She swiped her tears away, praying for strength to do what he asked. Standing on tiptoe, she kissed his cheek. "Yes, My Papa. I release you," she choked. But she hoped it wouldn't come to that and that another ship would arrive soon so everyone would be saved.

Her father held her close for a moment and kissed her cheek, his own eyes glistening with unshed tears; then he took her elbow and hurried her along. "You must live with your aunt for a time—only for a few years. After you turn twenty-one, you'll be entitled to your trust fund."

She stopped and shook her head, dazed from his words, certain she hadn't heard him correctly. "Trust fund?"

He hesitated, looking at the stairs as if he wanted to push her up them. "Your grandparents set up a trust fund for you in America when you were born—didn't I ever tell you? It's a good thing, in light of what's happened to the house. There's still some money in the account as well—enough to take care of you for a little while. But the trust is a sizable amount; it will take care of you for many years to come. Now, Annabelle, we really must get you into a lifeboat," he insisted.

Annabelle, feeling as if she'd been transported into some bizarre dream, allowed her father to practically pull her up the stairs, her sluggish brain trying to sort through this new set of startling facts. She had a trust fund . . . the *Titanic* was sinking . . . she may never see her father again. . . .

She remembered the few lifeboats; the call for women and children first; the order for men to stand back. Her eyes opened wide in sudden understanding as the mists moved away from her mind.

"Father, I must find Lawrence first! Please!" She tugged on his sleeve. "I have to see him!"

"He's looking for you on the boat deck. Come along, dear. We really must hurry."

16

$\mathcal{L}$awrence hurried to the port side of the ship, beginning to feel as though he was walking in never-ending circles. Where was she? How would he ever find her in this swarming sea of humanity? He nervously pushed a shaking hand through his hair and approached one of the lifeboats being boarded. Instantly an officer blocked his way.

"I'll have to ask you to stand back, sir. Only women and children allowed."

"I know. I'm looking for someone; I wanted to see if she might be in the boat," Lawrence explained calmly, though his patience had worn wafer thin.

The officer looked a bit uncertain, then nodded. "You can stand there, sir, but come no closer."

Lawrence nodded and quickly scanned the fearful faces in the boat. Some of the women had blankets over their heads and were shivering from the cold, but not one of them looked back at him with beautiful emerald eyes.

As he stood there, Mrs. Straus walked up with her maid. She reached the boat, then stopped, shaking her head firmly. "I will not be separated from my husband. As we have lived together, so we will die together," she told the officer in charge. She walked over to where her husband stood and looked up at him. Lawrence barely heard her next words. "We have lived together for many years. Where you go, I will go."

Several other gentlemen, one Lawrence recognized as Colonel Gracie, tried to persuade her to change her mind, but she refused, shaking her head. Mr. Straus gently took her arm and the couple moved toward two deck chairs and sat down.

Suddenly there was a commotion as someone yelled that a group of men was trying to take over one of the lifeboats. Along with a few others, Lawrence hurried to the bow, more than a little aware of its slight downward slope. He watched from the sidelines as an officer jumped in the boat, waving a gun.

The officer yelled at the men in the boat, cursing and calling them cowards. Then he added, "I'd like to see every one of you overboard!" The anxious men hurriedly climbed out, and the officer yelled to the crowd, "Women and children into this boat!"

Worried, Lawrence turned away from the scene; Annabelle wasn't there, either. Hadn't she heard the captain's order that everyone must go to the boat deck? That was more than an hour ago.

With long strides Lawrence headed back toward the middle of the ship, wondering if he should return to the starboard side and check there again. Suddenly a loud report sounded overhead.

Looking up, Lawrence saw the black night burst into a brilliant explosion of bright, dazzling light. A well-dressed gentleman walked past Lawrence and up to a nearby officer who stood at the rail holding a pair of binoculars to his eyes. "Excuse me, sir, but if the situation isn't serious, as you've told us, then why are we firing rockets into the air?"

The officer barely glanced at the man as he pointed to a white pinpoint in the distance. "See that light? It's a ship a few miles out. We're trying to attract its attention by sending signals; we haven't been able to reach it by wireless."

Lawrence hurried away. He knew there was a lot more the officer wasn't saying. Though the crew continued to assure the passengers that the matter wasn't serious, there was a heightening sense of impending doom in the frigid night air.

Glad he'd thought to bring his fur-lined overcoat upon leaving his room, Lawrence stuffed his cold hands into the pockets and continued his search. This was hopeless. It was obvious Annabelle wasn't on the boat deck. He wished he hadn't agreed to stay up here and look; she was probably on one of the lower decks, worried and wondering where everyone was. Making the decision to go below, he turned his head toward the companionway and inhaled sharply.

Annabelle hurried in his direction, her long dark hair streaming around her, her green eyes glued to him. He stood stock-still and blinked. When he finally realized it really was Annabelle rushing toward him and not a beautiful apparition, he took off running to meet her.

"Annabelle!"

"Lawrence!" His strong arms wrapped around her, hauling her close, and she threw her arms around his neck, burrowing her head against his chest.

Neither of them noticed Edward standing several feet away. He smiled sadly at the embracing couple, shook his head, then turned and disappeared into the crowd.

ই▶

"Annabelle," Lawrence breathed into her hair. "Thank God you're all right! I was so worried when I couldn't find you. . . . I didn't know what to think." She sniffled, her body trembling, and tightened her hold around him. "There's so much I want to say to you," he groaned in frustration. "I was going to speak with you tomorrow. . . . I was going to make you listen to me!"

She looked up at him, her eyes shimmering. At that moment another distress rocket burst into the starry night sky, casting brilliant white light over her face. "Tell me, Lawrence. Tell me now," she whispered.

"Oh, Annabelle," he said, his gaze moving lovingly over her features. "There isn't time. We must find you a lifeboat."

"We have all the time in the world," she insisted softly. "We have right now, this moment. This is our tomorrow." She lifted her hands to either side of his face, cradling it. "Tell me, Lawrence. Please tell me what I never gave you the chance to say a few hours ago."

He looked deeply into her eyes. For a few moments, time was suspended and there was no danger, no sinking ship, no people hurrying past. There was only the two of them.

"I love you, Annabelle," he breathed. "I love you."

He pulled her close and his mouth descended to hers as, gently, slowly, his lips moved over her lips, reveling in their warmth, their softness. He tasted the saltiness of her tears, and his heart lurched in pain.

His mouth moved to her temple. "I've received your father's permission to court you, and I hope one day to ask you to marry me," Lawrence breathed next to her ear. "And you're wrong about my family—they love you like the daughter they never had and would welcome you with open arms, even if you were poor as a church mouse. . . . I don't care about titles or dowries, Annabelle. I only want you to be my wife. And nothing you could say will ever change that."

His voice cracked with emotion, in spite of his desire to remain calm. He closed his eyes briefly as he tried to control himself and keep up the pretense that nothing was seriously wrong. She must have no cause to suspect the imminent danger.

"And do you want to know what I would say if you asked me, Lawrence?" Annabelle pulled away to look at him. At his hesitant nod, she replied, "I would say: 'I, Annabelle Christine Guinevere Mooreland, wilt take thee, Lawrence Caldwell, to be my lawfully wedded husband; to have and to hold from this day forward; for better, for worse; for richer, for poorer; in sickness and in health; to love and to cherish; forsaking all others, as long as we both shall live.'"

Tears glistened in his eyes, making them radiate with warmth, and a sad sort of smile touched his lips. "And if the blessed day should ever come when you stand beside me as my bride, Annabelle, it would give me great pleasure to reply: 'I, Lawrence Lancelot Caldwell, do take thee, Annabelle Christine Guinevere Mooreland, to be my lawfully wedded wife; to have and to hold from this day forward; for better, for worse; for richer, for poorer; in sickness and in health; to love and to cherish; forsaking all others, I plight unto thee my troth.'"

"Lancelot and Guinevere," she breathed, eyes wide in understanding. "I never knew your middle name was Lancelot. . . . That's why you acted so strangely when I told you my full name."

Lawrence nodded, swallowing hard. "Like the story of Camelot I read to you years ago underneath the apple tree. Do you remember,

Annabelle? All the time I read to you, I never dreamed I was reading to the girl who would one day be my Guinevere."

"I always wanted you for my Lancelot, even then, but I never believed it could really happen," she managed, trying not to cry. "Oh, Lawrence—I was a fool to say what I did when we talked earlier! Please forgive me. At the time I thought I was doing you a favor. . . . You're the only one I've ever loved. When I was a child you were my best friend, my hero. And as the years passed you became so much more."

Swallowing convulsively, he pulled the signet ring off his finger, then took her hand, lifting it. Carefully he slipped the gold ring onto her finger and closed her hand in a fist so it wouldn't fall off. "Keep this for me, Annabelle, until I can get you another. And know you will forever have my love . . .'til the end of time."

Her gaze flicked down to her hand, clasped tightly in both of his, and the ring, which bore his family crest. "Oh, Lawrence," she murmured, her voice trembling.

"Shhh." He placed two fingers against her lips. "Mustn't cry, Little Belle."

She barely nodded. His fingers moved to brush away the tears trickling down her cheeks, then he gently drew her to him and held her close one last time. "We have to find a lifeboat for you now," he said, trying to inject a casual air into his voice, though emotion threatened to choke it off. Reluctantly he pulled away and took her arm, but she refused to budge.

"No, Lawrence. I want to stay here with you."

He looked away from her, toward the bow of the ship. "Annabelle, we'll only be apart for a short time, I'm certain. I'll follow in another boat, after all the women and children—"

"Look at me," she interrupted. "Look at me and say that. Promise me you'll come later, Lawrence."

His eyes briefly closed; he knew she would see the truth there and knew that she must not. Yet he couldn't bring himself to lie to her, even if it was for her own good.

She spoke very softly, so softly that he almost couldn't hear her. "I know the truth. I know this isn't merely a precaution as they've told us. I know the ship is going down and there aren't enough lifeboats for everyone. I also know they're allowing only women and children onto those boats—and there aren't enough even for them."

He turned his head and looked at her sharply, anticipating what she was about to say. "Annabelle, I want you to go now," he ordered, his voice low but firm.

"No, Lawrence, I won't," she cried, the tears starting again. "I don't want to go without you! I love you so much!"

Briefly he closed his eyes, pain flickering over his features. "Oh, my beautiful, independent, stubborn Little Belle. What am I to do with you?" he murmured, his hands going to either side of her face, his fingers tangling in her long, dark hair.

"Please, let me stay," she begged, even now seeing the denial in his eyes.

"No, my love," he whispered. "No."

"But I don't want to live without you!"

His eyes searched hers, begging her to understand. "If this is my appointed time to leave this world, I could never die content, knowing your life wasn't spared. And if I don't make it—remember, my darling, we'll meet again. One day in the heavenly kingdom, we'll be together again."

His head lowered while he spoke. As he breathed the last word, his lips touched hers in a kiss—gently at first, then with more passion. They clung ever tighter, trying to make up for what they were about to lose. With painful clarity, they both realized there would probably never be another shared tomorrow.

A third distress rocket fired into the black, star-studded sky, temporarily flooding it with light and showering a dazzling glow over the couple locked in tight embrace. They were oblivious to the people running past—shouting, crying, beginning to realize this was no mere precaution as they'd been told.

Reluctantly, Lawrence broke away. "Come, darling. Before it's too late."

Annabelle tightly clutched Lawrence's arm as they moved down the crowded deck toward the lifeboat. She tried to walk slowly, wanting to prolong their last moments together, but he was determined and hurried her along, almost at a trot.

Could it be that her long-held crystalline dream of shared love between them had finally come to fulfillment . . . only to be smashed to smithereens all around her? She didn't want to be separated from him, never to see him again! She didn't want to live without Lawrence, without his friendship and his love; how had she ever thought she could? *God, where are You?! How can You let this happen to me? To us?*

Annabelle watched, horrified, as several men ahead of them, upon realizing their hopeless plight, jumped over the rail into the cold ocean below. They landed with a splash of white foam within a few feet of each other and set out swimming, obviously hoping to reach one of the lifeboats rowing away into the dark night. As Annabelle looked down, she noted with alarm that the ocean was much closer than before, and there were other heads bobbing in the freezing water.

All too soon they reached the lifeboat. An officer caught sight of Annabelle and motioned her over. "Quickly please, miss! There's room for one more."

Annabelle looked at Lawrence, her eyes wide and pleading, begging him to reconsider. But he only shook his head and delivered one last soft kiss to her lips. "Good-bye, my love," he whispered hoarsely. "It's time for you to go now."

She was tempted to refuse—to have her way and stay with him no matter how he argued. But the loving plea she read in his eyes curbed her selfish desire, and she realized just how important it was to him that she enter the lifeboat. She knew she must, no matter how it tore her apart to leave his side.

Heedless of the people who stood near, Annabelle threw her arms around his neck and kissed him hard, wanting to imprint his lips on hers, to remember their soft warmth in the cold future that lay ahead of her.

A few bittersweet seconds passed until Lawrence gently removed her arms from around his neck and broke away, hating the anguished look in her eyes but knowing his own expression mirrored hers. "You must go now," he whispered. "Hurry, my love. Pray for me, and remember the Psalms." He wiped another tear from her cheek. "Don't be sad, Little Belle; I promise we'll be together again one day. And in case I don't . . ." He broke off and swallowed hard. "Tell Mother and Father I love them."

Annabelle barely nodded as she looked up at him through her tears, trying to memorize every line of his handsome face, every feature, every expression, in the few seconds left before she must board the boat. Vaguely she heard the officer behind her urge her to hurry.

"Yes, Lawrence. I'll tell them. And you're right—we *will* be together again one day soon, darling. I love you, my Lancelot. I always have . . . and I always will," she added in a whisper. Hand shaking, she touched his lips with her fingertips and looked once more into his beautiful ice-blue eyes. She forced herself to turn away then, unwilling to say the dreaded word "Good-bye."

The officer hurriedly helped her over the rail and into the boat. She sat on the hard, narrow bench beside a woman who also was crying.

Annabelle lifted her head and spotted Lawrence through her tears. He stood next to the rail, his eyes glued to her. She kept her gaze fixed on him as the boat lowered past A-deck, where desperate people tried to lunge into the boat through the windowless openings, only to be held at bay by an officer who waved his gun at them.

The whole evening seemed like a bizarre nightmare, making no sense at all. This couldn't be happening; the *Titanic* was unsinkable! Any minute now, Annabelle would surely wake from this horrible dream and find that she was lying on her bed in her stateroom. She would breakfast with her father and Lawrence; then she and Lawrence would stroll along the promenade, talking about all sorts of things, sharing fond memories, and discussing the Scriptures like they often did. . . .

The boat slammed onto the water with a slapping splash, breaking into her thoughts and convincing Annabelle this was no dream. A nightmare, yes . . . but no dream.

As the lifeboat moved away from the doomed ship, Annabelle felt as if her heart had been wrenched from within her to remain behind on the *Titanic* with Lawrence. "God, please help him," she whispered into the dark night. "Please, please keep him safe."

Another distress rocket lit the air, causing Lawrence to pull his gaze away from the departing lifeboat carrying away the woman he loved. At least she would be safe.

He moved away from the rail, and instantly a man Lawrence recognized as Thomas Andrews hurried up to him. "Please, sir, where's your life belt? I must insist that you put it on!"

"I left it in my stateroom on C-deck," Lawrence murmured, still emotionally numb; he was unable to see the alarm in the other man's eyes.

"I'll try and find you another," Andrews hastily said, and within minutes, he was back with a life belt for Lawrence.

Lawrence thanked him and automatically shrugged into it, vaguely aware as Andrews moved down the deck encouraging others to do the same. But there was little need of that now. The passengers had at last realized the hopeless situation, and the majority of them needed no coercion to put on the padded jackets.

A thought came to Lawrence's mind. Where was Edward? Lawrence must find him and tell him that he'd found Annabelle and she was safe. Should he have looked for Edward and let the man say good-bye to his daughter before she'd left?

Lawrence looked around the crowded deck filled with panicked people and noticed how few lifeboats remained. Pistol shots sounded as one of the officers shot his gun into the air in a desperate attempt to hold back the milling, wild-eyed throng of men seeking escape in one of the lifeboats.

"Women and children only!" the officer screamed. "Stand back, the lot of you!"

Lawrence hurried to the companionway in search of Edward. As he walked down the grand staircase to the next level, he saw Benjamin Guggenheim. He was dressed in a silk top hat, black tails, and white gloves, his valet next to him. Benjamin spoke to a nearby steward. "We've dressed and are prepared to go down like gentlemen. Tell my wife that I played the game straight to the end."

Lawrence hurried past them through the crowded room, searching the anxious sea of faces. He walked through the lounge, past the other stairway, and on into the smoking room. Edward wasn't there, but he was surprised to see Thomas Andrews standing and staring at a painting of ships on the ocean that hung over the fireplace mantel. His life belt was now discarded and lay on the floor at his feet.

"Mr. Andrews . . . ?" Lawrence asked, puzzled.

Thomas turned to look at him with eyes that were infinitely sad and vacant and slowly shook his head. Even more slowly, he turned once again to stare up at the painting.

Lawrence backed out of the room, not knowing what else to do, and hurried down the staircase in search of Edward, a prayer for the mentally anguished Andrews—and for all who had been left behind— in his heart.

ॐ

Along with those in her boat, Annabelle numbly watched the great ship sink lower into the water. The hundreds of bright lights on the decks still above sea level made it easy to see those on board. Everywhere she looked, people were running, trying to find a way out of the trap they now knew they were in. Toward the stern, Annabelle caught sight of a blond woman in a long black coat over a white nightgown, holding tightly to the arm of a taller blond man wearing a steward's uniform.

Sadie! It had to be! They were still close, and Annabelle clearly saw that the woman wore her hair in a long braid. Annabelle tried to call out to her, but with all the noise on the ship, there was no way her maid could hear. *Oh, Sadie. Please find a lifeboat.* As Annabelle watched, the couple moved away, with the others, closer to the stern.

ৡৄ

Lawrence hurried down the staircase, noting that the ship seemed to slant even more. He rushed through the corridors calling Edward's name, then ran down another set of stairs to the next deck. What he saw froze his blood.

Several inches of green sea water flowed down the carpeted corridors and the floor next to the grand staircase. Lawrence hesitated only a moment before he stepped into the freezing water and sloshed his way down the corridors, calling out for Edward. By the time he returned to the grand staircase, the water was slowly but maliciously up to his knees.

Quickly he ascended to B-deck and heard what sounded like a small child crying. He located a small boy—no more than four years old—crouched behind a potted plant. He was dressed in a long nightshirt and coat, but his feet were bare.

"Where's your mother?" Lawrence asked softly. The boy only stared at him with wide brown eyes and cried even harder. Lawrence looked in both directions, undecided. He couldn't leave the boy here after what he'd seen on the deck below. The sea water was slowly but maliciously inching its way upward.

"There, there, lad. I won't hurt you." He lifted the boy, who clutched Lawrence's neck tightly. As Lawrence made a quick search of the corridors in a vain attempt to locate the child's parents, he noticed that the skinny child weighed next to nothing. Well, if he couldn't find the boy's mother, at least Lawrence would make certain the child was safe.

He headed toward the boat deck and stopped in his tracks. The ship was now much lower in the water, but with a pang of alarm, Lawrence noticed something else as well. Hearing a sudden commotion toward the stern, he turned his head to look.

The third-class passengers had just been released from steerage. Men, women, and children hurried toward the boat deck in hopes of escaping. But they were soon to learn the terrible truth that Lawrence had only just discovered.

All the lifeboats were gone.

ào

Everyone in Annabelle's boat watched in shock when the smoke-stack closest to the bow gave a terrible creak and groan as it fell with a crash to the deck. The screams from the ship could clearly be heard over the still, cold night by those who watched wide-eyed from the lifeboat.

Annabelle tightly clasped her frozen hands together, desperately hoping that soon she would wake up and find this had all been a bad dream, nothing more. Even the crewmen quieted their filthy talk and watched, unbelieving. They'd been allowed into the boat with the women on the assumption they knew how to row, which they didn't. One of them had tried, but had ended up rowing in wide circles. After a woman had hesitantly suggested he put the oar in the oarlock, he had looked surprised and muttered, "Oh, is that what that's for?"

Many of the women had taken over the job of rowing, which also helped to warm them. Nothing, though, could melt the ice encasing their hearts, as their eyes stayed glued to the *Titanic* and watched as she slowly submerged, foot by dreadful foot. Every one of them still had loved ones on board, and every one of them began to realize the truth: There weren't enough lifeboats. And, unless a ship came along soon, their loved ones were doomed to a watery grave.

"Pray for me, Annabelle. Remember the Psalms."

Lawrence's last words to her resounded through Annabelle's numbed brain, and she blinked as though she were coming out of a long, drugged sleep. Yes, she would pray. She would trust God to take care of Lawrence, as she should have done from the very beginning. Remembering the Psalm she'd memorized just a few short hours ago dealing with protection and deliverance from danger, Annabelle recited it for her loved ones on board.

ào

Lawrence tried to find another life belt for the boy, who tenaciously clung to his neck, but his search was futile. Now that the third-class passengers had been allowed to come to the top, any spare life belts had quickly been grabbed up.

Lawrence thought a moment, then decided. He set the boy down, prying his arms from around his neck. Quickly he undid his bulky life belt, all the while praying his idea would work. The boy was so thin and small . . . surely it could work.

Lawrence stooped down and placed the belt he was wearing over the boy, noting with relief that it just managed to cover them both. However, he hoped the child wouldn't smother—the opening at the neck was too small for both of them, and only part of the child's head came through. But there wasn't much he could do about that. Quickly he fastened the life belt. The boy clutched Lawrence's coat at the back and wrapped his legs around him, holding on for dear life. Lawrence straightened, his balance a bit unsteady, and prayed he would be able to swim carrying such a burden. But there was no alternative—he wouldn't leave the boy behind. Thank God he'd kept up with his physical fitness while on board. He was accustomed to hard, strenuous exercise and was certain he was about to be faced with the ultimate test of physical endurance.

Lawrence waited silently and listened to the musicians as they played the hymn "Autumn," listened to the frightened screams emanating from all over the ship, listened to the lap of icy water against the hull as it greedily waited to suck its mighty "unsinkable" victim to its dark depths. His hands gripped the rail and he waited, praying, meditating, trying to block out the sounds of terrible fear all around him, trying to remain calm and not panic, waiting until the boat had submerged another few feet.

Then, after a quick warning to the boy to hold his breath and a hasty but heartfelt prayer for protection on his lips, Lawrence wrapped his arms around the lad and jumped into the frigid ocean waters, which immediately closed over his head.

ु≫

Edward clutched the rail and watched as the lifeboat that carried his daughter became a white blur on a vast, dark ocean surrounded by ice floes. He had stood a distance away and sadly observed the parting scene between Lawrence and Annabelle, his heart rending at the thought that now Annabelle would have no one—except, of course, for a handful of distant uncles and a reclusive aunt who cared little about her.

Edward listened to the band play the melodic, slow strains of "Nearer My God to Thee" and looked out over the still waters, praying that God would spare Lawrence for his daughter.

A young, dark-headed lad of perhaps ten, obviously from steerage, by the looks of his worn clothes, rushed by, a terrified look on his face.

"Here, lad!" Edward called out. "Stop a moment, I say!"

The boy stopped and turned. Huge, fearful black eyes lifted to the elegantly dressed man standing at the rail, appearing to be calm and dignified, while everyone around him was in a state of panic. "You want speak with me, sir?" he asked shakily in a thick foreign accent.

The man nodded. "Where's your life belt, lad?"

"I no have one."

"You have now."

The boy watched, unbelieving, as the man unfastened his life belt and handed it to him. He was so stunned that for a moment he only stared. Shakily, he reached for it and slipped it on, crying his thanks and throwing his arms around the kind man.

Edward awkwardly patted the boy's head. "Hurry along, son. Run to the stern with the others, and God go with you."

"*Vaya con Dios*—God be with you, too, sir!" the boy managed before breaking his hold and turning to join the others for the mad rush to the stern of the boat.

"Oh, He is, son. He is," Edward said quietly as he watched the boy's retreating back. His mind on the upcoming reunion, Edward turned his peaceful face heavenward to look at the black velvet dome of sky sprinkled with thousands of diamondlike stars . . . while the cold sea water rushed under the soles of his shoes and the boat deck began to slowly submerge.

❧

In the cold, still air, those in Annabelle's lifeboat could clearly hear the musicians on the *Titanic* playing the moving hymn "Nearer My God to Thee." Then all music suddenly ceased as the boat tilted even more and the musicians could no longer stand.

The people in the lifeboat watched, horrified, yet unable to tear their eyes away from the nightmarish scene unfolding before them. The bow of the ship disappeared into the sea, and the *Titanic* steadily slipped down at an angle, its gigantic propellers slowly rising out of the water. Frantic passengers pulled themselves along her decks toward the stern, many people falling to the dark ocean below. Soon the middle of the ship disappeared beneath the surface, the bright lights beneath the dark waters giving off an eerie greenish glow.

A terrible crack rent the night air as the ship broke into two pieces. The stern slammed back onto the water, throwing several people into the freezing sea, but after a minute the section began rising steadily again.

"Dear God, there are so many, so many . . . ," the woman next to Annabelle whispered, mirroring Annabelle's horrified thoughts.

Rows of bright yellow lights all along the remaining two hundred feet of the ship made it easy to see what looked like hundreds of miniature people fighting for their lives. Many fell or jumped off the boat to the icy water below. Some slid down the deck at a terrific speed, bouncing off objects like broken dolls. Others desperately held on to the railing or anything else mounted to the decks.

There were continual screams and cries as the afterdeck slowly, steadily, rose even higher, its lights still burning brightly. Suddenly they began to flicker off and on, then they went out completely, causing all to go black. The dark stern of the ship rose even higher out of the water until it was completely vertical, a huge, thick black column standing upright against the glittering dome of sky. There was a terrible, mighty roar within the ship, easily heard by those in the lifeboat.

Annabelle watched wide-eyed, forgetting to breathe, while the *Titanic* hung suspended for almost a full minute, as if holding on, refusing to be sucked under. And then, with a powerful rush, the ship slid rapidly below the ocean waters in a terrible downward plunge and was no more.

"She's gone!" cried several women in the boat. Annabelle just stared, unheeding, at the vaporous mist above the still black water where the mighty *Titanic* had been just moments ago. It was as though a valve in her brain had been mercifully shut off and she'd watched it all without really being there.

And then the cries started. Men, women, children—all were crying for those in the lifeboats to come save them from the freezing water. Annabelle blinked as reality seeped in. "Oh, we've got to go back and help!"

"Are you crazy?" one of the crewmen snapped. "There's too many people in this boat now. If we go back, they'll swamp us."

"But we can't just let them stay there! They'll freeze!"

"We can't go back, I said. It would be suicide!"

Annabelle ignored the words of the cruel man and turned to the other women in the boat. "Those are your loved ones out there! Are we just going to leave them to die?" she cried, thinking of Lawrence and her father.

Several sided with Annabelle, but most agreed with the crewman.

"Our boat is so full already!"

"There's no room."

"If we went back and picked up even one, we'd likely tip over and sink."

Though the excuses were valid, they didn't change Annabelle's heart. Because their lifeboat was lowered toward the end, it was fuller than the ones that had left earlier. But surely there was some room; surely they could save a few. Above the hundreds of wailing voices pleading for attention, Annabelle thought she heard a child cry out to her mama, and she began to earnestly plead with the others.

"There are children out there! Oh, please, let's try," she begged. However, only a few others changed their mind. The rest, the majority, were adamant in their refusal and continued to row in the direction of the ship's light they'd spotted earlier from the deck of the *Titanic*.

Annabelle clapped her hands over her ears to drown out the desperate cries of those left behind. She prayed for every one of them, tears running down her face. She prayed for Lawrence, her father, Sadie, the men and women, the children. *Oh, dear God, the children!*

It was as though a soothing voice suddenly spoke inside her head, gently comforting her: *Annabelle, My daughter, do not fear for the little ones. Even now I am holding out My arms, ready to receive them into My loving embrace. Instead, pray for those who don't know Me, that they will open their hearts and receive Me before it's too late.*

The soft voice seemed so audible that Annabelle looked at the others to see if anyone else had heard it. But the solemn faces showed no evidence of having heard the beautiful voice.

Recognizing the call to intercede, Annabelle quietly did so and was aware of being filled by a soothing warmth, even though on the outside she shivered from the cold. She lifted her face to the twinkling pinpoints of lights and looked at the awesome beauty of the nighttime sky, almost able to imagine angels coming from above to receive those who'd died, taking them to heaven to be with the Lord. And as she prayed, the peace that passes all understanding soothed her spirit, even though she'd probably lost everyone dear to her heart.

෭ଈ

Annabelle tried several more times to convince those in the boat to go back and rescue some of the others, but she received the same answer each time: No.

Little by little the cries diminished until few were heard. Soon all was quiet across the still, dark ocean.

Annabelle bit the inside of her lip and closed her eyes, knowing she'd done all she could. But the thought brought little comfort. Now she could easily hear the water lapping against the hull of their boat, the sloshing sound of the oars as they lifted and dipped into the ocean, and the clunk of ice floes they sometimes bumped against. And those from the other lifeboats who'd sung, or whistled, or cheered to drown out the pitiful cries, stopped their racket, knowing there was no more reason to make noise.

The woman next to Annabelle, who'd also wanted to go back, whispered, "Oh, God. What have we done? What have we done!"

Annabelle reached for her hand and clutched it hard, offering comfort and sharing pain. She hoped someone had gone back, that there was a chance her loved ones were still alive.

To Annabelle's complete shock, the blanket next to her foot began to move, and a whimper could distinctly be heard, quickly escalating into a loud cry. She reached down and, to everyone's amazement, picked up a baby who'd been protectively swaddled in the thick blanket. She drew the bundle close and began to croon and rock the little one, trying to hush the pitiful cries while drawing comfort from the child. The tiny bit of life she held relieved some of the ache in her heart, and she wrapped her arms tightly around the baby, trying to keep it warm, trying to save one life.

Everyone began to question the others around them: "Is it yours?" "Is that your baby?" But the mother couldn't be found, and in the chaos of the previous two hours, no one could remember an officer handing a baby to anyone.

Eventually, the baby cried itself to sleep again, and Annabelle sighed in relief. "How could anyone sleep through the horror of tonight?" she said sadly, mostly to herself.

"Babies can sleep through most anything. She sure is tiny," the woman next to her said as she continued to row.

"How do you know it's a girl?"

The woman shrugged. "I don't. Just a guess."

Annabelle studied the woman, who'd said little all night. Though it was very hard to see, Annabelle could make out the lines of strain and exhaustion on her face. "Would you like me to take over for a while? You can hold the baby."

The woman readily agreed, and, with only a little difficulty and a warning from one of the crewmen never to do it again, they changed places. Annabelle took the coarse handle and clumsily began to row, at first clacking against the other oars in front of her and behind. But soon she achieved a certain rhythm and proved to be more help than hindrance.

"My name's Annabelle Mooreland," she told the woman who held the baby close and put her cheek next to its face.

The woman straightened. "I'm Maude Harper," she offered.

The women exchanged little conversation after that, but a bond of sorts had been established. An hour later, when they still hadn't reached the elusive light of the ship, Maude sighed and said, "You think someone will find us soon?"

"I hope so," Annabelle replied, continuing to row. Her hands stung from the biting cold and the coarse wood, and her muscles were weary, but at least the exercise helped keep her warm.

Twice the crewmen set fire to rolled-up pieces of paper, using them as beacons in an effort to signal their whereabouts to any ships nearby. Earlier, they'd seen a strange glow in the sky, and a crewman had informed them it was the Northern Lights. Many times they rowed toward what they thought were ship's lights, but they turned out to be stars rising on the distant horizon.

As the night wore on, muscles Annabelle rarely used screamed for relief. Maude must have noticed how she had begun to lag at the oar, for she offered to trade again. Despite the crewman's curses and threats for the women to stay seated before they capsized the boat, Maude handed the baby to the woman next to her and stood, allowing Annabelle to slide down the bench in her place. Annabelle steadied Maude while she carefully took a few steps, sat down, and took over the oar once again.

"And I had to get stuck with a bunch of simple-minded women," the crewman muttered to himself.

"You weren't forced to get into the boat," a woman in front of Annabelle responded bitterly. "Our men would have taken much better care of us than you've done."

"That so? Well, here's something to keep you warm then."

The burly crewman carelessly flicked his lit cigarette in her direction. There were screams and shrieks as the red-hot cherry tip landed in her skirt and was hurriedly extinguished.

"Aw, leave 'em alone, mate," another crewman said casually, trying to relieve the awful tension in the boat that had been building since the *Titanic* sank. "The ladies have been through enough as it is."

"An' I don't need your lip either, Marley!"

The one named Marley continued rowing as he quietly said a few more words and managed to calm his irate partner. Afterward, Annabelle heard a woman on the boat turn to him.

"Mr. Marley," she said softly, "I just want you to know, I appreciate all your help. And if I come out of this alive, I plan to send a letter to the White Star Line telling them what a valuable employee they have in you."

The woman on the other side of Annabelle, who was now holding the sleeping baby, said under her breath, "It takes a crisis to find out the true character of a man."

Her words made Annabelle think of Lawrence and her father. Had they also helped others before the ship went down? Annabelle liked to think so. She also liked to think they were in one of the other lifeboats out on the ocean.

≈

The sky lightened and the stars faded away. Pink tinged the eastern horizon as the sun made ready for its appearance.

The baby, who'd been passed around throughout the night—all the women wanted to take care of it—became hungry and began to cry. All in the boat were thirsty, cold, and exhausted. However, there were no provisions in the lifeboat, and many of the women were dressed only in their nightgowns and coats and wore slippers on their feet.

Annabelle still wore her fur coat over her evening gown from the night before, and as she looked down at it in the brightening dawn, she noticed a long tear in the skirt. She slipped her hand in the pocket of her coat and felt for Lawrence's ring. It was much too loose to wear, and concerned she might lose it, she had put it away. Finding it now, she grasped it tightly in the palm of her hand for comfort. She wanted to pray, but her mind was too numb to do so. She'd had little more than four hours sleep in the past forty-eight hours.

And then on the horizon they clearly saw something: a light . . . and one below that; it was the hull of a ship. Help had come at last.

Some of the women began to cry as they rowed toward the large ship that bore the word *Carpathia* on its hull. Annabelle later remembered little of what happened afterward, except that the crying baby was hoisted up in a canvas bag that had been lowered, and Annabelle was tied to a narrow "swing" of sorts and pulled upward. Once her feet touched deck, her legs buckled, and one of the officers caught her and lifted her in his arms.

Annabelle had a vague impression of going down seemingly endless stairs and being carried through a corridor, then laid on a cot. A warm, coarse blanket was tucked around her shivering form, and she gratefully nestled into the softness of the pillow under her head. When feeling began to return to her numb body, the needlelike, hot pain was so intense she almost cried.

Emotionally, physically, and mentally exhausted, Annabelle lay on the small cot, Lawrence's name escaping her lips before she fell into a sound sleep.

(18)

*S*creams and cries sounded throughout the night; so horrible were the wails that Annabelle pulled back in fear and clutched at the rough surface of the boat. As she watched, the huge ship, which blocked out most of the starlit sky, began to sink lower. Her father and Lawrence calmly stood on the deck and silently waved to her, but when she cried out for them to jump to the empty seats inside her boat, they slowly turned and walked away.

The great suction of the ship going under pulled her small lifeboat toward it with greedy watery fingers. She screamed and tried to row faster, but to no avail. Desperately she turned to those in the lifeboat with her, only to find that they'd been frozen; their hair and faces were encrusted with icicles, their eyes now vacant. She began to scream.

"Wake up, miss! Wake up!"

Annabelle's eyes fluttered open to find sunlight streaming through a porthole to the cot where she lay; a young stewardess was gently shaking her.

"Where am I?" Annabelle croaked in a raspy voice.

"You're on board the *Carpathia*, miss. You were rescued from a lifeboat."

"A lifeboat," Annabelle breathed, trying to force her brain to understand. "Yes, now I remember. The *Titanic* . . . Oh, dear God," Annabelle murmured, closing her eyes in horror.

The stewardess bit her lip. "I—I've brought you something to eat. 'Tisn't much, mind you. But there's not enough food for everyone on board. If you feel up to going to the dining room, you might be able to get some soup, though."

Annabelle looked at the plate with two pieces of brown bread slathered with butter. "Have all the lifeboats been rescued?"

"Yes, miss. Yesterday morning."

"Yesterday morning . . . ," Annabelle repeated. "What day is it?"

"Why, it's Tuesday, miss. You slept 'round the clock."

"Tuesday!" she exclaimed, sitting bolt upright; she ignored the wave of dizziness that assaulted her. She had to hurry and dress. She needed to search the boat to see if any of her loved ones were on board. Another thought immediately hit. She had no clothes, except for the torn velvet evening gown she wore. Though she was hardly presentable, she had little choice. Annabelle swung her legs over the bed, her head swimming. "I need to look for them," she muttered vaguely.

"You have to eat first," the stewardess urged. "You need the strength the food will give you to walk around the ship."

Reluctantly Annabelle agreed, and she hastily ate. Afterward, she had to admit she did feel a little better. She thanked the stewardess and hurried out of the room to start her search. Finding an officer, who asked her name and added it to a list of survivors he held in his hand, Annabelle questioned him concerning the whereabouts of her loved ones. He scanned the list for the names she gave him.

"I'm sorry, miss. But so far, no one with those names has been recorded." Seeing her distress, he quickly added, "But that doesn't mean there's no hope. I'm still adding names. I only just added yours. And there's another, besides myself, who's doing this as well."

Annabelle gave a small smile and nodded. Perhaps they hadn't had their names written in the ledger yet or the other officer had them on his list. She thanked him and hurried away, looking through all the public rooms and on the decks and studying every person, some of them huddled in blankets and many of them wearing nightclothes and wrappers.

Maude Harper, the woman in the lifeboat, was the first person Annabelle recognized. Maude told her that the baby they'd cared for had been joyfully reunited with its frantic mother, who'd somehow been separated from her child and put in another lifeboat, and Annabelle was happy for the unknown woman.

She was relieved to find Missy, frightened but in one piece, and her mother. When Annabelle asked about Maria, Doña Ortega informed her that Maria was unconscious in the officers' quarters below deck, but she would live. However, Annabelle didn't see any sign of Charlotte or Eric. Though she'd been uncomfortable around the two, she certainly didn't wish them dead! Now she felt bad for her earlier actions—especially toward Charlotte. Annabelle fervently hoped Charlotte had responded to the message of salvation Annabelle had shared with her . . . and she hoped someone had told Eric about Jesus, too. What happened Sunday night proved that no one knew when tragedy would suddenly strike and it would be too late; everyone deserved a chance to hear the message of the gospel and to make a choice.

Annabelle found the dispensary and decided to peek inside, but before she could open the door, a steward stopped her.

"You can't go in there, miss. There's two injured men inside in a state of undress. One of 'em was struck in the head with an oar when he swam to them, beggin' them to save his son. And the other is the young wireless operator, Harold Bride."

"Oh, dear. Did the boy live?" she asked.

"Aye. But the poor lad will likely be a cripple. He has severe frostbite in both feet, just like Mr. Bride does. They may have to cut off a few of the lad's toes."

"Oh, how horrible!" Annabelle's eyes went wide.

"That it is," the steward agreed. "But they're the lucky ones."

"What do you mean?" she whispered.

"Only a handful of them left in the water were rescued."

Annabelle looked at him in shock. Only a handful? But there must have been well over a thousand, from what Annabelle had seen!

"Mr. McKee," a gruff voice full of authority interrupted. "Haven't you duties to perform?"

The steward talking to Annabelle turned to the officer walking toward them. "Aye, sir."

"Then I suggest you get to them."

"Aye, sir. Right away, sir." McKee hurried away.

Annabelle put a hand to the officer's sleeve before he, too, could walk away. He turned, his bushy eyebrows raised.

"Excuse me, sir, but could you tell me . . . is it true what that steward said? Were only a few in the water rescued?" Annabelle asked, her tone pleading with him to say otherwise.

"Aye, miss. From what we've learned, it's so," he said, emotion coloring his voice.

Her heart turned into a heavy stone, threatening to block off her breathing. "Is there a chance there are more lifeboats waiting to be rescued?"

"No, miss. The last one was picked up at approximately eight-thirty yesterday morning."

"But—but maybe there are still some alive in the water, or perhaps some of the people may have climbed out onto an iceberg?" she asked hopefully.

He looked at her sadly. "We returned to the site of the sinking earlier and circled the waters. No one was found."

"Oh, my," she breathed, feeling as if she might faint.

His brows furrowed in concern. "Are you looking for someone?"

"Yes." It came out little more than a squeak.

"Perhaps they're on the boat deck in the third-class steerage section," he suggested helpfully. "In all the excitement, it's possible a mistake was made."

"Yes, thank you! I'll go and look now."

"Will you be okay?" he asked gruffly, noting her pale face.

"Yes. I'll be fine. Thank you for your help."

Annabelle hurried to the third-class section. But as she studied the huddled, dejected forms in hopes of seeing a familiar, loved face, she soon realized it was pointless. They weren't there.

She climbed the stairs and went through the gate leading back into first class. On her way to the boat deck, she ran into Maggie Brown. The two women hugged in reunion, and Annabelle tearfully told Maggie the situation.

Maggie patted Annabelle on the back. "It'll be okay, honey. In all the excitement it's possible you mighta missed them. You oughta try again later."

Annabelle barely nodded. Maggie studied her wretched expression. "Now, now." Maggie put her arm around Annabelle's shoulders, steering her down the corridor to the dining room. "What you need is a good meal. Things'll look better soon. I'll bet you find 'em all safe and sound—snug as a bug in a rug."

Annabelle nodded, then swallowed hard. "There were so many, Maggie. So many . . ." Her voice trailed off.

"I know, honey. I know."

Later that afternoon, Annabelle again searched the decks, but to no avail. The truth was becoming clearer; Annabelle was the only one who'd survived. But still she hoped. Later, she begged one of the officers to let her look at the completed list; but none of the names Annabelle hoped to see were written there.

She went through the rest of the day in a fog similar to the one in which the *Carpathia* traveled that evening. The weather was so much different than when she'd been on the *Titanic*, but it matched the way she felt inside. The seas were choppy, the winds bitterly cold, the skies stormy. Annabelle walked the deck. Cold needles of ocean spray stung her face.

"Oh, God," she cried to the dark skies. "How can I go on without him? Why did this have to happen?" Only the sound of the sea splashing against the boat answered her sad queries.

Hot tears running down her face collided with cold drops of saltwater. She thrust her hand into her coat pocket and pulled up the ring—Lawrence's ring. " 'Til we meet again, my love . . . ," she said softly, tears choking her voice. Putting the ring to her lips, she kissed it, then carefully dropped it back into her pocket.

She would never marry. There could never be another. She felt empty inside, drained, but she knew one thing. Like David had done in the Psalms—when his entire world was falling apart—Annabelle would simply have to trust God to be God and cling tightly to Him. She had no one else.

ॐ

"Excuse me, steward?" Annabelle called out to the white-jacketed man in front of her.

"Aye, miss?"

"I wanted to inquire as to how the boy in the infirmary is doing. The one with frostbite in his feet."

The steward grimaced. "Not very well, miss. Poor lad is little more than a babe, but likely he'll be a cripple for the rest of his life. And he lost his mama in the sinking, too."

"Oh, the poor thing," Annabelle said sadly.

"Likely when we reach New York and he's taken to a hospital, the doctor will have to cut off his toes."

She briefly closed her eyes, her heart hurting for the child. "I wonder, is there any way I could see him? I mean, I know his father is in there as well, and—"

"Oh, no, miss. He was released this morning, and Mr. Bride is also out of the room for the time being."

"Then may I see the boy?"

He looked uncertain. "I'll have to ask permission. Are you a relative by any chance?"

"No. Just someone who cares."

He eyed the calm woman with the beautiful emerald eyes, which were rather bloodshot from crying. Obviously she'd lost someone in the sinking. But then again, hadn't everyone? "I'll see what I can do."

"Thank you," Annabelle said sincerely. She watched him walk away. Ever since that morning, she'd felt a strong impression in her spirit to visit the child. She'd spent all day Wednesday in the officers' quarters below decks—where some of the *Titanic's* survivors slept at night—angry, crying, pleading, and finally, accepting her sad set of circumstances. This morning, she'd gone to God, begging Him to help her and give her the desire to go on without Lawrence. Almost instantly, she remembered the boy in the infirmary and knew she must go to him.

Fifteen minutes later, upon receiving permission, Annabelle entered the room and went to the small child who lay on a cot. Both his feet were wrapped in white bandages, which were awkward-looking on his sticklike legs. She looked down at the fearful, wide eyes in the pinched, narrow face. Slowly she lifted her arm and laid a hand on the curly blond head. The boy didn't flinch but only looked at her and blinked his eyes.

"Are you an angel?" he asked in a babylike voice that trembled a little.

"No, dear."

"My mama went to be with the angels," he said, the tears coming to his brown eyes.

"I know," Annabelle said softly. "I know."

Her heart wrenching at his pain, she knelt down and gently drew him to her. His thin arms wrapped tightly around her neck, and he began to cry.

❧

After promising to visit him again soon, Annabelle left the boy and walked down the corridor to the stairs that led to the upper deck. It was strange, but an instant bond of love and friendship had sprung up between them during the short visit. *Because we've both just lost a parent?* she wondered.

Annabelle had been told they would reach the shores of America soon, so she walked up to the covered deck to look for land, even though it was evening. Thunder crashed and lightning ripped open the sky; a sheet of blinding rain obscured any view.

Dismayed, Annabelle turned to go back down below, then stopped. Several yards away, a man stood at the rail watching the spectacular storm, obviously unconcerned about being splattered by a few slanting drops of cold rain. A white bandage was tied around his head, and Annabelle wondered if he could be the boy's father. She remembered that the steward had told her he'd suffered a head injury.

She almost approached him, then stopped. Certainly it wouldn't be proper to do so, even considering the unusual circumstances. Unmarried women simply didn't talk to strange men. Annabelle turned to go, then paused and looked at his dim form again. He lifted a hand to the back of his head as if to smooth his dark hair, though it only came into contact with the bandage. There was something familiar about that gesture. . . .

Her hand went to her throat and she clutched her mother's necklace. "Lawrence," she breathed.

The man's shoulders stiffened beneath his overcoat, as though he'd actually heard her whisper above the driving rain. Annabelle briefly closed her eyes in sad resignation; she'd already searched the whole boat and had seen that Lawrence's name wasn't on the list of survivors.

The man moved away from the rail. Perhaps she should go, she thought in the split second before they faced one another. She didn't want him to think she'd been staring—which she had, but for different reasons than he might guess. But before she could turn away, the man turned to face her. At that moment lightning brightened the sky, illuminating the man's face and a remarkable pair of silvery-blue eyes. Eyes like warm ice.

"Annabelle!"

Her shoulder hit the wooden frame of the companionway as she fell against it, scarcely believing what she was seeing and hearing. Only when his strong arms went around her and his hot tears fell against her temple did Annabelle realize her Lancelot had been spared. "Lawrence!" She threw her arms around him. "You're alive! You're really and truly alive!"

His hands moved to cradle her head, his fingers tangling in her dark curls, and he pulled back a fraction. His eyes hurriedly searched her features as if to make certain she were real, then his lips lowered to her upturned face, and he feverishly kissed her forehead, her closed eyelids, her teary cheeks.

"Annabelle," he breathed, and then his mouth found hers.

Locked in his embrace, she lost all sense of time. His warm lips on hers were demanding yet gentle, anxious yet relieved. She tightly clung to him, unable to believe he was really with her and not at the bottom of the cold, dark ocean.

"Oh, my Guinevere," he murmured into her hair after he'd broken the kiss, "I thought I'd lost you. I've been looking for you ever since this morning."

"I thought you were dead. . . ." Annabelle's voice wavered, and she felt as though she might cry again. "I didn't see your name on the survivors' list, and I couldn't find you."

"The list." He briefly shut his eyes. "I never checked the list." He moved with her inside the empty companionway, where they could hear one another over the sounds of the storm.

She shook her head in confusion. "How could I have missed you? I thoroughly checked the ship for you and my father and Sadie." Her voice trembled, and fresh tears came to her eyes. "They didn't make it."

He drew her to him and held her close. "Oh, my love, my Little Belle, I'm so sorry." For a few moments all was quiet as he gently comforted her, stroking her back, kissing her hair.

She lifted her wet face to him. "It's the way Father wanted it. He told me so before I left that night. He hadn't been happy since Mother died. But at least God gave us a few days to mend our relationship . . . I'm so thankful for that. And I take comfort in the fact Sadie was with the man she loved," Annabelle managed, her voice choked with tears. "But where were you?"

He smoothed the damp, straggled hair away from her face, unable to keep his hands off her. "I've been unconscious since the rescue," he explained. "I only awakened this morning."

Annabelle's eyes widened in understanding. "Then you're the one," she breathed. "The one who saved the boy in the infirmary. But they told me it was his father."

Lawrence studied her. "You mean Peter," he said softly. "But what's this about his father? I understood he's now an orphan."

Annabelle swallowed hard. "They told me—when I wanted to search the dispensary—that a man had been injured trying to save his son. And they and Mr. Bride were the only ones in the room."

Lawrence nodded. He looked to the stormy skies beyond the open doorway. "I found Peter before the *Titanic* went down. I jumped ship with him and was able to swim to a lifeboat. I begged them to take the child, but got struck with an oar—whether accidentally or on purpose, I don't know. I don't remember much after that. . . ." His eyes closed briefly, then opened to look at her.

"I suppose I finally got the taste of adventure I've always wanted," he said dryly, though his gaze was tortured.

"Oh, Lawrence, I just thank God you were spared," Annabelle said quietly, her fingers running along his bristly cheek; she needed to touch him, still hardly able to believe he was really standing in front of her.

Lawrence frowned. "But why me? So many were left to die in the freezing waters. I suppose they took me along with the boy, since we were laced together in a life belt, but I still can't believe all those who were lost. Women and children! Why was I spared?" His eyes closed in pain.

"Stop it, Lawrence!" Her hands went to either side of his face. "It wasn't your fault that there weren't enough lifeboats—you did all you could do. God answered my prayers—you're alive!" Her emerald eyes blazed with an inner fire. "I prayed that night, just like you asked me to do. And I'm so thankful you're here now! Instead of questioning why you were spared, just be grateful you were. God gave your life back to you, Lawrence. Don't wonder why—just be thankful."

"Yes," he said after a moment. "Yes, you're right. And I intend to spend every moment I have left remembering that and helping others in my Savior's name." He looked at her strangely, as if he wanted to say something but didn't quite know how.

"Annabelle, you know I love you. Everything I told you before you left the *Titanic* that night—I meant it sincerely. I want to marry you, to make you my own."

Annabelle's eyes were bright. "And I also meant everything I said, Lawrence. I want to be your wife. The reasons I had for staying away were foolish. *I* was foolish."

"My love," he breathed. Raising her hand to his lips, he kissed the open palm gently. He lowered her hand, not letting go, and looked down into her face, his eyes solemn. "I have something to ask you, Annabelle, something very important." He paused a moment, trying to frame his words. "Do you think you could share your heart with another besides me?"

She looked puzzled, then her brow smoothed. "You mean Peter."

"Yes," Lawrence said with a nod. "He has no one, from what I've learned. His mother obviously died in the sinking, and from what he told me, his father is dead also. He doesn't know what his surname is.

If no one claims him when we reach New York, I plan to adopt him. I've grown rather attached to the lad, and I don't want to see him end up in an orphanage.

"I plan to seek the services of a highly qualified doctor once we arrive in Manhattan—I only pray it's not too late to save his feet. I want to do everything I can to help ensure that he doesn't walk with crutches the rest of his life," he ended hurriedly, his words almost tripping over themselves, afraid of what Annabelle's answer would be. He didn't want to lose her, but he felt he must do what he could to help the lad.

She looked into his eyes steadily. "He's a sweet boy."

"You've seen him?" Lawrence asked in surprise.

"I just came from visiting with him before I found you," Annabelle explained. "And in the short time I was with him, he stole a little piece of my heart. I want to help you do whatever we can for Peter, even if that means only being his mother."

Tears came to Lawrence's eyes at her sincere words. "You will make a wonderful mother." His lips briefly lowered to hers. "Do you still have the ring I gave you, Annabelle?"

She nodded and pulled it out of her pocket. He took it from her and once again slid it on the third finger of her left hand. "After we reach New York," he said, "I plan to trade that for a diamond. You can give it back to me then."

"You certainly do have a great many plans, Lord Caldwell," she teased, suddenly lighthearted despite the fierce storm raging about them, despite the tragedy of the past few days. God had delivered the man she loved from a watery grave and brought him back to her arms. How could she not feel anything but happy?

He smiled, the first real smile she'd seen in a long time. "Yes, I suppose I do, Miss Mooreland. But they're all empty without you beside me to share them. . . . Thank God you were spared," he rasped, his voice again choked with emotion.

He lifted the hand with his ring to his mouth, kissing her fingers gently, his eyes locked with hers. "For as long as we both shall live, Annabelle, I promise to love you with every breath I take," he pledged softly. "This is our tomorrow, and may God give us many more besides."

"Oh, Lawrence," she breathed, unable to get anything else past the sudden lump in her throat.

He took her in his arms and kissed her, sealing his promise, while the Statue of Liberty dimly appeared on the horizon, bearing its famous motto: "Give me your tired, your poor, your huddled masses, yearning to breathe free. The wretched refuse of your teeming shore, send these the homeless, tempest-tossed to me. I lift my lamp beside the golden door."

Arm in arm, Lawrence and Annabelle looked past the stormy skies toward the bright beacon of hope standing in the harbor; toward a future together, with God's loving hand leading them along the watercourses of life; toward thousands of bright tomorrows to share side by side.

And in their hearts they thanked their Savior for making it all possible.

*E*PILOGUE

*A*nnabelle touched the diamond on her finger and smiled as she looked out the latticed window at the rolling green lawns of Fairview. It had been almost a year since she'd spoken the treasured vows in front of a minister, forever binding her to Lawrence. And God had blessed them both.

Peter, his blond curls bouncing, waved to her as he cantered past on the black pony he'd received from the earl seven months ago. Laughing softly, Annabelle waved back.

Though Peter would always need a crutch, he had learned to walk with it quite well. A skilled doctor had done all he could to help the boy, but despite his best efforts, Peter had lost two toes on his left foot. Yet the child seemed happy, wrapped up as he was in the love of his new family.

Several months after Lawrence married Annabelle, he received a wire stating that his father was ill—though his condition wasn't serious. Still, Lawrence felt the time had come to leave America. It had been difficult for Annabelle to board a ship, though she'd known all along that a return to England was inevitable. But she had secretly hoped she wouldn't have to face such an undertaking for some time.

Throughout the voyage she clung to God, trusting He would protect them as He'd done when the *Titanic* sank over a year earlier. And He did. Nevertheless, she'd been relieved when Lawrence promised she would never have to set foot on a ship again.

A mewling sound reached her ears, breaking into her reverie, and Annabelle's expression softened as she bent over the cradle and touched her infant daughter's rosy cheek. Blue eyes blinked open, and Annabelle was thrilled when a small smile appeared.

"Ah, little Gwen. You're happy to be here, too, aren't you?" she crooned, offering a finger. The baby reached for it and grasped it tightly, causing Annabelle to give a soft chuckle.

"Annabelle! What are you doing out of bed?"

Lawrence's hushed words preceded him as he quietly entered the nursery, coming up behind her. Putting gentle hands on her upper arms, he briefly looked over her shoulder at their tiny gift from heaven before turning Annabelle to face him.

"The doctor said you were to rest," he admonished, his voice soft.

"I grew weary of lying in my room." She gave a little shrug. "After all, it's been almost a week since the baby was born. I'm fine, Lawrence—really I am."

He emitted a long, drawn-out sigh. "Oh, my beautiful, independent, stubborn Little Belle. What *am* I to do with you?" he teased, shaking his head in mock frustration.

Quirking one eyebrow, she gave him a coquettish smile.

"Love me?"

He grinned, and his ice blue eyes warmed. " 'Til the end of time, darling," he murmured, drawing her close. " 'Til the end of time. . . ."

ℰLIZA

BY MILDRED COLVIN

———◆◆◆———

To my sister Jean Norval for her untiring help, making suggestions, solving problems, editing, and polishing. Without her input, I would still be struggling with stacks of unreadable manuscripts.

To my sister Pat Willis for reading *Eliza* twice—first to voice her concerns and then to okay the changes.

Also, to my daughter Becka del Valle who delights in finding and deleting unnecessary words. Plotting is a joy with your input, Becka.

Thanks so much Becka, Pat, and Jean.

1

October 1836

"*D*o you think Lenny will be all right?" Eliza looked back at the small frame schoolhouse as if she could see her ten-year-old brother inside.

"I wouldn't worry about Lenny." Her father slowed his steps to match hers.

The early October sun felt warm on Eliza's back as they turned down South Street toward the business square in Springfield, Missouri. "I suppose you're right. It's just that Mother always taught him."

Father laughed. "Lenny can take care of himself."

Eliza sighed. "I suppose."

Although her mother had been gone more than a year, the pain of her passing remained with Eliza. She missed her gentle ways and the love she had shown to each of her six children. Eliza thought of Nora, her baby sister, and a smile touched her lips. Nora's birth had weakened their mother and indirectly caused her death, but the sweet baby had brought so much love and happiness into their lives as well, and Eliza missed her.

Nora lived sixty miles north in the country with their oldest sister, Vickie. Eliza longed for the day when they could return to their old home and bring Nora to Springfield. She held to Father's promise that as soon as they were settled here, they would go after Nora.

A freight wagon rumbled by. They stepped up on a low boardwalk leading past a large, two-story shop. The sign over the door read LEACH'S GENERAL STORE.

Eliza's father waved across the square to a man coming from the bank building. He smiled and nodded at two women hurrying past on their way to the general store.

Eliza said, "Springfield is smaller than Saint Louis, but after living in the wilderness it seems large."

Her father smiled and nodded. "Three hundred inhabitants and growing."

They approached a small white building sandwiched between a millinery shop on one side and a larger empty building on the corner. A sign over the door read CHANDLER SHOP, ORVAL JACKSON, PROPRIETOR.

Eliza stepped inside, and the familiar odor of tallow assailed her senses.

Father watched her sniff the air. "There's nothing like the smell of a candle shop, is there?"

Eliza wrinkled her nose. "I can think of things that smell better."

He laughed. "Wait until nearer Christmas when I start using bayberry. You girls always liked it."

Eliza thought of her sister just older than herself. "I think Cora liked it best. I wish we could send her a bayberry candle for Christmas."

Father nodded. "But with no delivery service to our old backwoods home, she'll have to do without."

"I guess." Eliza ran her hand over the shiny dark oak counter that stood along one wall. Tall, slender candles lay on one end of it, sorted by size. Other candles hung by the wick from hooks on the walls and ceiling. Shelves along one wall held sconces, candleholders, lanterns, and snuffers. In one corner was a pile of cotton yarn waiting to be made into wicks. Sitting around the room were several candle stands made of walnut, cherry, oak, and the less expensive, pine. On top of each was a candle in a tall, brass candlestick.

Her father moved about, lighting the candles on the stands until a soft, warm glow filled the dark shop.

Eliza watched her father. "I guess it's time for me to go home and clean house."

"You can stay all day if you want, but I need to get to work. I've got an order to get out for Mrs. Wingate."

"Who's that? Someone important?"

"Her husband helped finance my business. His bank's across the street."

Eliza glanced toward the window as the front door opened.

A young man stepped into the shop. "Mr. Jackson?"

"Yes, may I help you?"

The young man's gaze met Eliza's for just a moment before he turned his full attention to her father. "I'm James Hurley. Mrs. Wingate sent me. She said you were thinking of adding a cooperage and would be needing help."

"Of course." Father stepped forward, and the men shook hands. "I'm glad you stopped by." He nodded toward Eliza. "This is my daughter Eliza."

James acknowledged her presence with a slight bow. "Mrs. Wingate mentioned that you and your brother would be arriving in town soon. I'm glad to meet you."

Eliza smiled at him. "We came in last night. I was just on my way home. I'll see you later, Father. For dinner?"

Her father nodded. "I'll pick Lenny up, and we'll be at the house about noon."

"All right." Eliza closed the door behind her and started across the square toward home. So her father was already adding on and would be hiring an employee. Perhaps the challenge of starting a new business was what he needed to heal his grieving heart from her mother's death.

She turned up the path to a large, two-story house set back from the road on the outskirts of town. She knew her father had bought the house by using most of his savings from some investments he had made years ago when they lived in St. Louis. The house had come completely furnished because the woman who had lived in it couldn't tolerate the frontier existence of Springfield. Eliza smiled as she wondered what the woman would have thought of the log cabin they had just moved from. Their nearest neighbor had been almost two miles away.

She let herself in, and an hour later she had fluffy mashed potatoes, fried pork, a pan of corn bread, and a bowl of leftover brown beans sitting on the table. She stood back and studied her work. Father liked fruit with his noon meal.

She looked around the well-ordered kitchen. Was there a pantry? When they'd come the evening before, she hadn't explored the house so she didn't know what treasures it held.

She opened the back door and went through a small anteroom lined with tools and a bin of firewood to the outdoors.

A long, white wooden door lay at an angle from the ground to the upper foundation of the house. She lifted the door, leaning it against the outside of the anteroom. Musty dampness filled her nostrils as she descended the steps. She stood at the bottom to light the candle she had brought.

The back door slammed. "Eliza, where are you?"

"Down here, Father." She turned, glad to run back up the steps to the bright, sunlit yard. "I thought there might be some fruit in the cellar."

"Well, what are we waiting for? Let's see if we can find a jar of peaches."

A flurry from behind him brought Lenny to the front. "I want to go, too."

"Great, you can keep the mice and bats away." Eliza grasped each of Lenny's shoulders and held him in front of her. "How was school this morning?"

"Aw, it was all right." He swiped at a spiderweb.

"Look at this." Father's voice brought her attention back to the cellar. "Mr. Wingate said it was fully stocked, but I didn't expect to find a cellar full of food."

"Father, you've been here more than two months. Haven't you even looked down here? How have you been eating?" Eliza looked from the full shelves to her father.

In the soft light of the candle, Father's grin looked sheepish. "There's a café in town for men like me who can't feed themselves."

Eliza took a jar of peaches off the shelf. "Well, you won't need to go there anymore." She left the cellar, calling over her shoulder. "Come on, our meal is getting cold."

෨

The next morning Eliza woke to a thick blanket of clouds and drizzling rain. The rain stopped midmorning, and by the time she had the noon dishes cleaned and put away, she felt she had been confined to the house long enough. About an hour after her father and brother left, she grabbed her shawl and headed out the door for town.

She hummed a hymn as her feet covered the damp ground. Not until she saw her father's shop did she slow her gait. There had been no real reason to come to town. As far as she knew, the house was well stocked. She didn't need to see her father about anything. Yet she would have to pass by his shop to reach the general store. Without a doubt he would see her and welcome the chance to tease her about neglecting her duties. She giggled. She wouldn't give him a chance. She'd tell him the clouds made it so dark inside she needed more candles.

Eliza pulled open the door and stepped inside. "Father, you wouldn't believe how dark it gets when the sun doesn't shine."

The man behind the counter was not her father. She knew it before he turned and looked at her with those clear, gray eyes that she remembered from the day before when James Hurley had first stepped into her father's shop. A slow smile lit James's face. His voice held a deep timbre, smooth and resonant. "Yes, but if the sun shone all the time, we'd sell very few candles."

Eliza glanced toward the back room. "Where is my father?"

"He stepped out for a few minutes."

"And left you here alone?" As soon as the words were out of her mouth, she wished she could call them back.

One eyebrow lifted as James pinned her with a glare. "I don't plan to steal the profits, Miss Jackson."

A flush spread over Eliza's face. "I'm sorry. I didn't mean that. I just meant it's only your second day on the job."

"Actually, it's my first." James grinned. "I'm a quick study. At least your father seems to trust me enough to leave me alone for ten minutes."

"Oh." Eliza had never found it hard to talk to anyone before. But there was something about those gray eyes looking at her and the way James smiled that made her want to leave and stay at the same time. She decided it would be best if she left when memories she had thought long buried rose in her mind.

Ralph Stark, a young man from her old home, had smiled at her in much the same way. When Ralph had looked at her with that same intense gleam in his eyes, she had felt special and pretty. She had loved him and thought he loved her. Then, during their courtship, he'd married someone else, leaving her with the pain of rejection. Strength gained through her newfound relationship with the Lord had brought her through that time, yet she wondered even now if she would ever forget her first sweetheart.

The cool, damp air felt good on her hot cheeks as she turned back toward home. Her appetite for browsing through the general store had been squelched.

ॐ

When Thursday morning dawned clear, Eliza decided it was time to wash clothes while she could hang them on the line. She worked hard all morning, barely finding time to fix the noon meal for her father and brother.

But she soon had stew simmering on the stove and was throwing the potato peelings into the slop bucket when she heard steps at the door. Moments later, Lenny ran into the kitchen.

"Look what I got this morning." He strutted up to her and lifted his face.

Dried blood lined one nostril. He squinted at her through his red, swollen left eye. Eliza looked toward the doorway where her father lounged against the frame.

He shrugged. "Ask him what happened."

She turned back to her little brother, her hands folded across her chest. "Well, are you going to tell me?"

"Ah, Eliza, it ain't nothin' to get upset about." Lenny looked pleased with himself. "It was just a little old fight."

Her father spoke proudly from the doorway. "If you think he looks bad, you should've seen the other fellow."

Eliza turned toward her father. How could he condone this?

He laughed. "Don't look at me that way. It was all over by the time I got there."

"Lenny, why did you get into a fight?" Eliza asked.

" 'Cause I ain't no teacher's pet."

"You're not the teacher's pet," Eliza corrected.

"Right, I ain't." He touched his eye tenderly. "Cletis sure can hit hard."

"Cletis?"

Lenny nodded. "Yeah. Cletis Hall. Can he come over sometime?"

"Here? To our house?" Eliza couldn't believe him. "Why do you want him to come here? I thought you just had a fight with him."

"Your sister doesn't understand a man's way of doing things, Lenny." Father pulled out a chair. He looked at Eliza. "You see, Cletis didn't have any respect for the teacher's pet, but he's got a lot of respect for the first boy in school who was brave enough to whip him."

Eliza could hear pride in her father's voice. She looked from him to Lenny. "So you made a friend by beating him up?" She shook her head. "You're right. I don't understand it. Bring your friend here to play if you want. Just make sure he doesn't mess my house up. And there'd better not be any more fighting."

Lenny grinned and as quickly grimaced. Father stood. "Come on, Lenny. Let's take care of that eye."

Eliza watched them go and shook her head. She reached for the long-handled spoon to stir her stew. She didn't need to worry about Lenny. Obviously, he could take care of himself.

2

*E*liza tilted the coffee canister and looked inside. Less than half full. She wanted to see what Leach's General Store had in stock, and this was as good an excuse as any.

She ran upstairs to change into her afternoon visiting dress. The black-and-pink-striped silk was terribly out of date, but she had nothing better. She shrugged, reaching for the matching silk bonnet. She went downstairs and out the front door, determined to enjoy her afternoon. Only this time she would avoid the chandler shop and James Hurley.

Red and yellow leaves, blending with the green of the trees overhead, provided a colorful canopy for her walk. In the distance a dog barked and another answered. Smoke from a backyard fire wafted by, teasing her nose as she passed a house.

She reached the business square a few minutes later. She tried to hurry past her father's shop, but before she reached the door, two women came out, each clutching a package.

"Thank you, and please come again." James smiled at the women as he held the door for them.

Eliza looked up and caught his gaze on her. She smiled. "Hello, Mr. Hurley. I see my father is keeping you busy."

He grinned. "Good afternoon, Miss Jackson. Could I interest you in candles, a new cherry candle stand, or maybe a snuffer?"

"No, thank you. I'm on my way to the general store."

"Ah, Mr. Leach's gain is our loss."

She smiled as she went on. Maybe her father's new employee was just being friendly when he smiled at her.

It took a moment for her eyes to adjust to the dim interior of the store. A potbellied stove held center stage with an open cracker barrel nearby. Elderly men took from its contents while they argued politics.

The aromas of tobacco, leather, and fresh ground coffee mingled with the familiar smell of the wood-burning stove. She hesitated a moment as she looked around. Mr. Leach must have the best-stocked store in town, with not an inch of space wasted. Everything from Bibles to medicine, coal oil to calico, and school supplies to candy had its own special place. A wide assortment of hardware, household goods, and groceries filled the shelves.

Eliza's heels clicked on the wooden floor as she moved down the center aisle past the grocery counter and dry goods shelves. Mr. Leach, busy behind his high counter in the back, greeted her with a warm smile. "Good afternoon. What can I do for you?"

Eliza smiled. "I need a pound of coffee."

"Then a pound of coffee you shall have." The storekeeper nodded toward one side of the store. "Have yourself a look around while I get it. We just got in some new calico the other day."

Eliza turned and wound her way past kegs and barrels of flour, sugar, vinegar, and molasses. Close to a half hour later, oblivious to the activity around her, Eliza picked up the corner of a blue-sprigged calico and rubbed it between her fingers. How she wished she could sew decently! But no matter how often her mother or her sisters, Vickie and Cora, had tried to teach her, she could never force her fingers to take the tiny stitches needed for dressmaking.

"Are you finding anything you like?" Eliza turned to see a middle-aged woman, her plump face wreathed with a friendly smile.

Eliza sighed. "Oh, there are so many, and I like all of them." She refolded the calico and turned away. "But I came for coffee, not fabric."

"A young girl can always use a new dress." The woman eyed Eliza's outdated frock. She extended her hand. "I'm Alice Leach, the storekeeper's wife."

Eliza placed her hand in the woman's strong grasp. "I'm glad to meet you. I'm Eliza Jackson. My father recently opened the chandler shop down the street."

"Oh, yes. Mr. Leach was telling me that the chandler's family had arrived. Welcome to Springfield."

Eliza nodded. "I guess I should be starting home. I'm sure your husband has my coffee ready by now."

"Come back anytime. Next time you need a new dress, let me know, and we'll find you something pretty."

Eliza took the coffee and turned to leave as another customer came in. She watched the girl breeze through the store to the high counter where Mr. Leach stood.

"Hello, Miss Vanda," Mr. Leach greeted her. "What can I do for you today?"

Eliza slipped out the door as the other girl gave her order. Vanda. What an unusual name. It was pretty, just as the girl was.

Eliza crossed the square and turned north on the road leading home. Dust swirled about her skirt as she hurried. She had spent most of the afternoon accomplishing nothing. She'd better be thinking of supper.

She set her package of coffee on the table in the kitchen and then went upstairs to change clothes. She had no sooner taken her bonnet and wraps off than a knock on the door downstairs startled her.

With her heart pounding, she ran downstairs and opened the door, surprised to see the girl from the store.

"Hello. Won't you come in?" Eliza smiled and stepped back.

Vanda stood unmoved. "Is your mother home?"

Eliza's heart constricted at the question. She shook her head. "My mother died a year ago."

"Your father isn't here, is he?" An uncertain expression crossed the girl's face.

Eliza shook her head. "No, he's at work."

"Then you are the only one home?"

"Yes, won't you come in?" Eliza repeated the invitation.

Vanda walked to the middle of the room and looked around. Her eyes rested briefly on the covered sofa with gleaming mahogany legs and two matching chairs. Her gaze swept past the fireplace, then dropped to the carpet before she turned to Eliza.

"Won't you sit down?" Eliza could scarcely believe she had company.

Vanda looked at the sofa but shook her head. "No, what I've got to say won't take long."

"Oh." Eliza wondered at the sharp tone in the girl's voice.

"You have a brother named Lenny, don't you?" Vanda's eyes bore into hers.

Eliza nodded. Surely Lenny couldn't have done anything to Vanda.

"Is he about nine or ten years old?" Vanda's hands were on her hips now.

"He's ten." Eliza was puzzled. "He's been in school all week, except at night when he's been home. We just moved in last week."

"I have a ten-year-old brother, too. Maybe you've heard of him." Vanda paused. "Cletis Von Hall."

"Cletis Von Hall?" Eliza repeated the name. She frowned, trying to remember. Lenny had said the boy he fought was Cletis Hall.

Eliza met the other girl's gaze. "Yes, Lenny told us about the fight he had with Cletis. He also said he and Cletis are now good friends."

"Good friends!" Vanda's eyes widened. "Good friends don't give each other black eyes."

"Oh, I don't think they were friends when they fought." Eliza wasn't sure she could explain what she didn't understand herself. "You see, the fight itself is what made them friends."

A sneer crossed Vanda's face. "My little brother was beaten black and blue, and you tell me he's friends with the boy who did it?"

"I know it doesn't make sense, but that's what Lenny said."

"It certainly doesn't make sense, and I don't want it to happen again." Vanda took a step forward, her forefinger lifted toward Eliza. "Either you see to it, or my father will."

Eliza watched the angry girl step to the door.

"I'm sorry Lenny hurt your brother." Eliza followed her out. "I'll speak to him about it."

Vanda paid no attention to Eliza. She stood on the porch, her hand resting on a post.

Eliza looked over her shoulder to see what had caught her attention. Coming up the road arm in arm was Lenny with another boy.

"Cletis Elliot Von Hall!" Vanda's exclamation brought the boys up short. "What on earth are you doing?"

The boy shook a heavy lock of blond hair off his forehead. "I ain't doin' nothin' wrong."

"What are you doing with . . . him?"

Cletis frowned at his sister. "Me and Lenny's buddies."

Cletis had gotten the worst of the fight. Both of his eyes were blackened. His lower lip had swelled, and a bruise marred his cheekbone.

The two boys stood in front of Vanda. Cletis looked up at her. "Ah, Sis, you ain't gonna make a big thing out of that old fight, are you?"

Vanda stood, her arms crossed, looking at her brother. Finally, she spoke. "Do you mean you let some boy beat you up, and then you made friends with him?"

Cletis waved his hand at her. "Don't worry, Sis. This is men stuff."

Vanda made an exasperated sound and turned to Eliza. "He got that from my older brother and my father. Every time they do something stupid, that's what they say. Sometimes I get so mad I could bite a nail."

Eliza smiled. "I had the same conversation with Lenny and my father last night. They told me I wouldn't understand."

For the first time since they met, Vanda's expression softened. "I'm sorry for the way I stormed into your house and for the things I said."

Eliza shook her head. "Don't be. You were only protecting your little brother. I'd have done the same."

Vanda held her hand out. "I'm Vanda Von Hall. I don't know your first name."

Eliza smiled and grasped her hand. "Eliza."

Vanda shook her hand. "I guess I'd better be getting home." She picked up her bundle of purchases. "I need to get supper before my father gets there."

Eliza laughed. "It sounds like you have the same job I do. My father will be home before long, too, and I haven't even decided what to fix."

She turned to Lenny. "Does Father know you came home from school without him?"

Lenny nodded. "Sure. We went by the shop, and he said it was all right."

"He was probably glad to get Cletis out of his shop."

Eliza laughed at Vanda's cryptic remark.

"Can I stay and play with Lenny?" Cletis looked at his sister.

"No, you'd better be home when Poppa gets there."

Cletis kicked at a rock and mumbled.

Vanda shook her head when Cletis shuffled away. "I'm so sorry. Sometimes Cletis gets out of hand, and my temper does, too. It's hard without a mother, but I guess you know that. Mine's been gone two years now."

"I'm sorry. About your mother, I mean." Eliza laid her hand on the other girl's arm. "I'm glad I got to meet you. When you have time, come back and visit. I get lonesome with just my father and brother."

"I know." Vanda smiled. "I've got to go." She walked away, calling over her shoulder, "I'll be back, I promise."

Eliza watched as Vanda grabbed her little brother's arm and pulled him down the road. When they reached the corner, they both waved. Eliza and Lenny stood on the porch waving until their new friends turned the corner and were lost to sight.

ও

Eliza woke early Sunday morning. She hurried through a breakfast of biscuits and oatmeal before getting ready for church.

Three hours later, Eliza sat at the end of the pew beside Lenny. She had hoped the Von Halls would be at church. But she saw neither Vanda nor Cletis.

As she turned her attention back to the sermon, the eerie feeling of someone staring at her crept up her backbone. She turned to meet the scrutiny of James Hurley. His gray eyes locked with her brown ones for only seconds before she turned away.

Eliza tried to pay attention to the sermon, but her mind wandered up and down the pews. There were several young people near her own age. Would they accept her? Would they become her friends?

She sighed, forcing herself to listen to the remainder of the sermon. When the last "amen" had been said, people began to stir. Eliza stood and stepped out into the aisle ahead of Lenny and Father. They made their way to the back door, nodding and speaking to everyone they saw.

Finally, they reached the minister. "We're so glad to see you again this morning, Mr. Jackson." He clasped Father's hand and gave it a hearty shake. "I haven't had the privilege of meeting your children."

As Father introduced them, Eliza saw James Hurley help a woman, who she assumed was his mother, into a farm wagon while a young girl climbed in the back.

The pastor smiled at Eliza. "We've got a good group of young people here. It won't be long until you have many friends."

"Thank you, Sir." She smiled. "I hope you're right."

As he turned to Lenny, she looked back toward the road and saw James climb in beside his mother. He picked up the reins, then looked at her and smiled.

Her breath caught in her throat. With a flick of the reins, the wagon moved out. Eliza watched until he turned the corner and drove out of sight.

"Mr. and Mrs. Wingate, so good to see you." The pastor's voice brought Eliza's attention to a fashionably attired, middle-aged couple stepping out of the church.

"Good sermon, Pastor. Just what we needed this morning." Mr. Wingate put a tall-crowned, brushed-beaver hat on his head. He stepped off the porch and shook her father's hand. "How's that chandler shop, Orval?"

Eliza moved with her father and the Wingates a short distance from the church. Lenny ran off to play with some other boys.

"Considering the condition of our pocketbooks at this time, not bad." Father smiled at Mrs. Wingate. "I appreciate your business and the customers you've sent."

Mrs. Wingate, a tall, blond woman smiled. "I recognize quality when I see it. I would never go back to making my own candles."

Eliza couldn't visualize the woman before her bent over a vat of foul-smelling tallow.

"Have you thought more about adding a cooperage?" Mrs. Wingate asked.

"Actually, yes." Father nodded. "I took your advice and hired the young man you sent. We've been working on getting the building next door ready. James is a good worker."

"Excellent." Mrs. Wingate looked pleased. "I thought he would be." She turned to Eliza. "You must be Mr. Jackson's daughter Eliza."

Eliza nodded. "I'm pleased to meet you, Mrs. Wingate." She felt dowdy compared to the well-dressed woman before her. In the country, it hadn't mattered, but here she felt keenly the difference between her dress and the clothing worn around her.

The woman linked her arm in Eliza's. "I'm so glad you've come to Springfield to live. We've enjoyed having your father here, and I know you and your brother will become dear to us as well." She didn't wait for a response but asked, "Have you met my son Charles?"

Eliza shook her head. "No, I've been here only a week and haven't met anyone." She thought of Vanda and added, "Except one girl."

"Oh? Who might that be?" A spark of interest shone from the woman's eyes as she centered her attention on Eliza.

"Her name is Vanda Von Hall. I thought she might be at church this morning, but I didn't see her."

"No, she wasn't here today." Mrs. Wingate frowned. "Her older brother, Trennen, is our driver. I've often wondered if we should have him drive us to church on Sundays just to get him here."

She smiled then. "How do you like living in Springfield?"

"It's very nice. I love the house Father bought."

Mrs. Wingate nodded. "Yes, it is a nice place. You were very fortunate to get it." She paused a moment before asking, "It must be hard trying to keep up with that large house and an active brother, too."

"Oh, no." Eliza shook her head. "I enjoy my work."

"But a young girl needs to get out and play once in awhile. Maybe your father will remarry someday, and you'll be free to pursue other interests."

Eliza had been close to her mother. She could never imagine another woman taking her place. She shook her head; her voice lowered. "No, I don't expect my father to ever marry again. I don't mind taking care of the house. He doesn't need a wife."

Eliza recognized the calculating look in Mrs. Wingate's blue eyes as she nodded. "I'm sure you do a wonderful job, Dear. My husband claims my worst fault is interfering." She glanced toward her husband and smiled. "Speaking of Mr. Wingate, I believe he's ready to leave." She patted Eliza's arm. "I'm glad we got to visit. You come see me sometime, all right?"

At Eliza's nod, the older woman turned away. Eliza collected Lenny, and they left, too.

"Winter will soon be here," Father commented as they walked home.

"Yes, that's true." When the snow and cold weather moved into the area, Eliza knew she would be confined to the house. She didn't look forward to that time.

"Seems someone is having a birthday before long." Father smiled at her.

"Is that right?" Eliza fell into his joking mood. "Are you going to get that person something nice?"

Father laughed. "Sounds like you know whose birthday is coming up."

Eliza laughed with her father. She was well aware that she would soon be nineteen. Plenty old enough to run a motherless household.

$$\textbf{3}$$

A week later, Father opened his cooperage in the building next to the chandler shop. Unlike the shops in St. Louis he had shared with his brother, there was no door connecting the two buildings, so he rigged a string and bell from one shop's door to the other. When either door opened, the bells would ring in both shops. It wasn't a perfect system, but it let Father and James know when they had a customer.

After working both shops for two days, Father came home exhausted. Eliza found him sprawled across the sofa after supper. Lenny lay on his stomach on the floor, reading a book.

She touched her father's shoulder. "I know it's early, but if you want to go to bed, I'll see that Lenny settles down at his bedtime."

"What would I do without you, Eliza?" Father pulled himself up. "I wouldn't be so tired except for running back and forth between those two shops."

"Can't you move them both into the same building?"

He shook his head. "No. Neither place is big enough. What I need is another person to run the candle shop until I get James trained."

"Is he having trouble learning?"

Father shook his head. "No. He's doing fine. It's just that there's so much to learn. I want him to learn the chandler trade as well. That way I can trust either shop to him if necessary."

"Father." An idea took shape in Eliza's mind. "Could I take care of the chandler shop?"

Father stared at her. Eliza's heart beat fast against her ribs. A log in the fireplace snapped, sending sparks into the room. They both rushed to step on them, crushing them out before they burned through the rug.

Father returned to the sofa. When he finally spoke, his expression was solemn. "For two weeks in the afternoon only."

"You mean I can?"

Father laughed. "You'd think I just gave you a gift." He patted the sofa. "Sit down here and let me tell you what you're getting into."

As Eliza listened to her father explain her new duties, she tingled with excitement. Finally, she would be in the hub of the town's activities. Every afternoon for two weeks she could visit with the women and girls who came into Father's shop.

Eliza's excitement continued into the next morning as she hurried through her chores. She heard a knock on the door downstairs just as she smoothed the covers on Lenny's bed.

"Oh, no." She groaned. "I have little enough time without someone calling." She smoothed her hair and ran down the stairs.

She opened the door to Vanda's smile. Eliza stepped back. "Please, come in."

"I intended to come sooner, but I've been busy." Vanda's gaze swept the room. "You have such a nice house."

"Thank you. We really like it." Eliza closed the door. "Won't you sit down?"

As Vanda sat on the sofa, Eliza took the chair and leaned forward, eager to share her news. "Oh, Vanda, you'll never guess what I'm going to do this afternoon."

Vanda relaxed back into the sofa. "What?"

"I'm going to work in my father's shop." Eliza's light brown eyes sparkled.

"When do you start?"

"Right after noon."

"Oh, then I'm probably keeping you." Vanda stood.

Eliza knew she should finish her work, but she and Vanda hadn't had a chance to talk. She shook her head. "All I have left to do is prepare dinner. That shouldn't take long."

"What are you fixing?"

"I've had beans on the back of the stove since early this morning. I need to bake corn bread and fry some meat."

Vanda nodded. "How long until your father comes?"

Eliza looked at the clock sitting on the mantel. "Almost an hour."

"Let me help," Vanda pleaded. "I'll leave before he gets here. He needn't ever know I was here."

"That won't be necessary." Eliza frowned. "I mean, you don't have to help. Just stay and visit with me. Why don't you stay for dinner?"

"Oh, I couldn't do that."

"Is your father expecting you?"

Vanda shook her head. "No, Poppa's gone all this week. He's working at a sawmill east of here."

"Then there's no one to worry about you, unless your brothers . . . ?"

"No, Cletis takes his lunch, and Trennen eats at the Wingates'."

Eliza took her arm. "Good, then it's settled. Let's go to the kitchen while we talk."

She led the way, and they were soon visiting like old friends. Vanda insisted on mixing the corn bread while Eliza fried meat and set the table.

When Eliza set four plates out, Vanda looked at her. "Are you sure your father won't mind?"

Eliza laughed. "He'll be glad I've found a friend."

Vanda pulled the golden-brown corn bread from the oven just as Father stepped through the kitchen doorway. His hazel eyes twinkled. "Well, what have we here?" He turned to Lenny, who had come in behind him. "You put a woman to work outside the home, and the first thing she does is get help with her household chores."

Lenny stepped around his father. "Are you going to be our housekeeper?"

Vanda's cheeks flamed as she looked at Eliza. Eliza took Lenny's shoulder and pushed him toward the sink. "Go wash your hands. You know Cletis's sister. She's our guest."

Father ran his hand over his hair. He smiled at Vanda. "I'm sorry. I sometimes get carried away teasing my daughter. I'm glad you're here with Eliza. Please, make yourself at home."

After that they enjoyed an uneventful dinner hour until time to go back to work and school. Eliza rushed through the dishwashing with Vanda's help. As they put the last dish away, Vanda glanced toward the door leading to the parlor.

"Your father seems nice. Is he always like that?"

Eliza made a face. "Actually, he was on his best behavior. The way he acted when he first came in is more like his true self. He's terribly fond of teasing."

"That's because he loves you."

"Yes, I know." Eliza started for the door. "What's your father like? Does he like to tease, too?"

A crease formed between Vanda's eyes as she frowned and followed Eliza. "No, Poppa doesn't tease. Especially not since Momma died."

"He must have loved her very much." Eliza picked up her cape as they passed through the parlor. Father and Lenny had gone ahead so the two girls would be walking by themselves.

Vanda shrugged. "I suppose." She followed Eliza out the front door and waited while she closed it.

A touch of dampness clung to the air under a canopy of gray clouds. Eliza pulled her cape close, glad for its warmth. She glanced at her friend, realizing for the first time that Vanda's clothing was as outdated as her own.

Several minutes later the two girls stopped in front of the chandler shop. After saying good-bye to Vanda and promising they'd get together soon, Eliza went inside. She didn't see her father in the store so she looked in the back room. No sign of him there, either. She stood in the doorway and looked at the disarray that made up his workroom. He and Lenny had left the house several minutes before she and Vanda. Where was he?

❧

James glanced out the front window of the cooperage and saw Eliza go past with Vanda Von Hall. He stepped closer to the window. They stopped in front of the chandler shop and talked a moment before

Vanda moved on. Eliza went into the shop, setting off the bells that were rigged to ring if either shop door opened. James ignored the ringing bell and turned back to his work. He didn't have time to stare at a girl when he had barrels to make.

The half-finished barrel he had been working on was the last of an order that needed to be delivered that afternoon. He'd better get it finished. He stepped over and around tools, metal rings, barrels, and tubs to the far wall where wood slats were stacked. He crouched down behind a large barrel to select the slats he needed from the pile on the floor.

The door opened with barely a jingle of the bell. James peered around the barrel and saw the blue of Eliza's skirt. His stomach turned somersaults as he watched her gaze sweep the large room. When she turned as if to leave, he stood up, afraid she would go and he wouldn't get to talk to her. In his haste, he bumped the large barrel in front of him, causing it to rock on its bottom. He grabbed a cloth to wipe his sweating palms and stepped out from the barrel.

Taking a couple of steps toward her, he asked, "May I help you, Ma'am?"

James couldn't keep the silly grin from his face when she turned back to face him, her eyes wide and beautiful.

"I'm looking for my father."

"Do you make a habit of misplacing him?" He couldn't resist teasing her.

"Oh, honestly!" She reached for the door.

Instantly contrite, James chuckled. "I'm sorry. He isn't back from dinner yet."

"I see. Have you eaten?"

James's smile grew wider. "Not yet. I'll eat when your father gets back. I brought my lunch. Thank you for thinking of me, though."

James admired the red that tinged Eliza's cheeks as she stammered, "I didn't . . . think . . . oh, that's all right."

As she jerked the outside door open and slipped out, he reached to stop her before he realized what he was doing. Eliza Jackson was his boss's daughter. He had no business teasing her or even thinking of her in a romantic way. Again, he turned back to work.

❧

Eliza hurried toward the chandler shop and almost bumped into her father.

"Well, have you been visiting with the new apprentice?" His eyes sparkled as they searched her red face.

"Father!" Eliza welcomed the cool breeze that floated by. "I was looking for you. I thought you'd be here by now since you left the house before I did."

Her father laughed as he opened the door to the chandler shop. "I stopped by the school. Lenny said his teacher wanted to talk to me."

Eliza stepped into the store ahead of her father. She turned quickly, her embarrassment forgotten. "What did he do?"

"Nothing." He chuckled. "She wants some of the fathers to build props for the school Christmas program."

"Christmas already?" Eliza gave him a skeptical look.

Her father laughed. "Yes, Christmas already. It's not a bad idea to get started early on the construction."

❧

After supper on Saturday, Father challenged Lenny to a game of checkers. He won the first game against Lenny, so Eliza played the second and also lost to him.

She set her pieces back on the squares. "Now it's time for the losers to play, Father. You may watch this game."

Father let Lenny take his chair and grinned at Eliza. "You think I can learn something from watching you two play?"

She nodded. "Certainly. If you watch closely enough, you can learn how to lose."

It wasn't long until Lenny jumped one of Eliza's pieces. She tried to concentrate on the game, but too much was on her mind. Finally, Lenny jumped her last piece. He sprang to his feet, twirling around. "I won. I won."

"Well, don't gloat about it." Eliza picked the game up and carried it across the room to the mantle.

Father laughed as Lenny fell down against him. "Eliza was right. I did pick up some pointers from her game."

Eliza tried to make a face at them, but it soon turned to a laugh. "All right, so I'm not a good checkers player." She sat in the chair opposite the one they shared. "Do you know what today is?"

Father nodded, his voice subdued. "Yes, it's Nora's second birthday." He pulled Lenny onto his lap. "She's old enough now to come home. As soon as we can, we'll bring our little girl here to live with us. I promise."

Eliza clung to his promise. She missed her little sister so much. Vickie had taken her right after their mother's funeral to care for along with her own son, Christopher, who was just a few months older. The arrangement should have been temporary, but the first few months had been hard as Father grieved for his wife. Then, Father gave his life to the Lord one day as his oldest son, Ben, prayed with him. After that, Father decided to move to Springfield, and the time never came to bring Nora home.

Father pushed Lenny from his lap. "Run and get my Bible. It's almost bedtime."

Father read a passage of Scripture and prayed. Then he stood, running his hand over his thinning hair. "I completely forgot. Lenny, your teacher said there'll be a spelling bee and social next Saturday night at the schoolhouse."

Lenny's eyes brightened. "Can we go? I bet I can outspell everyone in that school."

Father laughed. "In that case, we'll have to go and see. How about it, Eliza? Do you think you can outspell everyone in school?"

She smiled. "I don't know, but I'm willing to try if you are."

A wide grin set on Father's face. "I wouldn't miss it."

~

Eliza saw James Hurley come in to the crowded schoolhouse with his sister and mother. He smiled and spoke to her as he passed.

"I'm glad you came." Vanda took her arm. "Would you like to meet my poppa and Trennen? They're both here."

"Of course." Eliza followed her across the crowded room.

"Poppa, I'd like you to meet my friend."

"If you'll excuse me." Mr. Von Hall nodded to the men he had been talking with. He smiled at Eliza.

"Poppa, this is Eliza Jackson. She moved here a month ago with her father and brother."

"I'm pleased to meet you. I hope you'll like our town." Mr. Von Hall was a tall man with thick blond hair and blue eyes. He appeared warm and friendly. There was something about his carefree smile that reminded her of Ralph. Eliza decided that she liked him.

She smiled. "I already like Springfield very much."

"Poppa, where's Trennen? I want to introduce him to Eliza." Vanda searched the room and jumped when a masculine voice spoke behind her.

"Who are you wanting me to meet?"

Eliza turned with Vanda to see a tall, slim, dark-haired young man with an engaging smile. His gaze shifted from Vanda to Eliza as his sister started talking.

"Trennen, I want you to meet my friend, Eliza Jackson." Vanda smiled at Eliza. "This is my big brother, Trennen."

Eliza's smile froze as she met the blue eyes of Vanda's older brother. His look swept over her before resting on her face. Her heart thumped hard. Her lashes lowered. "Pleased to meet you."

She felt his hand close around her fingers as he lifted them for a quick handshake. "And I'm pleased to meet you."

Eliza noticed the personal tone of his voice. She pulled her fingers from his grasp and turned away, glad for Miss Fraser's shrill voice demanding attention.

"We're ready to start," the schoolmarm announced. "Please, let's have order."

The room grew quiet as all eyes turned toward the raised platform where Miss Fraser stood. "The children and I welcome you to our school for our annual community spelling bee. Everyone who wishes to compete, please form a line around the room. The rest are welcome to sit at the children's desks and watch. Thank you."

Again the hum of voices filled the room as everyone shuffled around, finding their places.

Eliza squeezed Vanda's hand. "You're going to spell, aren't you? I promised Father I would."

Vanda shrugged. "I might as well, I guess. But I'm not a good speller. I'll probably be put out the first word I get."

They were in line before Eliza realized that Trennen stood behind her. He cocked his eyebrows at her and smiled. "Good luck, Miss Jackson."

"Thank you." She tried hard to ignore his presence.

Miss Fraser stood behind her desk with a sheaf of papers lying before her. She raised her hand for silence and gave the first word to a small girl. "Miriam, give us the definition for the word *good* and then spell it, please."

One by one the words were given out, and the spelldown began. When either the definition or spelling was wrong, that person had to find an empty seat in the center. Several rounds later, the words grew in difficulty as the number of spellers diminished. One after another sat down when the word *stultiloquence* was given. Eliza knew it meant foolish talk, but she wasn't sure she could spell it. Surely someone would get it right before they reached her.

Vanda made a face, whispering, "Where'd she come up with that?"

Eliza shrugged and shook her head. "I don't know, but I hope someone spells it soon."

Her father was next. Eliza held her breath when the woman in front of him sat down.

Father said, "Stultiloquence means foolish talking, which I think has been established already." A ripple of laughter swept the room before he went on to correctly spell the word.

Eliza watched James step forward.

Miss Fraser looked up from her list. "Define and spell *serry*, please."

Eliza was aware of Trennen standing behind her, making occasional comments, obviously trying to hold her attention, and she compared the two. While James was at least three inches shorter than Trennen, he had a broader, more muscular frame. Trennen sported rakish good looks with his thick dark hair and expressive blue eyes. James, with gray eyes and light brown—almost blond—hair, was not as handsome, although he was far from homely.

Now he said, "*Serry* means to crowd and is spelled s-e-r-r-y."

Miss Fraser looked up and smiled. "It looks like our spelling is improving." She nodded toward James. "You may take your place at the end of the line."

As James passed Eliza, their gazes met and held for several seconds. He smiled and nodded.

Vanda missed the next word, passing it on to Eliza.

Miss Fraser smiled at her. "Miss Jackson, please define and spell *pulchritude*."

Eliza took a breath to calm herself. "Pulchritude means beauty. P-u-l-c-h-r." She stopped. A vowel must come next, but was it *i* or *e*? She said the word to herself and guessed. "I-t-u-d-e."

Miss Fraser beamed at her. "That is correct. Please step to the end of the line."

Trennen stayed with her through the next round, and then left Eliza with six others, including her father and James. She listened to James define and spell *pneumonitis* without hesitation and decided Father had been right when he said James was intelligent.

One more round brought Eliza to the front with only four people behind her. She felt proud of staying in so long. Even Father had taken a seat. She felt confident when Miss Fraser smiled at her and said, "Miss Jackson, your word is *timous*."

What an easy word! Eliza smiled. "Timous means timely. T-i-m-e-o-u-s."

"Oh, I'm sorry." Miss Fraser frowned.

Eliza's face burned as she took a seat with Vanda and Trennen. "I thought you'd never come sit by me." Vanda made light of Eliza's mistake.

Eliza sank into the seat, trying to compose herself. "I can't believe I did that. There's no *e* in timous. I must have had the word *time* on my mind."

"That's what it means." Trennen smiled at Eliza.

"Yes, but I knew better."

"Hey, you stayed in longer than I did." His easy grin soon had her feeling better.

Another competitor sat down. Vanda indicated the two remaining. "I wonder who will win—James Hurley or Mr. Stenson?"

"I don't know."

Miss Fraser threw out words that Eliza had never heard, and still the two men battled.

"This could go on forever." Vanda yawned.

Eliza nodded. "It certainly looks that way."

But it didn't. Whether he was tired or he really didn't know the word, when Miss Fraser called out *repudiation*, Mr. Stenson shook his head and frowned. "Don't reckon I know the meaning of that one." He looked up at Miss Fraser. "I could spell it though, I imagine."

"I'm sorry, but the definition must come first." Miss Fraser smiled. "Mr. Stenson, you've done a wonderful job of defining and spelling. Thank you."

Mr. Stenson nodded and stepped toward a nearby seat. Eliza watched James as he took a step forward and waited until Miss Fraser repeated the word. "Repudiation means rejection. R-e-p-u-d-i-a-t-i-o-n."

"That is correct." Miss Fraser shuffled her papers and laid them neatly to one side while the room erupted in applause. She smiled at James. "Mr. Hurley, I'm certain I speak for everyone here when I say congratulations on an excellent evening of spelling. Will you please step forward?"

Eliza watched James step on the platform beside the schoolmarm's desk. He stuck both thumbs in his pockets and waited while she spoke.

"I want to congratulate all of our participants. However, a spelling bee may have only one winner. Some of our leading citizens decided that the winner of tonight's spelling bee deserved a prize. Mr. Wingate, on behalf of his bank, donated a half eagle that I am presenting to our 1836 spelling bee winner, Mr. James Hurley."

James took his right hand from his pocket. His neck was red as he reached for the five-dollar gold coin. He cleared his throat. "Thank you, Miss Fraser." He turned to the crowded schoolroom and nodded. "Thank you."

As he started to step down, Miss Fraser stopped him. "Mr. Hurley, we want you to lead the way to the refreshments, with Mr. and Mrs. Wingate coming next." Miss Fraser's high voice cut into the rising hum of voices and shuffle of feet as people began to move about. "Reverend Appleby, will you ask the blessing, please?"

As soon as the prayer ended, Eliza turned to Vanda. "Shall we find a place in line?"

But at that moment, Cletis tugged on his sister's arm. "Come on, Vanda, Poppa wants to go."

Trennen smiled down at Eliza. "I'd be glad to escort you."

"Miss Jackson." Eliza turned at the sound of James's voice. "You did a fine job tonight."

She smiled at him. "Thank you, Mr. Hurley, but you are the one to be congratulated."

He shrugged. "Spelling was never a problem for me."

"You seem to do a great many things well. My father is very pleased with your work at the cooperage."

"I enjoy my work."

Eliza glanced at her father and saw Mrs. Wingate take him by the arm. She led him to a woman she had been talking to earlier.

"That's good. I think Father enjoys what he does, too."

"Is there something wrong?" James touched Eliza's arm to get her attention.

She lifted concerned eyes to his. "I don't know. Do you have any idea who that woman is my father is talking to?"

He looked across the room. "Do you mean Mrs. Wingate or Mrs. Hurley?"

"Mrs. Hurley?"

He smiled. "My mother."

"Your mother?" Eliza almost choked on the words. She looked again, and recognition dawned in her mind. Of course. That was the woman she had seen with James at church. Mrs. Wingate had said she was a widow. Her father could easily become attracted to such a woman. Eliza knew she attended church regularly, and for her age, she was quite nice looking. Eliza watched her father's smile and easy conversation with the women and felt the noisy, crowded room close in on her.

She turned to Trennen. "I'm sorry, but I don't feel like eating. Maybe some other time. Excuse me."

She grabbed her wrap, fleeing out the door into the cold night. She leaned against the front of the building and looked up at the black, star-filled sky. She thought of her mother and the love her parents had shared. Even after a year, she missed her mother so much. It didn't seem right for Father to look at another woman when he should still be missing Mother as much as she did.

She started as the door opened. "Are you all right?" James asked.

"Of course." Eliza spoke with a sharper voice than she intended and added, "I just needed some fresh air." She brushed past him as she went back inside, leaving James watching her with a puzzled expression.

$$4$$

The day before Eliza's birthday she went out back of the house to throw corn to the chickens. They squawked in protest, running a few steps away, only to hurry back and peck a staccato on the ground.

Eliza lifted her eyes to the fields in back of their property and beyond to a distant stand of trees. Autumn colors made a splash across the horizon. She loved fall. It was a time of harvest. A time of gathering in the bounty that God had provided. It was also her birthday.

Father was planning a surprise for her. He hadn't said anything, but she knew. She could hardly wait until tomorrow to discover what it might be.

Eliza ducked her head as she stepped into the dim interior of the small henhouse and gathered a half-dozen eggs. "Good. This is plenty for my cake."

She needed to hurry with dinner because Father wanted her at the chandler shop while he and James made a delivery.

She went in the back door, meeting Lenny in the kitchen.

"Where have you been?" Eliza set her eggs on the table and eyed her brother, dirt-streaked from his head down to his bare feet.

"None of your business."

"That's where you're wrong." Eliza's hands went to her hips. Father allowed Lenny entirely too much freedom, coming and going as he pleased. "As long as I'm the only adult in this house, your whereabouts are my business."

"You ain't no adult," Lenny sneered.

"I'll be nineteen tomorrow, and that's a whole lot more adult than any little ten-year-old boy." She took a threatening step toward him. "How'd you get so dirty?"

He shrugged. "Playin' with the guys."

"What'd you do? Roll around on the ground?"

He grinned. "Part of the time. We were playin' keep away with a wagon wheel rim. It ain't that easy to keep it a-rollin' with three or four guys trying to get it away from you."

"You'd better take a bath before we eat." Eliza pulled the washtub from the back porch. "There's some hot water on the stove. After we add cold, there'll be enough." While she talked, she filled the tub and then dipped her hand in. "This feels fine. I'll give you ten minutes to get that dirt scrubbed off, and then I've got to start cooking. Hurry and get in while I get you some clean clothes."

"Do I have to take a bath?" Lenny whined.

Eliza turned at the door. "Yes. Father wants you to go with him on a delivery this afternoon." Her voice softened at his crestfallen look. "If you stay clean, you won't have to take another bath tonight."

"Another bath?" His voice rose in panic.

Eliza laughed. "You want to be clean for church tomorrow."

When he stared at her, his eyes wide and his mouth open, she pointed toward the tub. "You'd better be in there by the time I come back, or I'll put you in myself. And don't forget your hair."

As usual, Lenny didn't tarry in the water. With his bath out of the way, Eliza had just enough time to mix a cake before she fixed the noon meal. She heard the front door open as she reached for the oven door.

A tendril of hair escaped the confining bun at the base of her head and flew into her eye just as Father came into the room. She brushed at her hair with her left hand while she wrapped her right hand in her apron and reached for the hot pan. Pain seared her finger. The pan clattered to the floor as she jerked her hand back.

"Ow!" She put her finger in her mouth. "Where's the butter?" Tears blinded her eyes.

"Cold water works best." The deep voice and gentle hands guiding her to the sink were not her father's yet were familiar.

She looked into James's gray eyes. What was he doing here?

He pushed her hand into a pan of fresh cold water. She closed her eyes, savoring the relief.

"Keep your hand in for a few minutes." He turned to her father. "Do you have any burn salve and bandages?"

"I think so." It was the first thing Father had said since he came in the door. Eliza could hear him rummaging in the cabinet. She heard someone pick up the cake pan.

"Is my cake all right?" She wiped a hand across her eyes.

"It's fine." James moved back to her side. "How's that hand coming?"

"The water takes the pain away."

He lifted her dripping hand and laid it on a towel. "Let's get your hand dry so we can wrap it."

"Here we go." Father handed James the salve.

Eliza kept her gaze away from James as he blotted her hand. She reached for the can of salve the same time he did. "I can do it."

"Are you sure?" He sounded doubtful.

"Of course. It's just a little burn."

She sighed with relief when the men moved away.

"Is your hand still hurting?" James asked when she joined them at the table.

"Not much." Eliza realized Mother would have been ashamed of her manners. "Thank you for helping me. The cool water took most of the burn out. I'll remember that if it ever happens again."

James smiled. "Let's hope it never does."

As soon as they finished eating, Eliza cleared the dishes from the table and stacked them by the sink. Lenny ran outside, calling over his shoulder that he'd be ready to go anytime.

James shoved his chair back and crossed the room to the sink.

"Do you need help? You don't want to get your hand wet."

Before she could stop him, he was at the stove, bringing the teakettle of hot water. She stepped in front of him to pump cold water into the sink. She pointed to the counter. "Just set it there. I can handle this."

"Are you sure? I don't mind helping." He hesitated. "At least let me pour the water in for you."

"No. I can do it myself." She knew her voice was sharp, but his presence so close made her jittery. It wasn't right that a man wash dishes.

"Aren't we going to get some of that cake for dessert?" Father asked.

Eliza looked at the cake James had set on the cabinet. She shook her head. "I made it for tomorrow. It isn't even frosted yet."

"That's right. Someone's having a birthday tomorrow, aren't they?"

Eliza turned toward her father in time to see the smiles that passed between the two men. So James knew what Father had planned for her birthday.

"I guess we'll have to wait, James. Eliza's quite a stickler for doing things up right."

Eliza stiffened. Had Father just invited James Hurley to her birthday party?

James went back to the table and pushed in his chair. "I've enjoyed the stimulating conversation and excellent food. Thank you. Maybe sometime you can all come out to my mother's home and share a meal with us."

Eliza heard Father's chair slide under the table. She turned to see him smile at James. "We may take you up on that one of these days."

Eliza frowned as her father and James went into the parlor. Mrs. Wingate should have minded her own business. Father didn't need a wife.

She hung up her apron, looked at the wet bandage on her index finger, and her frown deepened. Maybe she should have let James wash her dishes, after all. Her finger throbbed. She pulled off the sopping wrap and threw it away.

As she tried to wrap a clean strip of cloth around her finger, the kitchen door opened and James stuck his head in. "I thought you might need some help with the dishes. Your father is hitching up the wagon."

"They're all done." She turned her back toward him.

She sensed his presence beside her. "Here, let me do that for you."

"I can do it myself." She was ashamed of the sharp tone in her voice.

"Miss Jackson." He took the cloth from her. "I don't bite. Besides, your father wants to get started on that delivery, and you may as well ride to the shop with us."

Eliza's face burned as she submitted to his gentle ministering. As soon as the bandage was in place, she fled the room, pausing at the door long enough to say, "Thank you, Mr. Hurley."

❧

The chandler shop was quiet with no one next door in the cooperage; so, between customers, Eliza finished her current novel.

While she walked home, she thought of what to fix for supper. Father had said they might not be home until late. Maybe she could fix vegetable soup.

There was no sign of life in the house as Eliza stepped on the porch. She pushed the door open and went in.

"Happy birthday, Eliza." A chorus of voices met her.

Several matches blazed, bringing lanterns and candles to life. Father stood in the middle of the room, his arms outstretched. Eliza moved into his embrace. "Happy birthday, Sweetheart." He gave her a quick hug and kissed the top of her head. "Some of our friends have come to celebrate with you a day early. You don't mind, do you?"

"Mind?" Eliza looked around the room. "Of course I don't mind."

Except for the chairs from the kitchen, there was not a stick of furniture in the parlor. Instead, the walls were lined by people, some she knew and some she didn't. Her eyes met James's briefly. He smiled at her. His sister and mother were there. Miss Fraser. The Wingates. The pastor and his family. Everyone laughed, and the hum of conversation picked up. So this was Father's surprise. She looked at him and smiled. "Someone has been busy this afternoon. Did you really make a delivery?"

He nodded. "Oh, yes. Mrs. Wingate and Vanda spearheaded this renovation."

Vanda hugged her. "Happy birthday, Eliza. This is the first party I've gone to in a long time. We're going to have so much fun. My father couldn't come, but Trennen's here somewhere." She leaned close and whispered. "I think you made an impression on him at the spelling bee."

Others pressed close to speak to Eliza. One by one the older people clasped her hand, saying a few words before moving on through the open door into the kitchen. Eliza could see the table groaning under the weight of the food that had been brought in.

She turned to her father and laughed. "I was worried about getting supper ready, and look at this. There's enough to feed the entire town."

He smiled. "I think that's about how many we'll be feeding. Mrs. Wingate is in charge of serving. I'd better see if she needs anything."

"Oh, Father, shouldn't I help?"

Vanda grabbed her arm. "Not tonight. You're going to stay in here with us and play. We'll eat when the older people are finished."

More than a dozen young people and as many younger children laughed and visited in the parlor. Vanda clapped her hands together and raised her voice. "Mrs. Wingate said we couldn't eat until we've played at least two games." Amid laughter and token protests she continued. "Everyone knows "Skip to My Lou," so grab hands and let's go."

Trennen grabbed Eliza's hand. "I've got my partner." He smiled. "Happy Birthday, Eliza. You sure look pretty tonight."

Eliza returned his smile. "I might have fixed up if I'd known I was going to a party."

His gaze moved over her in a way that brought a flush to her face. "No need. You look perfect to me."

"Thank you." She glanced toward James. He paid no attention to her and Trennen. He was too busy talking to his partner, a girl Eliza hadn't met.

Vanda started singing with the others joining in. "Skip, skip, skip to My Lou, skip, skip, skip to My Lou, skip, skip, skip to My Lou, skip to My Lou, my darling."

Holding Trennen's hand, Eliza skipped around the circle, adding her voice to the others. She cast a side glance at Trennen. With his eyelids lowered lazily, he smiled, and her heart fluttered. After Ralph's rejection she thought she would never look at another man. Now, with Trennen smiling down at her as if she were the only girl present, she wasn't so sure.

ஓஒ

Eliza strolled toward town, her surprise birthday party of two nights ago filling her mind. She giggled as she thought of the look on Trennen's face when Joe Martin had grabbed her after "Skip to My Lou" ended. Joe lasted through the next game, then Daniel Ross stepped between them, and so on it went the entire evening. Every game had found her with a different partner. But never James Hurley. He had kept his distance, and she hated to admit, even to herself, that she was disappointed.

Then the adults had come into the parlor to join the fun. When they played "Pig in the Parlor," Eliza noticed that Father picked Mrs. Hurley for his partner.

She and Father had laughed and talked as if they'd known each other for years. Eliza didn't understand how Father could act that way toward a woman other than Mother. He behaved as though he didn't miss Mother at all. Eliza missed her, and seeing Father with another woman stirred the pain of her loss so much more. How she wished Mrs. Wingate had never interfered!

Eliza pushed through the door to Leach's General Store.

"Good morning, Miss Jackson," Mr. Leach's voice boomed from the back of the store. "How are you today?"

"Fine, thank you."

"Thought you might be feeling a bit old after that birthday party." Mr. Leach's broad face beamed at her over a stack of feed sacks.

Mrs. Leach bustled in from the back. "You had a lovely party." She smiled. "What can I do for you?"

"Father told me to buy some dress fabric as my birthday gift."

Mrs. Leach led her to the bolts of material on a counter against the wall. "That's a wonderful idea. Let's see what we've got." She picked one up, holding it next to Eliza's face. "How about this pretty blue sprig? You've just the right coloring to go with it."

The minutes slipped by while Eliza and the storekeeper's wife selected several pieces of fabric. Finally, they had the yardage cut and folded neatly in a tall stack beside her. Eliza looked at Mrs. Leach with a nervous laugh. "Do you know of a seamstress?"

"I certainly do. The Kowskis are about as reasonable as you'll find, and they're good."

A few minutes later, Eliza left the store with a large bundle in her arms and directions to the Kowskis' house. The package was heavy and cumbersome, so she decided to stop first by the chandler shop to show her father what he had given her.

She found him alone in the back room. She went in and dropped her bundle on the worktable. "What've you got there?" he asked. "It isn't dinnertime, is it?"

Eliza shook her head, smiling. "No, are you hungry?"

He rubbed his middle. "Now that you mention it . . ."

Eliza laughed. "You'll forget all about your stomach once you see what I bought."

Father wiped his hands on his big apron and moved to her side as she untied the paper, letting it fall away. "Well, I'd say you've picked out some pretty dresses. How are you going to get that all sewn up?"

"That's what I wanted to talk to you about." Eliza felt her face flush. "Mrs. Leach gave me directions to some women who do sewing for a living. She says they're very reasonable. But I didn't know if you could afford the extra expense."

Father patted her back. "I'd forgotten which one of you girls was so handy with a needle. It was Cora, wasn't it?"

Eliza nodded. "Cora and Vickie are both good. I couldn't sew a decent seam if my life depended on it."

She heard a noise and turned to see James standing in the doorway. He nodded to her. "Hello, Miss Jackson."

"Hello." She turned away to cover her fabric, her face burning. She hoped he had not heard her last words.

While James and her father discussed an order for unusual-sized barrels, she prepared to leave. Father hadn't said if she could hire the women to sew for her, but that was all right. She'd ask again later.

She waited until a lull came in their conversation and then spoke. "Father, I've got to get home. I'll see you at noon."

James took a step toward her. "I have a few minutes to spare. I'll walk you home."

Eliza frowned. "That won't be necessary."

"It is if you're planning to take that. You'd never be able to carry it all the way to your house." He took the bundle from her before turning to her father. "This shouldn't take long and then I'll get right on that order."

Eliza turned imploring eyes on her father. "I don't need any help, Father. Maybe he should start the order now."

The twinkle in her father's eye was unmistakable. "James knows what he's doing. Getting you home is more important than any order."

Eliza stretched to her full height. "Father, I've never needed assistance finding my way before."

"But you've never had such a big package to carry." He grinned, obviously enjoying her discomfort.

Eliza turned, defeated, toward the door. Her father's words followed her. "Go ahead and hire those ladies to sew your dresses for you."

Eliza went through the shop into the autumn sunshine without a backward glance. She turned toward home, walking in a near run.

ટ્રે

James followed Eliza, watching her ramrod-straight back with an amused grin. It was obvious she didn't want his company—just as obvious as it had been the night of her party. He'd been unable to get near her for all the other fellows.

Her package was heavy, but mostly it was cumbersome. Strong as he was, he felt the pull on his arms before they had gone far. Of course, it might be easier handled if he didn't have to go in a half run to keep up with her. He tried to think what he might have said to offend her but could think of nothing.

He shifted the package to his shoulder, taking the strain off his arms. How was she going to get it to the dressmakers'? He took a few running steps to overtake her as she started down the Booneville Road.

"Would you mind slowing down?"

"You may stop and rest if you're tired." Her cute little nose went into the air.

"Miss Jackson, I'd like to ask you something, and it's all I can do to keep up."

Her pace slowed.

She acted like his little sister in a snit. He tried again. "Once I get started on that barrel order, I won't have much time. Have you considered how you're going to get your dress goods to the dressmakers'? Right now, I've got the time to deliver it. Wouldn't it make sense to take it there instead of your home?"

As fast as she'd been walking, James wasn't prepared for her sudden stop. He also wasn't prepared for the flashing brown eyes she turned on him. "So you did hear."

He hesitated, uncertain what was wrong. "Hear what? When we left your father said—"

"That since I can't sew, I'll have to go to the dressmakers'."

Her large brown eyes glistened. He nodded—then shook his head—confused. "No, that wasn't exactly what he said."

She shrugged, straightening her shoulders again. "He might just as well, because it's true. But I don't think you should go with me."

"Why not?"

Her eyes met his. "Because I don't want you to."

"Oh, really?" He grinned, intrigued by her show of independence. "I'll tell you what I'll do. I'll carry your fabric to the dressmakers' house, and then I'll leave. Is that a deal?"

Her eyes never left his. "Do I have a choice?"

"No." His grin grew even wider, and he was sure he saw an answering one tug at the corners of her mouth before she twirled away.

This time, as she turned back, she slowed her gait. James walked behind and to her side. He didn't want to overstep the boundaries she had put between them until he was sure where he stood with her. Somehow, Eliza Jackson had caught his fancy. As he watched the proud set of her shoulders, he determined to find a way to break down the wall she had erected against him.

≥

When they reached the dressmakers' home, Eliza took the package from James and thanked him. His cheerful whistle as he tripped down the steps toward town brought a smile to her lips. She knocked on the door of the small cabin, hoping Mrs. Leach's directions had been correct and this was the right place.

A girl near Eliza's age opened the door. A smile of recognition crossed her face. "Eliza Jackson, how nice to see you again."

Eliza looked from the friendly green eyes to a sprinkling of freckles covering the girl's alabaster skin. Her deep auburn hair was long and curly, pulled back at the nape of her neck to hang free down her back. Eliza remembered seeing her at church and at her party, but she couldn't remember her name.

"Miss Kowski?" At least Mrs. Leach had told her that much.

"Oh, please, call me Kathrene." She stretched out a small, dainty hand and grasped Eliza's arm. "Come inside. I want you to meet my mother. She didn't go to your party. She had some work to finish and wouldn't take the time."

Eliza followed Kathrene into a cheerful sunlit parlor.

"Mother, this is Eliza Jackson. I went to her birthday party Saturday night, although I don't think she remembers me." An impish grin lit Kathrene's face as she looked at Eliza.

Eliza couldn't help blushing any more than she could stop the laughter that escaped at her own expense. "I'm sorry. It's just that there were so many there." She smiled at the woman sitting in a chair in front of the window. "I'm pleased to meet you, Mrs. Kowski. I'm in need of a seamstress, and Mrs. Leach recommended you."

Mrs. Kowski pushed the garment she was working on to the side and stood, stretching her back as she did. "How nice of Mrs. Leach. Here, set that package on the couch. It must be quite heavy."

Kathrene and her mother could have passed for sisters. *Almost twin sisters,* Eliza thought as she looked from one to the other.

"It is a little heavy." Eliza deposited it on the couch and untied the string.

"I love to look at new fabric." Kathrene pulled the paper back and lifted the first piece. "This is so pretty. You'll be beautiful in it."

Mrs. Kowski thrust a magazine into Eliza's hands. "This is the latest *Lady's Book*. See if you like anything."

"Won't you need a pattern?" Eliza wasn't sure, but she thought Cora had always used a muslin pattern for their dresses.

Kathrene laughed. "Don't worry, Mother will make a pattern from the sketches in the magazine."

"Oh." Eliza was impressed with a talent she knew little about. She perched on the edge of a chair and thumbed through the magazine until she found a dress that she thought would be perfect for church.

"Could you make this one from the blue print?" She held the page for Mrs. Kowski to see.

"Yes, I think the blue print is a good choice for it. Would you like to pick out the rest or wait and see how this one turns out?"

Eliza stood. "I'd like to look further, but it's time now for me to be home fixing my father's dinner. If you made your own dresses, I'm sure mine will turn out fine."

Mrs. Kowski smiled as she set the magazine aside. "Before you leave, may I take a couple of measurements so I can cut out your dress tonight?"

A few minutes later with the measurements recorded by Eliza's name and a price agreed upon, Kathrene walked out to the front gate with her. "I really enjoyed your party Saturday night."

Eliza smiled. "I'm glad you came. I'm sorry I forgot your name. We've been here just a month now, and I've met so many people I have trouble remembering everyone."

A warm smile lit Kathrene's face. "I'll just have to make myself more noticeable from now on."

"I thought you would be two older women, maybe sisters. Then when you turned out to be my age, I was a little nervous about letting you know I couldn't sew. I thought you might laugh at me." Eliza smiled.

Kathrene shook her head. "I could never laugh at someone else when there are so many things I can't do." She laughed softly. "My mother is a wonderful cook, but I think she's about despaired of ever teaching me."

Eliza took Kathrene's hand and squeezed gently. "Speaking of cooking, I've got to go. I'm really glad I got to meet you."

Kathrene nodded. "Let's make ourselves known at church, too. I've seen you each week, and now I'm ashamed I didn't introduce myself."

Eliza edged toward the road. "That's all right. I didn't do any better Saturday night." She waved as she started down the dirt road toward home. "Come over and visit me sometime."

"All right, I will." Kathrene stood by the gate to wave before turning back inside.

Eliza thought Kathrene was every bit as nice as her best friend, Grace Newkirk, from back home. Now she had two new friends, Vanda and Kathrene.

She hummed "Home, Sweet, Home" until she caught sight of her father's shop. Only to herself would she admit that James had been right. She would have struggled to carry her package as far as he did. She appreciated his help but wished she wasn't so attracted to him.

$\bigcirc$

5

*O*h, Eliza. It looks perfect on you." Kathrene clasped her hands under her chin and sighed. "You have such beautiful coloring."

After several fittings throughout the first part of November, Mary and Kathrene had finished the first dress.

Eliza smiled. "Thank you."

Mary Kowski bustled in from the other room. "Here are some more magazines you may look at for the rest of your dresses, Eliza."

Eliza smiled at Kathrene's mother. "Thank you. I love this one."

She still found it hard to believe that Mary Kowski was old enough to be Kathrene's mother. Mary's energy seemed boundless as she rushed from one project to another.

Several minutes later, Eliza hurried home with a light step. With Mary's and Kathrene's help, she had picked out the other three dresses.

That night just before bedtime Father said, "I've been doing some thinking about Christmas."

"Christmas is more than a month away, Father." Eliza looked from her father to her brother. Lenny just shrugged his shoulders.

Father smiled. "Yes, I know. But it may take us that long to get ready. I'm just getting started on the bayberry candles. Your dresses are not finished. We should be looking for gifts. And we mustn't forget, it's a two-day trip even in good weather."

Lenny's eyes grew wide as Eliza leaned forward. "What are you talking about, Father? A two-day trip where?"

"Oh, did I forget to mention that?" The twinkle in his eyes warned Eliza that Father had something special planned.

"Yes, you did."

Lenny looked smug. "I already know."

"How could you? Father, did you tell—"

"No." Father shook his head. "I didn't tell Lenny anything."

"All right, Smarty." Eliza turned to her brother. "Where are we going for Christmas?" The words had no sooner left her lips than she knew. She jumped from the chair and flung her arms around her father's neck. "Home. We're going home to see everyone for Christmas, aren't we?"

"Where else would we go that takes two days?" Lenny's look of scorn was lost on Eliza's enthusiasm.

"How can you do that? What about the shops?" Eliza asked.

Father made room for Eliza on the couch. "James can handle anything that comes, and if not, he can close up until we get back."

"Yeah, it'll probably snow, and we won't go, anyway." Lenny hid his eagerness behind a look of indifference.

"You've got a reasonable concern there, Son." Father's smile disappeared for a moment. "But the weather has been unusually mild so far, and according to the almanac, it should be for awhile."

"Oh, Father, you're right. There's so much to do." Eliza began counting on her fingers. "I'll have to prepare food for the trip. I want to bake something special to take. We need to take gifts for everyone. What do you think they'd like?" Before he could answer, she smiled. "We'll see Nora and Christopher, too. I just know they've grown."

She swung toward her father as a new thought entered her mind. "Are we bringing Nora home?"

Father shook his head. "I want that more than you know, Eliza. But I don't see how we can at this time. The shops are just getting started, and I need your help much too often for you to tend an active two year old, too. But soon we will."

They talked, making plans until it grew late and Father sent them off to bed.

ᙍ

Their coming trip dominated the conversation at breakfast the next morning. Father swallowed his last bite of biscuit and pushed his chair back. "I've been thinking we ought to invite our old friends for Christmas dinner."

Lenny looked up. "I'll bet the Newkirks will come because Ben's married to Esther. But what about the Starks? Aaron will come with Cora, so that just leaves Ralph and Ivy."

At the mention of Ralph's name, Eliza's spoon dropped to the table. She hadn't thought of him. In all the excitement of seeing her family again, she had forgotten Ralph. But of course he would be there. With his wife and baby. She gathered the dishes from the table while dread crept over her soul.

"It looks like your sister's ready for us to get out of her way, Lenny." Father stood and stretched. "I'll lay aside the next batch of bayberry candles to take back for the girls. I'll be working on them today. How'd you like to come down and tend the shop this afternoon, Eliza?"

"Fine." She pulled Lenny's spoon from his hand as he shoveled in the last of the oatmeal. He swiveled around with a frown. "Hey, can't you wait until a guy finishes?"

"Good, then I'll see you later." Father guided Lenny toward the door. "Tell your sister bye and thank you for breakfast."

Lenny turned to peek under his father's arm at Eliza. He crossed his eyes and stuck out his tongue. "Good-bye, Eliza, and thank you for what I got to eat before you jerked it away."

Father's back was turned as he pushed through the kitchen door into the parlor. Eliza lifted a heavy iron skillet as if to throw it at Lenny. "I'm glad you enjoyed it, little brother. Would you like some of this, too?"

Lenny ducked under his father's arm and ran through the door. By the time Father looked at Eliza she was drying the skillet. She smiled at him. "Bye, Father. I'll see you at noon."

When the front door closed behind them, the house grew quiet, allowing memories of Ralph to beat without mercy against Eliza's heart. How could she go see the man she'd thought she would marry when he was married to another? She finished the dishes and hung the wet tea towel on a rack to dry. She put beans on the stove to simmer, yet the image of Ralph would not leave. She moved to the bedrooms, making beds, straightening, dusting, and sweeping. Still Ralph haunted her.

With sudden determination, she ran to the kitchen, shoved the beans to the back of the stove, and grabbed a heavy, woolen shawl. There was plenty of time to see Kathrene and Mary Kowski before noon.

The fresh air felt good on her face as her feet carried her to the small cabin across town. Kathrene opened the door at her knock.

"Eliza, come in." Kathrene's smile of welcome gave a sparkle to her green eyes.

"I didn't intend to come today, but I have wonderful news, and I need some adjustments made." Eliza moved into the room past Kathrene.

"What is your news?" Mary gave Eliza a warm hug.

All thoughts of Ralph faded as Eliza sat on the couch between the two women and told of her eagerness to see her family at Christmas. "I'd like my other three dresses adjusted to fit my sisters."

"Oh, Eliza, how sweet of you." Mary patted Eliza's hand.

Eliza smiled at her friend. "I want the pink for Esther. It's soft and feminine just like she is."

Mary smiled and stood. "I'll get some paper and a pen to write down the changes we'll need to make. Are the girls much different in size from you?"

Eliza frowned as she brought each to mind. "No, not really. Esther's taller and a little thinner. Cora and I always wore each other's clothes, so there shouldn't be any changes to make there. Vickie is older, but she's probably an inch shorter than Cora and me. She has two children that she says have made her fat, but she really isn't."

Mary wrote, trying to keep up with Eliza's descriptions. "Then you think Vickie might be just two or three inches larger around than you?"

Eliza nodded. "Yes, that's about right."

"All right." Mary laid the pen and paper down. "I think I have enough here. Why don't you pick out the fabric you want for each sister?"

"I think Esther should have the pink, Cora the blue, and Vickie the green calico."

As she left, she touched Kathrene's arm. "Please pray for me while I'm gone."

"Of course. Mother and I both will. Besides safe travel, is there something special we should be praying about?"

With a sigh, Eliza met her friend's concerned gaze. "There was a young man." She hesitated as moisture threatened her sight. "He married someone else." She took a deep breath and brushed a hand across her eyes. "Just pray that if I see them, I won't make a fool of myself."

Kathrene gathered her into a hug. "I understand. I'll pray that God will show you He has something better for you than what you lost."

Eliza straightened and smiled. "Thank you. Now I've got to run home before Father gets there. I may have burned beans for him to eat if I don't hurry."

Kathrene laughed, calling after Eliza's retreating figure, "I burn them when I'm right there watching. Yours will be fine."

True to Kathrene's prediction, the beans had cooked down but were not scorched. Lenny and Father each had two bowls full.

At the shop that afternoon, Eliza kept busy most of the time. A customer left just as Vanda came in.

"I didn't expect to see you." Vanda smiled.

"Does that mean you wouldn't have come in if you'd known I was here?"

Vanda laughed. "Of course not. It means I'd have been here sooner so we could visit longer."

"You say all the right things, but that doesn't explain why I've scarcely seen you all this month." Eliza pretended to pout.

Vanda picked up a bayberry candle from the counter and sniffed it. "My father hasn't been working as much so I've had to stay close to home." Her smile didn't reach her eyes. "He has some old-fashioned ideas about women. He doesn't like for me to be away from home any more than necessary." She quickly changed the subject. "M-m-m. These really smell good, don't they? What are they?"

Eliza glanced toward the candle in Vanda's hand. "Bayberry. Father's making them for Christmas. I've sold several today."

A wistful sound came into Vanda's voice as she put it back. "Maybe nearer Christmas I can get one. But for now we just need the cheapest candle you have."

Eliza came around the counter. "You know, we do have a candle that costs a little more, but in the long run it's more economical because it lasts so much longer."

"Oh, really?"

Encouraged by Vanda's interest, Eliza reached for the special candles and handed one to her friend. "These are made with whale blubber and burn as long as three or four tallow candles. The light is brighter, too. But they only cost about twice as much."

"H-m-m. That sounds like a good deal." Vanda smiled. "I'll take two of them."

The bell above the door rang as Eliza wrapped the candles for Vanda. She looked up, meeting James's gaze.

"Good afternoon, ladies." His presence seemed to dwarf the room.

Eliza returned to her work, her hands trembling as she tied the string. Vanda smiled at him. "Good afternoon, yourself." She turned back and tapped Eliza's arm. "I believe he was speaking to both of us."

Eliza lifted her gaze to the gray eyes watching her. A half grin sat on his lips. She felt a stirring deep inside that she didn't want to feel. "Hello, Mr. Hurley."

His lips spread into a full smile.

She felt her face flush. Why did he have to look at her like that? "Is there something you need? My father is in the back room."

He shivered violently. "B-r-r-r. We may get that first snow before Christmas, after all." He grinned, doffed an imaginary hat, and strode across the shop. He stopped, turned, and nodded with a big grin at Vanda before disappearing through the back door.

As soon as the door closed, Vanda turned to Eliza. "Why did you treat him so cold? It's obvious he likes you."

"Likes me!" Eliza's voice rose. "Where'd you get an idea like that? He was rude to me."

Vanda laughed. "He wasn't rude. He was just reacting to the way you patronized him. Just because he's your father's employee—"

"Oh, Vanda," Eliza interrupted. "I didn't mean it that way. It's just that he makes me nervous. Here are your candles. I think you'll like them very much. They are about the only kind I use at home."

Vanda reached for the bundle, a smile softening her face. "James Hurley likes you, and I think he has caught your fancy, too."

Eliza didn't answer except to tell Vanda good-bye as she left. While her friend was right about Eliza's feelings for James, Eliza couldn't allow herself to like him. Ralph's rejection still hurt too much for her to trust her heart to another.

The shop filled with customers, so she was busy when James walked back through on his way to the cooperage.

6

*E*liza could scarcely sit still when Cedar Creek and then the log cabin came into view. A wave of homesickness for her mother swept over her. She watched the closed door of the cabin coming closer, half expecting Mother to be standing there, waiting with a welcoming embrace. But Esther opened the door.

Esther laughed as she stepped out to greet them. "Father. Eliza and Lenny. Oh, Ben will be so surprised."

Father gave her a warm hug. "Where is my oldest son?"

"At the barn. We have a cow down that he's taking care of." Esther looked as beautiful as ever. Her wheat blond hair, done up in a loose bun, fell in a soft wave across her forehead. Her lips, full and pink, curved up at the corners.

Father looked toward the building that had served as shelter when they first moved to the country. "Lenny, you can help me with the horses. We'll see what Ben's up to."

Eliza stepped through the heavy oak door ahead of Esther, allowing memories of the three happy years she had spent there to course through her mind.

"I'm so glad you came." Esther hugged Eliza. "Your sisters and Ben will be thrilled. We all talked the other night about how hard it would be to have a real Christmas with you gone. Why don't we invite everyone over to share Christmas Day with us? Grace will want to see you."

"That would be wonderful." Even as Eliza agreed, a twinge of fear struck the pit of her stomach. "Everyone" included Ralph.

"You must be worn out from your trip and probably hungry, too." Esther turned toward the kitchen. "Did you get any sleep?" Esther stirred the fire in Mother's old cookstove while Eliza stifled a yawn.

She laughed. "Some. I didn't feel tired until you started talking about it. Even now, I'm so excited I don't think I could rest."

Esther smiled. "That's good, because I expect Ben will have your sisters here before we finish eating."

"Is there anything I can help you with?"

Esther shook her head. "No, you go greet your brother."

Ben crossed the room in long strides and grabbed Eliza in a warm hug.

Father and Lenny followed him into the room. Ben turned to face them, his arm still around Eliza's shoulders. "I'm having trouble believing you're here. We'll have a real Christmas, after all."

"Yes, if gifts are not important." Esther's soft voice brought a groan from Ben.

"Oh, I forgot. We didn't know you were coming."

"Don't worry about gifts." Father laughed. "Eliza already said the best gift she could get is coming home for Christmas."

Eliza nodded as everyone looked at her. "That's true. I just want to be with my family. What could be better than that?"

Ben smiled. "Of course you're right." His eyes, so like their father's, twinkled. "The only problem is, I saw your wagon. It's loaded to the top."

"Yes, and we need to unload." Father jammed his hat back on his head. "Come on, Ben. Show us where you want these supplies. We need to lighten the wagon for our return trip. Then someone needs to tell Cora and Vickie we're here."

As soon as Cora and Aaron arrived, Eliza ran from the cabin with her father and Lenny behind her while Ben and Esther waited on the porch.

Aaron lifted Cora from the horse's back, holding her waist until he was sure she had her footing. Cora smiled up at him. "I'm fine, Aaron, really."

Eliza pushed past her brother-in-law to catch her sister in a fierce hug. She laughed. "Are you surprised to see us?"

"Yes and very glad."

Then Lenny and their father pulled Cora away, and Eliza stepped back. It was good to be home.

"How you been doin', Eliza?"

She looked up into Aaron's bright blue eyes. How much like his brother Ralph he looked! She ignored the pounding of her heart and smiled at her brother-in-law. "Just fine. I'm so glad we could come home."

"Yeah. Ben said we'd have a big Christmas dinner. Be jist like old times, won't it?"

Her heart lurched at the thought, but she managed a weak smile. "Yes, it should be really nice." She thought of Aaron and Ralph's sister. "How's Ivy getting along?"

Aaron smiled. "She's doin' real good. That little fellow of hers ain't no bigger'n a minute, but he sure runs her a merry chase. He's already crawlin'."

Eliza laughed. She tried to imagine Aaron's sister as a mother. It was hard to see anything but the sullen girl she had been before her marriage to Mr. Reid. "Is Ivy happy?"

Aaron grinned. "Happy as a pig in the wallow."

"I'm glad she's happy. It'll be good to see her."

"You're the one I want to visit with." Cora linked her arm in Eliza's as they turned toward the house. "We've got three months of catching up to do. You're going to tell me all about that big city you live in and what you've been doing there."

"Don't worry, I will."

"Here comes Nicholas." Lenny's excited voice drew attention to the trail behind the house. Although Lenny was several years older than his nephew, the two boys had always been close.

Eliza and Cora followed the others to meet their sister Vickie and her husband John. But it was their oldest son, Nicholas, who scrambled from the wagon before it stopped and ran past them to grab Lenny.

"Let me have those babies." Father reached for Christopher and then waited while John set Nora on his other arm and then turned to help Vickie.

After a warm hug from Vickie and John, while the others visited, Eliza watched the two little ones look at Father with solemn faces. She noticed his eyes were moist as he clutched them close. Nora lifted a tiny hand to her father's cheek. "You mine papa?"

A smile lit his face. "Yes, I am."

"Me, too." Little Christopher reached up to tug on his chin.

Father smiled down at his grandson and kissed his cheek. "I'm Grandpa to you."

"Eth. Bampa." Christopher nodded his head while Nora snuggled against her father's chest.

"Well, it looks like they haven't forgotten Father," Eliza said.

"Of course not, and they haven't forgotten you, either," Vickie spoke beside her. "It seems like a lifetime, but you've only been gone a short while."

Cora pulled Eliza by the hand. "Let's see if we can get Nora away from Father."

Nora stared at Eliza with wide brown eyes. Slowly a shy smile tugged at her mouth, and she leaned forward.

It wasn't hard to talk Vickie into letting Nora spend the night. Eliza took advantage of the short time with her little sister before John came midmorning the next day to take her back home so she wouldn't be in the way of Christmas preparations. Ben and Father made the rounds of the neighbors, inviting them to Christmas dinner, while Esther and Eliza cleaned house and baked a wide assortment of pies and cakes.

That afternoon, Cora and Aaron came. They hadn't been there long before Cora took Eliza's hand and pulled her toward the door. "Grab your wrap. We haven't had that talk you promised me." She nodded toward the ladder leading to the loft. "We can't share our secrets up there anymore. Now we have to go outside where we can find some privacy."

"Don't you girls be gone long. When Vickie and John get here, we'll open gifts." Their father's eyes twinkled. "You won't want to miss that."

Cora laughed. "You're right, we won't. We'll come right in when they get here."

"So tell me what it's like in Springfield," Cora said before they stepped off the porch.

Eliza described the house and shops. She told about the church and several of the people she had met. "I've made two friends. Kathrene Kowski helps her mother as a seamstress. They are both wonderful. I know you'd love them, too."

She went on telling about the friendship that had grown between herself and Kathrene. Then she said, "I have another friend, Vanda Von Hall. Vanda reminds me of a will-o'-the-wisp. I don't know where she lives, and she doesn't come to church often. I only see her when she comes to me."

Cora shook her head. "She sounds strange."

"Oh, but she isn't. Actually, she's very nice." Eliza defended her friend. "I've met her father and brothers. They seem nice, too."

"Brothers?" Cora smiled. "And how old are they?"

"One is Lenny's age."

"And the other?"

"About twenty-one." Eliza's face felt hot in the cold air.

"So have you met any other young men, or is this the one?" Cora grinned at her sister's discomfort.

Eliza turned to face Cora. "I don't have to settle for the first man who looks my way. Father gave me a surprise birthday party, and I'll have you know I was the most sought after girl there." She interrupted as Cora started to speak. "No, I wasn't the only girl."

Cora laughed. "I'm glad to see living in the city hasn't changed you."

Eliza relaxed as she laughed with her sister. "I don't know if I've changed, but I do know it's good to be home for awhile."

"Only awhile? Does that mean you're anxious to get back?"

Eliza thought of the well-furnished, roomy house awaiting them and shrugged. "I suppose in a way I am. It's nice having my own house to care for, even though sometimes I'd like to turn all the work over to someone else."

Cora didn't speak for several moments and then said, "Have you considered that Father might marry again?"

Eliza's heart lurched as she thought of Mrs. Hurley. She turned on her sister. "How can you even think such a thing? He loved Mother too much to desecrate her memory."

"But Father is still young enough to have . . ." She paused, then added, "Feelings."

Eliza stopped near a young apple tree, its bare branches moving in the cool air. "If you don't mind, I'd rather find out about all of you. And don't tell me Vickie is going to have another baby. I already know."

Cora laughed. "You always know." She paused. "Almost everything."

"Do you mean Esther?"

"How did you know she was, too?"

Eliza shrugged. "By the way she acts, and I thought I noticed a difference in the way she looks."

Cora shook her head. "You are a wonder, but you don't know everything."

Eliza looked at her sister. What had she missed? Then she noticed the protective way Cora's hand rested on her abdomen. With a glad cry she threw her arms around her. "You, too? Oh, Cora, that's wonderful. No wonder you look so happy. I thought it was because you're so much in love with Aaron."

Cora laughed. "Well, of course, I am." She patted the slight bulge under her coat. "But I already love this little fellow, too."

The jingling of harness and rumbling of a wagon announced John and Vickie's arrival. Eliza looked toward the west as they came into view and began to laugh.

"What's so funny?" Cora touched her arm. "We promised Father we'd come right in when Vickie got here."

"But that's just it." Eliza could scarcely get her breath. "We have to open gifts now." She wiped her eyes, trying to stop laughing. "I just realized I had dresses made for each of you, and not one of you will be able to fit in them."

Cora linked her arm through Eliza's. "If you think you're going to take the dresses back, you can think again. We'll just save them until we can wear them." She smiled. "Come on, let's beat Vickie and John to the house."

Eliza enjoyed the time spent with her family as they gathered around the Christmas tree and exchanged gifts. Both Father's bayberry candles and her dresses were welcomed. She sat on the floor with Nora snuggled in her lap. She couldn't resist squeezing her little sister, knowing that their time together was short.

❧

Eliza woke the next morning to a churning stomach that could be attributed to only one thing. Before the day ended, she would see Ralph.

Esther's father and mother came early with their seven children and more than enough food for everyone. Eliza grabbed her friend Grace in a welcoming hug. "It seems like ages since I saw you last."

Grace squeezed Eliza. "What do you mean, 'seems like'? It has been ages." She pulled away and looked at her friend. "This is the lonesomest place ever with you gone. What's it like where you live? You've got to tell me all about it."

The girls wandered off arm in arm, falling into the easy friendship they had known before. Eliza spent the morning close to Grace, watching and listening for Ralph. Each step on the porch or opening of the door caused her heart to quicken, but he still had not come by midmorning.

"Is that a wagon I hear?" Vickie pulled the kitchen curtains back.

Cora looked over her shoulder. "It's Ivy and Mr. Reid." She turned to Eliza. "They have the sweetest little boy."

Eliza saw Ivy, still seated in the wagon, hand down a blanket-clad bundle to her husband. "I can't see him. Ivy looks well, though."

"I think you'll appreciate the change in her, too." Cora laid a hand on Eliza's shoulder. "Becoming a mother made her a different person. Of course, the real change came when Ivy accepted Jesus last month."

"Oh, that's wonderful!" Eliza smiled as Ben opened the door.

Ivy's long, shiny black hair was done in a braided coil on top of her head. Her carriage rivaled that of a queen as she stepped into the house with a warm smile. "Ben, it's good to see you."

Ben nodded to Ivy and shook hands with her husband. "Good to see both of you, too. All three of you." He lifted the baby's tiny hand in his large one. "This little fellow gets bigger every time I see him."

Cora stepped forward to greet her sister-in-law with a quick hug. "Ivy, I'm so glad you came. Now Eliza can see you while she's here and get to meet my nephew."

Eliza started to shake hands with Ivy but was surprised when she received a hug instead. "You've given us all a nice Christmas gift by coming home for a visit."

"Thank you, Ivy." Eliza didn't know what to make of the changes she could already see. Ivy had always been beautiful, but now a look of radiance surrounded her.

As the Reid family mingled with the others, Eliza stole a quick glance through the window across the field to the woods.

"I think we're ready to set the table." Vickie's voice put Eliza back to work.

Several minutes later, Eliza stood at the end of the table with Grace and counted the place settings. "Will there be enough room for everyone? We squeezed in ten places here at the table. What about the others?"

"Howdy, folks." Ralph's cheerful voice rang out, sending a chill down Eliza's back. "Reckon you'uns thought we wasn't gonna make it."

"No, we knew long as there was food awaitin' you'd git here, Ralph," Aaron greeted his brother.

Eliza stood, her hands gripping the back of the chair in front of her.

"Eliza." Vickie's hand felt gentle on her shoulder. "We can eat in shifts or spread out into the other end. It's warm enough so the older children can eat outdoors."

Eliza nodded. Her senses numb, she heard the hum of conversation mingling with childish shouts. Yet through it all, Ralph's voice sent waves of warmth to her face. She turned slowly, hoping her cheeks were not as red as they felt.

He stood, as handsome as ever, talking with the other men. She almost hated him for being so good-looking. Then his eyes lifted to hers, holding her gaze for a heartbeat. She turned away. She was glad when the men moved outside.

"Do you mean you walked with the baby? I figured you'd hitch that old ox up to something." Ivy took the baby from Anna.

"Ralph broke the axle on that wagon you gave him, and he's never gotten around to fixing it." Anna shrugged. "It wasn't so bad, though. Ralph carried the baby part of the way."

"Oh!" Ivy's foot hit the floor. "Sometimes I have trouble believin' Ralph's my brother." Her voice softened as she turned back to Anna. "Mr. Reid and I will take you and the baby home."

"Thank you, Ivy." Anna's pale blue eyes looked tired. "I'm sorry we didn't bring anything. Ralph said not to. He said it'd be too hard to carry."

"He was right." Cora smiled at her sister-in-law.

Eliza kept her distance from both Ralph and Anna. In the crowded house it wasn't hard, yet their presence seemed more real to her than those with whom she visited.

The men and children came inside, and then Father prayed. The children took heaping plates to the porch, while the women relaxed in the parlor end of the large room to feed the babies, and the men sat at the table.

Eliza vied for the privilege of helping Nora. She soon found there was little she could do as Nora insisted on feeding herself.

But Ralph didn't appear to have the independence of a two year old. As Anna fed mashed potatoes to their nine-month-old son, Eliza heard him call his wife.

"Hey, Woman!" His voice carried over the steady hum of voices. "Get me some coffee."

Anna set the baby on the floor and made her way to the kitchen.

Aaron looked across the table at his brother. "Why don't you get it yourself? Ain't you got legs?"

Ralph grinned. "Sure do." He nodded toward his wife. "See 'em comin'?"

Aaron's dark brows drew together. "One of these days, Ralph, somebody's gonna set you down."

Ralph grinned and took the coffee Anna handed him.

Anna had her baby cuddled in her arms, nursing him, when Ralph called again. "I'm needin' some of that pie, Woman."

Ivy jumped up, handing her baby to Cora. She looked at Anna. "Doesn't he even know your name?"

Anna sighed. "It's just his way."

Ivy snorted. "You sit still. I'll take care of my lazy brother."

Eliza watched Ivy stalk to the sideboard at the far end of the kitchen. She picked up a pie and headed for Ralph. She lifted a piece of blackberry pie and slapped it upside down on Ralph's plate, juice splattering everywhere.

Her softly spoken words barely reached the women. "I know you're too lazy to scratch your own itch, Ralph, but if you bother Anna again, you'll be eatin' the rest of your food off your lap."

Ralph looked up at his sister in surprise. "What got your back up? Cain't a man eat in peace?"

"Just be sure that's what you do. And let Anna have some peace, too." Ivy rejoined the women, took her baby from Cora, and sat back down.

Anna gave her a wan smile. "Thank you, Ivy."

"I don't know why you put up with him." Ivy shook her head. "If Mr. Reid did me that way, I'd be hurt plumb through."

Anna shrugged. "I don't mind."

The women had to clean the table before they could eat and then clean again when they finished. Esther peered into the water bucket. "We're out of water for the dishes. I guess I'd better ask one of the men to get some."

"I'll go," Eliza said. A trip to the well by herself would be a welcome relief.

She picked up the empty bucket and, threading her way through men and smaller children, went outdoors. The cool air against her face felt good. She could see Lenny and Nicholas playing with the Newkirk children. Their childish laughter filled the air. She envied them their innocence.

Eliza lowered the water bucket into the well until she heard it splash and sink. She tugged on the rope to pull it up. When Ralph's voice startled her, she dropped the rope, turning to find herself less than a foot from him.

At the sound of the bucket hitting the water again, Eliza swung back and grabbed the rope.

"I said howdy, Eliza."

She fought to control the pounding of her heart.

"Ain't ya gonna say nothin'?" Ralph persisted.

Eliza set the full bucket on the rim of the well and faced him. "Hello, Ralph. It's nice to see you again."

A familiar grin spread across his face. "It's right nice seein' you, too."

Ralph was handsome, and he knew it. She stood under his spell, unable to control her heart.

"Come walk with me a ways. I'm full as a tick." He reached out.

She started to take his hand; then, as if a fog lifted, she saw him as she'd never seen him before. He needed a shave and a haircut. A bath wouldn't hurt. He had a wife, yet he asked another woman to walk with him. He was lazy and inconsiderate, with no respect for his wife.

The image of James Hurley filled her mind. He worked hard at his job. He was always clean about his person and in his speech. James was a Christian. Ralph was not. How could she have spent so much time yearning for a man who could never be faithful to anyone, not even his own wife?

She shook her head. "I don't think so, Ralph."

"Come on, Eliza. It'll be like old times." He grinned his most persuasive. "I missed you."

A sudden flash of anger struck her. "In case you hadn't realized, you're the one who up and got married."

"Now, Eliza, you know that weren't my idea."

She gave him a withering look. "I feel sorry for Anna. I wouldn't go across the yard with you, Ralph. Go back inside and get your wife if you want someone to walk with."

She pivoted away from him toward the well, shutting him once and for all out of her life. Freedom such as she hadn't experienced for almost a year released her heart.

She picked up the full bucket of water, turned around, and shoved it at him, splashing the front of his shirt. "Here, take this to the house so we can wash dishes. It'll make a good impression on your neighbors—and your wife."

Not waiting for him to talk his way out of it, Eliza went to the house. Happier than she'd been in a long time, she announced, "Ralph's bringing the water."

Ralph followed her with the bucket balanced in his right hand, a frown on his face.

Ivy laughed. "I don't know how you did that, Eliza, but you'd better tell Anna your secret."

Eliza smiled. "Oh, Anna, Ralph told me he wanted to go on a walk. Why don't you go? There's enough of us to do these dishes and watch your baby for you, too."

Anna's tired eyes shone as they met her husband's. He looked from Eliza to Anna, and a good-natured grin lit his face. "Guess I know when I'm whipped."

Anna took his hand. "Since I don't have to walk home, I'd be proud to go with you, Ralph."

$$7$$

inter remained mild with little snow. In the months following their brief visit, Eliza missed her family even more. Each day she longed for the time when Nora could come to Springfield where she belonged. Yet she had much to be thankful for. No longer did Ralph's image haunt her. How could she have thought she loved such a lazy, faithless oaf?

"Spring's just around the corner."

Eliza turned from the dishes at her father's voice.

"It doesn't look much like it." She glanced toward the window where the bare oak branches stood out cold and forlorn. "Of course, no more snow than we've gotten, it hasn't felt like winter, either."

"That's true." He grinned. "I ran into Miss Fraser downtown." He pulled out a chair and sat down. "Miss Fraser has decided the perfect way to raise money for the school would be a box social."

"When will it be?"

"She wasn't sure. The first month without an *r* in it, I think she said." He grinned at Eliza. "I've been thinking. You'll need a new dress to wear. Why don't you pick something nice out and take it to your seamstresses?"

"That sounds like a good idea." Eliza laughed with her father.

ॐ

The box social was set for the first day of May. Eliza woke early to prepare a tempting meal. A young fryer from the chicken coop went into her skillet, and potatoes boiled in a pan on the stove. She decided to make two blackberry tarts for dessert. Once they were in the oven, the potato salad could be made.

She tied the handles of her wicker basket together with a bright red hair ribbon, then stood back to admire her work. She nodded with satisfaction as her father came into the kitchen.

"Are you ready to go? I've got the buggy hitched."

Eliza smiled. "Oh, so we're going in style today."

"Of course." Father reached for her basket. "We don't want anything to happen to this." He lifted it, pretending to almost drop it. "What have you got in here? It weighs a ton."

"Oh, Father." Eliza laughed. "I know it isn't that heavy. It's just potato salad, chicken, and tarts."

"Can we go now?" Lenny ran into the kitchen, slamming the door behind him. "I'm starving."

"Which reminds me." Father set Eliza's basket back on the table. "Did you fix enough for Lenny?"

"Of course." Eliza stepped to the cook table and picked up another box. "This is for you and Lenny. It's a good thing you said something, because I almost forgot it."

Father took the box in one arm and carried the basket in the other. As he went out the door, he grinned down at his son. "Looks like you'll have plenty, Lenny. I'll be eating some other lady's cooking today."

Eliza's heart sank as she followed him to the buggy. She thought he had lost interest in Mrs. Hurley. By the time he parked among the other wagons and buggies, she decided that if there were any way possible to keep him away from Mrs. Hurley, she would do it.

Eliza's feet slowed as she neared the table set under a tree in the middle of the yard. Mrs. Hurley stood behind the table holding a white box with a sprig of goldenrod tied on the top. Eliza watched her place it on the table and walk away.

Eliza walked around the table. She set her basket in front of Mrs. Hurley's box. Then in one quick motion, she pushed the box to the center of the table between two others. To make sure it was one of the last auctioned off, she covered it with her own basket.

"Are you guarding the food, or did you just get here?" A voice at her elbow startled Eliza.

"Oh, Kathrene. And Mary. I didn't see you come up." Eliza smiled at her friends. She held out her skirt in a curtsy. "How do you like my new dress?"

Mary straightened the collar in a motherly gesture. "I do believe you look prettiest in blue."

"Thank you." Eliza watched as her friends added their colorful boxes to the growing pile on the table. "Everyone will want to eat with you. Your boxes are so pretty and clever."

"Well, they aren't so pretty underneath. That's why we covered them with fabric scraps." Kathrene adjusted the ribbon on hers. "Of course, the food is delicious since Mother wouldn't let me help."

"I believe they're about to begin." Mary touched Kathrene's arm. "Let's move to the shade of that tree."

Eliza saw her father nearby talking to James and his mother. Her emotions churned as she watched. Then her eyes shifted to Mary. Maybe she could talk Father into buying Mary's dinner. A smile sat on Eliza's lips. It might work.

After the minister prayed, the auction began. One after another, the boxes sold, and the couples separated from the others to share the contents.

Eliza saw James and Mrs. Hurley walk away from her father. Seizing the opportunity, she stepped to his side.

Father grinned at her. "See that big box on the end? I'll bet it's got a good meal inside."

Eliza had no idea to whom it belonged, and she didn't want to take the chance. She shook her head. "No, just because it's big doesn't mean anything. Look at those two on the other side."

"In brown paper?"

"No, in calico. One is Kathrene's, and the other is her mother's. I know they'll be good."

"Your seamstresses?" The tone of his voice made it sound as if a woman couldn't do two things well.

"I'll have you know Mrs. Kowski is a good cook," Eliza announced.

"In that case, I'd better buy her box." Father was joking, but Eliza grasped his words as a lifeline.

She smiled. "Oh, yes. You will, won't you? I know you won't regret it." The auctioneer picked up the one next to it and began his chant.

A frown touched Father's forehead. "Which lady is Mrs. Kowski?"

"She's standing over there by that tree with Kathrene."

He looked where she indicated, and his eyes widened. "Do you mean the two little redheaded women? I've seen them at church and thought they were sisters. Which one's the mother?"

Eliza laughed. "Mrs. Kowski is on the right."

Father turned back without a word as the auctioneer picked up one of the fabric-covered boxes. Eliza nudged him. "That's it, Father. That's Mrs. Kowski's."

"Now what am I bid for this pretty box. Why, if the food inside's half as good as the covering, it oughta be worth a dollar. How about it? Do we hear a dollar?"

Father raised his hand. "I'll bid fifty cents."

"I got fifty cents. Do I hear seventy-five?"

Eliza held her breath. If Father didn't get Mary's box, there would be nothing she could do to stop him from buying Mrs. Hurley's.

After bidding it up to one dollar and a quarter, the auctioneer stopped. "Sold to the gentleman who keeps us in light." Father claimed his meal amid laughter.

"I believe I just bought your box, Ma'am." He offered his arm to Mary.

Eliza was surprised to see a faint blush touch Mary's cheeks. She smiled up at him and slipped her hand under his arm. "Perhaps we should find a place to eat, then."

Kathrene giggled as they walked away without a backward glance. "Well, well, imagine my mother walking out with a man after all these years."

Eliza stared after the departing couple. Her victory left a bitter taste. "What do you mean, walking out? This isn't a social engagement. We're here to raise money for the school."

Kathrene's eyebrows raised. She turned back, clasping her hands. "Look, my box is next."

"Yes, and there's Charles Wingate waiting with a smug expression on his face." Eliza inclined her head toward the young, well-dressed gentleman. "We know who you'll be eating with, don't we?"

Kathrene just smiled.

"Well, looky here. If there isn't another pretty one." The auctioneer held up Kathrene's box. "Let's see if we can start this one at a dollar. How about it?"

Charles's hand shot up. "I'll bid a dollar."

"Make it one-fifty." A stranger spoke from the edge of the crowd.

"One-fifty it is. Do I hear two?"

Charles nodded.

"Two and a quarter." The stranger's dark eyes flashed a challenge.

"Two-fifty." Charles ignored the auctioneer.

Kathrene's face flushed as she watched the two men battle over her box. Eliza nudged her. "Who is he?"

Kathrene shrugged. "I've never seen him before."

"Well, he wants your box awfully bad." Eliza stared openly at the tall young man. His dark brown hair blew across his forehead in a gust of wind. Eliza could see that he was quite handsome.

Charles called out, "Five dollars."

The stranger bowed toward his opponent. "Enjoy your meal."

Charles smiled and nodded. He held out his hand to Kathrene. "Let's find a quiet place to eat."

Eliza watched Kathrene glance over her shoulder toward the stranger. He caught her gaze and smiled.

After a couple more boxes sold, the auctioneer picked up Eliza's basket. "A finer-looking container than this couldn't be found today, gentlemen. I hear tell the contents are just as fine. What'll you give for a chance at this good meal?"

"A dollar." Again the voice of the stranger called out.

Eliza's heart quickened. Would her basket go as high as Kathrene's? She glanced toward James. Would he counterbid?

He stood in a group of men, his arms crossed. His eyes met hers. He grinned and shook his head. Her face flamed. The nerve of him.

She hadn't asked him to bid on her basket. She turned her back to him.

"I was told you are the young lady I'm to eat with." A deep voice by her side spoke.

Eliza looked into the stranger's deep brown eyes. She'd been so busy fuming about James that she hadn't realized her basket sold. Without thinking, she asked, "How much did you pay?"

His eyes twinkled as his lips lifted in a lopsided grin. "Exactly one-fifth of my present assets."

At her blank look, he took her arm to lead her away. "This day finds me a poor man, Miss . . . ?"

"Jackson." Her heart quickened at his masculine good looks. "Eliza Jackson."

"Miss Jackson. I paid one dollar for your basket and from the weight . . ." He lifted it toward his nose and sniffed. "And the aroma, I'd say I got a bargain."

Her face grew warm as her lashes lowered. "You flatter me, Mr. . . ." She looked up at him. "I don't know your name."

"Stephen Doran, Miss Jackson."

⁂

Kathrene lowered her coffee cup and smiled at Eliza. "The box social yesterday was a success, wasn't it?"

Eliza stared across the kitchen table at her friend. "A success?"

Disaster would be a better word. James hadn't bid on her basket. Stephen Doran's bid was the only one she got, and then when they joined Kathrene and Charles, he scarcely noticed her. She couldn't even bring herself to think of her father and Mary.

Eliza tried to not listen as Kathrene chatted about how much her mother had enjoyed Father's company.

One thing was certain. Mary had kept Father away from Mrs. Hurley. The entire afternoon, Eliza had seen him only once when he'd told her he was giving her friend a ride home and would come back for her and Lenny.

"Don't you think so, Eliza?" Kathrene's voice cut into her angry musings.

"Think what?"

"Stephen Doran. Don't you think he is quite handsome?" Kathrene's green eyes sparkled.

Eliza stood and walked to the sink. "You know he only bought my box so he could get close to you."

"Why, Eliza!" Kathrene's eyes widened. "Have you taken a fancy to Mr. Doran?"

Eliza let out a short laugh. "How could I take a fancy to someone who spoke no more than two sentences to me? I notice he found plenty to say to you, though." She crossed her arms. "Didn't you feel sorry for Charles? I'm sure he felt as left out as I did."

"Left out!" Kathrene jumped up, setting her coffee cup on the table with a loud *thunk*. "I think you're jealous."

"Jealous?" Past hurts and frustrations boiled in Eliza, spilling over into words she didn't mean. "How could I be jealous of you? I have everything I want right here." Her hand swept out. "You can have your Stephen, and Charles, and James, and every other man in town if you want them. I certainly don't."

"And you think I do?" Kathrene's eyes flashed. Her freckles stood out against her white face. "If that's what you think of me, I won't trouble you with my presence."

Kathrene wrenched the kitchen door open and stomped through the parlor. The bang of the front door echoed through Eliza's head, accusing her.

A verse from the Bible came to her mind. "For jealousy is the rage of a man: therefore he will not spare in the day of vengeance." Tears welled in her eyes. Kathrene was right. She was jealous.

Before she could move, the door opened and Kathrene peeked around the edge. "I'm sorry, Eliza. May I come back in?"

Eliza nodded, meeting her embrace.

"I shouldn't let my temper get away from me," Kathrene said.

"No, I started the whole thing because my pride was hurt by a stranger we'll probably never see again." Eliza wiped her eyes.

"Let's agree that no man will ever come between us," Kathrene said.

Eliza nodded.

ै़

"We've been invited to dinner at the Kowskis' Sunday after church," Father announced that evening. His wide grin gave him a boyish look.

Sunday at the Kowskis' was all Eliza had feared it would be. Her father and Mary kept up a lively conversation about church happenings, discussing the sermon that morning and their hopes for the young man who came forward for prayer.

Lenny remained quiet throughout the meal except when he asked for more to eat. Eliza frowned at him, but he didn't notice. When he finished his second helping, she picked up her own and Lenny's plates. "I'll wash the dishes, and then we need to be getting back home, don't you think, Father?"

He groaned and patted his stomach. "I don't know if I can move. You've outdone yourself on this meal, Ma'am." He smiled at Mary. "It was even better than the box social."

"Thank you." She gave him a warm smile. "I enjoy cooking."

Eliza stood and moved to the wash table. Mary's hand on her arm stopped her. "Leave the dishes to Kathrene and me. You're our guest."

Kathrene laughed. "Yes, Eliza. I may not be able to cook, but I can wash dishes."

Eliza smiled before turning to her father. "Don't you think we should be going? I'd like to rest before church tonight." She stepped toward the door.

Father pushed his chair back and stood. "Come on, Lenny. You heard your sister." He looked at Eliza with an affectionate smile. "I don't know what I'd do without my little girl. She's taken over the running of the house and Lenny and me." He patted her shoulder. "Does a real good job, too."

She looked up at him with accusing eyes. "Thank you, Father, but Mother was a good teacher."

Mary met her stony gaze with a warm smile. "Your mother must have been a wonderful woman to have raised such a beautiful daughter."

Eliza's lashes lowered. "Thank you, Mary. Yes, my mother was a wonderful woman."

But was she the only one who thought so? Father seemed to have forgotten his late wife as his interest in Mary grew. At church that evening Father sat beside Mary.

8

*E*liza watched her father's relationship with Mary develop and knew she could only blame herself. One day, toward the middle of June, he came into the chandler shop and told her Mary had agreed to become his wife.

After he left, Eliza stood in the middle of the floor while the words *He doesn't mean it* kept running through her mind.

"Did I catch you daydreaming?" James's voice penetrated her befuddled brain.

"What do you want?" Did he always have to catch her at a disadvantage?

"I have a question for your father."

"He isn't here." Eliza didn't want to be rude to James, but she couldn't seem to stop.

"It's a good thing you don't have any customers." James lounged against the counter.

Eliza turned her full gaze on him for the first time since he came into the shop. "Why?"

A slow grin spread his mouth. His eyes twinkled merrily. "Because, Miss Jackson, an old grouch like you would drive a less brave person away. What's got your back up today?"

Her hands clenched at her sides. "My father."

Sandy-colored eyebrows arched above his gray eyes. "Your father?"

"He says he's getting married."

"To Mrs. Kowski?"

She nodded. Tears filled her eyes. "Oh, James . . ." Her voice broke, and she found herself leaning against his chest. His arms encircled her as the tears fell.

After awhile she stepped back and blew her nose. "I'm sorry. I don't usually cry in public."

"No one's here but me." James smiled tenderly at her. "Are you going to be all right now?"

She tried a smile of her own. "I don't think I'll ever be all right with my father remarrying. But I'm okay now. Thank you."

"I guess I'd better get back to work then." James moved to the door. "When your father comes back, would you tell him I need to ask him something?"

She nodded.

He opened the door. "And, Eliza . . ."

She looked at him.

"If there's anything I can do, you know where to find me."

When her father returned, Eliza told him James had been looking for him. He went to the cooperage and stayed there the rest of the day.

A couple of days later Eliza came into the house from the garden with her apron full of new potatoes and green onions. Father and Lenny sat at the kitchen table.

"You mean I get to stand up in front of the church with you?"

"That's right." Father smiled at his son. "I think you're old enough to do that, don't you?"

Eliza tried to ignore them as she set the vegetables out on her work counter. Lenny didn't understand what it would do to their lives if Father remarried. Eliza picked up a potato, washed it in a pan of water, and began scrubbing the soft skin off.

"What about Eliza?" Lenny asked. "She gonna do somethin', too?"

"Of course." Eliza could feel her father looking at her, but she refused to turn around. "Mary wants Eliza and Kathrene to stand beside her to demonstrate that we'll all be one family." Father cleared his throat. "Why don't you run along so I can talk to Eliza now?"

"Okay." Lenny slammed the door on his way out.

Eliza stiffened when her father moved to her side.

"I'd like for you to be happy for us, Eliza." Father's voice was low and pleading.

A flush moved over Eliza's body. So Father knew how she felt. She sighed. She never had been good at keeping her feelings to herself. "I don't want you to marry her, Father. How can you replace Mother so easily?"

Her father flinched as if she had hit him. "I loved your mother. I still love her memory and always will. Mary is not a replacement for Mother. I will never forget your mother, Eliza. But I love Mary for herself, and I intend to marry her for that reason."

"I don't want you to marry her, Father," Eliza repeated with stubborn determination.

When her declaration met with silence, she turned toward him. The saddest look Eliza had ever seen covered his face. "I love you very much, Eliza, and I'm sorry you feel this way; but in all honesty, I have a perfect right to remarry. I'm trusting God that in time you'll accept it. In the meantime, Mary is waiting for you to pick out your dress."

Shame for her thoughts and words filled her heart. Still, she could not bring herself to accept her father's decision to remarry. "I don't need a new dress."

Father frowned. "Go to Leach's this afternoon and get some fabric to take to Mary. She's got enough to do without waiting until the last minute to make your dress."

Eliza knew she had pushed her father far enough. She nodded and turned back to her vegetables.

$\delta\rightarrow$

Eliza walked to town that afternoon, kicking at every rock in her path. She crossed the square and entered Leach's General Store.

"Good afternoon, Miss Jackson," Mr. Leach greeted her. "What can I do for you?"

"I'd like to look around, if you don't mind."

"Not at all. Make yourself at home." He turned back toward the door as the bell rang again.

Eliza wove her way through the barrels and counters of merchandise toward the stacks of fabric along the far wall. She held a blue silk up to her face.

"That's very beautiful," Mrs. Wingate spoke beside her.

Eliza lifted her head in surprise. She hadn't heard anyone approach. "Yes, it is."

"I understand your father and Mary Kowski will be married in a few weeks."

Eliza shrugged. "Yes, I suppose so."

Mrs. Wingate laid a sympathetic hand on Eliza's arm. "Don't you think your father ever gets lonely?"

"He has Lenny and me. Why would he need anyone else?"

"You won't always live at home." Mrs. Wingate smiled. "Eliza, many older people who have lost their spouses remarry for companionship and to share the burden of living."

Eliza remembered her father's confession that he had eaten downtown before she and Lenny came. He loved Mary's cooking. Surely, Father's marriage would be one of convenience. When Mrs. Wingate left, Eliza turned back to the fabric with a lighter heart.

Mary finished Eliza's dress the day before the wedding. When she went to pick it up, Kathrene met her at the door. "Mother went to town with your father, but I guess you already knew that."

"No." Eliza frowned, hurt that Kathrene knew her father's whereabouts when she didn't.

Kathrene pulled her inside. "Come and see what I've got." She pointed at a small round table by the window. An assortment of wildflowers filled the vase sitting in the center.

"Where did you get those?"

Kathrene blushed. "Do you remember Mr. Doran, the young man who bought your box at the social?"

How could she forget?

"He gave them to me." Her voice dropped to a whisper. "He asked me to walk out with him."

"You didn't . . . ?"

Kathrene shook her head. "No, of course not. We know nothing about him."

"What about Charles?"

Kathrene flashed a smile. "What of Charles? He's a good friend, nothing more."

Eliza followed her into the bedroom, where her dress lay across the bed. She couldn't help noticing the sparse furnishings in the small cabin. Kathrene and her mother shared the double bed that took up most of the floor space in the small room. Her bedroom was twice the size of theirs.

Eliza scarcely noticed her dress as she looked around the small cabin. Her eyes rested on the cracked chinking in the walls, and she wondered how the women survived the cold winter winds. Mary had good reason to marry her father.

She smoothed the billowing blue silk skirt and smiled at Kathrene. "It's very lovely, as is all your work. I'll wear it proudly when I stand beside you tomorrow."

⅋

"Dearly beloved, we are gathered together . . ."

It was a lie—the five of them standing up together as one family. Eliza tried to forget where she was. She did fine until the minister turned to her father.

"Wilt thou love her, comfort her, honor, and keep her, in sickness and in health; and, forsaking all others, keep thee only unto her, so long as ye both shall live?"

A hard, empty ball expanded inside her stomach. Surely she had never missed her mother more than at that moment.

As in a dream, Eliza watched her father slip a gold wedding band on Mary's finger. The minister said, "I now pronounce you man and wife. What, therefore, God hath joined together, let not man put asunder."

Eliza bowed her head with the others as the minister prayed, but she did not anticipate his words when the prayer ended.

The minister nodded to her father. "You may kiss your bride now."

Father gathered Mary into his arms. Eliza stared hard at the floor. How could he kiss her? Mercifully, the moment was over quickly.

Kathrene elbowed her. "We're supposed to follow the bride and groom outside."

"How wonderful! You two girls are sisters now." Mrs. Wingate stopped them near the back door. "Congratulations."

"Thank you, Mrs. Wingate," Kathrene answered for them both.

Charles stepped around his mother as she turned away. He smiled at Kathrene. "May I have the pleasure of your company for dinner?"

"We would be honored, wouldn't we, Eliza?"

"You go. I'll eat alone." Eliza dropped Kathrene's arm and slipped outside into the fresh air. She had never felt so alone in her life.

She crossed her arms, leaning her shoulder against a tree. A slight breeze ruffled her hair. She lifted her face to it, closed her eyes, and let it cool her cheeks.

"Eliza," James's low voice intruded.

Again he appeared at the worst possible time. She opened her eyes to look at him. "What do you want?"

He laughed. "Your use of the English language never ceases to amaze me. Are you always so stingy with words, or is it just with me?"

She sighed. "I'm sorry. It isn't you."

He grinned. "Good. I wanted to ask you to eat with me." His voice lowered. "I know you're having a hard time today. I'd like to help if I can."

Eliza gave a short laugh. "I don't think that's possible. They're already married."

"Sometimes having a friend helps."

"A friend?" Eliza hadn't thought of James as a friend before and wasn't sure she wanted to. She suddenly realized that "friend" didn't sound like enough.

At his nod, she smiled. "All right."

She looked up, saw Vanda approaching, and called to her. "I was afraid you wouldn't be here."

Vanda's laugh brightened Eliza's mood. "Me? Miss my best friend's father's wedding? Not on your life."

She looked at James.

Eliza moved away from the tree. "James is eating with us. Is that all right with you?"

Vanda shrugged. "Sure, but I think we'd better be going if we're going to get anything."

They reached the grounds set aside for the dinner just as the minister prayed. Mary and Father led the line and then sat at a special table prepared especially for them. A white cotton tablecloth covered the rough wood, giving the table an elegant look.

Vanda peered closely at her friend. "Do you think you'll like having a new mother?"

Eliza's eyes narrowed. "You mean stepmother, don't you?"

Vanda nodded. "I guess that answers my question."

"I don't mean to be so snappish. This whole thing has been a strain."

"Maybe we should get in line." James touched Eliza's arm.

Lenny and Cletis ran past. "Hey, you gonna stand there and let all the food get ate up? Come on. We'll let you get in front of us."

Vanda lifted her eyebrows. "I wonder why they're so interested in us all of a sudden."

They wound around tablecloths spread on the ground picnic style and people with their plates piled high. Lenny and Cletis stepped back for each of the stragglers until the last guest was in line.

Vanda frowned. "They must be up to something."

James laughed. "They're boys. Boys are almost always up to something."

"I suppose you know from experience?" Eliza realized she felt better. James was right; she had needed to be with friends.

"Of course." He grinned down at her, making her heart do flip-flops.

Eliza smiled but agreed with Vanda. She knew her brother. Sometimes Lenny was more than she could handle, and as much as she liked Vanda, she realized his behavior had gotten worse under Cletis's influence.

As Eliza filled her plate, she saw Lenny and Cletis scramble from under the table where Mary and Father sat. The boys ran a short distance away. They stood behind a large oak tree, their hands stifling giggles, their eyes dancing in merriment.

She kept them in sight as she ate. She was certain they had pulled a prank on Father and Mary, but she couldn't think what it might be. With her attention divided, she kept up her end of a lively conversation with James and Vanda.

Vanda glanced over the crowd. "What happened to our brothers? I forgot to watch them."

Eliza nodded toward the oak tree. "They're standing over there." Even as she spoke, the merriment went out of the boys' faces. Lenny's eyes grew wide. Cletis grabbed his arm, pulling him back.

"What on earth are they doing?" Vanda sounded as puzzled as Eliza felt.

"Maybe we'd better find out what they've already done." Eliza looked toward the table where her father sat. Father and Mary were visiting with others who had joined them. Eliza let her gaze roam over the table, trying to find something out of place.

And then she saw it. A thin wisp of smoke curled upward from the end of the table. As she watched, the smoke disappeared in a sudden burst of flames.

"Fire!" Eliza's outcry created pandemonium. Father lifted Mary from her seat. With one arm around her, he tossed his glass of water on the flame. Others followed his lead as they scrambled back from the burning cloth.

"Cletis and Lenny did that, didn't they?" Vanda searched through the excited crowd. "Where are they?"

Eliza pointed. "They just ducked behind that tree."

The two girls set off in a run to catch their brothers. As angry as Eliza was at Lenny, she was even more angry with herself. She had known he was up to something, and she hadn't stopped him.

Vanda grabbed Cletis first and held tight in spite of his squirming attempts to escape. Lenny ran a few steps before Eliza caught his arm. He turned wide, fearful eyes on her. "We didn't mean to, honest."

"That's right. We didn't make any fire." Cletis tried to wrench out of Vanda's grasp. "Ow! You're hurtin' me."

"I'll hurt you a whole lot more if you don't tell the truth." As Vanda reached for a better grip on her brother, he jerked free. He stumbled from the sudden release, then took off running. Vanda turned a troubled face toward Eliza. "I hate to think what Poppa will do to him when he finds out. I'd better catch him." She left in a run, calling over her shoulder, "I'm sorry."

Eliza watched her for a moment before turning toward the crowd gathered around the table. She looked down at Lenny. "Well, are you going to tell me what happened, or would you rather tell Father?"

He shrugged his shoulders. "I told you we didn't mean to."

Eliza closed her eyes for a moment, then looked at her brother. "Lenny, you obviously did something, even if you didn't mean to. What did you do?"

He clamped his lips shut, looking defiantly up at her.

"All right, then." Anger welled up in Eliza as she pulled him toward their father.

9

*L*enny trembled beneath Eliza's hands. Her anger turned toward Cletis. How dare he run off and leave Lenny to take the blame for what he had instigated!

"Leonard Jackson, do you know what this is?" Father held a small object between his fingers.

Lenny nodded. "It looks like an old firecracker, Sir."

"It's a firecracker, all right, but it's not old, and you know it." Father pointed a finger at Lenny. "Go to the buggy and wait until we come."

Lenny jerked from Eliza's grasp and ran. Eliza looked up, meeting the gray eyes of James Hurley. "I hope your father isn't too hard on Lenny."

"Why? Don't you think he deserves to be punished?"

He shrugged. "Probably, but I doubt there's a man here that hasn't pulled a stupid trick like that at some time in their lives. It's part of growing up."

"Trying to blow up the table your father is sitting at is more than a stupid trick."

James laughed. "That little firecracker wouldn't have done much more than make a big noise."

"But it didn't make any noise. Instead it made a fire." She crossed her arms. "You know, what's bad is that Cletis Von Hall got away, and he was probably the one who did it. Lenny was just with him."

James lifted his eyebrows. "In that case we'd better hope that Vanda doesn't tell her father what happened."

"Well, I should hope she would," Eliza said. "He deserves to be punished even more than Lenny."

"I suppose, but—"

"Eliza, are you ready to go?" Her father stood with his arm around Mary's waist. "Kathrene is coming later with Charles."

Eliza looked at James. "I guess I need to go."

He nodded. "I'll see you at church tonight." He turned and walked away.

≈

As soon as they entered the house, Father laid a gentle hand on Eliza's shoulder. "Would you mind going upstairs? I need to talk to your brother alone."

Eliza sat on the stairs out of sight while her father decided Lenny's punishment. When Mary suggested he not play with Cletis for two weeks, she crept upstairs to her room.

Eliza felt the strain of the day especially at supper that evening. As soon as her father laid his spoon down, she pushed her chair back, picking up her bowl. "I'll wash dishes."

"No, Eliza," Father said. "The dishes can wait. Mary and I have something to say."

Father looked first at Eliza, then Lenny, and finally Kathrene, before his eyes met Mary's. She nodded slightly.

He smiled at her and began. "Mary and I have decided it would be good for us to go away for a short time."

"Where are we goin'?" Lenny asked.

"Not all of us, Son." Father ran his hand over his thinning hair in a nervous gesture. "I meant just Mary and me."

Lenny frowned. "What do you wanna do that for?"

Kathrene leaned forward, a smile on her face. "I think that's a wonderful idea. When will you be leaving?"

"In the morning." Father turned to her. "I just need to speak to James tonight, we'll pack a few things, and then try to get as early a start as we can tomorrow."

"Well, don't worry about us. We'll get along just fine." Kathrene shared a smile with her mother.

Eliza shrugged when her father's gaze met hers. "Sure, we'll be fine."

Father's hazel eyes darkened. He reached across the corner of the table to clasp her hand. His voice was soft. "Eliza, we're going after Nora."

Eliza sat in stunned silence until she pulled away from her father, her chair crashing to the floor as she sprang up and ran from the room, the dishes forgotten.

Emotions she didn't understand flooded her being as she stumbled up the stairs to her room. For almost a year she had planned to go with Father when he brought her sister home. Now Mary would be the one. Mary would take over her sister, her father, and even her house. She fell across the bed to release a torrent of tears into her pillow.

ঌ

Sometime later, a tap on the door brought Eliza upright. "Who is it?" Her voice sounded hoarse from crying.

"Kathrene. May I come in?"

Eliza scrambled from the bed and across the room to her washbasin. She splashed cool water on her face and blotted it with a towel. She moved to the door, smoothing her wrinkled dress with her hands.

If the remains of her crying bout were still on her face, Kathrene made no notice. She stepped into the room, a gentle smile the only evidence of her concern. "They sent me to tell you it's time to get ready for church."

"You're glad, aren't you?" Eliza struggled with the hooks on her dress.

"Glad about what?" Kathrene's hands felt cool against her back as she helped.

Eliza stood still to let Kathrene unfasten her dress. "All of it. Your mother. My father."

"In a way I am. Mother has been alone so long. I'm happy she has someone to love and to love her."

Eliza felt tears burn her eyes. "What about your father? Have you forgotten him? I haven't forgotten Mother and neither has my father. He'll never forget her. He'll always love her."

"Oh, Eliza, of course I haven't forgotten my father."

Eliza turned and saw the matching tears in Kathrene's eyes. "Mother will always love him. But I should hope there's room in her heart to love your father, too."

ع

The evening service passed in a blur until James stopped her after church. Concern softened his expression. "Are you all right, Eliza?"

"Do you know how many times you've asked me that in the time you've known me?"

He smiled. "No, it does appear to be a habit I'm developing."

"I don't know if I'll ever be all right again. When my mother died, my world was turned upside down. It just seems to get worse every day."

"I'd like to help if I . . ." His voice trailed off as Eliza's father placed a hand on his shoulder.

"Mr. Hurley, you are just the person I need to talk to."

Eliza backed away. She felt betrayed and cheated as her father made arrangements to return to their wilderness home without her.

When they got home, Mary turned toward Father's bedroom, her bonnet and their Bibles clutched in her arms. Eliza stared at her as she went through the door.

"Come on, Eliza." Kathrene tugged on her arm. "There's no towel in my room. Where do you keep them? Your father said he didn't know."

Eliza followed Kathrene up the stairs.

Kathrene led her to the guest room and stepped inside. Eliza pulled the middle drawer of the chest of drawers open to reveal neat stacks of towels and washcloths. She looked at the bed where Kathrene's dress of the afternoon sprawled where it had been thrown. A petticoat lay in a circled heap on the floor as if she had just stepped out of it. Even Cora hadn't been this careless with her things.

Kathrene pulled a washcloth and towel from the drawer and turned to the washbasin, a bright smile on her face. "This room is so wonderful. I've never had a room all my own before. And this is such a big, pretty room. I love it."

Somehow the idea that Mary had married Father for their house eased Eliza's pain.

಼

Eliza pushed her bedroom curtain aside and looked out. In the early morning light she watched her father's wagon move slowly out of the yard. A movement on the seat in front caught her eye. Father waved at her. Mary, sitting beside him, looked up and waved, too.

Eliza hadn't found it in her heart to see them off like Kathrene and Lenny had. As soon as breakfast was over, she had told them goodbye and retreated to her room. She lifted her hand for a moment and then let the curtain drop back into place.

She sank to her bed, where she stayed until a knock on her door interrupted her time of self-pity. "Eliza, please, may I come in?"

"What do you want?"

There was a moment's silence, and then Kathrene said, "It's Lenny. I can't find him."

"He's probably outside playing."

"I don't think so. He was in the house reading while I washed the breakfast dishes. I went out to feed the chickens, and when I came in, he was gone."

"Those chickens are mine. Father bought them for me." Eliza pulled the door open to glare at Kathrene.

"I know they're yours, Eliza. I was just feeding them." Kathrene's voice was soft. "I thought you might want some time alone this morning."

Eliza's gaze dropped to the floor, her conscience pricked.

"I've looked everywhere, Eliza. I don't know what else to do. Your father said Lenny was not to go anywhere without our permission. Don't you think we should do something?"

Eliza shrugged and met Kathrene's worried gaze. "He's probably run off to play with Cletis. He'll come home as soon as he gets hungry."

A spark of green fire lit Kathrene's eyes. "He's disobeying his father, and I'm not going to let him get away with it. We have a responsibility to see that Lenny obeys. If we don't stop him now, he won't listen to a thing we say the entire two weeks our parents are gone."

Finally Eliza nodded. "All right. Let me get my bonnet. I'll go downtown and see what I can find out." She turned back into the room.

"Shouldn't I go, too?" Kathrene followed her. "Isn't there someplace I could look?"

Eliza tied her bonnet under her chin. "No. I think you should stay here in case he comes back."

"I suppose you're right." Kathrene looked doubtful. "But if he isn't back by dinner, I'll go with you this afternoon."

Eliza laughed off Kathrene's concern. "Oh, don't worry, he'll be here when it's time to eat."

The midmorning sun warmed her back as she tried to imagine where little boys went on summer mornings. She knew they sometimes rolled wagon rims across the square. Maybe James had seen Lenny.

Eliza went to her father's shops. James was busy with a customer, so she stepped inside and waited.

After placing his order, the man left, nodding to Eliza. James looked up with a smile. "I didn't expect the pleasure of your company today. What can I do for you?"

"I'm looking for Lenny and thought you might have seen him."

James's smile disappeared. He shook his head. "No, I haven't seen him. Is something wrong?"

She shrugged. "Probably not. He just left home without permission."

"I'll close up shop and help you look."

"No, that's not necessary." She stepped back. "I'm sure he'll come home at noon to eat."

James shrugged. "All right. I'll keep an eye out. Maybe he'll come by."

"Thank you." She turned and ran from the shop. She asked Mr. Leach and looked everywhere she could think but didn't find him.

Kathrene and Eliza ate a hurried meal at noon. Eliza expected any moment to hear the front door open and see Lenny come in demanding food. But he didn't.

"Where should we go?" Kathrene placed her plate on the counter. She turned as Eliza started to speak. "And don't tell me I have to stay home again. I won't do it. I may be just a stepsister, but I care."

"All right, we'll go together." Eliza sighed. What if Lenny wasn't with Cletis? What if something terrible had happened? She didn't know where to look for him. Surely she had exhausted every possible place that morning.

"Where will we look?" Kathrene asked again.

"I guess we could go back to town." She stood and picked up her plate. "Maybe Mr. Leach has seen him since I was there."

But Mr. Leach shook his head. "No, I haven't seen him since church last night."

"Where do we go now?" Kathrene asked.

Eliza looked across the square at the cooperage. Should she check back with James? She knew he would willingly drop whatever he was doing to help them search. While she tried to decide, she saw Vanda walking toward them.

"There's Vanda. Maybe she knows something."

The girls met in the middle of the square.

"Have you seen Lenny?"

"Have you seen Cletis?" Both spoke at once.

"That settles it." Eliza sighed. "They're together, but where are they?"

"I don't know." Vanda frowned. "Cletis slipped out early this morning after my father left. I managed to keep his stupid prank yesterday quiet, but if he doesn't get back home before long, there'll be nothing I can do."

"Have you talked to Trennen? Maybe he has seen them." Eliza felt as if she were grasping for straws.

Vanda nodded. "I just came from the Wingates'. Where have you looked?"

Eliza's hand swept out in an all-inclusive gesture. "Everywhere we could think of. Do you know of any special places they might go?"

Vanda looked thoughtful. "Have you looked at the creek?"

"I didn't know there was a creek." Eliza's eyes grew wide. Until that moment she hadn't thought that Lenny might be hurt. "You don't think they've drowned, do you?"

"No, I didn't mean that." Vanda started across the square. "There's a creek just northwest of town. It has a quiet spot where the boys like to swim. As warm as it is today, they might be there."

The girls turned down the dirt road leading west out of town. Eliza sighed, and Kathrene looked at her. "It is terribly warm, isn't it?"

She nodded. "I understand if they went swimming in this heat, but Lenny's still in trouble."

"Cletis, too. It isn't much farther." Vanda pointed to their right. "Just beyond those trees."

Before they were through the trees, Eliza heard laughter. Her temper flared, and she ran into the clearing on the bank of the creek. Lenny was there, all right. So were three other boys, including Cletis. And all were stripped to the bare skin.

"Oh, my." Kathrene's soft gasp as she came up behind Eliza stopped the boys' horseplay, and all four dove under the water.

Cletis was the first to break the surface with a ferocious scowl. "Get outta here. Go on. Beat it." He hit the water toward them.

The other boys came up for air one at a time. Guilt sat on Lenny's face even as he frowned at Eliza. "Yeah. Go away." He copied his friend.

Eliza wasn't sure what to do. The boys' clothing was scattered along the bank where they had let it fall. She knew they couldn't come out of the water as long as the girls were there, yet how could they be trusted to come if someone didn't stay and enforce it?

Vanda planted her hands on her hips. "Cletis, if you don't get out of there, I'll come in and get you." She picked up some pants from a pile of clothing, then stepped to the edge of the creek, her feet just inches from the water. "Here, put these on."

"I can't. I'll get 'em all wet. What do we gotta get out of here for, anyhow?" Cletis asked. "We ain't hurtin' no one."

"Poppa's going to be home in a couple of hours, Cletis. You know that."

The change in Cletis's expression amazed Eliza. "Guess you guys heard. We gotta go home now."

At their outcry, he shrugged. "Can't help it. That's just the way things is. We'll come back tomorrow."

Eliza thought to herself, *Oh, no, you won't.* She kept her opinion quiet, though, saving it until she had a firm grip on Lenny.

"We ain't gettin' outta here with you standin' there," Cletis yelled at his sister. "Go on. I'll be along shortly."

"All right. I'll go, but you'd better follow me home. And the rest of you better go on home, too."

As she talked, Vanda tossed Cletis's pants to the side. What happened next took them all by surprise. Vanda stepped backward, landing on loose rock. Her ankle twisted under her. Her arms flew up as if to embrace the creek, and she fell full length, face forward into the water.

The boys' hoots of laughter as Vanda struggled to right herself released Eliza from her stupor. She rushed to the water's edge, shouting at them to be quiet. "Don't you know Vanda could be hurt?"

She reached her hand toward Vanda. "Here, let me help you out."

Vanda sat in waist-deep water, her clinging skirts draped about her bent knees. Her face flamed as she struggle to her feet. "I can do it."

Eliza asked, "Can you make it to my house?"

At Vanda's nod Eliza turned to the boys, still watching with smirks on their faces. "As soon as we're gone, you get out of there and go home. Do you understand me?"

"We done said we would, didn't we?" Cletis answered for them all.

She turned away, knowing she would have to trust them. Vanda needed her immediate attention, and she wouldn't worry now that she knew where Lenny was.

The three girls set out, walking quietly until they were past the grove of trees. Then a giggle came from Vanda. Eliza looked at her in surprise. Their eyes met, and the merriment in Vanda's expression was contagious.

"I must have looked ridiculous sitting in that water." She grinned.

As Eliza nodded, laughter burst from both girls. Before long all three were laughing hysterically.

As they neared town, Kathrene gained control first. She spoke between giggles, "Honestly, I'm just glad you didn't get hurt."

"So am I." Vanda looked down at her dress. She held it away from her legs as she walked. "I feel stupid. Dunking myself that way." She grew sober. "Maybe I should go on home."

Kathrene shook her head. "It'll be no trouble for you to stop by our house and change."

Eliza led the way upstairs to her room while Kathrene headed for the kitchen to wash the neglected dishes from their meal.

Eliza crossed to the bed and spread the quilt over it. "When we discovered Lenny gone this morning, our housework was forgotten." She apologized for her unmade bed in the otherwise neat room.

"Your house looks wonderful to me." Vanda stood in the middle of the floor. "I'm afraid I may drip on your rug, though."

"Don't worry about it." Eliza opened the door to her wardrobe. She reached for one of the dresses Mary had made, but Vanda stopped her.

"How about this one instead?" Vanda pulled one of Eliza's oldest dresses from the wardrobe.

"Take one of these new ones."

"If I can't wear this one, I won't borrow any." A determined light shone in Vanda's eyes.

"All right, but I don't feel like much of a friend letting you wear that old thing."

"You're the best friend I've ever had, Eliza." Vanda turned away, peeling out of her wet dress.

Eliza laid some underclothes on the bed and reached to take the dress. "Here, I'll hang your clothes outside to dry." She opened the door and started through it when a large yellow and green bruise on Vanda's back caught her eye. Vanda's wet, tangled hair hung down, covering most of it.

She spoke before she thought. "What did you do to your back? It looks like someone took a stick to you."

Vanda looked over her shoulder at Eliza and laughed. "Don't be silly."

"There's a huge bruise on your back."

Vanda appeared to be puzzled. She tried to see her back by twisting around. "Maybe I fell on a rock in the creek."

"Maybe."

Eliza vaguely remembered seeing old bruises on Vanda's face and arms before, but she didn't pursue the subject; because at that moment the downstairs door slammed, and Lenny's voice called out, "I'm home now, and I hope you're satisfied. You just ruined a good afternoon for me."

"Whoa, Fellow, I'd rephrase that if I were you."

Eliza's eyes grew wide as she recognized James's voice. "Your sister's not the one who took off without telling anyone where she was going."

Vanda grabbed up the undergarments and began pulling them on. "Oh, dear. It must be getting late. I've got to get home before Poppa does."

Eliza barely heard her as she traced James's and Lenny's voices going into the kitchen. What was James doing here? Her heart rate increased as she closed the door and moved down the hall to the stairs.

$$\textbf{10}$$

s Eliza carried Vanda's wet dress through the parlor, she saw Lenny curled up on the sofa, already engrossed in a book, munching a slice of bread. James straddled a chair in the kitchen. She didn't look at him, even though she could feel his eyes on her.

She pinned the garments to the clothesline, returned to the house, and walked back across the kitchen. James's voice, mocking, followed her into the parlor.

"Good afternoon, James. Thank you for closing up the shop while you looked for my little lost brother. You can't imagine how much I appreciate it."

Vanda ran down the stairs, her hair in wet ringlets down her back. "Eliza, thank you so much for the loan of this dress I'll be especially careful with it." She pulled the front door open. "I've got to get home now. Cletis and Poppa will be wanting supper."

Eliza closed the door behind Vanda. She took a deep breath, then pushed the kitchen door open.

Eliza caught the twinkle in his eyes as James grinned at her. She turned away to hide her own smile. "Vanda's gone. She had to hurry home to fix supper for her father."

Kathrene dried her hands and hung the tea towel by the sink. "I guess she found some clothes to wear."

"Yes." Eliza nodded. "She took one of my oldest dresses. I couldn't get her to take a nicer one."

James cleared his throat noisily. Eliza turned to see a wide smile on his face. "Good afternoon, Eliza."

The corners of her mouth twitched. "Good afternoon, James. I've been so busy I haven't had time to tell you how much I appreciate the help you gave us in finding Lenny. I'm sure we couldn't have done it without you."

James stared at her. His smile faded and then came back with a laugh. He stood, shoving the chair under the table. "All right. Maybe I didn't find him, but I looked. When Mr. Leach said you still hadn't found him after dinner, I closed shop and looked everywhere I could think of. I just didn't think of the creek."

Eliza's conscience smote her as she listened to James's deep voice. "I'm sorry, James. I didn't realize. Really, I thank you for being concerned."

"That's all right." He stepped around Eliza to the door. "I'd better get back to work. There are still a few hours left in this day."

He nodded toward Kathrene, his gaze returning to linger on Eliza. "I'll let myself out. Bye, Eliza. Kathrene."

The day Father, Mary, and Nora were due home, Eliza left the dishes to Kathrene while she took the butter churn and a chair from the kitchen to the back porch. Lenny had behaved himself after the creek incident, but first one thing and then another had brought James to their door the last two weeks. First it was milk and now cream. He claimed his cow was giving more than they could use. And twice he had come about shop business. As if Eliza knew anything about making barrels. Mostly they'd just talked about nothing in particular before he went back to work. Eliza smiled, thinking how much she enjoyed his company.

She poured in the cream, dropped the wooden lid in place, and sat with her legs straddling the churn. As she worked, butter slowly emerged from the liquid while her arms grew tired. She lifted the lid to peer inside. Pale yellow clumps floated in the cream. Her butter was done.

She dropped the lid back into place at the sound of a wagon on the road. Her butter forgotten, she hurried from the porch and around the house. Father pulled back on the reins, bringing the wagon to a stop before jumping off to catch Eliza in a bear hug.

He pulled back and looked over her head. "I see the house is still standing."

She acted indignant. "Father, you know I'm quite capable of taking care of things."

He laughed as Kathrene and Lenny rushed from the house. "Why didn't you tell us they were back?" Kathrene admonished Eliza as she brushed past to give Father a quick hug. He then swept Lenny up and hugged him close.

Lenny's wide smile belied his protest. "Hey, I ain't no baby." His thin arms circled his father's neck and squeezed tight.

Mary, holding three-year-old Nora on her lap, watched her husband's homecoming with a smile before calling to him, "I'd like my share of hugs."

Father set Lenny down and reached up to circle her waist with his hands. "I was being selfish, wasn't I?"

"Just a little, but you're forgiven." She smiled down at him. "Why don't you take Nora first? I think Eliza is aching to get hold of her."

Nora was fine when Father handed her to Eliza, but the minute Mary's feet touched the ground, she began struggling to be free. "Mama, I want Mama." Her little arms reached toward Mary.

Eliza felt as if she'd been slapped. "Nora, don't you remember me?" She stroked the little girl's velvety face.

A wail mixed with cries for "Mama" was her answer. Nora's large brown eyes became puddles of distress, filling and overflowing down her cheeks. Nora strained against Eliza's hold, leaning her little body as far as she could toward Mary.

Mary reached for Nora. "I don't know what is the matter with her. It's really hard to tell what little ones are thinking."

Nora snuggled her head against Mary's shoulder and popped her thumb into her mouth.

Eliza saw the look of sympathy on Kathrene's face, and her heart hardened. This wouldn't have happened if she'd been allowed to go with Father.

Mary walked toward the house with Kathrene close beside her. They disappeared inside while Eliza stood watching.

Father patted Eliza's shoulder as he turned toward the wagon. "Don't worry about Nora. She'll come around. Remember, it's been a long time since she's seen you."

Eliza shrugged from his hand. She didn't want sympathy. She wanted her little sister. She went back to the butter she had left on the porch.

She soon had the butter wrapped and stored in the cellar and the buttermilk in a half-gallon jar ready to drink for breakfast. She was closing the cellar door when Father found her.

"So there you are. I've been looking for you." He grinned at her, slipping his arm around her shoulders. "I was beginning to think you'd disappeared."

She shook her head. "No, just working as usual. Mr. Hurley's cow is suddenly giving more than they can use. I made some butter."

Father laughed, giving her a quick hug. "That's my Eliza. One day you'll make some man a good wife. You're a lot like your mother, you know."

"I am?" Eliza looked up at her father. He couldn't have given her a nicer compliment.

"Yes, you are, more so than either Vickie or Cora." He sat on the back steps. "Here, sit beside me. I have some things to tell you."

Eliza's heart constricted at the serious look on his face. She sat beside him, turning so she could watch his expression as he talked.

His smile gentled, not lighting his face the way it usually did. "I've got letters from the girls for you."

"What's wrong?"

He sighed, looking off to the horizon before he answered. "It's Ben and Esther. On the first day of May, three months ago, they had a little girl. They named her Agnes Danielle. She died before the sun set that same day."

"Oh." The one word rushed out with the air Eliza had been holding. Her eyes filled with tears of sympathy for her brother and his wife. "How terrible."

"Ben and Esther are strong. Their faith in God will see them through."

As she thought of Ben and Esther's loss, her own problems seemed trivial. If they could remain strong, so could she. She brushed at her eyes and stood. "I'm glad you told me. Maybe God will give them another baby."

"Yes, maybe so." Father stood and reached for the back door. "Come on inside, and I'll give you those letters. They wrote to Lenny and Kathrene, too."

Kathrene? Why would they write to her? She walked ahead of her father into the kitchen and took the letters from him. She smiled, holding them close to her heart. "I'll be in my room if you need me."

He grinned. "Don't worry. We won't bother you until you've finished reading."

"Thanks, Father." She reached up on her tiptoes to kiss him on the cheek. "I'm glad you're home." Then she turned and walked toward the parlor. She stopped, her hand on the door. "Father, what about the other two babies? Are they all right?"

"They're as fat and sassy as any two babies I've ever seen."

"And you're not proud of them?" She smiled at the obvious pride on his face.

"Of course I am. Now you get on upstairs and read your letters before I tell you everything that's in them."

Her smile faded when she caught sight of Kathrene on the sofa poring over the letters she had received. She looked up at Eliza, a wide smile on her lips. "You don't know how blessed you are to have sisters. All my life I wanted a sister, and now I have five."

Eliza forced a smile that she didn't feel and ran up the stairs to her room. She fell across her bed. She could hardly wait to read her letters. She placed them all in a neat stack to the side and reached for the first one.

As soon as Eliza opened her letter and saw the carefully printed script inside, she realized it was not from one of her sisters but from Grace Newkirk.

I miss our times together. I have no one to share my secrets with. My biggest news isn't much of a secret. Eliza, I'm going to be married. I wish you could stand with me at our wedding early next spring. I'll be Mrs. Jack Seymour. His family moved in this past spring. He's a wonderful Christian man. He's good, kind, and thoughtful. I know you'd love him, too, if you were here. (But not as much as I do!)

The ink on the page blurred as Eliza stared at it. So Grace was getting married. A gnawing pain pulled at her stomach.

She rolled over on her back, still clutching Grace's letter. Cora, Esther, and Ivy were all married, and now Grace had found the right man. Even Kathrene, who couldn't cook or keep a neat house, had two men clamoring for her attention.

A long, sad sigh escaped as she rolled back over. She read Esther's letter next. Like the woman who wrote it, it was filled with love and faith in God. Even her heartbreak over the loss of her baby was tempered by her faith.

A paragraph toward the end caught Eliza's eye.

Ben and I have been praying about God's will in our lives. We love it here in our cabin with most of our family around us. (You, Father, and Lenny would make our joy complete.) But it seems God is speaking to our hearts that He has work for us to do. Just as Father felt he must move on, so it seems, must we. We have talked to Brother Timothy, and Ben has written to the missionary alliance he recommended. Eliza, we are so excited that God has chosen us to be missionaries to the Indian people in Kansas Territory. We are preparing as much as we can now so we'll be ready to go next spring. From the way it looks now, we will be leaving here right after Grace's wedding. Isn't God good?

Eliza wiped tears from her eyes. Esther had just suffered the greatest loss a woman can have, yet there was no indication of self-pity in her letter. Instead it was filled with the wonder of God's love and of her desire to give herself to lost people. Eliza felt convicted of her own selfishness and lack of commitment.

She shrugged off the unwelcome mood and picked up Vickie's letter.

> *Hello, Little Sister, it seems forever since I've seen you. Can you imagine the surprise we all had when Father showed up with a wife? And what a wonderful woman! We fell in love with her immediately. Father said you introduced them. That must mean you love her as much as we do*
>
> *It didn't take long to see how much Father cares for her. I don't mean to say he has forgotten Mother. I'm sure he could never do that. But it's obvious this marriage is good for him. I remember how melancholy he was the first few months after Mother died. I worried when you moved to Springfield, not knowing if another location was what he needed. Maybe it wasn't, but Mary obviously is. I wanted to let you know that we all approve of your choice for a stepmother. If we can't have Mother, Mary is certainly our choice, too.*

Eliza tossed her sister's letter aside and jumped to her feet. She paced the length of her room and back. How could her sisters welcome another woman into their mother's place? Was she the only one who missed Mother?

She sank to the bed and gathered up Vickie's letter. The rest was about her two rambunctious sons, Nicholas and Christopher. Then she told of her new baby daughter, Faith Victoria.

> *I was quite ill while I carried this baby. John and I prayed and claimed the promise in Mark 9:23. It says, "If thou canst believe, all things are possible to him that believeth." That's why, when our baby girl was born healthy and strong, we had to name her Faith.*

Eliza was glad for the three children Vickie and John had but hoped they didn't have any more. As far as she was concerned, it was not worth the risk of her sister's life. She turned back to her letter.

Oh, yes, I must tell you that both John and I have accepted Jesus as our Savior. Brother Timothy is a powerful speaker and very good at tending to the needs of his congregation. He is a young man without a wife, but he seems to have wisdom beyond his years. It was through his influence that we found our way.

Again, Eliza wiped tears. Her oldest brother, Ben, had been first to accept Christ, and then their mother came to the Lord after Nora's birth. Cora was next. But it took their mother's death to bring Eliza and her father to the Lord. Now John and Vickie had joined their spiritual family. Eliza's heart sang.

Finally, she turned to the last letter—the one from Cora. She skimmed the part that told how much Cora liked Mary. Then Cora told of her new baby. Eliza read carefully.

Eliza, you don't know how much I've missed you. After my baby was born, I thought of you and was sad. My sadness is for both of you because you will not get to watch him grow, and he will not have the benefit of his aunt Eliza's guidance. After all, what better teacher could he have for arguing with his younger brothers and sisters? Could anyone have been better than the two of us, do you think? Truly, I would love to have one of our old verbal fights.

Eliza smiled at her sister's nonsense. She, too, missed the loving rivalry that had gone on between herself and Cora. She turned back to her letter to see what else she could learn about her new nephew.

Speaking of disagreements, Aaron and I had our first over our son's name. Can you believe that? For some reason, he wanted the name Jesse. I wanted Dane. Being the submissive wife that I am, I gave in to him. Our son's name is Jesse Dane. Of course, I call him Dane, and even Aaron is beginning to, as well.

Eliza laughed. She couldn't imagine Aaron disagreeing with Cora about anything. He doted on her and would give in to any whim she had. She sighed. If only she could find a man to love her half as much.

She gathered up her letters and put them in her dresser drawer. She knew in the coming months she would read them over and over, savoring each memory they brought of home and the ones she loved.

That night Nora slept in the downstairs bedroom with Father and Mary. Eliza kept silent about the situation, but inwardly she hurt. Nora treated her like a stranger. She ran to Kathrene and Mary with every need. By the end of the week, Eliza despaired of ever winning her confidence.

Then on Saturday evening after supper, the family relaxed together in the parlor. Father stood at the mantel, watching his wife sew by candlelight. "Why don't you put that down and see if you can win a game of checkers against me?"

Mary smiled up at him. "It's not likely I could do that."

"I'll go easy on you." Father picked up the set. "You'll be putting your eyes out, anyway, doing such close work in this dim light."

Mary lifted the garment and bit off a thread. "I've sewn in dim light for years."

"But you don't have to now." He moved a small table between Mary's chair and the end of the sofa. He opened the board on the table and started putting the pieces in place.

Mary laughed at his persistence. She laid the half-made garment aside. "I suppose Nora can wait for her dress."

Nora, who had been quietly playing on the floor with a doll, looked up at her name. She tossed her doll to the side and ran to Mary. "I can play, too."

"Of course, you may, Darling." Mary held her hands out. "Would you like to sit on my lap?"

Nora's shoulder-length hair bounced as she nodded. Eliza bit her lower lip as she watched her little sister. She looked so happy with Mary.

Father leaned back in his chair and tried to look sternly at his little daughter. "All right, you may play, but you wait until Mama tells you what to do."

Nora's big, brown eyes were serious as she nodded. "Yes, Fauver."

They played one game with Nora moving Mary's pieces, and Father won easily.

"See, I told you I couldn't play this game." Mary laughed and gave Nora a hug. "Even with my little helper, I lost."

"You need practice. How about another game?"

Mary shook her head. "I've had all the checkers I want for one night."

Eliza stood. "I'll play with you, Father."

"All right." Father grinned at Mary, teasing her. "Now I'll have some competition."

"No, me play." Nora grabbed a red playing piece in each hand.

Eliza's heart sank, but Mary came to her rescue. "Nora, I know if you talk nice to your sister, she'll let you help, just like I did. Would you like to do that?"

Nora looked from the checkers to Eliza and nodded. Mary stood with her, letting Eliza take her place.

Eliza held her little sister close for a moment. It felt so good to finally hold Nora's warm little body without her squirming for freedom.

Once her sister was secure on her lap, Eliza kept Nora as long as she could. Father won the first game. She found it hard to concentrate with Nora moving the pieces. She lost the second game, but she had two pieces crowned king before Father's kings jumped them.

When she won the third game, Father yawned. "Well, I think we'd better call it a night. Lenny, why don't you hand me my Bible?"

"Are you quitting because you finally lost, Father?" Eliza smiled at him.

He grinned back. "Do you think I'm that childish? No, don't answer." He laughed and took the Bible Lenny handed him. "Let's see what God's Word has for us tonight."

Eliza kept Nora with her throughout family devotions and afterward. She helped her into her nightgown as the family got ready for bed. She even carried her outside to the outhouse.

The sun was just sinking below the western horizon when they returned to the house. Eliza's steps were slow, trying to delay the moment her sister would go back to Mary.

"Nora, how would you like to sleep in my room upstairs tonight?" She tried to keep her voice light, although she felt as if her life depended on the answer.

Nora looked at her older sister. "Where you room?"

"You haven't even seen my room, have you?" Eliza's steps quickened. "How about we go look at it, okay?"

Nora's small head nodded. "Okay."

Eliza carried Nora upstairs without confronting anyone. "It's right in here." She pushed open the door and tossed Nora on her bed so that she bounced.

Nora's happy laughter thrilled her. She scrambled to her feet, her arms lifted. "Do again."

Eliza picked her up and hugged her before positioning her over the bed. "Here goes." She pretended to drop her but didn't.

Nora squealed and grabbed for Eliza's arms. "Do again."

Eliza laughed, this time letting go. Nora fell on the soft bed with a shriek of laughter.

"What's going on in here?" At her father's voice, Eliza turned, lost her balance, and sat down beside Nora.

Nora scrambled up, standing on Eliza's lap, her arms wrapped around her neck. Her lower lip stuck out. "Liza mine."

Father laughed and then slipped his arm around Mary's waist as she came up beside her. He grinned down at her. "It would appear that we've lost a roommate."

Mary's smile widened, "I'm glad to see that you two girls have made up."

Eliza met her soft green eyes and for the moment felt no antagonism. "So am I."

She looked up at her father. "Does that mean Nora can sleep here now?" Her arms tightened around the little girl.

He nodded. "If that's what you want."

"It is." Eliza's smile lit her face. For the first time in a long time, she felt happy.

As if to make up for her earlier behavior, Nora became Eliza's shadow. She sat on her lap all through church the next morning. Eliza kept so busy trying to keep her quiet that she had no idea what the sermon was about.

However, she was well aware of James sitting on the other side of the church with his mother and sister. He added to her happiness when he stopped to talk to her and Nora after church. "I won't ask if you are all right this morning. That sparkle in your eyes tells me you are."

Eliza laughed. "Yes, I'm feeling much better now that my little sister is here."

"I'm glad." James smiled and stepped aside as a couple of young women joined them and exclaimed over Nora. He waved over their heads and said, "I'll see you later."

*E*liza was glad to see Vanda slip into the back pew Sunday evening just before the minister opened his Bible.

"'Except a man be born again, he cannot see the kingdom of God.'" He paused, stepped to the side of the pulpit, and pointed a finger at the congregation. "Where will you spend eternity?"

Eliza had never heard him talk so fast nor so loud as he paced from one side of the pulpit to the other. She bowed her head and prayed for any who were in need of salvation.

When the altar call was given, Vanda make her way with four others to the front. Mary, Father, and Kathrene went forward to pray with those seeking salvation. Mary knelt beside Vanda.

Eliza held Nora on her lap and made sure Lenny stayed by her side. She felt shaken. She could think of no time she had spoken to Vanda about her soul. She hadn't even considered that Vanda might be in need of salvation.

Tears of repentance for her own neglect trickled down Eliza's cheeks. She bowed her head and prayed, asking God to forgive her for being so selfish with all He had given her.

After church, she waited by the door while Vanda made her way toward her. A wide smile dominated her thin face. Her large brown eyes danced with happiness.

"Oh, Eliza, I'm so glad you waited." The two girls hugged. Vanda pulled back. "Do you know how wonderful I feel right now?"

A flush covered Eliza's face. Had Vanda not known she was a Christian? She nodded. "Yes, I do."

Vanda tugged on Eliza's arm. "Let's step outside. I want to ask you something."

Eliza allowed the other girl to lead her to a tree near the side of the church. It was dark there, away from the lantern light on the front steps.

"Will you pray with me for my father?"

"Your father?"

Vanda looked down with her head bowed. Eliza had to strain to hear her voice. "Poppa is a good man when he isn't drinking. He had so much in Germany, before he came to America. But he's a younger son, and there was no inheritance for him." She looked at Eliza. "He thought he would be successful in America, but every business he tried failed. Then he met my mother. She was young and beautiful, and her family had money. She was a Wingate."

"You mean you're related to Mr. Wingate?" Eliza couldn't keep the surprise from her voice.

Vanda nodded. "Yes, he's my uncle."

"I didn't know."

Vanda smiled. "Trennen works for them, but other than that we don't associate. Poppa's pride won't let us." She seemed impatient to continue as several people came outside. "My parents eloped. In Pennsylvania, Poppa was able to find enough work to keep us alive. Then Uncle Charles came here, and Mama got sick. Poppa would have done anything for her. When she wanted to be near her brother, he packed us up and moved. His heart broke when she died. He won't leave now because she's buried here."

"How sad." Eliza didn't know what to say.

"Eliza, I'm sure you already know the rest." Vanda looked down. "You've seen the bruises. Poppa's always sorry when he's sober, but the drink turns him mean."

Eliza's heart went out to her friend.

She nodded. "Of course, Vanda, I'll pray."

"Thank you, Eliza." She laughed. "I am so happy tonight."

Eliza looked around at the departing congregation. Her father stood on the steps. He shook the minister's hand, then took Mary's arm and stepped off the porch. Nora sat on Mary's other arm as if she belonged there. "Vanda, you aren't going to walk home in the dark, are you? Why don't you come with us? I'm sure Father won't mind taking you home."

"Thank you, but I have a ride." Vanda smiled and indicated some young men standing in a group several yards away.

As Eliza looked, James Hurley separated himself from the others and came toward them. "It won't be out of James's way to take me, but I do appreciate your offer."

"Good evening, Eliza." James smiled.

"Hello, James."

He nodded. "Well, Vanda, are you ready to go?"

"Yes." Vanda took his offered arm. Eliza watched them walk toward his wagon. Her heart wrenched at the sight, and she realized she cared for James more than she should.

ৈ৵

One day in late September, Kathrene came home with news of a taffy pull. "It's at Barbara Martin's house." Her eyes sparkled in excitement. "Charles asked me to go with him."

Mary looked up. "That's wonderful, Dear. When is it?"

"This Saturday evening." Kathrene moved to stand next to Eliza. "Barbara said to tell you to come, too, Eliza. If you'd like, you may ride over with Charles and me. He said to be sure and ask you."

Eliza's rolling pin stopped in midstroke. She looked up at Kathrene, her brown eyes snapping. "Thank you, Kathrene, but if I go, I'll go by myself."

"Eliza," Kathrene spoke softly, pleading, "we really want you with us."

Eliza shook her head. "I don't think that would be wise." She lifted her pie dough and placed it carefully on the pan.

"Eliza, do we have any leavening?" Mary stood at the cabinet rummaging through the baking supplies.

"I thought there was some."

"Well, there isn't now." Mary turned and smiled. "Would you two girls mind running to the store?"

Eliza wondered if Mary asked them both to go in an effort to bring them together again. She felt the prick of her conscience as she realized that most of the problem was her fault. Walking to town with Kathrene was the least she could do to make amends.

They had just started down the road toward town when Eliza heard footsteps behind them.

"Hey, wait up, will you?"

"What do you want?" Eliza asked Lenny as he caught up with them.

"Ma, er . . ." He glanced quickly at Eliza. "Mary said I could go with you."

"All right." Eliza pointed her finger at him. "But you behave yourself. You either stay with us or go to Father's shop. Do you understand?"

He nodded. "I'm goin' to Father's."

After the girls left the store, they started across the square to Father's shops.

"Miss Kowski, wait a minute."

They both turned to see Stephen Doran hurrying toward them. Eliza stepped back, frowning at Kathrene's sharp intake of breath. Was she really so smitten by this penniless drifter?

"Miss Kowski." He smiled, and Eliza had to admit he was very good-looking. "I understand Miss Barbara Martin is having a taffy pull this Saturday evening. I would be honored if you would go with me."

"Oh, I can't."

Eliza smiled at the expression on Kathrene's face.

"If it's because I'm a stranger to your folks, I'd be glad to talk to your father . . . or mother." His expression was as woebegone as hers.

"No, it isn't that." Kathrene shook her head. "I've already promised someone else."

"Then you are going?"

"Yes, I'll be there."

"Well." He jammed his hands in his pockets. "I'll see you then." Again he smiled at her. "Until Saturday."

As soon as he left, Kathrene said, "Oh, I didn't think. Why didn't I suggest he take you?"

Eliza gasped. "Don't you dare! I don't need your charity. I'm going to see my father now. I'll come home later with Lenny."

How dare Kathrene patronize her just because she had two young men at her beck and call while Eliza had none? Tears stung her eyes, and she wiped at them as she neared the door to the chandler shop.

Father was alone in the shop when she entered. He looked up from the ledger he had been working on and smiled at her. "What a sight for sore eyes."

She smiled. "Is Lenny here? I thought I'd walk home with him."

"He's in the back. I thought he might as well do a little work before school starts again."

Eliza moved to a display of candles hanging from the ceiling and tapped at them, watching them swing back and forth

"Why don't you tell me what the problem is?"

She tried to laugh, but it came out as a sob. "Can't I hide anything from you?"

He pulled her around to face him, his hands on her shoulders. "I know you haven't been happy. Please, tell me what it is."

"It's so silly." At her hiccupy laugh, he pulled her against his chest, and she couldn't hold the tears back.

While his shirt grew damp, she told him of the party. "Kathrene has two beaux. I don't have anyone. I'm almost twenty."

He patted her back. "Maybe it just isn't God's time yet, or maybe it is, and you haven't recognized it."

"What do you mean by that?" She looked up at him as he handed her his handkerchief.

A jingle at the door warned them that someone was coming. He pushed her gently toward the workroom. "You step in there just a minute until I take care of our customer."

Eliza stood in the workroom, trying to repair the damage to her face with her father's handkerchief. Two large vats sat in the middle of the room. Candle wax and rolls of wick waited on the floor. Finished candles lay in piles on a table. Lenny was nowhere to be seen.

After what seemed a long time, Eliza carefully opened the door to the shop a crack. She couldn't hear anyone talking. She pushed it open a little farther. She didn't see anyone. As she pushed the door all the way open and stepped into the shop, Father came in the front door.

He grinned. "Oops! I got caught, didn't I? Sorry to keep you waiting, but I had to take care of some business next door."

"That's all right, Father. I need to go home, anyway."

He lifted her chin and gave her a quick kiss on the forehead. "Don't look so sad. Maybe things aren't as bad as they seem."

She smiled for his benefit. "Maybe not."

She hadn't gotten more than a hundred yards from the shops on her way home when quick footsteps sounded behind her. Thinking it was Lenny, she stopped and turned around.

James came within an inch of running into her. "What'd you stop so quick for?"

"I thought you were my brother." She stepped back to put some distance between them.

"No, I'm not your brother." The look on his face and the inflection in his voice caused a flush to spread across her cheeks. "I was trying to catch up with you so I could ask you if you're going to the taffy pull Saturday night at the Martins'."

She looked down. "I planned to, but I don't see what business it is of yours."

He threw his hands out in a helpless gesture. "Eliza Jackson, you are the most aggravating woman I've ever dealt with."

"Oh, and I suppose you've dealt with a lot of women?" She turned a saucy face to him.

His gray eyes twinkled above a grin that set her pulse racing. "Not so many you need be concerned."

"And who says I'm concerned about what you do?"

"Eliza." He grew serious. "All I want is for you to go with me to the party. How about it? Can we call a truce and go as friends?"

She nodded, surprised that her voice sounded so normal. "I suppose it would be all right. I should ask my father first."

James smiled. "Good. I'll be at your house around six thirty." He turned and walked back toward town, whistling.

ও

The promise of winter brought crispness to the September air Saturday evening as Eliza left the house with James.

They walked down the steps toward the road. Eliza noticed the absence of any vehicle in front. She glanced up at James as he took her elbow to help her over a wagon rut.

"You realize, of course, that Kathrene left ten minutes ago in a shiny blue Victoria pulled by a matched set of horses."

"My, a blue one, even." Knowing James, she assumed he was making fun of her.

"Yes. Cobalt blue with matching Morocco upholstery."

"Now, I am impressed. First the horses and now the upholstery. Everything must match." He grinned down at her. "What did you do? Come out and inspect it?"

He was making fun of her. She fell into his mood. "Why not? I'm not so lucky as Kathrene. I suppose I shall always have to walk wherever I go, unless I can somehow take Charles from Kathrene. He's the only man I know who can afford such luxury."

"And what's wrong with walking?" A frown set on James's face. "The night is warm enough, there's a full moon overhead, and we're both young and able."

Eliza looked up at James. She had been joking, but by an instinct peculiar to women, she knew that in his mind the joke had turned to criticism.

"There's not a thing wrong with walking. Actually, I quite enjoy it." She smiled at him and was glad to see his frown disappear.

The Martin house blazed with lights. Just before they went inside, James said, "Your father would have more business than he could handle if there were more parties like this one."

Eliza laughed. "I think you're right. They must have every candle in the house burning and a few lanterns as well."

Barbara opened the door at their knock. "Come on in. Make yourselves at home." She pointed toward a door off the parlor. "Pile your wraps on the bed in there."

James and Eliza shared a smile as she fluttered off to attend to someone's call. They tossed their outer garments on the bed and returned to the parlor just as Vanda came in, followed by her older brother.

Trennen nodded at James. When he turned to Eliza, a flush touched her cheeks at his scrutiny.

James's hand closed gently around her upper arm. "Come on, it sounds like they're starting the candy."

"Vanda." Eliza motioned toward her friend. "We don't want to miss out on the taffy pulling, do we?"

"We sure don't." Vanda smiled and joined them as they followed Trennen into the kitchen.

"Come on, everyone, it's just about ready." Barbara bustled about the large kitchen, setting out plates and butter for each of her guests. "This is going to be so much fun." She handed Eliza a plate.

"Hey, don't I get one?" James asked.

"Sorry, just one to a couple." Barbara turned to Vanda. "Here's your plate, but who's your partner? You don't want to pull with your brother. I know. Why don't you take mine?"

Before Vanda could answer, Barbara ran across the room and grabbed her brother's arm. He was talking to the Ross boys and resisted at first.

"I wish she wouldn't do that." Vanda looked embarrassed.

"Don't you like her brother?" Eliza asked.

"It isn't that. Joe's fine. But he doesn't look like he wants to come."

"I wouldn't be so sure about that." Eliza nudged her friend as Joe straightened and looked across the room. His frown of annoyance was replaced by a smile as he met Vanda's eyes. He nodded and followed his sister.

Joe Martin was at least six feet tall and thin. His hair, a dark brown, contrasted with his fair sister's. Eliza had never thought of him as anything more than Barbara's brother. Now she watched Vanda's face as he approached and wondered if the two of them might make a good couple.

She glanced across the room and caught Trennen's gaze on her. A slow, lazy smile crossed his face, and she looked quickly away.

She was glad when Barbara's mother lifted a large spoonful of candy from the pan and watched it sheet off. A sweet aroma filled the air. "The taffy's ready."

A chorus of cheers greeted her pronouncement. Eliza and James got into line with the other couples to get their plate of hot taffy. The atmosphere was festive and loud with everyone laughing and talking while they waited for the candy to cool enough to handle.

She avoided Kathrene and Charles as much as she could, but she noticed that Stephen Doran stayed close to them. He had come alone, and Barbara had agreed to be his partner, though Eliza knew she would have preferred David Ross.

Finally, someone decided the candy had cooled enough. James reached into the bowl and scooped off some butter. He inclined his head toward the only empty corner left at the moment. "Come on, Eliza, and bring the plate of candy."

"Yes, Sir." She followed him, ignoring his raised eyebrows.

"Set the plate down and take my hands." He spread the butter over his own hands and then reached for hers.

"As you wish, Sir." She set the plate down and started to stretch her hands toward his, but the look on his face stopped her.

"If you don't stop calling me *sir* . . ." If he had finished his sentence, she was sure she wouldn't have heard it for the pounding of her heart.

Her voice sounded small even to herself as she said, "James."

He grinned "That's much better." He took her hands then and rubbed them between his own.

"There, that should be good enough." Their eyes met, and warmth radiated between them. James dropped her hands and reached for the plate.

As they pulled the candy between them, it stretched and hardened. Barbara told them to make some thin, ropelike strands for a game they would be playing.

"All right, everyone listen, and I'll explain the game to you." Barbara clapped her hands for attention.

She held up a large bowl. "Break off a piece of your rope candy about one to two inches long. Put it in this bowl, and then we'll pick someone to start the game."

"Aren't you going to tell us how to play first?" someone called.

Barbara's long blond ringlets swished across her back as she shook her head. "I won't have to. You'll know soon enough."

The bowl made the rounds of the room and came back almost

full. Barbara giggled. "If we use all this, we may be here all night. Who wants to go first?"

"Why don't you go first and show us how?" Joe spoke from the corner. Several others voiced their agreement.

"All right, but I'll need a partner." Barbara turned to smile at David Ross. "I choose you, David."

David had brought a girl named Anna Johnson whom Eliza didn't know. He joined Barbara in the center of the room near the long trestle table. "Okay, what do I do?"

Barbara reached into the bowl and withdrew a piece of the short candy. "You remember this game, don't you, David? We played it before." She clamped one end of the candy with her teeth, her lips making an O around it. She then bent toward David with her hands clasped behind her back.

David grinned. "Sure, I remember." He put his hands behind his back and bent toward her. His mouth closed around the candy, and he bit it off, then straightened, chewing the piece in his mouth.

He grinned at the others and swept a bow amid laughter and hand clapping. As he straightened, he said, "All right, it's my turn now since I bit it in two." His eyes glanced about the room, settling on Anna. "Will you accept my challenge, Anna?"

Anna's face grew rosy, and she shook her head, a self-conscious smile on her lips.

"Come on, Anna, it's all in fun."

Anna allowed herself to be cajoled into playing. Her face was bright red by the time David again bit the candy off.

Since the same couple was not allowed to break the candy twice in a row, David chose Barbara next. When she broke the candy, she picked Stephen Doran. Eliza watched him bite the candy and then turn with a gleam in his eye toward Kathrene.

Kathrene's eyes sparkled as she placed her lips around the candy and they touched Stephen's. Eliza silently and slowly counted to five before she heard the snap of the candy in the quiet room. Kathrene picked Charles next, and on it went until it was Trennen's turn.

He turned slowly, his eyes taking in each girl until they rested on Eliza. He cocked his head to one side, his left eyebrow lifting slightly. "Well, come on."

Eliza's heart thudded in her chest. Trennen's good looks and confidence frightened and excited her. She leaned forward, taking the end of the candy in her teeth. Trennen's face was so close to her own. She looked down at the candy. Her vision blurred, and she became conscious of the many watchful eyes surrounding her.

Then Trennen's lips moved forward, across the fraction of an inch that separated them, and touched hers. She jerked back, and the candy broke off in her mouth.

Her face flamed as Trennen whispered, "That was nice. Let's try it again sometime."

"All right, Eliza. Pick another partner," Barbara called to her.

Eliza pointed at James. "I'll challenge you."

His grin showed his acceptance.

Again, Eliza's heart pounded. She picked the longest piece of candy that she could find and clamped the end in her teeth. With her hands clasped behind her back, she leaned toward him. The room grew quiet as he took the other end in his teeth.

Seconds ticked off as they stood, nose to nose, holding the candy. Then it snapped off in James's teeth. His eyes danced at her surprised expression. Their lips had not touched.

After a couple more games, Barbara stood up. "It's getting late, but I want to thank you all so much for coming. I don't know about you, but I've had lots of fun."

Kathrene caught Eliza and James as they put on their wraps. "Charles is bringing the buggy around. Would you like to ride home with us?"

James shrugged. "That's up to Eliza."

She thought of the plush Victoria and was tempted. But then she looked at James and shook her head. "We'll go home the same way we came."

Kathrene shrugged. "All right, if that's what you want."

"It is." James took Eliza's arm and guided her out the door.

They walked together, talking about the party, the town that was growing up around them, and James's plans for his life's work. Before she realized it, they had turned into her front yard.

"I like farming and hope to never live in town, but I also enjoy working with your father."

"So what are you going to do? Be a farmer or a cooper?"

"Both." James grinned down at her as they neared her house. "Unless your father runs me off for keeping you out too late. You know we'd have been here a lot sooner in that fancy blue Victoria."

She nodded as they stopped just short of the front porch. "I know, but it wouldn't have been as much fun."

"So you think walking is fun."

"Depending on the company."

He grinned and then became serious. "Eliza, I enjoyed this evening very much. So much that I hate to see it end." He searched her face. "Would you consider going with me next Saturday to see my farm? I'd really like to show it to you."

She smiled up at him. "Do I have to walk?"

He laughed. "I don't know. Do you think your father would loan me his buggy?"

"I don't imagine he'll say much against it. If he does, I might put in a good word for you."

James stepped closer, his hands on each of her elbows. "Does that mean you'll go?"

She nodded, unable to speak with him so near.

He leaned toward her. "Eliza, may I kiss you good night?"

Her heartbeat drummed in her ears. Without a word, she nodded.

As he pulled her into his arms and his lips lowered over hers, moisture came unbidden to her eyes. She had not expected such strong feelings to come with a simple kiss.

James smiled down at her. "You'd better go in before your father comes out."

Eliza walked into the house in a daze.

12

*T*he next morning at church, Eliza cast shy glances at James. He returned her smiles and after the service went out of his way to speak to her.

"I told my mother I was bringing you out next Saturday."

"I hope it's all right with her."

He smiled. "She's anxious to get acquainted with you. Now all I have to do is get your father's permission."

"Oh, no, you don't." She gave him a saucy grin. "I already asked, and he said yes."

James laughed. "Great, now I know what his answer will be tomorrow when I ask for the use of his buggy."

Lenny ran by, yelling over his shoulder, "Come on, Eliza. Father and Mama are ready to go."

Eliza frowned after him. "I can't believe he calls her 'Mama.' He just does it because Nora does. But Nora doesn't remember Mother."

"Perhaps you shouldn't be so hard on him. He's young, too, you know."

"Maybe." Eliza turned back to him with a smile. "Well, I've got to be going. I'll see you later."

Monday evening Father told Eliza he'd been approached by James and had given him permission to borrow his buggy on Saturday. He grinned at her with a teasing light in his eyes. "I always heard tell a boy was getting serious when he took his best girl out to meet his mother."

Eliza's face flamed. "Don't get your hopes up yet, Father. I'm afraid James just wants to show off his farm. It looks like you're stuck with me for awhile."

Father laughed, but Mary said, "I can't imagine a nicer thing than to have you right here with us always."

Eliza turned toward the stairs without responding.

ஜஒ

On Saturday afternoon, the air felt cool while sunshine brought the trees alive with color as Eliza and James rode toward his farm.

They hadn't gone far when he pointed to the left. "This is the north boundary. I've only added twenty acres since my father died. Someday, I'd like to have at least two hundred."

"That would make a nice-sized farm for this part of the country," Eliza said. "What do you raise? Cows, horses, pigs?"

He grinned at her. "Yes."

"Yes! You mean you have all of those?"

"All of those plus chickens, dogs, and cats."

"My, you do have quite a farm." Eliza laughed with him.

He pointed at a house sitting to the left of the road. "Here we are."

Someone had built onto the original log cabin, making a nice-sized house. It stood two stories tall with a fresh coat of whitewash. A dog curled up on the back steps wagged his tail as they walked toward him. He lifted his head, gave one sniff, and then settled back to complete his nap.

"He's not the best watchdog, but he's friendly." James patted the dog's head before opening the door for Eliza.

She laughed and stepped inside.

Mrs. Hurley took a pan of cookies from the oven. She smiled. "I thought you might like a warm treat. There's hot chocolate on the stove." She turned to her daughter. "Pour some out for each of us, Melissa. We'll sit here around the table and visit a spell."

"That sounds nice," Eliza said.

"How is your family, Eliza?" Mrs. Hurley placed the cookies on the table, then pulled a chair out.

James reached for another chair and pulled it from the table for Eliza. She smiled her thanks and then answered his mother. "They're just fine, thank you."

Eliza enjoyed the time she spent with James's mother and sister. Both made her feel at home as they talked about the weather, the town, and their farm. Eliza learned that the farm had been given to James at his father's death more than ten years ago. She was amazed that a boy so young would be trusted with such an undertaking. His mother assured her that he had proven himself worthy, getting up before light to care for the animals and do chores.

Pride set on her face as she smiled at her son. "He worked morning and night to make a living for us and still kept up with his studies. I worried that he couldn't do it with all the responsibilities he had, but James stayed in school until he knew as much as the schoolmaster." She smiled at him.

Eliza looked at James with shining eyes.

He laughed. "Don't let my mother fool you. I have a well-used fishing rod out in the barn to prove I didn't work all the time."

Mrs. Hurley laughed and patted James's hand. "Yes, all boys must play, or they don't make good men."

"Come on, Eliza." James set his mug down. "Let's go look around."

He grasped her hand, pulling her to her feet. She felt self-conscious when he kept her hand firmly in his as they went out the kitchen door.

Together they walked across his farm as he pointed out the various animals and crops. They were walking back toward the house when he pulled her behind a toolshed.

"What's the matter?" She grabbed her bonnet to keep it from slipping off her head.

He turned to face her. His eyes were dark as they looked deep into hers. "There's something I need to know."

She felt as if she couldn't breathe. "What is it?"

His hand touched her neck while his thumb stroked her cheek. "I want to know . . ." He paused a moment as his gaze dropped to her lips. "If I have to ask every time I want to kiss you."

Her heart thudded. She could not speak. All she could do was shake her head from side to side.

"Good." His hand cupped her chin, lifting it until their lips touched. Eliza responded as she hadn't the first time and experienced emotions beyond anything she had ever imagined.

When he pulled away, a grin set on his lips. "You know I plan to take advantage of this, don't you?"

"What do you mean?" Her breath came in short, quick spurts.

"I mean there's still that big tree between us and the house." He stepped around the corner of the toolshed, pointing to an old oak broad enough to hide the two of them from anyone looking out a window.

She walked past him, putting a little distance between them before she spoke. With her head tilted toward one side, she smiled. "That's true, but you'll have to catch me first."

Before the last word left her mouth, she was running as fast as she could toward the house. When she heard the pounding of his feet behind her, an unreasonable alarm gave her the impetus she needed to make it past the tree before he caught her.

He wrapped his arm around her and pulled her close to his side as they continued to the house. He grinned at her struggles to pull away. "If you think you're going to get away from me after that trick, you'd better think again."

"What will your mother think if she sees you holding me this way?"

"Probably that she raised her son to be as smart as she thinks he is." James laughed but removed his arm from her shoulders to hold her hand instead. He stopped at the back steps. "Your father may be worried about me keeping his horse and buggy out too late. I'd better get it back to him."

"What about his daughter?" Eliza pretended to be deeply hurt. "You men always put your possessions above us womenfolk."

"But, Eliza . . ." The twinkle in James's eyes gave away his serious expression. "Don't you know you womenfolk are our possessions, too?"

"You may consider your wife a possession, Mr. Hurley—if you ever find someone who will marry you—but I will never be any man's possession." Eliza lifted her chin defiantly.

James laughed. "That's one statement I can believe, Miss Jackson." He pulled her toward the door. "Come inside for just a minute; then I'll take you home."

Eliza sat close beside James on the way back to town. She scarcely knew what to think of the new emotions that he had awakened in her.

"You know, I just thought of something." James interrupted her thoughts. "We haven't had a good argument since before Barbara's party."

"It's rather nice, don't you think?"

He grinned at her. "Just being with you is nice."

Her face flushed, and she looked away. As she did, she saw a lone figure trudging toward town ahead of them.

"James, isn't that Vanda?" As they got closer, she gripped his arm. "It is. Please stop and let's give her a ride into town."

Vanda climbed into the back and leaned against the seat. "This is much better than walking."

"Where were you headed?" Eliza asked.

"I need to go to the general store, but my main reason for coming into town was to see you."

"Is something wrong?"

"I think so." Vanda looked to the countryside as it rolled by. "Before I was a Christian, I might have overlooked this, but now I realize how important it is that everyone comes to know the Lord in a personal way."

She looked at Eliza. "I'm concerned about Cletis and Lenny. They are young, but they're doing things they shouldn't, and I'm afraid it'll just get worse as they get older."

Eliza felt a sinking sensation in her middle. What had Lenny done now?

Vanda continued. "I thought you might tell your father that I caught Cletis and Lenny chewing tobacco the other day out behind our outhouse."

"Lenny was at your place?" Eliza was as shocked by that bit of news as she was at what he had been doing.

"Yes, he's been out several times. Cletis knows when Poppa isn't going to be there. The boys said it was all right with your folks."

Eliza sat in stunned silence. It seemed she had quite a bit to talk over with her brother when she got home.

🦆

Eliza saw her opportunity to talk to Lenny the next day when he went to the outhouse right after the family returned home from church. She waited until he came out. "I had a talk with Vanda yesterday."

Lenny just looked at her.

"She says she caught you and Cletis with some tobacco. Is that true?"

"So what if it is?" He glared at her. "You ain't my boss."

"I may not be your boss, but I could sure tell Father that Cletis is a bad influence on you. How would you like that?"

She saw fear come into his eyes and then change into something else. But she was unprepared for his next words.

"I guess you got reason to be jealous of me and my friends, 'cause Father don't have to get me no friends."

"What do you mean?"

"Father got you James, didn't he?" Lenny sneered. "I was in the cooper shop when he told James to ask you to that party. James didn't want to, either. He said he didn't think you'd go with him. But Father said he'd sure appreciate it if he'd try, anyhow, so James said he would."

Lenny's voice pounded in Eliza's head as a drum that would not stop. Never in her life had she felt so humiliated and hurt.

Eliza spent the rest of the afternoon in her room. James had told her he wanted to continue working as a cooper. Well, he had certainly earned that right. She reached for her pillow and buried her face in it as great sobs racked her body.

ۂ

Before church that evening, Eliza crawled into bed and went to sleep. The grief she suffered robbed her natural coloring, leaving her pale. It was not hard, when Kathrene came to wake her, to convince her and then Father that she would be unable to attend the service with them.

As soon as the door closed, she looked to be sure everyone had left her room before she threw the covers back and sat up, clutching her knees to her chest.

Her pride had been deeply wounded, but she couldn't hide away forever while James laughed at her. She would show him and Father, too.

ৡৢ

Trennen came to church the following Sunday morning. Although he sat quietly in the pew behind her, Eliza was aware of his presence almost as much as she was aware of James sitting across the church beside his mother and sister.

Before James could reach her, she left the building, and Trennen fell into place behind her. Without touching her, he leaned forward slightly to speak close to her ear. "Good morning, Eliza."

She turned around with a smile. "Good morning, Trennen. It's nice seeing you in church."

She was not the only one glad to see him there. Several stopped to shake his hand. Eliza stayed with him. She saw James heading their way, so she tugged Trennen's sleeve. He went with her without question. James caught up with them before they'd gone far.

"Eliza, could I talk with you?"

"If you have a question about your work, my father is over there." She inclined her head, refusing to look at James. "Now, if you'll excuse me, I'll continue my conversation with Trennen."

She turned away, pulling Trennen with her. James did not follow. Trennen looked down at her, a lazy grin in place. "I might've come to church before now if I'd known everyone wanted me to."

"Of course, everyone wants you to come." Eliza turned to look up at him and saw James join his mother.

"I suppose that's why no one ever asked me."

Eliza looked up at Trennen. "Do you mean the Wingates never asked you?"

"Well, yeah, but they don't count. Vanda, too, but that doesn't mean anything."

"Why not?" Eliza suddenly realized his sister hadn't been at church. "Where is Vanda, anyway?"

"Probably home with Pop." Trennen shrugged. "I think he was supposed to come in this weekend."

Eliza's eyes widened as she remembered what Vanda had said about her father beating her and Cletis when he came home drunk. Was it possible that she was suffering at her father's hand right now?

Trennen touched her shoulder, bringing her attention back to him. "I'll walk you home."

"I'd have to ask my father first."

"I'll go with you." Trennen took her arm, and together they caught Father and Mary as they headed toward their buggy.

"Father, would it be all right if Trennen walked me home?" Eliza looked hopefully at her father.

He hesitated, looking first at Trennen and then at Eliza. "I suppose if you come straight home, it will be all right."

Trennen nodded. "Thank you, Sir."

Trennen took her hand and placed it in the crook of his arm. Together they crossed the churchyard and started across the road just as James's wagon pulled out in front of them.

Eliza pushed James from her mind and tried to concentrate on the young man beside her. As they came up to the front porch, he stepped back.

"Why don't you come inside for awhile?"

He stuck his hands in his pockets. "Naw, I'd better not, but I'd like to see you again. How about tonight? Do you go to church at night, too?"

She smiled. "Yes, we usually do."

"Good. Then I'll see you there." With that, he turned and walked away.

From then on Trennen never missed a church service, and several times he walked Eliza home. She knew the people were pleased to see him. Many prayed for his salvation, hoping at each altar call that he would be the next to go forward. Eliza also prayed for him, but mostly she enjoyed having a young man interested in her because he liked her and not because he was afraid he'd lose his job.

James tried several times to talk to Eliza, but each time she managed to avoid him.

For awhile Eliza enjoyed Trennen's attention, but as the weeks went by she grew tired of his insincere compliments and chivalrous behavior. At first she pushed her discontent aside, but it would not leave. One Sunday morning she decided she would tell him she no longer wished to see him.

As usual, he sat in the row behind her. When church dismissed, he waited outside for her.

Lately, Father had not been as free with his permission for her to walk out with Trennen as he had at first. So she pulled her father aside. "Father, if Trennen asks to walk me home this morning, may I please? I'd really like to talk to him."

A frown creased Father's forehead. "I don't know, Eliza."

"Father, he's been a perfect gentleman."

"I'm sure that's true. But do you think his sudden interest in attending the house of God has anything to do with his concern for his soul, or is it the attraction he feels for one of God's children?"

Trennen had told Eliza that he started coming to church when he did because he enjoyed the kiss they had shared at the party so much. She flushed as she evaded her father's question. "I cant read his thoughts, Father."

Father sighed. "All right. Go ahead, but be careful."

"Don't worry. I'll be fine." She brushed off his concern. "We're just walking across town."

Before she made it to the back door, James blocked her path. "Eliza, could I talk to you?"

His eyes were dark gray as he looked down at her, his expression serious. She skirted around him. "I'm sorry, Mr. Hurley, but my *unpaid* escort is waiting for me. My father handles any problems with his businesses." She rushed past before he could stop her.

She waved at Trennen and walked toward him, wondering if James was watching.

Trennen smiled when he saw her. "May I walk you home?"

She nodded. "Yes, I've already asked Father, and he said it was all right. I wanted to talk to you."

When they were out of sight of the churchyard, he reached for her hand. She reluctantly curled her fingers around his.

Trennen squeezed her hand. "I thought you wanted to talk to me. You haven't said more than two words."

Eliza realized that they had already crossed the square downtown. If she were going to get this done, she'd have to do it now.

Her steps slowed. "Trennen, I'm flattered by the attention you've paid me. I enjoy our walks very much. But . . ."

His hand stiffened in hers.

"But I wonder if there isn't someone else you'd rather be with."

He laughed. "Are you jealous?"

"No." She looked quickly at him. "No, I didn't mean that."

His hand squeezed hers again. She winced at the pain, but he as quickly released her hand and, stopping in the road, turned to face her. "Are you wanting another man's attentions? Maybe Hurley?"

The anger in his voice and on his face surprised her. She shook her head. "No, that's not what I meant." How could she explain it to him? What could she say that wouldn't hurt him?

"Good. Then there's nothing to talk about." He took her hand again and continued walking.

They soon reached her front door, and she had accomplished nothing. Before he left, she tried again. "Trennen, I didn't mean to hurt your feelings."

As she hesitated, the front door opened, framing Kathrene. "Eliza, Mother says for you to invite Trennen in to eat with us. She says it's about time the family became acquainted with him."

Trennen's lazy smile softened his blue eyes as he looked down at Eliza. "Well, do I get to stay?"

$$13$$

*T*hat night when Eliza went to bed, she pulled the covers up to her chin. Trennen had been the most gallant, attentive guest she had ever seen. He'd complimented Mary on her cooking so many times Eliza had felt like gagging. That was one of the problems with him. He said all the right things so often that she questioned his sincerity.

She sighed. How was she going to stop seeing Trennen? Even Father said that he seemed to be a nice young man.

Just thinking about it made her thirsty. She threw the covers back, climbed from bed, and went downstairs to the kitchen.

"Kathrene seemed quite pleased, didn't she?" The muffled voice of her father came from his bedroom.

With her ear near the door, she was able to hear Mary. "I hope we did the right thing."

Father said, "I've heard nothing but good about the boy. I know he's closemouthed about his past, but I think he's everything he claims to be."

"I suppose."

Eliza realized they meant Stephen Doran.

Father said, "I wouldn't be surprised if this isn't the man Kathrene marries."

"You know, Orval, I love all our children. Yours and mine. Vickie and Cora are so sweet. And Ben. How could I help loving him? He's just like his father."

Mary paused for a moment. "Then there's Eliza. I think I began loving her when she walked into my house with that bundle of fabric that was almost as big as she is."

Eliza heard a muffled sob and Father say, "It's all right, Mary. Eliza's a good girl. She'll come around."

"I know." Mary cleared her throat.

"You're a good mother, Mary. You're good with Lenny, and Nora adores you. I'm proud of the way she took to you so quickly." He laughed softly. "And now God is blessing us with one that won't have to adjust to a new mother or a new father."

"Yes." Eliza could hear the smile in Mary's voice. "Our own little one to raise together. I know our baby won't be here until spring, but I get so anxious. I want to know what our child will look like."

Eliza's father spoke, but she didn't hear. How could this be? Surely Mary and Father were not expecting a baby. They couldn't be. Mary was supposed to cook and clean for him. She was not supposed to bear his children.

Eliza crept back to her room, her thirst forgotten.

ેન્

As November gave way to December, Eliza's worries grew. Mary's condition became more pronounced, and Trennen refused to leave her alone. Several times she tried to tell him that she didn't want his company anymore, but he refused to listen. And James stopped trying to talk to her.

Eliza didn't feel the freedom to tell her father that she didn't want to go with Trennen. So he gave permission for her to ride to the Christmas play with Trennen, just as he did for Kathrene to ride in Stephen Doran's well-worn buggy.

When the parts for the play were given out, Vanda was chosen to play Mary, the mother of Jesus. Her eyes shone as she turned to Eliza. "Poppa's away working. He said he'd be gone all month, and I hope he is because he would be angry if he knew what I'm doing."

"You mean he wouldn't want you in the play?" Eliza couldn't understand his problem.

Vanda nodded. "He doesn't want us going to church. Cletis comes out of rebellion, but I come because Jesus is my Lord. I can't turn my back on Him."

That evening when Trennen took Eliza home, he walked her to the door while Vanda and Cletis waited in the Wingates' buggy. In the two months they had been keeping company, Trennen had never done more than hold her hand. Now he stepped up on the porch with her and pulled her into a shadowy corner away from prying eyes. Eliza's heart pounded.

"Trennen, please . . ."

"I love you, Eliza." He stopped her protest, pulling her close to him. "All I want is one kiss."

When she resisted, he pleaded with her. "Don't you love me?"

All the time he talked, he held her close, his cheek against hers. Finally, his lips touched hers, and she felt she had no choice but to surrender. Maybe if she allowed him one kiss, he would let her go.

But Trennen's kiss deepened into something Eliza didn't understand. She shoved against him. "Trennen, no . . ."

"I love you, Eliza." He reached for her again.

"You can't do this, Trennen. It isn't right." Her heart pounded in fear.

She shoved him backward, making him stumble against the porch post. "I want you to leave, Trennen. And I don't want to ride home with you anymore."

He started toward her, a look of anger on his face. Then his expression changed, and his head bowed. "I'm sorry, Eliza. It's just that I love you so much. Don't tell me I can't ever see you again."

Eliza's heart began a hard steady beat. Her head felt light. She watched him standing dejected, and sympathy replaced anger and fear.

"I have to go inside now, Trennen. I'll see you later." She turned and let herself into the house.

❧

Eight days before the Christmas program, Trennen again asked her to let him take her home.

At first she said no.

"Are you afraid of me, Eliza?" Trennen looked sad.

She shook her head. "No, of course not. But I need to go. Father's waiting. He said they are working late on an order tonight so he needs to get back to the shop."

As she turned away, Trennen captured her arm in his hand. "Eliza, I need to talk to you. It's important." He pleaded with her. "I promise you, if you'll go with me tonight, I'll leave you alone from now on if that's what you really want."

She stood looking at him for several seconds, trying to decide what she should do. She didn't love Trennen, and she knew she never would. She loved only one man.

Pain seared her heart, burning the image of James Hurley in its depths. Hers was a lost love. Twice, she had been scorned, first by Ralph and then by James, but only once had she truly loved. She loved James and always would.

"Eliza, please say you'll go with me tonight." Trennen shook her gently, bringing her eyes to focus again on his face.

"Promise you'll leave me alone after tonight?"

His head drooped, but he nodded. "If that's what you want."

She shrugged. "All right. I'll tell my father."

Eliza's mood darkened like the clouds above when she climbed into the Wingates' buggy and sank into its plush cushions. Vanda squeezed her hand while Trennen settled into the front seat beside her.

"I'm glad you came tonight." Vanda smiled, oblivious to Eliza's unhappiness. "The play is coming along well, don't you think?"

Eliza nodded.

Vanda said, "I feel so unworthy playing the part of Mary. Can you imagine what it must have been like for her? She was just a young girl, but she became the mother of our Lord. Oh, how wonderful it would be to be used of God."

"You'd better not let Pop hear you talking that way." Trennen spoke across Eliza.

Vanda looked down at her hands. "I know. I keep praying for him, but . . . sometimes I get discouraged. I'm so afraid something will happen to him, and he won't know Jesus."

Trennen laughed. "You should worry about what happens to you if he finds out you're still coming here."

Vanda sighed. "I suppose." She was quiet as they dropped off three small children.

Eliza was glad the next stop would be hers, as she wanted desperately to close herself in her bedroom, climb in her bed, and have a good cry in her pillow.

But Trennen turned the horses south, away from her father's house. She looked at him in alarm. "Where are you going?"

He laughed. "Relax, Eliza. I have to take Vanda and Cletis home and then turn around and come back into town, anyway. You don't really mind, do you?"

Eliza did mind, but when she looked at Trennen's lazy grin and saw the determined light in his eyes, she knew it would do no good to protest. She shook her head and settled back.

They turned down the same road she had taken two months earlier with James. When the barn and the toolshed came into view, she remembered the kiss she had shared with James.

She turned her face away from the house as they drove past. James was in town, working with her father on a rush order, but she didn't want to be reminded of the wonderful day she had spent there.

Less than a mile farther down the road Trennen turned the buggy into a yard cluttered with various wagon parts and tools.

Vanda stiffened. "Poppa's home."

Cletis spoke from the backseat in a small voice. "Take us back to town with you, Trennen."

"Naw." He stepped down. "You wouldn't have anyplace to stay. Come on. I'll go in and talk to him."

Vanda lifted her chin as Trennen came around the buggy to help her down. "No, Trennen. You take Eliza home. We'll be fine."

"Vanda, why don't you come back to town?" Eliza caught her friend's hand as she climbed down. "You could stay with me. Lenny would love to have Cletis come."

Vanda shook her head. She gave Eliza a smile. "Thank you, but we can't. Someone has to take care of Poppa." She jumped to the ground. "Don't worry. We'll be fine."

As Cletis crawled from the buggy, Vanda turned to Trennen. "You go on and take Eliza home. It wouldn't do for Poppa to see you right now. You know he doesn't like you working for the Wingates. It'd just make things worse."

As Trennen guided the buggy back out onto the road and turned it toward town, Eliza looked over her shoulder to see the door close behind Vanda. "Are you sure she'll be all right?"

"Why wouldn't she be?" Trennen shrugged. "He probably won't lay a hand on her."

He turned and looked down at Eliza's worried expression. "Aw, don't worry about Vanda. What would your father do if you did something he didn't want you to?"

She spoke quietly. "When I was little, he spanked me. Mostly, he talks to me." She smiled. "I think the talks hurt the most."

His arm encircled her, drawing her close to his side. "Sit over here where it's warmer."

They were nearing the Hurley house. Eliza shrank against Trennen's side, turning her face away from the house.

He hugged her even closer, his hand rubbing her upper arm. His head lowered toward hers. They were in front of James's house. She turned away. "Trennen, we're in front of a house."

"You know who lives there, too, don't you?" His voice sounded angry.

She nodded. "But that doesn't—"

"Oh, it matters all right. I know all about you and Hurley. I've seen the way you look at him."

They were past the house now. Trennen's mouth covered hers in a rough kiss that frightened her. She pulled away. He let go of the reins, giving the horses their heads. They slowed to a leisurely stroll. "You are mine, Eliza. No one else is going to have you." He held her with both hands, his kisses now forceful and demanding.

She struggled for freedom. His voice sounded hoarse, his breathing ragged. "Don't fight me, Eliza. I love you."

She fought with everything she had. She screamed, but there was no one to hear. She beat at him, trying to push him back. He pinned her against the cushion. She kicked at him. He cursed.

The horses became skittish as the buggy bounced with their struggles.

Her head felt light and dizzy. She had to get away before she fainted. But Trennen pushed her into the corner of the seat. Fear rose within her.

Then as if a voice spoke within her head, she heard the words, *"Call upon Me in the day of trouble: I will deliver thee, and thou shalt glorify Me."*

"Lord Jesus, help me." Her cry came from the depths of her heart, and she knew her Lord would hear.

In the next instant she saw the buggy whip. She stopped struggling as her hand closed around it. She cracked the whip over the horses' backs, startling them. They reared and came down in a run, whinnying with fright.

Trennen fell off balance, landing on the floor with a cry of pain. Cool air rushed in where Trennen had been, and Eliza knew she was free. She scrambled to the side and, without thinking of the consequences, jumped from the racing buggy.

$\approx$

James stood outside on the street while Orval closed and locked the door of the cooperage.

"I sure appreciate you staying tonight," his boss said.

"That's all right. I'm glad to see it done."

The two men walked around the building to where James's horse and Orval's buggy waited.

James flexed his shoulders, then pulled his collar up around his neck before reaching for his horse's reins. A misty rain began to fall. "Think it might turn to snow before morning?"

"Could be," Orval said. "My girls always thought we should have snow for Christmas. Maybe they'll get their wish this year." He climbed into his buggy. "Take care going home. If this picks up before you get there, you'll be soaked."

James swung into the saddle and nodded. "I'll see you in the morning at church."

He rode at a brisk trot, glad that the cold mist fell against his back. He'd soon be home in the dry with a cup of hot coffee in his hands. His mind turned to the subject that had haunted him day and night for two months. What had he done to Eliza?

He shouldn't have taken the liberty of kissing her behind the tool-shed, but she hadn't seemed to mind at the time. His heart quickened at the memory.

He'd tried time after time to talk to her, but she always cut him off. He frowned as he thought of Trennen. What did Eliza think she was doing, walking out with a fellow like that?

As he turned down the road to his house, he saw buggy lanterns coming toward him. It seemed odd that someone would be out so late on such a miserable night. The buggy came fast and then veered toward him as if trying to run him off the road.

James pulled his horse to the side, narrowly missing a collision. As it whipped past, he recognized the Wingate buggy. He was almost certain Trennen sat bent over in the driver's seat. He must be in an awfully big hurry.

James went on, hunching his shoulders against the rain while he watched for any more surprises. Then several yards before he reached his house, he heard a soft moan from the side of the road. He reined in and dismounted.

ટ≫

Eliza lay in a crumpled heap. She heard the buggy go on without her and then a blackness, darker than night, closed in, taking her away from the terror she had just experienced.

"Eliza, what are you doing here? Are you hurt?" Gentle hands scooped her up, and she moaned in answer to the distant voice.

She tried to open her eyes, but her lids were so heavy. She laid her head on the man's shoulder, trying to burrow deeper into his arms.

He groaned. "Oh, Eliza, my love. If he's hurt you, as God is my witness, I'll make him pay."

She tried to respond, to tell him she wasn't hurt, but she was so sleepy. She couldn't keep her eyes open, and the words wouldn't come.

Then they were at his house.

౿

James struggled with the door, and his sister opened it. She looked at his burden with wide eyes. "What happened? What are you doing with . . . ?"

"I found her by the side of the road just outside," James interrupted as he brushed past. "Mother, can I put her on your bed?"

"Of course." She led the way and then pulled the covers back as James carefully lay Eliza down. He knelt by the bed to unlace Eliza's shoes and slip them from her feet. He pulled the covers up, pausing when he saw her torn dress. His gaze moved to her face where a new bruise marred one pale cheek just under her closed eyelashes. His eyes darkened and his jaw clenched as he gently tucked the covers under her chin.

"What happened, Son?"

He turned toward his mother and shook his head. "I'm not sure. I'm going back into town for her father and the doctor."

"I'll take care of her." Mrs. Hurley followed him back into the kitchen. "There's hot coffee on the stove. Won't you have a cup before you go back out?"

"I can't take the time. If anything happens to her . . ." He didn't finish, but he knew his mother understood.

James couldn't push his horse fast enough. The mist had turned to a gentle drizzle, and it hit him full in the face, but he hardly noticed. All he could think of was the girl in his mother's bed. Would she be all right? He prayed every step of the way that she would.

Lights blazed from the front of the Jacksons' house. The door opened immediately on James's knock. Mr. Jackson stood framed in the doorway. "James, have you seen Eliza?" Worry lines etched around his eyes.

"Yes, she's at my house."

"Thank God. I was just getting ready to go look for her." Orval visibly relaxed.

"Sir, something's happened to her. I think you'd better come."

Orval's face went pale. "What do you mean? Is she hurt?"

"Right now she's asleep. I'd like to get the doctor to take a look at her, if you don't mind."

"I'm going with you, Orval." Mary crowded close to her husband's side.

"It's raining, Mary."

"Orval, she's my daughter, too. I'll get my heavy cloak." She turned back into the house.

"May I go after the doctor, Sir?" James asked. He wanted to be on his way.

"I'd appreciate that, James." Orval nodded. "We'll be there as soon as we can."

When James reined his horse back into his own yard, the Jacksons had just arrived. He called to them before going to the barn. "Doc's on his way. Go on in."

James took care of his horse before he walked to the house. He stopped outside and looked in the direction of town. Right now Eliza was his primary concern, but tomorrow would find him at Trennen Von Hall's door.

She was still asleep. Mary sat beside the bed, holding her hand. Orval sat by his wife, his eyes never leaving his daughter's face.

The doctor came in a bustle of reassurance. He shooed all but Mary from the room. James paced the kitchen floor, finally throwing himself into a chair at the table when his mother pushed a cup of coffee into his hands.

He watched the closed door, willing it to open. How he longed for Eliza to look up at him again with her saucy little grin. He hadn't known how much he could miss her sharp tongue until now.

"James, I'm sure she'll be all right." His mother rested her hand on his shoulder.

"Trennen did this to her." He still watched the door.

Orval turned at his words. "I figured as much. He was supposed to bring her home. He must have decided to take his brother and sister home first."

"So he could get her alone." The words stuck in James's throat. "But he won't get away with it."

"There's the doctor now." Mrs. Hurley's hand tightened on James's shoulder as the door opened.

James tried to see past the doctor, but he pulled the door closed and crossed the room to the woodstove. He held his hands above it, warming them. "Before you go in, Mr. Jackson, I've a few words to say. She's awake now, but she's upset."

James's heart skipped a beat.

"The young man she was with suffered a broken arm when the horses got away from him. I set it just before James came to get me, although at the time I didn't know there was another casualty."

"Is she hurt in any way?" Orval asked.

The doctor shook his head. "Just a few bruises. She'll be fine. You take her home tonight and put her in her own bed. Let her take it easy a couple of days, and she'll be good as new."

Orval disappeared into the bedroom and closed the door behind him. As James sat there waiting, he knew without doubt that he loved Eliza Jackson. He determined that when she was well, if she would let him within shouting distance, he would tell her just how he felt about her.

*E*liza woke to a gentle kiss on her cheek. Mary straightened and smiled at her. "How are you feeling this morning?"

"All right." Eliza turned her face toward the wall. "Where's my father?"

Mary sat on the edge of the bed. "He's gone to church."

"Eliza . . ." Mary touched her shoulder. "Can you tell me what happened last night?"

Eliza pulled the covers close. "I have a headache. I'd like to sleep."

"All right, Dear." Mary stood. "But you're going to have to face this sooner or later. Your father plans to visit with Trennen today. If he hurt you . . ."

"No." Eliza shook her head and then winced with the pain. Tears sprang to her eyes. She blotted them with the covers, keeping her face from Mary. "I jumped from the buggy."

Mary reached out and smoothed Eliza's hair. "We have a lot to thank God for."

Eliza tried to sleep, but she kept remembering. She knew Mary was right. It had taken a miracle for her to get away from Trennen and another to keep her from serious injury when she jumped.

She prayed, thanking God for His love and help. Although she felt better, heaviness remained in her heart—deadness to her soul that she didn't know what to do about. She prayed again, asking God to remove the heaviness, but still it remained. Something was keeping her from full favor with God.

At noon Father came into her room. He sat on the edge of her bed. "How are you feeling, Eliza?"

"I have a headache."

"I need to know what happened to you last night."

"What difference does it make?"

"It makes a lot of difference." Father frowned. "According to Mr. Wingate, Trennen didn't come home last night."

"He took the Wingates' buggy?"

"No, it's there, but Trennen is gone. Mr. Wingate is on his way to the Von Hall home." He shook his head. "I don't think he'd go far. According to the doctor, his arm was broken last night."

The hint of a smile broke Father's serious look. "What'd you do to him?"

Eliza looked at her father. "I prayed. Then I saw the buggy whip and cracked it across the horses. Trennen lost his balance and fell to the floor. That was when I jumped."

"And you got this bruise on your face." He tenderly touched the bruise with the back of his fingers.

Mary knocked on the door and entered, carrying a tray of food. Father stepped out of her way as she placed it across Eliza's lap. He grinned down at Eliza pushing herself upright. "So we're feeding this girl in bed, are we?"

"Don't bother Eliza." Mary straightened and playfully shoved her husband toward the door. "Your dinner's waiting downstairs."

Eliza watched them leave. She hadn't told him what Trennen had tried to do to her, but she thought her father knew, anyway.

What would Father do to Trennen? He said he planned to talk to him. At the moment she didn't care what happened to him as long as he never touched her again.

§

James went home from church with a heavy heart. He'd hoped to confront Trennen, but it seemed the scoundrel had disappeared. He ate dinner, then went outside to care for his animals. A light snow had fallen in the early morning hours. He'd have to fork some hay down and check on his stock.

On the way to the barn, he saw the Wingate buggy drive past. His heart quickened until he realized Mr. Wingate drove it. He waved and went on to the barn.

He'd just finished with the hay when he heard his name called. "James. James, I need your help."

Mr. Wingate hurried toward the barn as James ran out. "It's Vanda. She's been hurt bad. Come, help me." His sentences came out in gasps.

James told his mother where he was going before jumping into the buggy beside Mr. Wingate.

Vanda lay on a small cot in the front room of the cabin, her face a stark contrast to her dark hair spread out on the pillow. A thin blanket covered her, and the room felt like ice. Her face, with one eye swollen shut, was bruised almost beyond recognition. She appeared to be sleeping.

James looked at Mr. Wingate's ashen face. "Where's Cletis?"

"I don't know. He's not here."

James reached out and touched Vanda's neck. A faint pulse beat under his fingers. "She's still alive, but she won't be if we don't get help."

Vanda moaned as he picked her up, blanket and all. He tried to carry her as gently as he could. He laid her on the back seat of the buggy, then climbed in and put her head on his lap. He tried to cushion her as best he could to help smooth the ride.

James breathed a prayer of thanks when Mr. Wingate stopped in front of the doctor's house. They hurriedly carried Vanda into the doctor's examining room. As the doctor probed for broken bones and internal injuries, Mr. Wingate's plump face turned red with indignation. "It's that no-good father of hers, I'll wager. We tried to help the children, but he wouldn't hear of it."

The doctor nodded. "I know you did what you could. No one in this town can fault you there."

James felt cheated when the blame shifted from Trennen, but he shrugged off his personal feelings and asked the doctor, "Will she be all right?"

"There are some broken ribs, and as you can see, she's badly bruised." He shook his head. "Whoever did this to her did a thorough job."

"That no-good—" Mr. Wingate started.

"Yes, I've no doubt you're right about that." The doctor nodded. "But it may be tomorrow before she's able to tell us for sure."

James saw Vanda's eyelid flutter. He took a step forward. "She's coming to."

The three men crowded near. Mr. Wingate got down on one knee near her head. "Vanda, honey, who did this to you?"

Her good eye stared at him, but there was no answer. He tried again. "Did your father hit you?"

A tear ran out of her eye.

Mr. Wingate looked up. "There's your answer."

He turned back to her. "What happened to Cletis? Do you know if he took him?"

"Now you've gone and done it." The doctor frowned at Mr. Wingate. "If she didn't know he was gone, you've given her something to worry about."

"Look." James watched the slow up and down movement of her head. "She knows."

Mr. Wingate insisted that Vanda be moved to his house. After the doctor bandaged her and gave her some laudanum for pain, James carried her to the buggy and then into the Wingate home.

&

Monday at noon, Eliza sat by her window to watch for her father. When she saw him, she pulled her dressing gown on and ran from her room. By the time she got to the kitchen door, she could hear Mary and Father talking. He said, "I suppose she's better than yesterday, but she's still in pitiful shape."

Eliza stopped, her hand on the door. She pressed close to listen.

"The poor girl." Mary sighed. "I can't understand how a father could do such a thing. Has she been able to talk yet?"

"As a matter of fact she has." A chair scraped across the floor.

Eliza pushed the door open a crack until she could see her father sitting by the table. Mary placed a buttered hot roll in front of him.

"M-m-m." He grinned his appreciation. "You're spoiling me."

Mary smiled before moving out of Eliza's sight. "What about Vanda being able to talk?"

Vanda had been hurt. Why hadn't they told her? Eliza pushed the door open and stormed into the room. "What's wrong with Vanda?"

"Should you be out of bed?" Father rushed to her side, taking her arm.

She jerked away. "I'm not sick. I want to know about Vanda. What's happened to her?"

Father told what he knew and that Vanda was now at the Wingates'.

"Father, I want to see her."

"I don't think so." He shook his head.

"Please, Father."

"Would it hurt for her to go just for a few minutes?" Mary intervened on Eliza's behalf.

He frowned. "She's been beaten, Eliza, almost to death. You won't recognize her."

Although Father argued, in the end, Eliza won.

She dressed with care in a blue dress made with thin balloon oversleeves. She selected the matching blue bonnet that looked like a hat with a wide rim framing her head. She tied the blue satin ribbons in a wide bow. She wanted to look her best for Vanda.

Yet when she saw her, she realized her father had been right. The purple, swollen face that turned toward her was unrecognizable.

"It's me, Eliza." The voice sounded like Vanda's, although slurred. "Sit here by me."

Eliza wiped tears away as she sat on the bed.

Vanda smiled and closed her hand around Eliza's. "It isn't as bad as it looks. I think he just hit me a couple of times in the face."

"Oh, Vanda, how can you joke about it?" Eliza wanted to cry.

"I'm not joking. I think that's what happened."

"But it looks like he ran your face through the sausage mill."

Eliza was surprised at Vanda's laugh. "Oh, that hurts." She quickly composed herself. "Here you sit, pretty as a picture, and tell me how ugly I am."

"I didn't mean that," Eliza quickly assured her and then saw the twinkle in the other girl's eye. "Oh. You're joking again. After what you've been through, I'd think you'd need to be cheered up instead of the other way around."

Vanda's eyes grew serious. "You have a bruise, too. I heard you went through a bad experience that same night."

Eliza's eyes widened. "How did you hear?"

Vanda's mouth twisted into a small, lopsided smile. "I'm learning to be quiet and listen." Her smile vanished. "At least Trennen won't bother you anymore."

Eliza's heartbeat increased. "What do you mean by that?"

"He left this morning on the stage."

Eliza frowned. "No one told me."

"They aren't telling me, either. I suppose they think I'm not strong enough." Again she smiled. "They don't know that the Lord is my strength."

Eliza smiled tenderly at her friend. "Father said the entire church is praying for your quick recovery."

"Then I will be out of this bed in time for the Christmas program." Vanda's eyes shone. "I want to see it even if I can't be Mary." Her hand moved to touch her side. "I only have a couple of broken ribs. That won't keep me down long."

"I'm sure it won't." Eliza wondered how Vanda could possibly be up and around in little more than a week.

Vanda reached out and squeezed Eliza's hand. "Do you remember I asked you to pray for my father?"

Eliza nodded.

"I'd like for you to pray with me even harder now." A tear rolled from Vanda's eye. "I don't know where he is or what he's doing, but I'm afraid he will die without knowing Jesus."

"Aren't you angry with him for what he did? You almost died. You would have if they hadn't found you."

Vanda shook her head. "He didn't know what he was doing. Don't you see, Eliza? My sins nailed Jesus to the cross. How can I help but forgive others when I have been forgiven so much?"

Eliza sat and stared at her friend. Vanda meant what she said. Eliza bowed her head. She nodded. "I'll join you in praying for your father."

Eliza didn't stay long after that. She needed the privacy of her room where she could think and pray. Vanda was a babe in Christ, but she had taught Eliza something that she would never forget as long as she lived.

For hours Eliza stayed shut away in her room, where the others thought she was resting. Instead she fell to her knees beside her bed, alternately reading God's Word and praying. At first unwilling to give up her own feelings, she finally saw herself honestly for the first time in many months as God revealed what she would have to do in order to be brought back to the right relationship with Him that she craved.

After a time, she arose and washed away the tears of her soul-searching. She glanced out the window and saw it was still too early for her father to be home from work. She needed to talk to Mary.

Mary sat at the table peeling potatoes for supper.

Eliza sat in a chair across the table, unsure of how to begin. How could she break down the wall she had built with a simple apology? But she knew she must try.

Mary turned to smile at her. "Did you have a nice rest, Dear?"

Eliza shook her head. "I was praying about something that's been bothering me."

"Is it anything I can help with?"

Eliza smiled at Mary. "I think I already have my answer. Do you have a moment?"

"Of course."

Eliza looked into Mary's kind, green eyes. "Do you love my father? I mean, really love him?"

A tinge of pink touched Mary's cheeks. She smiled and nodded. "I love your father very much. I thank God every day that He led you to introduce us."

Eliza bowed her head as moisture clouded her vision. "I've been terrible."

Mary's hand stretched across the table to cover Eliza's with a sympathetic touch. "You've had a hard time adjusting, but God has assured us all along that you would come through this."

"You've been praying for me?"

"I pray for you every day, Eliza. I care about you. I loved you before I loved your father, you know. You were my friend, and then you were my daughter."

Eliza looked up at Mary, disbelief covering her face. Mary had forgiven her before she even asked.

But Mary misread Eliza's expression. "No, I don't mean I'm trying to take your mother's place. No one could do that, and I wouldn't want to. She will always have a special place in your heart and in your father's. That's only right. But don't you see? It's the same with me. I already have one daughter, yet I have plenty of room in my heart to love five more. That doesn't mean I love Kathrene less. It just means I love you as much."

Tears streamed down Eliza's face. All she could do was choke out the words, "I love you, too, Mary. I'm so sorry."

She didn't remember moving out of her chair, but she found herself kneeling on the floor with her head in Mary's lap.

Mary stroked her hair, crooning words of forgiveness as the healing tears fell.

Finally, Eliza pulled away, her face wet with tears, a smile on her lips. She reached out and took both of Mary's hands in hers. "I'm so glad I came to talk to you."

"I am, too." Mary smiled through her own tears. "You don't know how glad."

"What's going on here?" Neither had noticed Father come in. He stood looking from one to the other.

Eliza jumped up and grabbed him around the neck. "I love you, Father."

His arms slipped around her as he held her close. "I love you, too, Eliza." He looked over her head at Mary, his eyebrows lifted in question.

Mary stood. "Eliza and I have just come to a wonderful understanding." She stepped to her husband's side, and he put one arm around her. "We've decided there's room in our hearts for each other and for you, too."

Father let out a long breath. "That's the best news I've heard in a long time."

ॐ

The next day Eliza returned to visit Vanda. She went every day that week, each time noticing an improvement in Vanda's condition. Still, no word came about Cletis and his father. Eliza knew Vanda worried about them. On Friday, as Eliza left, Vanda caught her hand and held it. "Eliza, would you pray with me right now for Cletis and Poppa?"

Eliza nodded. Still holding Vanda's hand, she knelt beside the bed, and together the girls prayed that God would protect the two and bring them to salvation.

The following week when Eliza prayed with her friend again, Vanda kept her hand. "Wait, Eliza, please."

Eliza remained on her knees.

"I know what Trennen did to you. I know Uncle Charles sent him away because of it. And I wouldn't blame you if you don't want to, but I think he needs our prayers, too."

Eliza hesitated only a moment. "I'll pray with you for your brother."

As Vanda's physical strength returned, Eliza's spiritual strength grew. She spent more time in prayer and Bible reading during those weeks than she had in the past two years. Her relationship with Mary became a treasure. Kathrene, when she wasn't with Stephen, responded to Eliza's encouragement to become the sister she had always wanted to be.

But there was still one dark spot in Eliza's life. She could not forget James Hurley. Every time she thought of him, a dart driven by Lenny's words pierced her heart. *Father got you James, didn't he?* It hurt more every day.

A light snow began to fall Sunday afternoon. That evening, buggies and wagons arrived early for the Christmas program. The church shone with candles and lanterns and buzzed with the excited voices of parents and children alike. Both front corners of the church had been partitioned off with sheets and quilts to make two small rooms where the actors could get into costume. Eliza wound her way behind Lenny through the crowded church.

Someone jostled her, and she fell into James. His hands closed over her upper arms to steady her, and he did not let go. She found herself eye level with his mouth. Her gaze lifted to his dark gray eyes frowning down at her.

"Are you all right, Miss Jackson?"

At the formal use of her name, she stiffened and pulled back. "I'm just fine, thank you, Mr. Hurley. Now if you'll excuse me, I'm supposed to be an angel tonight."

A slow smile spread across his face. "That should be interesting."

"Oh!" She jerked away and moved as quickly as she could to the corner where the angels were dressing. She slipped through a space between two quilts, glad to be out of his sight. She knew her face flamed.

"Eliza, here's your costume." Kathrene tossed it to her, then slipped into her own. Eliza carefully wrapped the sheet around herself, and Kathrene tied it into place. The halo and wings were harder to keep on, but finally all three angels were ready.

"Who's going to play Mary now that Vanda isn't able to?" Barbara whispered.

"I don't know," Eliza whispered back. Yesterday afternoon at their last rehearsal, a replacement still hadn't been announced.

The program began with the small children. One gave a welcome that brought a round of applause. Then several others sang "What Child Is This?"

The angels peeked through narrow cracks between quilts. Eliza could see the front of the church where most of the activity took place.

"What's going on?" She whispered to the other angels as a hush fell over the congregation and several gasps were heard. Applause filled the church. The girls could only look at each other and wonder what was happening. Then as quickly as the applause began, it stopped.

As a hush fell on the congregation, Eliza saw a hooded Mary and Joseph cross the pulpit area. Mary turned and, with Joseph's help, sank to the floor behind the manger. It was Vanda. Her face, yellow and green with bruises and still distorted by the swelling, had never looked lovelier to Eliza. A glow seemed to emanate from her serene expression. She kept her eyelids lowered in reverence. Then she reached out and lifted a doll from the straw-filled manger and cradled it in her arms.

While the shepherds came from the opposite corner, Eliza followed Barbara to stand behind Mary and Joseph. Kathrene stepped forward and sang "Angels from the Realms of Glory."

When Eliza blended her voice with Barbara's on the chorus, she felt God's presence. She was so thankful that God had given His only Son to become the sacrifice for her sins. There was no love greater than that.

James sat beside his mother and watched the Christmas program. He smiled at the small children and felt proud of his younger sister, but the one person he most wanted to see was hidden from his view in the front corner of the church. He brought to mind the snapping brown eyes that were becoming a regular visitor to his dreams. He remembered the feel of her satin cheek, the softness of her dark hair caught in his fingers.

He loved Eliza Jackson, but she wanted nothing to do with him. For the thousandth time he asked himself what he had done to turn her away.

And then she stepped from the curtains that hid her and stood behind Mary and Joseph. He had made fun of her being an angel, but as he stared at her, he knew he had never seen a more beautiful angel. Her eyes lifted above the heads of the congregation as if she looked into heaven. The yellowed bruise still covered her cheek, yet a soft smile touched her radiant face, making her appear beyond the reach of earth—and man.

The dull ache in his chest had become part of him. Because she was beyond his reach. He looked down at his clenched fists. He'd tried to talk to her, but she wouldn't listen. She went out of her way to avoid him. He had to find out what was wrong if he had to have a talk with her father to do it.

℘

Winter came with a vengeance after the Christmas program. One snowfall followed another until the drifts measured more than four feet deep. Father said Old Man Winter was making up for last year's mild weather.

Eliza was glad the weather kept her from seeing James. Maybe if she didn't see him, she could forget him. She spent most of her time in the house helping Mary and Kathrene or playing with Nora. She began to look forward to spring when she would have a new brother or sister.

Then, winter gave way to spring flowers and sunshine. A time of new growth. Kathrene accepted Stephen's marriage proposal, but Eliza's life seemed to stall as her heart refused to forget James. All winter she had tried to block him from her thoughts, yet the first day she went back to church, he was there. When their eyes met, she knew she would have to learn to live with the pain of her love for him.

One day Father came home from work at noon with some news. He came into the kitchen where the women were working, a large smile on his face. "You'll never guess who just arrived in town."

Lenny came into the kitchen from the parlor. Father reached out and ruffled his hair. "You'll be wanting to hear this, too."

"Tell us who before we burst with curiosity," Mary said.

"Cletis Von Hall."

"Cletis!" Eliza squealed before Lenny could react. "Was his father with him? Where had he been? Did he go see Vanda? Oh, she'll be so happy he's all right. Is he, Father?"

Father laughed. "Yes, Eliza, Cletis is fine. As soon as we told him where Vanda was, he went to see her." Then he grew serious. "His father wasn't with him."

Silence fell around the table as her father related the story told to him. "After Von Hall beat Vanda unconscious, he picked her up and put her on the cot in the main room of the cabin. He covered her with a blanket, but when she remained limp and unresponsive, he thought she was dead.

"Cletis said his father panicked and ran, taking him. By the time they got to a town called Rolla, Mr. Von Hall was desperate for more whiskey, but he didn't have the money. He shook like he had a chill, and then he broke down and cried. He was like that for hours until he slept. When he woke, he took Cletis into town. They stopped at the first church they came to. Cletis said he didn't know what happened there except his father talked to the preacher, and he wasn't shaking anymore. The preacher went with them to the sheriff."

"He turned himself in." Eliza frowned. "Why didn't we hear anything? Wouldn't they have checked to see if Vanda really died?"

"Yes, except before they could, the weather got bad. A fire broke out in a house next to the jail. The two prisoners were released to help fight it. Von Hall heard a little girl crying. He perished saving her life."

Eliza scarcely noticed the tears running down her face. God had granted Vanda's wish to be used by Him.

"Cletis stayed with the minister until the weather cleared enough to send him home."

&

The next morning, Eliza put on her nicest visiting dress and went with Lenny to the Wingates' house. Mrs. Wingate took Lenny back to the kitchen to eat a snack with Cletis, leaving the two girls alone in the parlor. They met in the middle of the room and hugged. Eliza couldn't stop the tears.

As they pulled apart, she said, "I'm sorry, Vanda, about what's happened."

Vanda nodded. "Thank you. God knows what's best for us. I'll always remember my father died a hero. And I have Cletis back."

"Yes, how is he?"

Vanda smiled. "I don't think you'd recognize him. Oh, he looks about the same, but he doesn't act it. He was so rebellious before, but now he's trying really hard to do right. He even asked me if I thought God loved him."

"That's wonderful, Vanda."

"Yes, and that's not all." Vanda sat on the edge of a chair. Her eyes shone. "Cletis and I are going away. We have an aunt in Boston who wants us to come live with her. She has no children. Uncle Charles says she and her husband are a wonderful Christian couple who will probably spoil us rotten."

"Oh, Vanda!" Eliza couldn't help the cry of dismay that leapt to her lips. "You can't leave."

"I know, Eliza." Vanda crossed to the sofa and sat beside her, putting her arm around her shoulders. "I'll miss you, but I believe this is for the best. I want Cletis to grow up in a home where there is discipline and love. I think he will have that with our aunt and uncle."

"Why couldn't he get that here?"

"Uncle Charles and Aunt Martha do love us, but they are too close to all that's happened. And they aren't as young as our other aunt and uncle." Vanda smiled. "Besides, I have a feeling Cletis will need a father young enough to keep up with him."

Eliza knew in her heart that Vanda was right, yet she knew she would never forget her friend.

15

*V*anda left the first week of April. Eliza stood by the stage-coach with her. Vanda wore a soft blue dress of the latest fashion, and Eliza knew several more new dresses were packed in her trunk. Mrs. Wingate had made sure her niece and nephew would not be ashamed when they arrived at their new home. Eliza waited while the others told Vanda good-bye, and then she stepped forward.

"I don't know how I'll ever get along without you." She hugged Vanda with tears in her eyes.

"You promised to not cry." Vanda hugged Eliza tight. "I'll write to you as soon as I get there."

"You'd better." Eliza forced a smile. "Because I can't write to you until I get your address, and as soon as you're gone, I'll think of a million things to tell you."

"Eliza, you're the best friend I've ever had. If it hadn't been for you, I'd never have found Jesus as my Lord."

"I didn't do anything."

"Oh, yes, you did. At first I only went to church because you were there. You were my friend, and I wanted to be with you. Then the message of God's salvation got through to me, and I went because I knew there was something missing in my life. If you hadn't been my friend, I'd have never heard that message."

Eliza could only say, "I'm glad."

"You're not going to leave without telling me good-bye, are you?" James's voice called from behind Eliza. Her heart began the hard quick pound that had become all too familiar in his presence.

"Of course not." Vanda extended her hand, and James shook it.

"This town will miss you two very much, you know." James smiled down at Vanda.

"Oh, I don't know about that." Vanda returned his smile. "But I do know we'll miss all of you."

"You take care." James turned as if to leave.

"I will." A twinkle entered Vanda's eyes. "And you take care of my friend."

James looked at Eliza. His eyes were serious as he said, "There's nothing I would like better." Then he turned and walked away.

"Better get aboard, Miss," the driver called from the open door of the coach.

"I've got to go." Vanda gave Eliza another hug. She whispered near her ear, "Be good to James." Then she and Cletis climbed on the stage.

Eliza stood by the side of the road, waving until Vanda disappeared in a cloud of dust.

&

The next day, Kathrene came in from an outing with Stephen. Her eyes shone. "Eliza, do you want to hear something funny?"

Eliza sank into a nearby chair. "It would probably be more entertaining than what I've been doing."

Kathrene sat on the sofa. "Stephen has been keeping things from me, but today he confessed."

Eliza sat a little straighter.

"We went out to look at the house." Kathrene clasped her hands in front. "Eliza, he's building a mansion for me."

Eliza frowned. She was sure Kathrene would think anything Stephen built was perfect. But really! How could a penniless beggar . . . ?

"Remember how we all thought he was poor?"

Eliza nodded.

"He isn't poor at all." Kathrene laughed. "He just wanted me to think that because he wanted me to love him for himself and not for his money."

"What would make him do that?" Eliza was as puzzled by Stephen as she had been the first time she'd seen him.

Kathrene sobered. "He's from New York where his father owns some factories and several other businesses. His father wanted him, along with his younger brother, to take over the businesses." She paused. "Stephen was engaged to be married before."

Eliza's eyes widened. "What happened?"

"He found out she was marrying him for his money. He was deeply hurt and angry. So he sold his share of the businesses to his brother, reinvested a lot of it in some regional railroads, and came west."

"But Kathrene, what if he wants to return to New York someday? Would you go with him?"

Kathrene shook her head. "I don't think I have to worry about that. Stephen has assured me that Missouri is where he wants to live and die. He knows I'm not marrying him for what he can give me. And he knows the people here like and respect him for himself, not because of his money."

She held up her hand. "Please, Eliza, don't ever tell anyone just how wealthy Stephen is. He loves it here, and he wants to make a home for us where we can be like our neighbors."

"Are you telling me that Stephen is even more wealthy than the Wingates?" Eliza could scarcely believe that.

Kathrene laughed. "I'm afraid so, but you'd never know it, would you?"

"What about your house? Is it really a mansion?"

"I might have exaggerated on that. It's a very nice two-story frame house." Kathrene smiled. "Eliza, I really love Stephen. I'd be content to live in a log cabin at the edge of town as long as I can be with him. I don't care about his money."

One morning in mid-April, about an hour before Father was due home for dinner, Mary called to Eliza, "Would you please run and get your father? Tell him I'm not feeling well."

As Eliza started to go, Mary called to her again, "If you see Kathrene, please tell her to come to my bedroom."

Eliza ran up the stairs as fast as she could and pounded on Kathrene's bedroom door before jerking it open. "Kathrene, your mother needs you right away in her bedroom. I think it's her time."

Eliza left the house in a run until she reached the business part of town.

With her breath coming in gasps, she passed the cooperage and stuck her head in the chandler shop. The front room was empty. She crossed to the back room. No one was there, either. As she turned around and started back across the showroom, James opened the door and came inside.

They stood for an eternity staring at each other. He spoke first. "I thought you were a customer."

How could she speak past her pounding heart? "It's Mary. Where's my father?"

Immediately he understood the problem. "He left just a minute ago to make a delivery. I'll catch him." He stopped at the door. "Do you want to wait here?"

She followed him as he went around the building where his horse stood grazing. She watched him saddle the horse, trying to decide what she should do. Kathrene was with Mary. Surely they wouldn't need her. Maybe she should stay and watch the shops until either Father or James returned.

"What about the doctor? Do you want me to leave word with him, too?" James swung into the saddle.

At her nod, he smiled. "Don't worry. I'll give your father my horse; then I'll make the delivery and come right back." He nudged his horse forward, calling over his shoulder. "If you decide to leave, be sure and put the closed signs in the doors."

She watched him spur his horse into a run before she turned back toward the chandler shop. She opened the door, stepped inside, and collapsed onto the stool behind Father's high counter. Her knees and hands trembled. She crossed her arms on the counter and laid her head on them, trying to still the tremors that passed through her body.

She prayed for Mary, asking God to give her a safe delivery and a healthy child.

"Are you all right, Eliza?" Mrs. Johnson stood in the middle of the shop, a concerned expression on her face.

Eliza smiled at the elderly lady. "Yes, I'm fine. Is there anything I can help you with?"

By the time Mrs. Johnson had made her selections and gone, Eliza figured James had caught up to Father. Maybe he was on his way home. And that was exactly where she should be going. If she waited around the shops, James would come back, and she'd be alone with him. She didn't want to take that chance.

But before Eliza could close the shops, Mr. Morrison stopped with an order for barrels. He finally left, and she put the closed sign in the shop window. As she turned to leave, James pulled Father's wagon in and stopped. As usual her heart pounded when she saw him.

James jumped from the wagon and moved to her side. "I'm glad you're still here. I was afraid you'd go home."

He stood too close. "I'd really like to talk to you, Eliza."

"Whatever would we have to talk about?" She stepped back from his overpowering height. If she didn't get away, she might cave in and cry.

"Your father seems to think you're unhappy." He got no further.

Her head snapped up. She glared at him. "How dare you and my father discuss me! I am not your concern."

She pushed past him, then stopped long enough to fling one last remark at him, "I am also not a charity case, and I'll thank you to remember that."

ɞ

James watched Eliza disappear around the corner. What had she meant by her being a charity case? He shook his head. There was no understanding a woman when she was riled. But what had he done to make Eliza so angry with him?

He glanced at the wagon and smiled. Maybe there was one way to insure she stayed put long enough to find out what had got her back up. He'd have to wait a few days until the Jackson family settled down, but at the first opportunity, he'd enlist Mr. Jackson's help.

≈

The entire family crowded around the bed where Mary lay propped up, her face beaming with pride as she looked at Father. He sat on the side of the bed, a small bundle of blankets in his arms.

"Eliza, come see our new sister." Kathrene took her arm and pulled her to Father's side. "We've all been promised a chance to hold her, but Father's being a hog."

"You'll get your turn." Father looked up with a grin. He pulled a tiny hand from the blanket.

Nora squealed as the miniature fingers curled around Father's big one. "I hold my lovey."

She jumped on Mary's knees, and Father laughed. "Whoa, Girl. You'll be hurting Mama doing that."

Immediately Nora stopped. "I sorry, Mama." She plopped down beside her father, her little legs stretched out. "I want my lovey."

"All right." Father passed the baby to Nora, keeping his hands under her head and back. "We'll start with the youngest and work our way back up to me."

"Be careful, Orval." Mary tried to see. "Don't let her drop her."

"Don't worry. I've got a good hold."

While Nora and Lenny got their turns with the baby, Eliza stepped to Mary's side. "Are you all right?" She clasped Mary's hand in both of hers.

Mary smiled. "I'm fine."

"Kathrene and I can take care of everything." Eliza remembered how tired her mother had been after Nora's birth. She had never regained her strength. She didn't want the same thing to happen to Mary.

Mary smiled and reached for Kathrene's hand with her other hand. "You don't know how much I appreciate both of you."

Eliza took her turn at holding the baby. The small bundle felt so light in her arms. She pulled the blanket back to see a tiny face framed by light brown hair with a hint of red in it. The little rosebud lips made a sucking motion and then grew quiet. The baby's eyes that had been closed in sleep opened and seemed to study her big sister's face. Love, as great as she had ever felt for Nora, swept through Eliza's heart. This baby was her sister.

She looked up at her father. "I wish Cora and Vickie and Ben could see her."

He nodded. "I know. I do, too."

"She's so perfect." Eliza was totally captivated. "What is her name?"

Kathrene reached for the baby. "Why don't you discuss a name with our parents while I hold my little sister?"

Eliza placed a kiss on the tiny forehead before relinquishing the baby to Kathrene. "Be careful with her."

"Eliza, I know how to hold a baby."

Father turned to Mary. "Have you picked a name?"

Mary shook her head. "Nothing I've thought of sounds right."

Eliza lifted Nora and sat with her on the bed. "How about you, Nora? Do you have any good ideas? What do you want us to call the baby?"

"Her's my lovey," Nora said.

Eliza squeezed her little sister. "Yes, she's a sweet little lovey just like you, but I don't think we want to name her that."

"Lovey, Lovelle, Lovena." Mary tried changing the word slightly. "Why can't we make our own name with some variation of that? I like the idea. It could mean sweet little loved one."

Father looked thoughtful. "What's wrong with Lovena?"

"Or we could spell it with a *u* so it's more like a name. How about Luvena?" Eliza suggested. "What about Luvena Anne or Luvena Marie?"

"Luvena Marie Jackson," Mary repeated and smiled. "I like it. What do you think, Orval?"

He nodded. "It sounds like our littlest girl has a name."

❧

Luvena, or Lovey, as Nora insisted on calling her, was a quiet baby. She slept most of the day, crying only when she had need of attention. And attention was one thing she had no lack of.

One day as Eliza rocked her little sister to sleep, she noticed Mary in the doorway of her bedroom watching them. A smile played around the corners of her mouth. "You are going to have that baby so spoiled no one can do anything with her."

"You don't really think love will spoil her, do you?" Eliza asked.

Mary reached down and took her baby. "No, and neither will rocking."

She stopped at the door, turning to say, "I'm going to put Luvena in her own bed, and then you and I are going to get your father's meal."

At dinner, Father looked across the table at Eliza. "How long has it been since you helped me with the shops?"

"Not counting the day Luvena was born?" At his nod, she thought back and couldn't remember the last time. She shrugged her shoulders. "I don't know. A long time, I guess."

He seemed interested in his food. "I've got a delivery needs to be made this afternoon. How'd you like to go along?"

"I'll go with you, Father." Lenny stopped chewing long enough to volunteer.

"No, this time I want Eliza to go. I'll tell you what, Lenny; you can go on the next delivery I have to make. How's that?" At Lenny's nod, Father looked back at Eliza. "How about it? There's a blue sky above and April flowers coming up all over the place. You couldn't pick a prettier day to go for a ride in the country."

She laughed. "All right. As soon as the dishes are done, I'll come."

"Eliza, I can do the dishes. Why don't you go on with Father now?" Kathrene urged her.

"Will we leave on the delivery right away?" Eliza didn't want to chance another encounter with James.

"Sure. The wagon's already loaded and sitting in back of the shops."

"All right, then." Eliza nodded. "I'll go." She knew Father had been concerned about her. If it'd make him feel better, she'd go with him. Besides, it was a beautiful day.

Her steps lagged as they approached her father's shops. Above all, she did not want to see James. She edged toward the side of the building. "I'll go around back and wait in the wagon."

Father nodded. "That's fine. I need to go inside for a moment." He waved her on as they parted. "This won't take long."

James was nowhere in sight. Eliza sighed with relief and climbed on the wagon. A bird scolded her from the branches of a nearby tree. She adjusted her skirts and tried to find the bird. The dense covering of green leaves hid it well. She tilted her head back and looked all the way to the top of the tree. The scolding went on, and still she couldn't see it. Slowly, her eyes searched for the bird, branch by branch. She became so engrossed in finding the bird she didn't realize her father had returned until she felt the wagon move as he climbed on.

A flicker of blue in the tree caught her attention then, and without turning to look at him, she pointed at it. "Look up there, Father. Do you see that bird? He's been making a racket ever since he saw me, but I've just now found him."

When Father didn't answer but flicked the reins over the horse instead, Eliza turned to see what was wrong.

James looked back at her.

"No," the cry tore from her throat. "I will not go with you. Where is my father?"

The wagon moved forward. James shrugged. "Your father's in the shop, and you are going with me."

"James, I assure you, if you do not stop this wagon now and let me off, I'll jump."

With the speed of lightning, James grabbed her arm and pulled her close to his side. "You're just the little spitfire who would do that, aren't you?"

They pulled out and turned north down the Booneville Road. James's arm slipped around her shoulders. "James, let go of me." Eliza spoke through clenched teeth. Her heart pounded hard in her chest. "This is not proper. People are looking at us."

He grinned at her. "If you promise to behave yourself, I'll let go."

She tried to sit as dignified as possible with her side pressed against James. "All right. Let me go, and I won't jump." At his triumphant look, she added, "I won't talk to you, either."

They were past the business part of town, where the houses spread out thin. James relaxed his hold on her, letting her scoot as far as she could get from him. He nodded. "I guess that's a pretty good bargain. With your mouth shut, I might be able to tell you a thing or two."

She turned to him with fire in her eyes. "Like how much my father's paying you for this little excursion."

He looked at her with a puzzled expression. "He doesn't pay me extra for deliveries. Besides, what's that got to do with anything?"

"It has everything to do with it, and you know it." She retreated back into silence.

James shook his head. "If you're ready to not talk now, I'd like to talk to you."

"I told you I wouldn't talk to you, didn't I?" She refused to look at him.

"Yes, but it doesn't sound like you're ready."

"I'm ready anytime. But I'll have to warn you. I don't plan to listen to anything you have to say."

James let a burst of air escape through his teeth. "Eliza, you are the most aggravating woman I have ever met." After a second, he added. "You're also the prettiest."

She swung around to look at him, but he stared ahead down the road. "In the last six months, I don't know how many times I've tried to talk to you. But every time I start to say something, you run away or do something to stop me."

"I don't see any reason for us to talk."

"Well, I do." James raised his voice as he turned to look into her eyes. "Were you in love with Trennen?"

Eliza gasped. How could he ask her such a stupid question? She glared at him and then shifted in her seat.

"Eliza! You either sit still, or you sit over here where I can keep hold of you." At his commanding tone she froze.

A smile curved her lips. "I wasn't going to jump, James."

"Then answer my question. Were you, or are you, in love with Trennen?"

"That's ridiculous." She looked out at the countryside they were passing through. "In the first place it's none of your business, and in the second place it's insulting to know that anyone would even think I possibly could be."

James let his breath out in a *whish*. Eliza looked at him and saw a wide grin on his face. For some reason his happiness just added fuel to her anger.

"For your information, James Hurley, I think Trennen Von Hall is an extremely handsome man." She felt victory as his grin disappeared. But she couldn't help adding, "At first I enjoyed his company, but it didn't take long for that to wear thin."

"Then why did you continue keeping company with him?"

"Because I couldn't get rid of him. I told him I didn't want to see him anymore, but he wouldn't listen. I was scared of him. I didn't know what to do."

"Why didn't you tell your father?" James's jaw clenched. He hadn't known the extent of Eliza's problems with Trennen.

"I didn't think of it," Eliza answered his question. "I kept thinking he would leave me alone if I asked him to."

"I would have been glad to take care of him for you."

"Thank you. But he promised to leave me alone if I went with him that one last time to take Vanda and Cletis home."

He pulled the wagon to the side of the road and stopped. He turned to her. "Eliza, I don't know what you think of me or if you ever think about me at all. I'm not handsome, and I don't have much worldly goods, but I've loved you ever since the first time you put me in my place." He picked up the reins. "Now I've told you what I've been wanting to, so I guess the rest is up to you."

"Put those down." Eliza waited until he laid the reins back down. "I don't believe you."

He stared at her. "You don't believe me?"

"No, I don't." She crossed her arms. "I know my father paid you to take me to that taffy pull. You didn't want to. Why should I believe anything you say?"

"Because I don't lie."

"Oh, you don't?" Eliza's voice rose. "And what do you call being paid to take a girl out and then acting like you enjoyed it?" She looked at him with accusing eyes. "You kissed me."

James's voice rose in volume to match hers. "I kissed you because I wanted to. And I did enjoy it. Both times." His voice suddenly dropped, and he frowned at her. "What are you talking about being paid, anyway?"

"My father, James." She spoke to him as if he were a child. "Lenny overheard him tell you to take me to Barbara's taffy pull. I would assume that was part of your job."

"Well, it wasn't." He doubled up his fist and hit his knee. "How you and Lenny could have gotten such a fool idea is beyond me. It just so happens that your father knew of my feelings for you."

Eliza's eyes widened as she listened to him.

"I told you I've loved you for a long time. I guess I wasn't too good at hiding it—at least not from your father. When Barbara invited me to her taffy pull, he asked me if I was going and who I would take. I told him I probably wouldn't go because you were the only girl I wanted to take and I didn't think you'd go with me. That day Lenny eavesdropped, your father told me you were in the other shop and would be leaving soon and I should ask you. Again, I told him I didn't think you'd go, but he was insistent that I'd never have a better chance."

He grinned at her then. "I decided it wouldn't hurt to ask. You couldn't do much more than bite my head off, and you'd already done that so many times I was getting used to it."

Eliza sat in stunned silence staring at him. Then she found her voice. "You mean you really wanted to take me? My father didn't talk you into it?"

He nodded, his eyes sparkling with amusement. "I mean I really wanted to take you."

"What about today? Whose idea was it to trick me into going with you?"

He grinned. "That was mine. Your father thought it was a good idea. Who knows? I may get a raise because of it."

"Oh, you." She halfheartedly hit at him, but he caught her hand in his.

They sat, turned toward each other, holding hands. Finally, he said, "I've told you I love you, Eliza. I need to know how you feel about me."

Her eyelids lowered, hiding her eyes. A spot of pink tinged each cheek. "I love you, James."

He moved across the seat closer to her. His forefinger cupped her chin, raising it until she had to look at him. "Please, say that again."

A smile played around the corners of her mouth as she obeyed. "I love you, James."

"Eliza, will you marry me?" James held his breath as he waited for her answer.

She nodded and uttered the one word he wanted to hear. "Yes."

His lips closed on hers in a long, sweet kiss. But when he lifted his head, Eliza's saucy little grin came back. "How much did my father pay you to ask me that?"

He groaned. His tone threatened. "Eliza . . ." But then he stopped and laughed. "I can see right now it'll take a heavy hand to keep you in line."

"And you're just the man for the job?"

He nodded. "That's right, and don't you forget it."

Her eyes widened as James leaned slowly and deliberately toward her. His right arm slipped around her while his left hand touched her cheek, then slid to the back of her head, taking her bonnet with it. When his mouth claimed hers, she felt as if she were floating, and she never wanted to come back to reality.

When the kiss ended, she saw that James was just as shaken as she was. He pulled her close, looking down at her with the light of love still shining in his eyes. "How soon can we get married?"

She pulled her bonnet back up and then leaned back against his shoulder with a sigh. "My birthday is in October. How about then?"

"October!" He pulled forward to see her face better. "I think my birthday would be a better time. It's in June."

"But Kathrene's getting married in June. I don't know if I can get ready that soon."

"Of course you can. What's there to do? We just stand up in front of the church and the preacher talks a little."

Eliza giggled. "Someone had better tell Kathrene she's doing it all wrong, then."

James let out a long breath. "Eliza, we won't need a bunch of stuff. We'll have to live with my mother."

When Eliza didn't say anything, James looked at her. "You don't want that, do you?"

She smiled, shaking her head. "We need to talk."

"What we need is our own cabin. How long would it take to put together a one-room cabin? A week or two at the most. That's all we'll need, and then after we're married, we'll build on to it. I know the folks around here would help us." He grinned. "We could get married the first of May."

Eliza laughed, then gave him a quick kiss. "You are wonderful, James Hurley. But you're going to lose your job if you don't get these barrels delivered, and then where will we be?"

"You don't have to worry about that." He laughed. "After all, I'm marrying the boss's daughter."

He picked up the reins and flicked them over the horse's back. This time, as the wagon rolled down the country road, there was no distance between its two occupants.

Precious Jewels

by Nancy J. Farrier

For Hunter, my grandson. He is so precious to me.

1

Dakota Territory—January 1888

esse Coulter hunched over in the saddle, clinging to his horse, praying for shelter from the blizzard raging around him. The howling winds tore at him with invisible hands. The cold ripped the very breath from his nostrils.

How long had he been struggling through this storm? It seemed like days, but he knew that couldn't be true. *Oh, God,* he sobbed from his very soul, *I've failed You. I'm so sorry. If I could do it over, I would follow You no matter how difficult. Forgive me, Lord.*

His horse had stopped. He couldn't see, but he could feel the still muscles beneath his hand. He swayed dangerously far to the side. *Tired, I'm so tired.* He could barely form the thought. Then the wind gripped him, lifting his exhausted body into the blackness. The wet snow formed a blanket about him. He felt warmth as the cold fingers of death wormed their way through his sodden clothing. *A whale might have been better, Lord,* he thought as the blackness closed about him.

ॐ

Megan Riley paused, her mittened hand resting on the door latch. Rising panic tightened her chest, making breathing difficult. She leaned her head against the door, listening to the gale outside trying to tear the house apart. *Where are they? Why aren't they home by now?* Tears she couldn't afford to shed if she were to go out in the frigid weather threatened to fall anyway.

She glanced at the curtain blocking her view of the bed she shared with her younger sister, Seana. Indecision reigned. As the outside temperature dropped through the day, Seana's fever had risen, then broken at last. She finally slept, but Megan felt a desperate need for their mother to be here.

"Meggie."

A sudden drop in the wind brought the hoarsely whispered word to Megan. She quickly crossed the room and opened the curtain. "What is it? I thought you were asleep."

"Is Momma home?" Seana's pale face gleamed in the lamplight. "Where are you going?"

"Hush, now. There's no need to worry. Pa probably decided to stay in town rather than head home today. Maybe he and Matt didn't get everything loaded in time. They're most likely still visiting with Pastor and Mrs. Porter. You just rest. I'm going outside for a little more firewood."

Megan watched her sister's dull gaze drift to the pile of wood along the inside wall. "But you've brought in enough wood, haven't you?" The soft words were full of fear.

"I suppose I have." Megan smoothed the hair from her sister's forehead. "But for some reason I feel the need to bring more."

Seana closed her eyes. "You're right, Meggie. I feel it, too. Hurry back." Her head turned on the pillow; her eyes closed again in sleep.

Megan swallowed against the lump in her throat. *God, please take care of her until I get back. Help me to be safe.* At nine, Seana was eleven years younger than Megan. She had followed Megan since she could first toddle on unsteady legs, always calling her Meggie.

Outside, the wind, a howling banshee determined to have its way, pushed Megan back against the side of the house. The bitter cold burned all the way down her chest as she breathed in. She adjusted her scarf to cover her nose, hoping it would warm the air a little. Tiny needles of snow did their best to pierce the few parts of her face exposed to its touch.

Megan groped for the wood sled, thankful once more that her father had made it. On snowy days, it was so much easier to pull a sled full of wood than to carry an armful of logs while crossing the treacherous ground. She fumbled for the rope that would guide her through the storm and growing darkness. Earlier this afternoon she had put up a guide rope to the barn and to the woodshed so she wouldn't get lost.

The heavy drifts resisted her efforts to move. Her feet felt like lead weights after only a few steps. *God, I don't know why You have me doing this, but please help me. A person could easily freeze to death in this. Keep me safe. And, Lord, please keep Momma and Papa and Matt safe. I don't really think they stayed in Yankton another day. This storm began so suddenly, they could have been caught unaware. I don't think they were prepared for it to get this cold. Please watch over them.*

Tucking her head down to block the arctic air, Megan plowed ahead. Used to the resisting tug of the snow, she didn't realize her foot had connected with something solid until it was too late. She lost her grip on the lifeline and tumbled forward into the snowdrift, freezing ice crystals coating her face. She braced for the impact, a jolt of surprise racing through her as her hands contacted something that didn't belong in the deep snow.

A bump against her shoulder knocked Megan sideways. She stifled a scream that wouldn't be heard in this howling gale anyway. She lifted her head, squinting to see in the dimness of the late afternoon. She saw the movement just before the horse's nose nuzzled against her shoulder. Heart pounding, she reached up to pat it, then bent to brush aside the snow at her feet.

Whose horse was this? Had her father or Matt ridden ahead? Had she stumbled over one of them? Frantically, she dug, blindly seeking whomever lay buried here. Ever so slowly, she managed to free the upper body from the snow. *God, help me! I can't do this on my own. How will I ever get him inside? I'm not strong enough, and the snow blows back as fast as I push it away.*

Calm began to replace the panic. Megan knew she had to think clearly or whomever this was would die before she could help him. She inched upright, patting the horse that stood so close it blocked a bit of the wind. A tug on her arm reminded her of her errand. The wood sled. Of course! If she could only get him on the sled, she could pull him to the house.

Megan hauled the long sled next to the inert body. *God, please don't let him be dead!* She yanked and struggled, wondering how her little bit of strength could move someone so heavy. She knew for certain this wasn't her father or Matt. They were both slightly built, and this man—for she was sure it was a man—had much broader shoulders. In fact, his stocky body was proving impossible to lift onto the sled.

God, he's going to die if I don't get him inside. Please, help me.

The horse leaned over and blew its warm breath in her face. Megan brushed the ice crystals from the horse's nose. She gasped as an idea dawned, then doubled over in pain as the cold air rushed down her throat. Straightening, Megan began to run her hands down the horse's neck. Frantically, she prayed to find what she needed.

Relief flowed through her as her hands connected with a circle of rope. She fumbled with the leather thong while tying it to the saddle, wishing she could take off her awkward mittens. The rope finally dropped into her hand, and she quickly tied one end securely to the pommel.

She knelt next to the man, brushing away drifting snow that accumulated in the last few minutes. Making a second loop, she see-sawed it over his shoulders and under his arms. Pulling it tight, she stood and groped for the guideline. She sighed with relief as her fingers connected with her lifeline to the house.

Snow swirled; darkness marched closer. Megan realized she had no idea which way the house was. In the midst of trying to rescue this man, she had gotten turned around. She spun one way, then the other, straining to see through the raging blizzard. Panic washed over her like a wave.

Think, Megan, a nearly audible voice spoke. *Remember where you were at the start.*

She dropped back into the snow beside the man. Her thoughts scrambled, and she tried to remember exactly where she had been when she first found him. She closed her eyes and peace crept over her. *On his right side. Yes, that was it.* Megan stood, grasped the rope, and began to lead the horse toward the cabin.

The door resisted her momentarily, as the wind pushed to keep it closed. Then, when she despaired of getting it open, the wind gusted a different way, and the door swung wide. Megan slipped in amid a swirl of snowflakes, leading the horse.

"Whoa." She patted the horse's neck as she unfastened the rope from its saddle. "Easy, now. I'll put you in the barn as soon as I take care of your rider."

The horse filled half the small room. Megan edged past him, hoping he wouldn't get feisty in the cramped space. She dragged the stranger farther into the room and swung the door closed, shutting out the nasty weather.

"Meggie, there's a horse in our house." Seana's awe-filled voice was nearly lost in the noise of the horse's whicker.

"Seana, what are you doing out of bed?" Megan looked over at her wide-eyed sister. "I know there's a horse here. I had to use him to bring this man in before he froze completely. Now go hop in bed. I have work to do."

"But Meggie, who is that? Did Papa come home?"

"No, it's not Papa. It isn't Matt, either," Megan said, anticipating the next question. "I don't know who it is. I found him in a snowdrift outside. I don't even know if he's alive."

Megan glanced up at Seana's gasp. She regretted her harsh words, but couldn't take them back. She slipped her fingers under the man's coat collar. "I'm sorry, Honey. I shouldn't have said that. He is alive. I can feel a pulse, although it's a little weak."

Megan stood and ducked under the horse's neck. She leaned over and gave Seana a quick kiss on her cool cheek. "You've just gotten over your fever, and I don't want you to get worse. Please get back in bed. I'll get this man over by the fire where he can warm up, then I'll come tell you all about it."

She turned to duck past the horse again. Puddles of melted snow were building around his feet and steam rose from his coat, filling the room with the rank smell of wet horsehide. "Come to think of it, I think I'll take the horse to the barn before I check on you."

As Seana disappeared behind the divider, Megan turned to the task of dragging the man closer to the fire. Once there, she set about removing his wet outer clothing. She brought dry towels and rubbed the snow from his face and hair. She tried to ignore the wide set of his shoulders, the strength of his arms, and the strange feelings inside her. His rugged, sun-brown complexion told her he spent plenty of time outdoors; but his smooth hands said it wasn't at hard, physical labor.

Drying his hair, she felt a lump the size of an egg on the side of his head. "You must have hit your head when you fell off your horse." Megan didn't know why she spoke the words aloud.

His full lips turned up, twitching his mustache. His eyelids fluttered. Megan found herself staring into a pair of eyes the color of the cinnamon sticks Momma grated for cookies.

His smooth-fingered hand brushed her cheek. "Angel," he whispered hoarsely. "You're my angel."

His hand fell and his eyes closed once again. Megan touched the place where his hand had been. Never had she felt anything like this.

2

In the dim lantern light, Megan's frost-numbed fingers struggled to loosen the cinch. Eerie shadows danced across the stable wall. The buckskin dipped his brown nose in the pile of sweet hay she had thrown in the feeder. For tonight he could have one of the stalls usually reserved for her father's horses. She leaned wearily against the horse's tawny side. Her legs trembled as she listened to the howling wind and felt the biting cold. Were her parents and brother out in this storm? Had they stayed in Yankton with friends? Where were they?

Plucking a handful of straw, Megan began to rub the tiny bits of ice from the horse. Grunting, as if in appreciation of the attention, the steed leaned heavily against her hand. His tail swished, flicking her exposed cheek with its wet strands.

"I'm not a fly you have to swat." She gave his flank a light smack. "I wish you could tell me a little of your master. Where were you heading that you ended up on our doorstep?" She sighed and patted his neck. Dumping a small amount of grain in with the hay, she hefted the saddlebags and lantern. Pulling her mittens back on, she adjusted her scarf to cover her face, steeling herself to fight her way through the cutting wind.

God, please help this storm to be over by morning. I know worry is a sin, but I can't help it. I want to know my family is safe, but deep down I feel like something isn't quite right.

The cold, wet flakes of snow stung her eyes as she stepped from the barn's shelter. The wind battered her back against the door, slamming it shut. Throwing the saddlebags over her shoulder, she groped through blinding snow until she found the rope that led to the house.

Only a little ways, she assured herself. *I can do it. Seana needs me, and so does that man.*

After what seemed like hours, she pushed open the door of the cabin and stumbled into the cheery warmth. The stench of wet horse had faded; the floor would probably dry by morning. Setting down her burden, she stripped off her icy outer clothes and hung them on pegs near the door.

The stranger lay still as death near the fire. She stared at him, feeling the rise and fall of her own breathing as she willed his chest to move likewise, relief flooding through her as she detected the slight motion. Turning, she crossed to Seana's room. *Oh, please, I don't think I could cope with a dead man on top of everything else that's happened. Help him live, Lord,* she prayed silently, realizing that it was a selfish thing to pray.

Megan touched Seana's brow, and Seana opened her eyes. "Momma?"

Megan winced at the scratchy sound. "No, Seana, it's Meggie."

"Where's Momma?" Tears welled up in Seana's eyes. "I want Momma to sing to me. When will she be home?" Megan smoothed her hand over Seana's forehead, wondering how she could soothe her sister's fears when she had so many of her own. "Momma and Papa haven't come home yet. Perhaps they've had to stay in town another day. If they suspected the storm was coming, I'm sure they would have stayed over."

"But I want Momma." Seana began to sob. "Please make her come home."

Tears stung Megan's eyes. Seana rarely cried or demanded her way. That she was doing so now only spoke of her sister's fear.

"Will you sing to me, Meggie?"

"Of course." Megan smoothed her sister's hair and began to croon their mother's favorite song. Seana's eyelids fluttered, then slowly drifted shut. Megan continued to sing until her sister's breathing deepened and she slept.

Back in the main room, she dug her fists into the small of her back to ease the ache from leaning forward for so long. A low moan beckoned to her from near the fireplace. Crossing the room, she knelt beside the stranger.

"What am I supposed to do with you?" She didn't expect an answer. "You need to be up off the floor, but I know I can't move you by myself."

She studied the man on her floor. He reminded her of the broad and sturdy oxen her father kept for plowing the fields. She smoothed back the toffee-colored hair from his face. He needed a trim in both his hair and his mustache, the latter an interesting blend of reds, golds, and browns.

I don't know why I care what you look like. I know God doesn't intend for me to marry. If He had, He would have made me a lot more appealing. There isn't a man around who would look twice at me.

Laying the back of her hand against his forehead, Megan checked for fever. "I don't know why I did that. I have no reason to believe you're sick. Most likely it's the lump on your head and the hours of exposure that are keeping you asleep." She sat back on her heels and frowned. "Although, if I don't find a way to get you off the floor and in bed, it's quite likely you will end up sick."

As if in answer, his eyes snapped open. His panic-stricken gaze swept the unfamiliar surroundings before coming to rest on Megan's face. For a long moment, his warm cinnamon eyes stared at her.

"Angel," he whispered hoarsely. "I'm sorry. I couldn't stay with her. It would have been wrong. I had to go or I would have hurt her worse than I did. Please tell me you don't hate me for it."

His eyes closed, and she thought he'd lapsed back into sleep. Then, eyes still closed, his hand stretched upward until his fingers brushed her cheek. She took his hand and tugged gently, wondering if, with his help, she could get him to her parents' bed. Like a sleepwalker, he stood and allowed her to lead him. Within moments, she had him tucked beneath warm quilts. As she turned to go, his hand wrapped around her wrist. Her heart hammered as she pulled against his soft grip.

His eyes flickered open, then closed. "Sara, I didn't mean to hurt you." His grip relaxed, and he closed his eyes in sleep.

Megan touched her cheek where she could still feel the brush of his fingers. He'd called her Angel. *It must be the bump on the head. Angels are beautiful. No one in his right mind would ever confuse me with an angel.*

The angel faded and Jesse labored up the hill on leaden legs. "Sara, wait." Each step took more energy than he thought he had. He gasped for breath, his lungs burning. Sara, her red-gold hair floating around her like a mantle, beckoned him from the top of the hill. Her tinkling laughter echoed across the fields.

"We must talk." He yelled as loud as he could, yet he knew it wasn't enough. The thick air grasped at him, slowing his progress.

Sara clapped her hands impatiently. The hill faded, and he stood before Sara's house. The street was lined with carriages and horses. People milled about the yard. As he strode toward the door, men moved to pound him on the back, and women smiled and giggled.

A feeling of dread settled in the pit of his stomach. He looked up to see Sara framed in the doorway. Captivating Sara. From the wealthiest family in town. This was his engagement party. He was the envy of all the young men around. He had everything going for him. No one else knew how he would break her heart.

"Sara, we have to talk." He shouted to be heard above the crowd. "I have to explain." People were staring at him. Sara gave a petulant frown and beckoned him to come closer. He backed toward the gate. "It isn't right, Sara. It won't work."

He ran. Anguish ripped at his soul. He had to escape. The faces of his family and friends flashed by. They all tried to voice their disapproval. Hands reached out to stop him, but he ran on. The town faded in the distance. Another voice called, beckoning him to follow. But he hurried on.

"You don't understand," Jesse shouted to the hills. "I don't want what she wants. I'm not the person she expects me to be. God, I'm not who You want me to be. I can't do it." A sob tore from his throat. "I'm a simple person."

He fell to the ground. The soft grass waved around him. The scent of summer faded and the warmth turned to a chill that crept into his bones. Snow raged. The tiny flakes became daggers piercing his skin over and over.

"Oh, God." Sobs tore at his chest. "I'm not worthy to follow You.

I can't do it on my own. Please, if You want me to follow You, then give me a wife willing to stay beside me when I falter. Help her to love You enough to encourage me. Help me, God."

Peace settled over him. The dream faded and he rested, sleeping deep for the first time in weeks. He wrapped the heavy quilts close, sighing in contentment.

The voice of an angel murmured at his consciousness. The sweet melody wove a spell around him, pulling him awake. He forced his eyelids up and regretted it immediately. His eyes felt as if someone had thrown a bucket of sand in them. He closed them, wishing for cleansing tears that never came. Instead, the heavenly music spun about the room on a magic thread. He drifted to sleep again, wondering if all heaven's angels sang like this one.

He stood in his father's study.

"What are you doing with your life, Jesse?" His father's stern tone startled him.

Jesse glanced around. The huge mahogany desk only emphasized his father's imposing stature. Sunshine coming in the windows glinted off the polished paneling. The thick carpet muffled his footsteps as he neared the desk, placing his hands on the back of one of the overstuffed chairs facing his father.

"I'm going to work in the mine fields." He tried to sound determined.

"What about your marriage to Sara?"

"She isn't right for me." His hands gripped the chair, feeling the smooth leather give beneath his fingers.

"You're giving up a secure future to follow some gold lust?" His father's angry roar rattled the window glass.

"I can't stay here and be forced into a mold where I don't fit. Sara and I would both be miserable."

"I'd say the young lady is miserable right now," Richard Coulter thundered at his son. "You're not only bringing shame to her, you're disgracing our family name."

"I'm sorry." Jesse tried to find the words to make it right.

Jesse heard a sniffle and turned to the door. His mother stood there, her perfectly coifed blond hair a contrast to the dark surroundings.

"We need you here, Jesse." She pressed a bit of lace to her nose. "How will we ever get by if you leave?"

The room faded. He started to stretch out his hand, then stopped. "God will take care of you, Mother," he whispered. "He'll watch over you when I'm not here."

The angel's soft melody drifted near, her voice weaving around his very heart. Jesse tried once again to open his eyes. The light was dim, but he could see a figure hovering near him. Was this heaven?

His angel leaned close. Blue-gray eyes, sparkling with life, gazed at him. She wasn't beautiful, but an earthy prettiness warmed him to her. She smiled, and he tried to lift his heavy hand to touch the dimple in her left cheek. His body wouldn't respond, and he drifted away again. Was the angel real or simply another figment of his tormented dreams?

3

*S*treaks of sunlight fought a losing battle with the cold of the room when Jesse woke again. Motes of dust swirled in the air. A small fire crackled in the hearth.

His head throbbed, but at least he could think now. Jesse gave the room a slow perusal. The bed stood close to the wall, an armoire and table with a washstand near the closed door. Lifting his head, he tried to discover why he couldn't move. Weights seemed to be attached to his body, holding him in place; however, he couldn't see them. His head dropped back against the pillow, a film of sweat covering him from the exertion. He gasped for air, every breath sending needles of pain through his chest.

The door creaked, the scent of fresh baked bread and stew making his stomach growl. Turning his head, he could see a pixie face peeking around the door frame. The girl stared at him, a look of surprise on her pale features. One long brown braid swung like a pendulum in front of her shoulder, the only movement in a frozen tableau. She jerked back. The door slammed shut. He could hear her crying out, but couldn't make out the words.

The door swung open again. This time the young girl rushed into the room, tugging on the hand of a young woman. Jesse had vague memories of seeing her face. He tried to push up. Sweat beaded on his skin. A chill swept over him.

"See, Meggie, I told you he was awake." The pixie's braids bounced as she clapped her hands in delight.

"Calm down, Seana. I don't want you to have a relapse." Meggie moved over to the bed, where Jesse could get a good look at her. A neat coil of dark brown braids framed her round face. She leaned over to touch his forehead, her blue-gray eyes full of concern. The light in the room seemed to surround her when she smiled. His angel. He'd thought he'd been dreaming, but she was real.

"How are you feeling, Mr. Coulter?" Her fingertips grazed his forehead. Her dimple faded as she frowned at him. "You feel awfully warm. Are you hot?"

"No, Ma'am." His voice sounded scratchy from disuse. His body throbbed. He wanted nothing more than to fall asleep again. Another chill coursed through him. Jesse thought about asking for another blanket, but the effort would be too much.

Sleep weighed him down. He fought the tug of it, wanting to ask how she knew his name. Did he know these people? How had he gotten in this bed? What was wrong with him? As if through a hollow tunnel, he heard Meggie talking to the young girl.

"Seana, fetch me a rag and some cool water. Quick. Mr. Coulter is running a fever." The covers over him were loosened. Cool air rushed across his neck, and he shook with the chill. Something pressed against his chest.

"Seana, slow down, you're spilling the water."

"What's the matter with him now, Meggie?"

"I'm afraid he might be getting pneumonia from being in the snow and cold for so long. His breathing is congested. We'll have to fix something so he can breathe easier."

Jesse remembered the snow now. Darkness closed in tighter. The weight on his chest pressed down, robbing him of the precious air he needed.

ॐ

Megan worked at a feverish pace. She had Seana bathing Mr. Coulter's face with cool water, while she peeled and sliced onions to make a poultice. Last winter her brother, Matt, had gotten pneumonia. She'd helped fight the sickness with her mother and could still recall the various remedies they'd used.

"Meggie, why are you crying?" Seana looked tired as she came out of their parents' bedroom. Megan wiped her cheeks on her apron.

"I'm peeling onions, Seana. They always make me cry."

"Momma always cries, too." Seana's voice got very soft. Megan could hear the tears her sister struggled to hold back. She, too, had been praying once more for her parents and brother. Although she hadn't lied to Seana, the tears weren't all from the onions. Her heart ached with the fear that something had happened to her family.

For two days now, the storm had raged. Only by staying in town could her family have come through this blizzard unscathed. Even if the snow stopped now, it would be another two to three days before anyone could hope to get here from Yankton. The drifts would be too deep to get through. Her parents had the wagon, not the sleigh. Some how, she had to distract Seana and keep her from worrying. Seana had never been strong. Megan hated to think how her sister would react if something bad were to happen to their parents.

"Do you need more water for Mr. Coulter?" Megan pasted on a smile.

"I didn't know if I should keep using the cool water. He stopped sweating and now his teeth are chattering." Seana set the empty bowl on the table. She wrinkled her nose as she leaned over the skillet of onions. "Are you making that evil-smelling poultice that Momma made for Matt?"

"Yes. I'd appreciate you not calling it evil smelling." Megan's lips twitched as she recalled those very words coming from her father's mouth last year.

"Papa said Momma stunk up the whole countryside." Seana's blue eyes were wide as she gazed up at Megan. "He said the crops would have died if Matt hadn't gotten well in time."

Megan chuckled. "Papa was just joking. The fumes from these onions will help Mr. Coulter to breathe. He's having trouble getting air. That's why his breathing is so loud."

"Will he die?"

Megan felt like someone had rubbed her face in the snow. She wanted to yell at Seana and tell her not to ask such a ridiculous question, but she knew she'd been wondering the very same thing. "We'll pray that he doesn't." She hugged Seana. "You know Momma always claimed Matt got well more from the prayers than from the medicines she gave him."

"Then let's go right in and pray for Mr. Coulter." Seana grabbed Megan's arm. Megan laughed.

"You need to rest first, and I have to finish this poultice." She couldn't help noticing the way Seana's freckles stood out against the paleness of her skin. "You go lie down. I'll get these onions cooking and then go pray for Mr. Coulter. When you get up, we'll pray for him together. Okay?"

Seana nodded. "Will he get mad at you?"

"Mad at me for what?"

"Because you looked through his saddlebags."

Megan sighed. "I hope not. I needed to find out who he is." She didn't want to tell Seana she'd been looking for someone to contact if the man died. Megan hadn't thought he would live through the first night. Now, with pneumonia setting in on top of his injury and exposure to the cold, she didn't know what the outcome would be. How she wished her parents were here. They would know what to do.

Throughout the night, Megan sat by Mr. Coulter, alternately using the cool cloth to bring down his fever and changing the onion poultice. As the hours passed, she thought his breathing eased, but she couldn't tell for sure. If so, the change was slight. He continued to labor at drawing in air. One moment he would be sweating and throwing off the covers. The next moment his teeth would start to chatter, and he would shiver from the chills running through him.

Megan prayed harder than she'd prayed for anyone or anything. Last year when Matt had been so sick, she'd asked God to heal him, but not with the fervency she did for this stranger. After all, both of her parents were praying for Matt. This time only Seana's sporadic prayers were added to hers.

"Meggie?" Seana's soft words drifted through the thick fog of sleep surrounding Megan. She lifted her head and blinked. She'd fallen asleep with her head resting on the bed beside Mr. Coulter.

"Meggie, he's still alive. I hear him breathing." Seana looked like a waif in her nightgown.

Surging up, Megan groaned at the ache in her back from the unusual position she'd slept in. Lifting the covers, she yanked off the cooled poultice. How could she have fallen asleep and left this to grow cold? She shook her head to clear the cobwebs and placed her ear to his chest. If the congestion had lessened, she couldn't tell. He still labored painfully to pull in the air he needed.

"We'll have to heat up some broth and try to get him to take a few sips, Seana. He can't fight this sickness if he is weak from lack of food. Why don't you help me with breakfast while the broth heats?" She held out a hand to her sister.

By the time Seana finished eating, the broth was warm. Megan managed to rouse Mr. Coulter enough to get him to swallow a few spoonfuls. Then he collapsed against the pillow, eyes closed, the sound of his struggle to breathe filling the room.

Megan thought he was asleep again. As she tucked the covers close around him, his hand shot out and grabbed her arm. His slitted eyes stared at her. "Sara, I can't do this. You have to let me go. Why do you keep following me?" He began to cough hard enough to shake the whole bed.

Eyes wide as saucers, Seana watched from near the door. Megan tugged at her arm, trying to break free from his tight hold. The coughing spell ended, leaving him weak and shaking.

"Sara, please, I have to leave." He gasped out the words.

"It's okay. You can go." Megan held her breath as he froze, watching her with glazed eyes. His grip loosened. She pulled free. His whole body relaxed, and he slept again. Megan covered him before turning to leave.

"Meggie?" Tears were running down Seana's cheeks. Megan hurried to her sister and hugged her.

"What's the matter?"

"I thought he would hurt you. I was so scared." Seana clung to Megan, her body shaking. Megan herded her sister out of the bedroom and closed the door.

"Sometimes when people are very sick, Seana, they see things that aren't there. Mr. Coulter must have thought I was this Sara whom he knows."

"Who is Sara?"

"I don't know. I only found his Bible in his saddlebags. His name was written in there, but he'd recorded nothing else. When he wakes up, he'll tell us about this Sara if he wants us to know."

Megan sank into her mother's rocking chair and lifted Seana onto her lap. The rhythmic movement soothed them both. Seana, small for her age due to all the sickness that plagued her, seemed to weigh nothing at all. Her head rested on Megan's shoulder just as Megan had seen her rest against her mother many times. In no time Seana's deep, even breathing told Megan her sister had fallen asleep. She had so much to do; but for a few minutes longer, she relished the feel of her sister and the comforting motion of the rocker.

Jesse drifted in a cloud of pain. Voices swirled around him, some making sense, others only a distracting noise. Through it all, the heavy weight continued to press down on him like rocks piled on one by one. He didn't know how much time had passed. He couldn't tell whether it had been days or hours since this pain enveloped him. Somehow time didn't matter, only the battle at hand: the battle for his life.

"You have to marry Sara. She'll be the one to bring this family into the society we deserve. It's your duty to us, Son." His father's stern tones rumbled through Jesse's head. Society had always been the unattainable carrot his father strove to reach. All his life Jesse had been schooled to marry right so they would have the name and fortune needed to propel them forward. He'd failed, and his father would never forgive him.

"Jesse, Dear, you simply must give up this infatuation with religion. It isn't fashionable to be so fanatic about God." His mother's dulcet voice rang in his ears. "Attending the right church is important to one's place, but you needn't run around talking about Jesus as if He's a friend to you. People will think you're a lunatic." He could see his mother smoothing her perfectly coifed hair as she prepared to attend another tea, wearing the latest fashion, acting as haughty as any society matron. She tried to hide her disappointment in him, but Jesse knew he could never live up to her standards.

"If you truly love me, you'll give up this silly idea of going to the gold fields in Dakota Territory." Sara gave a pretty pout as she twirled her parasol, the whirling colors as mesmerizing as a snake. *"You don't want to go to such a dirty place when you can be here with me."* She smiled and pursed her lips, tempting him with all she offered. The day he left her, she vowed to get him back one way or another. She would carry a grudge until the day she got her way.

More rocks were piled on him. Jesse strove for a breath; the weight on his chest made the drawing in of air almost impossible. Spikes of pain tore through him with each effort. *Jesus, help me.* His tormented cry brought to mind the scene of his Savior on the cross, struggling to push against the nails so He could breathe. Jesus knew his suffering. He'd endured worse. Tears burned in Jesse's eyes. *Please, Lord, give me another chance to serve You. I'll go anywhere You ask, even home.*

The darkness lightened. The boulders on his chest warmed. Heat spread through his body, helping him to relax. He felt as if the hand of God was touching him, easing his hurt, changing his life. Relaxing as the agony lightened, Jesse drifted closer to the light.

Murmured words wove through his consciousness. Someone was in the room with him, talking. He wanted to turn back to the darkness. He couldn't face disappointing someone else. The promise he'd just made to God drifted through his mind. How could he have forgotten so soon? This was the direction God was leading him. He had to trust.

"Jesus, please, I don't know what to do for him anymore. I don't know what Seana will do if he dies. I don't know what I'll do." The sound of a woman crying compelled Jesse to awaken. His eyelids were so heavy as he forced them up. The flickering light of a lamp made him blink. Tears welled up, trickling down his cheeks. He couldn't move to stop them.

He'd never been so tired, yet Jesse knew without a doubt he'd been healed. Trying to draw in a deeper breath, he set off a spasm of coughing. Spikes drove through his lungs, but he'd gotten enough air to know he could breathe better.

"Meggie, look."

The coughing fit eased. Jesse saw the pixie in the doorway staring at him. He rolled back over to see his angel rising from a kneeling position by his bed. She'd been praying for him. He stared at her, concentrating on taking shallow breaths so he wouldn't cough again.

"Meggie, will he live?"

His angel nodded. "I think so, Seana." Her touch to his forehead felt like the flutter of butterfly wings. Jesse couldn't tear his gaze from her. He wished he had the strength to return her touch.

$\mathcal{F}$ rigid air brushed his cheeks when Jesse woke the next morning. Embers smoldered in the fireplace. His breath puffed out in white clouds. Under the pile of blankets and comforters, he stayed warm. For the first time since arriving here, he wasn't too hot or too cold. Although his body still felt the heavy weight of exhaustion, he could draw in shallow breaths without pain.

The door swung open. The woman he'd seen earlier entered, her arms piled with wood for the fire. She glanced at the bed and froze. "Oh, I didn't think you would be awake. I'm sorry." Her cheeks reddened as she stared at the floor. "I would have knocked first, but you have been asleep so long."

"I just woke up. Go ahead." The effort to speak left him gasping. Racking coughs began to shake his body. He curled on his side, trying to hold his breath to stop the coughing. By the time he could breathe again, the woman had the fire going and stood over him, one hand slapping against his back. Jesse had never been so tired.

"When my brother, Matt, had pneumonia, he would cough like this. Momma said he needed to get rid of the congestion clogging his lungs." The woman backed away. "I'm guessing that's what you need to do, too."

He tried to speak, but she held up her hand. "Don't. Talking will only make you cough again. Maybe later, when you feel better, we can talk. Right now I want you to rest. I'll bring in something to eat as soon as I get it fixed."

Jesse's eyes drifted shut before she'd closed the door on her way out. He slept the sleep of exhaustion and sickness, with only vague memories of reviving enough to swallow a few bites of some delicious soup the woman fed him. When he roused later in the morning, a little girl sat beside his bed, a rag doll on her lap.

"Hello." The one word caused Jesse to cough, although this time wasn't as severe as earlier. She stood next to the bed and patted his cheek until he could relax. The well-worn doll hung limply over her other arm, its skinny arms and legs dangling in the air.

"Meggie said you aren't to talk, but I have to watch you." The girl held one finger up as if lecturing a recalcitrant child. "Since you can't say anything, I'll tell you all about us so you won't be bored." Jesse nodded. The girl perched on the edge of the chair, a prim little miss replacing the mischievous pixie he'd seen before.

"My name is Seana, and you're at our house." She arranged the doll on her lap. "My sister, Meggie, is outside feeding the animals. She says I can't go outside because it's too cold and the snow is too deep. I just got over being sick, too. She brought your horse in the house. He dripped water everywhere on the floor and made the house stink." Her freckled nose wrinkled. "I don't want you to be mad at Meggie. She had to look in your saddlebags. We needed to know your name. She said Papa would have done that, too."

Sadness clouded Seana's eyes. "Papa and Momma and Matt went to town. They still aren't home. Meggie says they probably stayed with the Porters. Reverend Porter talks a lot in church on Sundays. We don't get to hear him very often because Yankton is too far away." She leaned forward and lowered her voice to a whisper. "I'm glad because I never understand the words he says. He makes me want to sleep."

Jesse's lips twitched. He'd met a few ministers who put him to sleep, too. The one at his parents' church, for instance. That man spoke in such a pompous monotone that Jesse wondered if even God stayed awake to listen.

"This is my doll, Ennis. I named her after my grandmother." The doll's features were worn, with several of the stitches of her mouth missing. The matted yarn that made up her hair hung in various lengths. Her button eyes still shone, but Seana would have to be careful or the few threads holding them would come loose.

"My momma made this dress for her at Christmas. She made me a dress just like Ennis's, but I can only wear mine for church or weddings." She frowned. "We don't have many weddings, either, so I've only worn the dress when we went to church at Christmastime."

A gust of cold air rushed into the room. The sound of a door closing heralded the arrival of Megan from outside. Jesse opened his mouth to say something, but Seana leaped to her feet and held up that warning finger again.

"Don't you talk or Meggie will get mad at me." She looked so serious, Jesse wanted to hug her and laugh at the same time.

"Seana, have you been bothering Mr. Coulter?" Megan appeared in the doorway, her cheeks and nose bright red from the cold. "I told you he needed to rest."

"He woke up. He tried to talk and I told him not to. I've been telling him all about Momma and Papa. He even met Ennis." Seana held up her doll as if presenting evidence of doing right.

Megan's lips twitched. "You did just fine, Seana." She turned to Jesse, her eyes downcast. "Get some rest, Mr. Coulter. I'll fix you something to eat. You have to build up your strength." She began to back out of the door. "Come along, Seana. Let Mr. Coulter sleep while you help me."

Jesse closed his eyes. From the floating feeling washing through his body, he knew full recovery might take some time. As tired as he was, he couldn't seem to relax. A jumble of thoughts tumbled through his brain. The picture of Meggie and her refusal to look at him, as if she were ashamed of something. The question of where God wanted him to go to preach. He wanted to go the right direction, but didn't have a clear idea which way that would be. He sighed, drifting toward sleep. Due to this sickness, he would have plenty of time to seek out God's direction. Perhaps He wanted Jesse to continue his trek to the Dakota gold fields and begin preaching there.

ॐ

That night Megan couldn't sleep. Visions of her parents caught in the blizzard wouldn't leave. Although she'd assured Seana their parents and Matt probably stayed in Yankton, she wasn't sure. Her mother had been very worried about Seana's fever. She promised to make

Papa leave early so they could be back before dark, if possible. The trip took half a day; but if they hurried with the shopping, they could have been back on the road shortly after lunchtime.

The storm had come in the afternoon. Heavy clouds in the sky had given some indication of bad weather, but no one could have guessed the fast drop in temperature or the severity of the blizzard. Megan hadn't been sure she would have time to put up guide ropes because the snow hit so hard and furious. If her family had already begun the trip home, they may have been trapped in the open. Tears burned her eyes at the thought. Every day that passed made her think something was wrong.

This afternoon, while Seana and Mr. Coulter were both asleep, Megan had gone outside. In the bright sunlight, the white snow hurt her eyes. She'd gone to the barn and climbed up on a fence, trying to get as high as possible to see if her parents' wagon was in sight. Nothing marred the white expanse in any direction. She'd watched until her toes and fingers went numb, praying for a sign of life somewhere, to no avail.

What if something had happened to them? She didn't want to face that possibility, but inside she knew she might have to. What would happen to her and Seana? She didn't want to leave this country and go back east. They didn't have any close family there who would care for them. As harsh as this land could be, Megan didn't want to leave. She loved this place.

Please, God, let Momma and Papa come home tomorrow. Help them to be safe. Megan turned her face into the pillow and wept silent tears. She drifted off to sleep praying tomorrow would bring good news. The seed of an idea gave her hope. Mr. Coulter and Seana were both stronger. Perhaps she could take Mr. Coulter's horse and go looking for her missing family. On horseback, the trip to town wouldn't take nearly as long. Maybe right after lunch she could go while they rested.

The morning dawned bright and clear. The blue sky made a sharp contrast with the whitened ground. A few clouds scudded past, but nothing looked like more storms. Megan hurried with the feeding and once more climbed the fence, balancing precariously as she looked around. Nothing moved as far as she could see. She climbed back down, gathered a sled full of wood, and returned to the house. Pasting a smile on her face, she did her best to act as if nothing was wrong so she wouldn't worry Seana.

"Good morning." Megan's hands shook as she carried the bowl of porridge to Mr. Coulter. She couldn't meet his eyes. During his sickness, she spent hours praying for him and watching him. She'd never met a man so handsome and fascinating. She almost wished he were sick again so she could wipe his brow and watch again the play of emotions crossing his face as he slept and dreamed.

"Morning." The word came out a scratchy whisper. He cleared his throat and tried again. "Good morning."

Megan set the tray on the table in the room. "Would you like me to help you sit up some? It might make eating a little easier."

"Thank you." He eased up, and she plumped an extra pillow behind his back to prop him up. She'd never been so close to such an attractive man. Her heart pounded like it did when Matt used to chase her across the fields.

"Would you like me to feed you, Mr. Coulter?"

"Jesse."

Startled, she glanced up. His twinkling brown gaze held her captive for a moment. She looked down at the tray in her hands, her cheeks hot with embarrassment. "What?"

"My name is Jesse. Mr. Coulter sounds so formal." He started to cough, although the sound wasn't quite as alarming as it had been yesterday. By the time he stopped, his face had paled and he seemed tired.

"I'll feed myself. Thank you."

Placing the tray on his lap, Megan stepped back. "If you need anything else . . . Well, I guess you won't be able to call me. I'll come in to check on you or send Seana. She's almost done with her breakfast." She hurried from the room before she wore the man out with her chatter. Not in years had she said so much to a man. What had come over her?

"Mr. Coulter, would you like some more coffee?"

Megan stilled, listening for the answer to her sister's question. A low rumble told her he'd said something, but she couldn't make out the words.

"Meggie would be mad if I did that. Momma says I always have to call adults by their proper name." Seana lowered her voice to a loud whisper. Megan knew Seana didn't think she would hear. "I think Jesse is a wonderful name, though."

Soft, deep laughter sent a shaft of warmth through Megan. Although she didn't wish Mr. Coulter the inconvenience of being injured and sick, she was glad the Lord led him here. Seana needed the distraction of caring for him so she wouldn't worry about her parents and brother. In fact, she admitted, the diversion helped her, too.

The morning sped past. Megan could feel a knot of worry in her stomach. She needed to ask Mr. Coulter—Jesse—if she could use his horse this afternoon, but the thought of approaching the man with such a request terrified her. What if he said no? Would she have the courage to go against his wishes? The building concern for her family told her she must do something.

A knock sounded on the door as Megan popped some biscuits into the oven for their lunch. She'd just been building her courage to approach Mr. Coulter and stared at the door as if she hadn't heard the sound right. Seana skipped out of her parents' bedroom, where she'd been regaling their patient with a myriad of stories.

"Meggie, we have company. Maybe it's Momma and Papa." She ran to open the door, her braids bouncing. Dread crept up Megan's spine, knowing her parents would never knock on the door. They would just come in.

Cold air whooshed into the house as Seana threw open the door. Two people, bundled against the cold, stood waiting.

"Mrs. Porter, Reverend, please come in." Megan's heart pounded loud enough to be heard in town. Her knees wobbled. The Porters came in, stomping the snow from their boots. Megan stared at them as Seana backed toward her, eyes wide, her doll clutched tight to her breast.

"Please, sit down." Megan's voice shook. "Let me get you some coffee. You've had a long ride in the cold." Her hands trembled as she retrieved some cups from the shelves. Fear clutched at her throat with hard fingers. Tears pushed at the back of her eyes.

"Megan, Dear, sit down." Mrs. Porter took the cups from Megan and guided her to a chair. With one arm, she drew Seana to her side, while her other hand rested on Megan's shoulder.

Reverend Porter cleared his throat. "There isn't any easy way to say this. This was a mighty bad storm, the worst I ever recall. The sheriff found your parents and brother late yesterday." He lifted his chin and twisted his neck as if his collar had tightened. "Your family started home before the storm. We think they tried to make it back to town and got off the road in the heavy snow. I'm sorry, but they froze to death."

The world turned dark. Megan couldn't get her breath. She heard Seana scream something, and then her sister was crying, her thin arms wrapped around Megan's neck. Mrs. Porter made clucking noises as if that would help them with their loss. All Megan could think was that her fears had come true, and God hadn't answered her prayers. What would they do now?

As if sensing her uncertainty, Reverend Porter cleared his throat. "I know this is a difficult time, but I wanted to let you know as soon as possible. We told the sheriff we'd break the news to you and let you know that we'll be bringing the bodies out here in a few days, after we make some pine boxes." He cleared his throat again. "We figured you'd want to bury them here at your farm."

Megan did her best to stifle her sobs. The tears continued to flow unheeded down her cheeks. Seana still had her face buried in Megan's neck.

5

*T*he next two days were a blur. Megan occupied the time caring for Mr. Coulter. Seana moved about in stunned silence. Reverend and Mrs. Porter showed up again with Augustus Sparks—the banker—and the sheriff. The men carefully unloaded three pine boxes from the back of a wagon and placed them at the back of the barn.

Megan watched them, tight-lipped. *The last indignity. The ground is too frozen for them to be buried.*

When that task was finished, the men entered the house, stomping their snowy boots. Mrs. Porter fussed around, pouring hot coffee, murmuring useless sympathy.

Dully, Megan wondered why they had enlisted the banker to help, but he put a quick end to her speculation. Waving away the cup Mrs. Porter proffered, he stepped toward Megan. His double chin jiggled as he moved. Dark eyes narrowed as he gave Megan a lecherous grin. "Miss Riley, your father had a loan with my bank. The note is due this June. With all that's happened, I don't know how you'll ever be able to pay it off."

Megan felt as if her world dropped away. Knowing that her parents were dead—and that their bodies rested in the barn—was bad enough. Having this repulsive man tell her more bad news was too much.

"Now, Megan, Mr. Sparks does have a solution to your dilemma." Reverend Porter spoke in the same sonorous tones he used in church. "Mr. Sparks has generously agreed to marry you and take care of the note himself."

Mr. Sparks's grin widened.

Megan felt reality swirling away. "I . . . I can't marry you." Her tongue felt like a huge cotton boll. "I won't." The tremor in her voice lacked the conviction she was hoping to convey.

"Now, Dear." Mrs. Porter patted her shoulder. "I know this has all been a nasty shock, but you can't possibly expect us to leave you in such terrible straits. Mr. Sparks is making a very generous offer. He's willing to take on a new wife. He'll care for your sister, too."

The banker peeled the gloves off his sausagelike fingers and began to unbutton his coat. "I don't believe you have any other choice, young lady. You can't stay out here in the middle of nowhere with no man around to care for you. I'm sure you and your sister will enjoy the amenities that come from living in town."

"He's right." Reverend Porter gestured for his wife to serve the coffee, as though this were his own house and Megan's situation would be readily solved. "Yankton has a lot of young ladies your age. Your sister will be able to attend school. Augustus here has just about the best house in town. Now we can perform the ceremony here, or we can wait until we get back to town. Which will it be?"

Megan could feel all of their gazes boring into her. She couldn't seem to get her breath. How could they expect something like this to happen right now? Even her parents hadn't cared for the banker. They only dealt with him out of necessity. They would never approve of such a union.

Giving Seana a squeeze, she urged her to stand. "Seana, please go to your room for a little while. I'll be along shortly."

Seana opened her mouth as if she wanted to argue. Glancing around at the others in the room, she nodded and scuffed her feet as she left. With her sister out of sight, Megan stood and faced the men. Locking her knees, she hoped they wouldn't see the tremors quaking through her. She'd been taught never to speak up to adults; but if they were considering marrying her off like some animal going to the highest bidder, she would have her say first.

"I don't know how you can expect me to do this. I've barely learned my parents and brother are dead, and you immediately want me to get married as if I can forget something that important. What about a period of mourning? Mr. Sparks, I'm sure you intend this as a kind offer, but I will not marry you now or ever. My sister and I will stay here on the farm and care for the land. I've helped my parents for years now."

"But my dear, how can you possibly plant the fields?" Mrs. Porter handed coffee to the men and turned to face Megan. "You won't be able to support yourself."

"And there's the loan to pay off. June is only six months away." Mr. Sparks spoke as if he were already rubbing his hands together.

"We will manage." Megan spoke more firmly than she felt. "Our hogs have done well this year. We have several young ones. Yankton already knows that my mother and I make the best sausages and hams." Her voice cracked at the mention of her mother. "Seana and I can make things and bring them to town to sell them. Perhaps since Mr. Sparks is in such a generous mood, he'll be willing to extend our loan. After all, these are unusual circumstances." She didn't add that she wouldn't be able to make any more meat to sell until next fall, when the young piglets would be big enough. Her father had already done the butchering for this winter.

"I'm afraid that will be impossible." Mr. Sparks attempted a forlorn look, but his gaze still made Megan want to turn and run.

"What happens if some unsavory character comes along?" The sheriff leaned forward. "You won't have anyone out here to protect you. This is a mighty far piece from town."

"My father taught me how to shoot a gun, Sheriff. I'm perfectly capable of protecting my sister and myself." Megan wanted to stamp her foot. "I will not marry Mr. Sparks no matter how kind his offer is. You will have to accept that."

"My dear." Mrs. Porter patted her shoulder again, causing Megan to grit her teeth at the woman's conciliatory tone. "There's been talk in town. We know about what happened to you back East. I'm sure you've noticed none of the young men have come to call on you. With your past, Mr. Sparks is perhaps your only chance at marriage."

"That's true." The reverend frowned, his disapproving tone echoing off the walls. "I believe you have no choice here. The sheriff and Mr. Sparks had the foresight to have the wedding right here and now. This will save you some embarrassment. I know there'll be talk because of your reputation and all; but as people become used to you, they'll forget."

"I want you to leave now." Megan spoke through clenched teeth. "I have nothing in my past to be ashamed of, other than the lies people spread about me." She began to shake. "You can take your *generous* offer of marriage and get out of here and leave my sister and me to our grief."

"I'm afraid we can't do that." Reverend Porter extracted a book from a deep coat pocket. "My wife and I consider this our Christian duty to see that you're taken care of properly. Now, if you will join Mr. Sparks here. The sheriff and my wife can be the witnesses."

They weren't listening. Megan couldn't believe this was happening. She was going to end up married to this repulsive man, and no one would hear what she was trying to say. Frantic thoughts tumbled through her mind. What would her mother do? Her father? She knew how the Porters learned of the travesty that happened to her before they moved here, but what about the others in town?

The four adults moved to surround Megan. She could smell the wet cloth from the outdoor clothing they still wore. She understood their hurry if they wanted to get back to town before nightfall. The air grew close. She wished she could faint or do something drastic to delay the inevitable. Reverend Porter opened his book and cleared his throat.

"I believe the lady said she didn't want to get married."

Everyone's gaze swung to the door of her parents' bedroom. Jesse leaned against the frame, a quilt wrapped around his broad shoulders, his bare feet protruding beneath. Megan's face flamed as she realized how this would look to these townsfolk. Their eyes widened, and she knew they weren't seeing Mr. Coulter as someone recovering from a sickness, but as a drifter taking advantage of a young woman. Even his face, covered with several days' growth of stubble, gave him a lawless look—one she found very appealing, although she had no right to think such thoughts.

"What is going on here?" Reverend Porter's face had turned beet red. "Who is this man?"

Megan opened her mouth to answer, but nothing came out. She knew the truth wouldn't be believable. Hadn't she told the truth before they moved here and none of the townspeople believed her? Even her parents didn't seem to understand the wrong done to her.

"Jesse Coulter." Jesse nodded his head, but didn't offer to cross the room to shake hands. Megan almost groaned. She knew he didn't have the strength to walk across the room, but none of the others knew that. They would assume he was being insolent, as many drifters were.

The reverend's hard gaze bore into Megan. "I didn't want to believe what we'd been told. I know how gossip can hurt a person, but this is proof that your reputation has been sullied. Did you have this man waiting and rush him in as soon as your parents left for town?" His words hit Megan like a gale, almost knocking her from her feet.

ε♥

Jesse leaned against the door frame and watched Megan's face turn white. His angel. How could they do this to her? What had she ever done? In the few days he'd been under her care, he'd never met such a thoughtful, hardworking, God-fearing woman before. She defined godly compassion, yet these people were accusing her of being a horrible person. He couldn't allow that.

When he'd first heard the conversation through the partially opened bedroom door, he grieved with her when he learned of the death of her family. She hadn't said a word about it to him the last two days, though he'd been too sick with the fever to have known, anyway. But disbelief pushed away the hurt as he listened to Megan being railroaded into marrying some man she didn't want. He knew he had to do something to help her out. His clothes weren't available, so he covered himself with the quilt, thinking he would be presentable enough. He hadn't thought about how this would look. He only wanted to protect Megan. Now he'd made things worse.

He tried to make his muscles move. Before getting sick, he could have thrown these men from the house with no trouble. Because of the pneumonia, he'd barely made it to the doorway. He hadn't even said anything for a minute because he couldn't get his breath, and the room was spinning so bad he thought he might faint, throw up, or both.

"This is not what you're thinking." Megan's fingers were twined together tight enough to look painful. "Mr. Coulter is sick."

"I don't want to hear any of your excuses." Reverend Porter's brows drew together, giving him the look of a storm cloud about to burst.

The overweight banker stared at Jesse with a venomous gaze. The sheriff unbuttoned his greatcoat to reveal a holstered pistol strapped to his side. His huge mustache accentuated his frown. Mrs. Porter stood frozen beside Megan, her hand covering her mouth, looking as if she wanted to cry.

"Reverend, I would think you should recall Matthew 7:1." Jesse stood his ground as the angry minister glared at him. " 'Judge not, that ye be not judged.' " Silence stretched taut in the room.

"I'd like to know who you are and where you came from." The sheriff strode over to confront Jesse.

"My name is Jesse Coulter. I'm from outside the Chicago area. I was passing through on my way to the gold mines in the Black Hills when I got caught in the blizzard." He looked past the sheriff to where Megan stood pale, but strong. "If it hadn't been for the young lady you're accusing, I'd have been dead. She saved my life."

"The blizzard ended days ago. Why are you still here?" The sheriff leaned forward. "I agree with the reverend. This doesn't look very proper."

"I caught pneumonia." Jesse shrugged. "I've been too sick to leave." Weakness pulled at him. He longed to crawl back to that bed and sleep for a week. How much longer could he stand here before he fell flat?

"He's right. This is the first time he's been able to get up since he's been here."

Megan took a step toward him, but Mrs. Porter caught her arm, pulling her back. "You mean you took care of this man for several days? You're not married."

Megan whirled on the minister's wife. "Mrs. Porter, the man was dying. What would Jesus do in such circumstances? Leave him to freeze to death? Let him die of pneumonia?"

"This just wasn't proper." Mrs. Porter glanced at her husband. "What will the townspeople think? After all, they've all heard the rumors of that incident with the young man where you used to live."

"And just how did they *all* hear that?" Megan took a step closer. Jesse bit back a smile at the thought that Megan might throw these people out without any help from him. "Did you make sure they knew all about what happened? I know my parents talked to you and your husband. They trusted you not to spread that information all over." The chill in the room rivaled the freezing temperatures outside.

Mrs. Porter's face reddened. "I . . . I don't know how the townspeople learned of your misfortune. Perhaps your parents told others."

"They wouldn't have told anyone else." Megan took another step closer, her fists clenched at her sides. "The only reason they talked to you was because they believed in being open with their pastor. Our whole family was hurt by those false accusations, and they needed to talk to you."

Megan turned away, and Jesse could see the tears in her eyes. She half-turned to face Mrs. Porter. Jesse strained to hear what she said. "You betrayed my parents' trust. I think that's worse than anything you're accusing me of doing."

"That's enough." Reverend Porter towered over Megan. He yanked on his black coat and glared at her. "I won't have you maligning my wife. You're the one in the wrong here."

He faced the banker. "Mr. Sparks, I'm sorry, but I don't believe you'll be wanting to marry this young lady now."

The banker stuttered. Yanking a handkerchief from his pocket, he wiped his face, even though the room was chilly. "I realize the circumstances have changed somewhat, but I'm still willing to be wed. It's obvious to me this young lady needs a strong man to care for her and keep her in line."

Jesse couldn't see the look the banker gave Megan, but her reaction made his insides tighten. He longed to be able to help her. He wanted to force these people out of the house, but his body wouldn't respond to any of the commands he tried to give. Even his brain felt fuzzy from exhaustion. Something had to happen soon or he would end up in a heap on the floor.

"I will not marry you." Megan glared at the banker, and Jesse wanted to cheer for her.

"I'm astonished at Mr. Sparks's generosity toward you, Megan." The reverend's smile for the banker changed to a scowl as he faced Megan. "I refuse to leave here today without seeing you become a respectable woman. It's obvious to my wife and me that you need someone to care for you. Mr. Sparks is a good match. I'm appalled at your lack of enthusiasm over his offer." He stepped closer, his tone becoming threatening. "Would you rather marry that poor excuse for a man who's standing half-naked over there? Is a penniless drifter better than a respected man like Mr. Sparks?"

Hands on her hips, Megan matched him glare for glare. "I would rather marry anyone than Mr. Sparks. I don't consider this a generous offer. He only wants to get his grubby hands on my father's land, just as he's done with countless others around here. He makes generous loans and then forecloses on the land without any consideration for who lives there. My parents would never approve of a marriage between Mr. Sparks and me. Now, will you kindly leave my home?" She flung her arm in a gesture toward the door.

"You have no choice about the matter, Megan. With your parents dead and you alone, the sheriff and I have taken it on ourselves to look after you. Mr. Sparks says you won't be able to pay off the loan. We can't have you thrown off your land. You have your sister to think about, too. She'll need caring for."

"He's right, Dear." Mrs. Porter tried to pat Megan's shoulder, but Megan jerked out of her reach. "I don't know where you got those horrible ideas about Mr. Sparks. He's a fine, upstanding citizen. He'll take good care of you."

Reverend Porter opened his black book again and cleared his throat. The sheriff moved to stand beside the banker. Mrs. Porter took a firm grip on Megan's arm. Jesse could see the look of panic that crossed Megan's face. His angel. He couldn't allow this to happen to her.

"I'll marry her." Before he could glance around to see who had spoken, Jesse realized the words had come from his mouth.

6

believe that's highly inappropriate." Reverend Porter spoke first. "Since we are in charge of this young lady's welfare, my dear wife and I would never see her married to a common drifter."

"I am not a common drifter." Jesse tried to stand taller.

"And just who would you be?" The sheriff took one threatening step forward.

"My father, Richard Coulter, is the owner of the First Central Bank of Chicago." He gave a tight smile. "So you see, Megan would be changing from one banker to another."

"You said you were going to the gold mines." Sheriff Armstrong narrowed his eyes.

"I have recently taken a leave of absence from the bank. I wanted to do a bit of traveling." Jesse swallowed hard against the half-lie. He had wanted to travel, but he hadn't intended to ever return to the bank or to the Chicago area. He couldn't look at Megan, fearing to see a look of disappointment in her eyes. Most likely she didn't want to marry him, either, but he could see no other way to keep her from being tied to a man she despised.

"This is preposterous." Mr. Sparks huffed. "We have no proof that he is who he says. This man could be anyone posing as a banker."

"He's telling the truth." Megan's soft whisper caused a hush to fall.

"How do you know that, Child?" Reverend Porter asked.

"When he was so sick, I looked through his things." She hesitated, glancing at Jesse and then away. "I wanted to see who to inform if he didn't live. He was so sick." She squared her shoulders. "He had some papers in his bag from the First Central Bank. I didn't read through them closely, but I did see the name of Richard Coulter on the papers."

"He could be making this up." Mr. Sparks wiped at his face with his handkerchief.

"No, he had a Bible in his belongings. That's how Seana and I knew his name."

"Meggie?" Seana peeked around the curtain. Megan held out her arms, and her sister dashed across the room and flung herself at Megan. "Meggie, please don't marry Mr. Sparks. You know what Papa said about him." Seana gave Mr. Sparks a pointed look as she tried to whisper, but everyone could hear what she said.

"I won't marry him, Seana."

"You will have to be wed, Megan." Reverend Porter frowned at her. "Your virtue has been brought into question. We can't have your reputation sullied further than it is." He glanced at his wife. "However, I will give you the choice of which banker you will marry."

Megan's eyes sparkled with unshed tears. Jesse ached for her. How could these people be so thoughtless? To be forced to make such a decision, when her family wasn't even buried, was cruel. "Perhaps you would give the young lady a few days to consider the choice before she makes it."

"That would never work." Mrs. Porter looked horrified. "Megan either has to marry you in order to stay here tonight, or she has to marry Mr. Sparks and leave with us. Knowing that you are here virtually unchaperoned leaves us no other choice, isn't that right, Dear?"

Reverend Porter nodded. "Megan, you must choose now or we will make the decision for you. We have to get back to town before too much time passes."

"I will never marry Mr. Sparks." Megan repeated the words with such force that Jesse had no doubts, but he wondered why she didn't say she would rather marry him. Didn't she like him, either? Confusion swirled through his mind. He couldn't seem to focus on anything any longer. His legs turned soft, and he slid down to sit on the floor with a thump. He tried to force a smile when they all turned to look at him, but none of his muscles seemed to be in working order.

இ

"Jesse." Megan's heart thudded as she watched him slump to the floor. He'd been so sick. He shouldn't have been out of bed at all, let alone for this long. Eternity seemed to have passed as they stood here debating her future, as if she had no significance. Megan hurried across the room and knelt beside Jesse. Her fingers touched his brow to find him slightly warmer than he should have been. She hoped his fever wasn't returning.

"What's the matter with him?" Sheriff Armstrong knelt beside her.

"I told you he's been sick. He's had pneumonia from the exposure he suffered during the blizzard. He shouldn't even be up and about. Help me get him back to bed." Megan tried to get her shoulder underneath his arm. Jesse tried to stand, but he didn't appear to have any strength left.

"Here, let me help with that." Reverend Porter pushed her aside. Between them, he and the sheriff managed to get Jesse back to bed. Megan tucked the covers around him and wiped the sweat from his brow with a damp cloth.

"Now, you see, we can't possibly go through with this. This man is as sick as I told you."

"It's still improper for you to be here with him." Reverend Porter's chin jutted out. "We'll give him a few minutes to recover. When he's awake enough to repeat his vows, we'll get you married."

"She should marry me." Mr. Sparks's face reddened. "I offered to be her husband. It was a generous offer, considering her background. I won't see her wed to some stranger we don't even know."

"Sometimes God makes other choices for us." Reverend Porter gestured at the man on the bed. "If you were to marry her, you would always have this hanging over your head. People would talk about how she spent these days with a stranger in her house. Having her wed him is the best way, especially since we know he's a man of means."

A slight smile appeared on Jesse's face. Megan watched him open his eyes, although he didn't seem to focus. She couldn't help but wonder what little joke ran through his mind at the reverend's words. Had he lied about who he was? Her emotions swinging with the wind, Megan didn't know what to think anymore. All she wanted was to curl up in a corner and grieve for her parents and Matt, to hold Seana and not think about the future.

Hours later, only the glow of the fire lit the main room of the house. Flickering images danced across the walls, but Megan paid them little attention. Huddled in an old quilt her mother stitched for her years ago, she allowed the tears to flow unchecked. Pain, hard physical pain, flared through her chest as she thought of her mother, father, and brother, their frozen bodies waiting in the barn until the ground thawed enough to dig the graves.

Dear God, what are we supposed to do now? How will I ever manage without Momma? Fresh tears traced down her cheeks. She could clearly recall the morning her parents left for town, although it seemed a lifetime ago now. The smell of cooking breakfast, ham and coffee, clung to her mother as she hugged Megan. Her father kissed her cheek, the touch of his beard tickling against her skin as he bid her good-bye. Matt with his saucy grin, hopping into the bed of the wagon in one easy jump. She could see how the legs of his pants were too short already, knowing her mother had left a big hem for this reason. Matt sprouted up faster than they could keep him in clothes. Never again would she hug them or talk to them.

"Momma, I'm married now," Megan whispered the words aloud. "I'm not sure Jesse even knows or understands that we're married. He did say the words, but his fever was up and his eyes didn't quite focus." Megan closed her eyes and fought a wave of anguish at the travesty of being married on the same day her family's bodies were brought home.

If Seana hadn't been there to see Reverend Porter perform the ceremony, Megan would be tempted to tell Jesse he'd had a dream. He'd been so sick, he would probably believe her. He would leave when he got well, and no one would bother her again. The townsfolk would still believe her married.

"What am I to do about the loan, Papa? How did you plan to pay it off?" She shuddered at the thought of the greedy look in Mr. Sparks's eyes. The man wanted all he could get. He saw the possibilities for this area to grow, and he wanted to own as much of it as possible. He wasn't beyond doing anything to anyone to get his way. Her father had returned home one afternoon, grim and withdrawn after assisting a neighbor who'd been evicted by Mr. Sparks. The banker stood by with a smile on his face the whole time the family made haste to pack.

"Where will we go if we can't pay the loan? He'll throw us out the same as he did the Sheffields, especially after I treated him so poorly today." Megan pressed her fingers to her burning eyes. She couldn't let this get her down. Her parents always insisted that God was in charge and He could be trusted, but Megan was beginning to wonder. Their trust in God left them frozen to death in a blizzard, with the possibility of eminent foreclosure on their property.

God, I don't know how You could do this to people who loved You as much as Momma and Papa did. If You're in charge, why did You leave Seana and me without any family? Why did You allow me to marry a man I don't even know and who probably has no desire to be married to me?

No answers came, but then Megan hadn't expected any.

The smell of frying bacon tickled Jesse's nose. His stomach growled. He stretched, reveling in the warmth of the bed contrasted to the cold of the room he slept in. Drawing in a breath, he tested his lungs to see how much air he could pull in without coughing. When he felt the catch in his chest, he froze, then slowly breathed out.

His body didn't feel as sluggish this morning, and he wondered if he could get out of bed. He hadn't been up since this sickness weakened him. He frowned. Of course, there was that crazy dream he had last night. Shaking his head, he chuckled. Imagine him getting married. That had to be an illusion. He'd just promised God he would go wherever the Lord led, so he knew getting married and settling down wasn't for him. He might live his whole life without a wife. His thoughts strayed to Megan. Of course, if he had to become a husband to someone, she would be a good choice. He would always carry a fondness for his angel.

The bedroom door edged open, and Seana's face peeked around. At the sight of him awake, she lit up like a summer day. "Meggie, he's awake." She flung the door the rest of the way open and bounded into the room, her braids bouncing across her shoulders.

Sliding to a stop, Seana leaned her elbows on the bed and gave Jesse a peculiar smile. He couldn't begin to guess what was going on behind those sparkling blue eyes. "Megan sent me to see if you were awake and if you wanted some real food for breakfast. She's cooking bacon and eggs. I have to slice some bread, too, and there's coffee."

Jesse chuckled. When had he last felt such enthusiasm? No wonder Jesus mentioned coming to Him as a child. Who wouldn't be drawn to one like Seana? A loud rumble interrupted his thoughts. Seana covered her mouth with her hand and giggled.

"I guess that's your answer. The smell of that bacon woke me up. I can almost taste it from here."

"I'll tell Meggie." With that, Seana bounded across the room and disappeared from sight.

A few minutes later, Megan came in carrying a tray laden with his breakfast. She appeared more shy than usual, her gaze downcast, a hesitancy about her that hadn't been there before. Had he done something to offend her? Thinking hard, Jesse couldn't recall anything he'd said or done. He bit back a grin. Thank goodness, she wasn't privilege to his dreams. If she knew he'd dreamed about them having a wedding, she'd be running rather than bringing him food.

"Good morning."

Megan flinched at his words, sloshing coffee from the cup onto the tray. A flush spread over her round cheeks, giving her a rosy fresh appeal. Jesse wanted to do something to make her smile so he could see the dimple in her cheek. He picked up the fork instead, wondering why he would be thinking of such things when he would be leaving this place soon and never see these people again.

"Good morning, Mr. Coulter. Are you feeling better this morning?" Megan spoke so softly, he had to strain to catch the words even though she stood beside him. Her tone held a touch of something different. Fear? Uncertainty?

"I'm feeling much stronger, thank you. I believe I'll try to get up as soon as I eat." He scooped up a bite of eggs. "It will be good to finally get out of bed. I'll see if I can remember how to walk. Maybe by tomorrow I can get out of your way."

Megan paled. She stepped back. "I'll be back to get your tray." She rushed from the room. Jesse stared after her, wondering what could possibly be wrong. Up until now Megan had been sweet and caring. He'd enjoyed the way she sat with him, talking on occasion, but mostly watching over him. After breakfast he would have to find out about the sudden change in behavior.

Feeling stronger after eating, Jesse asked for some water to wash with and his clothes. Megan brought both, then retreated in uncharacteristic silence. This time he noted the dark circles under her red-rimmed eyes. Why had she been crying?

Seana waited outside when he opened the door. Standing up took more energy than he thought it would. Just getting washed and dressed drained him so much, he wasn't sure he could make the trek across the room to a chair. Sweat beaded on his forehead. Seana frowned at him as he rested one hand on the door frame.

"Meggie, I think he's gonna fall like he did yesterday."

Yesterday? When had he fallen yesterday? He hadn't been out of bed until now. Before he could question Seana's statement, Megan was beside him, helping him to a chair. He'd never felt so stupid as he did now having a woman assist him in walking. Jesse hated this sickness. He sank into the rocker with a grateful sigh.

"I'm not sure you should be up and about yet, Mr. Coulter." Megan wiped his brow.

"Why not, Meggie?" Seana patted him on the arm. "He got up yesterday right before he married you."

$\mathcal{L}$ifting another shovel of manure from the stall floor, Jesse tried his best to ignore the pine boxes in the back of the barn. In the past few weeks, since he'd learned he was married to Megan, he'd done his best to take over the chores and save her the heartache of seeing these reminders of her family.

Married! He thrust the shovel into the muck covering the floor. He'd made a promise to God, and now he couldn't keep it. When he recovered, he'd planned to leave and follow wherever the Lord led him, just like Jonah went to Nineveh. Under Pastor Phillips's tutelage, he'd learned a lot about the Bible. He could preach a sermon with the best of them and had, on occasion, assisted the pastor. This was God's call for his life. He'd been running from that call, yet now he wasn't running; he was at a dead stop.

Taking a handkerchief from his pocket, Jesse wiped the sweat from his face. He leaned against the post by the stall door and surrendered to the fatigue washing through him. This job should have taken him half an hour to do, but the lack of energy that plagued him made every chore stretch out three or four times longer than it should. Megan assured him her brother, Matt, had the same problem after he had pneumonia. Still, he felt like a useless old man most of the time.

The door creaked, then crashed against the side of the barn as a gust of wind caught it. Seana stumbled inside, her pale cheeks rosy from the cold, her doll, Ennis, clutched to her chest. Jesse hurried to grab the door and shut out the fierce wind.

"Seana, what are you doing? Does Megan know you're outside?"

Hugging her arms tight around her frail body, Seana shook her head. Jesse could see the snow clumped over the top of her boots. Her feet would be frozen if he didn't get her back in the house soon. He reached for her, but she backed away.

"Don't touch me." She held out her hand in front of her as if that would keep him away. "Megan won't let me come to see Momma and Papa, but I have to." Tears glittered in her eyes. Jesse could see all the hurt and anger she'd been holding back brimming to the surface.

He held out his hand. "I'll take you to them."

She sniffed. He could see she wanted to refuse. Sniffing again, Seana let him take her small hand in his. He led her to the back of the barn. A small barrel rested across from the boxes. Jesse knew about the times Megan sneaked out here after Seana went to sleep. He'd kept her secret so far, but he always watched the time, unwilling to let her stay too long in the frigid weather.

Easing down on the barrel, Jesse lifted Seana onto his lap. He snuggled her close, hoping to give her some of his warmth. A calico cat meowed and wound around his legs. Seana bent down to pet her.

"This is Mama Kitty. That's Shadow." She pointed to the gray cat hiding behind a pile of hay. "They help us keep the mice away from the feed." Seana leaned back against Jesse, her gaze on the pine boxes a few feet away.

"Why are they in boxes?" The small sound of Seana's voice made his heart ache.

"Remember what Megan told you about not being able to bury them until the ground thaws? Well, this is a way of keeping them safe until then. And even after they're buried." He rubbed her arm, tucking her head under his chin. "You know, Seana, your parents and Matt aren't in those bodies anymore. They've gone to live with Jesus now."

"In heaven?"

"Yep. Do you know what heaven is like?"

"There are angels there."

"That's true." Jesse took off his mittens and worked them over her hands and up her arms as far as they would go, careful not to make her drop Ennis. "The Bible talks about heaven being a wonderful place. No one gets sick there or hurt. They don't even have anything to cry about."

"They got hurt here." A small sob shook Seana. "Jesus didn't keep them from dying."

Jesse rocked Seana as she cried. He'd been worried about her lack of emotion over these deaths. She'd laughed and gone on like nothing had happened. He knew it wouldn't last, and now looked like the time for her to grieve. *Jesus, give me the words to help her.*

"You know all the times your parents have gone to town shopping and left you with Megan?" Jesse asked. Seana nodded, her head pressed against his chest. "Did you miss them while they were gone?"

"Yes."

"But you knew they'd be coming home, didn't you?"

"This time they didn't."

"That's true. This time they went to a different home. They went to stay with Jesus." He brushed the hair back from her cheek as she lifted her face to look at him. "But just like they used to come home to you, they're waiting now for you to come home to them."

A lone tear spilled down Seana's cheek. "I can't ever go there. Momma wanted to show me the way, but I didn't want to talk about it."

"Did she tell you the only way to get to heaven is through Jesus, Seana? Did she want you to ask Him to be your Savior?"

She nodded. "Momma talked about that, but I didn't want to. Now I don't know if I remember how to do it. Maybe Jesus took them away because I was so bad."

"This wasn't to punish you, Seana. Jesus loves you. He loves your whole family. Do you understand what sin is?" Jesse waited as she thought and then nodded her head. "Do you believe Jesus is the Son of God sent to die for our sins?"

"Yes. Momma told me about all that."

"Then all you have to do is ask Him to be your Savior. Jesus is just waiting for you to want Him." Bowing his head, Jesse led Seana in a prayer. This time the ache in his chest wasn't from sickness, but from joy that God had provided such a beautiful answer to his prayer.

"Can I go see them now?" Seana's blue eyes stared up at him.

Jesse gave her a hug and a smile. "Not just yet. You have to wait until it's your time to go to heaven."

"But they'll get lonely for me, won't they?"

"I imagine they look forward to the day you can join them, Seana, but God's time isn't the same as our time. Only a short time will pass for them while you grow up, get married, and have a family of your own. It will be more like a day gone to town to them."

Seana glanced at the bodies and back to him. She gave him a watery smile. "Can I go tell Meggie?"

He hugged her to him. "I think Megan would love to hear, especially about your decision to ask Jesus to be your Savior." Seana hopped off his lap and trotted to the door. Mama Kitty trailed behind her, purring as Seana gave her a final pat before slipping through the door. Jesse followed her, wondering how he'd come to love this little girl in such a short time. Had he also come to love her sister? His wife? Would he ever love her?

∂≫

Megan grasped behind her to pull the shed door shut as she balanced a basket in her other arm. Her breath blew out in a cloud of white in the chill afternoon air. A weak sun did little to warm anything. Juggling her basket of potatoes and dried vegetables for a stew, she didn't see Seana until her sister leaped forward, wrapping Megan in a fierce hug. Vegetables went flying as the basket dropped to the ground.

"Seana, whatever are you doing outside?" Panic flared through Megan. Her sister's health was always fragile. She couldn't take the extreme cold and had to be protected.

"Meggie, I have something to tell you." Seana's brilliant blue eyes twinkled with excitement.

"Seana, get inside. I'll pick up the vegetables and come in. Then you can tell me what you were doing outside when it's so cold." Megan regretted her harsh tone when some of the sparkle left Seana's eyes.

"Yes, Meggie." Seana let go and began to trudge off to the house, her shoulders slumped.

"Wait." Megan waited until her sister turned back. "Help me pick these up and you can tell me your news while we work."

Seana grinned and bounced back to help Megan. Megan knelt

down, grateful that the snow here had packed enough to keep their dinner from disappearing.

"I went to visit Momma, Papa, and Matt."

Megan froze at Seana's words. Anger welled up inside her. How could Seana do that? Hadn't she told her to stay away from the barn? Footsteps crunched in the snow, stopping beside her. She looked up as Seana continued to drop vegetables into the basket. Jesse stood there. For an instant their gazes met and held. Megan knew he understood her thoughts. He knew about the nights she slipped out to sit with her family. As if she could read his thoughts, she saw the hurt she'd done to Seana by not allowing her a time to grieve.

Reaching for a potato, Megan pushed away her roiling emotions. "I'm sorry I didn't take you out there before, Seana. I was so afraid you'd get sick." Her voice caught in her throat. "I couldn't bear for anything to happen to you, too."

Jesse bent over and picked up the basket. "Looks like you've rescued supper, Ladies. Shall we get inside?"

Megan allowed Jesse to take her hand and help her up. She frowned over his bare hand and opened her mouth to ask why he wasn't wearing any mittens. A glance at Seana gave her the answer. He'd given up his warmth to keep her sister from getting too cold. Gratitude she couldn't express flowed through Megan. In the past few weeks, Jesse had been such a gentleman. He'd worked hard as soon as he could get on his feet. She noticed the lines of fatigue on his face by evening. Not once had he complained about being forced to marry her. He hadn't even said anything about continuing on to the gold fields as she thought he would, and she hadn't had the courage to bring it up.

By the time Megan had the vegetables washed for the stew, Jesse had the fire crackling and the water in the pot. Seana's cheeks and nose were still cherry red when she came out from changing into dry, warmer clothes. Megan frowned, hoping her sister wasn't coming down with another of her fevers so soon. All her childhood had been plagued with sickness. Their mother always said the child caught every little disease that came within a hundred miles.

"I have something else to tell you, Meggie." Seana glanced at Jesse as if she wasn't sure how to continue. He winked at her. "I'm going to live with Momma and Papa."

"You can't possibly stay in the barn, Seana. It's much too cold and dirty."

"Not in the barn. I'm going to heaven." Seana clapped her hands, bouncing on the balls of her feet.

Megan felt as if she'd been kicked by a mule. She could feel the color drain from her face. Her mother had once told her that some people had premonitions of their own deaths. Is this what was happening to Seana? Her fingers gripped the edge of the table before her knees could buckle and send her to the floor.

Strong arms surrounded Megan. Jesse eased her back against his solid form. For once, she welcomed his strength.

"Seana, why don't you tell your sister what we talked about in the barn?"

Seana gave another bounce, oblivious to the turmoil she'd thrown Megan into. "We talked about heaven and how Momma, Papa, and Matt are there. Jesse showed me how to ask Jesus in my heart so I can go there, too." She wrinkled her brow. "He says it may take a long time to me, but to Momma and Papa it will be like a day before I'm there with them."

Tension drained from Megan, leaving her weak-kneed. She sagged back against Jesse, relief pouring through her. He'd known. He understood what she thought and had had Seana share her conversion so Megan wouldn't think her sister was going to die soon. How could this man be so perceptive? Her heart warmed. She'd never known anyone like Jesse.

Holding out her arms, Megan waited for Seana to come, then hugged her hard. "This is the best news I could hear. I believe Momma and Papa are rejoicing with the angels." She kissed her sister on the head before releasing her. Flashing Jesse a grateful smile, she busied herself with scraping the vegetables into the pot. If she wasn't careful, this man would become too important to her; and she knew there would come a day when he would leave. There wasn't a man alive who would want to be married to her. With her plump body and plain face, she'd known she would never marry. Jesse had shown his reluctance by his lack of desire to be around her. Every evening as soon as supper was finished, he retired to her parents' room. He never even kissed her like Papa used to kiss Momma. She couldn't blame him. After the disparaging remarks made on their wedding day and the way she looked, he'd have to be stupid to want her.

Quiet had descended on the house by the time Megan finished cleaning up from supper. Seana, tired from her afternoon exploits, hadn't argued at all when Megan sent her to bed. Jesse thanked her for the meal and returned to his room as soon as he finished eating. She mentally forced herself to begin thinking of her parents' room as Jesse's. After all, he was now head of this home. She would have to adjust.

Sinking into the rocking chair, Megan sorted through the mending basket, choosing one of Seana's dresses to work on. After turning up the wick on the lamp, she broke off a piece of thread. The quiet tread of footsteps startled her.

"Seana, what are you doing out of bed?"

A low chuckle greeted her words. "That's the first time I've ever been accused of being a little girl."

Megan's cheeks burned. "I'm sorry, Mr. Coulter. I didn't realize you were still awake."

"Jesse." Jesse scooted a chair close to hers and plopped down, causing the chair to creak in protest. Megan wanted to scold him for not sitting down gently, but held her tongue. "You need to start calling me Jesse. I sound like an old man when you say Mr. Coulter."

Megan knotted her thread, trying to keep her hands from trembling. What did he want? Why was he sitting so close? He'd almost ignored her until now. "Jesse, then." Her voice quivered.

"We need to talk, Megan. I've given you time to grieve for your family. I know it's been hard on you." Jesse leaned forward, his elbows on his knees, his hands almost touching her. "If we're going to save your farm from that banker you dislike so much, then we have to have a plan. I'll need a lot of help from you."

"I don't know what I can do." Megan couldn't seem to concentrate with him so close. "I don't even know how much we owe the bank."

"Then we'll have to take a trip to town as soon as the weather permits and stop in at the bank." Jesse rubbed his hands down his face. "Do you know if your parents had any money set aside to pay toward the loan?"

"They never talked about it. I don't know what Papa planned to do. He never mentioned any loan."

"Well, if we don't figure something out soon, we might just as well pack up and leave here."

Megan gaped at Jesse, forgetting, for the moment, her reluctance to meet his gaze.

8

*S*tanding at the edge of the open graves, Megan shivered in the raw wind that raced across the land. Tucked against her side, Seana stood silent and forlorn. Megan closed her eyes, trying to focus on the prayer Jesse was saying in remembrance of her parents and Matt, but his words jumbled together in her head, sounds too mixed up to make sense.

She hated the thought that her family would be buried here when they would most likely lose the land in June when the note came due. She and Jesse had scoured the house looking for money her parents might have set back or at least some paperwork on the loan, but they found nothing. In one of Papa's boxes, they found a small amount of cash and a list of seed needed for the spring. He must have planned to use this to purchase the seed for planting, but Jesse concluded there wouldn't be any extra. In one of the flour jars, Megan found her mother's stash of money that she always set aside to buy necessary items such as shoes or material. It wasn't enough, either.

Four weeks ago, they'd gone to town to talk with Mr. Sparks. He'd greeted them cordially enough, giving them the information they needed for the payoff. He refused to show them the original paperwork, saying Lee and Glenna Riley had agreed to the terms; and if Megan and her new husband wanted to keep the farm, they would just have to abide by the amount already listed. After they left, Jesse hadn't said anything all the way home. In fact, he'd been quiet since then.

Megan flinched as the first shovel full of dirt thudded into the grave. She widened her eyes, trying to keep the tears from falling. She'd cried enough in the past two and a half months. Today would put this difficult time to rest.

"Meggie, I'm c-cold." Seana's teeth chattered in the quiet.

"Take her on inside, Megan. I'll finish up here." Jesse tossed another shovel of dirt, his expression grim.

Wrapping her long coat around Seana to try to warm her, Megan began the slow walk back to the house. The wind pushed at her back like a mischievous child. The ground, freshly thawed, squished underfoot.

A picture of Jesse back there, working to bury her family, filled Megan's thoughts. She'd grown so accustomed to having him here, she couldn't imagine what life would be like when he left; but leave he would. She understood that. There wasn't anything to keep him here. He'd only been biding his time waiting for the spring thaw so he wouldn't have to travel in such miserable weather. She was sure of this, even though he'd never spoken of it. Why would he stay?

Yes, he'd spent hours repairing tools and harnesses, getting everything ready for spring planting. He'd fixed things around the house. When he found out they didn't go to church in the winter because of the distance and the cold, he even prepared Sunday lessons from the Bible so she and Seana wouldn't miss out on the chance to worship. As much as she loved hearing him teach from God's Word, she still didn't believe that God loved her or that anyone could love her. She would never measure up.

The warmth of the house washed over Megan as she removed her wraps. Seana kicked off her boots, then went to stand in front of the fire instead of taking off her coat and scarf.

"Meggie, will I always miss them?" Seana's shoulders slumped.

"I imagine you will. I know I will." Megan knelt in front of her sister and began to unbutton her coat. "We certainly don't want to forget them, do we?" She smiled. "Sometimes we can just talk about the wonderful things we remember about our family. I know they would be happy, and I'm sure Jesse won't mind." She gave Seana a hug, kissing her forehead.

"I'd better fix some hot coffee and get the bread in the oven. When Jesse comes inside, he'll be ready for something to warm him up." Leaving Seana to finish with her coat, Megan bustled around the kitchen, trying to keep her mind from straying to her husband. Why did it matter to her that he didn't act toward her like a husband should act toward a wife? She knew that no man would ever be attracted to her, didn't she? She'd come to that conclusion long ago.

So why did she find herself longing for Jesse's touch? The memory of her father kissing her mother, the two of them snuggling together when they thought no one could see them, tugged at her heart. Although she'd never admitted it, she'd yearned for that kind of relationship with a man. What a joy it would be to have Jesse look at her the way Papa had looked at Momma—like she was the most precious jewel in the world.

A burst of cold air tumbled in as Jesse stamped through the door. With a glance, Megan noted his rosy cheeks and the look of good health that made him glow. He'd recovered from the pneumonia, much to her relief. For weeks he'd been weak; but he refused to rest, working long hours, doing any little job he could find that needed done. There were always things to be fixed on a farm.

"Thank you." Jesse clenched his fingers around the cup of coffee Megan handed him. She loved the strong look of him. He wasn't tall or slender like many of the boys and men she'd known. Instead, Jesse was as sturdy as an oak. He didn't have fat on him. He worked far too hard for that, but he was solid. Sometimes she had trouble keeping herself from touching his hands or finding out if his arms were as rocklike as they appeared.

"Thank you." Megan couldn't look up at him.

"For what?"

"For all you've done." She gestured in the direction of the newly filled graves. "For caring enough to see to their proper burial."

"You're welcome." Jesse took a gulp, then sputtered and nearly choked. "Whew, this isn't left over. I didn't expect it to be so hot." He flashed a smile. "I want to take you to church tomorrow."

"But we can't." Megan backed up a step.

"The roads are passable. I've made sure all the tack is mended. If we leave early, we'll be able to get there on time."

Megan's heart pounded. Facing Mr. Sparks at the bank had been bad enough. To face the whole congregation, knowing what they thought she'd done, was more than she could do. "What about Seana? She'll get chilled."

"We'll wrap her up good. You can heat some rocks in the fireplace to keep her feet warm. I'll pack them around her myself." Jesse set the cup on the table. "My mind's made up, Megan. We need to go to church. I know why you don't want to go, but you have to face them sometime. If they're good Christian people, they'll be glad to see you."

જ

Clucking to the tired team, Jesse noted the number of wagons and carriages surrounding the small church at the outskirts of Yankton. He tried to ignore Megan's pallor as her whitened fingers gripped the seat beside him. Since the beginning of the marriage, he'd wanted to ask her about the comments made by Reverend Porter and his wife, but he hadn't been sure he'd even heard them right. Everything about that day faded into fuzziness as he tried to pin his thoughts down. He'd been so sick, he hadn't realized he was married until Seana said something. He could still recall the shock as reality took hold. Megan was his wife, although still in name only. For some reason he'd sensed fear and uncertainty in her. As much as he longed for a closer relationship, he wanted to wait until she was ready.

In almost every way, Megan was the opposite of Sara, the girl to whom he'd been betrothed. Where Sara was tall and blonde, Megan was short and well rounded. Sara's blond locks and fair complexion contrasted completely with Megan's mahogany hair and sun-browned skin. Even on the inside they were opposites. Sara thought only of herself and what others could do for her. Megan always thought of others first. Her constant attention to his every need testified to that. After knowing Megan, Jesse couldn't believe he'd ever been attracted to Sara. Of course, much of that attraction had been the result of his parents' insistence that she would be right for him. How wrong they had been.

"Are we there, Meggie?" Seana rose up on her knees to peer between them. Excitement made her eyes sparkle more than they had in some time.

"We're here." Megan's short response spoke volumes of her reluctance to face these people. Jesse wanted to help her, but he knew it was best for her to face her fears. That's why he had made her come. When she saw how friendly these people would be, she'd relax and enjoy the fellowship.

The tinny plink of a piano drifted from inside the building as Jesse hopped down to secure the team. By the time they walked up the steps to the door, the hymn was in full swing, the chorus of voices echoing the song in his heart. Oh, how he'd missed the fellowship with other believers. If only this church were close enough to attend every week.

Megan had a tight hold on Seana's shoulder. Jesse wasn't sure if she didn't want the girl to skip on ahead or if she needed the support. He took Megan's elbow in his hand, guiding her into the sanctuary. The floorboards creaked. The people sitting closest to the door glanced around. One by one they stopped singing and stared at the Coulters. Jesse urged Megan to continue down the aisle where there were empty seats. As they passed the rows, silence descended, except for one group of young people about Megan's age. One of the girls leaned over to whisper to her companion. Before the Coulters passed them, the whole group was staring at Megan and snickering. Megan acted as if she hadn't noticed, but Jesse could see the flush in her cheeks. By the time they arrived at the empty pew, even the pianist stopped playing, the air filled with silent tension.

Her face bright red, Megan stared at the floor. Jesse smiled at the grim faces around him. Reverend Porter, standing at the front of the congregation in a black suit that gave him the appearance of a vulture, stared at them with narrowed eyes. An uncomfortable silence stretched until Jesse thought he might explode.

Reverend Porter nodded. "It's nice to see the Coulters here this Sunday. Mrs. Porter, perhaps we could start this hymn over again."

Jesse couldn't begin to imagine the cause for the animosity he felt from these people. Mrs. Porter, seated at the piano, began to pound the keys with a force that threatened to ruin the instrument. This time the singing lacked conviction. Under the guise of the music, Jesse could hear the whispers as ladies and gentlemen alike tilted their heads together and passed on some bit of gossip. He ground his teeth together in an effort to keep quiet.

As the hymn drew to a close, Reverend Porter gestured for his wife to take her seat in the pew near the piano. He smoothed his dark coat and opened a huge Bible. Clearing his throat, he read, " 'Whither shall I go from thy spirit? or whither shall I flee from thy presence? If I ascend up into heaven, thou art there: if I make my bed in hell, behold, thou art there.' " He stared in silence, his gaze roving over the congregation and coming to settle on Megan. "Reading from Psalm 139, written by David, King of Israel."

His gaze never leaving Megan's downcast face, Reverend Porter pointed his finger. "There is nowhere you can go to hide from God. He always knows where you've been and what you've done. Your sin cannot be hidden."

Jesse listened in astonishment as the preacher continued to berate the congregation with a variety of possible sins they couldn't hide from the Lord. He made no reference to the forgiveness that comes from confessing your sins to Him. Instead, he consigned them all to an eternity in hell for the wrongs they'd done—or had he? Most of his message was directed at Megan, or at least in her direction. What had she done that these people felt so much hostility toward her? She had the best heart of anyone he'd ever met. She didn't raise her voice to him, didn't argue, and didn't demand her own way, even though she'd been forced into a situation she didn't want. Why did this preacher condemn her?

"Is it adultery or fornication you've committed? In some secret place you thought no one would know about?" Reverend Porter's voice sounded more like the hiss of a serpent than that of a man of God. "Not only does God know your dirty secrets, but He tells His people to be set apart from sinners."

Reverend Porter straightened. "I suggest if you're one of those living in sin that you refrain from attending this church. We do not want the reputation of the Corinthian church. They willingly put up with disgusting sins until the apostle Paul set them straight. We will not tolerate sinful behavior here."

Megan's hands were clenched in her skirts. Jesse could tell from the set of her shoulders that she was strung like a tight wire ready to snap. Anger filled him at the injustice of this man condemning someone rather than extending the forgiveness of Jesus. Who taught Porter about the Bible? They hadn't done a very good job. He couldn't wait to leave here. If he'd known the bigotry they would face, he would never have subjected Megan to this travesty.

The church meeting ended with a sonorous prayer by Reverend Porter, extolling the virtues of living a sinless life and condemning those who didn't. Jesse gritted his teeth. Reaching down, he covered Megan's clenched fist with his hand. He felt her start, and he could feel her trembling, most likely from the same anger that consumed him.

Outside, the congregation separated into small groups, speaking in hushed whispers and staring at the door of the church as the Coulters stepped out. Jesse still held Megan's hand. She seemed to be drawing strength from him. For the first time since their arrival, she lifted her chin and straightened. She didn't meet the gaze of any of the people clustered around, but stared off across the wide lawn toward where their wagon awaited. Jesse wondered if she were judging the distance and the time it would take them to cross over and be gone from here. He couldn't blame her at all. He wanted to leave this place and never return.

They were almost to the wagon when a voice halted them. "Megan, wait." Glancing over his shoulder, Jesse saw a short, heavyset woman hurrying to catch them. In her arms she cradled a sleeping baby. Four children trailed after her like quail after a mama. By the time she reached them, she had to gasp for breath before she could speak. Megan stiffened as if terrified of what the woman would say.

"Megan, Dear, I'm so glad we both came to church today. This is the first time we've been here since the blizzard." Her voice trailed off. Tears sparkled in her eyes. "I just wanted to tell you how sorry we are about your family and what happened. If there's anything William and I can do, please say so."

Megan relaxed. "Thank you, Mrs. Bright. I'm sorry I haven't been by to visit, but the weather has been bad." An awkward silence fell. "I don't believe you've met my husband, Jesse Coulter. Jesse, this is one of our neighbors, Mrs. Edith Bright."

"Mr. Coulter, it's a pleasure to meet you. Oh, there's William coming with the reverend. If you're like us, you have to head back right away. Perhaps we could travel together and stop along the way for our lunch." Edith raised her hand to wave at the approaching men. She didn't seem to be aware of the dark cloud hovering around the preacher.

9

*D*read filled Megan as she watched the preacher stalking toward her. This day looked like it might go from bad to worse. After the way Reverend Porter's gaze bored into her in church and the reaction of the congregation when she, Jesse, and Seana walked in, she knew the angry frown on Reverend Porter's face boded ill. She pasted on a smile as she smoothed the ruffle along Seana's collar.

"Good afternoon, Mr. Bright, Reverend Porter." Megan hoped they couldn't see how much she wanted to turn and run. She tightened her hold on Jesse's hand, almost unaware of doing so.

"I don't know what you're doing, showing your face here like this. Did you think we wouldn't have heard about your meeting with Mr. Sparks?" Reverend Porter said.

"What are you talking about?" Megan glanced at Jesse. He seemed as puzzled as she did.

"Mr. Sparks told me about you coming to town on the pretense of asking about the loan. Any decent Christian wouldn't have proposed what you did while your husband waited outside. Although reluctant to believe the rumors we'd heard about you, after talking with our esteemed banker, I can see they were true."

"Exactly what did I say to Mr. Sparks?" Megan tried to push away the feelings of impending doom. She wanted to climb in the wagon and drive away from here as fast as possible. Would she never be free of the vicious lies those young men told about her?

The preacher leaned over and glared at Megan. "I'm talking about how you told Mr. Sparks you regretted not choosing him for a husband. You even suggested the two of you could meet privately on occasion."

Edith's gasp echoed Megan's. "I said no such thing. In fact, I didn't speak to Mr. Sparks without my husband there." Megan paled as she remembered Mr. Sparks calling her back as they were leaving. He said he wanted a private word, then only offered again his condolences about her parents. Jesse had been right outside the open door. She hadn't thought anything of the interchange.

"Don't add lying to your list of other sins, Mrs. Coulter."

"Just a minute, now." Jesse stepped forward, pushing between Megan and Reverend Porter. "I was at the bank, too. When Megan spoke to Mr. Sparks *privately*, I was right outside the door watching them. Mr. Sparks asked to speak to her, not the other way around. I believe you should question your source before accusing my wife of anything." Jesse's fists balled at his sides, his whole body like a tight spring. A thrill raced through Megan as she realized no one had ever stood up for her like this before. In spite of the accusations, she wanted to smile.

"We've known the Rileys for several years now." William Bright stepped forward. "Megan has never done anything to deserve such treatment. I think you could have at least given her the opportunity to tell her side of the story."

Reverend Porter whirled on Mr. Bright. "You're stuck out there in the middle of nowhere. You don't hear the things I hear. This girl has a sinful reputation that's followed her here. Now we're seeing her true colors. As a member of my congregation, I'm going to have to ask you and your missus to not associate with her."

Mr. Bright's jaw tightened. "I don't believe you have the authority to tell me who I can or can't associate with. The Rileys were a fine couple. I intend to stand by their daughter. Lee Riley helped me out more than once, and Megan, here, stayed with us when Edith had so much trouble with the last baby. I don't know what we'd have done without her help. She's a fine girl."

"Her parents told me they had to move out here to escape all the problems she caused with young men. At least out here they were away from town and so could keep her in line."

"Reverend, I've never hit a preacher in my life, but if you don't turn around and leave us, you're going to be the first. If I'm not mistaken, you're gossiping about information told to you in private. In my Bible, gossip is a sin." Jesse tilted forward until his face was inches from Porter's. All across the grounds, people were silent as they watched the interchange.

The two men glared at each other for a long minute before Reverend Porter stepped back, easing the tension. Megan thought Jesse wanted to go after him, so she placed a hand on Jesse's arm. He glanced down. She gave a small smile. She could feel the muscles in his arm loosen. Taking her hand in his once again, Jesse faced the preacher. "You stopped a little too soon when you were reading from Psalm 139. What about the next two verses? 'If I take the wings of the morning, and dwell in the uttermost parts of the sea; Even there shall thy hand lead me, and thy right hand shall hold me.' I guess that part of the Scripture didn't fit what you wanted to say. That psalm isn't talking about hiding our sin as much as letting us know that God is always there to guide us. No matter where we go, He'll lead us if we allow Him."

Turning his back on the preacher, Jesse led Megan and Seana to the wagon. He handed them both up, then turned to Mr. Bright. "I don't believe we've been introduced, Mr. Bright. I'm Jesse Coulter, Megan's husband. We'd take it kindly if you would join us on the trip home. Megan has some lunch packed."

"I do, too." Edith Bright, surrounded by her wide-eyed children, took a step closer. "We can stop and combine our lunches. The company will be enjoyable." She sent a glare at the preacher.

"You go on ahead. I'll get my family loaded up." William Bright shook Jesse's hand. "If we're going to be neighbors, I'd like to get to know you. Living so far from town, we have to stick together." He, too, shot an angry look at the departing preacher, raising his voice on the last words so they would be heard by anyone close.

"Meggie, can I ride with Sally?" Seana enjoyed the rare visits she got with the oldest Bright girl. "Please?" At Edith's nod, Megan gave her permission and watched as her sister clambered down and skipped over to climb into the Brights' wagon, giggling with her friend as if there weren't any troubles in the world.

The small groups of people scattered around the church grounds began whispering together, their glances raking over Megan. Jesse clicked his tongue, and the horses began to move. Megan held her head high, unwilling to allow these people to know how upset she was. On the way home, she should explain to Jesse why there were so many rumors about her. She didn't know if she had the courage to bring up her painful past.

§➤

The horses snorted and tossed their heads as they drove away from Yankton. Jesse knew they were sensing the roiling emotions running through him. How could Reverend Porter call himself a Christian, yet treat someone the way he'd treated Megan? There were places in Scripture talking about discipline in the church, but this wasn't the way to handle it. Reverend Porter should have come to the house with Mr. Sparks in tow to talk to Megan, rather than confronting her in front of the whole congregation as if she were some common criminal unworthy of justice.

Besides, where had the esteemed Mr. Sparks been today? Wasn't he a member of this church? If he didn't even attend Sunday services, then Reverend Porter should certainly give Megan the benefit of the doubt, considering she and her family always attended when they could.

For the first mile, he allowed his feelings to stew, glancing back once to find the Brights about an eighth of a mile behind them. Megan sat board stiff beside him on the seat, her gaze straight ahead. He wanted to talk to her, but he didn't know how to start. Since their marriage, they'd only talked of farm-related concerns. The realization dawned that they hadn't ever talked about anything husbands and wives usually shared. He found he wanted to tell her about his call to be a pastor, and he wanted to know her likes and dislikes. He especially wanted to know what had hurt her so much and what dark cloud followed her when she moved out West with her parents.

A quiet sniff broke his concentration. From the corner of his eye, he could see the way Megan's fingers trembled as they clasped together in her lap. From the movement of the material in her dress, he knew her whole body shook with her effort to hold in her hurt. A single tear rolled down her cheek, but she still didn't relax or let her gaze drift his way.

The horses were going on their own now. They'd been over this road often enough to know the way home. Jesse loosened his grip on the reins. The tension and anger inside him flowed away, replaced with compassion and caring for his wife, something that he'd never expected to feel. Shifting the reins to one hand, he put his other arm around Megan's shoulder and drew her close. She resisted for a moment, then leaned her head against his shoulder.

Jesse marveled at how natural it felt to have Megan leaning against him. Her head fit just right in the curve of his shoulder. Closing his eyes, he breathed deeply, loving the scent of soap mixed with the fresh smell of outdoors and sun. He wanted to rest his cheek on her head, to caress her arm. He wanted to kiss her and care for her as a true husband should.

"Megan, I'm so sorry I made you go to church. I had no idea you would be treated that way." Jesse stroked her arm.

She shuddered. With a sob, she erupted in tears. He held her tight until the crying eased, murmuring soft words of comfort, praying God would guide him as a husband.

"I'm sorry." Megan pushed away from him, wiping at her cheeks. "I don't usually act like this."

"You don't usually get attacked in front of a crowd of people." Jesse pulled out his handkerchief and offered it to her. "I've never known a preacher to be so vicious."

"I've seen him do worse." Megan gave a slight hiccup as she wiped her eyes.

"Worse than this?"

Megan nodded. "A few years ago we had a family in town whose boys were . . . rambunctious." She glanced up at Jesse with reddened eyes. "The boys weren't bad; they were full of energy and life. They liked to play practical jokes, and some people didn't like that. Reverend Porter has always been stern and doesn't see amusement in much of anything."

She paused to blow her nose. "Anyway, the boys played a practical joke on the Porters. It was harmless, but the reverend took offense.

He called the parents up in front of the congregation the next Sunday and chastised them for not having control of their children. He read Scripture, although much of it out of context, according to my father. By the time he finished, the family was so humiliated, they left."

"They left town or church?"

"Church that morning. They tried to stay in town, but Reverend Porter has a lot of influence here. So many people were against them, the family ended up leaving. I only hope they found a good church and a pastor who will not be so condemning.

"Papa often said if there was any other church to attend, he would change in an instant. I know of others who agreed with him."

"I suppose there aren't any other churches close enough to ride to." Jesse pursed his mouth in thought. A seed of an idea began to sprout.

"No." Megan glanced behind them, a thoughtful expression on her face. "You know, you have a lot of knowledge of the Bible. Seana and I both appreciate the lessons you've done on the Sundays we stayed home." She fell quiet, nibbling at her bottom lip.

"What if—"

"I've been thinking—"

Megan blushed as she and Jesse both spoke at once. Jesse flashed her a grin. "Go ahead, you first."

She hesitated, smoothing her skirt with her gloved hands. "What if you started a church? I guess that would never work because we live so far from town, but I think a lot of people around here would welcome someone other than Reverend Porter. If only we weren't so far from Yankton."

Jesse nodded. "That's sort of what I wanted to talk to you about." He took her hand, needing the contact. She didn't pull away. "I've been thinking about how we don't really know each other. Ever since the wedding, we've talked about Seana or the farm, but we've never learned much about one another." He paused as she looked away. Had he seen a look of fear in her eyes? What was she afraid of?

"Yoo-hoo, Megan." Mrs. Bright called from behind them.

Jesse hadn't realized how close the neighbors had gotten to them. They must have pushed their team some to catch up. He tried not to show his disappointment. They could talk later. Jesse hauled on the reins, pulling the horses to a halt. He and Megan both turned in their seats to face the Brights.

"Megan, these boys are just about to starve to death." Mrs. Bright's laugh tinkled in the chilly air. "I think that includes William. Men and boys are always hungry. Are you and Jesse ready to stop for a bite to eat?"

Glancing first at Jesse, Megan pointed at a small rise of land. "We're ready. Momma and Papa used to have lunch at the next rise. The ground will be a little drier there. Is that okay?"

"Lead on." William clucked to his team at the same time Jesse did. The wagons rattled along the road for a few minutes to the small hill.

As soon as they halted, the children tumbled over the side of the wagon and scampered to the top of the hill. Seana and Sally climbed at a more sedate pace, the pair still in deep conversation. Jesse smiled, remembering how his sisters and their friends giggled and talked for hours.

Handing Megan a blanket, Jesse lifted the basket of food from the back of the wagon. One of the many things he appreciated about Megan was her cooking skill. Without the hard work needed to keep up a farm, he would be as fat as one of their hogs by now. She made the lightest biscuits and the tastiest stew he'd ever eaten. He knew she had packed a fried chicken in the lunch this morning, and his mouth watered at the thought.

"Here, let me take that." Megan stretched out her hand for the blankets Edith Bright was juggling along with the baby.

"Do you want the blankets or Henry?" Edith asked. "If you don't mind, I'd love a break from this one. He's done nothing but squirm all the way from town."

Megan held out her arms. Henry gurgled as he almost jumped at her. The look of utter delight on Megan's face as she cuddled the wiggling infant close in her arms told Jesse she would make a great mother. He'd never given much thought to being a father; but watching Megan, his heart filled with a longing so strong, he thought anyone would be able to see.

As the women strolled up the rise after the children, William

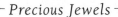

stepped up beside Jesse, lugging a much bigger basket. "I heard in town that you're about to lose the farm. Sometime soon I'd like to talk about Mr. Sparks and the shenanigans he's pulling around here. Something just doesn't smell right."

10

$\mathscr{B}$efore the man had a chance to say more, Edith called for them to hurry up and bring the food. The older boys raced back and forth between their parents as Jesse and William climbed the hill, toting the baskets. The two boys were full of energy, as only the young possessed. They settled down when the food was laid out, however, and everyone dug into the food with gusto.

"More chicken?" Megan lifted the bowl, still half full of fried chicken, and offered it to Jesse. He shook his head, then sighed.

"You're going to fatten me up, Megan. I think there is one more piece calling my name." Jesse felt a thrill of satisfaction at Megan's blush. "I don't know how I managed to be the one to have you as a wife." He leaned forward, noting the Brights were taking care of a fight between the boys. "You are a blessing." He winked. Megan's cheeks turned bright red. Jesse snatched a chicken leg from the bowl and took a big bite to hide his grin. He didn't want her to think him insincere, but he couldn't help being delighted to watch her. Giving her a compliment was like watching a rose blossom. He knew her parents were very good and loved her. The uncertainty must come from whatever hurt she'd endured before they moved here. He hoped someday she would be able to get past that pain.

"Jesse, we've heard you're from the Chicago area." Edith gave a frazzled smile, relaxing as her boys calmed down. "Do you still have family there?"

"Yes, Ma'am. My parents and two sisters still live there. Both of my sisters are married."

"Whatever made you decide to ride out West—and in the middle of the winter?" Edith served William a piece of chocolate cake.

"I . . . I guess I needed to get away for awhile." Jesse knew the excuse sounded lame. He didn't know these people well enough to go into detail about his personal life and failures. He wasn't even sure if he could share that with Megan, yet he felt he would have to, soon. "I didn't think about getting caught in a blizzard, though. I guess I should have waited until spring."

William scooped up the baby before he rolled into the cake. The tot chortled. William grinned. "Were you headed to Lead or Deadwood? I heard you planned to work in the gold fields."

"I hadn't actually decided which town to settle in. I thought I'd wait and get a feel for the place." Jesse began helping Megan pack up the lunch items. He didn't want to admit that his going out West had been a result of running from God, not a desire for adventure, as most people thought.

Giving the baby to Sally, William began helping Edith pack up their basket. The boys, faces pocked with chocolate cake crumbs, darted away across the rise, running as fast as their little legs could move. The baby let out a squall as Sally rocked him in her arms. Edith held out her hands for the screaming infant.

"Edith, why don't you and Megan sit here and visit while Jesse and I carry the baskets to the wagon? We can take a few minutes before we have to leave."

Jesse felt his stomach clench. He nodded his agreement to Megan and strode toward the wagon, the lighter basket clasped in his hand. He hoped William would have some sort of information he could use to help them get out of debt and keep the farm. He knew how much this meant to Megan, and now it meant a lot to him, too. He'd come to love this place, with its rolling hills and wide-open spaces. This wasn't at all like Chicago, where people were packed like animals in a pen. Neighbors were nice once in awhile, but he liked being able to go outside and stretch without everyone in a five-mile radius hearing about it.

Both baskets landed in their respective wagons with audible thumps. Jesse walked back to help William check the harnesses on his horses. He didn't know how to broach the subject, so he waited for the older man to speak first.

William cleared his throat. He ran expert hands over the traces and buckles, but Jesse could see his mind wasn't on the harnesses or horses.

"First the Sheffields, then the Murrays, the Reids, the Overtons, and last of all the Baxters." William leaned his arms over his horse's back as he stared at Jesse. "Those are the farmers who've had Sparks foreclose on their land in the last six months. Most of them were gone before anyone knew what had happened. I've heard the sheriff accompanies Sparks and escorts the family off their land before they even have a chance to pack much of anything."

"Why are so many people taking out loans they can't pay off? Have the crops been bad?"

William stared off into the distance. "I didn't know any of the families that well, except Megan's folks and Patrick Murray. They had the farm just past ours. Patrick and I talked on occasion, and the wives enjoyed getting together for a visit. Patrick mentioned having a loan, but I thought he said he paid it off with the proceeds from last year's crops. In fact, he had an exceptional year and said he would be ahead some because of it."

William combed his fingers through the horse's mane. "I know because, after harvest, he and his wife invited us over for a little celebration. He said this year would be the first he wouldn't have to borrow money for seed."

"So what happened?"

William shrugged. "I don't know. I went over one day a couple of months later. The house was deserted. Some of their belongings were still there, but no one had lived in the house for a long time. I rode to town, thinking something bad might have happened to them. The sheriff said they defaulted on their loan and had to be evicted. He heard they'd gone on west, but he didn't know where."

"I'd have thought they'd have contacted you before they left."

"I know." William gave the horse's neck an affectionate slap and led the way to Jesse's team. "That's when I remembered hearing about others being evicted. I asked some discreet questions and found out about the others I mentioned. There may have been more I haven't heard about. This is a big territory. Communication isn't always the best."

Jesse nodded, lost in thoughts of his own. Was this banker involved in something underhanded? If so, how would he ever prove that? He couldn't even find the papers from the loan Megan's father took out.

The chatter of the women and the squeals of the children drew Jesse back. He finished readying the horses and felt William's hand on his shoulder.

"Watch yourself, Jesse. I knew Lee Riley pretty well. I don't recall him ever saying anything about a loan he owed the bank that was due this spring."

The next few minutes passed in a flurry as women and children said good-bye and loaded into the wagons. In another few miles they would be parting ways and probably wouldn't see one another for at least a month. Unease filled Jesse as he thought of how little time he had to solve this dilemma before the sheriff paid them a visit and they wouldn't have a home anymore.

ૢ৶

The soft crackle of the fire soothed Megan as she relaxed in the rocking chair. Despite the difficult time at church, this had proved to be a wonderful day. She hadn't realized how much she missed another woman's company until she had the chance to visit with Edith. When she'd stayed with them last year, she and Edith had become very close. She loved those little rascals, too, and Sally.

The rhythmic scrape of Jesse sharpening knives, completing his evening chore, reminded her so much of her father that for a moment tears blinded her. Jesse worked so hard for her and Seana.

For the first time since they'd arrived home, she allowed herself the luxury of remembering the way Jesse stood up for her at church today. When they first walked into the church, she felt the animosity. She knew the instant Reverend Porter saw them and hadn't thought she could continue walking down the aisle. Then Jesse took her elbow, and strength she didn't know she had suffused her. She'd walked to that pew doing her best to ignore the townspeople who knew her terrible secret, or at least whatever version of that experience that had been spread about. Most likely the story didn't contain an ounce of truth.

The whole service had been directed at her, the sinful woman who dared to disrupt the meeting. She'd always felt sorry for those who had Reverend Porter's ire directed at them, and now she knew why. The man didn't know how to show any godly compassion. He passed judgment instead as if it were his God-given right to do so.

When they drove away from Yankton, she wanted to have the earth swallow her up. She didn't know how she could face anyone again, let alone her husband and her friends. Her body ached with the effort to hold in her feelings; but like a loose end, the thread of her emotions began to unravel. Then Jesse slipped an arm around her, urging her without a word to lean against him. He hadn't said anything, just let her cry while he comforted her. He hadn't asked why people treated her so poorly. He'd never asked about any of the references to her ruined reputation. He'd simply shown her God's love. She'd never had any man comfort her like that since she'd grown too old to sit on her father's lap. Something inside her warmed at the idea that Jesse might see her differently than others did.

On the way home after lunch, Jesse had continued to hold her hand, as if he wanted to have contact with her. From the feelings fluttering through her as his thumb circled on the back of her hand, Megan couldn't imagine what it would be like if they hadn't been wearing gloves. The thought made her flush. She ducked her head, hoping Jesse wouldn't notice and wonder what she was thinking.

She'd expected Jesse to notice the girls in town, but he hadn't. He hadn't even glanced at Belinda Parkins, with her gorgeous blond hair and slender figure. All the boys fought for the opportunity to sit with her. Even many of the older men earned angry nudges from their wives when Belinda walked past. Belinda had always been the one to laugh at Megan for her "cute chubbiness," making all the others their age laugh while Megan wanted to die. That's why she didn't enjoy trips to town or attending church.

Jesse sighed and arched his back, which must ache from bending over so long. He checked the edge of the knife blade and nodded. Picking up his sharpening stone and rags, he took them to his room to put them away. She could never fault Jesse for being messy. Like her father, Jesse always cleaned up after himself. She appreciated that.

"I don't suppose I could convince you to stop your mending for awhile." Jesse stood in the doorway smiling at her. Megan's heart thudded.

"Is there something you want me to do?"

"Yep." He grinned, his cinnamon eyes twinkling dark in the firelight. "Since Seana seems to be asleep, I'd like you to take a walk with me. I know it's cold, but we could check on the livestock and look at the stars."

Her breath caught in her throat. She didn't think she could answer. Stabbing the needle into the cloth, she set the piece aside before she hurt herself. Why did he want to walk with her? Did he plan to tell her he was leaving?

He must have taken her setting the mending aside as a yes, because he clomped to the door and plucked her coat from the peg. "Here you go." He held out the garment, waiting for her to put it on. Megan wasn't sure if she wanted to go along with this, but as she looked at Jesse, she couldn't see how she could say no. He'd been so kind and gallant today. How could she ruin that?

The night was clear and cold. Millions of stars shone against the black sky, some twinkling like tiny fireflies in the heavens. Her breath whooshed out white on the air, even after passing through her scarf. The last remnants of snow clung in dirty patches to the places that received the most shade during the day. Soon the snow would be gone and spring would arrive. The hills would be covered in green and dotted with bright flowers. She loved that time of year.

Jesse threaded her hand around the crook in his elbow and led the way to the barn. Tingles ran through Megan at the contact. Never before had he shown this desire to touch her. Why was he doing so now?

The warm, damp smell of livestock and hay greeted them when Jesse opened the barn door. At one end a sow grunted at the intrusion of light from the lantern Jesse carried. The horses snorted and stamped. Jesse's gelding moved to the front of his stall and gave a soft whicker of greeting to his master.

"They all look okay." Megan jarred the stillness with her words. She felt she had to say something.

Jesse smiled down at her. "Then let's go for a little walk. That is, if you can stand the cold."

"Sure." Megan tried to keep the apprehension from her tone. The night air chased away any shadows of exhaustion from the long day. She'd always loved the nights here. No factory smoke tinted the sky. The quiet spoke to her as if God Himself would come down here and walk with her. She'd always loved the feeling, but had never shared it with someone else.

The crunch of frozen ground told of their passing as they walked. Jesse didn't say anything, but he brought his arm closer to his side, tugging her along, too. She thought about removing her hand from his grip, but knew she didn't want to.

"Have you ever had a beau?" Jesse's question took her breath away. Had he heard rumors of what had happened? A tremor raced through her.

"No, I haven't." Her voice shook. "We don't get out much, and we live so far from town." She walked faster, not sure what she wanted him to believe.

Pulling her to a stop, Jesse turned to face her. He hadn't let go of her hand, but now took both hands in his. "Megan, I have something I want to say to you." He gazed up at the stars, his lips tight together as if he were trying to figure out how to phrase something.

"On the way home today, I realized that we haven't spent any time getting to know one another." He squeezed her hand, and she stopped what she was about to say. "I want to learn about who you are. There are things you need to know about me, too. I know we didn't plan to get married, but to me marriage is forever. If you're to be my wife, I want to know all about you."

Fear blazed through Megan. Would he want to know about her shame?

"Hey." Jesse waited until she looked up. "I know something happened to you before you moved out here. You don't need to tell me about it if you don't want to. Whatever it was, I know that right now you're a wonderful, caring person. I've seen the way you are with

Seana, the way you held that baby today. You were so hurt by your parents' and brother's deaths, yet you've carried on in a remarkable way. I admire you, Megan."

She stood frozen, staring up at him. What was he saying?

"Megan, I've come to care about you." Jesse drew her even closer. His arms closed around her, and she wondered if he could feel her pulse pounding.

"I like the way you look. You're not skinny and wasted like some girls. You aren't whiny or self-centered I like the way you feel in my arms." His voice trailed off. He bent his head and touched his lips to hers. Megan clung to him, wishing this moment could last forever.

11

*Q*uiet rang through the house. A few night birds called to one another outside, disturbing the late night peace. Seana's soft breathing in the bed across the room gave the only whisper of sound inside. Megan touched a fingertip to her lips, marveling at the remembered feel of Jesse's kiss. Conflicting feelings warred inside her. Would he, too, betray her and ridicule her? Hope flared up, fighting the negative emotions that threatened to drag her down. She'd felt hope before, but that hadn't stopped what happened. At long last the heaviness in her limbs drew her down into an exhausted sleep.

The voices began calling. Laughing voices. Young people having fun. Megan turned to see a door, cracked open, a shaft of light pouring out, inviting all who passed to enter.

Her feet dragged at the ground as she drifted toward the door. The voices grew louder. Girlish giggles mingled with manly chuckles and laughter. The clink of glasses added a tinkling quality.

As Megan approached, the strip of light widened. Megan could see through the opening. Instead of a room, a green lawn stretched out before her. The grass sparkled and waved in the sunlight. Huge trees made a rustling noise as the wind wove through their leaves. A pond glittered at the far end of the sloping lawn.

Close to where Megan stood, a group of young people was seated at a long table. The girls wore party dresses, the boys, their good suits. A huge mound of food rested on a nearby table. The young people had well-laden plates before them, although the food looked untouched.

Dread crept over Megan in a nauseating wave. She recognized them. Turning around, she groped for the door, wanting to escape before they noticed her. The door had disappeared as if it had never been there in the first place. She was trapped.

"Did you see her?" Hiram spoke. Handsome, sought after, Hiram. The boy all the girls wanted to notice them. Somehow Megan faced them again. She wanted to move, but her body refused to respond.

"Tell me about it." Susan leaned toward Hiram, giving him a coquettish smile. "I want to hear the story again."

Hiram laughed, his head tipped back, his blond hair falling in waves from his perfect features. "How could she have thought I would be interested in her? Truly, by the time she has a child or two, she'll be the size of a cow." Hiram paused as his audience crowed in delight.

"She was the easiest girl to dupe."

"You mean you've done this before?" One of the other boys leaned forward, listening with obvious interest.

"Of course." Hiram waved his hand in the air. "These poor young things need someone to give them attention. I saw her at every church function and dance, standing to one side looking like some chubby, forlorn puppy." The group howled again.

"I just wanted to give her a little excitement." He leaned forward. His tone took on a hushed note. "I didn't know she would respond so . . . um, enthusiastically."

The other boys grinned and prodded one another with their elbows. The girls blushed, hiding for a moment behind their fans.

"How did you get through that crusty exterior?" the other boy asked. "When I tried to talk to her, she turned out to be as cold as a fish."

"It takes finesse." Hiram smoothed his hair. "You have to show just the right amount of interest, yet leave some mystique that draws her into the net. I've mastered the technique."

"So what did you do?" The eager boy grinned in anticipation.

"Well . . ." Hiram frowned and rubbed his chin as if deep in thought. "I became vulnerable." He grinned at their puzzled expressions. "I pretended to be hurt. As she was leaving, I opened the gate for her. In the process I managed to—on purpose—get a splinter in my palm. Women can't resist a wounded man." He chuckled. "By the time she assisted me in removing the splinter, she agreed when I insisted on walking her home. One thing led to another from there." He shrugged, as if the conquest had been nothing.

"No." Megan opened her mouth to scream, but no sound came out. "He's telling you lies. This isn't what happened." How many times had she tried to convince everyone that Hiram had lied? No one listened to her.

"Did you . . . did she . . . ?" The boy couldn't get his question out in his eagerness.

"Of course." Hiram polished his fingernails against his shirt. "You saw what she looked like when we caught up with all of you. How could you doubt what we'd been doing? She was still clinging to me. I could barely get away."

Horror encompassed Megan. Why did she have to hear these lies again? Tears streamed down her cheeks. Even her parents hadn't been sure of her innocence in the face of the lies Hiram told. She'd tried to explain how she'd tripped and tumbled down a hillside. That's how her dress got the mud on it and her hair so disheveled. She clung to Hiram's arm because her ankle throbbed from the fall.

Even the bruise that developed there didn't convince anyone that she'd told the truth. Everyone said she was desperate for a young man's attention and willing to do anything to get it. Megan had never known such shame.

"So do I have a chance with her, too?" The young man rubbed his palms on his pant legs.

"All of you have a chance." Hiram's eyes twinkled. "If you have no success, then you aren't half the man I think you are. Let us know," he called after him as the boy dashed away.

"No." Megan wept in uncontrollable sobs. She had to do something to stop this. She hadn't before, and look at the results. She tried to push forward, to confront Hiram, but her body refused to move. Twisting and turning, she cried out again and again.

"Meggie, Meggie, wake up." Seana's small hands gripped her shoulders, shaking her. Megan couldn't seem to stop the sobs. Her pillow felt damp from the crying she'd been doing while dreaming.

"What's going on?" Jesse called from outside the door. "I'm coming in."

After the nightmare she'd just experienced, Jesse should have been threatening to Megan, but somehow a measure of peace descended with his arrival. Seana moved aside, and Jesse sat down, pulling her into his arms like he might comfort a young child. For a long time he stroked her back, whispering soothing sounds that she couldn't even make into words.

"Seana, I want you to go on back to bed. Your sister's fine." Jesse spoke only after Megan's trembling eased. "I'm going to take Megan out and fix her some warm milk. You go on back to sleep."

Crawling back in bed, Seana was asleep almost before Jesse could tuck the covers around her. He turned back to Megan and scooped her up, covers and all, and carried her out into the kitchen. She waited in silence, watching as he built a small fire in the stove to warm some milk for her.

The drink tasted delicious, warming her clear down to her toes. Her eyes opened in surprise at the touch of sugar he'd added. Her mother always added sweetener and cinnamon, but most people didn't. Even without the spice, the hot tonic was perfect.

"Thank you." Drowsiness overtook her almost before she took her last sip. She felt Jesse's strong arms lifting her from the chair as he carried her back to bed. The urge to talk to him, to tell him about the nightmare, plucked at her heart, but her tired body couldn't seem to respond. The gentle touch of his kiss on her forehead was the last thing she felt as she drifted off.

&

For a long time, Jesse sat at Megan's bedside, watching her sleep. He'd never felt such tenderness for another person. When he awoke from a sound slumber to hear sobbing, he couldn't imagine what was wrong. Hearing Seana cry out for Megan made him move faster than he thought possible. The sight of her white face awash in tears haunted him. All he'd wanted to do was hold her and keep her safe from whatever followed after her.

"God." His words were barely audible in the quiet. "Please help me to be a good husband to Megan. Help her to trust me with whatever hurt she's suffered. Give me wisdom, Lord. I know You brought me here for a reason. Let me help her."

ॐ

The cows were lowing their protest by the time Jesse got to the barn the next morning. "Sorry, girls." He patted the closest one on the rump. "Last night was a rough one. I missed the rooster this morning." He chuckled, wondering how anyone could rely on one of those feathered creatures that crowed whenever they felt like it, not just at the crack of dawn.

The quiet swish of milk into the pail brought out Mama Kitty. Jesse shot a stream of milk in her direction, which she lapped right out of the air. Shadow watched from the side, but didn't approach Jesse and the cow. When Mama Kitty began to clean her multicolored coat, Jesse lost interest and his thoughts turned to Megan. She'd looked so tired this morning. He wanted to tell her to go back to bed and get some rest, but he knew she wouldn't listen.

He set the milk pails near the door and began to fork hay into the feeders. The barn door creaked open. Megan stepped inside, pulling the door closed behind her. Jesse stopped, uncertain why she'd come out here. She usually fixed breakfast while he did the outside chores. She smiled, a rather strained one, but a smile nonetheless.

"Don't worry, I have Seana working on breakfast. I think she can fry a little bacon without burning it, and the biscuits are in the oven." She took a couple of hesitant steps. "Can we talk for a few minutes?"

Shoving the pitchfork into the pile of hay, Jesse gestured at a small bench. He tried to give her a smile that would put her at ease. "I can't think of anyone else I'd rather be talking to."

Megan blushed and ducked her head. She perched on the edge of the bench as if she wanted a quick getaway. She took off her mittens, and her fingers kneaded her coat buttons. "Thank you for last night. The milk and all . . ." She cleared her throat and looked away for a moment. "You said you wanted to learn more about me."

He covered her fidgeting fingers with his hand. "You don't have to tell me if you don't want to, Megan. But I want you to know I'm willing to listen if you do want to talk."

"I wanted to tell you last night, but I got so tired. The nightmare and all the old fears wore me out, I guess. Will you listen to the story now?"

He nodded.

"It isn't pretty. I want you to know that if you want to leave after hearing what I have to say, I'll understand." Her voice caught. She closed her eyes for a moment.

Leaning back against the stall behind them, Jesse slipped his arm around her shoulders. With a gentle tug, he leaned Megan back against his chest. This way she wouldn't have to face him, and it might be easier for her to tell the story.

In almost a monotone, Megan told him about the dream. She told him what happened, how no one believed or listened to her. Jesse felt her anguish and burned with anger at the young men who did this as a prank.

"Just that easily, my reputation was ruined. Hiram's lie cost me any hope of being treated decently. Even though I didn't accompany any of the other boys involved, they reported that I had. Rumors flew all over town. The pastor from our church came calling." Megan paused, lost in thought, her body strung as tight as the strings on a fiddle. "He looked like the Grim Reaper, and when he got done talking with my parents, they looked the same. It wasn't long after that when Papa announced we were selling our house and moving to the Dakota Territory."

Jesse tightened his arm around her. Her story hadn't turned him away. Instead, he wanted all the more to show her the love she deserved. She began to speak again, and he leaned forward to catch the soft words.

"In the last two months, I've thought often how I could be the cause for their deaths. If I hadn't been so blinded by that cad Hiram's good looks and sweet words in the first place, I'd never have gone with him. Then those boys never would have lied, and my family would never have had to leave."

"Megan, don't you do this." Jesse put his hands on her shoulders and turned her to face him. "Don't you ever blame yourself for what happened to your family. None of you could have predicted that blizzard."

She nodded. "I know. I guess sometimes I just feel sorry for myself." She shrugged. "That's not a very Christian way to act."

He brushed a piece of hay from her hair. "Maybe not, but it's very human." He stood and helped her to her feet. "I'd better finish these chores before Seana eats all that bacon she's cooking, and I don't get any."

"I meant what I said, you know." Megan stepped away from him, her hands twisting her coat.

"And what's that?" Jesse had no idea what she meant.

"I won't make you stay here. You were forced to marry me when you didn't even know what you were doing."

"Wait right there." Jesse held up a hand. "I may not have known, but God did. He's the one in charge of my life. I believe you're the right wife for me."

Tears glittered in her eyes. "I'm fat. I'm ugly. Why would you want to stay with me? You're so handsome. There are other prettier girls who would love to marry you."

"That is the last time I ever want to hear those words coming from your mouth." Jesse couldn't keep the anger from his voice. Megan looked up, wide-eyed.

"Megan, you are a masterpiece created by God." He lowered his voice. "He knit you together and made you who you are. You are perfect for me. God knew that." He wiped a tear from her cheek.

"One of the things I prayed after leaving home was that if God wanted me to marry, He would send a godly woman, just the right person for me. You, Megan, are that woman."

Tears were flowing unchecked down her face. Jesse pulled her close and pressed his lips against her hair. "I didn't have to marry you,

Megan. I could have stayed in that bed and let them railroad you into marrying Mr. Sparks, but that wasn't God's plan. Can you see that?"

She nodded against his coat, and he stroked her back and her hair until she quieted in his arms. Tilting her chin up, Jesse smiled at her. Megan gave him a tentative smile.

"I think we'd better take the milk on in. What do you think? I can finish the chores here after breakfast."

Megan drew on her mittens and swiped at her cheeks with her mittened hands, nodding. Jesse followed her to the door, grabbing the bails of the buckets on his way. The sky was beginning to lighten in the east as they stepped outside. Jesse matched his steps to Megan's as they walked toward the house.

The door to the house flung open. Seana stumbled out. "Meggie, help me." A billow of smoke followed in her wake. Flames danced up the sleeves of Seana's dress, getting larger as the girl ran. Jesse's heart thudded as he quit thinking and sped toward Seana.

*S*eana." Megan froze, staring in horror as her sister ran toward them. Flames leaped up her arms, reaching greedy fingers to her face and hair. Beside her, Jesse dropped the buckets with a clunk. The milk sloshed in the pails, but didn't spill over. Jesse raced for Seana, his feet churning up clumps of wet earth from the well-worn path.

Screams tore through the air. Megan's throat ached, and she knew she and Seana were both screaming. Jesse reached Seana and tackled her in midstride. He fell on top of her, covering her with his body. As if she'd suddenly been loosed from bondage, Megan leaped forward, her heart pounding. What was he doing? Jesse should be helping Seana, but he was going to hurt her worse than the fire!

Rolling back and forth, Jesse looked like he was forcing Seana deeper into the damp ground. Megan wanted to weep. Minutes before she'd trusted this man; now he was trying to kill her sister.

"Stop." Megan grasped Jesse by the collar of his coat and dragged at him. "Get off her. What are you doing?"

"Megan, it's okay." Jesse glanced back over his shoulder. "I'm not hurting her. It's what I had to do to get the fire completely out."

He rolled to the side. Seana's sobs turned to quiet hiccups. Mud coated much of her. Her hair was singed; and the smell of smoke, burnt clothing, and scorched flesh made Megan nauseous. Jesse lifted Seana up from the ground and hugged her to him. Megan realized he had tears on his cheeks. Where moments before she'd felt anger, now a fierce love poured through her. Jesse had saved Seana's life with his quick action.

"Take her." Jesse thrust Seana at Megan. He leapt away to snatch up the two pails of milk and dashed for the house. Megan and Seana hurried after him. Smoke still billowed from the doorway. Fear lodged in Megan's throat, making it difficult to swallow.

"Jesse." She trembled at the thought that he might be burned trying to put out the fire. She stopped in the doorway, letting her eyes adjust to the dimness and the billows of smoke. Across the room, Jesse stomped on embers burning into the wood planks of the floor. Moving fast, he rolled up the rag rug her mother had made and headed for the door. Megan stepped aside as he tossed the smoking rug into the yard.

Jesse turned to survey the room, his chest heaving, sweat beading on his brow. Megan began to cough. Her lungs burned with each breath she took. Beside her, Seana also began to cough.

"Take her out of here, Megan. This smoke isn't good to breathe."

Grabbing the sleeve of his coat, Megan stopped him as he started to cross the room. "You come, too. I don't want you to get hurt."

Jesse smiled and squeezed her hand. "You go on out. I'll be right there. I just want to check and make sure all the fire is out. Leave the door open to let the place air."

Holding her breath, Megan led Seana outside. Seana doubled over in a fit of coughing. By the time she finished, she was shaking so hard, she could barely stand. Megan led her to a bench along the wall of the house.

Easing the charred, sodden cloth away from Seana's arms, Megan had her first glimpse of the burns. They were bright red and already blistering. Smears of brown mud would need to be washed away. "Wait right here, Seana. I'll be back."

Going to the side of the house that saw the least sun, Megan dug through the mound of snow that bordered the edge. The crust had hardened, streaked with gray and black from the dirt. Underneath the crust, the snow was mostly clean. Megan scooped up a double handful and carried it back to her sister. Putting the snow on the bench beside Seana, Megan began to spread it over the singed flesh. She hoped this would stop the burning and cool Seana's arms. She also prayed the melting snow would help wash the dirt from the burns without doing further damage.

"It hurts, Meggie." Seana's sobs made Megan wish this pain could be hers instead. Why did this have to happen? Seana leaned forward and groaned as agony ripped through her. A few times Megan had received minor burns from cooking. From that experience, she could only imagine how painful these severe ones would be.

Megan was returning with her second handful of snow when Jesse stumbled from the house. He bent over on the stoop, hacking and gasping for air for a minute before he straightened.

"You're doing good." Jesse knelt beside Megan as she applied more snow to Seana's arms. "I'll get your coat, Seana, so you don't get too cold." He returned in a moment and draped the heavy outerwear over Seana's shaking shoulders. Megan felt like crying. How could she have forgotten how cold her sister must be? All she'd thought of was treating the wounds.

"You did fine." Jesse must have read her mind. His arm wrapped around her shoulders for a quick hug. "You needed to get the burns cooled off first. There's some salve in the barn that should help take the sting away and keep infection from setting in. I'll go get it as soon as you get her cleaned up enough."

"What happened?" Megan glanced up at Seana and Jesse as she realized things had been moving so fast she hadn't asked how the fire began.

"A log rolled out of the fireplace." Jesse sounded grim.

"It's my fault." Seana spoke so low, Megan wasn't sure she heard her.

"Nonsense." Megan looked up to see the tears swimming in Seana's eyes. "Sometimes the logs shift, and one will roll out. You know that's happened before. That's why we're careful to keep the rug away from the front of the fireplace."

"I don't think these logs shifted on their own." Jesse stared at Seana, who studied the ground.

"I did it." Seana looked at Megan, desperation in her gaze. "You were gone so long and the room was getting colder. I thought I could help by putting on a couple of logs. I knew you'd be cold and the warm fire would be nice. Then that one log moved and fell out. It rolled across the floor to the rug. I tried to roll it back, but my dress caught on fire." Her eyes filled with tears. "I'm sorry."

"Oh, Seana, I'm sorry, too." Megan leaned forward and kissed her sister's cheek. "I should have come back in the house sooner. I didn't mean to leave you for so long."

Seana glanced at Jesse. "I did get the biscuits out of the oven and I finished the bacon. At least you can have some breakfast."

Smiling, Jesse stood and swept her into his arms. "Then let's see if the smoke's cleared enough. I'm starving." He paused and gave Megan a sheepish grin. "I do hope we can just drink water today, though. I threw the milk on the fire to put it out."

Megan managed a smile. "I don't think I've ever heard of using milk that way."

§≈

"Megan, I think we need to take Seana to town to see the doctor." Jesse stepped up behind Megan as she washed the breakfast dishes, speaking softly so Seana wouldn't hear him. "Those burns are really bad. The doctor might have something to give her for the pain. I don't know if the salve I have will help enough, either."

Turning so her back was to her sister, Megan swallowed hard before speaking. "Couldn't you just ride to town and bring the doctor here? The trip might be too hard for Seana."

"That would take too long. I wouldn't get back before nightfall, and even that's not guaranteed. What if the doctor can't come right away?" Jesse brushed a stray lock of hair from Megan's face. "I know you don't like going to town, but for Seana, we have to. She isn't strong, anyway. I'm also worried about the smoke she breathed. She's still coughing, even though you and I stopped a long time ago."

Finishing the last of the dishes, Megan wiped her hands on a towel. Walking away from Jesse, she began to wash the table, swiping at non-existent crumbs. Jesse had seen her clean the table already. He waited. She needed something to do while she considered their options.

"I've got some water warmed to wash her." Megan came to a stop beside him, but didn't look up.

"Don't make it too warm on her arms and face. Use cool water only on the burns. Don't rub, either."

Megan nodded. Jesse watched her face turn a little paler as she ladled water out of the kettle. He didn't know if she was worried about Seana and caring for her burns or if she was afraid of going to town. After Sunday's fiasco, he couldn't blame her for wanting to wait a long time before returning. Jesse knew Megan cared too much about Seana to forego seeing the doctor just because she didn't want to be seen in Yankton.

"I'll see to the stock and get the wagon hitched up while you're getting Seana ready to go." Jesse glanced down at his still-muddy clothing. "Then I'll come in and change before we leave." He touched Megan's shoulder. "I've seen someone burnt like this. They didn't get help, and the wounds got infected. I couldn't stand to see Seana go through something like that."

The drive to town seemed to take forever. Megan rode in back with Seana. Jesse had put down a mattress and several blankets to keep the young girl as comfortable as possible. Even so, the constant motion of the wagon caused her ceaseless pain. Megan had to keep Seana's arms uncovered so the blankets wouldn't pull any more skin away from her burns. Bits of cloth still clung to the worst of the injured areas. When Jesse tried to peel away her sleeves, the pain had been too great.

Lunchtime had passed when Jesse drove the wagon down the main street of town, following Megan's directions to the doctor's office. He felt bone weary. The travel wasn't as hard as knowing every jolt in the road hurt Seana. She'd passed out more than once on the trip here.

The doctor, a tall, thin man who looked more like an undertaker than a healer, took one look at Seana and motioned them to bring her right in. A middle-aged woman with a hat that held more feathers than a bird jumped from her seat in the waiting room, stared open-mouthed, then huffed her way out. Jesse didn't miss the distress that crossed Megan's face as she tried to ignore the woman. He would have to ask about her as soon as they saw to Seana.

"Martha." The doctor's bellow echoed off the walls. "Martha, get down here." He acted as if Jesse and Megan weren't even in the room as he went about gathering items he needed. A woman as tall and thin as the doctor rushed into the room. Her hands were busy tying an apron over her gray dress.

"Yes, Myron. What is it now?" Her voice squeaked to a stop as she focused on Seana, who had once more passed into unconsciousness.

The doctor swiveled around from his rummaging. He started to speak when his gaze caught Megan and Jesse standing by the table where Seana rested. "Oh, this won't do. You'll have to wait outside. I'll let you know when I'm done."

Martha made little shooing noises and motions with her hands, as if she were urging the chickens to leave the pen. Jesse took Megan's arm to lead her from the room. She gave him a panic-stricken look that shot a shaft right through his chest.

"Megan, she's in good hands. The doctor will do the best he can."

Like a sleepwalker, Megan followed in silence. As soon as they cleared the threshold, Martha slammed the door shut. The waiting room, empty now, offered a variety of seats. Jesse chose a ratty sofa and gave Megan's shoulders a gentle push. He sat beside her. She didn't seem to know he was there. Putting his arm around her, he rubbed her shoulder in a soothing motion. With his free hand, he tipped her head until she rested against him. For a few minutes she stayed stiff; then bit by bit, she relaxed. He didn't try to talk, but offered her comfort by his presence. He hoped that would be good enough.

Screams erupted from the other room. Megan jolted upright. Her eyes filled with tears. Jesse caught hold of her. She turned to him.

"I have to go to her."

"You can't."

"She needs me." Megan choked on a sob. "Why can't Momma be here? I can't do this alone."

Jesse hauled her to him, hugging her tight. "Oh, Megan." His whispered words stirred the wisps of hair that had worked free from the braids wrapped around her head. "Since your parents died, you've tried to be both of them to Seana and to yourself. You can't be someone else." He kissed her temple as silent tears slipped down her cheeks. "All God wants is for you to be you and to follow Him. You are so precious to Him, Megan. He didn't allow this as a punishment."

"Then why did He allow my parents and Matt to die?" Megan sounded so much like a little girl that Jesse wanted to pull her onto his lap and snuggle her close.

"I can't answer that." *Lord, please help me here,* Jesse prayed. "I know many of the prophets and people in the Bible asked similar questions about why injustice is allowed. Why do good people die and bad people prosper?"

"And what did God answer?" Megan tilted her head back to look up at him.

Jesse thought of the examples in Scripture for a moment. "Do you remember what he said to Job?" Megan shook her head. He almost forgot what he was supposed to say, at the trusting look in her blue-gray eyes. Jesse cleared his throat and scraped his thoughts together.

"When Job questioned Him, God asked if Job had been present at the beginning of the earth. He asked if Job continued to maintain it."

Megan's brow furrowed.

"You see, Megan, God's ways are so much different than ours that we can't question what He allows or doesn't allow. We have to trust that He will work everything out the right way. God always wants the best for us."

For a moment Megan was silent as she stared at the wall, a faraway look in her eyes. With a sigh, she smiled at Jesse and nodded. "You're right. I've read those verses before. Job suffered much more loss than I have. If he could end up praising God, then who am I to question what's right?" She gave him a watery smile. "That's much easier to say than do."

"You are so right." Jesse grinned.

The office door opened. Dr. Stanhope stepped out and pulled it shut behind him. He finished brushing the sleeves of his shirt down over his arms as he walked toward them. Jesse could feel Megan's tension as she rose to stand next to him. He placed his hand on her elbow to let her know he was there for her.

"The youngster should be fine." Doc smiled, losing his undertaker image. "Those burns are pretty nasty, but Martha will give you some medicine for them and give you instructions for her care. She'll cough for a few days until all the smoke clears out of her lungs. Try to have her drink plenty of liquids to keep her throat from getting too sore."

His brow creased. "She might be in quite a bit of pain for the next few days while the healing starts. I'll give you something to help with that, too."

Jesse breathed a sigh of relief a few minutes later as he helped Megan and Seana settle in the back of the wagon. He planned to get a little something they could eat on the way home and then head out. They should be able to be home in time for the evening chores.

Piling the blankets close to Megan so she could cover up Seana as the weather cooled, he felt her stiffen. He glanced over his shoulder to see Reverend Porter and the banker glaring at them from the sidewalk.

Mr. Sparks rubbed his hands together and gave them a feral smile. "Weather's turning nice, don't you think, Reverend? June will be here before you know it."

13

he extra blanket tucked around Megan's shoulders did nothing to ease the bone-deep chill. She shook, not from the cold as much as from the fear invading every part of her. *God, what are You doing? First, Momma and Papa and Matt. Now Seana's hurt and Mr. Sparks is going to get our farm. Where will I go? What will I do? I have no future.*

From the corner of her eye, she caught a glimpse of Jesse's broad, straight back as he guided the team toward home. Did she even have him? Yes, he'd been wonderful lately, but what about when they lost the farm? What would he do then? Did he truly want to be saddled with her as a wife, or would he continue with his life without a backward thought for her or Seana?

God, there's no one I can turn to. Everyone I know thinks I'm an awful person. Even the preacher in town wouldn't let me into his home. An image of the Bright family popped into her mind. She could feel the weight of the baby in her arms and remember the softness of his skin, the way his round eyes crinkled in laughter as he looked at her. Shame washed over her. God hadn't left her alone. She had no right to question Jesse's allegiance, either. So far, he hadn't given her any reason to believe he would turn his back on her. *Jesus, forgive me. I've been wallowing in self-pity, whining like a little child. Instead, I should be thanking You for saving Seana's life.* With sudden clarity, she could see Jesse throwing himself on top of Seana and rolling to put out the fire. Her throat tightened. If he hadn't been there . . .

"Jesse." His name caught, coming out too soft for him to hear. She cleared her throat. "Jesse."

He turned and flashed her a smile that made her heart dance.

"Getting hungry? The rise where we ate with the Brights is right up ahead. I thought we could stop there and rest a minute while we eat." He glanced at the sun. "We won't be able to stop for long, though. I hope you don't mind."

"That's fine." The words Megan wanted to say wouldn't come out. Jesse turned back around. She watched him lean forward, doing the little that needed doing to guide the team over the rutted road. His hands were strong and capable, yet she knew they could also be gentle. She touched her cheek, recalling the feel of his fingers there. A flood of warmth washed over her at the memory.

Jesus, have I been blind? I've been so caught up in my grief and complaining that I didn't realize You sent Jesse to me, knowing I would need his love and support. Yes, Lord, I do believe he loves Seana and me. I don't know why or how, but he does. Lord, I love him, too. Help me to show him that. Help me be the wife he needs.

"Here we are." The wagon rattled to a stop. Jesse swung down from the seat and held out his arms to help Megan. Seana still slept, so Megan put a blanket under her sister's head and reached out to Jesse. As he lifted her over the side, her breath caught at the feelings flowing through her. The look in his cinnamon eyes held her fast.

When Megan's feet landed, her legs buckled. She would have fallen if Jesse hadn't pulled her against him. She could feel his heart racing almost as fast as hers.

"I guess I sat too long." She tried to laugh, but couldn't.

Jesse's arms tightened. Megan's hand seemed to have a life of its own as her fingers caressed his cheek. The very air around them vibrated with emotion. Megan couldn't breathe. Her small hand slid behind Jesse's head as she tilted her face. Afterwards, she could never be sure who initiated the kiss; she only knew she didn't want it to end.

"Megan." Jesse's husky whisper told her more than a long discourse. He cupped her cheek with his hand and kissed her until she was breathless. Even then she didn't want to stop. She'd never experienced feelings like this before.

Jesse trailed a line of kisses across her face, then rested his cheek against her forehead. His rapid heartbeat and breathing told her he was as affected by the kisses as she was. *This must be what Momma and*

Papa felt for each other. Megan smiled at the memory of her parents' moments of affection, the clear adoration they had for one another.

"We'd better get out our lunch." Jesse stepped back, retrieving the package of sandwiches he'd purchased. Megan checked on Seana, still sound asleep, before walking hand in hand with Jesse up the rise to have their lunch. She felt almost like a shy schoolgirl on a first outing as her husband spread one of the spare blankets on the ground and helped her to sit.

The food was delicious, although Megan wasn't sure what she'd eaten. All her senses seemed to be heightened. She noticed the brush of the breeze against her cheek and smelled the fresh scent of spring in the air. The cushion of dried grass beneath the blanket felt like a feather pillow. Every movement Jesse made, every word he spoke, every smile and look of love in his eyes echoed inside her.

"We'd best be going." Jesse stood and held out his hand to help her up. "I want to be home before dark." After folding the blanket, Megan followed Jesse to the wagon. She didn't want this time to end.

Seana's soft breathing told Megan she still slept. Jesse finished checking the harnesses and helped Megan into the back.

"Wait." Megan placed her hand on his chest. Once more his closeness stole her breath and her thoughts. "I . . ." She glanced again at Seana, then back to Jesse. "Would you mind if I sat up with you for awhile until Seana wakes up?"

Jesse grinned. He slid his hands from her waist to around her back, tugging her close. He gave her a tender, heart-melting kiss. "I wouldn't mind at all." In one swift move, Jesse lifted her to the seat. Megan fussed with her skirts, trying to calm her racing pulse. How could one man be so strong that he could lift someone like her as if she were nothing?

The horses seemed eager to resume the journey. They set off at a good clip, and Megan could almost see pictures of the barn and food in their thoughts. Jesse slipped his arm around her shoulders. She stiffened in surprise for a moment, then relaxed and gave him a shy smile. Leaning her head against his shoulder, she sighed in contentment.

"Why were you passing through here last January, Jesse?"

Silence stretched as he stroked her arm. She felt the light kiss he pressed against her hair. "I was running away."

"From what?"

"From *whom* would be the better question." Jesse paused for so long, she wasn't sure he would answer.

"All my life my father tried to fit me into a mold that wasn't right for me. He wanted me to be a banker just like him and his father before him. Money and status are the two things that matter most to him. We always attended the right functions, with the right people, and wore the right clothes. My parents are well respected."

"Didn't you like banking?"

Jesse shrugged. "I have a different view of life and wealth than my parents or my sisters. Besides, I like being outdoors too much to be cooped up in a building all the time."

"Tell me about your sisters." Megan twisted to look up at him.

"They're both older than me. They married the right men. My father picked them out. Amanda and Patricia both attend the right church and do everything the way Father expected them to. They're perfect—to him."

"He picked out their husbands?" Megan straightened, alarm racing through her. "What about you? Was it Sara?"

Jesse's brow furrowed. "How did you know about Sara?"

"You talked a lot when you were sick. You thought I was Sara." Megan felt heat creeping up her neck to her face. Maybe she shouldn't have said anything.

Sadness settled over Jesse. "Yes, he had Sara picked out several years ago. She was from a family that would be an excellent match, increasing our wealth and holdings." His eyes darkened as if he were begging Megan to understand. "I couldn't marry her. I couldn't spend my life living a lie." He flicked the reins to urge the horses on. "You see, Someone else had a call on my life."

Taking his arm from her shoulders, Jesse wrapped his fingers around Megan's hand, bringing it to his lips for a brief kiss. "I was never like my family. I hated church."

She gave him a startled look. "You hated church?" Megan couldn't help thinking how she dreaded ever going to church again. She'd struggled with separating her feelings about church from her feelings about God.

"The church my family attends is about show. You wear the proper clothes and sit in the designated pew for your status. It's like everything is orchestrated for the congregation's benefit and nothing is there for God." Jesse flicked the reins again. "I didn't realize that until I met Pastor Phillips."

"Who's Pastor Phillips?"

Jesse grinned. "You have to remember you're married to a black sheep. I tended to disappear any chance I got. I'm not sure how it happened, but I found myself in a poorer section of town one day. In looking back, I know God guided me there so I could meet Pastor Phillips." He chuckled. "You would never have guessed the man was a pastor. He was playing a game with some of the neighborhood kids. Even though I dressed differently, they invited me to join them. That was the most fun I'd had in my life.

"From that time on, every chance I got, I slipped off to Pastor Phillips's church. He's the one who taught me who Jesus really is. I had no idea there was more to religion than wearing your best clothes to church once a week."

"Did your parents get angry when they found out where you were going?"

Jesse groaned. "*Angry* doesn't describe them. By the time they found out about Pastor Phillips, I already accepted the call to become a preacher. My father stopped those ideas fast. He even hired a man to follow me to make sure I didn't run with unsavory characters anymore." Jesse stared off into the distance, lost in thought. "He couldn't stop my thoughts, though. I did that all by myself."

"What do you mean?"

He sighed. "I bent to my father's will rather than following God's call."

"You were so young to go against your parents, though." Megan wanted to hug away the hurt she could see in his eyes.

"That's no excuse. Look at all the young men in the Bible who gave up everything to follow God's call: Samuel, David, many of the prophets, the disciples. I was more like Jonah. I ran from what God wanted me to do, and I knew I was running."

Seana moaned. Megan leaned over the seat and placed her fingers on her sister's forehead. Seana quieted. Megan sat back up to find Jesse studying her. She blushed, as thoughts of kissing him again rampaged through her. "Was . . . was banking so awful?"

Jesse gave her a wry smile. "Yes. I hated being cooped up inside that stuffy old building. I loved taking care of the animals and helping the gardener with the plants and grounds." He gazed around at the land spread out before them. "I think God used my willfulness to bring me here. I'm so excited about doing farming as soon as the weather warms up. I found some seed your father had stored in the barn. I thought I'd ride in and buy some more next week so we'll be sure to have enough." He paused.

"I don't know a whole lot about farming. Maybe I'll visit with William Bright and see if he can give me some advice."

"He could help a lot." Megan tried to keep the bitterness from her voice as her fears rose up in a suffocating cloud. "The problem is, why should we go to the trouble to plant the fields when we won't have a farm after June? I don't think we should do Mr. Sparks any favors. He won't take care of the crops."

§

"Meggie, oww!" Seana began to cry.

Jesse halted the team and grabbed Megan's arm to steady her as she climbed into the wagon bed with Seana. Seana's eyes were wide with fear and pain. She held her body very still, as if simple movements hurt too much to do. Jesse hated the thought of starting the wagon moving, knowing the motion would bring discomfort to the child.

He waited until Megan was settled with Seana's head on her lap. She spoke softly to her sister, calming her down. After a few minutes, Megan looked up at Jesse and nodded. He turned away with the image of her fear and hurt evident in the look she'd given him. More than anything, he wanted to erase those worries; he wanted to see her smile and laugh.

The wagon jounced down the rutted track leading to their farm. No matter which way Jesse guided the team, he could still feel every bump in the road and imagine how those felt like jolts of pain to Seana. With Megan beside her, the young girl was putting up a brave front. She hadn't cried out once since they started off again.

A few minutes later, Seana slept. Megan didn't want to leave her, so they rode in silence. Megan's words came back to Jesse. What about the bank taking back the farm in June? What could he do about that? He had some ideas, and he thought now would be the time to act on them. He'd tried hard to think of some reason Megan's father would have such a large outstanding loan due at an awkward time, but he couldn't come up with anything. He mulled over the information William Bright shared with him and what he knew of banking practices, but nothing made any sense. A gnawing unease deep inside told him something wasn't right here.

He'd gone through Megan's father's papers time and again looking for something about the loan. The only bank papers he'd found showed the loan Mr. Riley took out for seed and equipment three years ago, but there was also documentation that it had been paid off. Had he taken out another loan and not kept the paperwork? That didn't seem to fit with the little he knew about Lee Riley. The man had kept careful records of everything, from what he planted to how the crops produced, valuable information for Jesse or anyone who followed his example. He had a book about the animals and their offspring. Jesse didn't think very many farmers kept track of things like that, so why did Lee Riley not have anything about a loan that meant he would lose the farm he loved if he didn't pay it off?

The sun was sinking low by the time Jesse drew to a stop in front of the house. His muscles ached as he climbed down. Megan looked as tired as he felt. As his hands circled her waist, he recalled their kisses earlier this afternoon. If only Seana weren't watching them, he would be tempted to steal a few more of those kisses. Megan had no idea how desirable she was, but he intended to show her. He couldn't believe how much he'd grown to love her in the short time he'd known her. She'd become like a precious jewel to him, something of great value that he didn't want to lose.

14

*S*tepping out of the bedroom, Megan arched her back to ease the ache of weariness. Seana finally slept. Megan didn't know how long this would last. The medicine Doc had given them had lessened the pain enough for sleep to claim her sister.

If only she could take some of the medicine herself. Megan shook her head. The ache inside her was completely different. She knew she would have trouble sleeping tonight because of Jesse and the longing he'd awakened in her. Her cheeks warmed as she recalled his kisses this afternoon. She hadn't wanted him to stop. The way he looked at her, as if she were the most delectable sweet he'd ever seen, made her heart pound and her insides tremble.

Lord, I've fallen in love with him. Is this what You intended when You brought him here? Megan thought back to those first days when she cared for Jesse while he was so sick. Had she even been falling in love with him then? Is that why she hadn't fought marrying him as much as she could have? She knew deep in her heart that she wouldn't have agreed to marry Mr. Sparks that easily. *Jesus, help me to be a good wife to Jesse. Help me encourage him in the calling You've given him.*

A slight movement across the room drew her attention. Jesse squatted in front of the fire. Megan's breath caught in her throat. The firelight flickered and moved like a caress over the planes of Jesse's face, highlighting his toffee-colored hair. His strong hands were still, his eyes staring into the flames as if he were a million miles away. Was he thinking about the girl he didn't marry? Did he have regrets about Sara? Megan didn't want to consider that. She wanted to trust what she'd seen in Jesse's gaze today.

Although she didn't think she'd made a sound, Jesse turned and smiled at her. Megan thought she might melt.

"Would you like me to get you some coffee?" She almost groaned. What a stupid thing to ask. Who would want coffee this late? In fact, why was Jesse still up? He usually went to bed early. She thought he might still be worn down from his bout with pneumonia, but he wouldn't admit to it.

Jesse straightened and brushed at some wood chips on his pants. "I think a glass of warm milk might be better."

"Do you want me to throw it on the fire for you?" Megan slapped her hand over her mouth. She couldn't believe she'd said that.

Tipping his head back, Jesse laughed harder than she'd ever seen him laugh. She couldn't help it, she had to join in. Crossing to the kitchen, Megan hoped their mirth wouldn't wake up Seana.

"I think this fire should stay lit." Jesse gasped, his eyes twinkling. Still chuckling, he strode across the room to join Megan. "I'm glad you can laugh. I was so afraid you'd be beaten down by all that's happened. You're a strong woman, Megan Coulter."

"I only do what I need to do." Megan tried to ignore the rush of excitement that shot through her at his approach.

"I know what I see." Jesse took another step closer. "You're always polite, but you don't give an inch to anything that's wrong. Remember when the reverend tried to make you marry Mr. Sparks?" He grinned. "I think if I hadn't stepped in, Sparks would have been flying—right out the door."

Megan felt her lips twitching. She'd always enjoyed this sort of repartee with her parents, but she'd never been comfortable enough with anyone else to let go and be herself. She chuckled. "Now that would have been a sight to see."

Jesse took another step. She could almost feel the warmth of his arms as she imagined them around her again. Megan gestured at the stove. "Do you still want some warm milk?" After studying her for a long moment, Jesse nodded.

Within a few minutes, they were seated across the table from each other, sipping the warm drink. Megan had added a little sugar and cinnamon.

"Mmm. This is delicious. What kind of cow gives milk like this?" Jesse's eyes crinkled.

"This is my mother's recipe. We do have sweet grass around here, but nothing with these spices." She met his gaze, then looked away. He made her feel things she'd never felt before. "None of us liked warm milk, so on nights when we couldn't sleep, Momma fixed it this way so we would drink it."

"Did it help you sleep?"

Megan chuckled. "I think sometimes we worked at staying awake just so we could get a sweet treat. Momma and Papa probably knew what we were doing, but they still spoiled us. A lot of parents would have used a switch instead." Megan ran her finger around the rim of her cup. "I hope if I ever have children, I can be half as good a parent."

She jumped as Jesse's warm hand covered hers. "You'll be the best. Look at the way you are with Seana. Anyone who can get along with her sister like you do will make a great mother."

Megan leaned across the table and spoke in a low whisper. "You just haven't seen the times I pinch her when you're not looking."

Jesse grinned. "I may not see them, but I would have heard."

They laughed and Megan straightened. She wondered if she should pull her hand out from under Jesse's and decided not to. His touch felt so right. She wanted more. They should be getting sleep so they'd be ready for tomorrow, but neither one of them seemed eager to end this time together.

Jesse cleared his throat. "Tomorrow I'll ride over to the Brights'."

"That's fine." Megan nodded. "You said you wanted to talk to him about planting. It'll be time soon."

Their conversation wasn't comfortable now, but stilted. The warmth of Jesse's hand covering hers had grown to something more. Megan found herself wishing the table wasn't between them. She wanted him to hold her.

"Do you think Seana will be okay for the night?" Jesse's soft question startled her. His voice sounded funny, almost strained.

Megan nodded. She didn't trust herself to speak. Her mouth felt dry. Jesse stood, never letting go of her hand. He rounded the table, and Megan, too, rose. At his slight tug, she moved toward him as if in a dream. The look of love in his eyes surrounded her, taking away thoughts of anything but her husband.

When he kissed her this time, Megan felt like a princess. She'd given Jesse the opportunity to leave and he hadn't wanted to. He loved her—something she never thought a man would do. She loved him, too, with a deep aching love that she'd never known would be a possibility.

"Megan." Jesse's kisses strayed from her mouth along her jaw. Shivers of delight coursed through her. His arms tightened. The next thing she knew, he swung her up and strode to the bedroom. Her heart thundered loud enough to be heard miles away. Jesse glanced down, a question in his eyes. Megan smiled, her fingers tracing the outline of his face. She barely noticed when he kicked the door shut behind them.

A slight breeze lifted the strands of hair that had worked loose from her braids, sending them dancing across her forehead and cheeks. The fresh scent of spring was in the air. Bright green shoots of grass were poking up from the ground, as if overnight an artist had run his brush across the landscape, adding color to the brown. Megan wanted to throw her arms in the air and twirl in a wild dance of delight that winter was at an end. She settled for taking a deep breath and thanking God for the new life He'd given them.

"Meggie, wait." Seana darted after Megan, her long braids flying behind her. One month had passed since Seana had been burned. Except for the slight pink color on her arms, you couldn't tell where the burns were. Seana scampered up to Megan, her eyes sparkling, her cheeks flushed with excitement. "Meggie, can I go to the creek and play? I finished the chores you gave me. Please?"

"You know you can't go to the creek by yourself. Especially this time of year, when we've had so much rain." Megan stretched out her hand to Seana. Her sister's health had been improving as winter faded. As she felt stronger, Seana had also been showing some rebellion. Megan thought Seana missed their parents more than she would let on, but she hadn't been able to get Seana to admit that.

"I'm old enough to go there. Matt could go by himself." Seana put her hands on her hips. "I know how to swim if I fall in. I only want to see if I can find some frog eggs. Matt showed me how."

"Matt was a lot older than you. When he was your age, he couldn't go to the creek by himself, either." A lump wedged in Megan's throat. Matt had always taken Seana with him on his jaunts to fish or hunt for tadpoles and frogs. Their age difference didn't seem to matter. Matt doted on his younger sister.

"Why don't you come with me? I'm taking some water and a piece of corn bread out to Jesse."

"Why?"

"He's been working hard, and supper is still three hours away." Megan studied Seana's defiant stance. "Don't you think he deserves a little something? Remember how Momma used to do this for Papa?"

"Jesse isn't my papa." Seana hurled the words like stones. Megan flinched. Seana whirled and ran back to the house, but not before Megan could see the tears brimming in her eyes.

Jesus, I don't know what to do here. She's hurting so bad. Do I just wait, or do I punish her for insolence? I'm not a parent, Lord. Help me.

The joy seemed to have gone from the day as she trudged on to the field where Jesse plowed the soil. Megan attempted to erase the concern from her face, pasting on a smile when Jesse waved at her, then strode in her direction, leaving the team to rest.

"Hey, Beautiful. This is a pleasant surprise." Jesse brushed a sweet kiss across her lips.

"It is not a surprise." Megan couldn't help the giggle that escaped. "I do this every day."

Taking a long drink of water, Jesse winked at her. "Maybe the surprise isn't seeing you, but realizing how much more I love you every day."

Megan waved her hand in front of her face. "Whew, it's getting hot out here. It must be all the blarney floating around."

Jesse laughed and drew her close for another kiss. "That was the honest truth, even if you don't believe it." He released her. "Now why don't you give me that piece of corn bread before it's completely squashed and tell me what has you so upset."

Megan glanced down at what had once been a beautiful square of corn bread, but now looked more like something the horse stepped on. She flushed and handed the flattened piece to Jesse. "I'm sorry."

"You're avoiding the real issue." Jesse undid the cloth covering and took a huge bite. He didn't seem to care about the shape of his food.

Megan sighed and glanced back toward the house. "It's Seana again. I don't know what to do, Jesse. She's so moody lately. I thought she would have been rebellious over losing her parents months ago. Instead, she acts like they died yesterday."

Jesse took another long drink of water. "Hey." He pulled her close. Megan rested her head against his chest, listening to the steady thump of his heart. "She's been sick and hurt, Megan. I don't think she felt well enough to understand the loss. Give her time, Angel. She'll come around."

"But she resents your being here."

"That's natural, I think. She sees me as trying to take her father's place. Maybe in her child's mind, she wonders if she gets rid of me, maybe they'll be able to come back." He gave her a tight hug, then handed her the water container. "I'll try to quit a little early tonight. Maybe I can take her to the creek and do some fishing. Fresh fish for supper might be a nice change."

"Okay." Megan sniffed and wiped her nose. She gave Jesse a sly smile. "If she pushes you in, can you swim?"

"Nope, you'll have to come along and rescue me." He gave her a quick kiss and headed back to the horses. "I'll stop in about an hour. Don't say anything to her. She might think of an excuse not to go."

ও

His hair still wet from washing up, Jesse whistled as he opened the door to the house. Seana sulked in the corner while Megan chopped something for supper. The tension in the room could stop a train.

"Seana, I need some help." Jesse didn't glance at Megan, not wanting to give their conspiracy away.

"I'm busy." Seana grabbed up her doll, pretending to do something important with the toy.

"You can bring Ennis with you." Jesse paused to frown and rub his chin as if in deep thought. "The problem is she might get dirty and wet." He shrugged. "Oh well, I'm sure you can clean her up."

"What do you need me to do?" Seana was trying hard not to be interested.

Jesse sighed. "Well, there's some fish down in the creek, hollering to be caught. I hoped to find someone who could show me the best place to dig up worms and maybe even the best fishing holes."

Seana stared down, silent and still. Jesse turned to Megan. "Will you go with me, Megan? I really don't know where to go, and I'm hungry for a mess of fresh fish. I've been thinking about that all afternoon."

Megan opened her mouth to answer when Seana jumped to her feet. "She doesn't know. She never wanted to go fishing. Only Matt and me did that."

Jesse swung back around to face Seana. "Well, if you won't help me out, then Megan's the only hope I have. Will you help me?"

Seana shot a look at Megan that might have been triumph. "Come on, I know the best spots. Matt showed me all of them."

"Do we have some fishing poles?"

"They're out in the shed." A seed of excitement shone in Seana's eyes. "There's a can for worms out there, too."

"Why don't you go look for them while I instruct your sister on the fine art of getting ready to cook fish?" Jesse winked at Seana. She did her best to wink back, then darted out the door.

He heard the sniffle before he turned around. Megan wiped at her eyes with a corner of her apron. "Thank you."

"Thank me for what?" He went to her and wrapped his arms around her. He arched his brow. "Say, have you been chopping onions? You seem to be crying."

Stretching up, Megan dragged his head down and gave him a kiss. Jesse kissed her back. "I'd better go before I forget what I'm doing."

"Aren't you going to instruct me in the fine art of cooking fish?" Megan's gaze was wide and innocent.

He chuckled and kissed her again. When she was breathless, he stepped back. "Those were my instructions. Now you have to figure them out." Laughing, Jesse headed for the door. "We'll be back in an hour, Angel." He winked. "If you hear me hollering, come to my rescue."

$\mathcal{T}$ give up." Jesse sank down on the bank of the creek. "There aren't any worms to be found here. The only way to catch a fish is to try to grab one out of the water, and I'm no good at that, either."

"Matt did that once." Seana perched on a rock near the creek, her arms crossed, her back rigid. She'd been bouncing and excited until they stood on the small hill leading down to the winding stream. She froze, and Jesse could almost see the memories of fun times spent with her brother parading through her mind. He'd tried everything he could think of to reach her, but nothing worked. Acting as if he couldn't do this was his last resort.

"I've heard of people being able to do that, but not when the water is so cold."

Seana's chin tilted up a notch. "Matt did it in the summer. If it was warmer, I could show you how."

"Did you catch fish with your hands, too?"

She shook her head. "No, but I watched how Matt did it."

Jesse could see the sheen of tears in her eyes. "Me, I have to have a fat, juicy worm, or I can't catch a thing." Jesse plucked a blade of grass, taller down here by the water, and stuck it in his mouth. "Of course, I didn't have much chance to fish in the city."

"Matt said city folk don't know nothing about living."

"Matt could be right." Jesse's thoughts strayed to the values embraced by the people he knew. How many of them were miserable trying to keep up with fashion, wealth, and the status of their neighbors? They didn't have any idea how precious life could be until too late.

"Why don't you go back to the city?"

Jesse stilled. He'd almost missed the words, they were so quiet. *Lord, what do I say?* He studied the set of Seana's shoulders and thought of all she'd lost since he'd arrived. How could he have been so insensitive? She needed love and understanding—attention. That's why she was lashing out.

"Seana, I don't want to take Matt's place or your papa's."

"Then why did you come here?" Her chin trembled.

"Because this is where the Lord brought me. I was lost in the storm. He led me to you."

"Why?"

Jesse sat up. "Maybe because I needed your help. Maybe because you needed mine, too."

"I don't need you. I need Papa and Matt and Momma. They can take care of me just fine. I want them." She bent her knees and wrapped her arms around them, huddled in a ball. "Megan doesn't want you, either."

"I don't believe that's true, Seana. Have you talked to Megan about this?"

Seana shook her head and swiped the tears from her face. "It's true, I know. We don't want you here."

"If I leave, who will plow and plant the fields for you?"

"I can do it." Seana gave him a fierce look. "I've watched Papa."

Jesse quirked one eyebrow. "You can hitch a team to the plow? Have you ever done that?"

"No, but Momma always says there's a first time for everything. I know I can do it."

"Okay, I'll make you a deal." Jesse waited as Seana narrowed her gaze a moment before nodding. "You help me find a worm and catch a couple of fish for supper, and tomorrow I'll let you help me do the plowing."

He tried not to hold his breath or look anxious as she considered his offer. Seana jumped down from the rock and walked over to him. "Deal." She held out her hand. "Then when you see how good I am, you'll leave, right?"

"Fair enough." Jesse nodded. "But only if Megan wants me to go. She has a say in this, too."

They shook hands, and Seana walked to the edge of the creek bank. Taking a stick, she pried a rock loose and dug in the soil for a minute. With a grunt of triumph, she slipped a couple of fat worms free from the dirt, holding them aloft for his inspection. Jesse prayed he'd done the right thing. He wanted to reach Seana and help her through her hurt.

Threading a worm onto his hook, Jesse followed Seana downstream. She pointed to a spot in the creek, and he landed his bait there on the second try. The water swirled and eddied around the rocks and brush, the sound as soothing as a mother's crooning to her infant. He settled back against a tree, the rough bark poking through his shirt. Seana sat on a rock, her gaze glued to the spot where his line dipped below the surface of the stream.

Within minutes Jesse felt a hard tug on the pole. He sat up, his gaze going to Seana. She leaned forward, an excited expression making her look like the child she was. Jesse fought back a grin and began to work the fish to the edge of the water, where he could flip it up on the bank.

A squeal escaped Seana as she pounced on the flopping fish. For the moment, she seemed to have forgotten her dislike of Jesse. He could see her having done this many times in the past with Matt. She held the trout as high as she could.

"Bring him over here." Jesse pointed to a spot away from the creek in case the fish wiggled loose from the hook. He'd had many fish flop right back into the water before he could grab them.

Putting a new worm on the hook, Jesse ignored the wriggling fish and looked at Seana. "Do you think we can catch another one in this spot?"

She frowned at the swirling water, then nodded.

"All right. You toss the worm in, and I'll work on cleaning this fish while you catch the next one." He tried to act nonchalant about the proposal, but didn't miss the widening of Seana's eyes as she glanced from him to the worm dangling from the hook to the stream. It took her several tries and a little assistance to land the bait in the right spot, but Jesse couldn't help the satisfied feeling that welled up inside as he went a little way downstream to clean the first fish.

"Jesse, I got one." Seana's voice squeaked. Jesse crashed through the brush just in time to see her flip a trout onto the bank.

"This one is even bigger than the one I caught." Jesse placed his cleaned fish alongside hers. "I think you beat mine by at least two inches."

Seana clapped her hands. Jesse was amazed that the sulky girl of a few minutes ago could be so changed. Maybe her anger would pass as she learned he wasn't trying to replace her family—or the cause of them being gone. Jesse determined he would have to win the girl over. She deserved loving, and God sent him here for a purpose.

They caught two more fish before Jesse declared they had plenty for supper. Both of Seana's fish were bigger than Jesse's. She skipped ahead of him all the way back to the house. The sun hung low in the west. Chores needed doing before supper, so Jesse sent Seana to the house with the catch while he headed for the barn. Although tired, he worked fast. He couldn't wait to eat some fresh trout. Plus, the thought of seeing Megan again made the chores a breeze.

ᣟ

"Meggie, look." Seana rushed through the door, a string of fish in one hand, poles in the other.

Megan shut the oven door and set the pan of biscuits out to cool. "Those are nice, Seana." She left the kitchen to admire them.

"I caught two of them all by myself. These two." Seana pointed out the two biggest trout. "Jesse couldn't even figure out how to find worms. I had to show him where they are and then show him the best spots to fish."

"Sounds like without you we might not have had any supper tonight." Megan bit back the urge to caution her sister not to brag. Right now Seana needed encouraging, not discouraging. "Why don't you wash up? You can help me with supper. We should try to have everything ready when Jesse gets in from doing the chores."

Seana's face clouded over. Her lower lip stuck out a bit. "All you ever think about anymore is Jesse. You don't care about me. You don't even miss Momma, Papa, and Matt." She threw the fish on the table. "Well, I hate him." Seana rushed to her bedroom, leaving Megan stunned and in tears.

Her hands shaking, Megan picked up the stringer and carried it to the basin of water she had prepared to wash the fish. It wouldn't hurt them to soak for a little while so she could take care of this matter. Taking a deep breath, she headed for Seana's room, wishing that she could take with her some of her mother's wisdom in handling these matters. This was going too far and needed to be addressed.

"Seana?" Megan stepped into the bedroom. Her sister huddled on the bed, rolled into a ball. Her shoes, still damp from being near the creek, dripped pieces of dried grass on the bed and floor. "Seana, take off those shoes. You know better than to have them on the furniture."

"You're not my momma." Seana's voice was so muffled, Megan wondered if she'd heard right.

Taking a deep breath, Megan tried to count. She shouldn't have begun this conversation by pointing out her sister's faults. Her mother and father both told her she was too bossy with her sister and brother. Closing her eyes, she tried to think of how her mother would have handled this. "What did Momma say right before she left for town?"

A sob racked Seana's thin frame. "She said you were in charge while they were gone."

"That's right, Seana. I'm still in charge."

"I don't want you to be. I want Momma and Papa."

The bed rustled as Megan sat down beside her sister. "I don't want to be in charge any more than you want me to be. I want Momma and Papa and Matt home, too." She smoothed Seana's hair away from her tear-streaked face. "The problem is, they won't be coming home. We have to be brave and live like they want us to. Do you think they would be happy to see you acting like this?"

A hiccupping sob shook Seana. "No." She flung herself at Megan. "Meggie, it's his fault. I know it."

"What? Whose fault?"

"Jesse's." Seana's eyes met Megan's. Megan could see her sister pleading for understanding.

"You think our family died because of Jesse?"

Seana nodded.

"Why would you think that?"

"Because he came here the day they died. It's his fault."

Megan hugged her sister close, aching inside for the loss that was just now catching up to the young girl. She'd had trouble dealing with this, too, but all along she'd assumed Seana was too young to understand death. Her assumption that Seana would go right on despite missing their parents and brother had been wrong. What should she do now?

"Jesse was lost in the storm. He nearly died before I found him. How could he have done any harm to our family?"

"I don't know, but he did." Seana shook with sobs. Megan began to rock her, hoping to ease the girl's pain.

"Seana, you're looking for someone to blame for their deaths, but there isn't anyone. Sometimes things like this happen. Death can come to us all—it will, in fact. We have to be ready to accept that even when it hurts."

"I want them back." Seana pushed free. "You have to say those things because you married Jesse."

Weariness settled over Megan. She didn't know what to do. She had no idea what Momma and Papa would have done. "I have to fix supper. You stay in here. Take off those muddy shoes. Think about what you've said. Jesse has done nothing but be kind to us since he's been here. He doesn't deserve your nastiness."

Megan's legs trembled as she walked from the room. Her stomach tensed with the feeling that she'd failed her parents when they left her in charge. Her earlier question to Seana now haunted her. What would her parents say about how she was doing?

She didn't hear anything from Seana as she prepared the fish for cooking. By the time Jesse came through the door, the smell of supper permeated the air. Megan's stomach rumbled. They hadn't had fresh trout in months.

"Oh, that smells so good." Jesse drew in a deep breath, his face split in a wide grin. After hanging his hat on a hook near the door, he clumped into the kitchen and swept Megan into his arms. She couldn't get over how affectionate her husband was. She loved the attention he lavished on her. Whenever she approached him, he gave her his immediate consideration, no matter what else he was doing.

"How's the most beautiful girl in a hundred miles?" Jesse nuzzled her neck, sweeping kisses up to her cheek.

"You are going to be eating burned fish if you keep this up." Megan tried to sound fierce, but her giggles spoiled the effect.

"I'll catch more," Jesse murmured against her ear. "You taste better than any old fish, anyway."

"Jesse." Megan slapped at his shoulder. He grinned and landed a kiss on her lips. She quit fighting, even if she hadn't been protesting in earnest. His kisses were so sweet. She couldn't seem to get enough.

"Stop that. You're killing her, too." Seana's scream from across the room jerked Megan and Jesse apart. Megan blinked and stared at her sister, whose face had turned red with rage.

"Seana, we were kissing."

"No, he was gonna kill you like he did them."

Anger coursed through Megan. "Jesse did not kill anyone, Seana. You've seen Momma and Papa kissing like that. What's wrong with you?"

"I hate him." Seana clutched her doll tight to her chest. Her eyes shone bright with unshed tears. She looked like a forlorn waif, but her emotions were coming out as hatred toward Jesse. Megan knew they couldn't allow that to continue.

"Seana, that's enough. I want you to apologize to Jesse."

"I won't."

"Do you remember what Momma would do when you behaved like this?"

Seana stared at her for a moment. The fight seemed to trickle out of her until she hung her head. "She whipped me with a switch."

"That's right." Megan's heart was breaking as she tried to remain firm. "Jesse is my husband, your brother-in-law. I was wrong earlier when I told you I was in charge. Jesse is the one in charge here, just like Papa was the head of the house before." Megan waited a moment to let that sink in. "You will treat Jesse with respect."

Her tone softened. "I know you're missing our family. I am, too. But you can't blame Jesse for something he didn't do. All right?"

"Yes." Seana's braids shivered as she nodded her head.

"Now get ready for supper." Megan forced a light tone, hoping to ease the tension. "The fish you caught are almost ready for you to eat them."

Seana shuffled back to her room to put up her doll. Megan could see the glint of moisture in Jesse's eyes. He looked so gruff sometimes because of his size, but he had a tender heart.

"She wants me to leave." Jesse's voice told the hurt he felt. He tried to smile, but failed. "At the creek she told me you don't want me to stay anymore."

16

he evening air carried a chill, making Megan glad she'd brought a shawl with her when Jesse suggested they take a walk. Her whole body cried out with exhaustion from the tension of the evening. Seana had calmed down, but they all still felt her rejection of Jesse. Now her sister slept, and Jesse walked silently by Megan's side. She could almost feel his hurt and frustration.

"I'm so sorry about what Seana said."

Jesse squeezed her hand. "She's a child. I'm sure she'll be okay in time." They walked in silence for a few minutes.

"I should have seen this coming." Megan fought to speak around the lump in her throat. "She cried when my parents and Matt were gone, but it's slowly sinking into her that they're gone for good. She always did want Momma to hold her for hours when she was sick."

Stars twinkled across the expanse of the sky. On the horizon, the moon was just peeking above the hills. Megan felt choked by the responsibility weighing down on her. She felt guilty over her anger at her parents for leaving her with this mess. What kind of daughter was she to feel this way?

"I don't know what to do." The words came out on a sob.

Jesse halted, pulling her close. "Seana's gone through a lot, Megan. Give her time. She's also a Christian now. You can use Bible verses to guide her. I'll be there to help, but she already resents me. I don't want to turn her away completely."

Her head rested against his broad chest, and she closed her eyes. The steady beat of his heart calmed her. "You're better than warm milk."

"What?" Jesse tipped her head back and smiled down at her.

Megan could feel the heat warming her face. "I meant . . . when you hold me." She struggled to find the right words. "When you hold me like this, I forget all about my troubles. You make me relax. I feel so content."

He chuckled and let her lean against him again. "I could say the same for you. You know, I really thought I'd never get married, but now I can't imagine life without you." The kiss that followed stole her breath. The next one made her forget everything.

Jesse broke the kiss and stepped back, his breathing ragged. He caught hold of her hand. "I brought you out here to talk. If we don't start walking again, I'm going to forget what I had to say and just suggest we return to the house." He paused, then stepped closer. "Come to think of it, maybe we can talk tomorrow."

"Oh, no you don't." Megan gave a breathless laugh and swatted at him. "You can't tell me you have something important to talk about, then put it off. I won't be able to sleep."

"Maybe I was just wanting to get you out here where we could be alone."

Megan tilted her head and tried to hide a smile. "That won't work. We were alone in the house, since Seana sleeps like a bear in hibernation."

"Perhaps I wanted to be romantic." Jesse gestured up at the millions of stars. He drew her close and lowered his lips toward hers.

"Won't work." As she murmured the words, she sighed with longing. She didn't know if she wanted to continue with this intimacy or hear what he had to say.

"You're right." Jesse held her tight for a few minutes. "I need to talk to you about this."

Megan waited, content to remain in his embrace forever. She couldn't imagine what would be so important. They'd already discussed Seana, the plowing was underway, and Jesse had visited with William Bright a couple of times for advice on managing the farm.

He cleared his throat. Stepping back, he took her hand and began to walk. "The other day when I was at the Brights', William and I got into a discussion about church and religion."

Megan tensed, but remained silent, waiting to see what Jesse had to say.

"William and Edith haven't been back to church since the last day we were there. Reverend Porter did come to visit them." Jesse squeezed her hand as she tried to pull away. He wouldn't let go.

"Porter spouted some religious jargon, trying to convince them that he was in the right that day. They didn't fall for it. In fact, William told Porter to leave and never come back when he started telling them all the rumors about your reputation being sullied."

Anger made Megan feel taut as a strung bow. She wanted to say something in her defense, but knew there was nothing to say. Her hand began to ache, and she realized how tightly she had gripped Jesse's fingers. She made herself relax the hold she had on him.

"I didn't say this to make you mad or to bring up hurtful things." Jesse sounded anxious that she understand. Looking up into his dark eyes, Megan attempted a smile, but failed.

"William and Edith both miss the fellowship with other believers."

"Then they need to go back to church. They shouldn't stay away on my account."

"They aren't, Angel." Jesse embraced her. "William says they won't go back to a church where the reverend spreads gossip and treats the parishioners like you were treated."

"There aren't any other churches close enough to attend." Megan thought about how much she missed church functions. Even though she didn't care to be around people a lot, she still liked hearing the Word of God preached to a group of believers and nonbelievers. She wanted to feel a part of God's family.

Jesse took a deep breath. "That's what I wanted to talk to you about. We've discussed the idea of starting a church a few times, but haven't done anything yet." He hesitated as if gathering his thoughts. "I invited the Brights to come over on Sunday and worship with us." He stopped, turning her to face him. Megan had to fight a smile at the hopeful look he gave her. He reminded her of Matt as a little boy, begging to do something he wasn't sure would be allowed.

"That is the best idea I've heard in a long time." Megan's excitement began to grow. "Edith will probably bring something, and we can share a meal after the service. I can't wait." She hugged Jesse. "I don't know why you were so worried. The Brights are good friends. We don't get to see each other often. I'm always happy to have them visit, and worshiping together will be even better."

Pushing her back a step, Jesse took hold of her hands. "That's not quite all." She quieted as he paused. "William wants to invite some of the others who live within traveling distance of our place. Most of them live too far to get to Yankton, but they could come here on a Sunday."

Fear gripped Megan. She closed her eyes. Having close friends over to worship with was one thing. Having a crowd was another. Who knew what someone might have heard? Then more rumors would be spread, and she would be the target of those looks and comments that hurt more than any physical pain she'd ever experienced.

"Megan, look at me." He waited until she opened her eyes. "You have nothing to be ashamed of. There are always people who will gossip. That's why gossip is mentioned right alongside of murder in the Bible." He pulled her into his embrace. "Don't let your fears hinder what we should do for Jesus. I've promised Him to serve wherever and however He wants. I thought that meant going somewhere far away." She leaned back to gaze up at him. He kissed her and gave her a reassuring smile. "Now I understand He wants me right here. That's one of the reasons I'm here, or God is using me here, despite my willfulness. There's a need for a church and I'd like to start one. Will you help me?"

Megan leaned her forehead against Jesse's chest. He was so strong and sturdy and tender. She loved him so much. Could she stand with him? Would God give her the strength and courage to do so?

For the first time, Megan realized how much she depended on her parents' faith. Although she'd always believed, she never had to stand on her own before. She could almost feel God ask, "Whom will you serve this day?" Lifting her head, she met Jesse's gaze as tears filled her eyes.

"Whatever God wants you to do, I'll be right there."

"Thank you." Jesse whispered the words as he leaned close for a long kiss. By the time the kiss ended, they were both breathless again. "Now, I think it's time for the two of us to go back home, don't you?" His eyes twinkled with love and excitement. Megan knew her eyes must reflect those same feelings.

ૐ

The yard held a scattering of makeshift tables on one side. The other side was lined with benches waiting for the neighbors to arrive for their first church service. Jesse yanked at the collar of his shirt and tried to pray harder. He'd never led a complete service before, although he'd helped Pastor Phillips several times. Megan assured him the people would love his preaching, but he still had the tingling of nerves letting him know he was depending too much on himself and not enough on God.

A wagon rattled into sight. William and Edith waved, their boys and Sally jumping down almost before the wagon had a chance to stop. Seana, delighted at the chance to spend the day with her friend, dashed from the house. Every day, Seana made several trips to the barn to see if Shadow or Mama Kitty had their babies yet. Now she grabbed Sally's hand and dragged her in that direction, most likely hoping to have kittens to show her.

"Mornin', William." Jesse greeted the man he'd come to think of as a friend. William was steady, a hard worker, and willing to give advice, not ridicule, to a newcomer.

"Mornin', Jesse." William took the baby and helped Edith to the ground. "There are two more wagons behind us. I think it's Harry Price and Joseph Martin, with their families. Caleb Duncan promised they'd come, too." William gave a slow grin. "With their fourteen young 'uns, they'll about fill up the benches."

Jesse shook his head. Fourteen. That was a passel of children, for sure. "Once we have the service, we can take the benches to the tables while the women set out the food." Jesse slapped William on the back. "Thanks for all the help yesterday. I couldn't have gotten ready without you."

William studied the makeshift tables and benches thrown together from scraps. Jesse knew he was thinking of the work they'd put in, when William showed up unexpectedly with a wagon full of scrap lumber, a hammer, and some nails. He wanted this church to work out as much as Jesse did.

"I've been praying for years that God would send us someone who could preach a good Bible-based message and who would be willing to meet with folks who couldn't make the drive to Yankton." William stared off in the distance, not meeting Jesse's gaze. "You're an answer to prayer."

"I don't know. You haven't heard me preach yet." He watched as another wagon came into view.

William turned and lowered his voice, although no one else was near. "Before the others arrive, I wanted to ask if you'd heard anything back from the letters you sent."

"I haven't been to town to check the mail. I should be going this week sometime to get supplies. If I hear anything, I'll be over and let you know." Jesse stepped forward with William to greet the new family driving into the yard. He hadn't told Megan that Mr. Sparks had stopped by William's place, offering to buy it from him. Sparks told William if he didn't sell, they would be neighbors soon when he took over the Riley place. The man refused to think of it as the Coulter place. He wouldn't even acknowledge Jesse when they passed on the street in Yankton.

Another wagon clattered to a stop. Jesse busied himself unhitching horses and directing the older boys to where the stock could be watered and penned up for the day. Women called greetings to one another as they herded toddlers and carried food to the house. The older children squealed in delight as they played a game of tag to pass the time until everyone arrived. The peace and quiet that usually filled Jesse's day turned to chaos, but he didn't mind a bit. The Holy Spirit had given him a message for these people, and now that the time had come, he couldn't wait to share God's Word with them. As he watched the chatter and joy these people who lived in isolation exhibited as they met with one another, Jesse felt a welling up of love and compassion. For the first time, he began to understand what Pastor Phillips meant when he talked about loving his flock. With God's help, these people would become Jesse's flock of believers.

In no time the horses were cared for, the food put in the house, the children gathered, and everyone seated on the rough benches, waiting for Jesse to begin. He looked out at their eager, expectant faces and thrilled to the work God had prepared for him to do.

"Good morning. Thank you all for coming." Jesse cleared his throat and glanced at Megan. He'd been afraid she would be uncomfortable with the gathering, but with Edith arriving first, Megan had relaxed and seemed to be enjoying the company.

"Pastor Dan Phillips taught me most of what I know of the Bible. I enjoyed many of his services and would like to pattern this one after some of his." He grinned. "That means I'd like to start off with some singing, and I'm looking for one of the men here to volunteer to lead the songs."

The men glanced at one another from the corners of their eyes, looking as if they'd rather be a hundred miles away than here. Jesse had no idea who to call on because he didn't know anyone other than William well enough to elect them. William admittedly had trouble carrying a tune in a bucket.

"Caleb's oldest boy, Samuel, has a fine voice. I've heard him singing in the fields." William pointed to the boy in question. The youth's face turned bright pink, and he ducked his head.

"Samuel." Jesse waited until the boy looked up at him. His bright eyes held a mixture of longing and embarrassment. "Would you like to come and help me with the singing this first time? Then, if you like, you can take over the other Sundays."

With Samuel's help, they sang several verses of "Amazing Grace" and "Rock of Ages." Without an instrument to guide them, they were probably a little off-key, but Jesse didn't mind, and he knew God didn't care, either. These people were having a great time worshiping together.

"Before you sit down, Samuel, I'd like to do one more song. Do any of you know 'The Church's One Foundation'?"

Samuel frowned and shook his head, as did the others. Jesse nodded, knowing they might not have heard the song yet. "I'd like to teach this one to you because, as we begin a church here, I want us to remember who the founder of our church is. I'll sing through the first verse to show you how it goes. Then you can join me the second time."

> The Church's one foundation is Jesus Christ her
> Lord;
> She is His new creation by water and the word.
> From heaven He came and sought her to be His holy
> bride;
> With His own blood He bought her and for her life
> He died.

By the time the people finished singing, there wasn't a dry eye in the crowd. Blessed by how they longed to worship, Jesse hoped he would be able to deliver the message God had given him for these believers.

*T*hroughout the singing and introductory statements he gave, Megan couldn't take her eyes off Jesse. She forgot her discomfort with the crowd of people. She forgot her concern about Seana. Some change had transformed Jesse into a confident leader. She'd never seen that side of him before. His very demeanor took her breath away, and his words put a longing in her heart to know Jesus better.

"I'd like to read a portion of one of the psalms. Those who have their Bibles can follow along." Jesse held his Bible in one hand while he flipped through the pages. "I'll be reading from Psalm 90, verses 14 through 17. 'O satisfy us early with thy mercy; that we may rejoice and be glad all our days. Make us glad according to the days wherein thou hast afflicted us, and the years wherein we have seen evil. Let thy work appear unto thy servants, and thy glory unto their children. And let the beauty of the Lord our God be upon us: and establish thou the work of our hands upon us; yea, the work of our hands establish thou it.'"

Closing his eyes, Jesse prayed a simple prayer, then studied the people who waited in silence for him to begin. For some reason Megan could feel something different about this morning. Many Sundays Jesse shared Scripture with her and Seana. He'd taught her a lot, but today felt different somehow. She sensed a presence that hadn't been here, or at least as noticeable, before.

"Those four verses hold a wealth of wisdom I could talk about." Jesse stood tall, the slight breeze ruffling his hair. "I could talk about being satisfied with God's mercy or rejoicing and being glad all our days. I want to speak to you instead about the years wherein we have seen evil and the choices we have to make because of that."

Silence fell heavy over the group. This wasn't what Megan expected for a first service. She leaned forward to hear what he would say next.

"We've all experienced hard times: crop failures, disease, loss of loved ones. How many of us are able to walk away from tragedies without anger or frustration? How many of us are glad that those things happened?" A murmur rumbled through the group. Jesse waited a moment for it to die down.

"Look again at verse fifteen. Moses is the writer of this psalm. We all know Moses suffered a lot in his life. He didn't have an easy time, but here he is asking God to make him glad that he's been afflicted. Why is that? Take a minute and think about some difficult time you've gone through. Have you been able to thank God for that trial? Are you glad you experienced it?"

The breath seemed to drain from Megan's body. She thought of the deaths of her family, the lies spread about her both back East and out here. How could she be glad any of that happened? God couldn't expect that.

Jesse's tone softened. "That's hard to do. I believe it's only through God's grace and the working of the Holy Spirit that we're able to be glad in such circumstances. Why should we do this? Look at verses sixteen and seventeen."

Glancing down at her Bible, Megan drew in a sharp breath. Her heart pounded. The hairs on her arms stood up. She tingled as if a presence surrounded her. She listened as Jesse spoke, knowing his words speaking to her heart were a message from God to her. The fact that God chose to speak to her in any form or fashion made her want to weep. He loved her. It didn't matter what happened to her then or now, God loved her. He sent Jesse to be her husband because He loved her. Jesus would give her the courage to be right for Jesse, to encourage him in all that God had planned for him to do.

"When we choose to be glad for the afflictions God allows in our life, we will see the glory of God every day." Several heads nodded as Jesse continued. "Do you want to be beautiful? Then be glad at what the Lord's done in your life. Let Him establish the work of your hands and all you do will hold His beauty."

Jesse shut his Bible and looked at each person. "God has called me to preach His Word—to be a pastor. I'd like to be your pastor. I would like for the Lord to establish a work for me here in this community for those who aren't able to travel farther." He smiled at Megan. "My wife and I invite all of you to come every Sunday and hear the Word of God preached. You're all welcome to worship with us every week."

They were dismissed after William led them in prayer. The men moved to shake hands with Jesse and carry the benches to the tables, while the women rushed inside to set out the food. Megan lost count of the number of people who told her how much they appreciated the service and how they looked forward to next Sunday. Seana and her friends raced around the yard like young colts finally free from a pen. Megan couldn't seem to stop smiling. She hadn't had the chance to speak with Jesse, but every time he looked at her, it was like a physical touch of reassurance and love.

୧

"Did you ever wish for a smooth road without any ruts?" Jesse grinned at Megan as the wagon rocked through another pothole. With the recent rains, the road to town had grown increasingly more difficult to navigate. Sometimes Jesse feared they would break a wheel in the places he couldn't avoid.

"Do they have streets like that in Chicago? I can't remember such luxuries." Megan smiled up at him, her cheeks flushed with a healthy glow. Her eyes sparkled. Jesse wanted nothing more than to stop the wagon, hold her, and kiss her.

"Would you please stop that?" He guided the team around another hole.

"Stop what?"

"Stop looking so beautiful. We'll be late getting to town and late getting home, if you don't."

"How will my looking at you a certain way make us late?" Megan gave him an incredulous look.

"Because I might do this." Jesse pulled on the reins and stopped

465

the horses. Taking Megan in his arms, he kissed her with all the desire he felt.

"Ick. I can't look." Seana made sounds from the back of the wagon like she was going to be sick. Jesse chuckled and released Megan, whose cheeks were even more flushed now.

Megan fanned her face with her hand. "Seana, you should pray for a wonderful husband like Jesse."

"Not if he makes me sick like you've been."

"You've been sick?" Jesse studied his wife's healthy glow. He'd never seen her look so good.

Megan shrugged. "I've been sick a couple of mornings this week. Certain smells seem to be upsetting my stomach." She smiled and raised her voice so Seana could hear. "The sickness has nothing to do with Jesse."

"Tess Duncan says it does." Seana crossed her arms, looking defiant. Her attitude toward him had improved, but Jesse knew they still had a ways to go before she would want him around for good.

"Why does Tess think Jesse is making me sick?" Megan's eyes twinkled with mirth.

"Tess told me her mother says her father is the reason for some of her sickness. Her mother gets sick to her stomach and tired, then she gets fat, and then they have another baby in the house."

Jesse felt the breath whoosh out of him. Megan's eyes widened. He could see that she was considering if it were true. He sat perfectly still, watching the play of emotions across her face. When her eyes began to glitter and her hand covered her lips as they formed an *O* of wonder, Jesse knew. Megan's hand strayed to touch her abdomen. Jesse couldn't resist covering her hand with his, as awe filled him at the thought that they would have a child. In a few months, he, Jesse Coulter, would be a father.

"Is it true?" At his whispered question, Megan looked up. Her eyes shone.

"I think it is." She sounded shocked and delighted at the same time. "I hadn't considered this as the reason I was getting sick. It hasn't been bad. Edith was so sick, she couldn't get out of bed."

"I love you so much, Megan." Jesse gave her another long kiss. A quiet sniffle from behind interrupted them. Jesse glanced down to see Seana swiping at her eyes.

"Hey, what's the matter?" He ruffled her hair. "You're going to be an aunt. Don't you like the idea?" Seana shrugged.

"What else did Tess say, Seana?" Megan lifted her sister's chin. "What did she tell you?"

Seana tried to turn away. A tear trickled down her cheek. "She . . . she said you won't want me around anymore and will probably put me in an orphanage since Momma and Papa died."

Megan gasped. "That's the craziest thing I've ever heard. Why would we want to get rid of you?"

"Because I don't belong to you. I'm only a sister. Tess says you'll only want your children around you now." Seana's lower lip quivered. Megan's mouth opened and closed as if she were so shocked she couldn't think of anything to say.

Jesse turned farther on the seat. "Seana, do you understand what it means to be an aunt?" Seana shook her head, looking as miserable as a child could.

"Well, I know something about it because I'm an uncle." He waited until Seana gazed up at him, a glimmer of hope in her expression. "My sisters both have children, and while I lived back home, I often went over to play with them. I took the older ones fishing or hunting. I even escorted my oldest niece to a church social. She wanted to go with a boy and her parents agreed she was too young for such a thing. I volunteered to take her, and everyone was happy with that. We had a wonderful time.

"As our child's aunt, you will have the responsibility of loving the baby and helping to guide her as she grows up. You can teach her games and show her how to do different jobs."

"Ahem." Megan tapped him on the chest with her finger. "What if this baby is a boy?"

Jesse grinned. "Then she'll help show *him* how to do things." He looked back at Seana, whose face had lit up. He could see she was considering how important her job would be.

"Does Sally like her baby brother?" Megan asked.

Seana nodded. "She likes them all most of the time. She says it's fun to have someone to play with or to dress up like a doll."

"See?" Megan smoothed some flyaway hair from Seana's forehead. "You'll have fun with this baby, too."

Seana wrapped her arms around her legs and gazed off into the distance. Jesse could almost read her thoughts. She loved playing with Ennis, and this baby would be one more doll to attend to. Turning back around, he drew Megan close for a brief hug before continuing on to town. A father. The thought filled him with awe, fear, and joy all at the same time.

As they drew closer to town, Jesse could sense Megan tensing. She still hated coming to town, although she seemed to be enjoying the church services and the fellowship they had with those who attended. Jesse knew she still felt uncomfortable around the reverend and Mr. Sparks. Today they would be facing Mr. Sparks at the bank.

Jesse had finished the early planting. Despite all the chores that still needed doing, he and Megan couldn't afford to wait any longer before talking with the banker. There had to be some way to extend the loan until fall, when the crops would sell and they would have the money to pay the bank.

He would also need to go by the post office and see if his letter had been answered. William had asked last Sunday if he'd heard anything. Another family had been put out of their home by the bank. William knew them some and thought they had paid their loan. Just like many of the previous people, this family was there one day and gone the next. Something wasn't right, and Jesse intended to find out what.

Yankton appeared sleepy in the late morning. Most of the residents were working or at home preparing meals. The students whose families could spare them were at school; the other children worked alongside fathers and mothers in the fields and gardens. A light breeze took the heat from the sun, not making the air cold, but providing a freshness that felt good. The fresh scent of rain hung in the air from an early morning shower. Jesse drew in a deep breath, enjoying the smell.

He caught Megan's hand in his and held on, hoping to give her some support. Her face had paled as they reached town. Most likely she was nervous, but after the news shared on the road, he wondered if she was feeling sick again. He stopped the wagon in front of the bank.

"You okay?" Megan jumped as Jesse spoke close to her ear to keep Seana from hearing.

Her attempt at a smile didn't last. "I'll be fine."

Before Jesse could tie the horses, Seana had scrambled from the wagon. He helped Megan down, gave her a quick hug, and stepped back. "Ready?"

Megan took a deep breath, nodded, and lifted her chin. Jesse grinned and held out his arm.

When they entered the bank, there was only one customer, an old man doing more talking than the teller seemed to want to hear. Mr. Sparks stepped from his office as the door closed behind them. He rocked back on his heels and patted his generous paunch. Jesse could feel the anger curling up inside him. Sparks had the look of a predatory animal about to pounce on its prey. Jesse knew he and Megan were the prey.

"Good afternoon, Mr. Coulter. Have you come to pay off that loan?" The smirk on Sparks's face told Jesse the man knew he wouldn't be able to come up with the money.

"No, Sir, but we would like to speak with you about the loan if you have the time." Jesse kept one hand on Megan. Seana stood behind them, subdued for the moment. The old man had ceased talking to the teller. The only sound in the bank was the ticking of the grandfather clock against the back wall.

"Come right on in." Sparks gestured at his office door. "Maybe we can make this transfer early and fast."

Jesse ignored the insinuation and guided Megan toward the office. He nodded at a chair along one wall, and Seana plopped down to wait for them. Sparks lumbered across the floor and settled into a protesting chair behind his desk. Jesse and Megan sat close together, a united front against the injustice of what Sparks had planned.

Opening a drawer, Sparks brought out some papers. He put them on the desktop and narrowed his eyes as he examined Jesse and Megan. "Well, are you ready to sign over the farm and admit you can't pay off the loan? That will save a lot of grief. If you do that, I'll even give you two weeks to pack up and move."

18

*H*er fingers gripped the edge of the chair so hard, Megan wondered that the wood didn't crack. She wanted to scream. She wanted to throw something at this pompous windbag who thought he knew so much and had so much power. Her tongue refused to work. Bit by bit she calmed enough to ease her grip on the chair. The clock in the corner began to annoy her as each steady tick sounded like a stroke of thunder.

"My father did not have a loan with this bank, Mr. Sparks." Megan blinked in amazement at her controlled tone of voice. Ice crystals should have been sparkling in the air in front of her.

"I have the papers right here, Mrs. Coulter. I'm sure your parents didn't share such privileged information with you." Sparks riffled the incriminating papers with his meaty fingers.

"We found no papers or notes of any sort when we went through my parents' things. My father always kept perfect records of everything. Why would he not have an account of something like this loan when it meant he could lose the farm?"

"I can't answer that, Mrs. Coulter, and I'm afraid it's too late to ask your father."

Megan gasped. The blood drained from her face, leaving her light-headed. How could the man be so cruel?

"I'd like to see those papers." Jesse stood, stretching out his hand to the banker. Megan could see the ticking muscle in his jaw, the only indication of the anger he must feel.

"These are private records for the bank only, Mr. Coulter. I can't allow you to see them." Mr. Sparks opened the drawer and slipped the evidence out of sight.

"I believe when I married Megan, I became the owner of her father's farm. You consider me in charge of paying off the loan. Why won't you allow me to see the agreement you had with Mr. Riley?"

"You can take my word for what is written there. That's all you need." Sparks's chair creaked in protest as he leaned back. "All you need to do is come up with the money or sign the farm over. Which is it?"

A muscle in Jesse's jaw jumped. "Due to the rough winter and the death of Megan's parents, I'd like to ask you for an extension on the loan. We could pay you back in the fall when the crops come in."

"I'm afraid I can't do that." Mr. Sparks frowned. "If I let one person have an extension, then everyone will want one. It's bad for business."

"Mr. Sparks, my father is a banker. I've worked with him for years. You can't fool me." Jesse's eyes flashed. "I know you can hold off on payments without being hurt. An honest banker wouldn't withhold information or force people off the land when they've had such a difficult time."

Sparks stiffened. His eyes narrowed. "Maybe out here in the Territories we do things differently than you do in the big city, Mr. Coulter." He leaned forward, his meaty hands spread on the top of his desk. "I don't like your accusations. Because of Megan's difficulties, I will extend the loan for two weeks. That will give you six more weeks to come up with the money. On that day I will be at the farm and you will either pay me or be ready to leave."

He stood and gestured at the door. "I don't think we have any more to say to one another."

Stunned, Megan didn't think her legs would carry her from the office. She was going to lose her home. All the memories of her parents and brother, all the good times they shared were still there in that house and the land. She couldn't leave.

She felt a hand grip her elbow. As if in a dream, Megan looked down to find Jesse's strong fingers lifting her up. She didn't want to leave. There had to be some way to convince Mr. Sparks to let them have more time. They just couldn't lose their home. Where would they go?

Jesse let go of her elbow and gently touched her waist. He held her close like he was trying to shelter her from hurt. Her heart swelled with love for this man. What had her mother said when they left their home to move to Dakota Territory? Home is not a place, but a group of people. As long as she had Jesse, Seana, and now the baby, she would be at home. Her memories of her family would always be there, no matter where Jesse took them to live.

As they stepped out onto the street, the sun dipped behind a cloud, bathing everything in shade for a few minutes. Down the street a man carried a child into the doctor's house. The sheriff stood in front of the jail, an imposing figure even from this distance. A man hurried along the walkway, most likely heading home for his lunch. Megan thought life seemed to go on for others no matter how the current crises made her feel as if time were at a standstill.

"I need to check on some mail." Jesse managed to give her cheek a chaste kiss as he spoke close to her ear. "Do you want to go with me or wait in the wagon? As soon as I get done, we'll head home."

"Seana and I will wait for you." Megan forced herself to move closer to their horses. "I don't want to sit down. We'll be doing enough of that on the trip home."

Jesse gave her arm a light squeeze. "Okay. I'll be back as soon as I can. This shouldn't take long."

Time seemed to stretch as Megan and Seana walked a bit, then stood by the wagon. The sun played peekaboo with clouds that were growing larger and darker. Megan pushed away the worry that they would be caught out in a storm on the way home. She hated for Seana to be exposed to weather like that. Her sister had been getting stronger and hadn't been sick for weeks now. She didn't want that to change.

"Ready to go?"

Megan jumped as Jesse spoke from behind her. She hadn't heard or seen him coming. One glance at the frown on his face told her his news hadn't been good. She could see at least two letters protruding from his pocket. With his help, she climbed aboard the wagon, trying to wait patiently for him to tell her what he'd heard.

They rode in silence for the first hour. Seana, tired from the long morning trip, lay down in the wagon bed and took a nap. Megan wished she could join her sister. The past couple of weeks she'd been so tired. A thrill flowed through her as she remembered the cause of her unusual exhaustion. She would be having a baby this winter. From her reckoning, the little one should arrive around Thanksgiving or Christmastime.

In the midst of plans for making baby clothes, knitting stockings and such, Megan didn't realize Jesse had been talking until he touched her arm. She jumped. "I'm sorry, did you say something?"

"Were you asleep or doing some heavy thinking?" A slight smile let her know he wasn't upset with her.

Her face warmed. "I . . . I was thinking about the baby." She stared down at her feet, not sure why she was so embarrassed.

Jesse slipped his arm around her shoulder. "I haven't gotten used to the idea of me being a father, but I am happy." He paused, his fingers caressing her arm. "In fact, I haven't been this content before in my life. I know the situation with the bank looks grim, but I can't help feeling as if I'm right where God wants me to be. Does that make sense?"

Megan's vision blurred. She blinked as she gazed up into Jesse's serious face. Staring into his eyes, she thought she could see into the very depths of his soul. Emotion welled up, almost choking her. *Jesus, You blessed me so much with this man. Thank You.*

"It makes perfect sense." Megan touched Jesse's cheek. "I do get afraid sometimes, but right now I'm looking forward to seeing how God will work this out. After all, He's the one who got you to start the church out here. I don't believe He'll ask us to quit before we truly get started."

Jesse hugged her close, a slight smile easing his serious expression. "I need to talk to you about something." Thunder rumbled in the distance. Jesse flicked the reins to urge the horses to keep moving. Megan knew this had something to do with the letters he'd gotten. She tried to relax, but had the feeling bad news would follow.

"I need to leave." Jesse's arm tightened as Megan flinched.

"What?" She pushed away from him, half-turning so she could see him better.

"I have to go back home. I have some business there." He touched the envelopes protruding from his pocket. "My father is very sick."

Megan gasped. "I'm sorry. Of course, you'll want to go."

"Thank you for understanding. While I'm there, I also need to attend to some matters I've been looking into." Jesse dwarfed her small hand with his large one and gave a comforting squeeze. "This is a bad time for me to be gone, but I'll get back as fast as I can. At least I won't have any blizzards to contend with this time." His attempt to lighten the moment failed.

"How long will it take you to ride all the way to Chicago and back?" Megan tried to act like she wasn't scared.

"I'm not going to ride there. William suggested I go to Sioux Falls and take the train. That way my travel time will be cut. I'm hoping to be back in two weeks at the most. Sparks gave us six weeks, so I'll be here in plenty of time to keep him away."

"Keep him away? William suggested the train?" Megan shook her head, feeling like there must be cobwebs keeping her from thinking straight. "I think maybe you should explain what you're talking about."

Raindrops spattered around them. Jesse reached back and wrestled the tarp over the edges of the wagon so Scana wouldn't get wet. Then he pulled a smaller piece over Megan and himself for shelter.

"William and I have been talking about the problems with the bank. We have some ideas that something isn't right. I think I know why. I had planned to go back east soon anyway, depending on what I heard after I wrote to my father." He gave Megan a cocky grin. "I have a plan for saving our farm, but I really wanted to surprise you. What I have in mind may not work. Will you trust me?"

Gazing into his love-filled eyes, Megan couldn't do anything else.

ॐ

Jesse stared out the window as the train chugged into the station. People hurried every which way, trying to find the right person or the right train. Porters stood by piles of suitcases. For the past few miles, all Jesse had seen were buildings, houses, and people. How he missed the wide-open spaces and rolling hills back home. He smiled. Already this place felt foreign, and his heart longed to be back with his real family.

Joining the line of people inching their way off the train, Jesse prayed as he had most of the trip here. He wanted so much for his plan to work out, but more than that, he wanted to be in God's will. The upcoming confrontation with his family wouldn't be pleasant. He needed to be firm, but loving. What did the Bible say? "Wise as serpents, and harmless as doves?" That's what he would have to become and that would only happen with God's help.

"Jesse. Jesse. Over here."

Glancing around, Jesse could see the arm waving over the crowd. One of his sisters must have come to greet him. He'd sent a telegram letting them know what train he would arrive on. The throng parted. Instead of his sister, Jesse stood face-to-face with Sara, his ex-fiancée. She threw her arms around his neck, kissing his cheek with enthusiasm.

"Oh, Jesse, I missed you so much. I can't believe you're home." She leaned back a little to bat her impossibly blue eyes at him. "I begged Amanda to let me be the one to meet you. I wanted it to be a surprise, though. Surprised?" Her beauty hadn't diminished, but her effect on him had. Jesse let his satchel drop, removed her arms from around his neck, and gave her a gentle push.

"Now look at me." Sara laughed, her eyes sparkling, her cheeks flushed. "Here we are in the middle of a train station, and I'm throwing myself at you. I'm surprised you weren't so embarrassed you jumped right back on that train." In a swirl of skirts, she turned and wrapped her arm through his, standing so close a curl of her long, red-gold hair rested on his shoulder. "I didn't mean to overwhelm you. I just missed you so much."

"Sara, that's enough." Jesse stepped aside, loosening her arm. "Didn't Amanda tell you I'm married?"

Sara waved one hand in the air. "Oh, that. She said something about you thinking you were married to some country bumpkin.

Don't worry, Amanda's husband already has the legalities figured out. You'll be free in no time. Then you and I can continue with our wedding plans."

"I have no such intentions of getting out of my marriage. My wife and I are expecting a baby."

Sara paled and took a step back. Her gaze narrowed. Jesse remembered how she didn't like to have her plans changed or thwarted. With a sharp snap, she flipped open a fan and began to wave it in front of her face. She gave him a dazzling smile, one designed to render men speechless. "Come along. Let's get you home and your father can try to talk some sense into you."

"I thought my father was extremely ill."

"He may be sick, but he's not dead." Sara grabbed his arm, ushering him away from the platform and out to the line of carriages. "Come along, your family is waiting."

The ride to his house seemed interminable. Jesse sat as far from Sara as he could, but she ignored his discomfort as she repeatedly brushed her fingers across his hand or arm as she pointed out ways the city had changed in the months since he'd been gone.

At the house, Jesse's mother seemed to be the only one eager to see him. His sisters and their husbands maintained a cool attitude, as if his return wasn't at all welcome. His nieces and nephews, busy with their games, greeted him, then dashed away.

"Your father is in the bedroom." Jesse's mother drew him into the parlor away from the rest. "He isn't as strong as he used to be, Jesse. Try not to upset him. The doctor says his heart can't stand the strain anymore." She smiled and patted his hand. "He's better, though. As soon as he heard you were coming home, he began making wedding plans for you and Sara. He even has a surprise or two for you that he wants to announce tonight."

The bedroom door swung open soundlessly. His father, seated in a comfortable chair, surrounded by pillows and blankets, looked as gray as a blizzard sky. Jesse knew without any doctor's learned opinion that his father was dying. His father roused up, peering at Jesse, his gaze probing and intense as always.

"Jesse, you've finally come. I always knew you would come to your senses and return home to take up the business before I die." He indicated a chair near his. "Sit down. Let's plan your return to the bank and your wedding."

$$\textbf{19}$$

*S*leep evaded Jesse again. His bare feet made little noise as he padded down the hallway to his father's room. Two weeks had passed since he left home. Part of him longed to be back with Megan and Seana, yet another part needed to be here with his dying father. Although they disagreed on so much, Jesse didn't want to give up the hope that he could lead his father to a true knowledge of Jesus Christ before he died. He couldn't bear the thought of his father not having the chance to go to heaven.

The hinge gave a slight squeak as he eased the door open. A lamp turned low cast the room in a shadowy light. Jenkins, his father's butler, sat in a chair close to the bed, his light snores telling Jesse he was asleep. In the past few days, his father had grown noticeably weaker. The whole family knew he didn't have long to live.

"Jenkins."

The butler jerked awake at Jesse's whisper and light touch on his shoulder.

"Go to bed. I'll sit with him until morning."

"But, Sir, you have the meetings at the bank in the morning." Jenkins held himself ramrod straight. "I'm sorry I fell asleep. It won't happen again."

"Jenkins, you've done enough." Jesse clapped his hand on the man's shoulder. "I can't sleep. I'll be fine. Go on to bed."

For a moment Jesse thought Jenkins would protest again. He could see the indecision warring within the man. With a quick nod, Jenkins glanced once more at his employer, then marched from the room. Jesse watched until the door closed, then moved the chair closer to the bed. Throughout the exchange, his father hadn't stirred. Only the shallow rise and fall of his chest showed any life in him.

His silent vigil gave Jesse plenty of time to think and pray about the upcoming days. So far, his time at home hadn't gone as planned—not his plan or his father's. The major upheaval had been over his marriage to Megan. His parents insisted on an annulment, saying he'd been railroaded into marrying the girl. They didn't understand his explanation of God's design and that all the events in his life were working according to what God wanted for him. Refusing to agree to an annulment brought his father's ire and his mother's tears, but Jesse stood firm.

He'd found the information he needed, but couldn't leave as long as his father was so sick and the bank was in turmoil. For the past week, Jesse had been meeting with his brothers-in-law and the other officials at the bank, trying to get the paperwork done to transfer the leadership. His father wanted him to become head of the bank, but Jesse had no interest in doing so. He wanted to return to his family, his farm, and the church the Lord called him to start. Several times he and his father had spoken on the subject. Jesse assured him that his brothers-in-law were very capable of managing the business. To his father, their years of experience were nothing compared to his desire to have his only son inherit everything.

Jesse's thoughts turned to Megan. He never dreamed he would miss her so much after the short time they'd been married. The last five months had been the best of his life, despite the pneumonia. He grinned. Maybe because of the pneumonia. He knew that wasn't true. For the first time in his life, he was trying to follow Jesus in every way. Because of that, he'd been blessed with the woman of his dreams. Life might not always be easy and there were sure to be plenty of rough spots ahead, but he looked forward to living through everything with Megan beside him.

Every day Jesse wondered if he would get a letter from Megan. He'd written to her twice to let her know about his father and the situation with the bank. Before he left Dakota Territory, he'd made arrangements with William to check on the mail when he was in town and deliver anything that came for Megan.

His father groaned. Jesse raised the wick on the lamp as he leaned over the bed. Something had changed. His father's breathing sounded more labored; his color didn't look as good.

"Jesse." Richard Coulter's fingers felt like claws as they gripped Jesse's hand.

"I'm right here." Jesse touched his father's forehead, wiping away a film of perspiration. "Let me send for the doctor."

"No." The forcefulness of the word seemed to cost his father strength. He panted for a moment, but didn't let go of Jesse. "I want to talk with you. Must talk."

"What is it?"

"The papers. Are they done?"

"Yes. You signed the last of the papers today. At tomorrow's meeting your sons-in-law will take over the bank. Mother has been provided for, as have all your grandchildren. You can relax and not worry about a thing."

"You?" His father coughed and grimaced in pain.

"I'll always be on the board at the bank. Everything has been arranged as per your instructions."

His father's eyes seemed to clear. "It's time, Jesse."

A knot formed in Jesse's throat. As much as he and his father disagreed on almost everything, he didn't want to lose him, either. "Let me go get Mother. I'll send Jenkins for the doctor."

"No." His father's grip held. "Talk first."

"What do you want to talk about?"

"Is it true? What you believe?"

Jesse's heart leaped. "You mean about Jesus? About His dying for us so we have a way to heaven?" His father nodded. "Every word I read to you from the Bible the other day is true. Jesus paid the price for your sins and mine so we would have eternal life with Him."

"I've thought a lot about what you said. I think you may be right."

Jesse knew what those words cost his father. Richard Coulter had never been a man to admit to anyone else being right when it meant he might be wrong about something. The Holy Spirit must have been working on his heart to bring him to this point.

"Go get your mother while I spend some time alone."

As his father released him, Jesse stood. Two days ago he'd explained to his father how to accept Jesus as Savior. *Please, God, help him to be able to humble himself. Help me to know, too, Lord, please.*

ع

"Megan." Seana's cry was almost drowned out by the crashing of the door as she flung it open. "Megan, Mama Kitty, come quick." Tears tracked down Seana's cheeks as she grabbed Megan's hand and lunged back toward the door.

"Seana, stop. What's wrong?"

"It's Mama Kitty. She's hurt. You've got to help her." Seana swiped at her cheek with the back of her hand, leaving a dirty smear.

"Let me dry my hands." Megan wiped the water from her hands and hurried out the door after her sister. Seana flew to the barn, not slowing as she ran inside. Dread filled Megan as she saw the still body lying in a pile of hay. Mama Kitty had been missing since last night. Her newborn kittens were crying, most likely so hungry they were getting weak by now. Megan dropped down beside Seana.

"Seana, I'm sorry, there's nothing we can do for her." Megan blinked back tears.

"But the babies. They need their mama. How will they eat?" Seana's shoulders bowed as if she carried the weight of the world.

Wrapping her arm around her sister's shoulders, Megan tried to comfort her. "I don't know what to do, Seana. It looks like Mama Kitty was attacked. She managed to crawl back here, but she didn't live." Megan fell silent as Shadow, their other mother cat, slunk forward to sniff at Mama Kitty's body. The feeble cries of the kittens scraped at her nerves.

"Seana, let's pray. The Bible says God even knows when a sparrow falls, so He cares about these kittens. Let's pray for them." Megan took Seana's hand and waited for her sister to bow her head. "Jesus, You know how these little ones needed their mother. We're asking You to provide the help they have to have to survive since their Mama Kitty died. Please, help them. Help us, too, Lord."

Seana sniffled. For the past few days she'd been out in the barn every chance she could get free to see the baby kittens. She would watch them for hours. Shadow had kittens, too, but she wasn't as tame and would move them every time Seana found them.

"Seana, look." Megan nodded her head at Shadow. The cat had backed away from Mama Kitty and was staring at the place where the kittens were huddled in a writhing ball.

"Is she going to hurt them?" Seana whispered.

"I don't think so." Megan wasn't sure what the cat would do. Shadow inched closer to the yowling babies. She stopped and glanced back over her shoulder at Mama Kitty, as if trying to decide what to do. Taking another step, she leaned close and sniffed at the kittens. Their cries became more fervent, like they were begging for food from this stranger. With one more backward look, Shadow climbed in with the orphans. Making small comforting mews, she lay down and began to nudge and lick them as they sought the nourishment they needed.

As quiet settled over the barn, Seana turned to look at Megan, her eyes wide. "Shadow is feeding them. Do you think God sent her to help Mama Kitty's babies?"

"I sure do." Megan hugged her sister. "God has a way of knowing our needs and providing for them."

Seana turned back to watch the little ones nurse. "Just like God sent Jesse to us."

Megan tightened her hold on Seana's shoulders. She couldn't speak for a moment. "That's right. When we lost Momma, Papa, and Matt, God already had Jesse there to help us. God always watches out for us, Seana."

"I still miss them." Seana's voice trembled, but she didn't sound angry, only sad.

"I miss them, too. That's all right."

They sat quiet for several minutes, watching the miracle before them. Megan's legs began to ache. She stood and brushed the hay and bits of dirt from her skirt. "Come on, you can help me bury Mama Kitty. Then we'll fix supper together."

As Megan picked up the shovel, Seana stopped her. "I'm sorry I was so mean to Jesse. I do like him. I wish he would come home."

Megan hugged her again. "I know. Four weeks is a long time."

As they walked out of the barn, William rode into the yard. He waved an envelope at Megan. "I had to go to town today. I picked this up for you." He handed her the letter. "Sorry I didn't get there sooner. You doing all right?"

"We're fine, Mr. Bright. How are Edith and the children?"

"They're fine, except for that little one. He's getting some teeth and is fussier than a runt piglet." He tipped his hat. "I've got to get on home and do the chores."

"Can we get you something to eat or drink before you go?" Megan was torn between wanting to be neighborly and wanting to read her letter. She hoped this would be word from Jesse saying when he would be home.

"No, thanks, but we'll be seeing you on Sunday. Edith and the young 'uns sure do look forward to worshiping together."

"We'll see you then." Megan waved as William's big roan cantered from the yard. Glancing at the envelope, she felt disappointment that the handwriting wasn't Jesse's. The neat letters looked like a more feminine hand. Shading her eyes to look at the sun, she stuffed the missive in her pocket. Reading this would have to wait until chores were done.

She didn't remember the letter until Seana was already asleep. Megan sank into the rocking chair to relax a moment before heading for bed. The crinkle of paper reminded her, and she brought the envelope from her pocket. Turning the lamp up, Megan still had to squint to read the fine writing.

Dear Megan,

My brother, Jesse Coulter, asked me to write to you and inform you that he won't be returning to Dakota Territory. He apologizes for any inconvenience this causes you. He has many obligations here at home and will be staying to run the family business. Due to the unusual nature of your marriage, he's been advised to apply for an annulment. The papers will be coming to you as soon as possible, and you will be free to remarry.

Sincerely,
Amanda Coulter Bradley

Megan couldn't breathe. Her chest felt as if she would explode from the hurt. Jesse wasn't coming back. He was leaving her, Seana, and the baby. Deep down she'd always known this would happen. How could a girl like her attract someone like Jesse? Oh, how she loved him, but she understood, too. His family, and probably the girl he'd been engaged to, needed him more than she did.

Crumpling the letter in a ball, she thrust it into her pocket. In a haze, she went about her bedtime ritual: checking Seana, blowing out the lamps, making sure things were ready for morning. After closing the bedroom door, Megan flung herself on the bed, still in her clothes, and cried until the covers were soaked. She'd never hurt so much in her life. What would they do? She and Seana couldn't hope to pay the loan. They would be thrown off the land, and she could picture Mr. Sparks smirking as he watched them leave. Where would they go?

Oh, Jesus, help us. You will have to perform a miracle for us to stay here. Help me to not worry, but to leave everything to You, Lord. She hesitated a moment. *And, Lord, please watch over Jesse. You know how much I love him. No matter what he's done, I still love him.*

She fell asleep and dreamed of being in a green pasture. The flowers smelled sweet, the grass was like a thick carpet. She lay there with her head on Jesus' lap as He stroked her hair and told her everything would be according to His plan. The morning sun peeking in the windows woke her. Megan sat up and stretched, surprised to feel so refreshed and content. She had no idea how, but she knew Jesus would bring them through this.

Megan worked hard, hoping the effort would keep her from dwelling on her problems. After all, she reminded herself time and again, these weren't her worries, but the Lord's. He could take care of anything.

"Megan, someone's coming." Seana stumbled into the house, her face flushed, eyes shining with excitement.

Following her sister out the door, Megan shaded her eyes, trying to see the approaching visitors against the late morning sun. One drove in a buggy, the other on a horse. Her heart sank as she recognized the sheriff and Mr. Sparks.

"Good morning, Mrs. Coulter." Mr. Sparks began to talk before he even had the buggy stopped. "Have you got the payment for the loan? This is the first of June."

"You gave us a two-week extension. We came to the bank and talked to you about it." A surprising calm enveloped Megan.

"Yes, well, I don't believe we have any paperwork to that effect, do we?" Sparks heaved his bulk from the buggy. The sheriff swung down from his horse and stood behind the banker. Mr. Sparks stepped forward. "Have you got the money?"

"No, I don't." Megan drew herself up tall.

Mr. Sparks leered at her. "Where is this husband of yours?"

"He's gone back east. His father is very ill."

"That's too bad. Sounds to me like he left you when times got tough. You should have taken me up on my offer." Mr. Sparks chuckled. "Now, you'll have two hours to get the things you want and leave. The sheriff is here to see that you do go. We'll wait inside." He strode past Megan and Seana, entering the house like a king going into his castle.

20

*T*don't want to leave here." Seana sniffed as she wrapped her clothes in a blanket to carry to the wagon.

"I don't want to leave, either, but we have no choice. We can't fight the sheriff on this. If we don't go, he'll arrest us. Then what will we do?" Megan tried to swallow around the lump in her throat. For the past hour, she and Seana had worked feverishly to pack what they could and load the wagon. Sheriff Armstrong offered to hitch the horses for her, but Megan refused his help. The man was guilty of helping Sparks throw families out of their homes. She didn't want him doing anything for her.

"I need to load that chair in the wagon." Megan tried hard to keep the disdain from her voice as she faced Mr. Sparks, sitting in her mother's rocker.

Sparks rubbed his fingers over the armrest, stroking the dark wood, "Why this is one of the nicest rockers I've ever sat in. I think I might like this chair to stay with the house."

Megan held her clenched fists tight against her sides. "You can't do that."

Narrowing his eyes, Sparks gave her a look intended to freeze her in place. "You have no idea what I can do. You should have married me. Then you wouldn't be in this predicament." He settled back in the chair and began to rock. "Of course, I know you're regretting your decision by now." His feral smile made her shudder.

"Why would I do that?"

"Because your new husband isn't planning to come back, is he?"

"How did you . . . ?" Megan snapped her mouth shut.

Paper crumpled as Sparks dragged a wrinkled envelope from his pocket. Megan's hand slapped her apron where she'd stuffed the letter this morning. It was gone, fallen out when she hadn't noticed.

"That is private. Give it back." She held out her hand, trying to keep it from shaking. Seana came back in and stopped. She could probably feel the tension in the room and wondered what was going on. Megan gestured for her to leave, but Seana ignored her.

"I just found this lying on the floor. I couldn't be sure who it belonged to." Sparks smoothed open the paper. "Sounds to me like you'll be in the market for a new husband soon. Mr. Coulter seems to have found better prospects."

"No!" Seana raced across the room, flinging herself in Megan's arms. "He's lying. Jesse's coming back. He won't leave us and the baby."

Sparks's eyes widened. "Baby? Oh, this is interesting." He heaved his bulk up from the chair. "I intended to make you an offer again, but I won't take on another man's child. Your time is as good as up. You've loaded enough of your things. Sheriff, see that they leave."

"But they haven't finished packing." Sheriff Armstrong frowned. "They still have about an hour left to gather their belongings."

Sparks's face reddened. "I said their time is up. I pay you to obey my orders. Now get them out of here."

Megan could almost see the thoughts warring in the sheriff's head. If Sparks admitted to paying him to do this work, then the sheriff wasn't evicting them for legal reasons. Her mind raced as she tried to think of something to halt this travesty.

"Come on." Sheriff Armstrong gripped her arm and propelled her past the smirking banker to the door. "I'll help you in the wagon, then load your chair for you."

"How does it feel to be a pawn?" Anger welled up in Megan at the injustice. "I thought you took an oath to uphold the law, not to work for whoever could pay you the most money."

"Quiet!" Sheriff Armstrong jerked her arm as he stepped outside. His reddened face and narrowed gaze told her she should be quiet, but she was too angry to stop.

"Someday you'll have to answer for what you're doing here, for what you've done to all the people you've put off their land illegally."

"This isn't illegal. Sparks has papers saying you can't pay up on the loan your parents took out at the bank."

"My parents didn't take a loan out at the bank. They did not owe him any money. Those papers are forgeries. I'm sure of it."

"Are you saying our esteemed banker is doing something illegal here?"

"That's what she's saying, Sheriff." They both jerked around at the new voice. "And if you don't take your hands off my wife in the next two minutes, you'll be in more trouble than you can handle."

"Jesse." As the sheriff let go, Megan ran to her husband. He swung off his horse and pulled her into his embrace. The two men with him also dismounted.

"Jesse." Seana barreled into her sister and Jesse, laughing in delight.

"Hey, Seana, I missed you." Jesse leaned down and gave her a kiss on the forehead before straightening to face the sheriff and the banker. "I'd like to introduce you gentlemen to some new acquaintances of mine. This is Marshall Trumble and Mr. Owens, an auditor. They're here to check into the practices of the bank and the way people have been losing their land and homes."

Jesse's arm tightened around Megan. She rested her head against his shoulder. "It seems Mr. Sparks isn't really Mr. Sparks. He comes from back East, where he lived as Mr. Wiggins, then as Mr. Burns. Marshall Trumble has been tracking him for some time. This isn't the first time he's forged papers and forced people out of their homes. He's good at copying signatures of people who have done business with him."

Marshall Trumble stepped forward. A big man, he looked like someone used to getting his way. "Wiggins, you thought you got away, didn't you? Well, you're coming with me. We're going over your bank records. If this place is like the last two, you've been skimming off these people's accounts, too. Mr. Owens will help us get it all sorted out."

Stunned, Megan watched the marshall escort Mr. Sparks to his buggy. Sheriff Armstrong followed, looking like a boy caught with his hand in the cookie jar. She guessed he would be accountable for helping with the fraud. Her heart was so full of thanksgiving, she couldn't say anything as she walked to the house with Seana and Jesse.

"What's this?" Jesse bent to pick up the letter his sister sent Megan. It lay in the dirt where Mr. Sparks must have dropped it. Jesse scanned the writing, his face darkening in anger. "I can't believe she did this." He crushed the letter in his hand. "Did you believe her?" Jesse turned Megan to face him.

"Mr. Bright brought the letter yesterday. I read it last night. Yes, I believed it at first, but after I prayed, I knew that everything would work out fine, and it has."

Jesse drew her to him. "Megan, I love you so much. All I could think of back there was coming home to be with you, Seana, and the baby. I wrote to you twice, but I gave the letters to Amanda to mail. I'm guessing she didn't send them."

Megan couldn't stop smiling. "I have you home. The letters don't matter that much."

*E*PILOGUE

October 1888

cacophony of sounds brightened the sunny fall day. Children laughed as they chased each other over the hills and around the new church building. Women chattered in excited voices as they set baskets of food on tables, ready to be opened and shared after the services. Men stood in groups discussing the weather, the harvest, or admiring the way the steeple of the church gleamed in the light.

Jesse thought his chest would burst as he stood at the top of the steps and watched the gathering. The last few months had been busy. He and William Bright agreed to donate a piece of property where their land joined for a church, which could also be used as a school. The women were thrilled, since they lived too far from town for their children to attend classes. The new schoolteacher should be arriving any day. The harvesting would be over soon, and the children would be free to come.

Megan moved among the women, comfortable in her role as pastor's wife. She loved greeting each one and was adept at finding out little ways to help each family. Her caring nature brought the women to her when they had problems or needed something. Megan always seemed willing to pray with them and offer what help she could. As her faith deepened, Jesse had come to depend on their discussions of Scripture. He didn't know how he lived so many years without her.

Running her hand over her bulging stomach, Megan glanced up at Jesse and sent him a brilliant smile. They were both anxious to become parents. Jesse didn't think a baby had ever been wanted more than this one. They spent hours talking about names and planning things to teach and do with the baby. Megan insisted that since the death of Jesse's father, they should take time to visit his mother after the baby came. She was careful to point out to him how important family would be to her.

"Jesse, can I ring the bell?" Seana hopped up the steps, her cheeks flushed with all the running she'd been doing. This summer had seen a change in her. Megan said her mother tended to keep Seana in the house, afraid the frail child would get sick and die from exposure to the elements. Jesse insisted she needed the exercise and allowed her outside except in the worst weather. He thought that was the reason she had filled out and looked so healthy now.

"Looks like everyone is here." Jesse ruffled Seana's wind-blown hair. "Go ahead and ring the bell. We'll get everyone in and see if the building stands up to our singing."

Seana laughed as she skipped through the church doors. Jesse nodded at Mr. Owens as the man tied his horse to the hitching rack. Mr. Owens had taken over the bank. Jesse helped him some with business matters he wasn't sure of, but it had taken the two of them weeks to straighten out the mess created by Sparks. The banker now resided in prison. Sheriff Armstrong insisted he was innocent and hadn't known what Sparks was doing. Payment records spoke differently. Sparks had kept meticulous records, which helped convict Armstrong to a lesser degree and returned many properties to their rightful owners.

The bell pealed, the sound rolling across the prairie. People began moving toward the church steps. Megan hurried to Jesse's side to help greet everyone as they entered. After they were all seated, Samuel Duncan led them in several songs. In the past months he'd lost his awkwardness and embarrassment. Now he led the singing with an enthusiasm that often brought people to their feet.

Stepping up to the podium, Jesse gazed out over the congregation. He'd come to know and love these people. They welcomed him and Megan, eager to have a place to truly worship Jesus. Although not everyone agreed with every word he said, they agreed on the essentials of the gospel. The one thing he appreciated was that they were willing to talk with him about their disagreements rather than gossiping among themselves.

"I'd like for you to look in the book of Malachi with me, chapter 3, verses 16 through 18." Jesse waited for a minute until the sound of turning pages ceased. Not everyone had a Bible or knew how to read, but he encouraged those who could to bring their Bibles and follow along with him.

" 'Then they that feared the Lord spake often one to another: and the Lord hearkened, and heard it, and a book of remembrance was written before him for them that feared the Lord, and that thought upon his name. And they shall be mine, saith the Lord of hosts, in that day when I make up my jewels; and I will spare them, as a man spareth his own son that serveth him. Then shall ye return, and discern between the righteous and the wicked, between him that serveth God and him that serveth him not.' "

Every eye watched him. Jesse took a deep breath and began. "Every one of us has something precious that we value above our other possessions. I have my wife, Megan, our baby, and Seana. They are priceless to me. Today, I want to encourage each of you to remember that to God, you are a precious jewel. When you listen to what God has to say to you, and when you speak to one another of those things, when you fear Him and seek His will, then you will become one of God's gems. He can take what to others appears to be an ordinary rock and make something very special. I would like to see a whole church full to overflowing with jewels dedicated to following Jesus Christ."

As Jesse glanced down at his Bible, he couldn't help remembering how he'd run from God's call, yet Jesus had been faithful to draw him back. He could see Megan's shining face; and feeling the peace in his heart, he knew he was right where God wanted him.

Thanks to a Lonely Heart

by Elaine Bonner

Dedicated to my mother, Louzell Bonner.
You've been my biggest fan and critic.
I love you.

*H*e glanced around as he tied his horse to the hitching rail. Steven Barnes had looked down this dusty little street many times in the past few years. There was the feed store with the wagons out front waiting to be loaded with seed and grain. Across the street stood Hall's General Mercantile and as usual Mr. Hall was standing at the door leaning on his broom visiting with a customer. The bank, the café, every building in town was like a familiar friend to him.

The Coffee Cup Café had been painted white many years ago but the sand storms of west Texas had taken their toll. The steps creaked as Steven's boot made contact, and the wooden porch seemed to groan under the weight of a lone man walking across its weathered surface. Steven removed his cowboy hat and slapped it against the leg of his jeans sending sand flying in every direction before he opened the door of the café.

The little bell above the door of the Coffee Cup Café tinkled, and Emily Johnson looked up to see who her next customer would be. Steven Barnes was a familiar sight. He had come into the café many times over the past five years, but something about him was different this time. Emily could sense something was wrong. He rode his horse into town from the Bar Eight Ranch a couple of times a month, and he'd always been willing to pass the time of day with her before. She didn't know a lot about him except that he was married and had some children. For some reason, he had left them back in east Texas. He never talked about them much and would change the subject quickly if anyone mentioned them.

Occasionally, he would sit at one of the tables and read what appeared to be a letter. Emily couldn't help noticing the faraway look that would come over him at those times.

Today, as he seated himself on one of the stools at the counter, Steven Barnes was definitely preoccupied. Although she didn't know a lot about his personal life, he was always friendly, and she had always been fond of his sense of humor. But today there was no laughter in him. She poured him a cup of coffee and asked, "How are you today, Steven? Sure is a beautiful day, don't you think?"

"I'm okay, and the weather's fine I guess," he responded as he picked up his cup and took a sip.

Emily busied herself wiping tables for a few moments, then walked back behind the counter and tried again to engage Steven in conversation. "I noticed the big annual barbecue for the Bar Eight is next Saturday." She wiped her hands on the white apron covering her blue gingham dress as she continued. "I guess things are pretty busy out your way. Must be a lot of hustle and bustle to get ready for an event like that."

"I reckon there is," he replied without enthusiasm. "I don't get involved in that sorta thing too often. Chances are I won't be here next Saturday anyhow."

"You planning a little trip out of town, Steven?" Emily asked.

"Not just a trip," he confided. "I'm leaving for good."

A look of surprise flashed on her face as she inquired, "I don't mean to be nosy, but I know you have family in east Texas. Are you going home?"

His face turned pale. "Well, I'm going back to east Texas. I don't know if I can call it home anymore. Maybe I don't have a right to call it home." Steven's voice became shaky, and Emily could see his hands were trembling as he continued. "At any rate, I got word that my wife passed away a few weeks ago. A friend wrote me. He said that if I didn't get in touch with the county judge soon, my kids would become wards of the county. Seems a neighbor lady is helping take care of them now, but I've got to get back."

"Steven, I'm so sorry to hear about your loss," Emily said sincerely. "It must be very hard for you being so far away at a time like this. How many children do you have?"

"Five," he replied. "Four boys and a girl."

Emily could not tell by looking at his face what he was feeling, but she was hearing something in the sound of his voice. She thought it sounded like sheer terror. He must be scared stiff to think about going home to five children he hadn't seen for at least five years, having to take the sole responsibility for raising them.

"Have you ever been married, Emily?" Steven asked, drawing her out of her thoughts.

"Yeah, I was once," she answered. "My husband was killed right after the turn of the century in an accident. I guess that makes it about eight years ago now." It didn't seem like that long, and yet, in some ways, it seemed like a lifetime. "That's when I started working here." Emily paused and refilled Steven's cup.

"Thanks," he said, then looked at Emily as he asked, "Have you ever thought about getting married again?"

"Sure I have. But I guess I'm just too picky. And besides, the pickings aren't so good here," Emily answered.

On the outside she was smiling when she answered him. But the truth of the matter was Emily was so lonesome sometimes that she could hardly stand it. She had no children and no family, and she ached for a man in her life. She had loved her husband very much, and after his death, she had thought she would never be able to love again. But for quite some time, she had felt she was ready to welcome someone into her life. The trouble was, no one was beating down her door. The only so-called proposal she'd had was from a man twice her age. He lived in a shack on the edge of town and was looking for someone to take care of him in his old age. He was probably the only person in town worse off than she was. At the age of thirty, Emily was beginning to give up hope of ever finding anyone. She was trying to accept her lonely heart and learn to live with it.

"Do you like kids, Emily?" Steven asked.

"Yeah, I like kids," she replied. "My husband came from a big family. I loved to help care for his nieces and nephews before we moved out here."

Emily was saddened once again, thinking about Jim's family. She had completely lost touch with them after his death. They seemed to just forget all about her. Maybe she was a sad reminder of the son they had lost.

Again Steven's voice brought her back to the present. "Emily, I have a proposition for you," he stated matter-of-factly. "I need someone to help me care for my children and take care of the house. Would you consider marrying me and coming to east Texas with me?" Steven stared into his coffee cup as he continued. "Now this would be a marriage in name only. I wouldn't expect you to be a wife to me, just a mother to my children."

Emily dropped the cup she was holding, shattering it into pieces. The breaking glass startled the two older gentlemen seated at the table in the corner, the only other people in the room. One of them called out, "Hey, Emily, Lon'll dock your pay for that." Emily forced a smile back at the old fellow, but she couldn't speak. She looked at Steven. "What did you say?"

"I offered you a job and asked you if you'd be willing to marry me," he responded. There was no emotion in his voice and his face was void of all expression.

This certainly was not the proposal she had hoped for. There was no soft moonlight and certainly no bells ringing. Just a straightforward business deal. She knew Steven didn't love her, and she had known from the start he was a married man, so she had never thought of him in such a way.

"Of course I'd provide for you," Steven said. "I have a pretty good farm, and with a lot of work I think it could pay off. You'd get your room and board and whatever else you needed. I'd provide for you like a wife. I just wouldn't exercise my husbandly rights."

"Steven, you can't be serious. We don't know each other well enough to get married," Emily finally choked out.

"Like I said, I'm not asking you to be my wife. This is strictly a business deal. I'm really just offering you a job. I'm just offering to marry you to make it look respectable."

Stunned by his blunt reply, Emily muttered, "Steven, I don't know what to say. An offer like this needs some thought. Can you give me a little time?"

"I'm leaving early Friday morning. I need to know soon enough to arrange things with the preacher. I'll be back in town Wednesday morning. Can you decide by then?"

"I'll have my answer for you Wednesday."

Emily watched as Steven left the café, got on his horse, and rode off. She couldn't believe she had asked for time to think about his proposal. Why hadn't she just given him an answer then and told him no. What a ridiculous proposition! How could she even consider it?

Sure she wanted to get married, but she was hoping for a better deal than this. Steven wasn't even actually proposing marriage; he just wanted a mother for his children. After being alone all these years, she couldn't see herself raising five children. Wednesday she would just have to say thanks but no.

After the supper crowd was gone and the café cleaned and ready for breakfast the next morning, Emily locked up and went to the boardinghouse. Although Mrs. Jenson, the owner, invited her to play a game of cards, Emily politely refused, saying she was too tired.

She entered her lonely room, which had been her home for almost eight years. It wasn't fancy, but it was clean and comfortable. She had an iron bed frame with a soft mattress. The table by her bed held a white glass lamp with pink roses on the base; beside the lamp sat a picture of her and Jim on their wedding day. She sat on the bed as she picked up the small frame.

Staring at the picture and touching Jim's face, she said in a soft voice, "Oh, if only you hadn't left me. We had such a perfect love. I want that same feeling again. I ache to be loved like you loved me. To know that someone cares about me." Tears began streaming down her face, and with a trembling voice, she continued to speak to the picture. "Jim, I don't want to spend the rest of my life alone. What do I do? I know Steven doesn't love me, and I'm not in love with him, but what if this is my last chance? I don't want to spend the rest of my life alone and lonely. What should I do?"

She was tired and began to get ready for bed, but her mind kept racing. Steven and his unique proposal dominated her thoughts. As she lay in bed, she asked the Lord for guidance. This afternoon as she had stood in the café and watched Steven ride away, she had made up her mind to tell him no. But as she lay in the darkness talking with Jesus, she started to get confused. Surely God couldn't want her to marry a man she barely knew and didn't love.

She lay awake most of the night. *This is crazy*, she thought. *I've got to work tomorrow. I have to get some rest.*

The ache of loneliness continued to fill Emily's being. There were many questions to consider. She and Steven didn't love each other, and that was no basis for a marriage. Emily didn't even know if Steven believed in God. How could she even consider his proposal? Loneliness was the only reason she could come up with to leave Abilene and marry a man with whom she shared no love.

Of course, she wasn't real sure of her future here. Lon Blackstone had mentioned several times lately that he was getting too old to keep running the café. What if he closed it; then what would Emily do? Maybe if she thought of Steven's offer as just a job, she could make a better decision. After all, Steven had made it very clear that it was a job, not a marriage he was offering her.

Emily didn't know what time it was when she finally drifted off to sleep. She was abruptly awakened by a loud knock on her door and a voice yelling, "Emily, are you sick? You're late for work."

Startled, Emily answered, "No, I'm fine, Mrs. Jenson. I just over-slept. I'll be down in a minute."

Jumping from the bed, Emily splashed some water on her face and hurriedly dressed. She pulled her hair up in a quick bun and ran out the door. As she walked into the café, Mr. Blackstone, the proprietor, was already frying bacon, and a customer was seated at the counter.

"You're late," Mr. Blackstone smiled. This was the first time in the seven and a half years Emily had worked for him that she hadn't been on time. "Did you have a late date last night?" he asked.

"You know me, always out on the town," she laughed. "I'm sorry I'm late. For some reason I couldn't get to sleep last night."

"Have a lot on your mind, do you?" he questioned.

"Oh, something like that," she answered, turning to the customer seated at the counter. "Can I get you a refill on that coffee, Pete?"

"You need someone to talk to or a shoulder to cry on, Emily?" Lon asked seriously.

"Maybe later." She went to wait on the two gentlemen who had just entered the café.

Emily knew if there was one person in the world she could talk to and count on it was Lon Blackstone. He had been almost like a father to her over the past few years. She knew she could tell him her dilemma, and he would be straightforward and honest with his opinions.

The little café had a very busy day, and Lon stayed until three o'clock, instead of leaving as usual at two. Before he left, he poured two cups of coffee and turned to Emily. "Girl, let's sit down and rest a minute. We deserve it."

After they seated themselves at a table, he looked at Emily and asked, "Care to tell me what's going on?"

"Someone asked me to marry him yesterday." That was the first time she had said it out loud, and it sounded strange.

"That's wonderful! But who is it? I didn't know you were seeing anyone special."

Emily sat quietly without responding to his questions.

"If you don't mind me saying so, you don't seem as excited as a girl should be when she gets a proposal of marriage," Lon observed.

She looked at Lon. "Let me tell you the whole story and please don't say anything until I'm finished."

Lon nodded and Emily cleared her throat as she began. "Steven Barnes came in here yesterday and told me he had just found out his wife had died. He said he has to go back to east Texas to take care of his children. Seems they will become wards of the county if he doesn't get back there soon. Well, he asked me to marry him. Actually, he offered me a job. He wants me to help him raise his children. He said we would get married for appearances only. It would be a marriage in name only."

Lon listened patiently as she finished the story. "What are you going to do?" he asked.

"Right after he left I thought, 'how stupid, why didn't I just tell him no.' I decided right then and there that I would tell him no thanks when he comes back for his answer. But, for some reason I couldn't stop thinking about his proposition. That's why I didn't get any sleep last night."

Lon, a dedicated Christian, asked the question she expected: "Have you prayed about this?"

"Yes, I have," she answered. "And the more I pray, the more confused I become. I have thought about getting married again for a long time. But silly me, I always thought in terms of marrying someone I was in love with. I thought God promoted that idea. One thing I do know for sure, Steven Barnes is not in love with me. I have never thought of him in terms of marriage, either. The thought of five children really scares me, too."

Lon looked thoughtful. "God does want there to be love in a marriage. But you said Steven made it very clear that this would be a marriage in name only, that he was really offering you a job. I have known a few couples whose love came after marriage. They got married for some good reason or another without being in love, but the love grew with time."

"So are you saying that if I marry Steven just to help him raise his children, that eventually we might fall in love?"

"That could be a possibility. You know some folks start out in marriage just being friends. As a matter of fact you have to be friends with the person you marry for a marriage to last. Do you like Steven? Are you friends?" Lon asked.

"I like him," Emily responded. "I don't know if you could say we're friends. The only place I've ever seen him is here."

"When do you have to give him your answer?"

"Tomorrow," she replied. "You sound as though you think I should accept."

"Not at all," he stated. "But I do think you should consider all sides. Since you didn't give him an immediate no, then the proposition must not have sounded all bad to you. You said the more you pray about it the more confused you become. Maybe God knows something you don't. Just make the decision you think is right for you, and I'll stand by you all the way. There is something for you to consider—do you know if Steven is a fellow believer?"

"That is a concern; I don't know. But since this is a job and not a marriage, if he isn't a Christian, his children might really need me. They would need someone to instruct them in the ways of the Lord."

Lon left her alone with her thoughts. Emily had really thought Lon Blackstone would think that Steven should be horsewhipped for making such a proposition to her and that she should tell him no thanks! Instead, she was even more troubled, if that were possible. It looked as though it would be another long night in her lonely room.

§∂∙

Late the next afternoon, Emily heard the door open. Looking up from the counter, she saw Steven. Maybe for the first time in all these years, she really looked at him. He stood a little over six foot tall and he had brown hair and blue eyes. He was not the best-looking man she had ever seen, but he wasn't bad, not bad at all.

What was she thinking? She had to keep everything in perspective. She had to remember he didn't want her for his wife, just as a mother for his children.

Steven walked over and sat down on a stool at the counter. "Could I get a cup of coffee?"

"Sure." She wasn't about to say anything first; he had to bring up the subject. With trembling hands, she poured his coffee.

He drank almost the whole cup before he spoke again. "Well, have you thought about my offer?"

"Yes, I have. Actually I have thought of nothing else the past two days," she replied.

"Have you come to a decision?" he asked calmly.

Her heart was pounding and her knees were shaking. She felt as though she was gasping for air. When she finally found her voice, she answered weakly, "I have a couple of questions first."

"Okay, what are they?"

Still with trembling voice, Emily asked, "Steven, are you a Christian?"

Steven drank another sip of coffee and then answered. "I believe in God. Used to even call myself a Christian. But I don't go to church much. Guess I sorta got out of the habit."

That was not the answer Emily had hoped for, but it would have to do. She went on to her next question. "Why are you here and your family still in east Texas?"

"I left to find work," he choked out.

"But why did you never go back home?" Emily pried.

"I kept thinking just a little more time, a little more money to send home. Before I knew it, too much time had gone by, and I wasn't sure I had a home to go to anymore."

"Surely your wife and children wanted you back more than they wanted the money you were sending," Emily suggested.

Steven looked aggravated. "Don't be too sure of that. Are you concerned about my leaving you someday?"

"To be honest, that did cross my mind. I'm not sure I'd want to be left alone with children that weren't mine."

Reaching into his jeans pocket, Steven pulled out a wad of bills and shoved them across the counter to Emily. "That's my month's wages. Take it and put it away. You can use it for a little security. I know I can't convince you that I would never dump my kids on you, but at least that would be enough to get you by for a few weeks. As soon as we get back to east Texas, I'll have the judge draw up papers as to who will care for the children in the event of my death or disappearance. Does that ease your fears?"

"I guess so," Emily mumbled. "But you don't have to give me this money. I know you'll probably need it for the trip."

"No, you keep it. I hope I've answered enough questions." Steven sounded agitated. "Now, are you going to accept the job or not?"

Emily hesitated just a moment, then answered, "Yes, Steven. I'll accept the job and I will marry you."

She had said it! She had accepted his proposal. She could hardly believe her ears. Had she really told Steven Barnes she would marry him?

His expression never changed. "I'll go talk to the preacher and see if he can marry us tomorrow. Can you be ready to leave early Friday morning?"

"Sure, I guess so."

He never said *I'm glad you said yes* or even *thank you*. It really didn't seem to matter at all to him one way or the other. She hadn't expected him to kiss her or even embrace her, but he could have at least smiled. Instead she got nothing!

"I'll be back after I talk to the preacher to let you know what time the ceremony will be," he stated as he walked out the door.

Emily had to sit down before she fell down. Her knees were about to buckle under her, and the butterflies in her stomach must have turned into birds. Really big birds. She couldn't believe she had actually said yes. Well, there was still time to change her mind.

She was still sitting down when Steven returned a few minutes later.

"The circuit judge is in town. I ran into him on my way to the preacher's. In light of the circumstances of our marriage, I decided to ask him to perform the ceremony. Is that okay with you? He can do it about three o'clock tomorrow."

Still in a state of shock, Emily replied, "That's fine with me. Where will the ceremony be held?"

"That's a problem," he said. "There isn't a courthouse here, so I guess we'll have to use the sheriff's office. It really doesn't matter. Do you want me to pick you up here or at your boardinghouse?"

"The boardinghouse, I guess," she responded. "I'll go and talk with Lon now and tell him I'm quitting. I sure hate to leave him in a bind, but maybe he'll understand."

"I'll see you tomorrow about fifteen 'til three," was all Steven said before he left.

Emily closed the café and walked over to the Blackstones'. As she walked, she tried to sort out her feelings. She didn't know what to say to these people. They had been so good to her. She sure hated not being able to give them more notice. She knew they would be happy for her if she were truly in love, but as it was, she couldn't explain why she was marrying Steven. Loneliness was the only explanation.

Emily arrived at the house, summoned up her courage, and finally knocked on the door. "Emily, my dear, do come in. What brings you by here tonight?" Helen asked as she invited Emily into her home.

By this time Lon had come into the room. Emily made herself as comfortable as she could on the sofa, then she began. "I have come to share some news with you." She tried as best she could to put a smile on her face and enthusiasm into her voice when she added, "I'm getting married."

"Oh, my dear, that's wonderful! Who is the lucky fellow?" Helen wanted to know. When Emily didn't immediately reply, Helen added, "I didn't know you were seeing anyone."

Shyly, Emily began to explain. "It's Steven Barnes. He asked me to marry him, and I accepted. The problem is, we're getting married tomorrow, and then we're leaving early Friday morning for east Texas. I'm so sorry I couldn't give you more notice. You two have been so good to me; I really hate leaving you in a bind."

"This is all very sudden, isn't it? I didn't know you and Steven had feelings for one another. You never mentioned it," remarked Helen.

Lon had not said a word. "I might as well tell you the whole story," Emily said. "Steven asked me to marry him so I could go and help him raise his children. It seems his wife recently passed away, and now he's left with the task of being a father and a mother. As you know, he hasn't even been a father lately. I guess he just didn't want to face them alone, so he asked me to help him. This will be a marriage in name only. I am to help with the children and take care of the house."

"It seems to me those are jobs he could have hired someone to do. He didn't have to marry himself a nanny and housekeeper," Helen angrily stated.

"Actually Helen, he did hire someone to do those jobs—me. The marriage is just for appearances," Emily informed her.

"But—" Helen began before Lon cut her off.

"Helen, that's enough. I know Emily has considered this very carefully. I know she feels she's doing what's right for her. What time is the wedding?" he inquired. "We'd like to be at the church to see you married—if that's okay?"

"There is no one I'd rather have at my wedding than the two of you," Emily answered. "The wedding is at three tomorrow afternoon, but it isn't going to be at the church. Steven thought under the circumstances he'd ask the circuit judge to marry us. The ceremony's going to be in the sheriff's office."

"At the sheriff's office!" Helen exclaimed. "That will never do!

Lon, you get in touch with that judge and tell him the wedding will be here. At least a living room is more pleasant than a sheriff's office. I'm sorry, Emily. I know I'm butting in, but we'd love for you to be married in our home."

"Oh Helen, that would be so wonderful. It would be a lot nicer and warmer here. Thank you so much," Emily said with tears in her eyes.

"Lon, you find the judge and tell him about the change in plans," Helen instructed.

"I'll tell him. I know where to find him. He always stays at the same place. You don't worry about a thing, Emily. Helen and I will take care of every detail. You just bring Steven over here."

"You don't think Steven will mind the change in plans, do you?" Helen asked, with concern in her voice.

Emily looked at her and replied, "I don't think so. But after all, it is my wedding, too. I should at least get to pick the place for the ceremony. You two are so wonderful. How can I ever repay you for your kindness?"

"Kindness never has to be repaid," Lon stated. "You just be happy. That's all we want for you."

Emily hugged both her friends and left. She would have never made it these last seven and a half years if it hadn't been for Lon and Helen. Not only had they given her a job, but they had been like parents to her. She would miss them terribly.

Back in her room at the boardinghouse, she began to load her few personal belongings into her trunk. Mrs. Jenson had been very surprised to hear her news. She'd wished Emily well and even refunded the balance of her month's rent as a wedding gift.

Emily had very few possessions, and she didn't need long to pack. She didn't know where she would be spending tomorrow night. Steven hadn't mentioned it. She figured she would stay here, but just in case, she would be packed and ready to go. She laid out her best blue dress to be married in. This was nothing like her first wedding when she was so in love.

She had hardly been able to wait to marry Jim. He was her handsome prince and loved her with all his heart. She had been sure of that. She had worn a traditional white dress, and her father had walked her down the church aisle. It had been a wonderful day.

Her mother wasn't there, for she had died when Emily was a baby. Her father had never remarried, and he passed away just a year after her marriage to Jim. Still, she and Jim had a wonderful but short marriage. They had shared only five years together, but she had been left with nothing but happy memories. It seemed those memories would have to last a lifetime now. She was sure there would be no happy memories made tomorrow.

ಎ

Emily was awakened by the sun shining through the window onto her face. She didn't know how long it had been since she had slept this late. Of course she had no idea what time she had finally fallen asleep; she hadn't slept much in the last two nights.

She got up and washed her hair so it would have plenty of time to dry. She had decided to try to fix it a little special today. Although it wouldn't matter to Steven, it might make her feel better.

Mrs. Jenson was more than willing to help, but there was nothing Emily could think of for her to do. They spent the morning visiting together, but Emily couldn't bring herself to tell Mrs. Jenson all the details of her marriage. She loved her, but she knew Mae Jenson was one of the biggest gossips in town. Emily let her think that she and Steven had a mutual affection for each other and had decided to get married since he was having to leave town. Mae thought Emily was very noble for having said yes to a man with so many children.

After lunch, Emily went upstairs to dress and work on her hair. She fixed it, looked at it, then took it down and tried again. After a couple more tries, she noticed it was getting late. This time would have to do.

When she put the last pin in, she admired her handiwork. She had pulled most of her hair up but had let some soft curls fall around her face. The outcome was rather flattering. No one except Jim had ever accused her of being pretty, much less beautiful, but today she didn't look half bad.

She put on her dress and made a final inspection, pleased with what she saw. She would try to feel good about herself, no matter what happened today.

Mrs. Jenson called to her from the foot of the stairs. Knowing Steven must have arrived, Emily took a deep breath and started down the steps.

He was waiting for her in the parlor.

"You look lovely," Mrs. Jenson said, giving Emily a hug. "I wish you and Steven the best."

Steven looked on and said nothing. Finally he told Mae good-bye, then turned to Emily. "We'd better be going."

He opened the door, and Emily walked out into the sunlight. Once outside and safely out of earshot of Mae, Emily said, "There's been a small change in plans. The wedding is going to be in the home of Lon and Helen Blackstone. When I went over there last night to tell them I was leaving, they just insisted. I hope you don't mind."

"No, that's fine with me. You did tell the judge, didn't you?" he asked.

"Lon said he would take care of that for us."

They walked the rest of the way in silence. Emily was praying the entire time, *God, please let me be making the right decision.*

Lon greeted them at the door, extending his hand to Steven. "Congratulations, Steven. You're getting a wonderful girl."

Steven shook his hand and thanked him weakly. Emily noticed the vase of fresh flowers on the mantel, and from the fragrance in the air, she detected that Helen had baked this morning. Emily certainly hoped they hadn't gone to a lot of trouble. She didn't know how Steven would react.

The judge was already there waiting for them. Steven turned to him and said, "I guess it's time we get started."

"An eager bridegroom. I've never met a man yet that wasn't in a hurry to get the wedding ceremony over," the judge teased. He walked over and stood in front of the mantel. "If you two would just stand in front of me here, we'll get started."

Emily was in a daze, not from happiness but from fright. She still couldn't believe she was doing this. But she must have answered all the judge's questions to his satisfaction, although she didn't really hear what he was saying. When the judge asked Steven for the ring, Steven's face went pale. Getting a ring had never crossed his mind. Emily saw his despair and discretely slipped the small gold band that Jim had given her off her hand, then handed it to Steven. He in turn handed it to the judge, who was somewhat bewildered by this time. The judge continued with the ceremony, and Steven slipped the ring on her hand. Then came those words: "By the authority vested in me by the state of Texas, I now pronounce you husband and wife. You may kiss your bride."

What would Steven do now? Just ignore it, shake her hand, what? To Emily's surprise, he leaned down and kissed her lightly on the cheek. Her stomach did flips. She was completely amazed that his faint kiss could do that to her. Emily reminded herself she had to keep her emotions in check. This was not a true marriage, and she must not forget that.

"I hope you two don't mind, but I took the liberty of making a small cake and fixing some punch," Helen announced. "If you'll excuse me, I'll go get it."

"May I help you?" Emily asked anxiously.

"I'd be delighted for you to keep me company in the kitchen if you'd like," Helen answered.

Once in the kitchen, though, Emily sat down. She was relieved to have the ceremony over and to be away from Steven for a moment.

"You shouldn't have gone to so much trouble for us, Helen," said Emily. "But I really do appreciate it. You have made this day much more pleasant."

"You are very welcome, my child. I'm just so sorry that this day isn't more special for you in every way," Helen remarked. "Now let's go join the menfolk and enjoy some of my cake."

The cake and punch were delicious. The conversation on the other hand was lacking. The judge excused himself as soon as he finished his refreshments. Lon then began questioning Steven about east Texas and his farm. Emily learned for the first time that his place was near a town called Tyler. Steven said Tyler was about the same size as

Abilene. She also learned that it would take them almost two weeks to get there. At least now she had a little more information about her future.

Steven announced that it was time to leave and turned to Emily to ask, "Would you like me to walk you back to the boardinghouse or do you want to stay and visit with your friends for a while?"

"I think I'll just stay here," she said, fighting back the tears. He seemed so cold and unfeeling.

"Okay. I'll pick you up at sunup in the morning." He thanked Lon and Helen for their hospitality and left. He said no more to Emily.

It was a few moments before Emily could gain her composure and speak. "I want to thank you both again for everything you've done. I'll be going now. I just wanted to say good-bye to you in private."

Lon wished Emily well, gave her a big hug, and walked into the kitchen. Helen just stood there a moment before she spoke. "I'm afraid you've cut a very rough road out for yourself. Please remember we love you and are here for you if you ever need us. I know Steven said he didn't expect you to be a wife to him, but you'll be on the road for almost two weeks. You never know what can happen in that length of time. You take care of yourself and be prepared for anything."

"I believe Steven will hold true to his word about this being a business deal instead of a marriage. I'll just take it one day at a time and leave it all in the Lord's hands," Emily assured her. "I love you both, and as soon as we get there, I'll write you. I'll send you my address because I expect you to keep in touch." Emily hugged her friend, then turned and walked out the door.

She could no longer hold back the tears as she walked toward the boardinghouse. She wondered what people would think about a bride staying alone on her wedding night. This was not the normal chain of events, but this had not been the normal wedding.

ॐ

Back at the boardinghouse, Mae inquired if her husband would be joining her later.

"No," Emily replied, trying desperately to hide the fact that she had been crying. "He still has some things he has to finish up at the ranch. We'll be leaving at first light in the morning. I probably won't see you then, so let me say good-bye now. Thank you for everything you've done for me. You've always gone above and beyond a land-lady's call of duty."

They wished each other farewell, then Emily walked up the stairs to her lonely room one last time. It was early, but she was very tired and didn't feel like eating any supper. As she changed into her night clothes, the tears that had just started to flow on the walk home began to come in a storm now. She couldn't remember ever feeling so lost and alone; no one should feel this way on their wedding day, or any day for that matter. Lying across the bed, she sobbed and tried to pray, but the words would not come. Night had fallen when she finally drifted into a restless sleep.

$$\textbf{2}$$

*E*mily awoke with a start, disoriented for a moment. She shook her head and wiped her eyes to clear the cobwebs away. Maybe she had just had a bad dream. But no, letting her eyes open, she realized she was in her room at Mrs. Jenson's boardinghouse. And the cold hard fact was that she was married to Steven Barnes.

She stood and walked over to the window. Gazing out over the sleepy little town, everything looked the same. Nothing much ever changed here, but she knew her life was changing completely.

The sun was just barely appearing over the horizon, and she knew Steven would be there soon. She still couldn't believe she was Mrs. Steven Barnes. Her stomach churned. She couldn't remember ever being this frightened. *God,* she prayed, *please give me strength for whatever lies ahead.*

Hearing a buckboard pull up, she raced down the stairs, hoping to let Steven in without waking Mrs. Jenson. As she reached the bottom of the stairs, however, she heard Mae greet Steven.

"Come in, Steven," Mae was saying. "You certainly are out early this morning. I guess you're anxious to pick up your bride and be on your way."

"Yes'm, I am. We have a long trip ahead of us. Is Emily up?" he asked.

"I'm here. I heard you pull up." Emily came into the hallway. "Mae, I'm sorry we got you up so early."

"You didn't wake me," Mae replied. "I wanted to see you off. I have breakfast ready if you'll eat a bite."

"You shouldn't have gone to all that trouble," Steven responded. "I had something before I left the ranch."

Mrs. Jenson turned to Emily. "Well, you haven't eaten, and you need something in your stomach before you start off on such a long trip."

Emily could tell by Steven's expression that he didn't want to wait while she ate breakfast. And as nervous as she felt, she was afraid that food would just make her sick. She turned to Mae and tried to smile and sound excited. "You really shouldn't have gone to so much trouble. I'm so excited this morning, I'm afraid I couldn't eat a thing."

"I'll tell you what I'll do. I'll just wrap up some biscuits and bacon for you to take. You may get hungry in a couple of hours." Mae headed for the kitchen.

"That would be wonderful," Emily said. "Steven, I'll show you where my trunk is." They turned and started for the stairs.

Emily opened the door to her room and pointed to her trunk. "Is this all you have?" Steven asked.

Emily chuckled and said, "Yeah, I travel light."

Steven apparently failed to notice the humor in her statement, as he ignored her. *This is going to be a very long trip*, Emily thought to herself.

Steven picked up her trunk and left. Emily looked around one last time, then walked out and closed the door. She silently said farewell to Emily Johnson and hello to Emily Barnes. Whoever Emily Barnes was or would turn out to be was still unknown.

Mrs. Jenson was waiting on the front porch with a small basket. Emily hugged her, thanking her for all she had done.

Steven looked impatient when Emily finally walked out to the wagon. He helped her up onto the seat and then climbed up beside her. Popping the reins, he started the horses down the street. Emily turned and waved good-bye to Mrs. Jenson and to her life in Abilene.

The March morning was clear and bright as they started their journey. A nice breeze was blowing, and Emily was grateful that they were traveling now rather than during the blazing hot summer. After they had traveled several miles, however, Steven still had not said a word. Emily tried to decide how to start a conversation with him.

"How long do you think it will take us to get to your place?" asked Emily.

"Barring any trouble, and if we don't have to stop too many times, we should be there in about twelve days," he replied.

"Tell me about the place. What's it like?" Emily hoped this question would lead to more than a one-line answer.

"Not much to tell. It's a farm."

Emily was very frustrated. She could not bear sitting next to this man for twelve days in this wagon and not at least be able to carry on some kind of conversation. She continued to ask questions, and he continued to give as brief answers as possible. Finally the sun was high in the sky. Her stomach was beginning to let her know that she hadn't sent it any food since the wedding cake and punch yesterday.

"It must be about noon," Steven finally said. "I guess we can stop and rest a spell and have a bite to eat. I need to water the horses."

"That would be wonderful," Emily replied. "I would really like to stretch my legs. And I am getting hungry."

There weren't a lot of trees in this part of Texas, but they stopped near a small patch of grass by the side of the road. Emily was glad for time to walk around. Steven said he was going to take a walk down the road a little piece, and Emily decided that was very considerate, since it allowed her a little time to herself.

By the time Steven returned, she had spread a blanket in the small shade cast by the wagon and gotten out the food that Mae Jenson had fixed. Steven sat down on the edge of the blanket and helped himself to a biscuit without saying a word. She wondered if it was her or if it was just the time and place; maybe he was so used to spending time alone out on the range that he had forgotten how to converse with another human being.

The afternoon was the same as the morning: They rode in silence. It would have at least been nice if she could have enjoyed the view, but there wasn't much to see here, for the land was flat and empty. Occasionally she would see a jackrabbit or a tumbleweed would blow by, but that was about as exciting as it got. It was a long afternoon, and

Emily decided she would have to find some way to occupy her time or she would go crazy before they arrived in east Texas.

At sundown, Steven stopped for the night. He gathered wood for a fire, and Emily started to prepare supper. She fixed a small stew, and they enjoyed it with the last of the biscuits from Mae. Much to her surprise, Steven did tell her the stew was good.

"You can sleep here," Steven said, laying out a bedroll close to the wagon. "I'll be over there if you need me." He walked over about fifty feet and laid out the other bedroll.

Emily pulled her Bible out of her trunk and sat down. She was reading the Bible through as she had done several times before, and tonight's passage was Psalm 23. The verses had never meant so much to her or seemed so real. Tonight she thought she knew just what David had felt when he wrote this psalm; this trip was like walking through "the valley of the shadow of death." David couldn't have felt any lonelier when he wrote those words than she was feeling right now. *Lord, please be my Shepherd,* Emily prayed. *Please follow me all the days of my life.*

ॐ

Every day was the same. Emily tried desperately to carry on a conversation and each time failed miserably. She had known loneliness before, but nothing compared to what she was feeling now. Emily realized that loneliness seemed to intensify when you were with someone who apparently didn't want to be with you.

To occupy her time, she began to keep a journal, recording her thoughts and observations along the way. On day seven of their journey, she observed that at least the scenery was beginning to change. There were trees along the roadside and a lot of grass. The green was beautiful, and the wildflowers added a sprinkle of color here and there.

Emily had been so caught up making entries in her journal that she almost didn't realize Steven was speaking. "We should get to Fort Worth late this afternoon. I thought we would get a hotel room and spend the night there if that's okay with you."

Emily couldn't believe her ears: Steven was talking to her! She was sure he didn't actually want her opinion, since she knew he had already made up his mind. "That sounds great to me!" she responded almost too enthusiastically. "To tell you the truth, it won't hurt my feelings at all to get to sleep in a real bed for a night. And a bath sounds like heaven."

&

They arrived in Fort Worth about four-thirty that afternoon. The town was bigger and busier than Abilene, with lots of shops and, of course, a saloon or two. Steven stopped the wagon in front of the hotel, then helped her down, and they walked inside. It wasn't fancy, but it did look clean and well-cared for.

After Steven registered, Emily followed him up the stairs and into a room. She looked at the big double bed. One room, one bed.

"I'll go get your trunk and bring it up." Steven started toward the door.

"There's no need to bring the whole trunk," Emily replied. "There's a small blue cloth bag on top that has everything in it that I'll need."

Steven was back in just minutes with the bag Emily requested. "I'm going to take the wagon to the livery stable and get the horses taken care of. The clerk said the bath was two doors down, and he already had the girl fill the tub with clean hot water. You get cleaned up, and I'll be back later."

Steven left, and Emily immediately headed to the bath. She locked the door and took off her clothes. Quickly, she climbed into the tub. She couldn't remember ever having felt so dirty, and it was heavenly to sit in a tub of hot water. She lay back in the tub and closed her eyes.

She couldn't help but wonder about the one room and the one bed. What did Steven have in mind? He had talked to her more since their arrival here than he had the whole trip. Could he have decided that he would exercise his rights as a husband after all? He certainly had made no attempt out on the trail. What would make him decide to now? She couldn't help but be a little nervous about it, but right now a bath and getting her hair washed was all she cared about.

When she got back to her room, the bed looked so inviting she decided to stretch out for a little while. She didn't know how long she'd been asleep, when she heard a knock at the door. Sleepily she asked, "Who is it?"

"Steven," answered the voice from the other side. "May I come in?"

She walked over and quietly replied through the closed door, "Steven, I'm sorry. I fell asleep. I'm not dressed."

"Well, I'll be in the dining room. Why don't you get dressed and join me there," he invited.

"That would be nice. I won't be long."

She listened as he walked away. *Did he just ask for my company,* she wondered. *Don't be silly, he just knows you have to eat, and you can't very well cook for yourself in a hotel room.* Emily dismissed her thoughts as she hurriedly dressed and fixed her hair. She looked in the mirror and was not too displeased with what she saw. Seven days on the road had given her a rosy complexion.

She walked into the dining room and saw Steven sitting at a table alone. As she approached the table, he stood and pulled a chair out for her. She noted he did have good manners and also that he had taken a bath and shaved. She couldn't help but notice how nice he looked, and she got that strange feeling again. A kind of nervous, jittery feeling. When she came back to reality, she realized the waitress had approached and Steven was giving her his order.

"Emily, what would you like?" Steven asked.

"Oh, a steak sounds good to me, too," she replied, then added, "with potatoes and greens."

The waitress left, and Emily looked around the room. "This is a nice place. It's much larger than our little café back home and much nicer."

"I guess so," Steven stated. "I just hope the food is as good. I hate to spend money on bad food."

Emily watched him for a moment and realized he appeared as nervous as she felt. Her mind began to play tricks on her. Did Steven get the same little funny feelings she got from time to time? Could he be thinking about her as a woman?

Stop it, Emily, she thought to herself. *You knew from the start this was not a real marriage. Don't start kidding yourself now. He's never given the slightest indication that he's interested in you as a woman. Yet he did get just one room with one bed, and after all he is a man. . . .* She was once again lost in her own dream world when the food arrived.

They exchanged very few pleasantries over their meal. The food was good, and Emily just enjoyed the fact that she didn't have to cook or clean up afterwards.

"How much farther to your farm?" Emily asked.

"It's still about a five-day journey from here," he replied. Looking at his watch, he noted, "It's getting late, and we need to get an early start in the morning. I'll see you to the room."

Steven pulled her chair out, and she stood and started toward the door. That funny feeling was back again. Was he just walking her to the door or was he planning on going through the door? Her hands were sweating and her knees were weak. Her heart was racing like crazy. She could handle sleeping fifty feet from him in the wide open spaces, but sleeping only a few feet or possibly a few inches from him was something else entirely. Why was she feeling this way? *This is not a marriage—it's a job,* Emily reminded herself. She had never had any special feelings for Steven Barnes. He was just a man who came into the café from time to time. Why was she feeling this way now? Maybe simply because it had been a terribly long time since a man had held her in his arms, and she ached to be held and loved again.

They arrived at the door, her heart still pounding. What should she do? What was he going to do? "You get a good night's rest, and I'll call for you first thing in the morning," Steven said. "Be sure and lock the door," he added as he walked away.

Emily walked inside and locked the door. *How stupid of me,* Emily thought. *Of course Steven had no intentions of coming into the room and staying the night. The man barely speaks to me.* She slowly got ready for bed, on the verge of tears, though she really didn't know why. Was she relieved he didn't come in? Or was she disappointed?

She lay in bed and tried to figure out what was going on with her. All those years she had known Steven, she had thought of him as a married man and therefore unavailable. She had never looked at him with romantic eyes—but now she was married to him. Although he had made it perfectly clear that theirs was a marriage in name only, her lonely heart apparently had not totally accepted that.

She remembered her marriage to Jim and how much in love they had been. She remembered how very special those first few days and weeks were and how they could not get enough of each other. That was the only standard for marriage she had, and this was nothing like that. She guessed her heart just remembered and wanted that kind of relationship again, but she seriously doubted she would ever know that kind of love with Steven Barnes. Apparently, it would take a miracle to even get him to carry on a conversation with her.

She would just have to make sure she kept her emotions in check so she would not get hurt. She would learn to be as indifferent as Steven and remember that this was a job, not a marriage.

ह&

Emily awoke early the next morning, glad to have slept in a real bed. She knew she had the cold, hard ground to look forward to for the next few nights.

She was dressed and ready to go when Steven knocked on the door. "Good morning," she said as she opened the door. "Did you sleep well?"

"Morning," he replied. "I slept okay. Are you ready to go?" His usual impatience was showing.

"All ready," she answered, trying to keep a happy tone in her voice.

"Thought we'd get a bite of breakfast before we head out," he offered. He picked up her bag and led the way to the dining room.

They had eggs, bacon, and biscuits with cream gravy for breakfast, a hearty meal that left Emily stuffed. When they walked outside, the wagon and team were waiting, and they began the day's journey.

ह&

The scenery was getting prettier. More greenery and more trees. The day went by as the days before had.

On the morning of the eleventh day, Emily asked, "Steven, tell me about the children. I'd like to know a little bit about what to expect."

He sat quietly for a few minutes, then he cleared his throat and began. "It's been five years since I've seen them, you know." Emily sat quietly and let him continue. "The oldest is Matthew. He'd be about sixteen now, a man. Probably he has been doing a lot of the work around the farm. I figure he's been the man of the house. The next boy is Mark. My wife—Becky—had a thing for Bible names. Mark's fourteen. He was always real quiet, liked to read a lot. Then there's Luke and John. They're twins. Luke is the leader of the two, John follows him. When you see one of them, you see them both. They're ten. Then comes Sarah. I guess she's seven now. She was just a baby when I left. I can't tell you much about her. She was the spitting image of her momma the last time I saw her. Becky told me in her last letter that Sarah really liked school."

Steven sat quietly. Emily thought she had seen a couple of tears run down his cheek as he talked about his children. She knew he had left to find work, but why had he stayed away so long? Would she ever learn the answer to that question and all the other questions she had about this man? She could see a lot of hurt on his face. Possibly a lot of regret. All she could do for him at this point was pray for him, and maybe God would heal the hurt. She knew she had to pray for the children, too. She wasn't sure what she had gotten herself into, but she knew whatever lay ahead would not be easy for any of them. Emily pulled out her pad and pencil and began to write.

Day 11

Steven told me about the children today. I am very nervous about the prospect of becoming caretaker of five children. I wonder what they will think of me. This is the most frightening thing I have ever faced thus far in my life. I hope I never face anything worse. According to Steven's timetable, we should be arriving in Tyler tomorrow. So I will have to face the five judges either tomorrow or the next day. I pray for God's guidance and comfort.

≥∾

Late in the afternoon, they came into the small town of Tyler. Steven turned to Emily and explained, "We're gonna spend the night here. It's about a half day's ride from here to the farm. I thought we could stay here and get cleaned up so we would be presentable when we get there. I also have to let the judge know I'm back and am gonna assume full responsibility for my kids."

Steven checked them into a hotel. It was much smaller than the one in Fort Worth, but it was clean. Once again Emily got to soak herself in a nice tub of hot water. She just sat and relaxed, for she knew, starting tomorrow, her life would change. She wasn't sure it would be for the better.

"God, give me the courage to get through tomorrow," she prayed. "I lift Steven and all five of his children up to You. Give us all the courage to survive whatever lies ahead."

3

$\mathcal{T}$he wagon came to a stop. The house was large, with a front porch that stretched the length of the house. A swing hung on one end of the porch, and firewood was stacked on the other. The house looked as though it had never been painted. Toys were scattered across the yard's patches of grass, and a lone rosebush stood at the end of the porch. The one redeeming factor was a large oak tree beside the house that would shade it from the hot afternoon sun.

Emily looked around, realizing that everything familiar was gone from her life. Here she sat in front of a strange house, beside a man she hardly knew, about to embark on a life filled with uncertainty. The trip had been a long one, and it seemed years, not weeks, since they left Abilene. Now, sitting in front of this dark house in east Texas, she wondered once again if she had made the right decision.

The front screen door opened and out walked five children, their eyes fixed on the wagon, their faces cold. There was not a smile among them. Steven helped Emily down from the wagon and then opened the gate. As she walked toward the porch, no one said a word.

A heavyset woman stepped out the door, her hair pulled back in a bun, her face lined by years of hard work. She dried her hands on her apron as she spoke. "Heard you were coming home. You're a little late, don't you think?" She turned and walked back into the house.

Steven looked at his children. His faced showed sheer terror. Emily could tell he had no idea what to say or do.

The terrible silence was finally broken by Sarah. "Are you our daddy?" she asked.

Steven cleared his throat and with an unsteady voice answered,

"Yes, I am, Sarah. My, how you've grown. You're a beautiful young lady now."

He then spoke to Luke and John and received a quiet hello and weak handshake from each of them. Steven extended his hand to Mark. "Hello, Mark. It's good to see you." Mark stood still and stared at his father.

Matthew finally spoke. "Are you here to stay or just passing through?" His tone was bitter.

"I'm here to stay," Steven replied. He hesitated, chewing on his lip. "I–I'm sorry about your mother. I would like for all of you to meet Miss Emily Johnson. She has come to take care of you."

Emily couldn't believe her ears. How could he be so cruel as to say sorry about your mother, here's someone to replace her, all in the same breath? And what was that he called her, Emily Johnson? He hadn't even introduced her as his wife. Well, that was fine with her.

"Hello, children, I'm happy to meet each one of you," Emily said.

The children never moved and never said a word. They looked as though the wind had been knocked out of them, as though their world had just come to an end.

Emily glanced around as they entered the house. Some of the furnishings had obviously been in the family for years. The place had a homey atmosphere, and some people would probably find it cozy and welcoming. But Emily didn't. She didn't know if she would ever feel welcome in this house.

"Come on, I'll show you where the kitchen and the washstand are so you can freshen up," Steven said.

Emily followed close behind him. In the kitchen she saw the plump lady from the brief encounter on the front porch.

"Emily, I'd like for you to meet Alice Bentley. Alice, this is Emily Johnson. Emily will be taking care of the kids."

"Pleased to meet you, Miss Johnson," Alice responded. Then looking at Steven, she asked, "If she's gonna take care of the kids, what are you gonna do?"

"I'm gonna see if I can make a go of this farm and support this family," Steven answered sharply.

"Do you know how many times Rebecca prayed that she would

hear those words from you?" Alice asked. "No, you don't, because you haven't been around. She worked herself into an early grave trying to hold on to this place, waiting for the day you would come home. Well, now you're here, but she's not here to see it." Alice turned to stir the pot on the stove.

Steven's face reddened. He turned to Emily and said, "Through that door on the back porch you should find water and a wash pan."

Emily left the room, and Steven sucked in a deep breath. He turned to Alice and stated firmly, "I don't have to explain anything to you or anyone else. What happened was between me and Becky. I'm back. I will resume my role as father and head of this household. Is that understood?"

"Oh, I understand you all right. I just don't think you understand. Those kids have lost the only parent they have known. They don't know you or that woman you've brought here to raise them. The job will require a lot of patience, care, and understanding. I've never seen much of that in you. I can't judge her; I don't know her." Alice kept right on preparing dinner.

"You don't know me, either," Steven remarked as he walked out on the back porch. He turned to Emily and said, "See if you can help Alice with dinner. I'm gonna unhitch the team." As he walked away, Steven tried to hide the tears he knew were filling his eyes.

§≈

"Can I help you with anything, Mrs. Bentley?" Emily asked.

"The name's Alice. You can peel those potatoes if you like. Tell me about yourself, Emily."

"There's not much to tell. I've been a widow for eight years. I was working in a café in Abilene when I met Ste—I mean Mr. Barnes," Emily answered.

"When did you and Steven get married?" Alice inquired.

Emily dropped the potato she was peeling and turned as white as a sheet. She finally found her voice and replied, "What makes you think we're married?"

"That little gold band on your hand for one thing. And, no matter what I think of Steven, he isn't going to bring an unmarried woman into this house to live with him and his children and cause more gossip," Alice answered. "Of course there will be talk that Steven brought a new bride home when his wife was barely cold in her grave."

Emily could tell that was Alice's opinion, and she couldn't blame her. She didn't know why she hadn't thought of that sooner. Of course people would think she was the reason Steven didn't come home to his family. They would think she was a home wrecker, that Steven had met her while he was away, and they had probably lived in sin.

"It's not what you think," Emily began. "We are married, but in name only. Steven used to come into the café a couple of times a month and drink coffee. We'd pass the time of day, but that's all. I hardly know him. There was nothing between us before our marriage, and there has been nothing between us since. He married me, but only so I would come here and take care of the house and help raise the children. I'm not sure we're even married in name, since he introduced me as Emily Johnson."

"If it's not love, what made you marry him and come all this way to raise five kids you don't even know?" Alice asked.

With a faraway look in her eye, Emily said, "I don't know. I have asked myself that a million times over the last couple of weeks. I guess part of it, or maybe all of it, was loneliness—and the fact that it's not really a marriage but a job. I'm a nanny and a housekeeper, with just the title of wife."

Emily paused; she didn't know how much she should share with this woman, but for some reason she decided to continue. "I have no children and no family, just me. For the first few years after Jim died, I didn't want to find anyone. I had been so in love with him, I didn't think I could ever love anyone else again. But, after a time I began to long for someone in my life. But for some reason I remained alone. I had begun to resign myself to the fact that there would never be anyone for me. I guess when Steven made me his proposition, I thought this might be my last chance at having a family and not dying a lonely old woman."

"I'm afraid you've cut a very rough row to hoe for yourself. It's hard enough raising children with two parents who love each other and support each other. I'll just have to pray extra hard for each one of you," Alice said.

"I know prayer is the only thing that will help this situation." Emily sighed. To change the subject, she asked, "Tell me something about yourself, Alice."

"I've been a neighbor and friend of the Barneses since they first moved here about fifteen years ago. Matt was just a baby. I helped deliver the other four. Rebecca Barnes was one of the finest women I've ever known. I love these kids just like my own grandchildren. I've been helping out ever since Rebecca got sick. My husband and boys have helped out around the farm ever since Steven left."

Alice paused and turned the chicken she had frying on the stove, then continued. "I've been taking care of the kids since Rebecca died, but the county decided since I wasn't blood kin, they'd have to step in and take over. That's when Steven was contacted."

Very timidly Emily asked, "Tell me about Steven."

"I'm afraid anything I tell you will be biased," Alice said, "but here goes. As I said, they moved here about fifteen years ago. They tried to make a go of the place and for the first few years did pretty good. Then I don't know just what happened. We had a drought one year and their crops failed. They had the five kids, and I think it was just more than Steven could take."

Alice took a sip of coffee, then continued. "There seemed to be a change in Steven about that time. He had seemed like a pretty happy fellow, but he got to where he was gloomy all the time. They say you don't know what goes on behind closed doors, but I don't see how anyone could not have loved Rebecca. Anyway, Steven just up and left one day. Rebecca said he had gone to find work, and just as soon as they got a little ahead, he'd be back. That was five years ago. I never heard her say one bad word about the man in all that time. She'd just say he was doing the best he could."

"I knew he had a family," Emily remembered, "but he never spoke much about them. He never spoke much about anything. Our conversations usually consisted of the weather and local events."

Alice looked at the clock. "We'd better get dinner on the table or those kids will be starving."

&

Out in the barn, Steven had unhitched and fed the team. Now he just sat there on a bale of hay with his head in his hands, tears running down his cheeks.

Lord, I have no earthly idea what to do. I don't know if You even hear me after all I've done. I deserted my family, and now after all this time I have to be a father to my kids. How can I expect them to respect me after what I've done to them? I don't ask anything for myself, Lord, but show me what to do for the kids.

How long had it been since he prayed? He wasn't a churchgoing man. Oh, he had gone on occasion, and he did believe in God. As a boy he had followed Christ, but he hadn't prayed in years. Now it seemed the only thing he could do.

He thought about his situation. Why did he marry Emily and bring her here? What on earth could he have been thinking? He didn't know her and his kids certainly didn't. But it had seemed like a good idea at the time. He knew she was a good woman and a God-fearing woman. But why Emily? Why didn't he just wait until he got here and then find someone to help out around the house and with the kids? Maybe somebody that the kids knew. He had just made everything harder by bringing her. But, it was too late now. He would just have to make the best of a bad situation.

He had made things clear to Emily that this was a marriage in name only. She shouldn't expect him to be a husband to her, and he wouldn't expect her to be a wife to him. He doubted he could ever be a husband to anyone again, not after he had failed so miserably with Becky. He had lived with the guilt of being a poor husband and father for so long it had become a permanent companion to him.

His next step would be to tell the kids that Emily was his wife. He didn't know why he hadn't told them up front, but now he had no choice. He knew they wouldn't take it well—but then they weren't going to take anything about this situation well. He heard the dinner bell and slowly headed toward the house.

ॐ

The kitchen table was long, with chairs at each end and benches along the sides. Steven walked to the head of the table and pointed Emily to the chair at the foot of the table. "Emily, you sit there."

With rage in his voice, Matt cried, "That was Momma's place."

Without any emotion in his voice, Steven stated, "Now it will be Emily's place."

Trying to calm the angry seas, Emily responded, "I'd be happy to sit on the side or anywhere. It really doesn't matter to me."

"You kids might as well know now. I should have told you in the beginning. Emily is my wife and will be treated with the respect the woman of the house should have." Steven's voice was emphatic. He looked at Emily as if he were giving a command. "Emily, sit at the foot of the table."

The silence was deafening; you could have cut the air with a knife. Finally, the children took their usual places around the table, with Sarah sitting to Emily's right. Alice sat down to Emily's left with the two older boys. Steven picked up the fried chicken and served himself, then began to pass the plate.

"Aren't we gonna say the blessing?" Sarah asked.

Steven flushed and looked helplessly at Emily, then at Alice. Alice took the cue and asked, "Whose turn is it to say grace?"

Very shyly, Luke replied, "It's mine."

"Okay, bow your heads, and, Luke, you say the blessing," Steven instructed.

Luke began, "Dear Lord, we thank You for this food and for the hands that prepared it. We ask Your blessings upon this house." He hesitated a moment and cleared his throat as if trying to decide whether to continue. He then finished, "And everyone that dwells herein. Amen."

The meal was very quiet. No one seemed to know what to say or do. Emily wasn't even sure of what she was eating. She and everyone else went through the motions of the meal.

Steven finally spoke. "What's your usual routine around here after dinner?"

Bitterly, Matt replied, "We do our chores."

"I was hoping you'd be a little more specific," Steven replied.

"Okay. Mark and I have been trying to fix the fence around the garden. Some of the posts have rotted out and the fence is falling down. We were going to work on it this afternoon." In a short tone, he added, "Is that all right with you?"

Looking him in the eyes, Steven answered, "It's fine with me. Do you need some help?"

Staring right back at his father and never batting an eye, Matt replied, "We've gotten along without your help for all these years. I think we can manage this afternoon just fine! We can certainly mend a fence without your help!"

Nothing more was said. Steven finished and left without saying anything to anyone. Emily was probably the only one that noticed he barely touched his food. He certainly didn't have the appetite of a farmer. Alice began clearing the table. As soon as she and Emily had washed the last dish, she turned to Emily and said, "I sure hate to do this to you, but I have to get home and care for my own family. They made do with sandwiches for dinner, so I need to fix them a good supper. You should have plenty of leftovers for supper. You'll just have to heat them up."

"Thank you for everything," Emily told her. "I do hope we can become friends. I know I can't take Rebecca's place, and I don't want to. I would like to create a place for myself, though, and I hope folks will give me the chance."

Alice just smiled. Emily could tell she had reservations and that it would take time. Based on the brief time she had known Alice, though, Emily believed her to be a fair-minded person. "If you have any questions, give me a holler," Alice said. "I just live up the road a piece."

Emily walked Alice to the front door and watched as she disappeared down the road. Now she was truly on her own, and she was terrified. She turned around and wondered what to do first. She was sure Steven had brought in her trunk, but she had no idea where he had placed it. It would feel good to get out of her traveling clothes, but she didn't know where to go. This was supposed to be her new home, and she had never felt more like a stranger anywhere.

The front door opened into a large hallway. In the hall was a daybed, hat rack, and small dresser, neat but dusty. She turned and to her right was a large family room, with a big fireplace on the opposite wall. A large braided rug lay on the floor in front of it, with a sofa, two big overstuffed chairs, a rocking chair, and several straight back chairs scattered throughout the room. The room looked lived in but not messy. It, too, was a little dusty.

Pictures stood on the mantel. One of the whole family showed that Rebecca had been a pretty woman, small, a little frail looking in the picture. Steven had been a handsome young man. He didn't smile in the picture; as a matter of fact, only the children were smiling, while Steven and Rebecca looked very solemn. Emily wondered how long before he left this picture had been taken. Sarah was in the photograph, so it couldn't have been long, Emily deduced.

Another picture caught her eye, a wedding picture. In this picture the two people had big smiles on their faces. Steven was even more handsome here and Rebecca more beautiful. Emily knew she could not compare with Rebecca. Emily was anything but beautiful, and she certainly wasn't small and frail, though she preferred to think of herself as being from much hardier stock. She could just hear the folks now, asking each other what Steven could have seen in her when he had Rebecca waiting for him at home. Oh well, somehow she would get through all this and folks would realize she didn't steal Steven away from Rebecca.

She walked across the hall and opened a door. Her trunk sat in the middle of the floor, near an iron bed. This must have been Rebecca's room, Emily realized, looking at the silver comb and brush with a small hand mirror that lay on a dressing table. The room Steven had shared with her when he lived here. She opened the wardrobe and found it filled with clothes. The room had apparently not been touched since Rebecca died.

A trunk stood in one corner, and Emily thought about exploring it, but she decided against it for now. The wardrobe was full, so she would just leave her things in her trunk for the time being. As she removed one of her work dresses from the trunk, she knew she would have to talk with Steven about Rebecca's things. She frowned uneasily while she changed her clothes. This must be the room Steven intended her to use, but she wasn't sure it was big enough for both her and the memories she could feel here.

Exploring the rest of the house, Emily found one other small bedroom downstairs that appeared to be Sarah's. Upstairs were two rooms where obviously the boys slept. She decided to look around outside next. She would have liked a guide for this tour, but apparently that was not to be.

She found the well-stocked smokehouse, then walked through the chicken yard. From the looks of things, fresh eggs and fried chicken would be plentiful. She could see a couple of milk cows out by the barn, so there would be fresh milk and butter.

Emily could see the two older boys working on the garden fence, but she decided not to approach them. She heard children laughing in the distance. The noise sounded as though it was coming from the front of the house, so she moved that way. When she rounded the corner, the children spotted her and immediately stopped their play.

A big collie dog was in the yard with the children. "What's the dog's name?" Emily inquired.

"Precious," answered Sarah. "She's my dog; we got her when she was a baby and I help feed her and take care of her, so she's mine."

Emily smiled. "She's a beautiful dog. It looks like you've taken very good care of her. I can tell she loves you very much."

"She follows Sarah everywhere she goes," Luke added. "Momma always said she didn't have to worry about Sarah if she was off somewhere because Precious would take care of her."

"It's nice to have a friend like that. One you can depend on to always be by your side," Emily replied. She had a sad faraway look in her eye. Right now she would love to have a friend, just someone she could talk to.

Her thoughts were interrupted by Sarah's voice. "Since our father married you, are you our mother now?" All three children looked very anxious to hear the answer to that question.

"I know you children loved your mother very much, and I know I could never take her place," Emily said gently. "I just hope that in time I can become your friend. I would like for each of you to be my friend. I don't know anyone here, and I sure could use a friend right now."

John looked very puzzled. "I didn't know grown-ups had friends," he remarked. "What do they do with friends? They're too old to play games."

"There's lots of things to do with friends besides just play. Friends are people you can share all your secret thoughts with. Someone you can just talk to when you're lonely. Grown-ups need friends just like children do," Emily answered.

The children sat in silence, then Luke finally spoke. "I guess maybe we could be friends. What is it you would like to talk about?" he asked.

"Why don't each one of you tell me about yourself and what you like to do. What foods you like to eat. Just anything you can think of about yourself," Emily said.

The children started sharing their likes and dislikes, and Emily was enjoying their visit so much that she completely let the time get away from her. Suddenly, she realized it was getting late, and she had better get supper on the table.

She had just gotten everything warmed and ready when Steven came in, followed closely by Matt and Mark. Matt yelled for the younger children and soon all were seated around the big table. Supper was just as quiet as dinner had been. When they finished eating, only Sarah stayed to help Emily with the dishes. Emily wondered where Steven was; she really needed to talk with him and get a few things settled.

She found him sitting alone on the front porch and she cleared her throat before she began. "I don't mean to intrude, but there are a few things I need to know. Little things like what time do you want meals served? Where am I to sleep? Also, how much authority do I have with the children and assigning them chores? I just want to get things clear from the start so we have as few problems as possible."

In his usual monotone fashion, Steven began, "We'll get up about sunup, and you can start breakfast. We'll eat after the milking's done. Dinner will be about noon and supper about sundown."

He let out a long sigh, then continued. "You'll sleep in the front bedroom, the first door on the left. You have complete authority with the kids. You can assign them whatever chores you feel necessary. You'll run things like the lady of the house would do."

Steven had answered all of her questions, but he never looked at her. He just sat there staring down the road. Emily wondered if he was wishing he could take off down that road again and never look back, because right at this moment that was what she would like to do.

Emily decided this was not a good time to approach the subject of Rebecca's belongings. She sat in silence, looking up at the heavens and thanking God for getting her through this first day. She was dreading going to bed in that room.

$$\textcircled{4}$$

$\mathcal{E}$mily lay in bed for hours wondering how she would ever make things work. She may have made a little progress with the three youngest today, but she knew it would take a long time to make friends with Matt and Mark. Steven, well, that was a whole different story. How would she ever break through the barrier he had built around himself? Even though Emily considered this a job, she hoped to bring the children and their father together, but she could not foresee this group becoming a family anytime soon.

The loud crow of a rooster awakened Emily the next morning. She found Steven straining milk as she walked into the kitchen.

"Good morning," she said. "I'm sorry if I overslept."

"You didn't. I'm just up a little early," he replied

"I'll get breakfast started." Emily put the coffee on to brew, found the flour, and started to make biscuits. The door opened and in walked Matt. He grabbed the milk pail and started for the back door.

Steven stopped him. "The milking's done for this morning."

Matt gave him a long, cold stare, then turned and walked out of the room. Steven poured himself a cup of coffee and sat down at the table.

Emily fried bacon and scrambled eggs. Her biscuits turned out exceptionally well, she thought. The kids straggled in one by one and seated themselves at the table.

"Momma always gave us a choice of how we wanted our eggs cooked," said Mark under his breath. "And her biscuits were a lot better."

"I'm sorry if the breakfast is not to your liking. No one was here when I cooked the eggs, so I couldn't ask anyone how they wanted them," Emily said as nicely as she could. "Mark, how would you like your eggs prepared next time?"

Mark flushed, and his eyes shot daggers at her. "I prefer them fried."

"If everyone will be patient with me, I will try my best to learn your likes and dislikes." Emily's voice was polite but firm.

Steven acted as though nothing had transpired. Emily knew for now she was on her own with the children. He certainly wasn't going to help her in any way.

Pausing between bites of egg, Steven said, "I noticed all the fields have been plowed and planted except that back five acres. Is there some reason it was left out?"

"We're not going to plant it this year. The cotton we planted back there didn't do good," Matt answered. "Uncle Clyde said to let it rest a year, and that's what we're gonna do."

"What kind of deal do you have with 'Uncle Clyde' on the rest of the crops?" Steven inquired.

"A seventy-thirty split. We get the seventy cause we take care of the fields. He just helps us till and plant and harvest," Matt replied. "Do you have a problem with that?"

"No, I don't have a problem with that. But now that I'm home, I think we can do the work ourselves and we won't have to impose on him." Steven's tone was firm. He then added, "And we are going to plant the back five acres."

Matt's face turned red. He slammed his fist on the table and yelled, "We haven't been imposing on him. He has been paid for his help from the sale of the crops. Uncle Clyde said let those back five acres rest this year, and that's what we're gonna do. I think he knows more about farming than you do. He didn't run away when his farm flopped the way you did!"

Steven just sat there and let his son finish. Then he spoke. "I think you're forgetting who owns this farm, young man. And I also think you're forgetting who the father is around here. I will not tolerate this kind of behavior from you."

Infuriated by his father's remarks, Matt blew up again. "Me and Mark have been doing all the work around here while you've been gone. And doing a good job of it, too. Now, you just waltz in here and take over and expect us to bow to your wishes and respect you as a father. Well, that's not gonna happen, mister. You walked out on us and left us to fend for ourselves, and we did. No thanks to you."

Matt had to catch his breath, but he continued. "You couldn't handle it when things were bad. Now that things are going good, you expect to come back and take up where you left off. You weren't man enough to turn things around yourself. You let us do it for you. Now you want the benefits from it. We've worked hard for this place, and we're not gonna let you ruin it or take it away from us."

Matt was shouting at the top of his lungs. Steven didn't try to defend himself. He didn't do anything. Matt stomped out of the room and slammed the back door. Steven sat there a moment, then he, too, got up and left. Emily noticed his shoulders seemed to sag a little lower than usual. She couldn't help but wonder why he had let his son talk to him that way. She surmised that Matt had probably put into words a lot of the feelings Steven had about himself.

Slowly, everyone filed out one by one except Sarah. "I'll help you with the dishes," she said. "I always used to help Momma."

"Thank you, Sarah." Emily smiled. "I would love to have your help and your company. After we finish the dishes, maybe you could help me round up the dirty clothes. I need to do some washing."

"I'd be glad to, but we shouldn't have too much. Miss Alice washed day before yesterday," Sarah said. "You should know that Monday is wash day."

True to Sarah's word, the children didn't have a lot of dirty clothes, but Emily needed to wash hers anyway. She was sure Steven had some as well. She saw something sticking out from under the daybed in the hall. Pulling up the spread, she noticed Steven had pushed his things under it. This must be where he had been sleeping. Emily was surprised to find it a little unnerving to know that just a wall separated them at night. She pulled his clothes out and added them to her pile.

Sarah helped her gather wood for the fire and get the wash pot set up. After an hour, the washing was finished, and it was time to start dinner.

"Sarah, would you like to help me get dinner ready?" Emily asked. "I sure would! I like to cook." Sarah grinned from ear to ear.

It was the first genuine smile Emily had seen in quite a while, and it was really nice to see. "Since you're gonna help me, I think I'll have time to make a big peach cobbler for dessert."

Sarah's smile got bigger and brighter. "Oh, boy. Let's get started. I can hardly wait for dessert."

"Sarah, don't you kids go to school? I love having your help, but isn't this a school day?" Emily inquired as they began their meal preparations.

Softly and rather shyly, Sarah answered, "We do go to school, and this week is the first time we've missed in a long time. Uncle Clyde found out in town last week that Daddy should be getting here real soon, so Matt said we were gonna stay home for a few days and keep an eye on things. I don't know what we're supposed to keep an eye on, but I guess Matt and Mark do."

Emily got Sarah started washing potatoes. "Miss Emily," Sarah asked after a moment, "what is my daddy like? I don't remember him at all, and Momma never talked about him much. I used to ask Matt about him, but he would just say he didn't remember. Will you tell me about him?"

Emily was silent. She didn't know how to answer the child's question. She didn't know Steven herself. What could she say to this little girl? Sarah looked at her with such a trusting face. Emily couldn't tell her she just married her daddy without knowing him and came here to take care of them—or could she? She said a quick prayer and asked the Lord for guidance.

Emily began, "Sarah, I haven't known your father very long. He is a very nice man, and he loves you children very much. Right now he just doesn't know how to show it. He has been away so long and all of you are kind of like strangers to him. Just like he's a stranger to you. You'll have to give each other time. You'll all have to try to get to know one another again. Just like you will all have to get to know me, and I will get to know you. We all just have to be patient." Emily knew she had not answered the little girl's question, but she hoped Sarah would drop the issue.

"I like you, Miss Emily," Sarah said. "But I'm not sure about Daddy. He doesn't seem very friendly. He seems mad all the time. And Matt's mad now, too, since Daddy got here. I don't think Matt and Mark like him very much."

The child seemed to have a lot of insight into the situation. "They have a lot of things to work out between them. I don't think your daddy is mad, Sarah. He just has a lot on his mind right now." Emily added, "We'd better get that peach cobbler started if we want it to be ready for dinner." She hoped that would get Sarah's mind on a different subject, at least for a while.

After they had gotten the cobbler in the oven, Sarah set the table. "Would you like me to ring the dinner bell?" Sarah asked. "I'm really getting hungry."

Emily laughed. "Yes, of course. I'd forgotten we had to do that. You go right ahead."

Sarah went to the back porch and gave the dinner bell a nice long ring. Emily dreaded for everyone to come in. So far mealtime had not been the most pleasurable of experiences around here.

The boys all came in, washed up, and took their places at the table. Steven was nowhere in sight. They waited a few minutes for him until finally Emily asked, "Whose turn is it to say grace?"

"It's mine," Sarah said, and she began. "God is great; God is good; let us thank Him for our food. And please help Daddy and Matt not to be mad at each other. Amen."

Emily looked up and saw Steven standing in the doorway. "We waited, but the food was going to get cold, so we started without you. I hope you don't mind."

Visibly shaken by his daughter's prayer, Steven took his seat at the head of the table. "I'm sorry I'm late."

He picked up the ham, took a piece, and began to pass it around the table. He said nothing else. No one talked. *You'd think that the silence would be better than the yelling at breakfast was,* Emily thought, *but it's the loudest quiet I ever heard.* If this continued, no one would ever get to know anyone around here.

"Can we have dessert now?" Sarah asked with a big smile on her face. "Miss Emily made peach cobbler."

"Of course we can. Will you help me serve it?" Emily asked.

"Boy, that sure was good," Sarah said as she finished her cobbler. "It was as good as Momma's."

Matt shot daggers at Emily and shook his head. Under his breath he mumbled, "Not everybody will be that easy to win over."

Another appetizing and nourishing meal was over. Once again, Steven had eaten very little, and Emily's appetite certainly wasn't what it had been. At this rate she and Steven would both lose a few pounds. She did note that although Matt and Mark were not friendly toward her or complimentary to her food, they left little on their plates.

ℒ›

By twilight, the kids were all in their rooms. Steven had disappeared right after supper. Emily went out on the front porch for a while to get some fresh air.

She was sitting in the porch swing when she heard someone whistling, not a tune, just a monotone whistle. She looked up and saw Steven come around the corner of the house. As he rounded the corner, he spotted her and stopped.

"Beautiful evening," Emily observed.

"Yeah, I guess so," he hesitantly answered as he started to walk off.

He stopped when Emily spoke again. "Steven, could I talk to you for just a moment?"

He turned. "Go ahead."

"Steven, I feel uncomfortable in Rebecca's room. All of her things are still in there. Her clothes are in the closet and even her comb and brush on the dressing table." Emily didn't know what to say now. She hoped he would jump in and help her out.

After a considerable silence, he finally said, "I'll take care of it." Then he walked off.

Steven would take care of it—but when? She would just have to wait and see. She got up and went to her room. She read her Bible, then turned out the light. As she lay in the darkness, she once again asked God to help her through another day. She also prayed for Steven and each one of the children. She asked God to please help Steven show some love and affection toward his children.

She heard the front door open and footsteps in the hallway. Steven was going to bed right outside her door. She had gotten that strange feeling again that morning as she washed his clothes with hers. This cold, seemingly unfeeling man was causing her all kinds of grief and discomfort.

She couldn't help but think about him lying in this very bed with another woman, and that disturbed her. Why should that bother her? She had no claims on the man. With the darkness surrounding her, she wondered what it would be like to be held by Steven. She tried to make the feelings go away, but loneliness lay heavy on her heart. Emily began to pray for God to keep her heart pure. Although legally she was married to the man, she wasn't sure she was in God's eyes.

❧

Emily was awake early. This morning she would start her duties on time. She was glad there was a connecting door from her room to the kitchen, so she didn't have to go through the hall and pass Steven's sleeping form if he were still in bed.

She was making biscuits when Matt came in with the milk. He had apparently been determined Steven wasn't going to do his chores this morning.

"Good morning, Matt." Emily smiled warmly. "How would you like your eggs this morning?"

Matt grunted something unintelligible without looking at her. He finished straining the milk and left the room without a word.

Watching him as he exited, Emily whispered to herself, "Good morning, Emily. I'll take my eggs any way it's easier for you to fix them. You're so kind to ask." Then she thought, *Lord, please keep me from popping that rude young man up beside the head.*

Steven came in and poured himself a cup of coffee and sat down at the table. He looked very tired, like he hadn't gotten much sleep, either. She couldn't remember ever seeing anyone look so unhappy.

"Good morning, Steven," she greeted. "Did you sleep well?"

After a big yawn, he said, "Morning. I slept okay."

She would ask him the magic question and see what kind of response she could evoke from him. "How would you like your eggs cooked this morning?"

"Any way's fine with me," he responded, not to her surprise.

The children all wandered in as she set a plate of fried eggs on the table. Mark looked at the eggs, then at her, but there was of course no thank you from him. After the first bite, he did whisper softly, "I prefer them sunny-side up."

There was just no way to please this crew, so why did she try? She might as well make some more trouble, so she remarked, "I know this may be none of my business, but today is a school day. Since all of you have missed the last couple of days, don't you think you should go today?"

"We're taking the week off," Matt quickly replied.

"Is this some kind of a holiday?" Steven inquired.

"No, we're just taking the week off to be around here," was Matt's response.

"Well, that's very kind of you to want to be home with me and Emily, since we just got here," Steven said nonchalantly. "But I would much rather you kids go to school. An education is very important."

Emily was stunned. Was there a hint of humor in his voice? This was wonderful. She couldn't help but throw a little smile his way when he glanced at her. Be still my heart, she thought. Was that a little grin she saw almost touch his lips?

Matt started to argue, but Steven stopped him before he could begin. "There will be no discussion. You kids will go to school today."

They all got up to leave, but Sarah was the only one that said anything. "The breakfast was real good, Miss Emily." With her head down as she passed her father's chair, she said, "Bye, Daddy."

Steven turned her way. "Bye, Sarah." His voice trembled.

After the children left the kitchen, Emily prepared lunches to send with them to school. Steven rose from the table when the front door slammed behind the children. As he started out the back door, he called, "Don't fix dinner since the kids aren't here. I'll grab something when I come in later."

Emily watched him go. Then she turned to her chores. After spending the morning cleaning, she decided to take a break and explore the lane she had seen behind the barn.

ॐ

Steven came in to grab himself a biscuit and a piece of bacon and found the house deserted. This would be a good time to clear Becky's things out of the bedroom. He found an empty trunk in the attic and took it into Becky's room. He took down her dresses one by one from the wardrobe and neatly folded them and placed them in the trunk.

Lying on the top shelf was something wrapped in an old sheet. Pulling it down, he accidentally dropped it on the floor. As he picked it up, he noticed it was Becky's wedding dress. Holding it, he remembered how beautiful she had looked wearing it the day they were married. They were so happy then. What had happened to them? Fighting back the tears, he knew the answer to that question and blamed himself for the whole thing.

He had to finish this task before Emily returned. He cleared off the dressing table and looked around for anything else that might need removing. He picked up a small box from the table and looked inside. There he found a small locket. Opening it, he saw a picture of himself and one of Matt. He had given this to Becky right after Matt was born. More tears threatened.

He sat down in the rocking chair, clutching the locket in his hand. He and Becky had been happy at one time. The day he married her, he thought, was the happiest day in his life. But the day Matt was born, that was so special. When he held that little bundle in his arms, he had never felt such joy and love.

They had a good happy life until he forced Becky to move here to the farm. This had been his dream, not hers. He had wanted a farm and had sold everything they had to make his dream come true. Then he had run out on his dream and his family. Tears flowed freely. How could his family ever forgive him? How could he ever forgive himself?

Quickly, he closed the locket and tucked it back in its little hiding place. He put it away inside the trunk. Seeing nothing else he felt he should remove, he closed the trunk and carried it up to the attic.

৯৯

As Emily sat in the living room that evening, mending a pair of John's overalls, Sarah came in and asked, "Emily, do you go to church?"

"Why yes, I do, Sarah," Emily replied. "What makes you ask that?"

"Well, we go to church, too, and this Sunday is Easter. I was hoping you would go with us." Sarah took a long breath, then began again. "I usually get a new dress for Easter. Momma always made me one, but I guess this year I'll just wear my old one."

Emily looked at the little girl standing there so innocently. She was the only friend Emily had here, and Emily could already tell she was a treasure among treasures. Emily had a lump in her throat when she responded to Sarah's plea. "Sarah, I would love to go to church with you Sunday. I appreciate your thinking about me and asking me to go with you. Maybe if we talk to your daddy, he would give us enough money to buy some material, and I could make you a new dress for Sunday."

"Oh, Emily that would be wonderful! But we don't have to talk to Daddy. Momma had lots of material. It's in a trunk in her room. Come on, I'll show you." Grabbing Emily's hand, Sarah pulled her through the door into the bedroom.

Sarah walked to the trunk sitting in the corner by the fireplace and opened the lid. She began pulling out piece after piece of material. The little girl's excitement grew with each new discovery. Emily wondered why anyone would purchase so much material, but she guessed that didn't matter. Sarah was so excited that Emily couldn't help but get carried away in her enthusiasm.

They looked at every piece in the trunk. There was every color imaginable, plus the notions to go with them. Some of the material looked to be the weight and texture for heavy curtains or upholstery. Sarah finally decided upon a piece with small pink flowers in it. It was a good choice because it would be lovely with her soft blond hair and her sky-blue eyes.

Sarah smiled. "There should be enough material here for you to make you a dress, too. Momma and I always had a dress alike on Easter."

Emily was completely caught off guard by Sarah's comment. The little girl was so sincere, and she surely didn't want to hurt her feelings. "Sarah, that is very sweet of you. I would love to have a dress to match yours, but since this is Friday, I'm afraid I'll only have time to make one dress. I want you to have a new dress, and I'll make me something later."

That satisfied Sarah for now, and Emily was grateful for that. Emily took Sarah's measurements, then asked the little girl to bring her one of her dresses so she could fashion a pattern. Sarah rushed from the room and was back in no time with her Sunday best in hand. Emily noted the stitching; Rebecca had been very handy with a needle and thread. Well, Emily would just do her best and she considered that to be pretty good. She had never sewn for a little girl before, but she looked forward to the challenge.

Sarah told her good night, and Emily decided to start her project tonight. Her little nap after her walk had rested her, and she wasn't tired right now. She had noticed the treadle machine sitting in front of the window, and now she would check it out and see if it was in working order.

As she walked toward the machine, she noticed Rebecca's vanity set was missing from the dressing table. She opened the wardrobe and found it empty. Steven must have cleared everything out while she was gone this afternoon. He said he would take care of it, and he had wasted no time in doing so. She must remember to thank him for his consideration.

She quickly unpacked her belongings, hanging her clothes in the wardrobe. She placed her comb and brush on the dressing table, and she gently picked up the wedding picture of herself and Jim. Running her fingertips lightly across Jim's face, her mind began to wander again to days gone by. The what-ifs came back. Like, what if Jim hadn't died? Would they have had a place like this, maybe a little girl like Sarah? What if Jim were here right now? She knew her life would be different. Happiness would have filled her life if Jim were here.

Stop it! she said to herself. Jim was gone; she was here, and she would have to make the best of things. Emily could not change the past and had very little control over the future, but she could do something about the present. She could get started on a dress and make one little girl very happy.

Emily found the sewing machine in good working order. That would make her job much easier. She began to fashion a pattern in her mind, and using Sarah's dress for guidance, began to cut what she saw in her mind's eye. She got each piece cut to her satisfaction, then moved a lamp close to the machine and started to put the pieces of her puzzle together.

She heard the screen door open and knew that Steven was going to bed. She couldn't stop her heart from skipping a little beat, but she did try to ignore it. She forced herself to keep her mind on her sewing, not on Steven.

The clock struck 2:00 A.M., and she realized she had been at this for about six hours. She was pleased with what she lay out on the bed. This morning she would have Sarah try it on so she could pin up the hem and make any alterations that might be necessary. Emily could hardly wait to see the expression on the little girl's face. But right now she had to get some sleep.

ৡ৶

The rooster crowed all too early. It seemed Emily had barely laid her head on her pillow when she heard his unwelcome cry. It was Saturday, and the morning routine would be the same except that the children would not be going to school.

Steven was sitting at the table drinking a cup of coffee when she walked into the kitchen. "Sorry if I overslept," she apologized.

He looked up from his coffee and remarked, "I heard you up late last night. I thought I heard the sewing machine."

"You did. I hope it didn't bother you. I was making Sarah an Easter dress."

"Easter dress. Is it almost Easter?" Steven queried.

"Tomorrow's Easter Sunday," she answered. "Sarah invited me to go to church with her. I'm thankful she's warmed up to me. She is really a precious little girl."

Emily finished the biscuits and slid them into the oven. The kids straggled to the table one by one, except for the twins, who always came in together.

When breakfast was drawing to an end, Steven said, "I would like you boys to help me finish plowing and planting that back five acres this morning."

Then came the expected silence. Finally, Matt broke the tension by saying, "I thought I told you Uncle Clyde said not to plant that part this year."

"Matt, I thought I made it clear to you that I'm the father around here. I know what Clyde says. I agree that we don't need to plant cotton in that area, but I was thinking of planting corn there. And that's what we're gonna do."

"If you want to plant it fine! But don't expect us to help you," Matt argued.

Steven looked at Emily, then around the table and said, "If you'll excuse us, Matt and I need to step outside and have a little talk." Steven stood and motioned for Matt to join him.

"What's he gonna do?" asked Sarah after they had gone. A look of fear showed on her face.

Mark mumbled something about his father trying to prove who was boss. The twins looked almost as frightened as Sarah. Emily tried to calm their fears by saying, "It's okay. Your dad just wants to talk to Matt, and he didn't want there to be any more yelling at the table. You kids go on and play while I clean the kitchen."

❧

Outside, Steven and Matt stood toe to toe and stared at one another for what seemed like an eternity. Steven finally began. "Matt, we need to get things straight right now. I know you've been the man around here for quite a while. And from what I can tell, you've done an excellent job, but I'm back now. I'm back whether you like it or not, and we need to learn to work together."

Steven stopped. He really didn't know what to say to the young man at this point. He remembered a lot of long talks they had when Matt was a boy, but now he was grown. He wouldn't have let any man talk to him the way Matt had talked to him, but Steven couldn't help but think that he deserved Matt's wrath. For the sake of the farm and the others, though, they had to at least come to an understanding.

Steven started again. "Look, I know you're mad at me and probably at this point you even hate me. And I can't say that I blame you. But we need to learn to at least work together. We both want to be able to take care of this family, and for that to happen, this farm has to make it. Let's just try to work the fields together and harvest the crops when the time is right. You don't have to like me to do that."

"I don't have to do anything with you," Matt responded. "You have no right coming back here and trying to take over. You walked out on us without so much as a good-bye. We never heard from you until you showed up here Tuesday. Don't expect me to welcome you with open arms." The contempt in his voice came through loud and clear.

Steven never batted an eye. "Well, let me put it to you this way. I am the father; you are the son, whether you like it or not. My word will stand. What I say goes. Is that clear?"

"Yes, sir!" Matt turned and fled.

For a moment, Steven just stood there. What did Matt mean, they never heard a word from him? He had written Becky regularly, at least at first. And he had sent money every month since he left five years ago. Did she not ever tell the kids that or show them one of his letters? Maybe someday he could talk to Matt about that rationally. But he doubted that it would be any day soon.

5

$\mathcal{E}$aster Sunday, and what a glorious day! The sun was bright; the birds were singing; the flowers were blooming; all was right in God's world. At least those were Emily's first thoughts when she awoke that morning. Then she remembered where she was, and she knew hardly anything was right in this house.

She looked at the clock and realized she had plenty of time before anyone had to leave for church. Maybe a special breakfast this morning. The family arrived as she set a steaming plate filled with light fluffy pancakes on the table.

"Good morning. And a glorious Easter morn it is," Emily said in the most cheerful and convincing tone she could muster.

"Good morning, Miss Emily," Sarah chimed. "I'm gonna wait until after breakfast to put on my beautiful dress. I didn't want to get it dirty."

Emily looked around the table as she asked, "What time do we have to leave the house in order to get to church?"

Matt and Mark looked at each other, then Matt sharply questioned, "Do you plan on going to church with us?"

"Yes, Matt, I do," Emily answered firmly. "I always attended church back in Abilene. Sarah asked me to attend with her this morning, and I'm going to."

Silence once again struck the Barnes clan at the dining table. Matt and Mark both looked as though they might be ill. Sarah looked confused by the whole exchange, and Steven and the twins appeared not to notice anything but the pancakes.

Emily decided to break the silence. "I'm really looking forward to meeting some of my new neighbors. Is church at eleven here? What time do we have to leave?"

"Church starts at eleven, and it's two miles down the road. It depends on how fast you can walk as to how early you have to leave," Matt replied.

"Matt, we always take the wagon to church," Sarah reminded him.

"If I have to go to church, I'm not riding in the same wagon she's in. We'll take the wagon, but she can walk." Matt left the room.

Nothing more was said. Emily cleaned the breakfast dishes, then went to her room to dress. She guessed she had better leave by ten-thirty. Maybe someone would at least tell her which direction the church was. She didn't remember passing one when they arrived here, but she had been so nervous that day she could have missed it.

Emily walked out on the porch. Sarah was dressed and sitting in the porch swing. "Emily, could you help me with my hair bow?"

The wagon pulled up at the front gate as Emily finished Sarah's hair. Matt yelled, "Ya'll come on. It's time to go."

Just as he yelled, Steven rounded the corner of the house and walked up to the wagon. "Matt, it's really nice of you to drive everyone to church this morning," he commented, opening the gate for the twins.

"I told you I'm not riding in the same wagon as that woman!" Matt said angrily.

"Then I guess you'd better step down from there because Emily's riding to church in this wagon." Steven stepped up on the wheel and took the reins from the young man.

Matt refused to budge. In a commanding voice, Steven declared, "You either get down on your own, or I'll pull you down."

"I'd like to see you try." The words were barely out of Matt's mouth before Steven grabbed him by the collar and in one fell swoop picked him up and set him on the ground.

Everyone gasped, but no one was as surprised as Matt himself. He was on the ground before he knew what happened. He stood there dumbfounded.

"Now, young man, you can walk to church." Steven turned and looked at Mark and the twins, who were already in the back of the wagon. "If there's anyone else who feels he is too good to ride in the same wagon with Miss Emily, this would be the time for you to step down."

The twins stayed right where they were, but Mark climbed down from the wagon. He walked over and stood beside Matt.

"Emily, Sarah, I'm driving you to church," Steven called to where they stood on the porch.

Steven assisted Emily up into the wagon, then picked up Sarah and set her on the seat beside Emily. He climbed up beside the ladies and slapped the reins. The horses started down the road.

&

The church was a small white building with a tall steeple. Just as it came into view, the church bell began to peal out the call for all to come worship. Emily wasn't too sure any of this family was in a worshipful mood, but she knew there couldn't be a family there who needed it more. Steven pulled the horses to a stop and jumped down from the wagon. He lifted Sarah out and set her down gently on the ground.

After helping Emily down, he said, "I'll be waiting out here when the service is over to drive you home."

Without another word, he climbed back up in the wagon and drove away. Sarah took Emily's trembling hand and led her toward the open doors of the church.

A hush fell over the crowd gathered outside the doors as they approached. Emily deduced that the tall slender man standing on the steps greeting everyone was the minister.

Sarah pulled Emily toward him. "Brother Kirkland, this is Emily. She's living with us now and taking care of us."

The minister extended his hand. "Hello, Emily. I'm Thomas Kirkland. I'm very happy to have you worship with us this morning."

The tone of his voice and the kindness pouring from his eyes almost made Emily feel welcome. "Thank you, Reverend Kirkland. I'm happy to be here," was all she could manage to respond.

When the service was over, Sarah shot out the door with her friends and Emily was left standing alone in the midst of strangers. Finally a familiar face, Alice Bentley, walked up to her.

"It's good to see you, Emily," Alice greeted as she extended her hand. "How's everything going?"

"I guess it could be worse, but I'm not sure how," Emily answered honestly.

A crowd of curious onlookers had joined them. Alice began to introduce Emily to each of them. There were no warm smiles among them, just a few grunts. She noticed Alice introduced her just as Emily, never mentioning her last name. Oh well, she would try not to be judgmental. It would take time for these folks to get to know her. She had to be patient and give them the time.

Outside, Steven waited by the wagon. A couple of men had wandered over and were talking to him, seeming genuinely happy to see him. She thought she even spied a grin on Steven's face, but she didn't want to keep him waiting, so she strolled over to where he stood. As the men left, Steven called the children. They all boarded the wagon and started home.

"Everyone just loved my dress, Emily. Thanks for making it for me." Sarah looked up at her father, as if wanting him to say something to her. But as usual, he maintained his silence.

Emily had caught a glimpse of Matt and Mark just as the service ended. They were headed out the back door. She was glad they had come to church even if they didn't want to be seen with her. Today's message was one everyone needed to hear. It was too bad Steven hadn't joined them, but she would continue to pray for all of them.

Emily had tried to make Easter dinner a special occasion. She had put a tablecloth and the fancy dishes on the table. But nothing she did made any difference. The boys never refused to eat, but there was always some whispered comment about how their mother did things. Of course they whispered it loud enough for Emily to hear. Steven never ate much and never commented on the quality of the food. Sarah was the only conversationalist during mealtime.

Emily was determined that she would not let this gloomy family bring her spirits down today. She would keep in mind that this was Easter, that her Lord arose from the dead today, and she would rejoice and be glad.

ُ ﹏

The days dragged on. Nothing seemed to change. The children would go off to school, and Steven would head out for the fields. He would always tell her not to worry with dinner for him, but she would always make sure she left something easily accessible to him. She filled her days with household chores and long walks exploring the territory.

She had been in this place a month, and the only friend she had made was Sarah. Today she decided she must do something about it. She had attended church every Sunday, but no one had made an effort to become her friend. Alice greeted her each time she saw her, and today Emily decided she would make the first move to win Alice's friendship. She changed into a clean dress, grabbed her bonnet, and started down the road.

The Bentley residence was a well-kept white house with a white picket fence around the yard. Emily knocked on the front door, and Alice welcomed her inside.

"I hope you don't mind me dropping by unexpectedly. I just had this terrific hunger to visit with another woman," Emily explained.

Alice replied warmly, "Not at all. I should be ashamed of myself for not getting by your place to see how you were getting along. Let's go out in the kitchen. I just made a pound cake and some fresh lemonade."

The kitchen was a large room, much like Emily's. But something about it felt much different. The cabinets were painted white and a pretty curtain hung over the window. Some fresh-cut daffodils sat in a vase in the center of the table. The room and the lady reigning over it made you feel at home. That was the difference between Emily's kitchen and this room.

Alice poured them each a glass of lemonade and cut two pieces of cake, and the two ladies began to talk. Emily poured out her heart to Alice. She told her about the power struggle between Matt and Steven. How they all seemed to hate her, with the exception of Sarah and maybe the twins. She told Alice how lonely and miserable she felt.

Emily was really struggling and suffering to make a family out of complete turmoil. Her heart was showing on her face as she shared with Alice.

"You've mentioned how everyone feels about you and how you

feel about them. That is, everyone except Steven. What's going on with the two of you?" Alice questioned.

"Absolutely nothing," Emily replied. "There's no conversation, no nothing between us. Most of the time it's as though he doesn't even notice that I'm there."

Surprised, Alice asked, "You don't talk about anything? Not even the children?"

"He occasionally gives me some kind of instruction. And if I ask him a direct question, he'll answer it with as few words as possible."

"We've got to get you out of that house and involved with other people," Alice announced. "Day after tomorrow is our quilting day at the church. You're going with me. We all take a sack lunch and quilt and visit all day. It'll be a good chance for you to get to know some of the ladies and for them to get to know you."

"I'm not so sure they want to get to know me," Emily replied timidly. "They're pretty standoffish at church."

"Oh, hogwash. If I can change my mind about you, anybody can. I'm one of the most stubborn old women there." Alice laughed.

It was good to share laughter with someone again. They spent the rest of their visit just getting to know one another.

"Oh my, would you look at the time. I've got to get home. The kids will be coming in from school, and I've got to start supper," Emily said. "You'll never know how much this visit has meant to me. You'll have my friendship for life because of the time we have spent together today."

Alice embraced her newfound friend, then walked her to the door. "Don't forget, day after tomorrow. I'll pick you up about nine o'clock."

"I'm looking forward to it," Emily called as she opened the gate.

ॐ

As Emily finished her chores the next morning, she made another resolution. Her visit the previous day with Alice had turned out so well she decided to try something new today. Today she would make a picnic lunch and take it out to Steven. She knew where he was today. She had seen him working the field behind the barn.

Filling the basket with fried chicken, potato salad, and fresh baked bread, she headed out to find him. She stopped by the well first and pulled up the bucket where she had lowered a jug of freshly brewed tea earlier to cool. She wrapped it in towels and started toward the barn.

Emily found Steven hoeing the rows of cotton just as she had expected. Hearing her call his name, he laid down his hoe and walked over to her.

"Something the matter?" he asked.

"No. I was in the mood for a picnic. It's no fun to have one by yourself, so I hoped you'd join me," Emily explained.

She spread the blanket in the shade cast by the barn and began to unpack the tempting morsels. She never gave Steven a chance to refuse.

Taking the large glass of cool tea she offered him, he drank it down without taking a breath. "That really hit the spot," he remarked.

She filled his glass again and handed him a plate of food. He actually seemed to relax a little.

"I don't know much about cotton, but those plants certainly do look healthy," she observed.

"Yeah, as long as we get a little rain now and then, we should make a good crop."

Steven ate more than she had seen him eat since they arrived here over a month ago. He even grinned a little when she offered him a piece of the pound cake she had baked that morning.

"Pound cake's my favorite," he said softly.

This was the most pleasant meal Emily had enjoyed in a long time. The conversation wasn't extensive, but it was pleasant. The thing she enjoyed most was there was no arguing and no one commenting under their breath about how Momma would have done it.

She packed up the basket while Steven folded the blanket and handed it to her. He seemed very nervous and was fidgeting like a schoolboy on a first date. She almost laughed, but she thought he was very cute.

"The meal was very good. Thank you," he said as he picked up his hat and started back to work.

Emily was pleased with the way this new adventure had turned out, too. Not nearly as dramatic as yesterday, but the least little improvement with Steven was progress. She could hardly wait until tomorrow. Maybe meeting the ladies of the church at a social function would be friendlier than at the worship service. She could only pray her third new adventure would turn out as well as the first and second.

৯৯

She was waiting on the front porch with her sack lunch when Alice drove up in her buggy the next day. When they pulled up in front of the church, Emily could tell by the number of buggies that quilting days must be well attended.

Inside, the quilting frames had already been set up and a couple of ladies were already busy stitching. As Emily and Alice entered, a hush fell over the crowd. It wasn't just Emily's imagination; all eyes in the room were on her. Alice took a firm grip on her arm, probably to keep her from fleeing the lion's den.

Alice pulled her forward as she spoke. "You girls remember Emily Barnes. I asked her to join us today. She's been in our community for a while now, and we all need to get to know her better. And we have to give her a chance to get to know us, too."

Alice directed Emily to the chair next to hers. "Emily, I'm sure you don't remember everyone's name, so let me introduce you again. To your left is Suzie Atwater, and the lady next to her is our preacher's wife, Rosemary Kirkland."

Alice continued until she had introduced her to everyone seated at the quilt. Emily picked up her needle and thimble and began to stitch. All eyes were still glued on her. She knew that not only did she have to win approval for herself at these quilting functions, but her stitches had to pass their critical eye, too.

Apparently her stitches met with their approval. Their eyes finally were drawn to the squares in front of them and they began to sew. Conversations could be heard all over the room, but Alice was the only person who talked with Emily.

Emily decided to try another daring adventure and proceeded to engage Suzie in conversation. This adventure failed miserably, so she continued with her quilting. At Rosemary's suggestion, they broke for lunch. Most of the women went outside and sat under the shade of the big trees to eat their lunches. Much to Emily's surprise and delight, Rosemary Kirkland joined Alice and Emily as they sat down.

"I hope you don't mind my butting in on the two of you." Rosemary's voice was friendly.

"No," Alice said. "We're delighted to have your company."

The ladies opened their lunches and began to chat. It seemed a big revival was planned for the month of June and Alice was in charge of arranging the meals to feed the pastor and visiting preacher. Emily gathered that the church family took turns feeding the ministers during the two weeks of the revival.

Emily had sat quietly during the ladies' conversation and Rosemary finally addressed her. "Alice tells me you're from Abilene. I've never been that far west. It must have been a hard decision for you to leave your home and come so far to start life all over."

"It was a very hard decision. One I didn't take lightly. But it seemed like the right thing to do at the time," Emily told her.

"Did you grow up in Abilene?" Rosemary inquired.

"No. I grew up in El Paso. My husband and I moved to Abilene about ten years ago. When he was killed, I just stayed on there. It's been home to me for quite a while," Emily confided.

Rosemary had a natural way of making folks feel comfortable. Emily hadn't meant to share so much of her personal life with her so soon, but she was glad she had.

Rosemary continued. "You certainly were young to be left a widow. It must have been hard on you. I'm sure your family would have loved to have you move back to El Paso."

"I didn't have any family left there. My mother died when I was a baby, so it had just been me and my dad. Daddy died right before Jim and I moved to Abilene." Emily couldn't believe she was sharing so much of her past with this woman. Before long she would be telling her the truth about her relationship with Steven.

The trio looked up from where they were sitting and noticed that most of the ladies had gone back into the church. Deciding that they had better do the same, they picked up their belongings and went inside.

&

The quilting bee ended about two o'clock. As Alice and Emily were getting ready to drive off, Rosemary yelled for them to wait. Running out to the buggy, she said, "Emily, that big white house you see over there, that's the parsonage. I want you to come and visit me anytime. I would truly love to be your friend."

Emily found it difficult to respond. She felt the tears welling up inside. "Thank you. I would love to be your friend, Rosemary."

"I'll be looking for you to stop by before long," Rosemary called as the two drove away.

Alice waited a few minutes before she said anything. "Emily, Rosemary is very serious. She wants to be your friend. She's a wonderful person, and I figure a lonely person at times. You may have noticed she and Brother Kirkland have no children, so I'm sure she gets lonely. She tries to keep busy with church activities, and she's always the first one there during an illness or a crisis. You'd do well to cultivate her friendship."

"I could tell that she's a very special person. I hope we can become good friends. I think it might take a while before anyone else wants to call me their friend. The other ladies didn't overwhelm me with their eagerness to get to know me."

"Give them time. They're all nice ladies, just prone to be a little gossipy and nosy. They'll come around once they get to know you."

&

The next day, Steven rode into Tyler and went directly to the bank, where he was shown into Calvin Meyers's office. Calvin was president of the bank and probably one of the most influential citizens in town.

"Steven Barnes, I'm glad you're back. It sure is good to see you," Calvin greeted as he extended his hand.

"It's good to see you, Calvin. I just need to know what the finances look like for the farm."

"It's in good shape. Just like the last report I sent you. Actually you may not have gotten that report. I mailed it a little over a month ago, so you'd probably left. I'll show you my copy of it." Calvin pulled a pad out of his desk and handed it to Steven.

"Thanks. I also want to tell you how much I appreciate you looking after things all that time I was gone." Steven looked over the figures on the pad Calvin handed him. "Things are in much better shape than I'd hoped. Looks like the place did much better without me around."

"You wait just a minute. You might not have been here, but you had a lot to do with the success of that farm," Calvin quickly pointed out. "When you left and stopped by here and appointed me guardian of your place and your family, I took that job very seriously. I've known you all your life. We grew up in the same community, and I knew if you were leaving you had good reason. Not a month went by that you didn't send money to care for your family. You had a big part in how well the place did."

"Oh, I know I sent money. Anybody could do that. I wasn't here for my family. I should have come home."

"Yeah, you should have come home. But I know better than anyone why you didn't. If you had left Rebecca in charge of things, you wouldn't have had anything to come home to. That woman could go through money faster than anyone I've ever seen." Calvin shook his head. "I also know she made your life miserable after you bought the farm. She sure was good at pouring on the charm for everyone else, though. After you left, she played the part of deserted female to the hilt."

"I did desert her. She had a right to play that part. When I left I only planned to stay gone just long enough to get us back on our feet financially. But as time went by, I couldn't bring myself to come back. I felt like such a failure. Not only as a farmer, but as a husband and father, too."

"When you wrote and asked me to find someone to share crop

or rent the land, I knew then you weren't coming home," Calvin confessed.

"You really picked wisely when you chose Clyde Bentley to farm the place."

"I talked to Clyde, and he agreed to do it and to teach the boys to farm so they could eventually take over. Clyde is your friend, Steven. He knew what Rebecca was really like, too. He could see how she rode you and never let you forget how you dragged her to that godforsaken place."

"Look, Becky's not all to blame here. I knew what she was like when I married her. I should have never taken her from the life she was accustomed to. She never wanted to be a farmer's wife. The farm was my dream. And I couldn't even hold on to it," Steven sadly admitted. "There is something I don't understand, though."

"What's that?" Calvin asked.

"Matt told me the other day that they never heard from me after I left. That's just not true. In the beginning, I wrote to Becky regularly. I didn't write so much the last couple of years, but I did at first. Now why would Matt think I didn't keep in touch with them?"

"I'm sure Becky planned it that way. Most anybody you ask will say she never said an unkind word about you after you left. She got more sympathy that way, and everyone thought she was a martyr." Calvin paused a moment. "Now she talked a different story to me. She didn't like having to come to me for money, and she called you some rather choice names in this office. As for the kids, she just let them think you left without a word, and that she didn't know where you were."

"She always knew how to get in touch with me. I have her letters to prove it." Steven sighed.

"You better hold on to those letters. You may be forced to prove it to your kids some day." Calvin grinned just a little as he asked, "Tell me about this new Mrs. Barnes I've been hearing about."

"And what have you been hearing?"

"Gossip is that she's the reason you didn't come home. Most folks have you living in sin with her for the past five years," Calvin informed him.

"Boy, they couldn't be farther from the truth on that one." Steven sighed again. "I don't care what anyone else thinks, but I'll tell you what really happened."

"You don't have to. You know I don't believe rumors," Calvin assured him.

"I know I don't have to, but I want to. I really need to talk to someone about this. A couple of days after I got your letter about Becky's death and about the kids, I went into the café where Emily worked. I used to go in there whenever I'd go to town. We were acquaintances, that's all. We'd pass the time of day, and she always had a smile for everyone who came in. Anyway, that day I just asked her to marry me. Actually I made her a business proposition. I knew she was a good, God-fearing woman, and I explained my situation to her. I told her this would be a marriage in name only. She accepted. I don't know why, but she said yes. I knew Becky would want the kids raised by someone like her."

"Are you sure you asked her to marry you because Becky would want the kids raised by someone like her? Or do you want the kids raised by someone like her?"

"I was sure at first now I don't know. She is a remarkable woman." Steven smiled as he thought about Emily. "I have to stand firm, though. I can't be a husband to anyone. I'm no good at that job."

Calvin frowned. "Steven, you made some mistakes. We all make mistakes. You can't beat yourself up forever over the past. The past is gone and you can't do anything about it. You can, however, do something about the present and possibly make the future better for yourself and your family. Don't throw your chance for happiness away. You deserve to be happy."

The men sat in silence for a short while. Steven was thinking about what Calvin had just said. He didn't feel he deserved to be happy. He had been a lousy husband. Becky had told him that often enough. He knew he would never be father of the year, either, but he could keep his children fed, clothed, with a roof over their heads. He would expect nothing for himself. He would have to pay for his mistakes.

Calvin interrupted his thoughts. "As for you not being a good husband, well, I thought it took two to make or break a marriage. I know you did your best. Maybe if you would have had more support from Becky, things would have been different. Look, Steven, you made some mistakes, but God forgives. All you have to do is ask for His forgiveness. He'll wipe the slate clean for you if you'll let Him. He'll allow you to forgive yourself, too."

"Calvin, I messed my life up, and now I've got to live with it. I think God gave up on me a long time ago. Thanks for the sermon and everything else." Steven stood and extended his hand to Calvin.

As Calvin shook Steven's hand, he replied, "Just remember, I'm your friend. I'm here if and when you need me." He smiled. "I'm gonna come out to your place one of these days and meet that remarkable woman that's your wife in name only."

Steven shot him a half grin as he turned to go. He had one more stop to make before he started back to the farm—the judge's office, where he needed to fix out a paper on the kids just as he'd told Emily he'd do. He had broken a lot of promises in the past, but from now on he would do his best to keep all promises he made, starting with this one to protect Emily.

Afterward, in no big hurry to get home, Steven kept the horse at a slow trot. His mind was spinning as thoughts of Emily filled his head. He had done remarkably well until now at keeping her at a safe distance; he couldn't start thinking of her as his wife. He couldn't fail at marriage twice.

Feeling the sunshine warm on his back and smelling the clean fresh air lifted his spirits a little. "The picnic the other day was really nice," he thought out loud. He could picture Emily as she came out to the field with the basket. It was such a relaxing moment, and so peaceful. Emily seemed to have a way of making things peaceful for him.

"Stop it, Steven," he said to himself. "You can't do this to yourself. She's just here to help with the children and take care of the house. She never agreed to be your wife. You've got to remember that!"

The other thing nagging at him was what Calvin had said about the Lord forgiving him and allowing him to forgive himself. He just couldn't see how that was possible. He had made such a mess of things, no one could forgive him. His kids certainly hadn't, and God

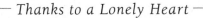

couldn't, either. Maybe if he worked hard enough and the farm continued to have success, maybe he could earn his children's forgiveness. But at this point he just wasn't good enough to be in God's presence. He had no right to ask God for anything.

*O*n Sunday after church, Alice approached Emily. "Would you consider having the ministers over for a meal during the revival?" she asked.

"Oh, Alice, I don't know. Our meal table is still a battlefield. I sure wouldn't want a preacher hit by a stray bullet."

"Just think about it. I have one spot left and I can't seem to get anyone to fill it. It's the noon meal on the first Friday. The visiting preacher is coming alone, so you would just have him, Rosemary, and Brother Kirkland. Maybe you could talk it over with Steven."

"I'll do my best. How soon do you have to know?"

"You can let me know Wednesday at prayer meeting. The revival starts next week. If I don't get someone else to take that spot, then I'll have to feed them three times instead of two."

It seemed silly not to be able to invite guests to your home. But Emily still didn't feel like it was her home. She took care of the house and prepared the meals, but she didn't feel at home. She would talk to Steven, but Alice hadn't given her much time.

The children were all in bed or at least in their rooms. The house was quiet, but Emily wasn't ready to turn in. She slipped out on the porch and sat down in the swing. Nature's symphony was in fine form that evening. The crickets and frogs appeared to be having a competition to discover who could sing the loudest.

The sound of Steven's monotone whistle grew louder, and Emily looked up to see him walk around the corner. He jumped when he saw her sitting there.

"I'm sorry if I scared you," she apologized.

"I just wasn't expecting anyone to be out here this time of night," he said. Sitting down on the edge of the porch, he remarked, "The breeze sure is nice tonight."

"It certainly is."

Steven gave her a long look, and Emily caught a glimpse of something in his expression, something she could put no name to. He wiped his forehead, as though he were suddenly hot. The evening was rapidly getting warm, Emily thought as she looked at Steven sideways. She was suddenly very aware of every little movement he made; she fought a sudden crazy yearning to be held close to him in his arms. The air that was once cool and inviting now seemed a little stifling.

She cleared her throat. Someone had to break this spell before it was too late. "Steven, I need to ask a favor of you."

"What is it?"

"Alice asked if I would have the preachers over for a meal during the revival. I would really like to do it for her. She's been so kind to me, I would like to help her out with this."

"Emily, you don't have to ask my permission to have people over. This is your home, too, you know. It may be a little awkward, but this family should be able to behave for one meal."

"Thank you very much, Steven. I'll let Alice know."

This was a side of Steven Emily hadn't seen. Being sensitive was not a trait he had been putting on display recently. It was very nice, very nice indeed. She noticed that the air hadn't cooled off at all.

"I guess I'd better turn in. It's getting late," Emily said as she rose from the swing. She felt weak in the knees.

"Good night," Steven whispered as she walked by him.

"Good night," she returned.

ॐ

The revival began. The visiting preacher, Brother Lemons, was a dynamic speaker, and the brush arbor that had been built for the revival was filled every night. The whole community seemed to have turned out—except for Steven. He drove them to the services and picked them up, but he never stayed. Emily was very disappointed. On Friday morning, Steven told the children that the ministers and Rosemary were coming for dinner. He instructed them to be on their best behavior.

The clergy and Rosemary arrived and were shown into the living room, where Steven played the gracious host. Emily was very proud of him.

"Whatever you're fixing smells delicious," Rosemary said, coming into the kitchen.

"It's ham. I hope you haven't eaten it every day this week."

"As a matter of fact, we haven't had it at all. It will be a welcome change. Although all the meals have been great," Rosemary acknowledged. "Sarah, the table looks lovely."

"Sarah is my right hand around here," Emily said, giving Sarah a smile. "I think everything is ready. Sarah, do you want to ring the dinner bell for the boys while I go get the menfolk?"

The meal was not as bad as Emily had feared. The children were quiet but well behaved. Brother Lemons was a wonderful conversationalist and drew everyone in at one time or another.

After the meal, Brother Lemons turned to Steven and commented, "I don't believe I've seen you at the service this week, Steven."

Emily almost dropped her cup of coffee. She couldn't believe the minister was so blunt. She wondered what Steven was going to say.

"No, sir. You haven't. I don't go to church much. Brother Tom can testify to that," Steven chuckled. Brother Lemons's question didn't seem to offend him at all.

"I want to ask a favor of you. You've shared your home and the bounty from your hard work with me, and I want to share my service with you. Actually it's not my service, it's the Lord's, but He and I want you to come. Will you do that for me?" Brother Lemons was looking directly at Steven, waiting for an answer.

"I'm not gonna lie to you and tell you I'll come. But I will think about it."

☙

Emily was glad to have some time alone with Rosemary. They had become good friends over the past weeks, and Emily had been able to share her heart with Rosemary.

"Tell me, are things any better? Steven seemed real relaxed at dinner," Rosemary said, as she and Emily washed the dinner dishes.

"There's been no major breakthrough, but there hasn't been as much quarreling, either. Steven was very nice about me having you over to eat. He really surprised me. I've never seen him talk to anyone as much as he did at lunch with Brother Lemons and Brother Tom," Emily confided.

"I really hope things work out with the two of you. I think you could make a good life for yourselves and the kids. I know you're in love with him. And from what I saw today, I think he may be falling in love with you."

Emily's stomach flip-flopped. She carefully dried the soap from her hands before she answered. "What makes you think I'm in love with Steven?"

"The way you look when you talk about him. You may not realize it yourself but you love him."

Emily poured them both a glass of lemonade and sat down at the table. "Oh, I realize it all right. I just don't like to admit it to myself, much less anyone else." Emily took a sip of her lemonade, then continued. "At first I thought my feelings were just because it had been so long since I had a man in my life. You know the kind of feelings I'm talking about."

Rosemary laughed. "Yes, I know. Just because I'm married to the preacher doesn't mean I don't experience those kind of feelings. We are very much in love with each other, and we are very loving."

"I tell myself I shouldn't have those feelings for Steven. I know we're married, but yet we aren't. I also realize that it is probably next to impossible for anything to change between us. He has built a wall so high and so thick around himself that no one can get through." Emily sighed.

"I wouldn't be so sure about that. I noticed him looking at you a couple of times when he thought no one would see, especially you, and what I saw has possibilities. I say the man is falling in love with you. He probably won't admit it even to himself right now, but he certainly has feelings for you," Rosemary told her friend.

"Steven is carrying around a big load of problems that he has to work out before he can love anyone. Right now he can't even let anyone love him," Emily commented as she prepared a tray with glasses and a pitcher of lemonade. "We'd better carry some of this lemonade out to the men."

They visited with the men on the porch, and just before the visitors left, Brother Lemons once again asked Steven to the services. Steven still wouldn't commit himself; he just smiled.

"I'll be praying for you, Steven," Brother Lemons called as he mounted the wagon.

ह∾

That evening Steven drove the family to the service as usual. He dropped them off and left, but before he got very far down the road, he abruptly stopped the wagon. He kept hearing a little voice telling him to turn the wagon around and return to the meeting. The little voice was insistent. It nagged him until he finally obeyed.

He returned to the meeting, but he parked the wagon out of sight. He stood under a tree near the arbor, where he could still hear and see but yet remain undetected. There was singing and shouting the likes of which he hadn't heard in years. When Brother Lemons started to speak, Steven stood spellbound.

The preacher spoke of forgiveness. He said that God would forgive all our sins. We don't have to clean ourselves up for God—God does the cleaning for us. His message said all a person has to do is to ask God's forgiveness and He gives it freely. God will take our burdens and carry them for us. We don't have to be weighted down anymore.

Steven stood there thinking. Could this be true? Would God forgive him for all he had done? This preacher had said almost the same thing Calvin had told him that day in the bank. Could it be that someone was trying to get through to him?

The final hymn was being sung. "Just As I Am" was ringing through the night. The words of the song were almost the same as the preacher had spoken: God takes you just as you are. Steven wanted forgiveness. He wanted to know peace in his life. He had lived with this guilt long enough, and he didn't want it any longer.

Steven fell to his knees right there beside the tree. He prayed, "God, forgive me for all my sins and my mistakes. I want peace in my life. I want You in my life." That was all he could get out. The tears began to flow like rain washing his soul clean.

The service ended and Steven made his way to the wagon. A part of him wanted to shout from the rooftops what had happened. Another part wanted to keep silent and enjoy the peaceful feeling for a while. The silent part won.

ॐ

The next week everything was the same around the farm except for the look on Steven's face. Ever since Friday night, he'd been wearing a peaceful look that Emily had never seen before. He even smiled occasionally, which was a rather unusual condition for him.

Sarah noticed the change in her father. "What's happened to Daddy?" she asked Emily. "He doesn't look so unhappy anymore."

"I'm not sure," Emily answered. "But I noticed something different about him, too. I think maybe he has asked Jesus to come into his life."

Sarah looked confused. "Wasn't Jesus his friend before? I thought Jesus was everyone's friend."

"He is," Emily assured her. "But you've heard the preacher talk about forgiveness and asking Jesus into your heart. Jesus doesn't just force Himself into your life. You have to ask Him to come in. A person also has to ask forgiveness for their sins and wrongdoings before Jesus can forgive them."

"And you think that's what Daddy did? He asked God to forgive him for his sins?" Sarah puzzled. "Did Daddy do something real bad?"

"No, sweetheart, I don't think your daddy did anything real bad. I think he just had a lot of problems on his mind. And I think he thought he did some things he shouldn't have done."

"I sure hope he feels a lot better now. Maybe I'll ask him if Jesus is his friend now."

"Maybe we had better wait until he feels like telling us about it. It may be something he wants to keep to himself for a little while," Emily said.

"I don't understand. If Jesus is his friend now, shouldn't he want to tell people about it? The preacher said that you should tell people about Jesus being your friend."

This was turning into one of those discussions with questions that could become difficult to answer to a child's satisfaction. But Emily would try.

"Some people have a hard time talking about their friendship with God. It's much easier for them to show other people by the way they live their lives. You know—by going to church, helping other people, loving their family. Even by the look on their face. You and I noticed a different look on your daddy's face."

"Yeah, but Daddy doesn't go to church."

The questions continued to get tougher. "Well, it's not absolutely necessary for a Christian to go to church. They should go so they can fellowship with other Christians and renew their faith. You know church for a Christian is like food for your soul. You have to eat food to stay alive, and if you go to church, it helps you grow stronger in your faith."

"Well, shouldn't Daddy go to church so he can grow stronger?" Sarah continued her inquisition. "Will his faith die if he doesn't go?"

Emily was going to have to come up with some answers that didn't lead to more questions. This child's curiosity was getting the best of her.

"As I said, church is good for you, but you don't have to go. You can read your Bible and pray without going to church. That can help you grow as a Christian also."

"I've never seen Daddy read his Bible and he only prays real short prayers at the table." Looking thoughtful, Sarah quietly added, "I wonder if Daddy has a Bible?"

"It isn't necessary for someone else to see you read your Bible or hear you pray. It's only necessary for God to see and hear you."

Sarah seemed satisfied with Emily's answers for the time being, but Emily was afraid a lot more of these endless question sessions lay ahead.

&

Steven drove the wagon to service every night the next week but left as usual, or so it appeared. He would park the wagon out of sight and walk back and stand in the shadow of the trees.

Friday night came, and the revival would be over after the service that night. When Emily walked out to get into the wagon, she noticed Steven had on a clean shirt and pants. He had never cleaned up to drive them to church before. Emily prayed that this was a sign that he would join them for the service that night.

Arriving at church, Steven helped the women from the wagon. He then offered Emily his arm. The duo walked to the brush arbor, with the younger children following close behind them. A large crowd had already gathered, which meant the back pews were filled. As the procession marched down the aisle, all heads turned, and a hush fell over the congregation.

Emily had been in a state of shock from the moment Steven had offered her his arm. She realized that she had a very tight grip on him, but she was afraid to let go for fear of falling over.

Steven stopped at a pew close to the front, and everyone sat down. Emily was finally able to take a deep breath, but she was still unable to speak. She just looked up at Steven and smiled. This was the first glimmer of hope that someday they might actually become a family.

Brother Lemons preached a powerful message that night. He talked about the meaning of families and the obligation of the father to be the spiritual leader. Emily saw that Steven listened intently, a puzzled frown on his face.

≈

When the service ended and the invitation was given, Steven fought an incredible battle. He felt the pull to go to the altar and confess before God and this company his newfound hope. But his pride and the devil were standing in his way. Finally, just before the last verse of the closing hymn, he made the short walk to the altar. He fell on his knees, and the ministers joined him.

"Thank you for caring enough to pray for me," Steven said as he embraced Brother Lemons at the altar.

"Steven, my boy, I'm not the only one that cares for you. You will never know how many prayers have gone up for you," Brother Lemons informed him. "Although your battle is just starting. I know you still have a lot of things to get straight at home. It won't be easy and it won't happen over night. You will have to be persistent, even when you feel all is lost. Just remember, in the end the victory will be worth the battle. My prayers will remain with you and your family. Also remember, Brother Kirkland will be here to help when you need him. And you will need him." Brother Lemons smiled. "So be man enough to ask him to be your friend and to allow you to cry on his shoulder."

After the service, most of the folks made their way to Steven and shook his hand. He was welcomed warmly back into the fold by the majority, although there were obviously a few skeptics in the crowd.

The ride home that evening was very quiet. Steven didn't think he had ever seen the stars shine brighter. The moon lit up the way like a brilliant torch. It was a grand and glorious evening! If only this feeling could last forever. He felt as though all of his problems had melted away. That of course was not true. Four of his problems were riding in the wagon with him, while two walked home. He would just have to pray for God's guidance on how to make things right with his family.

Unable to sleep that night, Steven walked out onto the porch and found Emily sitting in the porch swing.

"It's beautiful tonight. Don't you agree?" Emily asked.

"One of the prettiest I've seen in a very long time," Steven confessed.

"Your decision tonight was the answer to a lot of prayers. I'm real happy for you," Emily said as her eyes filled with tears.

Steven wanted to share his contentment with this woman who shared his name. But no matter how much he wanted to, he wouldn't allow himself to do it.

"Thank you," was all he managed to respond

$$\left(7\right)$$

*I*t was a hot and humid summer day and nothing pressing had to be done. After breakfast Steven told the twins that if they would help him dig up some worms, they would head to the creek for a little fishing. He had decided that a fishing trip might be a way to start winning over the twins.

Emily had never witnessed so much excitement from the two little boys. They grabbed their hats and headed to the barn to fetch a shovel. It was difficult for Emily to picture so much enthusiasm over little crawly things.

Watching the three of them almost running down the lane lifted Emily's heart. She was glad Steven was finally making an effort to get to know his children.

"Since the boys are fishing today, you and I should think of something special to do," Emily told Sarah.

"What could we do? I don't like to fish," Sarah informed her.

"I don't care much for fishing, either." Emily smiled. "I was thinking more of something we girls enjoy doing. Why don't we look through all that material in the trunk and see if we can't find enough to make you new curtains for your room."

"Really? You mean I can help make them?"

"Sure. I was about your age when I started to learn to sew," Emily said.

"Sarah, do you know why your mother had all of this material?" Emily questioned, as they looked through the trunk.

"Somebody sent it to her. Every so often a big package of material would come. I asked her who sent it and she just said it didn't matter."

"Why didn't your mother make it up into clothes?" Emily asked.

"I don't know. She made us new dresses at Easter and the boys a new shirt sometimes. I guess she didn't like to sew very much. Now what about my curtains?" Sarah's tone told Emily she didn't want to answer any more questions.

Emily removed one of the worn curtains from the window to use as a pattern and let Sarah cut the first panel as she watched. Sarah was almost as excited about her curtains as she had been months ago about her Easter frock. They cut and stitched until time for dinner. Sarah rang the dinner bell for Matt and Mark, but the two older boys never came in.

ॐ

After the fishermen returned with a bountiful catch, Sarah went out on the back porch and found her father washing up. Grabbing his arm, she cried, "Daddy, come to my room. You've got to see what Emily and I did today."

"Let me dry my hands," he answered, taking the towel from the hook.

"We made new curtains, Daddy, see," Sarah instructed as the two entered her room. "Aren't they beautiful? Emily let me sew a whole bunch on them."

"They certainly are pretty," Steven said, looking into the innocent face of his daughter. "Looks like the two of you did a terrific job."

Steven smiled at his little girl as she took his hand and started pulling him back toward the kitchen.

"Daddy likes my curtains, Emily," Sarah announced.

"They're really nice," Steven said, then asked, "None of you would happen to know where my horse is, would you? It's not in the barn."

"Maybe the boys let it out to pasture," Emily suggested.

"Where are Matt and Mark?" Steven asked.

"We haven't seen them all day," Emily responded. "They didn't come in for dinner and they haven't been around the house all afternoon."

When the family sat down for supper, Matt and Mark still hadn't arrived. They waited a while and then started eating without them. They were just finishing their meal when the two strays wandered in.

They had begun to help themselves to the food on the table when Steven asked, "Do you boys know what time meals are served around here?"

"Yes, sir," Mark replied.

"When the dinner bell rings you know to drop what you're doing and come in. Do you not?"

"We didn't hear the bell," was Matt's reply.

Steven asked them where they had been and if they had taken his horse. The boys gave limited responses to his inquiries and he informed them that if they made it a practice to be late for meals, they would go hungry.

"The meals are prepared and on the table on time. The least you can do is show up on time to eat them," Steven stated firmly.

The boys offered no response to his proclamation. They continued to fill their mouths and their stomachs.

ẽ❧

As Steven relaxed on the porch after supper, Sarah came out to join him. She had her hands behind her back as she approached her father.

"Daddy, would you read me a story?" she asked in her sweetest tone.

Delighted, Steven responded, "I guess so. Do you have a particular story in mind?"

Sarah held her hand out to her father as she said, "I'd like to hear a story out of here."

Steven took the book from her and smiled as he read the words "Holy Bible" on the front cover. "What story would you like to hear from this book?"

"It doesn't matter to me. You pick one," Sarah told him.

"Let's go into the living room, where we can sit by the lamp to read," Steven suggested.

As he sat himself in the large rocking chair, Sarah climbed into his lap. He opened the Bible to First Corinthians, the thirteenth chapter, and began to read. As he read the words of the chapter on love, a warmth began to fill his being, yet a sadness lingered there also.

Sarah had laid her head on his shoulder. He hadn't held this child in his arms since she was two years old. Tears falling from his eyes, he put the Bible on the table and hugged his daughter.

Seeing his tears, Sarah asked, "Daddy, why are you crying?" Getting no response, she added, "I love you, Daddy."

As she laid her head on his shoulder, he softly kissed the top of her head and whispered, "I love you, too, Sarah." He continued to hold her until she fell asleep in his arms.

This man who had been so unfeeling, so isolated within himself, had finally let someone into his world. Sarah lay limp and peaceful in her father's lap. Apparently, she had finally gotten what she had wanted: a daddy. The thought made new tears prick Steven's eyes.

"I'll get her dressed for bed if you'll take her to her room," Emily offered as she walked into the living room.

Steven smiled at her and stood with Sarah in his arms. He carried her to her bedroom and laid her gently on her bed. For a moment he looked down at the angelic face. He could never make up for all the years he had missed, but he would try to make the future the best that he could.

Leaving Sarah's room, Steven went upstairs and found the twins wrestling on the floor of their room.

"It's time for you boys to be in bed," he said.

"Yes, sir, we were headed that way. Just got a little sidetracked," John confessed.

"Well, save some of that energy for tomorrow. I need you two to help me in the fields," Steven told them.

"You mean we can go to the fields with you?" Luke asked. "We never got to do that before. Matt always said we were in the way."

Steven leaned over to tuck the boys in and assured them, "You won't be in my way. I think it's time you boys started to learn how to farm. Now get to sleep." He blew out the lamp on his way out the door.

Steven paused a moment in front of Matt and Mark's door, but he didn't feel he would be welcome in that room. *God,* he prayed, *please show me how I can win their respect. Maybe even their love.*

ॐ

Emily was in the swing when Steven stepped out on the porch. "Get everyone tucked in?" she asked.

"Well, three of them. The other two will have to tuck themselves in," he responded.

"Oh, they'll come around," she assured him. "You just have to be patient with them."

"I have a feeling those two will push patience to the limit. I'm not sure Job could have survived them. They make pestilence look pleasing."

"Steven, they're not that bad. They just have a lot of anger built up inside. We just have to get through that wall of anger and then we'll find the young men inside."

"I think anger is too mild a word. Hate seems to fit better," said Steven.

They sat in silence for a while before Emily bid him good night and went inside. The same little voice that had made him stop the wagon and go back to the camp meeting started nagging him again. This time it was talking about Emily. It told him he was an idiot to treat such a special lady this way. It told him that he needed to work on his relationship with Emily before it was too late.

It was a very persistent little voice, but for tonight he managed to ignore it, or at least put it off. He kept telling himself, and the little voice, that it was much more important to get everything straightened out with his kids first. Steven's experience told him that this would not be the last time he heard the not-so-gentle nudging from inside his soul.

ॐ

After breakfast the twins left for the fields with Steven, and Sarah ran out to play. Emily found herself alone in a house where she still felt like a guest. There had to be something she could do to make it feel more like her home.

She decided to start with the living room. Rolling up her sleeves, she gave the room a good scrubbing. Then she rearranged the furniture. The windows were covered with worn shades, and she decided to make curtains. She would start on that right after dinner.

After dinner, Emily set about her task. If she worked really hard, she could get most of the curtains finished so she could surprise everyone after supper.

Using the material from Rebecca's trunk, she made simple, straight curtains. She devised a way to hang them on the windows with some nails and heavy string. She made tie backs so she could pull the curtains open and let the light into the room. Pleased with her handiwork, Emily could hardly wait for everyone to come home.

Emily had supper ready when the family came in. As everyone started eating, Sarah commented, "I like the new curtains in the living room and the way you did the furniture."

"Thank you, Sarah," Emily responded.

With a look that could kill and a voice to match, Matt asked, "What did you do to the living room?"

"I just rearranged the furniture and made some curtains," Emily replied.

Matt jumped up from the table and ran to the living room. Angrily, he began to rip the curtains from the windows. Steven went after him and grabbed his son by the shoulders.

"Matt! Stop this!" he demanded. "What do you think you're doing?"

"What gives her the right to change my mother's house? She has no right to be here at all, and for that matter neither do you! Why don't you just get out?" Anger and hatred flowed from the bitter young man.

Without thinking, Steven spun Matt around and almost hit him, but Emily grabbed his arm before he could deliver a blow.

Looking Matt in the eyes, he demanded, "You will apologize to Emily for this outburst and for destroying her hard work."

"I'll never apologize to her!" Matt shouted as he struggled to release himself from his father's grip.

Steven took Matt by the collar and escorted the young man to the barn where the razor strap should be hanging.

&

After Steven and Matt left the house, Emily began to pick up the curtains. Matt had only torn them off two of the five windows, but as Emily picked up the last panel, she sat down on the floor and began to sob. She couldn't hold back the tears any longer. Tonight was the last straw. She didn't know if she could go on, or even if she wanted to.

Sarah walked over to Emily and put her little arms around her shoulders. "Don't cry, Emily. I'll help you put the curtains back up."

Emily looked up and saw the twins standing before her. "Yeah, we'll help, too."

These precious little children! She knew she had to keep trying for their sakes. Drying her eyes on her apron, she said, "Thank you, all of you. I would really appreciate your help."

Evaluating the damage, Emily realized all Matt had done was break the string that had been supporting the curtains. They were easily fixed and reattached to the windows.

"What do you think Daddy's gonna to do to Matt?" Sarah asked.

"He's gonna belt him good," Luke proclaimed.

"Now, kids, you have to leave the discipline up to your father. Matt behaved very badly and your father will talk to him about it," Emily said.

"Yeah, he'll talk to him with a belt," John chimed in.

About that time the back door opened and in walked Matt, followed closely by his father. Matt did not give the impression that he had enjoyed his conversation with his father. Steven stopped and washed his hands before he entered the kitchen.

Matt was headed out the doorway leading into the hall when Steven's voice stopped him. "Matt, just where do you think you're going?"

With a stubborn cutting edge to his voice he replied, "To my room, sir!"

"I don't think so. My memory appears to be better than yours. I think you've forgotten to do something."

"And what might that be, sir?"

"Matt, do we need to make another trip out to the barn to refresh your memory?"

Giving his father an "I'll get you for this one day" look, Matt turned to Emily and bitterly spit out, "Sorry."

It was apparent to everyone that he really wasn't sorry. But he did say it. Clearly, Matt was in a power struggle with his father. Whether Steven wanted it that way or not, he would just have to prove he was man enough to handle the job of father.

ॐ

Steven came around the corner of the house and spotted Emily sitting in the porch swing as usual. He sat down on the edge of the porch.

They sat for a long time in silence before Steven finally spoke. "I want to apologize for what Matt did tonight. The room looks really nice."

"There's no need for you to apologize. You didn't do anything. I should have been more sensitive to their feelings. I should have realized how hard it is for them to have someone else come into their mother's home and take over."

Steven couldn't hear her crying, but he could see her body tremble in the moonlight. "Emily, you've bent over backwards to be sensitive to everyone and not hurt anyone's feelings. This is your home now. Rebecca doesn't live here anymore."

Emily's sobs seemed to deepen with every word Steven said. Crying women had never been a specialty of his, and Steven didn't know what he should do. What he wanted to do was take her into his arms and hold her, but he couldn't allow that. Instead, he reached into his pocket, pulled out his handkerchief, walked over, and handed it to her.

Emily took it and tried to dry her eyes, but it was no use; the tears wouldn't stop flowing. The main valve had been turned on and there was no way to shut it off this time. Steven stood helpless. She looked like a child sitting there. What had he done to this lady? He had brought her from her well-known world to a world that was strange to them both. He could stand it no longer; sitting down beside her in the swing, he took her into his arms. He held her while the rest of the water flowed over the dam. He could feel the dampness of her tears through his shirt. He had no words of comfort; he just held her.

Neither of them knew how long they sat there. Emily's tears eventually ceased, but Steven continued to hold her. She finally lifted her head and looked into his eyes. "Thank you. I needed that."

"I didn't do anything," he replied gruffly.

"You did more than you'll ever know."

Looking into her eyes, she looked so helpless and vulnerable. He wanted to kiss her, but before he gave in to the urge, he stood up and left her sitting alone in the swing.

"If you're feeling better, I'm going to make one last round to check on things and then I think I'll turn in," he stated.

"You go ahead. I'm okay. I'll turn in soon," she told him.

Steven walked off. There was nothing to check on; he just needed to walk some of this tension off. He could hear his little voice in the distance, like it was coming up behind him. He turned and said out loud, "Now you just wait. Don't start with me tonight. I still need to take care of my children first before I can think of myself and my needs." Why had he said that? Was he beginning to need Emily?

His little voice couldn't help but answer his question and it stopped Steven in his tracks, for it was as audible as if someone was standing right there. "Yes, Steven. You are beginning to need Emily, and furthermore, you're in love with her." His little voice had a lot of nerve to tell him something like that and then just leave, but that's exactly what it did, and Steven was left alone with his thoughts.

ॐ

Emily found it difficult to fall asleep that night. Her mind was swirling and her heart was pounding. It had felt so good and so right to be in Steven's arms. She was proud of the way he was getting close to his children, the younger ones at least. If they could get close as a couple, maybe they could become a real family. She was in love with the man and there was nothing she could do to change that now.

$$8$$

*E*mily was in the midst of her morning chores as her mind replayed the events of the night before, over and over again.
That morning at breakfast Steven had acted no differently toward her. She didn't know what she had expected, maybe a smile.
There was nothing. She really needed to talk with someone. Maybe
she could visit Rosemary Kirkland this afternoon.

Steven had some work to do around the barn that afternoon, and
this gave Emily the perfect opportunity to visit Rosemary, as he would
be close in case the children needed anything.

Steven was repairing a harness when she entered the barn.
"Steven, I'm going to visit Rosemary Kirkland for a little while," Emily
informed him.

"Okay," he said. "I'll hitch the buggy for you."

Steven hitched his little gray mare to the buggy and brought it
around to the front of the house, where Emily waited. He took her
arm and helped her up into the seat.

As she started to drive away, he looked at her and smiled. "You be
careful."

It was such a little thing, such a common statement. But his smile
and his concern meant the world to Emily. She was a goner, and she
knew it.

Rosemary was sitting on her front porch shelling peas when Emily
arrived. Emily greeted her, then pulled up a chair and sat down.

"It's good to see you. What brings you up my way in the middle
of the week?" Rosemary asked.

"I just needed a little female conversation," Emily confided. "Have
you got another pan? I'll help you shell these peas while we talk."

Rosemary disappeared into the house and returned with a pan for Emily. Emily quickly filled it and began shelling the peas.

"Is there something special you wanted to talk about?" Rosemary asked.

Emily blushed as she spoke. "Oh, nothing special."

"Let me guess. Could the subject be about six-foot-three and weigh about 190 pounds? Tell me, has there been some new development?" Rosemary questioned.

"Am I so obvious? You always seem to know when Steven's on my mind."

"It's not that hard to figure out. I'd bet Steven's on your mind most of the time," Rosemary teased.

Emily blushed again. She told Rosemary about the events of the past few days, beginning with Steven's newfound affection toward Sarah and the twins. She ended with Matt's outrage the previous evening.

"It sounds as though Steven's beginning to take his role as a father seriously. I'm very happy to hear it," Rosemary noted. "I agree that he still has a long way to go before he wins over Matt and Mark, but I think he can do it. My question now is, has he started taking his role as a husband seriously?"

"I had a small glimmer of hope last night. I'm probably making too much out of it, but it really meant a lot to me at the time. After the fiasco ended and all the kids were in their rooms, I went out and sat in the porch swing. The whole evening had been a nightmare. I had only wanted to turn the house into a home and all I accomplished was to turn it into a battlefield again. Steven walked up and sat down on the porch." Emily paused for a moment; she didn't want to start crying now.

"He apologized for Matt's behavior and I told him he had nothing to apologize for. I should have been more sensitive of everyone's feelings. I know it's hard for the children having a stranger come into their mother's home and take over."

"You told Steven that you should have been more sensitive?" Rosemary wanted to know.

Emily nodded, then continued. "Steven tried to make me feel better by telling me that I'd tried to protect everyone's feelings and that it was my home and I could fix it like I wanted. He said Rebecca didn't live there anymore. Well, that's when I couldn't hold it in any longer. I sat there and cried like a baby. I was so embarrassed, but I couldn't do anything about it."

"You shouldn't have been embarrassed. Steven was right. It is your home now, not Rebecca's," Rosemary tried to comfort her friend.

"You're both wrong. Rebecca Barnes lives in every corner of that house. She lives in the faces of her children and she still occupies the place in Steven's heart that I'm rightfully entitled to. I didn't want to cry in front of him, but with every word he uttered I cried harder."

"What happened next?" Rosemary asked.

"Steven offered me his handkerchief, then he sat down beside me in the swing and held me in his arms until I finished crying. For just an instant I felt safe and secure and maybe a little loved." Emily had tears in her eyes once again.

"I don't think you're making too much of this. Steven has to care about you. If he didn't, he would have just let you cry alone. Tell me, how did he act this morning to you?"

"Like he always does. It was as though nothing had happened last night. But this afternoon when I left to come over here, he hitched the buggy for me. And when he helped me up onto the seat, he smiled and told me to be careful." Emily giggled. "Boy, I'm really grasping for straws now, aren't I?"

"Not really," Rosemary affirmed. "If it were anyone else smiling and telling you to be careful, I'd think nothing about it. But this comes from a man who, up until very recently, barely acknowledged you existed. Any small gesture becomes very significant when it comes from him. Now about his holding you last night—did he release you as soon as you stopped crying, and what happened when he did let you go?"

Emily thought a moment, then answered, "Well, actually he held me for a little while after my crying had stopped. And just for a moment, after he released his hold, I thought he was going to kiss me. But he didn't. He excused himself and left."

"That's very promising." Rosemary set down her pan of shelled peas. "Let's go have some lemonade and move this conversation into the kitchen."

Rosemary poured two glasses of lemonade and set a plate of cookies on the table. "I told you I saw something in Steven's eyes the day we had lunch with you," Rosemary said. "I really believe he's starting to have feelings for you but is afraid to act on them. I think maybe he's afraid of marriage."

She took a cookie, then continued. "Most folks around here thought Rebecca Barnes was wonderful, but I've got a hunch that all was not what it was made out to be. There was just something about her attitude. I heard her make a few comments about Steven that made me wonder if he didn't kind of have a rough time at home. It could be he feels like a failure as a husband and is afraid to try it again."

"Rosemary, how do you come up with all this insight on people? I know there's something in his past that's haunting him. And I know there was some reason why he didn't return home after he earned enough money to get the farm out of debt. But I just don't know what the answers to those questions are." Emily sipped her lemonade, then thoughtfully added, "If a man's happy at home, then why would he stay away for five years?"

"That's my point exactly. If Rebecca was such a wonderful wife, then why didn't her husband come home? Now either she wasn't so wonderful or he's just a scoundrel. I didn't know Steven before he left, but from what I've seen of him since his return, I don't think he's a scoundrel."

"Okay, so his marriage was far from perfect and he's afraid to try it again. So where does that leave me? Looks like my chances might be pretty slim." Emily sighed.

"Not necessarily. You know a horse can be a little skittish, but he can still be broken. You just have a fellow who's a little gun-shy, but he can be brought around with proper handling."

"Look, you're talking to the wrong woman. I'm about as inexperienced as they come at handling men," Emily confessed.

"You were married before, so you had to have won at least one man's heart. That makes you experienced. Anyway, mostly you just have to be yourself. Steven is falling for you already. You just have to give him a little push."

"And how do you suggest I push?"

"Take every opportunity when you're alone to flirt a little. Let the man know you're interested. He's probably afraid of rejection, so he won't make a move. Let him know in subtle little ways that he won't be rejected."

"Do you want me to throw myself at him?" Emily asked.

"No! You know how to flirt, surely. Just be extra nice to him. Give him the opening and see what happens. This man's your husband, not some total stranger."

"He's almost a total stranger. I know very little about him. And just because we have a piece of paper that says we're married doesn't mean we're husband and wife."

"Look, you'll figure out what to do as the opportunities present themselves. Just follow your instincts. Pray about it; I have a strong feeling that the Lord is on your side."

Emily heard the clock in the other room chime the hour. "I've got to go. It's almost suppertime. I didn't realize we'd talked so long. Rosemary, thank you for listening and for all your advice."

Rosemary stood and gave her friend a hug. "Everything is going to work out. You just wait and see. You two are in love and love always finds a way."

As Emily drove home she thought about Rosemary's advice. How could she flirt with Steven? She hadn't flirted in so long she was afraid she would make a fool of herself. Well, she would just play it by ear, and she knew praying about it certainly wouldn't hurt.

෫෨

It was a hot July evening and Emily really wanted to sit out in the porch swing, but this evening she was nervous. What if Steven was out there? How would she act? She went to her room, but it was too warm to go to bed. She peeked out the door before she walked out on the porch and saw no one. She eased onto the swing. Finally a little wind began to stir, and she relaxed until she heard that familiar whistle. But there was something a little different about the whistle this time. It was no longer monotone; Steven was actually whistling a tune.

"Sure feels hot this evening," Steven said as he sat down on the edge of the porch.

"Sure does," she replied. She hoped they were both talking about the weather. "How are the crops doing?"

"Pretty good, considering. The corn should be ready to gather next month. I'm gonna have the boys clean out the corn crib next week. Looks like we're gonna have a good year. We should sell enough cotton to take us through the winter and planting next year."

This was very nice, Emily thought. They were actually having a conversation. "The twins were really excited about helping you today, and Sarah's thrilled at the attention she's been getting from you."

"It feels good to be a father again. I didn't realize how much I'd missed them," Steven said. "I'd tried for so long not to think about the kids too often. Of course they have changed so much." His voice broke and he stopped talking.

Even in the moonlight, Emily could tell he was crying. She didn't know what to do. He might be embarrassed if he knew she could see his tears. "Steven, you have to put those years you were away behind you. You can't change the past, and you can't control the future. You just have the present, so make the best of the time you have now."

"I just wish there was something I could do about Matt and Mark. I wish they didn't hate me so much. Emily, what can I do to make things up to them?" Steven lifted his head and looked toward her.

Taken off guard by his question, she took a moment to respond. "Why don't you try sitting them down and talking to them. Just let them say what's on their minds and then you tell them what's on yours. Once everything is out in the open, maybe it won't look quite so bad and at least you'll know what you're dealing with."

"I don't know if I've got enough courage to sit down and talk to them face to face. There's so much anger there. It might be dangerous."

"Maybe you need a third party to be present. Someone who could be impartial. You might think about talking to Brother Kirkland.

Maybe he would sit down with the three of you or at least give you some advice on what to do."

"That sounds like a good idea. I'll think about it. Well, it's getting late. I guess we'd better go in." Steven stood and stepped up on the porch. He opened the door and allowed Emily to walk in first.

Emily stopped when she got to her bedroom door. "Good night, Steven."

"Good night, Emily. I hope you sleep well." Steven smiled at her.

Emily lay awake for hours. That strange feeling wasn't just in her stomach tonight; it was in her heart as well. They had talked on the porch almost like a husband and wife would. He had even asked her advice. It had been wonderful.

"Oh Lord, just let our relationship grow. Let us become a family in every sense of the word," Emily prayed. She also hoped and prayed that in the not too distant future she would feel Steven's arms around her again. And she couldn't help but wonder what it would be like to be kissed by this man she was falling in love with more and more every day.

After church on Sunday, Steven approached Brother Kirkland and invited him to drop by that afternoon. Steven explained that he needed to talk with the preacher.

It was about two o'clock when Rosemary and Brother Kirkland arrived, and Steven suggested they all sit on the porch since it was such a warm afternoon.

After chatting a few moments, Brother Kirkland suggested, "Steven, why don't you give me a little tour of your place. I'd like to see what you've done with it."

"Sure, I'd love to. If you ladies will excuse us," Steven said as he stood to leave.

Emily watched as Steven disappeared toward the barn. "I think

Steven wants to talk about Matt and Mark. He even asked my advice the other night about what he should do with them. I suggested he talk to Brother Tom."

"That sounds hopeful, him asking your advice about something," Rosemary observed.

"We had a very nice talk. It was the first time we'd ever really carried on a conversation. But those few isolated moments on the porch are still all we share." Emily's tone was wistful.

"Well, that's better than it was. Maybe those few moments will become more frequent, until they just happen all the time," Rosemary encouraged.

The men had passed the barn and headed down the lane. There was a fallen log by the side of the path and Brother Kirkland stopped and took a seat. "Steven, what's on your mind?"

"A lot of things," Steven confessed. "But mostly what I wanted to talk to you about was Matt and Mark. I've made real progress with the younger children, but those two are so bitter, I can't break through the wall they've built around themselves. Brother Kirkland, I need some advice on how to handle them."

"First of all, call me Tom. I don't want to be just your pastor—I want to be your friend. Secondly, can you give me a little background? I wasn't here when you left. I'll admit, I've heard various stories about your departure and why you stayed away. But I don't believe much unless I hear it from the source."

Steven really needed to unload on someone and maybe Tom Kirkland was the right person. "Well, this farm had always been my dream," he began. "My parents ran a little general store and were very successful at it, but I wanted to be a farmer. When I finally got my dream, I thought everything would be wonderful from then on. How wrong I was. Everything went pretty well for the first few years, but then it all fell apart. The weather didn't help. Most folks lost money that year. Anyway, the only thing I could come up with was to leave here and go find work so I could meet the mortgage. So that's what I did."

Steven paused, then continued. "I just kept drifting farther west until I wound up in Abilene. That's where I spent the last five years. Sarah was just two when I left, and Matt was eleven. I'm sure it was the hardest on the older boys. The younger ones were too young to know what was going on. I wrote to Rebecca regular at first, but I sent money every month the whole time I was away. I just couldn't make myself come home. I really missed the kids and wanted to see them, but I guess not bad enough, or I would've come back."

"Steven, when you left, you did what you thought you had to do to keep body and soul together. I don't see that you did anything wrong by leaving. I'm sure it was hard on everyone at that time," Tom stated. "You said you really missed your kids, but I noticed you didn't mention your wife. I get the feeling maybe your marriage wasn't as happy as most folks thought it was. Am I right?"

"It wasn't Becky's fault. I forced her to move out here. She didn't want to be a farmer's wife. Life was real hard for her. She had grown up in a rather well-to-do family, and farm life wasn't her cup of tea."

"Why didn't she go back to her family after you left and didn't come home?"

"After we moved here, her father turned the family business over to her brother and he squandered it all away. It broke her parents' hearts. I guess you could say they were left penniless. She blamed me for that, too. Her father didn't like me from the start, so even if we had been there, he wouldn't have given his business to her. He didn't want me getting my hands on any of his money."

"Did Rebecca blame you for all her misfortunes?"

"I was to blame for most of them. She never wanted a big family. But I'm the one that kept getting her pregnant. She didn't want to live on a farm, but I moved her to this place. Then I left her alone to raise five children that she didn't really want in the first place." The burden of guilt was so great that Steven couldn't continue. He had ruined Becky's life, and now he had to pay for it.

"Steven, you're not to blame for everything that was wrong in Rebecca's life. It takes two people to have children. Did you force yourself upon her?" Steven shook his head. "Well, she was a consenting adult and your wife. Maybe the farm was your dream, but did you force her here at gunpoint? Did you discuss it with her before you made the move here?" Tom asked.

"We talked about it a great deal. I sold my father's store after he died and we agreed to try this for five years. After the five years were up, we talked about it again and decided to stay."

"Sounds to me like she willingly made a decision to stay here. You didn't force her, she made the choice."

"Then why did she blame me for everything? When times were hard, why did she tell me it was all my fault?" Steven questioned.

"Some people find it impossible to accept responsibility for anything. They always have to put the blame on someone else for their misfortunes. Maybe that's what Rebecca did and you were the only one around she could blame."

"She seemed to delight in telling me what a lousy husband and provider I was. But when we were out among folks, she would act like the perfect obedient wife." Steven hesitated, then continued. "Something has bothered me since I got back: In an argument one day, Matt said that they never heard from me after I left. That's just not true. I wrote. Becky always knew how to get in touch with me. Is it possible she never told the kids?"

"That's entirely possible. That would have let her continue to blame you for any problems she had. To the general public, she never said an unkind word about you, and of course that won her a lot of sympathy. But it sounds to me like that was just her normal routine. At home she was telling you what a terrible husband you were, but in public she was singing your praises. Then she just continued the same pattern after you left."

"I let that woman destroy all of my self-confidence. I knew I was a terrible husband and would never be able to make any woman happy." Steven sighed.

"What about Emily?" Tom asked. "What kind of husband does she think you are?"

Steven couldn't help but chuckle. "Emily doesn't think of me as a husband. I don't know how she thinks of me. Probably as the biggest heel in the world."

Tom looked completely baffled. "What do you mean?"

"Emily and I are married in name only. When I found out I had to return to be father and mother to my children, I guess I was just too scared to face it alone. Emily worked in a little café I used to go to occasionally. I knew she was a kind and good woman, so I asked her to marry me and help me raise my children. I made it clear to her that she and I would have no relationship. I don't know how that woman has put up with me and these kids. Matt and Mark are rude to her, and I haven't treated her much better. For the most part, I just ignore her, although that's getting more difficult every day."

"What do you mean?" Tom asked.

"Maybe it's just the fact that I'm lonely or that there hasn't been a woman in my life for a very long time. But I find myself drawn to her. And right now, I need to work things out with my kids before I do anything about my personal needs."

"I'd say the first thing you need to do is to forgive yourself for your mistakes. God has already forgiven if you've asked Him to. Next, quit blaming yourself for Becky's unhappiness. I'm sure you made some mistakes as a husband; we all do. But you couldn't be the cause of everything wrong in her life. Steven, it's okay for you to be happy. You don't have to be miserable the rest of your life. You missed a lot of time with your kids, and you can't make up for that time. You need to ask their forgiveness. Tell them you're sorry for staying gone so long. Then you all have to get on with living today."

"But do you think Emily and I could possibly have a future after all this?"

"Yes, I do. You may have gotten married without really knowing each other, but you can make this work if you really want to," Tom encouraged.

"And just how do we do that?" Steven questioned.

"Maybe you need to court your wife and get acquainted. Who knows, you might realize you like each other. You might even find yourself in love."

Steven wanted to get off the subject of Emily and back to the original topic. "We've talked about everything but what I originally wanted to talk to you about. What do I do about Matt and Mark? Emily suggested I sit them down and get everything out in the open.

But when they hate me so much, that's a pretty scary proposition. So she suggested maybe a third party should be present."

"I think sitting down with them face-to-face is a splendid idea. And if you're asking me to be the third party, I'd be happy to. Do you have any proof that you and their mother corresponded during those years you were away?"

"I still have the letters she wrote me. I don't know if she saved any of the ones I wrote her or not. Calvin Meyers, at the bank, can verify I sent money each month. He also knew where I was the whole time. Before I left, I asked him to be in charge of the finances of the farm. Becky wasn't very good at managing money."

"We will allow the boys to vent all their anger, then you can present them with your side. We don't want to destroy their feelings about their mother, but they have to know that their father does care about them and always has. It'll be rough on everyone, and things may not get better right away. But at least the boys will have the truth and can sort out their feelings."

The men sat silently for a time before Tom spoke again. "Steven, you have a rough time in front of you, but you've already come through a very hard time. Now that you have God on your side, you will survive. Why don't we pray together? Then we'll go back to the house and join the ladies."

ε

On Tuesday morning, Calvin Meyers came out to the farm. Emily led him into the living room and he took a seat in one of the big over-stuffed chairs. "Is Steven around today?" Calvin asked. "I knew I'd be taking a chance finding him nearby—but I would really like to talk with him."

"You're in luck. He's in the field behind the barn," Emily informed him. "I'll get Sarah to run out and tell him you're here."

They chatted until Steven entered the room a few moments later. "Calvin Meyers, what brings you out this far? Are you here to foreclose on my farm?" Steven joked.

"I might just try that. The bank could make a good profit off this place. It's really looking good," Calvin teased.

"Have you been telling my wife any nonsense about me? Emily, don't believe a word this fellow tells you." Steven smiled at Emily.

Emily was too shocked to respond. She couldn't believe Steven had actually referred to her as his wife. Maybe they were making progress.

After talking for a while, Steven asked, "Since your bank has quite an investment in this place, would you like to take a little look around?"

"You bet. Emily, will you excuse us?" Calvin asked.

"Sure, I've got to get dinner finished. You're welcome to stay for dinner if you'd like," she offered.

"That sounds wonderful, but I have to get back to town. Maybe another time. It's been a pleasure meeting you." He shook her hand.

Once out of earshot, Steven asked, "So, what do you need to talk to me about?"

"Matt and Mark came to see me the other day," Calvin replied.

"That must have been the day they were late for supper and the day my horse was missing out of the barn. They were very vague about their whereabouts."

"Well, they came to see me. It seems they're concerned that you aren't very sincere in your dedication to them or this place, and they wanted to know how they could protect their interests. And of course their mother's money." Calvin paused to see what Steven's reaction to this bit of news would be.

"Those boys really dislike me. I knew their anger was strong, but I didn't know it went this deep. What did you say to them?"

"I hope I didn't overstep my boundaries. I told them you had sent money every month you were away. I also told them you'd made me caretaker of your finances. That you didn't have to come home if the money was what you were interested in, since it was your money and you could've gotten it anytime."

Calvin paused again and waited for a response. When Steven offered none, he continued, "Just as you suspected, the boys are under the impression that their mother didn't know where you were or how to get in touch with you. I explained that their mother and I always knew how to reach you and that I sent you a monthly statement on the finances of the farm. I also informed them that their mother heard from you, too. That didn't go over too well."

"I'm sure it didn't. They're so angry with me for leaving and then you tell them something they don't want to hear about their mother, the only parent they've had for a long time. I know it's got to hurt to think the one person you could count on lied to you. Calvin, why would she do that?" Steven puzzled.

"I don't know. Rebecca did some strange things. I guess she thought that if you ever came home, she'd have some leverage with the kids. She would be the good guy for hanging around and you'd be the bad guy for deserting them. The only problem is, now she's gone—so the boys don't think there is a good guy."

"Any suggestion on how I might become the good guy to those two?"

"I think you need to sit down and talk to them. Show them the letters you have from Rebecca. Let them know you didn't just desert them. That you stayed in touch."

"I hate to have to destroy their image of their mother."

"Steven, you can point out that although their mother's judgment wasn't the best in the world, she did love and care for them. But the bottom line is, their mother's gone and you're here. You're all they've got now. They have to forgive you and get on with their lives." Calvin turned to his friend. "I don't envy you this job, but you've got to talk to them."

"I know I do. Emily gave me the same advice. I also talked to Tom Kirkland about it. He has agreed to sit down with me and the boys and be a mediator. After what you've told me, I guess I shouldn't put it off any longer. I know how Daniel must have felt before he was thrown into the lion's den."

"You can handle it," Calvin said. "I've seen you weather tougher storms."

9

*S*teven drifted in and out of a restless sleep, thinking about the upcoming talk with Matt and Mark. But what really kept him awake was the thought of courting Emily. When morning finally came, he wandered into the kitchen. Breakfast smelled especially good this morning, and Emily looked especially nice. Steven was sure she probably looked this way every morning, but he had just been too blind to notice. Well, maybe he could throw a little courting in on the side while he arranged to have his talk.

"Good morning, Emily. Breakfast smells almost as good as you look," Steven announced as he took a cup from the cupboard and poured himself some coffee.

"Thank you," Emily said softly.

Steven gave her a big smile as he sat down at the head of the table.

❧

Emily couldn't help but smile as she did her morning chores. She even found herself humming a joyous tune. She was amazed at how the slightest attention from Steven made her mood brighter.

"Emily, you sure are in a good mood," Sarah noted as she threw the chickens another handful of corn. "Did you get some good news or something?"

"No. I'm just in a good mood today. It's such a lovely day, it makes me want to sing."

❧

Brother Tom was away from home when Steven dropped by the parsonage, so he left a message with Rosemary. Since Steven could do nothing about his boys today, he decided to try a little more courting. Stopping at the general store, he got Wilma Jenkins, the storekeeper, to pick out the notions Emily would need to make a dress with the material he chose. He would surprise Emily this evening after the children had gone to bed.

As Steven approached the corner of the house, he realized that he looked forward to seeing Emily sitting on the porch swing. In the early days he had been somewhat uncomfortable when he found her sitting there. But he had to admit that he could have ended his evening strolls elsewhere if he'd been that uncomfortable.

That evening, instead of sitting down on the edge of the porch, Steven went into the house. In a few moments, he reappeared with a small bundle in his hand.

He handed the package to Emily. "This is just a little something to thank you for everything you've done since we got here. I'm sorry it's taken me so long to say thanks."

Emily slowly reached out for the package. "Steven, you shouldn't have, but thank you. I don't think I've ever received a gift when it wasn't a special occasion." Her trembling fingers struggled to untie the string.

She ran her fingers lightly over the soft material. The moon was bright, but she couldn't distinguish the color. Smiling, she said, "I'm sure it's lovely, but I'll have to go in to the light to see the color."

"It's lavender, with little white flowers," Steven informed her as he sat down on the edge of the porch. "I realized you hadn't asked for anything since we got here. I thought you might like a new dress."

"That's very thoughtful of you. I can hardly wait to get it made. I hope I can finish it before Sunday." Steven could hear the excitement in her voice as she spoke.

"I've been very thoughtless toward you. If you need anything for yourself you can charge it at Jenkins' store. If they don't have what you need or want, then we can go into Tyler to get it. If you ever need money, don't be afraid to ask. Actually, I've been thinking, why don't you keep the money from the sale of the eggs? That way you'll have a little cash you can call your own, to do with as you please."

"That's very generous of you, but it's not necessary. I make do okay."

"I know it's not necessary, but I insist. I don't want you to do without things." Steven chuckled as he added, "I'm a successful farmer and my wife shouldn't have to make do. She should have whatever she wants."

"My, all this wealth could go to my head," Emily chuckled.

Looking at her he said, "Seriously. I'm sorry for not being more sensitive to your needs. And I'm eternally grateful for everything you've done for me and my family. You've also taken more than your share of abuse not only from me but my kids as well."

By the time Steven finished, Emily was in tears, but they were happy tears this time. They sat in silence for a while, neither knowing just what to say.

After a moment, Steven said, "Emily, I never did ask you, but did you spend your own money on the material for the curtains in the living room and Sarah's Easter dress? If you did, I want to pay you for them. I know I should've asked sooner, but it didn't really dawn on me until today, when I was looking for that material for you."

Emily shook her head. "There's a big trunk in my bedroom full of material. Sarah showed it to me when I told her I would make her a dress. I asked Sarah about it, and she said that someone had sent it all to her mother, but Sarah didn't know who it was."

Steven was quiet for a short time. "I thought it looked familiar. I sent a lot of material home through the years. Stuff to make Becky and Sarah dresses and the boys shirts, you know, for their birthdays and Christmas and such. I even sent a few pieces for curtains and slip covers to brighten the place up. I guess Becky didn't like my taste in fabric."

"You have excellent taste. But you either sent an awful lot of material or Rebecca made up very little of it."

"Well, before I take all the credit for the selection, I should tell you that Mable Truman, the dressmaker in Abilene, helped me pick out most of it. I had thought Becky would make it up into things for the kids and then she could truthfully tell them that their daddy hadn't forgotten them on their special days."

Not knowing what else to say, Emily finally asked, "Steven, have you thought anymore about having a talk with Matt and Mark?"

"I talked to Tom about it last Sunday, when he and Rosemary came by. I went to see him today to set up a time to talk to them, but he wasn't home. Calvin told me yesterday that the boys had been to see him, both of them mad as hornets. From what he said, I need to talk to them as soon as possible."

They talked a little longer, neither of them in a hurry to go inside. They both agreed that he couldn't put off his talk with his sons any longer.

ও

The family was seated at the breakfast table the next morning when they heard a knock at the door. "I'll get it," Steven said.

Opening the front door, he saw Tom Kirkland standing on the porch. "Rosemary told me you stopped by yesterday. I figured it was about the boys, so I wanted to get here as soon as I could," Tom told him.

"Thanks for coming so quickly. I've got a pretty urgent situation on my hands," Steven explained.

As the two sat down on the porch, Steven began to explain what Calvin had told him. "So the boys think you've come back for the money and are going to run off with everything they've worked so hard for?" Tom observed.

"Yeah, I guess so. Plus, they think I completely deserted them."

"Well, let's see if we can straighten any of this mess out." Brother Tom squared his shoulders.

The men went into the kitchen and found the family just finishing breakfast. Emily poured coffee for the two men as they seated themselves at the table.

As Matt and Mark rose to leave, Brother Tom stopped them. "Would you boys mind staying a few minutes? Your father and I would like to talk to you."

Hesitantly, the boys sat back down. Emily took the three younger children with her outside to do the morning chores, keeping them occupied while the others talked.

Steven had no idea how to begin, so he was grateful when Tom broke the ice. "Boys, your father spoke with me the other day. He's very concerned about the relationship—or I should say the lack of a relationship—between the three of you. It seems since his return you three have not been able to come to terms with your feelings. So this morning we're gonna try to get everything out in the open so we can deal with it." Tom paused and looked at the Barnes men before going on.

"I know you boys are angry," Tom continued, "and that's only natural, but keeping that anger inside doesn't do anyone any good. Least of all you. Matt, you start. I want you to tell your father just how you feel about him and this whole situation."

There was silence. Finally Matt began; once the feelings started to surface, the words rolled out like water flowing over a dam. "I'm mad, real mad. You walked out on all of us. You didn't care what happened. We worked hard to save this farm and to have a place to live. All boys my age have to help out around their places, but I didn't just have to help out—I had to run the place. I had to do your job. Momma told me I was man of the house and I had to take over for you, so I did."

Matt caught his breath and continued. "You left without so much as a good bye. I just woke up one morning and you were gone. Momma said she didn't know why or where you went. She said she guessed you went to find work. But we never heard from you again."

Steven listened as his son vented his anger and hatred. His heart broke to think that Rebecca had been so bitter as to turn his children against him. He didn't know if he could find the words to explain his feelings and actions; he didn't know if he could change their minds about him. But he had to try.

Silently, Steven said a prayer, and then he began. "I didn't just run out on you. Your mother and I talked about my going for a long time, and it seemed to be the only solution. The drought had wiped us out that year and our savings were gone. I had only one choice as far as I could see—leave here and go find work so we wouldn't lose the farm and our home. I looked in on you boys before I left. You were sleeping so peacefully, I just couldn't bring myself to wake you. I wanted to remember that peaceful look on your faces."

The boys appeared to be listening, but Steven couldn't tell much from their blank faces. He continued, "I started working my way west, and each time I went through a town I would mail your mother a letter. When I finally settled in Abilene, I wrote her on a regular basis and she answered my letters."

Brother Tom didn't have to ask for a response; Matt jumped right in. "No one heard from you. Momma said she didn't know where you were. Why would she lie to us?"

"I don't know why your mother said that, but it's not true. She always knew where I was. I also sent messages in my letters to you kids. And I sent money every month to Calvin at the bank," Steven defended.

Finally, Mark spoke. "Why did you wait until Momma died to come home? Was Emily the reason you couldn't come home sooner?"

"I don't know why I didn't come home. The longer I stayed gone, the easier it was to stay away and the harder it became to think of coming back. I had asked Calvin to get someone to farm the place, and he asked Clyde to do it. Clyde was willing to take on the job and to teach you boys. From Calvin's monthly reports, I knew the place was doing much better without me than it ever did with me, so I just stayed gone. I was a coward and I was wrong for staying away."

Mark wasn't satisfied with his father's answer. "What about Emily? Is she the reason you didn't come back?"

Steven shook his head. "Emily is not the reason. I've heard the gossip about her and me, but that's what it is—gossip. Emily and I are just now starting to become friends," Steven told his sons. "I hope someday that our friendship will grow into something more. Emily is, and will continue to be, a part of this family. I pray that you two will learn to accept her as such. You can't blame her for my faults and shortcomings."

His answer hadn't fully satisfied Mark's curiosity. "If Emily isn't the reason you stayed away and you had no other reason, then why did you come back at all?"

"I got news that your mother had died and that you children were gonna become wards of the county. I couldn't let that happen. Whether you believe it or not, I never stopped loving you kids."

"Then why didn't you stay in touch?" Matt wouldn't drop that issue. He just couldn't believe his mother had lied to him all those years.

Tom had remained silent throughout the conversation so far, but now he spoke. "Steven, go get the letters."

Steven went out into the hallway. As he got down on his knees and reached under his bed to retrieve the bag that contained the letters, he noticed a small box shoved all the way back against the wall. He had pulled the bundle of letters from his bag and started to walk back in the kitchen, when his little voice told him to look inside that box.

He pulled the bed away from the wall, picked up the box, and looked inside. There were his letters to Rebecca, tied neatly with a small ribbon. Stunned for a moment, he stood there in silence, staring at the contents of the box. Rebecca hadn't told the children about his letters, but for some reason she had kept them. Now he had absolute proof that he had not completely forgotten his family—but what was his proof going to cost his sons? Steven finally managed to make his legs carry him back to the kitchen where his judges awaited.

He laid the letters Rebecca had written him in front of Matt and then sat down. Matt began to thumb through them. Frowning, he picked up one, opened it, and read. When he had finished reading, he laid the letter down. His hands were trembling and the tears had started to trickle down his face.

"Why would she lie to us? She was our mother. Why would she make us think our father didn't love us anymore?" Matt asked between sobs.

"Son, I don't have the answer to those questions. But I can tell you, I do love you and I always have. I never stopped loving you and I never forgot about you." Steven cleared his throat. "I found this under the bed in the hall when I went to get the letters your mother wrote to me." He set the little box containing his letters on the table.

Mark began to examine the letters his mother had written while Matt opened the box. Matt picked up the neatly tied bundle and flipped through them. There was letter after letter that his father had written to the family while he was gone. His tears began to flow even more furiously.

"Why would she lie?" Matt cried.

"Matt, we don't know why she did it," Brother Tom explained. "No one can explain it. But I know your mother loved you. She was very wrong in not telling you the truth about your father's where-abouts, but you have to forgive her. You have to forgive your father, too. It's time to put the past behind you and start over."

"Forgive?" Matt choked. "You want me to forgive? I find out I've been lied to by the one person I thought I could trust, and I'm sup-posed to forgive her? My father deserts me without so much as a good-bye, much less an explanation, and I'm supposed to forgive him, too. Preacher, you're crazy!"

Matt gathered all the letters from the table and placed them in the little box, tucked it under his arm, then walked out the back door. Steven started after him, but Tom stopped him. "Steven, let him go. He needs some time alone to sort things out."

Steven turned around. Mark was still seated at the table, and Steven walked over to him and sat down on the bench beside him. He placed his hand on his son's shoulder. "Mark, I love you," was all he could say. Mark fell into his father's arms. Steven held him as they both cried. At least one son had forgiven him.

Tom stayed and talked with Steven and Mark until almost dinner-time. Matt had still not returned when Tom finally had to leave.

"He'll be back when he gets things straight in his mind," Tom said. "You come get me if you need anything." Looking at Mark, Tom added, "If any of you need to talk, feel free to stop by the parsonage anytime."

As Steven walked Tom outside and watched him leave, Emily ap-peared. She looked up at Steven and he dropped into the swing, his shoulders slumped. Quietly, she sat down beside him.

"Well," Steven sighed, "Mark seems to forgive me but Matt just walked off. I showed them the letters their mother had written to me, and by some strange coincidence, I found the letters I had written to Rebecca. They had been under the bed in the hall all this time. I showed them to the boys, too. Matt took all the letters and left. Tom says he just needs some time alone to sort things out. I sure hope that doesn't take too long."

"I'm sure that's it," Emily said. "It's just a lot for him to digest all at once. We'll pray he works things out soon."

"Emily, he looked so unhappy. His whole world came apart. He doesn't feel he can trust anyone anymore. I'm afraid I've lost him for good."

"Remember the prodigal son? He came back, and so will Matt. You just have to pray and have faith."

Steven frowned. "The prodigal son left because he was greedy and wanted to try things on his own. He didn't leave because he felt everyone had betrayed him. And he also knew he would be treated fairly by his father when he returned. Matt feels alone and betrayed. He doesn't trust me. What if he doesn't come back?"

Emily reached over and took Steven's hand in hers. Looking into his eyes, she said, "Steven, he will come home."

&

Matt still hadn't returned when the family finished supper. Steven looked around the table. "Do any of you have any idea where Matt might have gone?"

"There's a spot down by the creek where he goes a lot, but I already looked there. There was no sign of him," Mark answered.

"What about friends? Does he have any friends that he might go see?" Steven continued his interrogation.

"He doesn't have many friends," Mark answered. "He's been too busy being the man around here. He hasn't had time for friends. The only place he might go would be Uncle Clyde's and I checked there, too."

After the children left, Steven looked at Emily with desperation in his eyes. "Emily, I can't just sit here. I've got to do something. I'm gonna go have a look around."

"It's getting late. You be careful," she warned as he went out the backdoor.

Emily checked on the children, trying to reassure them that Matt would be okay. Even Mark seemed to welcome her attention tonight.

Emily was really more worried about Steven at this point than Matt. She knew Steven was still blaming himself for everything that was wrong in this family. She couldn't sleep, and since the evening was so warm, she kept vigil from the porch swing. As she waited she lifted Steven and Matt up to God in prayer.

The hours went by and there was still no sign of Steven or Matt. The mosquitoes forced Emily to move her vigil to her bedroom. She lay down, but sleep would not come, so she continued to pray. Somehow God would make this right; He could take an impossible situation and make it work out for everyone. She didn't know how He would turn this one around, but she knew He could and she continued to pray.

The clock on the mantel had just chimed 1:00 A.M. when Emily heard the front screen door squeak. She jumped up, put on her robe, and rushed out into the hallway. Steven stood there all alone. His mood seemed even darker than it did when he left.

"No sign of him?" Emily asked.

"Nothing. But I didn't really have much hope of spotting him after it got dark. I sat down by the creek and prayed and tried to figure out why I'd done the things I did. Why didn't I come home? I knew my kids needed me even if Rebecca didn't."

Steven slumped down on the side of his bed. "I would cry, but the tears are all gone. I knew winning the hearts of my older sons wouldn't be easy, but I never expected this. I've never felt so helpless in my life. Emily, why did I desert my family?"

"Steven, I don't have any answers for you. You're the only one who can answer all those questions. If you search deep down inside, I think you'll remember why you acted as you did."

Emily's voice was tender, and Steven knew the words she spoke were true. No matter how much he loved his children, he realized, his love for their mother had died a slow, painful death. Once he was away from her destructive criticism, he just couldn't force himself to come back. Not for anyone. He would have stayed and continued to endure her bitter remarks if the opportunity had never presented itself for him to leave; he would have even continued to defend her right to say them, and he would have gone on taking the blame for making her life miserable. But the opportunity came to go and he took it. Deep inside, he had been relieved to escape. Now he had to take responsibility for his actions.

Steven looked up into Emily's understanding face. Seeing the love in her eyes, he didn't feel quite so alone. He stretched out his arms and Emily walked into them. He held her around the waist and put his head on her chest. She stroked his cheek tenderly as she placed a soft kiss on the top of his head.

"I really made a mess out of everything," he sighed.

"There's nothing you can do about the past. It's done. You have to start from now. God has forgiven you because you asked Him to. Now forgive yourself. Start right now being the best father you can and your children will accept you for what you are now."

Afraid to look up into Emily's eyes, Steven asked, "What about being a husband? Can I start that from right now, too?"

"I don't see why not," Emily answered.

Steven stood and tilted her head up toward his face, then placed a warm tender kiss on her soft lips. He felt comforted just holding her in his arms. Steven released his hold and gave her one more gentle kiss before telling her good night. As he settled into his bed, he said one more silent prayer for Matt's safe return.

10

*S*teven was saddling his horse to go search for Matt when Mark came up behind him. "Dad, I want to go with you."

Steven was startled by the sound of someone behind him, but he was more startled by someone calling him Dad. He turned around.

"I'd like for you to come. You know Matt's hiding places better than me." Steven put his arm on his son's shoulder. "It'll be good to have you along, son. Families have to stick together at a time like this." Mark's arm around his waist told Steven that the young man agreed.

❧

Steven and Mark had searched everywhere. They had enlisted the help of Clyde Bentley and his boys, but they still had had no luck. Steven knew it was well past suppertime, for the sun was setting over the trees. He had sent Mark home earlier and given him instructions to tell Emily he would be in later.

"Steven, we're losing the light," Clyde said. "We'd better call it a day. Matt's a smart kid. He knows how to take care of himself. He'll come home just as soon as he has everything straightened out in his head."

"Unless he's better than his father at straightening things out, he may be gone a long time. I still can't seem to get things straight in my mind. Clyde, you didn't see his face when he left. His whole world had been destroyed. He doesn't think he can trust anyone anymore."

"I'm sorry about that. I didn't know Rebecca had told those kids she didn't know where you were. I knew Matt was very angry at you, and he didn't want to talk about you at all. But I just thought he was mad about your leaving. I had no idea she was filling their heads with such nonsense." Clyde shook his head. "Seems she told everyone whatever story best suited her fancy. She had most of the community believing she was the deserted wife. Poor Rebecca, they all thought. My Alice was a staunch supporter. She wouldn't even listen to me when I tried to tell her different."

"Well, Clyde, I did desert her. I left and didn't come back."

"Yeah, you left all right. But you didn't desert her. She knew you was going, and she knew why you was going. She also knew where to find you. Deserting is when you just up and leave without a word to anyone. You didn't desert. I caught Rebecca's temper a few times myself. That was one vicious woman when she got mad or things didn't go her way." Clyde looked thoughtful. "If she'd been my wife I'd probably left long before you did."

"I didn't know anyone but me had ever seen that side of her. She was always the loving and charming wife out in public. It was only in private that she would show her more emotional side," Steven remembered.

"Well, she showed it to me. She got real mad the first year I farmed your place. She wanted to pay me a small wage instead of sharing the profits, and she was fit to be tied when she found out she had no say in the matter. She raked me and Calvin over the coals."

"I'm sorry. You shouldn't have had to go through that. I should've come home and taken care of my own responsibilities, not pawned them off on you and Calvin," Steven said.

"Look, you're not responsible for Rebecca's actions. If she treated you anything like she treated me and Calvin, you had to go for your own sanity."

"Oh, her wrath was something I endured every day. It wasn't so bad until we moved here, to the farm. Before that it only happened occasionally. But she hated this place so much that she despised me for bringing her here. Before things got so bad I offered to try and sell and move back to Henderson, but she refused. By then her brother had taken over the family business and lost everything. I guess torturing me seemed like a better alternative than going back to her hometown and facing her family's shame." Steven paused; these were not pleasant memories.

"If Rebecca had only been willing to work with you, ya'll could've had a good life. You have five beautiful children and you could have really made a go of this place. A marriage can't work, though, if the partners aren't willing to work together and do a lot of compromising. A man needs a good woman behind him, and a woman needs an understanding and loving man."

How right Clyde was. He and Rebecca had never had the ingredients for a happy marriage. She had made him feel worthless and he had made her miserable. Now he was trying to salvage what was left of the mess they had made of their lives. Their marriage had never been good, but they had produced five wonderful children, and with God's help, he would be a father to them at long last. And maybe, just maybe, he could be a husband to Emily.

"We'd better head toward home. We'll get an early start in the morning if that kid doesn't show up tonight," Clyde suggested.

"Thanks for all your help," Steven said. "We've pretty much covered this area. There's no telling where he's at by now. I guess I'll go into Tyler tomorrow and talk to the sheriff. Maybe he can contact some of the surrounding areas and turn something up."

The men said their farewells and Steven headed home along the creek bank, leading his horse. He had walked about a mile when he heard a rustling in the bushes. Cautious, he stopped and watched for some wild animal to appear. Instead, Matt walked out of the darkness and almost ran into his father before he noticed he was there. Startled, the two stood in silence, staring at each other.

"Matt!" Steven finally cried. "Son, we've been looking everywhere for you. I've been worried out of my mind." He started to embrace his son, but Matt pulled away.

"I've just been trying to sort things out in my mind," Matt replied.

"Well, were you able to do that?"

"Not really. I still have a lot of unanswered questions."

Steven picked up a small twig and began to nervously break it into small bits. "Can I answer any of your questions?"

"Will you be honest with me and tell me the whole truth?" Matt quizzed.

"I'll try," Steven promised.

"Well, I remember how much fun we used to have. You would take me fishing, and we even camped out by ourselves a few times. Then one morning I woke up and you were gone. I didn't know why. You were just gone. Why didn't you tell me good-bye?"

Steven leaned against a tree for a moment, then squatted down and picked up another twig. As he raked the stick across the ground, he said, "I have those same fond memories."

His voice trembled as he searched for the words to explain his actions to his son. "It was just as I told you. The drought that year almost put us under. I had sold the general store I had inherited from my folks and put a down payment on this farm. The rest of that money I had put in savings and it saw us through even when the farm wasn't doing so good, but it was all gone. Your mother and I talked about our options and together we decided that I should leave and go find work. I could work to get enough to pay off the mortgage and set a little aside for a rainy day. So I left."

Matt sat down on the ground in front of his father. He said nothing, but Steven knew he was waiting for the rest of the explanation.

"I don't know why I didn't talk to you. I have no excuse. I was terribly wrong. Things were really bad for me. I felt like a complete failure. I had failed your mother, you kids, and myself. I was so caught up in self-pity that I couldn't see what anyone else might be feeling. I did go into your room the morning I left. You and Mark were sleeping so peacefully, I just didn't have the heart to awaken you."

Steven stopped. He had to be completely honest. "That's not exactly true. I was too big a coward to wake you up. I knew if you were awake I would have to do a lot of explaining before I left and I was too big a chicken to do that. That peaceful expression of your faces was a whole lot easier to live with than the questions would have been. Your mother told me she would explain everything to you after I left."

"I read your letters," Matt muttered.

"Then you know I did try to explain some of my actions to you in the letters. Of course that didn't do much good since you never saw them until yesterday."

"I blamed myself." Matt's voice quivered. "I thought that if I'd helped out more around the farm, then things wouldn't have gotten so bad and you wouldn't have run away."

"Matt, none of it was your fault. No one could help the drought. It was just one of those things farmers sometimes have to face. I did what I had to do about the farm. Where I fell short was in the way I handled things with my family."

"After you got enough money to pay the mortgage, why didn't you come home then?"

Steven sighed heavily. He knew he couldn't whitewash things and make them believable. He had to be perfectly honest with his son. "Your mother and I had a very bad marriage. It wasn't all her fault, and it wasn't all my fault. As I told you, I felt like a failure. Your mother never liked living on a farm, and she never let me forget I was the one who insisted we move here and give farm life a try. As time went by, we grew further and further apart. I felt like I had ruined her life."

Steven sighed. "Everything I touched I ruined. My marriage, the farm, everything. So the farther I got from east Texas and the bad memories, the easier it was to stay gone." He looked at his son. "Now don't get me wrong. You kids were never bad memories. You were the only things in my life that made sense. But for me to come back to you meant I had to come back to your mother, and I wasn't man enough to do that."

The night was still. Steven could hear Matt's slow breathing, and once or twice he thought he detected a sob. The quiet surrounded them for several minutes.

"Matt, you're too young to understand the relationship between a man and a woman. My staying away had nothing to do with you kids. It was all because I felt like a failure. Your mother made me feel that she would have been better off if she'd never laid eyes on me." Steven paused before he added, "When Clyde started helping you boys farm the place, you did so much better than I'd ever done, I decided all of you were better off without me. It was self-pity. I was full of it. I know that now. I felt really sorry for myself, so I stayed away."

"So you didn't love Momma and that made you stay away from all of us."

"That's putting it bluntly, but in a way I guess it's true. But if you read my letters, then you know I never stopped loving you kids. It was just your mother. If someone continually tells you what a loser you are and what a lousy husband and father you are, you eventually start to believe them. I had finally started to believe Becky. I thought you would all be better off without me around. So when I left, I just stayed gone."

Once again silence hung over them for a few moments while Steven struggled and prayed about what to say next. "Matt, I was wrong. I made the biggest mistake of my life. Not coming back to my family was the worst mistake ever. Please forgive me. I can't change the past, but maybe if we start over, start from right now, we can have a good future."

Matt was silent a long moment. Then he said, "I guess I can understand a little about why you did what you did. I thought all night about why Momma lied to us. Either she wanted to make our lives miserable or she really hated you. I noticed in your letters each time you wrote a special note to us kids. You said you missed us, but you never said you missed Momma. I also noticed in her letters, Momma never said she missed you or asked you to come home. I read the ugly remarks she made about being better off without you. Then I started remembering a few times I'd overheard the two of you."

Matt stood, then walked over and leaned against the tree behind Steven. "I remember one time before you left. She called you a lousy husband and provider and said that you were worthless. I didn't understand it all, but I knew she didn't like you very much. You never said anything back to her. You never defended yourself. You just let her yell and call you names."

"I'm sorry you heard any of our quarrels. A child shouldn't have to hear his parents argue."

"I didn't really hear you argue. You never said anything. She did all the yelling. Why didn't you defend yourself?"

"It's like I told you. I'd come to believe that what she said was true. I believed I was a lousy husband and father. I no longer felt like a man."

Steven stood and faced his son. "That's not true any longer. Several weeks ago, I gave my life to Jesus and He's showing me I am worth something. I know with His help we can be a family. And I can learn to be a good father. It won't happen overnight, and it'll take a lot of patience and understanding on all our parts. It will also require some forgiving on your part."

"So if I can forgive you, then everything will be okay?"

"No, Matt. Everything won't be okay. But it will be a start."

"So, after I forgive you, do I have to accept Emily as my mother?"

"Emily doesn't want to replace your mother. But I think if you would give her half a try, she could be your friend. She is a part of this family now."

Matt frowned. "I can't make any promises, but I'll work on forgiving you. As for Emily, that's a different story."

"Well that's not exactly what I'd hoped for, but we'll consider it a start. Now what do you say to going home before they send out a search party for the two of us?" Steven suggested.

11

*S*teven awoke with the sound of the rooster crowing. A multitude of tasks awaited him since he had abandoned his chores for the last couple of days. He dressed, then headed to the barn to do the milking. Just as he reached the barn door, it opened and out walked Matt with a pail full of milk.

"Well, good morning. You're certainly up early," Steven observed.

"I decided that since I'd probably been the cause of you getting a little behind in your work I'd get started early and help you catch up," Matt stated. "I noticed that the wood pile is really low. We'd better get started laying some in for the winter."

"You're right about that, son," Steven said. "Let's go in and get the milk strained and have breakfast so we can get started. I thought I'd let the twins help today," he added as he took the pail of milk from Matt.

&

Emily and Sarah hurriedly cleaned the kitchen. Emily was anxious to get started on the new curtains for her bedroom and a new dress for herself from the material Steven had given her. Sarah took her doll and went outside to play. Precious, her faithful dog, stayed continually at Sarah's heels as she baked mud pies for her doll.

Emily put a pot of black-eyed peas on to cook and a pound cake in the oven to bake before she pulled out her sewing. She knew her pound cake was Steven's favorite. She spread the cloth out on the kitchen table and carefully cut each piece. She would do as much as she could this morning and hoped that as soon as dinner was over she could finish at least one of her projects.

Stopping her sewing for the morning, Emily, finished the preparations for lunch. She prepared baked squash, new potatoes, fried okra, corn on the cob, and a big pan of cornbread. She still had fresh tomatoes and cantaloupe to complete the meal. Sarah rang the dinner bell as Emily lay the spread on the table.

Once the dinner dishes were washed and put away, Emily returned to her sewing. She cooked enough that morning so all she would have to do to get supper on the table was warm the food, that would enable her to sew right up until the last minute.

When her curtains were at last complete, she stood back and admired her handiwork. She was very pleased with what she saw. Her old bedspread still covered the bed, although it didn't go with the curtains as well as she would have liked. At least now the room felt more like it was hers. She hoped that before long the room would no longer be just hers.

Emily thought back to the night before last when Steven had kissed her. There had been no more such displays of affection. She knew he had been very hurt and upset that night, and she prayed that his turning to her had not been just because of the misery he felt. She hoped he kissed her because he wanted to.

It was a very hot day and Steven was having trouble keeping his mind on his work. Not because of the heat, but because his thoughts kept going to Emily. She had been so loving and understanding the other night. Emily had been there for him during his time of need. But most of all he couldn't get that kiss out of his mind.

As he picked up an armload of firewood and started toward the wagon, he very distinctly heard his little voice, *Steven, now that you have things basically under control with your children, are you going to get started on building a relationship with Emily? You keep stalling and making excuses. You have a terrific lady just waiting to be your wife and you keep acting like an idiot. It's time to get into the game.*

"I know. I know," Steven said aloud before he remembered there was no one there. He then began to develop a plan. He and Emily were married, but they didn't really know each other. He would continue with what he had halfheartedly started and court his wife. Maybe a walk after supper would be a good way to begin.

ॐ

After making sure the younger children were ready for bed, Emily let herself relax. The sun was low in the sky, but there was still at least an hour of daylight left as Emily walked out the front door. Steven was seated on the edge of the porch, leaning against one of the posts.

Before she could sit down in the swing, Steven asked, "Are you too tired to take a little walk with me?"

A little surprised by his question, she softly replied, "No. That's sounds nice."

"From the looks of those clouds in the distance, we may get a little shower later tonight," Steven observed, as they started down the lane toward the creek.

"We could use some rain. Maybe it would cool things off a little," Emily returned.

Their words were few and far between, but the silence was not awkward. As they continued their lazy stroll, Steven reached over and took Emily's hand in his. Just the touch of his hand made her stomach flip and her heart race. They stopped at the widest part of the creek, just a few yards upstream from the spot Emily had come to think of as her private sanctuary. Steven picked up a small stone and threw it across the water.

"I guess you think that was pretty good," Emily teased.

"It skipped three times even on this narrow creek," Steven returned. He offered her another stone. "Think you can do better?"

Emily took the stone and closely examined it before she gave it a toss. "Five skips," she bragged.

"Four and a half. That last one fizzled out, so I'm being generous even calling it a half," he returned.

"That's still one and a half better than you," she quipped.

Steven searched and found two more flat stones. "Okay, let's throw together and go for distance and number of skips."

The two stones made five skips each across the water, but Emily's outdistanced his and landed at the water's edge on the opposite bank.

"Just where did you learn the skillful art of stone skipping?" he asked.

"On the banks of the Rio Grande. My daddy used to take me to the river. He could skip a stone farther than anyone I've ever seen."

Steven seated himself on the soft grass and Emily joined him. "Tell me about your father," he said.

"There's not much to tell. My mother died when I was a baby and Daddy raised me. He worked hard all his life and never had much to show for it. He was a kind, honest, loving man. He couldn't give me much in the way of worldly possessions, but he gave me lots of love. He kept the two of us fed and sheltered. He never remarried, although he had lots of opportunities. Every widow and old maid in town was after Daddy and he took advantage of their eagerness to please him. He got them to teach me to sew and cook. He could cook, and he taught me all he knew, but he thought I could benefit from a woman's influence." Emily couldn't help but chuckle.

"The most important thing about my father, though, was the fact that he was a Christian. He loved God, and you could see that love in everything he did."

Night had fallen as they started back toward the farmhouse. Steven held her hand for the entire walk home. The house was dark with the exception of a light shining through Matt's and Mark's window. Hidden in the shadow of the house, Steven took Emily in his arms and kissed her soundly.

"Emily, why did Matt run away?" Sarah asked Emily as they were doing chores the next morning.

"He was upset," Emily responded. She didn't know how much she should explain. Stepping on Steven's territory was not what she wanted to do, but knowing Sarah, she would have to give the child a fairly thorough explanation.

"What was he upset about?" Sarah continued.

"I guess he was sort of mad at your daddy," Emily said, still certain the child would not be content with that answer.

"Why was he mad at Daddy?" Once again, Sarah's relentless pursuit of the truth was at work.

Emily decided she might as well give Sarah the only explanation she could. "You probably don't remember when your daddy lived here before with you kids and your momma. But Matt does, and he has been very angry with your daddy for leaving. Your daddy and Brother Tom sat down and had a long talk with Matt and Mark the other day, and your father tried to explain to the boys why he left. Matt got really upset and went off by himself to think things through. Now he's home, and maybe everything will be better between your daddy and Matt."

"Why did Daddy leave?" Sarah prodded.

"Sarah, I can't answer any more of these questions. You will have to ask your father why he left. I wasn't around at that time and he's the only one who can tell you that."

That must have satisfied the little girl's mind, for the persistent questioning stopped for now.

&

Emily laid aside the garment she was sewing and started outside to round up the kids for bedtime. She only got as far as the front door when she heard Steven's and Sarah's voices on the front porch. Sarah had her father cornered and was grilling him on the reasons for his disappearance.

Steven obviously didn't know how to answer Sarah's questions. Emily prayed for his guidance, and then quietly returned to her sewing for a little longer.

&

Steven explained about the drought and why he left to find work, but nothing he said seemed to satisfy Sarah. Her questions kept coming. She was like a hound that had a coon treed, and Steven was the coon. No way was he leaving that porch until she was satisfied with his answers.

"Sarah, I don't know how to explain to you why I didn't come home for so many years. Sometimes grown-ups make bad mistakes and bad decisions. My staying away was a bad decision. I love you children very much and I never stopped loving you. I thought about you all the time I was away. I wondered what you looked like and how big you had grown. But I just couldn't come home. I should have, though." Steven looked into Sarah's eyes.

He looked for reassurance that she was understanding what he was trying to tell her and that she was satisfied with his explanation. Instead, he saw confusion in her face.

"But why couldn't you come home?"

Steven was beginning to sweat now. Oh, how he wished someone could get him out of this hot seat. He looked around, hoping to see some help coming from somewhere, but he was alone with his interrogator. Where was that little voice when he needed it? It had been persistent about butting into things in which Steven didn't want interference, but now when he could use some help, the voice was silent.

Steven decided to try a slightly different approach. "Sarah, have you ever been afraid?"

"Yeah. I'm afraid of snakes. Mark scared me with one once. It was just a garden snake, but I was really scared," Sarah offered.

"Okay. Do you know what it means to let someone down? To have someone disappointed in you?"

"Uh-huh. One time I was supposed to help Momma fix supper, but I was playing and forgot to come in. She was really mad at me and said she was disappointed in me. It made me feel really bad." Sarah's little face was sad.

"Well. When I left here I was really scared. I was afraid I would lose the farm. And I thought I had let everyone down. I thought your mother was very disappointed in me. So I stayed away. I guess you could say I was hiding. I was afraid of facing your mother and you kids because I thought I let you down." Steven stopped talking and looked once again at Sarah.

Her face showed signs of understanding. "You must have felt really bad. I'm sorry you felt that way." She got on her knees in the swing so she could hug Steven's neck. "Daddy, you didn't disappoint me. I love you and I sure am glad you're home." She released her hold on her father.

Tears filled Steven's eyes. If everyone could be as forgiving as this small girl, the world would be a much better place. Giving Sarah a hug and a warm kiss on the cheek, he said, "I love you, too, Sarah. Now, I think it's time you went to bed. It's past your bedtime."

The little girl gave her daddy a big smile as she hopped from the swing and disappeared through the front door.

⁊❧

Emily heard the screen slam and laid down her sewing. Steven was still seated in the swing when she walked through the door. Looking up at her, he motioned for her to come sit beside him. After she had seated herself next to him, Steven reached out and took her hand.

"I wish you'd come out a little sooner," Steven proclaimed.

"I heard you and Sarah talking and thought I'd leave you alone. I thought you might need some time to yourselves," Emily returned.

"That child doesn't let up when she wants an explanation about something," Steven remarked.

"I know. I've been through a couple of her relentless question sessions. It's about time you had your turn," Emily said as she let out a soft giggle.

"There's an evil side to you that I've never seen before," Steven responded as he turned to look at Emily.

His smile told her he was joking so she quipped, "I think it's only fair that you get your share of answering her questions."

"Well, you could have at least come to my rescue when you heard her interrogating me," Steven continued with the lighthearted teasing.

"You weren't around to help me. Turn about's fair play, I always say."

"Like I said, you have an evil streak," he joked as he dropped her hand and slipped his arm around her shoulder.

Emily struggled to keep her voice steady as she asked, "Well, did you satisfy her curiosity?"

"I hope I did. She seemed satisfied. At least for now," Steven answered as he drew Emily just a little closer to him.

It felt good having Emily next to him. The emptiness he had felt for so many years was beginning to lessen. Without removing his arm from her shoulders, Steven reached over with his other hand and picked up Emily's left hand. He ran his finger over the gold band on her third finger. A cold shiver went through him. He had slipped that ring on her hand, but it wasn't his ring. He had been so unfeeling that day. How could a fellow ask a lady to marry him and then forget to buy a ring?

As the memory of that day began to flood his mind, Steven wondered why Emily had ever consented to marry him. He recalled the look on her face as she slipped Jim's ring off her finger and handed it to him to place back on her hand. He didn't understand why she hadn't fled out the door at that very moment.

Sitting there beside her now, he was certainly glad she hadn't. With her beside him, his lonely heart was being warmed and filled. As he continued to stroke her hand, a new and very unexpected feeling overcame him. He was jealous. The ring on her finger wasn't his; it had originally been placed there by another man. Emily had probably never taken it off until the day she slid it off for him to place back on her finger.

For the first time Steven realized he didn't like the thought of her ever being with another man. He knew from what she told him that she had loved Jim very much. Would she ever feel that way about him? He would do his best to make sure she did. And someday, someday soon he prayed, he would replace the ring she now wore with one of his own.

Emily's voice broke into his thoughts. "It's getting late," she said. "I guess I'd better go inside."

Steven wasn't ready to let her go, but for now he knew he had to. "Yeah, I guess you're right," he responded.

Emily stood, but Steven didn't go of her hand. He rose from the swing and pulled her into his arms. As she looked into his eyes he covered her mouth with his.

"Good night," Steven said as he released his hold on her. "Have sweet dreams," he continued as he opened the screen door.

"Good night," she whispered. As she passed in front of him through the door, she paused and gently touched his cheek. She gazed deeply into his eyes as she murmured, "My dreams should be very sweet tonight."

As Steven watched her disappear into her bedroom and close the door, he knew his dreams would be very sweet too. That is, if he was ever able to get to sleep.

12

*O*n Saturday evening, Steven walked out behind the barn and found Emily sitting on a fallen log.

"So this is where you are," he said as he sat down next to her.

"I just wanted a little quiet time, so I started to take a walk. I got this far and realized that maybe I didn't want to be completely alone after all. So I sat down here to try and figure out a way to get you to join me for an evening stroll."

"You didn't have to work so hard at figuring out how to get me to join you. All you had to do was ask."

"Well, I knew you were tired so I didn't think you'd be interested in a walk this evening," Emily said softly.

Taking Emily's hand in his, Steven told her, "I am tired but not too tired to take a walk with you."

Never letting go of her hand, Steven stood and pulled Emily to her feet. They strolled farther down the lane, hand in hand. Steven couldn't remember ever enjoying time like this with anyone. Becky would have thought evening strolls down a country lane were boring. Steven was learning that nothing he did with Emily was boring.

As they walked, Steven began to tell Emily about his dreams for the farm. He spoke about someday building a bigger barn. He hoped to have several cows to milk and more horses, just for the pleasure of raising horses. His voice became excited as he talked.

"I want this place to shine. I want my kids to be proud of their home. And someday I want at least one of them to want to take over and call this home for their family." Steven stopped and stood still a moment. He gazed up at the stars, then turned to Emily. "Emily, what kind of dreams do you have?"

Emily was quiet for what seemed like a long time. Finally she spoke. "Your dreams sound very nice. I'd kind of like to share them if that's okay."

"I sort of had that in mind," Steven replied shyly. "Someday I'd like to build us a new house. One with a big kitchen. Lots of space for the family to gather. One that is bright like sunshine. One so that when anyone walks into it, they can tell that it is your kitchen."

Emily was silent for another long moment. At last Steven prompted her, "Emily, would you like a new house with a big kitchen?"

"It sounds wonderful." He thought her voice trembled a little. "But I'm happy with what I have now. I don't have to have anything big and showy. I don't think the kids do, either. It's not the house that makes the home."

"I know. And I realize we still have a long way to go before we can call our place a real home. I also know we have a lot of work left before we're a family. But, Emily, sometimes you just have to dream." Steven took a few steps away from her and began to survey his surroundings. "Emily, I like what I see here, but there's still a lot of work to do. Not only to the farm but to the people that live here. Sometimes I get so anxious I have to just stop and visualize things the way I would like them to be. Do you know what I'm talking about?"

"I think I do."

"I can see a big white house. A pretty white house, with flowers all around. A big front porch. The perfect place to gather with the family. And for the grandkids to play later on."

He took Emily's hand and started back toward the house. He spoke again, but this time in a much softer tone. "Emily, I have other dreams, too. I also picture that someday we'll be a family, a real family. That my children will be proud to call me Dad. That Matt and I will work side by side, together in harmony, and that he'll even enjoy it."

"Well, that dream seems to be getting very close to being a reality," Emily observed.

"Yeah. We've made progress, but we've still a ways to go." He hesitated, then added, "In my dream, you're a part of the family, too."

"That part may be a little farther away. At least as far as Matt and Mark are concerned. Luke, John, and Sarah all accept me and even love me. But Matt and Mark are different stories."

Steven squeezed her hand. "They'll come around. It'll just take a little more time." Steven wanted to continue with his dream and tell Emily that his dream included her in the role of his wife, but he lost his nerve before the words would come out.

&

As they ate dinner on Sunday, Sarah asked, "We are going to the social at the Spragues', aren't we? It's a lot of fun. Last year was the first time I ever got to go. They have games and everything for the kids. And dancing for the grown-ups. We are going, aren't we, Daddy?"

"I hadn't thought much about it," Steven replied. "But I guess we can if everyone wants to."

"Oh boy! Emily, you want to go, don't you?" Sarah asked.

&

Music filled the air as Steven and the family arrived at the Spragues' big red barn. The laughter echoed as the fiddle rang out with the beginning chords for a square dance. The wagon had barely come to a stop before the twins and Sarah were off to join their friends. As usual, Matt and Mark had refused to come with the family. Steven helped Emily down, and then with pride on his face, he escorted her inside.

As the square dance ended and the first notes of a waltz came through the air, Steven took Emily in his arms and guided her across the floor; everyone else seemed to disappear; it seemed as though they were the only two people in the place. Sometime between the time Steven had asked Emily to marry him and now, they had fallen deeply in love.

They shared dance after dance with one another, waltzes and square dances alike. Steven did manage to tear himself away from Emily long enough to dance with his young daughter, and Emily in turn shared a dance with both Luke and John. Matt and Mark were both in attendance having ridden their horsed to get there, but they didn't acknowledge that their dad and Emily were present.

Steven was abruptly torn away from his wife for a few moments by some of the men who wanted to discuss the upcoming harvest. Rosemary found Emily sitting alone and joined her.

"You and Steven look really happy," Rosemary commented.

"Yes, we are. I'm starting to feel like a wife. Well, almost. At least I'm starting to feel like someday soon I'll be a wife."

"How are things with the boys?" Rosemary asked.

"Things seem to be pretty good between them and Steven. But I'm still very much an outsider as far as they're concerned. They only speak to me when they absolutely have to. I don't know what else to try to win their friendship."

"I don't have any advice for you. I've never been in that situation. All I can do is tell you to keep trying and continue to be patient. I'll keep praying for all of you."

"Thanks. I need all the prayers I can get."

"And just why do you need so many prayers?" Steven asked as he walked up beside his wife.

Smiling broadly, Emily replied, "Just because I'm married to you."

Steven took her teasing in stride and returned, "Just for that remark, you may need even more prayers. How about another dance?"

&❧

The entire crowd was disappointed when the Spragues announced the final song of the evening. Steven pulled Emily into his arms and whirled her around the floor. He wished he could make this evening last forever. He wanted her in his arms always. As the music ended, he reluctantly released her and they bid farewell to their hosts and friends.

A full moon lit their way home and cast a romantic glow on the evening. The children were fast asleep on some blankets in the back of the wagon before they had gone a mile down the road. Steven slowed the horses to a walk, then pulled Emily close to him.

Softly he whispered, "You really looked beautiful this evening."

"Thank you."

"I really had a good time. It was wonderful to hear you laugh so much." Steven stammered as he continued, "I wish I could make tonight last forever."

A lump as big as Texas filled Emily's throat as tears of happiness began to trickle down her cheeks. She finally whispered, "So do I."

She laid her head on Steven's shoulder and he lightly kissed her hair.

"I know it's late, but could we go out on the porch for just a few minutes?" Steven inquired after they had gotten the kids tucked in for the night.

"Sure. I'm so happy I don't think I could sleep anyway."

Matt and Mark arrived home just as they walked outside. "Did you boys have a good time?" Steven asked. "I sure did."

"Yeah, everyone could tell you had a good time. You made a fool of yourself with her all night," Matt snarled as he went into the house.

"Wait just a minute, young man," Steven snapped.

Emily grabbed his arm and said, "Let him go. Don't let him ruin this evening, please."

"You're right. I'll have a talk with him tomorrow. I don't want anything to spoil my mood tonight."

They sat in the swing and Steven held Emily in his arms. As they gently swayed back and forth, Steven confessed, "I guess it's become pretty obvious how I feel about you. My son says I made a fool of myself over you. Well, that's fine with me. I plan on making a fool of myself on a regular basis from now on." He pulled Emily closer and encircled her with his arms. "I love you, Emily."

He'd said it. He had finally put what was in his heart into words. "I love you," Steven repeated. He then turned her face to his and kissed her gently.

"I love you, too, Steven," Emily whispered, and they shared another kiss.

After she went inside, Steven walked back out into the night air and took deep breaths of the clean fresh air. Each night it got harder and harder to tell Emily good night at her door. And knowing that only a wall separated them made his heart beat out of control every night. Tonight he had to get control of himself before he did something he would regret later. He loved Emily; he didn't doubt that for a minute, but he wanted to give that love time to grow before he took her as his wife. He prayed for God to give him the strength he needed, and he thanked God for the love that he had found with this very special lady.

&

Emily leaned against the closed door of her empty bedroom. Never before had the room felt more empty or her heart more full. She longed to have Steven come through that door with her, but she knew they weren't ready for that yet. Their love was young, and they had to give it time to grow before they could consummate it as husband and wife.

As she lay in bed, Emily thanked God for the love she had found with Steven. She even thanked Him that she had been so lonely that she accepted Steven's outrageous offer when he had made it

&

In the morning Emily was in the kitchen preparing breakfast when Steven came in and set the milk bucket on the cabinet. He walked up behind Emily and encircled her waist with his arms. He placed a kiss on her cheek and whispered, "Good morning. Did you sleep well?"

"Good morning to you. I slept very well, thank you. How about you?"

Emily turned to face Steven as he informed her, "I had very pleasant dreams."

Steven and Emily were engaged in a warm good morning kiss when Matt entered the room. "Don't tell me we have to start putting up with this disgusting behavior?" he griped.

Upset at being so rudely interrupted, Steven returned, "I don't consider what I was just doing disgusting behavior. It's perfectly normal for a man to kiss his wife good morning. And it's not any of your concern in the first place."

"Well, if you have to do it, you could do it somewhere where the rest of us don't have to watch," Matt shot back.

"Excuse me. But this is my home and I'll kiss my wife wherever and whenever I please. You'd better get used to it because there's gonna be a lot more of it from now on."

Matt gave the back door a slam as he left the kitchen. Emily had remained silent throughout the confrontation, and Steven noticed the bewildered look on her face.

"I'm sorry about that. I didn't mean to embarrass you." He reached to take Emily in his arms.

Emily pulled away. "I wish my presence didn't cause such a problem for Matt. It made me very uncomfortable to have him catch us kissing and make such an issue out of it."

"Look, Matt will just have to learn to deal with it. Please don't let his attitude cause you to pull away from me. I love you, Emily. We're just getting our relationship on a solid footing. Don't back off now. I don't think I could take that." He paused a moment, then continued. "I'll slow down if I'm going too fast for you. I don't want you to be uncomfortable about anything. I won't demonstrate my feelings for you except in private if that's the way you want it. I guess I was still just a little carried away from last night."

Emily could hear the sincerity in his voice and see something akin to panic in his eyes. "Emily, just tell me what you want," Steven pleaded.

"I want our relationship to grow. I like for you to kiss me. It just made me a little uncomfortable for Matt to make such a big deal out of it. He made me feel like a kid getting caught by a father."

"I'll try to be more discreet from now on. It won't be easy, though. I've fallen deeply in love with you and I'd like to shout it from the rooftops. I want the whole world to know that I love Emily Barnes and she loves me. You do still love me, don't you?"

"Very much," Emily answered.

Steven took a look around the room, then gave Emily a quick kiss on the lips.

13

*O*ne more day of logging and they would have enough wood to take them through the winter, Steven estimated. He and Clyde had carefully calculated what the two farms would use and had decided that if they did as well today as they had the past few days, they should have wood to spare.

Matt and Clyde's son Jacob were using a two-man saw to fell a tall pine tree. They had made their cut and thought they knew exactly which direction the tree would fall. As they cut, the tree cracked and started falling in the opposite direction from what they had anticipated. Matt cried, "Timber!" Steven looked up just in time to see the massive tree coming down on him. He turned to run but stumbled. The tree fell, pinning him underneath.

Clyde dropped his ax and hurried to Steven's aid. Matt was already there. "Steven, where are you hurt? Can you tell?" Clyde called.

"It's my left leg. I can't move it at all."

Clyde began to shout instructions, and with his expertise, they skillfully cut the tree away and freed Steven's leg. One look told Clyde that his friend's leg was badly broken, but his first concern was to stop the bleeding. A branch from the tree had punctured Steven's thigh and he was losing a lot of blood. Clyde used his bandanna for a tourniquet and tried to get the blood flow under control. He also put a splint on the lower part of Steven's leg. Jacob and Matt unloaded the firewood from the wagon so Steven could be taken home.

ৡ

Emily saw the procession coming up the road, and her heart dropped to her feet. She ran down the road to meet them and saw Steven lying in the wagon covered with blood. "I don't think it's as bad as it looks," Clyde tried to assure her. "I've already sent for the doctor."

Once at the house, Emily had them carry Steven into her room. After making him as comfortable as they could, Emily cut away what was left of Steven's pants leg.

Steven had remained conscious throughout the whole ordeal. The pain was excruciating, but he was obviously determined to be strong. He reached for her hand. "Kind of a mess, isn't it?"

She looked into his eyes. He couldn't hide the pain from her, but she loved him for trying to make her feel better even now. "Yeah. You really did a good job. Now let me try and get this wound in your thigh cleaned and dressed."

"How about a little kiss first? A kiss would help the pain go away."

Emily smiled as she leaned over and gently kissed her husband. "I'm afraid my kisses aren't that powerful, but if you think they help, I'll be more than happy to oblige you."

She tenderly began to clean the wound in Steven's thigh. The bleeding had almost stopped for the time being. Dr. Emerson arrived and examined the wounds, then sent Emily out of the room when he got ready to set the bone. She cringed when she heard Steven's cry as the doctor pulled the bone into place.

Clyde and the doctor emerged from the room. Dr. Emerson gave Emily instructions on how to care for Steven's wounds and handed her some powder that would help ease his pain. "Be careful with that powder, but he'll need it for a couple of days," Dr. Emerson said. "Give him some now and he should sleep for a while. I'll be by tomorrow. If you need me before that, send for me."

Emily pulled the rocking chair up next to the bed that evening and made herself comfortable. Steven was asleep. She had no intention of leaving Steven's side this evening. She reached over and took his hand in hers and drifted off to sleep still holding his hand.

She was abruptly awakened by Steven's moaning and thrashing about. Quickly she spooned more of the medication into his mouth. When she did, she noticed his head was hot. The wound on his thigh had started bleeding again, she discovered, and she changed the dressing as the doctor had instructed. Then she began to bathe Steven's face with a cool washcloth. Steven continued to toss and turn and started to mumble in his restless sleep.

"Emily, where are you? Don't leave me," Steven cried.

Tenderly, Emily whispered, "Steven, it's okay. I'm right here."

She continued to bathe his face with the cool cloth. As she gently stroked his forehead, she spoke softly to him in a effort to calm his restless slumber. Steven would relax for brief intervals, but then the thrashing, moaning, and mumbling would start again. Emily couldn't understand everything he said, but at times she knew he was telling Matt it was okay, he knew he didn't mean to do it. She didn't know what Matt didn't mean to do, but it seemed very important to Steven that his son know he understood.

Other times Steven called Becky's name. He kept saying something about being a lousy husband and father. Once he told Rebecca that things had changed and he could be a good husband now to Emily.

Then there were times that he cried for Emily. He continued to beg her not to leave. Emily did her best to comfort him. She had tried for what seemed like hours to get his fever to come down, but her efforts were in vain. The doctor had told her to expect him to run a temperature, but he was burning up, and it became evident that the medicine the doctor had prescribed was doing little to ease the pain.

Emily quietly opened Matt's door and walked over beside his bed. She softly called his name. "Matt. Wake up."

Sleepily, Matt opened his eyes and grunted, "What do you want?"

"It's your father. I think he's getting worse. I need you to go get Doc Emerson."

Without another word, Matt jumped out of bed and grabbed his clothes. He was out of the house in no time and headed for the barn to saddle the horse.

Emily continued with her futile efforts to comfort Steven and ease his pain. Time passed very slowly as she waited for Matt to return with the doctor. When they finally arrived, Dr. Emerson once again cleaned Steven's wounds. He pulled out several more fragments of tree bark. Then he poured something that smelled like whiskey into the wound. When he did, Steven screamed with pain. Emily quickly answered the cries of the children and offered comfort and explanations to them.

"Will Daddy be okay?" the three younger siblings asked.

"The doctor's here now. Your daddy will be fine. Let's all pray and ask God to make him well soon." Emily was doing all she could to comfort the children and ease her own mind at the same time. After the little family group had asked God to pour out His healing blessings upon Steven, Emily left Matt and Mark in charge of the smaller children and went to be with her husband.

"How is he, doctor?" Emily asked as she entered the bedroom.

"That leg's got a pretty nasty infection, but he's a strong fellow. He'll be all right."

The doctor stayed until well after sunup. He cleaned and dressed Steven's wound several times during the course of his visit. By the time he left, he was satisfied with the way the injury looked and Steven appeared to be resting comfortably.

Emily was exhausted on her feet, but she was not leaving Steven's side. Matt and Mark had fixed the children's breakfast and had taken care of the morning chores. Clyde and Alice also came by early that morning.

"Emily, I'm here to help," Alice announced. "Just tell me what you want me to do first."

"That's very sweet of you, but I know you have your own family to look after," Emily returned.

"We'll get by. You need me right now, so here I am. That's what friends are for. I'll start lunch." Alice finished her little speech, then left the room.

Emily continued to sit in the rocker at Steven's bedside. She would hold his hand and bathe his face whenever he became restless. Occasionally, during his quiet moments, Emily would drift off into a light sleep, but the slightest movement from Steven would awaken her.

"Emily, you have to get some rest. You won't do Steven any good if you collapse," Alice stated when she brought Emily a glass of lemonade. "It's almost lunchtime, and I'll bet you haven't had any sleep since before Steven got hurt."

"Oh, I nap here in the chair when he sleeps," Emily said.

"Why don't you go lay down. I'll keep an eye on him," Alice offered.

"Thanks. But I can't leave him right now. I have to be here when he wakes up."

After lunch Brother Tom and Rosemary stopped by. They both tried without any success to get Emily to rest; she still insisted she had to be by Steven's side.

Emily stayed at Steven's bedside that night, and finally she fell asleep with her head lying on the edge of the bed beside him. The clock on the mantel had just chimed 3:00 A.M. when Emily felt Steven's hand caressing her hair. She lifted her head, and for the first time in almost two days, she looked into his blue eyes.

"You look very tired," he whispered.

"Well, you look wonderful." She took his hand in hers and gently kissed his fingers.

"How long have I been out?"

"Almost two days. You gave me quite a scare."

Steven gently stroked her cheek. "I'm sorry. I didn't mean to. Have you been here the whole time?"

Smiling, she looked into his eyes and whispered, "Where else would I be? I had to make sure you were okay."

"I love you, Emily Barnes."

"And I love you, Steven Barnes. Don't you ever scare me like that again."

"I'll do my best not to. Come here." Steven motioned for her to sit on the bed beside him. She carefully sat down on the edge of the bed and Steven pulled her into his arms. She gently put her head on his chest.

"You have to get some rest," Steven instructed Emily. "Who'll take care of me if you collapse?" He smiled.

"I'll get some rest. Don't you worry. Now that I know you'll be all right, I can rest."

"Good. I have to be all right. I have too much to live for now."

Emily slid back into the rocking chair. Seeing a grimace flood Steven's face, Emily asked, "Did I hurt you?"

"Just the jiggling of the bed. I'll be okay," Steven assured her as he took her hand.

For the most part he held her hand gently but rather frequently would give it a firm squeeze. Emily could tell by the expression on his face and the glassy look in his eyes that he was in pain. She picked up the powder the doctor had given her and mixed it with water, then spooned a dose into Steven's mouth.

Steven insisted that she go lie down, and she assured him that she would just as soon as he fell asleep. She sat by his side and held his hand until the medicine lulled him into a restful slumber. Finally assured that Steven was doing okay for the moment, Emily went out into the hallway and stretched out on the bed. She left the bedroom door open so she would be sure to hear Steven if he called out or became restless. Before she drifted off to sleep, she thanked God that Steven was better and prayed for his speedy recovery.

§⨾

The next morning Emily was awakened when she heard Steven moving around in his bed. His soft moans continued to make her heart ache. She wished desperately that she could take his pain away.

As she entered the bedroom, Steven opened his eyes. "Good morning," she whispered as she leaned down and kissed him gently on the cheek.

"Good morning. You look a little more rested. You did lie down like I asked, didn't you?"

"Yes. I stretched out on your bed. I feel just fine. Now, would you like a little something for breakfast?"

"I am a little hungry," Steven acknowledged.

"That's a good sign. I'll go see what I can find for you to eat."

"Oh, would you tell the kids that I'd like to see them. Especially Matt."

"Sure." Emily started into the kitchen.

"How's Daddy?" The question came from all five children seated at the kitchen table.

"Well, why don't you go ask him yourself. He wants to see you."

Everyone but Matt jumped to their feet as Emily cautioned, "Now keep the excitement down. Your daddy still doesn't feel very good, so be quiet and don't bounce on the bed."

Matt sat in silence and continued to pick at his breakfast.

"Matt, aren't you going in? You father especially asked to see you," Emily stated.

"He probably wants to yell at me."

"Matt, I don't know what the problem is, but he kept calling to you in his sleep the other night. He kept repeating over and over that it wasn't your fault. He wants to see you. I think you should go in and talk to him. Whatever it is you think you've done might not be so bad if you talk to him."

Matt leaned his elbows on the table and buried his face in his hands. "I caused his accident. I'm the reason he almost died."

Matt's shoulders began to tremble. Emily didn't know what to do. This young man had always shown such contempt for her, she didn't know if he would accept her consolation.

Emily finally walked over to Matt and placed her arm around his shoulder. "I'm sure it's not as bad as you think. I know your father doesn't blame you. Even if you were responsible in some way, your dad would forgive you. Matt, he loves you."

Surprisingly, Matt didn't pull away from Emily's touch or her comforting words.

"I am to blame. The tree fell the wrong way and pinned him under it. I must not have made the cut right or it wouldn't have fallen like that."

By now his whole body shook with sobs. Emily drew him into her arms. "Matt, it's okay. Your daddy's going to be fine. You can't keep blaming yourself. You have to go talk to him. You can't avoid him forever, you know. I know you'll feel better if you just talk to your father."

Emily wasn't sure Matt was aware of what he was doing, because he turned, wrapped his arms around her, and laid his head on her shoulder while the last of his tears spilled down his face. When the other children entered the kitchen, Matt quickly came to his senses and pulled away from Emily.

"Matt, Daddy wants to talk to you," Mark informed him.

Matt drew in a deep breath and walked toward the bedroom door.

୬

"Matt. Son, come over here and sit down." Steven indicated the chair next to his bed.

Reluctantly, Matt took the chair his father offered.

"Matt, you're probably feeling pretty bad, but I just want you to know this isn't your fault."

"How can you say that? I must have made my first cut wrong, so the tree fell on you."

"Matt, sometimes those pine trees have a mind of their own and fall where they want to. You didn't do anything wrong. You couldn't help what happened. Now quit blaming yourself. Once again I won't be able to live up to my responsibilities, so I need you to take over for me."

"It's not your fault this time that you can't do your job. Just tell me what you want me to do."

"Well, harvest starts next week. It'll be up to you to handle it. I know you can do it, because you've done it before. I really wanted to help this year, but that's out of the question now."

Matt lifted his head and met his father's eyes. "It's okay, Daddy. You worked hard in the fields. Whether or not you help harvest doesn't matter. The crops are still yours."

"Thank you, son. That means a lot coming from you. I'll be counting on you to see that everything gets done."

Steven extended his hand to his son and this time Matt grasped it firmly. They had come a long way since that first day on the front porch.

14

*M*att and Mark worked from sunup to sundown in the corn fields. The corn had dried and was ready to be pulled. Some of it they would store in the corn crib to use to feed the livestock through the winter; the rest they would shell so it could be milled into cornmeal. Clyde and his sons helped out, splitting their time between their own crops and the Barneses' fields.

Emily and the twins shelled corn until their hands were bleeding. Emily didn't realize how many years a person had to shell to fill a five-pound bag with kernels. She was very grateful when Clyde brought his corn sheller over for them to use. Luke and John took turns placing the ears of corn into the contraption and pulling the handle down to remove the kernels from the cob. Sometimes it took both of them to pull the handle, and Emily relieved them from time to time.

Doc Emerson dropped by at least once a week to check on Steven. After two weeks of bed rest, Steven was getting restless, and he was grateful when Doc Emerson brought him a pair of crutches. He then could go out onto the porch and do more than his fair share of corn shelling.

As the weeks passed, Steven's leg improved, but the doctor still insisted that he keep his weight off it and use the crutches. The cotton was ready to pick, and Matt and Mark went at it with a vengeance. On the second day of picking, Emily stated that she would be joining the boys in the fields. After listening to the many protests from the Barnes men, she put her foot down and went to the field just as she planned.

Emily had picked a little cotton in her youth, but very little. She had forgotten what a difficult and backbreaking job it was. Matt and Mark were each finished with a row before she got halfway down hers. But nothing discouraged her; she refused to give up. She would not let these little cotton balls get the best of her.

She felt Matt and Mark watching her. "Even Luke and John pick faster than she does," she heard Matt mutter.

"Yeah," Mark answered. "But I never saw Momma out in the fields, no matter how little help we had. She never pitched in the way Emily does."

§❧

Steven accompanied his family to church on Sunday. He couldn't manage getting up onto the seat, so he rode with the younger children in the back of the wagon.

Just as they started to drive off, Matt and Mark came out the front door and Matt called, "Wait up. Mark and I want to ride with you."

Steven was so overcome that he couldn't speak.

As the boys got to the wagon, Emily looked at Matt. "Matt, would you drive?"

"Yes, ma'am, I'd be glad to," Matt answered. Then he climbed up into the seat next to Emily.

Steven was bursting with joy. It seemed at last they would be a family. When they arrived at church, Steven noticed the tears on Emily's face.

Steven offered thanks to the Lord for the blessings of the day. He prayed that they would become a close family, that his children would love and accept him as their father, and that they would love and accept Emily as their friend, if not their mother. He also prayed for God's guidance in the final step of making Emily his wife.

§❧

The next morning as the family finished breakfast, they heard a loud commotion out front. When they went to investigate, they found most of their neighbors standing in the front yard.

"Steven, Emily, we're here to get the rest of your cotton picked. You're our friends and our neighbors, and we're here to help," Brother Tom said as he walked up on the porch.

"That's very kind of you," Stephen said to the crowd, "but I know most of you have harvests of your own. You don't have time to do mine, too."

"We discussed it after church yesterday. We decided that if we all pitch in, we can get everyone's done and no one will lose anything. We'll start with yours, then move on to the next field. We're a community, and for this harvest at least, we're going to work as one. After everyone's cotton is picked, then we'll pitch in and get it to the gin," Clyde explained.

Alice stepped forward. "Don't think you're getting off for free. You have to feed this bunch. But we ladies are here to help cook. Can you handle that, Emily?"

"With pleasure we can handle that," Emily answered.

The men headed to the fields and the ladies went into the kitchen. The old adage that too many cooks spoil the stew certainly failed to be true that day. The ladies talked and laughed as they worked to prepare a meal that would feed the field hands. Preparations were well under control when Emily decided to slip away for a few minutes and see if she could find Steven. He had disappeared right after the men left for the fields.

She found him in the barn sitting on a bale of hay. "What are you doing out here all alone?"

"Actually, I started out to feel sorry for myself but instead wound up counting my blessings. When we first arrived here, would you have ever believed that something like this could have happened?"

"Things were different then. It did appear hopeless and dark. Thank God, He is still able to change lives and mend broken hearts. He's also able to change folks' opinion about other people and circumstances."

Steven was silent for a moment. "You know, the day we arrived here, I sat in this very spot and had a long talk with the good Lord. That was the first time I had talked to Him in years. I asked Him to help me be a father to my children. At the time I was just praying that I would be able to keep food on the table, clothes on their backs, and a roof over their heads. I didn't think I could ever be a real father to them. I didn't think I deserved to be a real father to them. But look how He answered that prayer."

He paused, then said, "Emily, it's amazing. First He saved my soul and forgave me of my sins. Then one by one, He gave me back my children. Isn't God good?"

"Yes, Steven. God is very good. He has given me the family I didn't think I'd ever have."

He turned to face her. "There's one other thing. That first day, I talked to God about you. I couldn't figure out why on earth I asked you to marry me and come back here with me. I was certain that day that I could never be a husband to you, not when I had felt like such a failure as a husband. I didn't believe any woman could ever love me or want me as her husband. But look how God answered that prayer. He gave me back my confidence and He gave me you. He knew before either one of us that we were meant to be together."

"God does work in mysterious ways."

The dinner bell rang, and Steven sighed. "Emily, I have some things I want to say to you, but right now is not the time or the place." He stood with the aid of his crutches and offered her his hand, then pulled her to him and kissed her. "I love you, Emily."

"And I love you, Steven."

మ

The weeks passed. Harvest was just about over and everyone would have a good year. Doc Emerson had been out and told Steven he could start bearing weight on his leg. Slowly, he graduated from crutches to a cane.

Since he was no longer confined, Steven insisted on helping get the cotton to the gin. Everything was getting back to normal in the Barnes household. Actually it was better than what had been normal.

Matt and Mark had become a part of the family since the Sunday they had ridden in the wagon with the rest of the group. There was still some tension between the boys and Emily; the boys had been so angry at her for so long, they had never gotten to know her. They couldn't help but act as though she were still a stranger among them. But at least now they were willing to give her a chance.

Steven had begun calling the family together each evening after supper to have a short family devotional. God was bringing them together at long last.

By late November, the weather was cool but not freezing, since east Texas didn't have a lot of miserably cold weather. Emily remembered the day in the barn when Steven had told her he had some things to say to her but it wasn't the right time. That had been almost two months ago, and she was beginning to wonder if he had changed his mind. They hadn't spent much time alone since then. Sometimes she wondered if he was avoiding her.

The devotion time was over and the kids were all tucked into their beds, or at least safely in their rooms. Emily was making sure the firebox in the kitchen was sufficiently stocked for the morning when she turned and saw Steven standing in the doorway staring at her.

"Do you need something?" she asked.

"No. I was just watching you." He hesitated, then added, "That's not the truth. I do need something."

"What?"

"You. I need you, Emily Barnes. Would you be willing to put on a sweater and join me on the front porch for a little while?"

Emily gave him a big smile. "Sure."

Once seated in the swing, Emily noticed that Steven appeared nervous. He fidgeted in the swing, seemingly unable to get comfortable.

Finally, Emily asked, "Steven, is something wrong?"

Steven didn't answer right away. He fidgeted in the swing and shuffled his feet on the floor some more. Emily was beginning to worry, when he finally spoke.

"I've been wanting to talk to you, but I haven't been able to get my courage up until now."

"What's so important that you have to rake courage up before talking to me? You should know by now you can talk to me about anything."

"I know that. But this is different. It's about us."

Emily's heart began to pound. She didn't know if she was excited or nervous or a mixture of both. Not wanting to interrupt his train of thought, she sat silently and waited for him to continue.

"Emily, I'm very much in love with you and I want you to be my wife." Steven paused again, picked up Emily's left hand, gazed into her eyes, and asked, "Emily, will you marry me?"

"Steven, I'd be happy to marry you, but have you forgotten? We're already married."

"I know we stood before a judge and that legally we are man and wife. But I don't want that cold, heartless ceremony to be the start of our marriage."

Steven began to run his thumb over the gold band on her hand. "And I want my ring on your finger. It hurts me to think that I was so unfeeling that day that I would take another man's ring and place it on your finger. I want a new start. I want to forget that time ever happened. We met, and now we have fallen in love. I want you to be my wife in every sense of the word, but I can't take you as mine until we've been married in a church by a minister of God. I want to proclaim my love and devotion for you before God and everybody. Emily, will you marry me?"

"Oh, Steven. I feel the same way. Yes, yes, I'll marry you!"

Steven pulled Emily into his arms and kissed her. "When do you want to have the ceremony?" Steven asked.

"Anytime. The sooner the better."

"Let's go talk to Tom first thing in the morning."

When Emily got to her room, she removed Jim's ring from her finger. She gently placed it inside her small jewelry box, knowing she would never wear that ring again.

She walked to the bedside table and picked up the wedding picture of her and Jim. She gazed at it lovingly, then tucked it away in a bureau drawer. She had no feelings of emptiness or remorse. Emily knew Jim was smiling down on her. He would be happy that she had found true love once again.

15

he next morning, Steven and Emily went to see Tom Kirkland. Tom answered Steven's knock. "Come in. What brings you two to my doorstep?"

"We need to talk to you if you have a minute," Steven answered as they followed Tom into the house.

Emily blushed a little as Steven explained, "We'd like you to marry us."

"I thought you were already married," Tom said with a puzzled look on his face.

"Legally we are. But now we would like to be married in God's eyes. You see we want to start our marriage out right. We want to be married in church with our friends and family present."

"That's wonderful!" Tom exclaimed. "I'd be honored to marry you." He stood and offered his hand to Steven as Rosemary embraced Emily.

"When do you want to get married?" Tom inquired.

Steven looked at Emily and asked, "How much time do you need?"

"Well, I'd like to make myself a new dress for the occasion. A couple of days at least."

Rosemary jumped up and exclaimed, "Just a minute! I have a wonderful idea. Emily, follow me."

Emily followed Rosemary down the hall into a bedroom. Rosemary opened the wardrobe and pulled out a hanger covered with a sheet. As she pulled the sheet off, she revealed a beautiful ivory-colored dress covered with lace.

"Emily, I'd be honored if you'd wear my wedding dress. It should fit you. Here, try it on."

"Oh, Rosemary, it's beautiful. But I couldn't."

"Sure you could. Come on, try it on."

"But I can't get married in a dress like that. I've been married before."

"That's nonsense. Anyway, this dress is ivory, not white. And you and Steven are already married, you're just repeating your vows. This would be your something old. Please, it would make me so happy."

"It's beautiful. If you're sure it'll be all right, I'd love to."

Emily slipped off her dress and slipped into the wedding gown. "It's perfect," Rosemary said. "You look beautiful. Now let's get a date set, and the sooner the better."

"My feelings exactly," Emily responded. "I have one more favor to ask of you. Will you be my matron of honor?"

"I'd love to!" Rosemary exclaimed.

When they returned to the living room, Rosemary's eyes were shining. "Well, the dress is taken care of, so let's set a date."

"Well, tonight's prayer meeting, so we could announce it then and ya'll could be married Friday night. That's day after tomorrow. Can you be ready by then?" Tom asked.

"Sounds good to me," Steven answered.

Emily gave her approval as Rosemary said, "Why don't you leave the arrangements up to me? I want to decorate the church and I know Alice will want to help. You two don't worry about a thing. Just let me handle it."

As they got up to leave, Rosemary gave one last instruction. "Emily, why don't you plan to spend Thursday night with us? You know you're not supposed to see the groom on your wedding day."

"But . . ." Steven started to speak but Rosemary cut him off.

"Now, no buts about it. You can survive one day without her. Besides, it'll take us most of the day to get her prettied up for the wedding."

&

Emily and Steven called the children into the living room that same day after school. After everyone was seated, Steven said, "As I told you kids when Emily and I came here, we were married in Abilene. But now we want to be married again and this time in church. We want to really be husband and wife, and we want to start our marriage out right. So we're getting married Friday evening at six o'clock at the church."

Steven had barely finished his speech before the three younger children started to cheer. Even Matt and Mark extended their hands in congratulations, and then they embraced Emily.

Steven asked Matt to stay for a moment after the family meeting broke up. When they were alone, Steven asked, "Matt, I would like for you to be my best man."

"You want me to stand up for you at your wedding after all the trouble I caused you and Emily?"

"I can't think of anyone I'd rather have. You're my eldest son, and I want you at my side when I marry the woman I love."

"I'd be happy to stand up with you, Dad." Matt glanced toward the mantel and saw the wedding picture of Steven and Rebecca. Walking over, he picked up the little framed picture in his hand. "Dad, if you don't mind, I'd like this picture. She will always be my mother, and I'll always love her. I'll probably never understand the things she did, but I think I can live with that now. Your and Emily's picture should be here now."

With tears in his eyes and a lump as big as Texas in his throat, Steven hugged his son. "Thanks, Matt. You have become a young man who I'm very proud to call my son."

"And I'm proud to call you Dad," Matt returned.

ào

As soon as supper was over Thursday night, Steven brought the buggy around to drive Emily to the parsonage.

"I'll miss you tonight," Steven said as they slowly made their way down the road. "I've become accustomed to knowing that you're just in the next room."

"I'll miss you, too," Emily replied.

"After tonight I don't plan on spending any more nights without you. And I won't be sleeping in the hall."

Emily blushed, but he could see that the thought had great appeal to her. She tucked her arm through his and put her head on his shoulder.

"Matt has finally accepted both of us," Steven said softly. "I don't know if you noticed or not, but yesterday he removed mine and Becky's wedding picture from the mantel. He said that that place now belonged to you and me."

"Oh, Steven, isn't God wonderful? We will truly be a family now."

When Steven stopped the buggy in front of the house, he jumped down and then helped Emily to the ground. "I'd like a good-night kiss now. I probably won't be able to get one later." Emily obliged him, and then he walked her to the door. After briefly greeting Rosemary, Steven stepped off the porch. He stood alone in the darkness and watched Emily as she disappeared into the house.

"Thank You, Father God, for all the blessings You've poured out on this undeserving farmer," Steven prayed. He mounted the buggy and drove off into the crisp autumn night.

ॐ

Emily awoke. It was her wedding day. This time she was very much in love with the man and he was in love with her. Life was wonderful. Before she ever got out of bed, she thanked God for all the blessings He had bestowed upon her. And she especially thanked Him for Steven.

There was a gentle knock on her door, and Rosemary entered carrying a tray with pancakes, syrup, eggs, and coffee. "I think a bride deserves breakfast in bed," she said as she set the tray on the table beside Emily.

"This is just too much to ask for. I've never had breakfast in bed before," Emily acknowledged.

Rosemary sat with Emily while they planned out their day. Emily would get her hair washed while Rosemary went over to the church and helped Alice and a couple of the other ladies get everything ready.

Then Rosemary would come back and help Emily style her hair. They would have the afternoon to talk and visit like young girls.

☙

Steven didn't think he had slept a wink all night long. He was up early and got the milking done. He even managed to prepare an edible breakfast for his family. It was unbelievable to him that after all these years he found himself so desperately in love.

All day his thoughts were of Emily. Early in the afternoon, he slipped into the bedroom that tonight he would share with his wife. He filled the wood box so they would be able to have a cozy fire all night and moved in his few personal belongings and put them away. Although it was the room he had once shared with Rebecca, he was amazed to discover no unhappy memories were lingering anywhere. In the past few months, this had truly become Emily's home. He could feel her presence in every corner, like a warm and loving feeling. His heart raced with anticipation at the thought of spending the rest of his life with Emily. Once again he thanked God for Emily.

☙

The church was filled with friends. Steven nervously waited outside for his cue that the ceremony was about to begin. He repeatedly asked Matt if he had the ring. Each time Matt patiently assured him he did, but his efforts to calm his father were in vain.

As the music started, Tom, Steven, and Matt entered the church through the side door. The front doors opened and Rosemary slowly walked down the center aisle.

The wedding march resounded and the congregation rose. Emily appeared at the door holding on to Clyde's arm. As Emily walked toward Steven, the love he had for this woman poured out from him. Tears sparkled in Emily's eyes.

This ceremony was nothing like the first. Their love for each other not only surrounded them but touched everyone gathered there. On this perfect autumn Friday evening, they discovered the true meaning of the vows they were pledging to one another. Their love had truly made them one.

After the ceremony, everyone was invited to Clyde and Alice's for cake and punch. Before the evening got too late, Steven suggested to Emily that they say good night to everyone and make their way home. To Emily's surprise, the children gathered around them and kissed them good night and wished them well. It seemed that Steven had arranged for the kids to stay with Clyde and Alice until Sunday.

Steven tied the buggy to the fence when they got home and walked Emily to the door. Once at the door, he picked her up and carried her across the threshold. He built a small fire in the fireplace in the bedroom, then excused himself and went to unhitch the team. Emily took advantage of the time alone to change into her nightgown and robe.

When Steven returned, he removed his tie and coat, and he and Emily sat on the rug in front of the fire. As they sat facing one another, Steven gently stroked Emily's cheek. "I'm so thankful I asked you to come with me to east Texas. Whether it was misery, loneliness, or just plain fear of facing my children alone that made me ask you to marry me the first time, I don't really know. But I'm very thankful that you agreed. I'm also grateful that I've had the opportunity to get to know you, first as my friend and now as my wife."

"Yes." Emily sighed with contentment. "I'm thankful that I accepted your offer, even though I tried to think of it as just a job in the beginning. Because I was so lonely for a family again, I agreed to come to a strange place with a man I hardly knew. But God in His great wisdom and mercy has made something beautiful out of something that could have turned out so bad."

Emily reached into her robe pocket and pulled out an envelope. She handed it to Steven.

"What's this?" he asked.

"Remember the month's pay you gave me before we left Abilene? That's it. It's now the start of our savings to make the dreams we have for this place a reality."

A smile covered Steven's face as he took his bride in his arms. "I guess we can say thanks to lonely hearts, we're together. But a relationship that started out of loneliness and misery is ending in love. I do love you, Emily Barnes."

"And I love you, Steven Barnes."

*E*PILOGUE

*E*mily stood in the doorway of the living room and watched her husband talking to their six-month-old baby girl. Could it have been almost three years since she came to this house? And three years ago that's what it was—just a house, full of unhappy people. Now it was a home full of love.

"I hate to interrupt your conversation with Mary Elizabeth, but if we don't hurry we'll be late. The train is due in at three o'clock you know," Emily told Steven.

"I know. Mary and I were just discussing how excited we were that Matt was coming home from college. He hasn't gotten to meet his little sister yet." The baby gave her daddy a big smile because he spoke every word directly to her instead of looking at his wife.

"Well, let's go. The others are in the wagon," Emily said, trying to rush the stragglers.

"Daddy, Momma, are you two coming?" Sarah called from the back of the wagon. "We're gonna be late."

"We're coming," Steven called as he and Emily walked through the front door. "Matt will wait if we're not there when the train comes into town."

છે

"Do you see him?" Mark asked. He was craning his neck, trying to see past each passenger who was exiting the train.

The last passenger off was Matthew. He was a handsome young man and cut a magnificent figure standing there in his boots, jeans, cowboy shirt, and hat. As he stepped onto the platform, he was accosted by the happy group of family eager to greet him.

"It's good to have you home, brother." Mark grabbed Matt and gave him a bear hug.

"It's good to be home. Luke, John, you two must've grown a foot since I left last fall," Matt told the twins.

"Only about six inches," John replied with a grin as he and his twin brother greeted Matt.

"Matt," Sarah squealed as she jumped into the arms of her big brother. "I missed you."

"I missed you, too, baby sister. And you have turned into a pretty young lady since I left."

"Thank you, but I'm not your baby sister anymore. Come on. You've got to see Mary Elizabeth." Sarah pulled her brother by the arm over to where their parents stood with the baby.

"Welcome home, son," Steven said as he hugged Matt.

"It's really good to be home," Matt returned. "Now let me see my little sister."

"Mary Elizabeth, this is your big brother Matthew," Emily introduced. Emily handed the bundle to Matt.

"You're beautiful," Matt exclaimed. Right on cue, the baby gave her brother a warm smile. "Oh, look, she likes me and she's already got a tooth!"

"Of course she likes you. We've told her all about you. She's been very anxious for you to get here. She's ready to be spoiled by someone new," Emily told Matt.

"Thank goodness she looks like you, Emily." Matt gave his stepmother a smile, then leaned over and kissed Emily on the cheek. "Are you doing okay?"

"I'm fine. Especially now that all my family is back together. Even if it is for just a few weeks," Emily returned.

"Hey, enough of this. I think we can continue the rest of our reunion at home over some of Emily's chocolate cake," Steven said as he picked Matt's bag up off the platform.

"Emily's chocolate cake? I think I can handle that." Matt started toward the wagon with Mary Elizabeth in his arms.

"It's good to have our family together again," Steven whispered to his wife.

"Yes. I'll treasure these weeks since Mark will be leaving with Matt when he goes back to school," Emily wistfully commented.

"I guess the new house will just have to wait until we get our kids educated," Steven said.

"That's okay. I don't need a new house. I've already got the perfect home."